*Readers everywhere are loving each
of the stand-alone books in
the popular Beach House series...*

THE BEACH HOUSE
By Sally John

"I was immediately drawn into the story and didn't want to stop reading. Sally's expert characterization compels the reader to care about each one from the first word. The story swept me along, involving me in each of the characters' situations as if I had been included in that circle of friends staying at the beach house. Sally's books never disappoint, but always satisfy!"

Deborah M. Piccurelli, *author of* In the Midst of Deceit

"I loved reading this book about the friendship between these women and how the years and their current lives have slowly defined them. I think you'll really enjoy reading this one too."

Five-Star Book Reviews

CASTLES IN THE SAND
By Sally John

"*Castles in the Sand* is not only a book about God's forgiveness and redemption, but it is a captivating story of how God can reconcile a family that seems to have lost all hope."

BookBargainsAndPreviews.com

"Sally John has penned another novel with a poignant and challenging message. This book is beautifully written, tackling hard issues with sensitivity and integrity. The author contrasts the different attitudes of the Starr and Carlucci parents to a situation neither family condones, showing the results of both compassion and unforgiveness. The characters are appealing and their struggles real, giving the reader plenty to ponder long after the last page is read."

Narelle Mollet

BEACH DREAMS
By Trish Perry

"There are some powerful truths behind the humorous delivery, and while I laughed, I also shed a tear or two over the tender moments of revelation. Novel Reviews and I give *Beach Dreams* a high recommendation."

"In *Beach Dreams,* Trish Perry has written a fabulous story that combines a modern backdrop with an old-fashioned romance. The story deals with situations that are current and compelling and remind the reader that commitment to God's will is an important basis for a lasting romantic relationship. Not only does Ms. Perry show the romantic love of a man and a woman, but she also shows us the importance of having loving friends and family as well. While definitely a romantic story, there is also a strong underlying theme of dedication to God, friends, and family. A pleasure to read!"

Sunset Beach

Trish Perry

Based on an original concept by Sally John

HARVEST HOUSE PUBLISHERS

EUGENE, OREGON

Pier

Cover by Garborg Design Works, Savage, Minnesota

Cover photo © David Crockett / iStockphoto

Published in association with the literary agent of Hartline Literary Agency, Pittsburgh, PA

This is a work of fiction. Names, characters, places, and incidents are products of the author's imagination or are used fictitiously. Any resemblance to actual persons, living or dead, or to events or locales, is entirely coincidental.

SUNSET BEACH
Copyright © 2009 by Trish Perry
Published by Harvest House Publishers
Eugene, Oregon 97402
www.harvesthousepublishers.com

Library of Congress Cataloging-in-Publication Data

Perry, Trish, 1954-
Sunset Beach / Trish Perry.
   p. cm.—(The beach house series ; bk. 4)
ISBN 978-0-7369-2675-1 (pbk.)
1. Young women—Fiction. 2. Mothers and daughters—Fiction. 3. Family—Fiction. 4. Family secrets—Fiction. 5. Life change events—Fiction. 6. Seaside resorts—Fiction. 7. San Diego (Calif.)—Fiction. I. Title.
PS3616.E7947S86 2009
813'.6—dc22

                                         2008053345

Printed in the United States of America

09 10 11 12 13 14 15 16 / DP-NI / 10 9 8 7 6 5 4 3 2 1

For my sisters,

Donna Hawley,
whose friendship I cherish,

and

Noreen Hawley,
whom I miss more than I can express.

Acknowledgments

Many wonderful people influenced this book. I give my heartfelt thanks to:

Tamela Hancock Murray, for being a delightful, hardworking agent and friend.

Kim Moore and Nick Harrison, for your creative ideas, kind diplomacy, and keen eyes.

The Harvest House family, for being there, always, to support me and my books.

Sally John, for creating the beach house and allowing my characters to visit.

My readers, for your support, encouragement, emails, and reviews. I love hearing from you!

Mike Calkin, Vie Herlocker, Betsy Dill, and Gwen Hancock, my selfless critique partners, whose time, advice, and friendship are invaluable to me.

My wonderful experts, for helping me to keep it real:

    Jessica Gopp of Santa Clara University (life in Oakland)
    Gail Heideman (Russian orphanages)
    Kara McKenzie (violins and all things musical)
    The helpful staff at IslandExpress.com (Catalina helicopter flights)
    Dr. Bill Bushing (StarThrower.org), marine biologist extraordinaire, and SnorkelingCatalina.com (Catalina marine life)

Barb Turnbaugh, Michelle Sutton, and Wendy Driscoll, for being such fantastic cheerleaders, friends, and idea people.

Angie Breidenbach, Jill Bitzer, Vie Herlocker, and Betsy Dill, for brainstorming help.

The Saturday Night Girls, The Open Book Club, and my friends at Cornerstone Chapel, for laughs, encouragement, and prayers.

American Christian Fiction Writers, Romance Writers of America (FHL), and Capital Christian Writers, for your friendship, support, education, and commiseration.

Chuck, Lilian, John, Donna, and Chris Hawley, for being such a loving and whacked-out family.

Stevie, Tucker, Bronx, and Doug, for making life way too fun.

My heavenly Father, for keeping His promise to uphold me with His righteous right hand.

Dear Reader,

Welcome to The Beach House series, the continuing saga of an odd little cottage and the myriad characters who cross its threshold. Visitors come, hopeful for respite from life. What they receive instead is a dose of profound reality.

Located on the San Diego coastline, the house offers comfort in its old-fashioned decor, the refreshing scent of salt air, and the rhythmic whoosh of surf. Just outside the door, a colorful array of people move along the boardwalk. Nearby restaurants, shops, and tourist attractions complete the ambience of leisure time.

But other forces are at work. People bring with them their luggage, both in the form of suitcases and of heartache. Time at the beach house becomes less one of escape and more one of unpacking those emotional bags.

Neighbor Julian and his friend Zeke are an integral part of each story. Quirky as the house itself, they alternately delight and vex others with their keen discernments. Visitors find themselves nudged into realms they would sooner avoid. Start over? Forgive? Tell the truth? Fall in love? Grieve? Speak out? Believe God cares? *Surf?* No way!

The beach house is a place of epiphanies, flashes of insight that lead to healing of relationships. Come visit with the other guests. Laugh and cry. Be filled with hope. And be nudged toward the healing that God alone offers everywhere, every day.

Peace be with you.

Sally John

The Spirit himself testifies with our spirit
that we are God's children.
Now if we are children, then we are heirs—
heirs of God and co-heirs with Christ.

ROMANS 8:16-17

Prologue

Sunset Beach, California

Sonny watched Grig run back into the waves and tried to keep from crying. She knew why he needed to feel the slap of the cold water again, and she completely identified. He was the most beautiful boy she had ever dated, and it killed her to think she would never see him again after today.

But they were both practical, despite being smitten. They had been frank about this being a summer romance. He had plans; she had plans. This month had been exciting, tender, and full of temptation.

But if Sonny learned nothing else from her mother, she learned to put her education and career first. She would get her college degree—degrees—and stand on her own two feet before allowing love to sweep over her.

That was one reason Grig had been the perfect summer love. He was just as determined to stick to his career plans. He was already two years into his degree, and he needed to work when he wasn't in class. There would be no time for a long-distance romance. They had known that from the start.

Sonny studied him now, and he laughed almost self-consciously as he ran back to her, his dark-rimmed blue eyes playful. His hair, the color of grain, was darker when wet. He shook his thick bangs, and they both laughed when droplets of water splashed onto her warm skin. He hesitated for a second and then wrapped her up in a hug.

"Grig! You're freezing cold!" But she hugged him back just the same. He pulled away enough to look into her eyes, and she struggled again to remain sensible. This wasn't love. They barely knew each other. But she just had to use the word and get it out of her system.

"Oh, man, I love your eyes. Don't look at me like that or I swear I'll crumble."

He rested his head against hers and then leaned down to kiss her. She tasted the saltwater on his lips. She didn't refrain for a moment in kissing him back. Grig had been the strong one of the two, and she knew nothing else would happen between them.

He released her and took both of her hands. He had the most beautiful long fingers. "When do you have to leave?"

She looked over her shoulder, toward the house she had stayed in this month with her best friend's family. "I think I have to go pretty soon. Pam's dad said five o'clock, and I still have a little more packing to do."

He pulled her hands to his lips and planted kisses all along her knuckles. "Will you remember what I told you about Campus Life or Youth for Christ when you get to school?"

She sighed. This again. "Yes. I'll look into it. I swear. But I can't promise any great awakenings or anything, okay?" She knew this religious stuff meant a lot to him. And she knew that was why he had managed to be so firm about their relatively chaste behavior this month. She appreciated that, but she just didn't think the whole religion thing fit in with her plans.

They walked silently back to her friend's rental, holding hands and gently swinging their arms together. Before he left, he stood straight, like a soldier, his lean, muscled torso searing itself into Sonny's memory. He spoke crisply, with a perfect Russian accent.

"We must be brave."

She laughed softly, and so did he. But her eyes suddenly stung, and she shut them quickly to lean in and give him one last kiss. He kissed her back, his lips smooth against hers, and she heard a small sound—as if he were struggling—as he pulled away. She thought she'd burst into full-blown sobbing when she saw tears in his eyes too.

He lowered his head, gave her hands a squeeze, and whispered, "I'll never forget you, Sonny." Then he turned and ran toward his own beach house before she could respond or study his face further.

She watched until she couldn't see him anymore, wiping away her tears and hoping no one from Pam's family watched through the windows. She knew she and Grig had done the right thing to sever ties now, but she couldn't remember ever feeling her heart break quite like this before.

One

June 10, four years later
University of California, San Diego

The moment Sonny released the envelope, she had a change of heart. Again. She gasped as if she had been pinched and reached into the mail shoot to try to retrieve her letter.

"Sonata Miller, what in the world are you doing?" Anne Hutchison pulled her friend's hand back and laughed. She darted her eyes around them like a criminal. "I think it's a federal offense to steal mail from the post office, girl."

Sonny groaned. "I think you're right. Maybe I should camp out and ask the carrier to give it back to me." She leaned against the cold tiled wall, her shoulders slumped.

"Uh, no. They don't do that."

Sonny's sigh signaled her resignation. "I guess I'll take this as the Lord's will, then. He wanted me to go ahead and send it, and He didn't want me to be able to chicken out."

"You and the Lord." Anne looped her arm through Sonny's and pulled her toward the exit. "Come on, I need to pick up my cap and gown. Did you get yours yet?"

"No, and don't give me grief about the Lord." The sun made Sonny squint when they walked outside. She removed her sunglasses from the neck of her T-shirt and slipped them on. "Between you and my mom, I'm worn out with the whole defensive thing."

"Hey, you brought Him up." They walked across campus toward the Student Services building. Anne bumped her shoulder against Sonny's. "I just wonder if God isn't maybe too busy to be wringing His hands over whether or not you posted a letter."

"*Not* gonna do the defensive thing, Anne." Sonny flipped her straight blond hair behind her shoulders.

"What's the deal with the letter, anyway? You didn't write to Brad, did you?"

Sonny rolled her eyes. "Please. Over and done. The timing couldn't have been better. This way I'll start grad school fresh and focused this fall. Nope, the letter was to my aunt."

Anne stopped still and released Sonny's arm. "You found your aunt?"

"The investigator did." Sonny brushed her bangs out of her eyes. "At least I think he did. I gave him a picture of Mom, along with what little information I had about her sister, and he says the woman he found looks exactly like her. And her name is Melanie, which is one of the few details I was ever able to get out of Mom. She must be married. Melanie...um... Melanie Hines, it was. She lives right around here, if you can believe it."

"Get *out!*"

"Well, not La Jolla, but it was a Spring Valley address, so she can't be far."

They resumed their walk. "Did you tell your mom you hunted down her sister?"

"Not on your life. This reunion will never happen if I warn her."

"Oh, mama."

"I know." Sonny bit at a catch in her fingernail. "Why do you think I tried to grab the letter back? I just started something in motion that could destroy the one family bond I have. It might be a whacked-out relationship, but it's all I've got."

They wove around several groups of students sitting on the lawn. "Yeah, but you're all she has too." Anne's smile gave Sonny confidence. "She'll forgive you, Sonny."

Sonny straightened and gave Anne a single nod. "You're right. I'm all she has. Anyway, Mom had twenty-four years to fill me in. I'm tired of not knowing who I am and what I came from. I don't care if I came from a long line of criminals, a bunch of do-nothing couch potatoes, or a funny car full of circus people. I want to know. And I've run out of ways to ask her. I mean, at this point I'm practically begging her, and she's obviously decided not to tell me anything about my family. Now it's my turn."

The Student Services building teemed with seniors picking up their caps and gowns. Sonny and Anne joined the line directly behind a lanky kid shrouded in black and listening to what sounded like a tinny funeral dirge on his iPod. Someone in the vicinity had eaten a lot of raw onions at lunch.

Sonny wrinkled her nose and searched in her backpack for her gown receipt. "Besides, how can I hope to become an effective counselor when I'm so clueless about myself? How am I supposed to help people 'find themselves' if *I'm* totally lost?"

"I don't know about that," Anne said. "You seem pretty self-aware to me."

"Me?" Sonny found her receipt and tucked it into the pocket of her jeans. "Right. I don't know who my father is. I don't even know the circumstances of my birth. I've never met either set of grandparents. My mother has a sister she hasn't spoken to in decades, and she won't tell me why. I feel like she'll never trust me with my own history."

"So you're going to trap her into revealing it." Anne folded her arms across her chest.

"Absolutely. One week after graduation."

The line moved slowly forward.

"Mmm-mmm-mmm," Anne said. "Well, I'm not much for praying. But, girl, I *will* pray for you."

Two

June 12
Spring Valley, California

Melanie Hines stared at the letter and had to place it in her lap to still her shaking hands. Several rays of sunlight peeked through the window, but the warmth missed her. She vaguely registered Bailey's voice behind her—her husband had taken a client's call in the office they shared at home.

She tucked a wave of blond hair behind her ear and reread the letter. She pressed her fingertips against her breastbone. A sudden case of indigestion, maybe.

Bailey's victorious whoop startled her, but she didn't look him in the eye when he playfully dropped onto the couch next to her. She tried to focus her attention on what he said—something about the sale of another house.

Finally he stopped talking. He put his arm behind her on the couch. "Hon? You okay?"

"I just…I'm…just kind of shocked, I think." She passed the letter to him.

He held it far enough from his eyes to see the words without getting his reading glasses.

"'Dear Mrs. Hines. I hope this letter finds you well, and I pray it doesn't dredge up too painful a past for you.'"

He stopped. "Whoa. Are you sure you want me to read—"

15

"Don't be silly, Bailey. I have no secrets from you."

"Um, okay, so, '...painful past for you. I believe you and I are related, and I want very much to meet you. I know no one in my family besides my mother, Teresa Miller.'"

Even though she had already read the letter, hearing Bailey say her sister's name caused Melanie's eyes to water.

He let out a low whistle. "Well, what do you know? The elusive Teresa." He squinted his eyes and continued to read. "'I have gone to great lengths to find you, and I have to admit I'm not certain I've found the right Melanie Miller. But I suspect I have. The investigator—' What in the world, Melanie? Someone had you *followed*?"

She shivered for just a moment. His shock made her more nervous than she was when she first read that sentence. She did feel a little creeped out, knowing some shady character had probably observed her without her being aware. But then she handed Bailey the photograph that had come with the letter.

"Look, Bailey. She's just a kid."

The girl looked to be in her early twenties. Pretty. Petite. Long, layered blond hair. Cocoa brown eyes. A beautiful smile, which popped her cheeks forward like delicate little peaches.

He studied the picture. "She looks like you."

"Read the rest. She sounds desperate."

Bailey looked back at the letter. "'The investigator said you looked exactly like the picture I gave him of my mother. I know this sounds weird, and I'm probably invading your life and you'd probably rather I didn't, but I've been denied any information about my family for my entire life. I love my mother very much, but I want to know more than she's willing to tell me. Aunt Melanie, I want to know you.'"

Bailey stopped abruptly. He had that look on his face—the one he got whenever he heard about something sad, especially if it involved a child. Melanie put her hand on his knee.

"She's our niece, Bailey."

He nodded. "Poor kid. Okay, what else...'I've just graduated from college and I begin work on my masters in counseling psychology in the fall.'"

"Well, good for her," he said, a twinkle in his eye.

"'My mother's graduation gift is a week with me at a little beach house in San Diego from June 27 through July 3. I've written the address below. I know this is a lot to ask, but maybe you would like to make the family connection as well? No need to reply. I know this is short notice, so if you show, I'll feel honored. If you don't, I will understand and hope for a chance to meet you in the future. Only…well, *please* come. Yours truly, Sonata (Sonny) Miller.'"

Melanie watched Bailey lower the letter to his lap just as she had done. They both sighed at the same time, which led them to chuckle together. Bailey took her hand, and she relaxed, absorbing his warmth.

"Sweetie, I'll support whatever you decide," he said. "But you have some time to consider this, and I think you should use that time."

She looked into his open, loving face and sighed again. How in the world had she merited this guy? She leaned forward and gave him a kiss, placing her hand behind his head. When she pulled away she saw his surprised, goofy smile and laughed. "You're right, of course. I need to weigh the pros and cons, and I need to feel confident that she's who she says she is."

She stood, took the letter, and walked it over to her desk. She rested her chin on her hand and shot a lopsided smile at Bailey. "But we both know I'm going to go, right?"

"Yep." He stood and ran his hand through his short dark hair. "You wouldn't be the woman I love otherwise." He approached her. He lifted her loose curls away from her neck and gave her a quick peck. She breathed in the comforting, clean aroma of his aftershave.

Bailey looked at his watch. "I've got to go get Micah from lacrosse practice. Be right back."

"I'll get dinner started. Remind him to bring home his jersey. That thing is nasty."

After Bailey walked out she turned and picked up the letter again. "Sonata Miller." How like Teresa to think of music when naming her child. Melanie scanned what Sonny had written and realized Sonny didn't say her mother knew about the invitation for Melanie to join them.

She grimaced and pressed against her breastbone again. She hoped they had some antacid tablets upstairs.

It had been years, but she didn't remember Teresa dealing well with surprises. Especially those she hadn't orchestrated herself.

Three

June 20
UC San Diego

"Stop fidgeting, Sonny. You're more restless now than you were before the ceremony. Just hold still a minute." Teresa held her cell phone up to snap a few pictures of Sonny in her cap and gown. "There we go."

"I'm not restless, Mom." Sonny removed her cap. "I'm just excited. Relieved!"

"You'll make sure to get me that shot of them handing you the diploma, right? I can't tell you how much I've looked forward to this day, baby."

Sonny wore sandals under her gown, and her mother was in Gucci pumps. So Sonny looked up when they hugged. "Me too, Mom. Thanks so much."

"For what?"

"You know. All the support all these years. And four years of college expenses."

Teresa looked into her daughter's warm brown eyes and marveled. Was this the same little girl she carted with her to chorus rehearsals, left with sitters, disappointed so many times by staying after hours to perfect her solos?

"It was the least I could do, honey. You're going to make an excellent counselor."

Sonny sighed. "Maybe after my master's, anyway."

A girl with rust-colored hair ran up to them. "We *did* it, Sonny!"

18

They nearly smashed into each other to embrace, and they laughed as they tried to remain balanced. Teresa glanced around to see if anyone had a problem with their theatrics, but no one seemed to notice.

"Mom, you remember Anne, right?" Sonny kept one arm over Anne's shoulders. "She's been one of my best study partners ever."

Anne put her hand out. "Hey, Mrs. Miller."

"Ms." Teresa shook her hand. "Ms. Miller. Yes, I think we may have met before. I'm not very good with faces, I'm afraid."

A sizable group of people walked up behind the girl, and she turned and smiled. "Mom and Dad, you know Sonny."

The woman—with hair as red as her daughter's—lunged forward and hugged Sonny with hefty bare arms resembling freckled jelly. "Come here, you! We're so proud of you two!"

Really. You would think the woman lived on campus with the girls. Teresa could smell the thick scent of Shalimar wafting with her every move.

Before the father could speak, Anne nodded toward Teresa. "And this is Sonny's mom."

Teresa smiled. "Teresa Miller." She met mater and pater with a firm handshake, and then Anne proceeded to introduce her various siblings, her aunt and uncle, and a cousin or two. What a gaggle! And they all seemed to speak at once. It was like sharing a cramped elevator with a crowd just leaving a party.

"We're heading over to Tapenade for a celebratory lunch," said Anne's father, getting a word in edgewise, his voice raspy like a smoker's. "Would you two care to join us?"

"How kind of you, but no." Teresa answered without looking at Sonny. If Sonny was disappointed, she didn't want to see it. "We already have lunch plans."

More embracing ensued and a rather drawn-out session of farewells. When Sonny and Anne finally hugged each other goodbye, Teresa heard Anne speak in a lowered voice.

"You be sure to fill me in about the beach trip, okay?"

Teresa was sure Sonny looked uncomfortable about that comment, so the moment Anne left, she addressed the subject.

"You haven't invited Anne and her enormous family tree to the beach house, have you, baby?"

Sonny laughed. "Of course not, Mom. I wouldn't—" She abruptly looked down at her graduation gown and gave it an unnecessary straightening. "No, I definitely didn't invite them. Anne's just making conversation."

Teresa sighed. "I still don't know why you wouldn't rather have something a bit more grand for your graduation gift." She gave Sonny's cheek a single stroke and smiled. "Summa cum laude! I'm so proud of you. After all your hard work, I would have given you a car if you had wanted it. A trip to Europe!" She tilted her head at her girl. "It's not too late to change your mind, you know."

She didn't know if the flush on Sonny's cheeks was the result of the hot afternoon sun or something more complex.

"No, Mom. This beach trip with you is what I want. What I…need."

"But—"

Sonny took Teresa's hand. "And part of the gift is that you have to trust me on this and not expect me to give you my reasons." Sonny gazed at her, her eyes wide and intense.

Teresa couldn't help responding with suspicion, and she knew it showed in her own narrowing eyes. So she gave Sonny a crooked smile.

"It's not like you to be secretive, baby."

No response from Sonny. Just a polite smile and an absentminded scratch of the nose. Hmm.

Teresa sighed. "All right. Part of the gift. No more questions."

They made their way through the thinning crowd toward the parking lot. Teresa had to tiptoe to avoid her heels sinking into the lawn. Sonny launched into a story about something that went on behind the scenes as she waited to walk across the commencement stage earlier, but Teresa struggled to pay attention.

No questions allowed about the beach trip. She would *really* much prefer making car payments for the next five years.

Four

June 27
Mission Beach
San Diego, California

"All *right*!" Sonny beamed with pleasure when she pulled up behind the beach house. Mom would love this place. Even from behind, it was stunning.

Sonny got out of the car and breathed in, all the way to her belly button. Ahhh, she loved the hot, salty, *clean* smell of the beach. She checked her watch. Her mother would arrive in about an hour. Sonny left her bags in the car and bounded along the side of the house toward the front door.

Gorgeous. Two stories of white stucco and glass, with a beachfront balcony on the top floor. Maybe she would insist on her mother using that room, if it was a bedroom. That might take the edge off of an otherwise tense week. And the waves and sand were right outside the door, once you crossed the boardwalk.

But something was off. There was no lock box on the door, as the rental agency had promised. Maybe it hung somewhere else.

The front door opened and an older, dark-haired man stepped out. When he saw Sonny standing there, he looked as startled as she was. Then he adjusted his rimless glasses and smiled.

"Ah, you're this week's renter, I take it!"

What a nice accent he had. Like James McAvoy's, only deeper. Scottish, if Sonny guessed correctly.

She returned his smile, relieved he was on his way out. Must have been last week's renter. From the tan he sported, he appeared to have spent most of his visit sunbathing.

"Yeah, that's me. This week's renter!" She reached out to shake his hand. "Sonny Miller. And what a cool place!"

"Welcome, Sonny. I'm Julian." He shook her hand. His smile brought a twinkle to his friendly brown eyes. "Are you staying on your own this week, then?"

"Oh, no. My mother will be joining me. And—" She had better not mention Aunt Melanie. She couldn't exactly tell this guy her whole story, just in case her mom arrived before he was totally gone. "This place is so much nicer than I expected!"

"I think you'll love your stay here."

She nodded. "Yeah." Okay, she was ready for him to leave now so she could move on in. "Um, so, have you moved all of your stuff out?"

He tilted his head, a slight frown forming. "I'm sorry? My stuff?"

"Yeah, you know, so I can—" She jerked her thumb toward the house. "Wait. Didn't you rent this place last week?"

Julian looked at the house and then back at Sonny before he smiled. "Ah. I think we have a misunderstanding. I'm not a renter. I own this house."

She smiled right back. "Sorry!" She started toward her car and spoke over her shoulder. "Okay, I'm just going to go ahead and get my bags."

"Here, let me help." He followed Sonny and pulled her larger bag from the trunk, grunting in the process.

"Rather weighty, this. You don't usually come across such heavy packers at the beach."

"That's just my…um…I have some of my college textbooks in there. You know how heavy those can be."

"You don't have to spend your week studying, do you?"

"No, I just graduated, actually."

"Congratulations." His eyes crinkled at the corners. "And what's your degree?"

"Thanks. Psychology." Sonny grabbed her smaller bag and the fresh flowers she bought on the way over. "I thought I might have occasion to review some stuff this week." That was all he would get out of her. She appreciated his help, but she felt a little weird about his hanging around, owner or not. She hoped he wasn't going to be showing up at the house at odd hours.

He simply smiled. "I see."

Good, he knew to drop the subject. He walked ahead of her. But he didn't walk toward the house. He veered to the right.

"Hey!" Sonny felt momentary panic. Why did she just assume this guy was who he said he was? He might have just burgled that house when he walked out. And now he was walking away with all of her clothes for the week. And her counseling textbooks! All she had in her arms were flowers and a bag containing footwear and her beauty arsenal. Unless she was pulling a Lady Godiva for the next seven days, she needed to stop him. "Hey, where are you going?"

She took a couple of quick steps after him, but he slowed to a stop.

He turned and gave her that enigmatic smile again. "Is something wrong?"

Her arms were full, so she cocked her head toward the rental. "You're heading in the wrong direction, aren't you?"

He looked at the stucco house again, and then back at Sonny. He lifted his eyebrows as if an idea had just pushed them up. "Ah, *now* I see." He set her bag down and pointed to the stucco house. "No, that's my home. I live there. All year long." He turned toward the house next door, the one to which he had walked. The one Sonny had ignored until this moment. "*This* is the beach house."

Sonny instantly remembered the time she tried to make a chocolate soufflé as a teenager. The soufflé had been high and light when she removed it from the oven. Moments later it fell into a saggy, schlumpy mess. Not only did her emotions suddenly feel that way. This beach house looked that way.

It wasn't dirty looking or anything like that. It was just worn out and unattractive enough to need a big old brown bag thrown over it. Especially since Julian's house and another equally gorgeous house were on either side of it. Why hadn't this pitiful eyesore been demolished yet, she wondered?

She knew her face had gone sour. "You're kidding." She set down everything in her arms and rifled through her purse. She pulled out the rental agreement. "But look, it says right here, 'Thirty-four hundred—'" She looked back up at the stenciled sign above the door, and her voice diminished. "'Oceanfront Walk.'"

Julian's gentle laugh sounded like something a father might do if his child had said something adorably amusing. Not that she'd ever experienced that.

"Come now. I guarantee you're going to love this house. You and your mother—"

A gasp. "My mother!" Sonny had forgotten about that. Teresa Miller didn't do yucky. This was not going to start the week off well.

"Your mother will quickly grow to like the place, I promise. Everyone does."

Sonny pushed her sweaty blond bangs away from her forehead and squatted down to retrieve the flowers and her bag. "You have no idea. My mother will probably be knocking on your door five minutes after she arrives, a wad of money in her hand, making you an offer you can't refuse."

He lifted her suitcase again and grinned at her. "Well, my door is always open to visitors."

"I'd keep that to myself this week if I were you." Sonny walked with him to the door and punched in the lockbox code the rental agency had given her.

Julian put his hand out for her flowers so she could free her hand and turn the doorknob. "I'll leave you to it, then."

She sighed, pushed the door open, and took the flowers back. "Thanks, Julian. Sorry for the mistake."

He shook his head. "I think you'll find this isn't a mistake. You and your mother are where you're meant to be, I'm sure." He placed her suitcase inside the doorway. "If a slightly less than perfect beach house is your biggest problem this week, I think you have a lovely week ahead of you. I'll pray to that effect."

He gave her a wave and headed toward the boardwalk.

Sonny had to admit that he had a point. She had tricked her mother into spending a week with a sister she had deliberately avoided for twenty-five years. A bag-ugly beach house was the least of her problems.

Five

Sonny took in the house after she had shut the door. "Whoa." How could a place be so chaotic and yet charmingly funky at the same time? She saw stuff everywhere. Not litter, like trash and papers, but mementos galore.

She muttered to herself, "A regular souvenir shop." But souvenirs of where? Certainly not Southern California.

She set her bag and the flowers on the kitchen counter and walked around the living room, picking up knickknacks and trinkets representing half of the European Union. And not a one was displayed without a lace doily beneath it, unless it hung on the walls.

None of the furniture matched. The decor looked as if the owner had chosen one item from each era of her life and planted it here in memoriam. Afghans draped lazily over each couch and chair like terry cloth nightgowns covering aging women who had seen better days.

Sonny realized she was smiling. This place was cute in a little old lady way. Even if its walls were wake-up sunflower yellow, she liked it. And it smelled good, which wasn't always the case with old homes. She sniffed. Lavender?

A quick walk down the hall led to her discovery of themed bedrooms. Asian, country, seaside, and desert. Whoever owned this place had fun decorating it.

Sonny decided she would let her mom choose a room before settling in herself. They would have a full day before Aunt Melanie arrived. Maybe Sonny could guess correctly which room Melanie would prefer.

She returned to the kitchen and pulled Aunt Melanie's RSVP note from her purse. The handwriting looked as if Sonny's mother could have written it. But Sonny heard a distinct difference in Melanie's choice of words.

> Dear Sonata,
>
> I was surprised and pleased by your letter. You have, indeed, reached the correct Melanie Miller, and I suppose that makes me your aunt. What a blessing for me! I would love to join you at the beach house you're renting. I know the spot. As you know, we live in Spring Valley, and we go to the beach on occasion. I won't be able to head out, though, until church services end on Sunday.
>
> I look forward to getting to know you.
>
> Much love,
> Melanie Hines

Sonny had read the note so many times that she practically knew it by heart. Still, her stomach fluttered every time she read it. It sounded as though Aunt Melanie was a Christian, maybe. That might help keep the week civil, if she would bend the extra inch in the middle of a conflict. But Sonny noticed Melanie never mentioned her sister, Teresa. That couldn't have been an accident. What in the world happened between those two?

She sighed. "Well, that's what we're going to uncover this week, if I have anything to do with it."

She set the note on the counter and searched for vases and scissors to trim the flowers. This had been a good idea, bringing flowers. Not that the place needed more color, but nothing beat fresh-cut flowers for bringing cheer to a setting. And they might need help in that department this week. She had pink asters, creamy calla lilies, blue irises, and rose-colored freesia. There were enough to put flowers in each of the bedrooms and even some in the living room, if she could find enough vases. Something told her this house had plenty of vases.

She was halfway through her task before she realized she hadn't even given the beach much consideration. She opened windows and let the sound of the waves fill the house. She stepped out the front door. Perfect, really. The house faced the beach, so they would be able to sit on the front porch and enjoy the waves even when they didn't feel like walking along the water's edge.

But Sonny hoped there would be plenty of walks along the boardwalk and down by the water. She envisioned a few off-the-cuff counseling sessions during those walks. After all, she had her psych degree. Surely she would be somewhat effective in opening up long-stifled feelings.

She placed her floral arrangements in each bedroom and was admiring her work when she heard her mother's voice in the front room.

"Yeesh. Looks like *The Antiques Road Show* just threw up."

Sonny grimaced and scurried out to meet Teresa. She brightened her expression before her mother saw her. "Mom! Isn't this little place fun? It's kind of campy, don't you think?"

"Do you mean campy as in rustic, inconvenient, summer campy or so-vulgar-it's-fun campy?"

Uh-oh. "Um—"

Teresa waved her hand. "I'm just teasing, baby. It's sort of like those puppies that are so ugly they're cute." She surveyed the whole room while Sonny quietly watched. "Yes, it looks like a little old lady with a traveling streak owns it."

"Is that okay?" Sonny was flabbergasted at how quickly her mom had accepted the surroundings.

"Sonny, if I can't be flexible, what good am I, right?"

Sonny wondered for a second if her mother had been drinking. But she wasn't a drinker. She just wanted to be...flexible, as she said. Maybe this week wouldn't be as difficult as Sonny feared.

A sound at the front door caused both of them to look over. A tall, beautiful, model-thin woman stood at the door. She cast down her crystal blue eyes, but then she looked at Sonny and smiled. They were about the same age. And the young woman had a suitcase with her.

"Oh, there you are." Teresa's speech picked up speed. "I'll step out and get my bags as well. Come on in, Irina, and meet my brilliant daughter." She stepped toward the girl and ushered her inside. "Sonny, I may have mentioned my protégée to you, Irina Petrova? She's an absolute gem, and she joined us—us being the Oakland Symphony Chorus, of course—just a short while ago. She has one of the purest soprano voices I've ever heard. And she's got her first solo, her *debut*, sweetie, in a couple of months, so I thought she could come along and I could coach her a little this week. I knew you'd be flexible. Like me!" A nervous laugh. "And Irina's been so anxious about the solo. She could use the relaxation, couldn't you, Irina?"

Irina stared at Teresa with the same blank look Sonny probably had on her face. Then she looked back at Sonny and simply said, "Hi."

The girl looked like a corralled sheep. Not that she truly looked like a sheep. On the contrary, she looked like something off of a Milan runway. But it was clear her "coming along" hadn't been her own idea.

Sonny realized her jaw was as tight as a fist. She tried to shake off the tension. She stepped toward the girl and extended her hand. "Irina, was it? I'm Sonny. Welcome to the beach house."

"I'll just run out and get my bags," Teresa said, stepping out the front door.

"I'll help you." Sonny heard her own anger and tried to quell it with a deep breath.

Teresa spoke over her shoulder, nearly running away from the house. "No, no, baby. You show Irina where she can put her things. I'm fine."

Sonny put her hands on her hips. Unbelievable. If her mother thought this would keep them from having heart-to-hearts, she was in for a rude (and she did mean rude) awakening. She was determined to hash out her past this week, regardless of whether or not her mom's protégée buffer was around.

"I can sleep on the couch, if that's okay."

Sonny spun around and sighed. Talk about rude. "I'm sorry, Irina. There's plenty of room for you. You can even have your own room. Come on back and tell me which one you prefer."

But when Irina saw the smallest room—the one just off the kitchen— she insisted it was the one she wanted.

"I love the lace curtains. And the pretty armoire." Irina smiled. "They remind me of someone, but I'm not sure whom."

When she gave it thought, Sonny decided the slight separation from the Miller women might prove an advantage for Irina once Melanie arrived.

Sonny left her there to unpack, and she headed back into the living room area.

Teresa had quietly returned with two bags and got herself a glass of water at the kitchen sink. Sonny walked toward her, ready for a quiet confrontation, when she saw what her mother casually picked up from the counter.

Aunt Melanie's note.

Six

"Mom!"

Sonny's voice was full of panic as she rushed toward the kitchen.

Teresa jumped and nearly dropped her glass of water. "What? What's wrong, baby?"

After the briefest hesitation, Sonny squinted one of her eyes and reached up as if she'd been punched. "My eye!" She groaned and almost walked right into her mother before Teresa freed her hands to stop her.

"My eye!" Sonny repeated. She grabbed blindly at the counter and thrust her face close to Teresa's. "Look here! Do you see something in my eye?"

"Hold still, for crying out loud. You're fussing like a two-year-old. I can't look in your eye if you're squirreling around like that. What did you do?"

"Nothing. I just...just...do you see anything in there?"

Teresa waited for her to calm down, but apart from some redness from rubbing her hands all over her face, Sonny looked fine.

"There's nothing there, sweetie. I'm sorry, but I can't see a thing."

"You sure? Did you look really well?"

Teresa checked again. "Nothing, baby. You've smeared your mascara, but I don't see anything actually in there. Maybe it's a grain of sand. Why don't you cup some water in your hand and—"

"No, no." Sonny went to her purse and rummaged for a moment, her back to her mother. She turned around with a tissue in her hand. "I think it's okay now." She dabbed at her eyes and recovered quickly. "Yeah. I'm fine. Thanks. Come on." She slung her purse over her shoulder and picked up the smaller of her two suitcases. "Let's see which room you want back there. And by the way," Sonny put her hand on her hip again and spoke in a lowered voice, "what's with you bringing your protégée along? I thought this trip was your gift to me."

Teresa slowly picked up one of her bags and forced herself to look her daughter in the eye. She had already considered the complaints Sonny would make upon Irina's arrival. "Well, of course the trip is my gift to you. I think you two will have a lot in common. You could become friends."

Sonny sighed. "Mom. Nothing against Ivana—"

"Irina."

"Sorry, Irina. Nothing against her at all—she seems really nice—but I didn't ask for a new friend. I asked for this time with you."

Teresa put her arm around Sonny's shoulders and gave her a squeeze. "And that's exactly what you're going to have, sweetie. But it's an entire week. I'll bet you'll be sick of me—completely irritated—by tomorrow night."

"I'm a little irritated right now, Mom."

Another squeeze. "There, you see? Irina will fill in the blanks at those inevitable moments."

Sonny pulled away enough to give Teresa that once-over she tended to do. Through the years Teresa had learned to recognize when her daughter suspected her of withholding information or harboring ulterior motives. Sonny would put on her analytical face and peer into Teresa's brown eyes with her own, as if she could see past them and clear into Teresa's mind or heart. The gesture still made Teresa perspire. She set her bag down and dabbed at her upper lip with the back of her hand. Then she tried to propel Sonny forward. She would carry her bags back later.

"Come on, show me what's up with the bedrooms. More knickknacks, I assume?"

Sonny sighed and looked toward the bedrooms. "A few. And one of the rooms has a double bed, while there are twin beds in—"

Teresa turned back toward the kitchen. "Hang on, baby. I want to get that glass of water. This beach air makes me so dry." When she retrieved the glass from the counter, something niggled at the back of her mind.

"What's wrong?" Sonny stepped toward her. "You're frowning."

"Hmm? Oh, I'm just trying to remember…I was going to do…*something* before you walked into the kitchen and freaked out about your eye. Something captured my attention."

She put her finger to her chin and looked around the kitchen, trying to trigger her memory. "You know how you have an unfinished feeling that won't go away until you remember what you didn't take care of? I was about to do something when you came storming at me. What was it?"

Sonny suddenly dropped her luggage. She took the water from Teresa and put her arm around her. Now Sonny seemed driven to head toward the bedrooms. "I'm sure it will come back to you if it's important. Come on, Mom. Come pick your room."

"Fine, fine, fine, I'll pick a room." She sighed. "Did you say there was a double bed in one of these rooms? I'll take that, if you don't mind."

"Okay, then you get the desert room, right here."

Teresa stepped in. "Desert? Ah. A ceramic gecko on the dresser and camel pictures on the wall."

"Not to mention the pyramid-patterned bedspread." Sonny smiled. "It's cute, the themed-room thing."

Teresa sat on the edge of the bed. Firm enough for a good night's sleep, she was sure. She felt a lift in her mood over the prospect. "I can't tell you how much I'm looking forward to a week away from serious rehearsals and such, Sonny. A full week free of conflict? This idea of yours wasn't so bad after all."

It might have been Teresa's imagination, but for a second she thought she saw Sonny's smile flatline, right before Sonny brought it swiftly back to life.

Seven

June 27
Spring Valley, California

Melanie hummed along as Billy Joel sang "Honesty" from the clock radio on her nightstand. She gently layered several cotton blouses on top of one another in her suitcase. The delicate floral-scented sachet from her last trip still held enough fragrance to keep the case smelling fresh. She wanted to have everything packed and ready to go so she could drive to the beach house directly after church tomorrow.

She pulled two semi-dressy shifts—her emerald green one and a pink patterned one—from the closet. These would do in a pinch, should they go to a fancy restaurant or even a concert. She wasn't sure what to expect, but there was always the chance Teresa was scheduled to perform somewhere this week.

Melanie stood still and stared at the dresses. Did Teresa still sing? That had always been her driving ambition, to sing professionally. But if she had a daughter old enough to graduate from college, she must have changed her plans somewhat. Otherwise, when had she found time to fall in love? Or get married? Those choices hadn't seemed high on her list when they were last in touch.

"Whatcha doing?"

Melanie turned from her thoughts and smiled at her handsome teenaged son in the doorway. "Hi, honey."

Micah must have grown a foot taller this past year. He had Bailey's dark hair and her dark eyes, and he had been shaving long enough to have a genuine five o'clock shadow now.

"Come on in. I'm packing for my trip."

She knew she was biased, but as far as she was concerned, her son was as striking as any movie star.

"What trip?" he asked.

She chuckled. Striking, but with the focus of a spastic squirrel monkey.

"Remember? My trip to the beach? To meet your surprise cousin?"

"Oh, yeah." He came in and flopped back on the bed.

"Up!" Melanie tugged several pairs of shorts out from under him as he lifted off of them for her.

"Sorry, Mom."

"It's okay. Shoot, I should really have packed the shorts first. Here, Micah, put those long arms of yours to good use for me. Just scoop all of this out of the suitcase, forklift style."

The ticktock rhythm of a Chicago song filtered from the radio. Micah stood and approached her suitcase robotically, in time with the music. He made his own version of machine noises as he stiffly scooped her layers of clothing from the suitcase in one fell swoop.

She laughed and laid the shorts in the case. "Oh! I should put my sandals and shoes in too. Hang on."

Micah stiffly rocked from foot to foot. "Danger. Holding time elapsed. Must. Deposit. Cargo." He started lowering the clothes.

She swatted him on the back. "Stop playing, Goofy. Everything's going to slip out of your arms, and I'll have to start all over."

He resumed his real voice. "How long are you going to be with this runaway cousin, anyway?"

"A week." She placed her shoes and sandals in the suitcase. "Okay, put that stuff back in. And she's not a runaway! Where do you come up with this stuff?"

"Well, where's she been all this time?"

"With her mother, I guess." Melanie shrugged. "And at college."

"Ah. The mother's the runaway. The estranged sister you told me about."

"Yeah, but she wasn't really a...hmm. I guess she was sort of a runaway.

She ran away from me, your grandparents, and everyone I could think of who might know where she went. We tried to find her, but I think she chose not to let us do that. And she was an adult, so—"

"So she wasn't an official runaway."

"Right."

He sat back on the bed. "She was just weird."

Melanie laughed. "Micah, is there *anyone* in my generation you don't think is weird?"

"Uhhh…Will Smith is pretty cool."

"Will Smith. Anyone else?"

"Nope. Just him." A frown suddenly marred his expression. "Did you say you were going to be gone a whole week?"

"Mm-hmm." She walked into the bathroom to get whatever toiletries she could pack in advance.

"Mom! You can't be gone the whole week. I told you I need you to do dinner with Chelsea's parents on Thursday!"

Melanie walked out of the bathroom, tubes of sun block and body lotion in her hands. "What are you talking about? You never said anything about a dinner."

"Well, I meant to! Mom, I was counting on you."

"Maybe a little too much, sport. Don't you think you should check with me before you make plans for me?"

"But you never do anything in the evening. I was sure you'd be available."

She tucked the lotions in the zippered compartment of her bag and placed her hand on Micah's shoulder.

"Sorry, honey. Guess my life isn't as boring as you thought."

He covered her hand with his. When had his hands become so much bigger than hers?

"Mom, really. This is so important. I'm sorry I took you for granted, but can't you come back early?"

"Micah, I already committed myself to Sonny. What's the big deal? Just reschedule for next week. I can do any evening you want then. I'd love to meet Chelsea's parents." She frowned. "As a matter of fact, it would be nice to meet Chelsea."

"That's just it!" He stood and ran his fingers through his hair. "Next

Saturday is supposed to be our first, you know, real date. Not a group thing. I invited her to the lacrosse awards dinner, and then there's a party after. Her parents are really strict and won't let her go with me unless they spend a little time with you and Dad first."

Melanie hesitated for moment. "Your awards dinner is Saturday night? You didn't tell me that, either."

He put his palm out, as if she had just offered him something he was eager to take. "See, that's another thing. I thought you'd be here for the awards dinner. You know, in case I win something." His eyes suddenly widened and actually looked younger and more vulnerable than the rest of his seventeen-year-old body.

She laughed. "Nice try, buddy. I can get back in time for the awards dinner. The beach house rental probably ends Saturday morning." She lifted a sweatshirt jacket from the bed and folded it.

Micah's sigh reflected defeat. He sank onto the bed, next to her luggage. "Okay. I'll figure something else out." He absently lifted an errant blouse sleeve that hung out of her suitcase and placed it gently inside.

Melanie's heart softened a little at that. He was always so much more convincing when he didn't try to be. She draped the folded jacket over her arms.

"Look. I'll see what I can do. The beach house is probably just half an hour or so from here. Maybe I can meet you and Dad and Chelsea's parents in town for dinner, and then drive back to finish my week with Sonny."

Micah jumped up and grabbed her. He lifted her off the ground in an awkward yet wonderful hug. She smelled his cologne. Her baby wore cologne. Or was it deodorant?

"You're the best, Mom!"

She had to grunt out her next words. "Have you talked with Dad about this dinner date on Thursday?"

He set her back down. "No, but he's always home at night—"

Melanie arched one eyebrow.

"Going." He marched out her bedroom door.

She called after him. "And tell him about the awards dinner too."

"Right!"

Melanie smiled and looked at the crumpled jacket, still draped over her arm. She could easily smooth out the wrinkles before packing it.

She hoped it would be as simple to smooth out this new wrinkle she put in her "surprise" niece's plans.

Eight

June 27
Mission Beach
San Diego, California

Sonny watched her mother go directly to Irina's room before they walked out of the beach house.

"Irina, put down your music and take a walk with us on the beach. That's why we're here. So you can relax."

Sonny struggled to keep from frowning. That might be why Irina was here, but that wasn't why Sonny and her mother were here. At least not as far as Sonny was concerned, and wasn't this supposed to be her graduation gift?

When Irina joined them, Sonny did a double take. They had all changed into shorts, and Irina was all leg—very thin leg. Sonny flushed when Irina caught her staring.

"Whoa, Irina, have you ever modeled?" That sounded so much better than the word "skinny" that flashed through Sonny's mind. Sonny would love to have that word thrown her way, but most of her truly thin friends found the word hurtful.

Irina's smile looked shy, rather than wide open and happy—this demeanor seemed to be the norm for her. "No," she said. "I've been asked to model a few times, but I don't have time for that. Singing has always been more important to me."

"And rightly so. You're certainly beautiful enough to model, but any svelte beauty can put on strange clothes and walk gauntly down a strip of carpet and back. What you do is magical."

Irina glanced quickly at Sonny before they walked out the front door.

Was she worried Sonny was jealous? Sonny supposed she *was* a little covetous of Irina's ability to floor her mother the way she obviously did with her voice. But Teresa had always showered Sonny with plenty of praise and support. The only thing bothering Sonny about Irina's presence was the polite facade she and her mother had erected between themselves for Irina's benefit. Sonny needed to undermine that facade before it managed to settle too firmly into place.

She suspected her mother brought Irina specifically to prohibit Sonny from discussing anything confrontational.

"This is a nice little porch out here." Teresa inspected the white picket fence, the flagstone porch, and the wrought iron table and chairs. She gave Sonny a nod of approval and pointed to the grill. "Maybe we could do a little grilling some evening, huh, Sonny?"

"Absolutely." Sonny gave her mother her sweetest smile. Grilling was exactly what she had in mind, once Aunt Melanie showed up.

~

The three of them enjoyed a leisurely walk down the beach. The sky morphed from blue to pink as the sun slowly wended its way toward the horizon. The women let the cold waves lap at their ankles, and they weaved around children and parents who finished the day with a few last dips in the water.

"What's the name of your solo, Irina?" Sonny had to look up to the girl in order to meet her eyes. She was surprised at how blue Irina's eyes looked out here in the waning light. Sonny felt she had seen those dark-rimmed eyes somewhere before.

"I have a few solos." Irina looked down at the sand, her light brown hair falling like a veil around her face. "'Pie Jesu,' by Andrew Lloyd Webber. 'In Trutina,' from *Carmina Burana*—"

Sonny looked at her mother. "I should probably know which those are."

"You know them, baby." Teresa rested her hand on Sonny's shoulder. "You've heard me sing them a million times. Irina, sing 'Pie Jesu' for her."

Irina stopped and darted her eyes at the few people around them. "I...I can't do that."

Teresa turned and faced her, so Sonny stopped too.

"Nonsense. Of course you can," Teresa said. "You'll be singing in front of far more people than this in a couple of months."

"But at the concert hall I'll be singing for people who came to hear me sing. To hear *us* sing." Irina's shoulders seemed to shrink into her arms.

Sonny looked at her mother. "Mom, don't push her. It's okay, Irina."

Teresa took Irina's hands. "I'm pushing you a little, I know. But you're a stunning singer. Trust me. This is good for you."

"It's rude of me to—"

"It's a gift. You're giving these people a gift. The song is short and lovely and the perfect accompaniment to that gorgeous, dusky sky out there on the horizon. Come on. I'll sing the alto part with you. Close your eyes and just start."

Sonny squirmed almost as much as Irina did. She watched Irina close her eyes and saw moisture on her forehead that definitely wasn't there before. Sonny looked at her mother and was about to interrupt on Irina's behalf again.

But suddenly Irina started to sing, and Sonny fell still.

Yes. She knew this piece. Sung in Latin, asking the Lord to have mercy on us and grant us peace. She remembered reading the translation before.

Irina's voice was angelic and clear, less operatic sounding than Sonny knew Teresa's to be. But when Teresa added the alto line, and the evening waves washed gently toward them, the beautiful mingling of their voices and their surroundings transfixed Sonny. She looked at the setting sun and nearly cried.

The song was far too short, and despite the fact that their voices couldn't have traveled far, everyone around them had stopped and now erupted in clapping and cheering.

Irina's eyes shot open and filled with joy at the spontaneous show of appreciation.

So Sonny's mom was right, after all. Irina still looked shy and nervous, but Teresa seemed to know what Irina needed to feel better about herself.

Sonny watched her mother, who patted Irina on the back and spoke quiet words of encouragement to her. If she understood Irina so well, why couldn't she accept what her own daughter needed?

Maybe Sonny should try some of the same pushiness her mother had just used. Take her mother by the hands and order her to close her eyes and just spill about their family history.

Talk about a gift! That was the gift Sonny hoped to receive, whether her mother wanted to give it to her or not.

Nine

Teresa spotted an attractive man with dark curly hair standing on the beach just outside their rental. He wore a Hawaiian shirt and cutoffs. As she and the girls approached, she could see he had a gorgeous tan. He was with a dreadlocked man—rather Jamaican looking—and a pale heavyset man who seemed to be saying goodbye to the other two.

She heard the black man speak with a singsong lilt as they approached. "You take care of yourself, brother." He hugged the big man and gave him one of the most beautiful smiles Teresa had ever seen. He turned that smile in her direction when his Hawaiian-shirted companion called Sonny's name.

"Hello, Sonny!" He stepped in their direction and glanced at Teresa. "This must be your mother, then." He extended his hand. Scottish or Irish, Teresa wasn't sure which.

She looked at Sonny, her eyebrows raised.

"Yeah, this is Teresa, my mom." Sonny bit her lip. "Mom, Irina, this is our next-door neighbor. I'm so sorry. I've already forgotten your name."

"Julian." His smile was nearly as appealing as his friend's, and he shared it with both Teresa and Irina.

"Oh, right," Sonny said. "Julian. And Irina is my mom's, uh, friend."

Teresa rolled her eyes. Good grief. Sonny made it sound like she and Irina were, well, together.

"She's my protégée, actually." Teresa allowed a hint of appreciation in her eyes when she shook Julian's hand. He was pretty dishy, but not the slightest bit flirtatious. Ah, well.

Irina mumbled a soft greeting. When she didn't enunciate, she still had a trace of her Russian accent. Teresa actually thought that was a nice touch, professionally. Maybe she should encourage Irina to hang on to what little accent she could.

Julian put his arm across the shoulders of the dreadlocked man. "I guess you could say I was once this fellow's protégé. This is Zeke."

Zeke chuckled at Julian and shook the women's hands with open delight. "Welcome, sisters, welcome." He looked directly at Irina, and Teresa saw an immediate reaction in Irina's expression. She couldn't quite put her finger on it, but Irina looked better somehow. She smiled back at him as if he had said something beyond "Welcome."

"So tell us, sister," Zeke said to Irina. "What gift has the good Lord given you? Why are you this lovely lady's protégée?"

As was usually necessary, Teresa was about to speak for Irina. The girl was so amazingly shy. But Irina responded quickly.

"I sing a little."

"A little?" Sonny looked from Irina to the two men. "She sings like an angel."

This was something Teresa loved about her daughter. If there was ever something kind to say, Sonny would say it.

Julian seemed to appreciate Sonny's comment too. He looked at her and smiled as if she were his daughter. For the second time in as many minutes, Teresa noticed how attractive he was.

"So, Julian," she said, "how were you Zeke's protégé? Are you musically gifted as well?"

Julian and Zeke looked at each other and their grins grew wide. Zeke presented his palm to Julian in an invitation to explain for both of them. Julian turned to her.

"Definitely not musically gifted, Teresa, no. But I assume you are? Also a singer?"

Was he charming or what? She loved how he turned the topic right back to her.

"Yes. I'm a soprano with the Oakland Symphony Chorus. We both are."

Irina seemed eager to participate in the conversation when she could. "She's amazing. She teaches me so much."

Teresa found herself intrigued about Julian. "But what about you? As Zeke said, what's your gift?" She didn't feel comfortable with Zeke's whole *good Lord* thing, so she decided to paraphrase.

Julian actually hesitated before speaking. "I don't want to overwhelm anyone with my life story, but I suppose you could say I was at death's door when I met Zeke. And I was there willingly."

Teresa's eyes widened. Well. Yes, that was just a tad overwhelming for polite conversation. Apparently Sonny didn't feel the same.

"You mean, you were suicidal?"

Teresa shot a look at Sonny. They were, after all, just chatting on the beach. Didn't anyone else think this was an inappropriate—

"Yes. But Zeke and Faith Fontaine—she was the owner of the house you're renting—they made all the difference for me." Julian chuckled. "Well, I say *they* made the difference, but what I mean is they made a difference because—"

"They told you about Jesus," Sonny said, pointing at him, her mouth slightly open and smiling.

"Sonata Miller!" Teresa was appalled that Sonny would impose her religious beliefs on people so bluntly. This was something she *didn't* love about her daughter.

Zeke laughed out loud and pointed back at Sonny. "You spoke the truth, sister!"

The three of them laughed together.

"I *knew* it!" Sonny sounded as if she had just solved an Agatha Christie mystery.

Teresa broke out in a sweat. The moment had turned completely uncomfortable. Could she bolt out of here without drawing too much attention?

This was just wonderful. The handsome Scot turns out to be a suicidal Jesus freak, and Sonny and the dreadlocked dude are ready to set up a podium and shout hallelujah up and down the beach.

And one thing made the moment even worse. She looked at Irina, expecting the poor girl to be in the process of curling up, armadillo style, at this brash display of religious histrionics. But what she saw instead was her innocent young pupil, looking from one to the other of these two men, as if she had just heard the answer to all of the world's ills.

This would not do.

Ten

In the dark hour before dawn, Teresa finally gave up on sleep. Maybe the problem was the unfamiliar bed, but that certainly never kept her from sleeping when she was on tour professionally. Nevertheless, she was wide awake now and didn't have time to bore herself back to sleep before the girls awoke. She figured she might as well get up.

The sunrise peeked over the horizon by the time she tidied herself up and fixed a pot of coffee. The coffee beans smelled toasty and fresh—must have been left by the last tenants—and there were enough already ground to make a pot without having to wake the girls. They would need to do a grocery run today, though. She didn't really want to cook much this week, but they needed some breakfast items, at least.

She stepped outside to relax on the front porch and felt a renewal of energy just smelling the cool morning air from the ocean. The only sound, beyond the breaking waves, was the squeak of seagulls searching for breakfast. She saw Julian sitting on the seawall beyond the boardwalk. When she pulled one of the wrought iron chairs away from the table, she made enough noise that he looked in her direction.

Shoot. He smiled and waved. She should probably go exchange a few pleasantries with him. Though she was too tired to be "on" this morning, she ran her hand over her hair and sauntered over.

"You must have gotten up even earlier than I did." She sat on the wall next to him and noticed he held a cup of coffee too.

"Sometimes I get up early enough to watch the sunrise," he said. "But our sunsets are even more spectacular. Oh, I imagine you already know that. You said you were from Oakland, didn't you? You probably get to the beach often enough."

"Yes. But you live here year round, is that right? With...your family?"

"No. Rather, yes, I live here year round. Have done for years. But not with my family. My son and daughter are adults now with their own families." He smiled. "And I'm a grandfather. Quite a blessing."

No mention of the little woman. Widower? Divorced, maybe. "Then it's just you and Zeke here?" She cocked her head toward his house.

Julian chuckled. "Just me. Zeke lives in East County with his wife and child."

"So we're not likely to see him again this week."

"You never know with Zeke. He often seems to show up at the perfect moment."

Hmm. What was that supposed to mean? They seemed like such an unlikely duo. "And he's what, a friend? Oh, but you said you were his protégé—" She stopped abruptly, remembering where that line of conversation went yesterday. "Just a friend, is he?"

"And we work with each other, to an extent."

She tilted her head and gave him a crooked smile. "You work together, but Zeke lives in East County while you have this amazing beach home. Sounds as if you got the better end of that deal."

He had a nice smile, but she thought she saw a hint of chastisement in it just now. He glanced back at his home.

"You know, when I bought this place, I suppose you could say I was at the top of my game. I had rather a windfall as a result of some highly successful software designs I did. That's why I was able to afford such a comfortable home. But the price was higher than it should have been."

"You bought in a bad market?"

He shook his head. "Not all prices are monetary, are they?"

Ah. The suicidal tendencies. My, he was awfully forthcoming. Teresa certainly didn't find herself so open with relative strangers. Or with relatives, even.

Julian continued. "I achieved lofty goals, professionally, but my health and my family were casualties. I had a couple of heart attacks and lost my wife and kids." He looked out to the sea. "I've been forgiven for quite a lot."

Teresa's laugh was a short burst of breath. She had just *met* this guy. "You lay it all out there, don't you?"

When he turned to her, he looked as if he found himself as amusing as she did. "I do, yes. When your neighbors only live next door for a week or two, you tend to dispense with small talk and dive right into the substance of life, I suppose."

She sipped her coffee, which was already too cool. She didn't like the fact that she wouldn't feel odd right now, blurting out something entirely too personal for this man to hear. Why should she tell him anything, if she had managed to keep her missteps to herself all these years? She shouldn't.

"What's your family situation, Teresa?"

In an uncharacteristically spastic move, she tipped her coffee mug too quickly and completely missed her mouth. It was as if she had deliberately poured her coffee down the front of her shirt and into her lap. She yelped and jumped off of the sea wall and landed in the sand. In a ridiculously pointless gesture, she held her empty coffee mug away from her body.

Julian jumped down directly after she did. "Are you all right? Are you burned?"

"No, no, I'm fine." She looked down at herself. "What a dolt." When she looked back at Julian and saw his kind concern, she laughed softly. "Really. My coffee had cooled off too much to drink."

He gestured toward her clothing. "Ah. Well, this makes sense, then."

She laughed, and he did too. Behind his glasses, he had marvelous brown eyes, which crinkled at the corners. Despite his ability to make her feel unsettled, she thought she liked this man just fine.

"I should go change. The girls are probably up by now, anyway."

He checked his watch. "Right. And I need to take off for church soon. Maybe we'll chat later."

He easily pulled himself back over the low wall and onto the boardwalk. He helped Teresa do the same.

Before she got too far away, he called out again. "I'll be boogie boarding later, if any of you are interested. There are boards in the storage shed there." He pointed toward her house.

"Okay, I'll mention it." She waved and turned away again. It occurred to her that her spill had happened at the perfect moment, if it had to happen at all. Otherwise, either Julian would eventually talk about suicide and Jesus, or she would talk about things she had no intention of discussing with anyone.

Of course, Sonny would probably say the spill hadn't been an accident at all. Such Freudian nonsense. As if Teresa would deliberately pour coffee down her shirtfront to escape an emotionally intimate moment.

She had managed to escape such moments all of her adult life. She didn't need to ruin a perfectly good outfit to pull that off.

Eleven

Sonny finished stretching, her muscles loose and warm. She stood at her dresser mirror and pulled her hair into a ponytail. A quick adjustment of her sports bra and straightening of her shorts, and she was nearly set for her morning run. Before she strapped her iPod to her arm, she chose her "Worship Instrumental" playlist, so no lyrics would distract her thoughts.

A nod at her reflection in the mirror. "Ready."

Someone came in the front door. Before Sonny finished tying her shoes, she heard her mother shut her bedroom door.

She tapped at her mother's door and spoke softly, in case Irina was still asleep down the hall. "Hey, Mom, I'm going for a quick jog on the beach. I'll only be maybe thirty minutes."

"Yeah, okay." Sonny heard her opening a dresser drawer. "I need to wash up and change. I spilled coffee on myself, like a klutz. We'll get breakfast after you come back."

Sonny was pleased to see very few people on the beach this early. Since she would miss church today, she planned to spend the next thirty minutes in quiet time with God. The fewer diversions, the better. Her music would simply set the mood.

She loved running on the beach in the morning, before the heat became too intense, but she knew better than to make the run a long one. Too many long runs on the deceptively uneven sand had given her problems with her ankles several years ago. So she would treat the few beach runs she took this week the same as she treated chocolate—one of her loves, but enjoyed in cautious moderation.

Fifteen minutes into her run, she broke a good sweat. She turned back toward the beach house. She had prayed for guidance and an understanding attitude this week, and now she would cease praying and simply keep her mind open for anything God might want to drop in there.

She wasn't always aware of any great communication from God during times like this, and sometimes she would suddenly realize her mind had latched onto some thought and run with it. She was seldom sure whether her mind had wandered there or if God wanted her to think on that particular subject, but she didn't worry about that anymore. She knew from experience that her days simply progressed more smoothly when she began them with Him in this fashion.

She slowed to a walk once she reached the seawall and boardwalk in front of the beach house. She found the porch roomy enough for her to stop and stretch her legs. When she pulled her earbuds loose, the whoosh of the ocean waves filled her ears.

Sonny kicked the sand, and then her shoes, from her feet before she walked back into the house. She heard a blow-dryer running, either in her mother's room or the bathroom. A quick splash of water at the kitchen sink would tide her over until she could get in the shower.

She heard a quick knock at the side door, just off of the kitchen.

Before she could take a step toward the door, it opened, tentatively. A blond head eased in.

"Hello?"

Sonny chuckled. "Mom, what are you doing? I thought you were back there in the—"

The feeling of disorientation was swift and shocking. This was her mom. Yet not her mom. Same blond hair, but fuller, in loose curled waves. Same face, but with more natural color, the way she would expect her mother to look after a few more days here in the sun. Dressed in a more casual, less designer, style of clothing.

The woman smiled politely, and then her grin grew wide. "You're Sonny, aren't you?"

For a moment Sonny said nothing. Of course this was Aunt Melanie. The private investigator had told Sonny she looked just like Teresa's picture. Still, Sonny would have thought someone would have warned her about this.

She heard a sudden absence of sound. What was it? The blow-dryer had stopped. A door opened. Sonny's eyes never left Melanie's face, even when Melanie's attention turned to someone else entering the room.

Sonny finally spoke, whispering in a tone befitting a secret more than two decades old. She turned to see her startled mother. "Mom, you never told me."

Then she looked back at her aunt. "Nobody told me you were twins."

Twelve

For a moment Melanie stopped breathing. She may have stopped blinking, as well. She was only aware of the utter strangeness of seeing her sister after twenty-five years and seeing how much she had changed. And yet she looked as familiar as the face in Melanie's mirror.

Melanie forced herself to speak. She looked at Sonny, her niece who barely knew about her. Her niece who didn't even know her mother was a twin. "Twins, yes," Melanie said. "Identical." And then she recognized the clarifier as inane—obviously they were identical. She looked back at Teresa, who appeared completely disoriented.

"Hello, Teresa."

No answer.

"I take it you weren't expecting me." Melanie looked at Sonny and widened her eyes slightly.

Sonny went immediately to her mother but stopped short of actually touching her. The poor girl looked as anxious as a trapped felon. "Mom, I'm sorry. This was my idea. I just couldn't take the secrets anymore."

Melanie watched them. Teresa turned her head toward Sonny and looked at her as if she were a stranger, or as if Sonny had rendered her mute through some unimaginable feat. Then she looked back at Melanie, swallowed audibly, and spoke on an exhaled breath.

"Melanie."

A door at Melanie's side opened, and a tall, beautiful girl walked out of a small bedroom, rubbing her eyes. She smiled at Melanie.

"Morning. I slept late. Sorry." She walked past Melanie and into the kitchen.

"That's…okay." Melanie wasn't sure what else to say.

The girl got herself a glass of water from the sink and looked up at Sonny and Teresa as she drank.

"Irina." Sonny gestured toward Melanie. "This is my Aunt Melanie."

Irina looked from Sonny to Teresa and frowned. She drew the glass away from her lips. Then she swiftly shifted her eyes to Melanie and back at Teresa. With a thud, her glass dropped the last few inches into the sink. She blinked several times.

"Wow."

Melanie almost laughed when Sonny nodded vehemently at Irina. "I *know!*" Her eyes wide, she blurted with indignation. "They're *twins!*"

But Teresa was so still and hard to read, Melanie was certain laughter was out of line.

"Look, Aunt Melanie," Sonny said, "let me show you to your room. It's this way." She stepped back and beckoned Melanie toward her.

Melanie looked directly at Teresa before deciding her next move. "Teresa? Is that all right with you?"

Teresa appeared startled and then quickly composed. "With me? Of course it's all right with me. Make yourself comfortable."

As Melanie approached her, in order to follow Sonny, Teresa turned away, toward the windows, and looked out at the beach.

Well. This wasn't uncomfortable at all.

But Sonny's expression was full of pleading, so Melanie followed her back to the bedrooms. Still, Sonny spoke as if all was well, possibly in an effort to convince others that was the case.

"I'm in the Asian bedroom, and Mom's in the desert one. Irina wanted the little country-themed room near the kitchen, so that leaves the seaside one available." She pushed the door open to reveal pale blue walls and an abundance of shells and ocean pictures in the room. "But I'll be happy to trade with you if—"

They heard a door slam. They both glanced in the direction of the living room before looking back at each other.

"This room is fine, Sonny. Go check on your mom."

"I think I will." Sonny took two steps and stopped. "You're sure the room is all right?"

Melanie gave her the most assuring smile she could muster. "It's perfect."

Sonny returned the smile and then ran toward the living room.

Melanie put her suitcase on the bed and sank down beside it with a sigh.

"Perfect."

Thirteen

Sonny was nearly at the side door when the anxiety in Irina's voice stopped her.

"Sonny, wait!"

Irina stood in her bedroom doorway. She almost looked as if she had hurt herself, or as if she were cold. She gripped her elbows and scrunched her shoulders stiffly forword.

"I'll be with you in a minute, Irina," Sonny said, reaching for the door.

But Irina's tension was hard to ignore. "You should wait, I think."

Sonny stopped and turned, her heart still beating swiftly. She didn't have time for this. What did Irina know about anything? A shy, probably privileged, diva whose greatest problem involved sharing her perfect voice with adoring fans in a month or so. Her very presence here had probably ratcheted up the stress between the Miller women by a few degrees.

"Irina, I need to go after my mother. You have no idea what she's done to me."

If Irina were in physical pain, she couldn't have looked less comfortable. "I think your mother lied to you. All your life, maybe?"

Sonny sucked in her breath so quickly her chest hurt. To hear a near stranger describe her circumstances so clearly, so easily—how obvious must her pain be? Had others seen it so plainly?

"Has she...did she ever tell *you* anything about my past? My family history?" Sonny readied for the answer, knowing how betrayed she would feel if Irina knew more than she did.

"No. We don't know each other to talk like that." Irina glanced in the direction of Melanie's bedroom. "But your aunt. You didn't even know your aunt and your mother were twins? And your mother, she avoids your aunt's eyes." She studied the floor. "Family is too important for such...deception."

So, even the protégée was savvier about these things than Sonny's mother was.

"Well, you can understand, then, why I need to go talk to her." She started for the door again.

"But maybe it's good for her to be alone right now. To calm down. And to think."

"Right. To figure out how she can get out of this jam is more like it. To continue avoiding me."

"Or to think about what's at stake."

Sonny stopped still. Now that was quite a thought. Maybe her mother wasn't angry at being tricked, so much as afraid of what would happen next. Surely there were reasons she had avoided her sister all these years. And now that Melanie was here, those reasons might come to light.

Did her mom actually think Sonny would disown her because of anything Melanie might divulge? Sonny couldn't imagine any secret being that horrible.

She wouldn't go after her. She would try to wait for her mother to come back on her own, once she'd had some time to think, as Irina said. Considering her mother's past behavior, Sonny could only hope she wasn't already on her way back to Oakland.

As if she had followed Sonny's thoughts, Irina said, "She left everything here when she walked out. She didn't take her purse, car keys, nothing. She'll come back."

Sonny sat on an afghan-covered couch in the living room. Its cushions were soft, and it formed around her like a pillow. "You're right. I'll wait."

Irina's posture remained tight, despite her success in convincing Sonny to stay. She perched on the edge of a chair near the couch, her hands clenched together at her knees. "I was adopted when I was ten. From Russia."

Sonny sat up straight. Well, now. That was kind of random. Or maybe not. "You're Russian?" Actually, now that she thought of it, Sonny had noticed a slight accent every once in a while. Something a little different about how Irina phrased things at times.

Irina nodded. "My brother and I, we were both adopted. My brother is twenty-four, a year older than I am."

"So you were both adopted by the same family? Did you grow up together? Here? In the United States, I mean?"

Irina spoke toward her lap. "Yes, for the last thirteen years. Our father was in prison in Krasnodar since we were very young. I was just a baby then. I don't remember him at all."

"Whoa."

"I was five when our mother died, and there was no one to take care of us. We lived in the orphanage until we were adopted by my mother and father. An American couple." She looked up. "I can't remember my Russian mother's face anymore."

"You don't even have pictures of her?"

A minor shrug of one shoulder. "Maybe a picture existed when we first went to the orphanage. But not anymore."

Sonny said it again. "Whoa, Irina. I'm sorry."

"You did nothing wrong," Irina said, smiling shyly at her.

"Yeah, I know. But, man, four years ago I was so eager to go to college, to get away from Oakland, because I was sick of my mother being so—" She stopped and smiled back at Irina. "I think you know how, um, involved she can be."

Irina's smile traveled up to the corners of her eyes, but she said nothing.

"And by comparison, I mean, there you were, torn from your parents so early in life, living in an orphanage—"

"This is why I say how important family is. And honesty. I know what happened to my Russian parents. I know my birth father remains in prison. I know my mother died. And I know my adoptive parents loved me enough to travel from the other side of the world to make me their child. Me and my brother. And we are all very close. But how can you be close if you don't know anything about each other?"

Sonny nodded and ran her finger along a pattern on the afghan. "Yeah. My mother knows all about me, so I guess she thinks she's close enough with me. But not only don't I know much about her—not her history, anyway—I don't know much about myself. She doesn't want me to know."

Irina sighed and almost made Sonny laugh when she parroted what Sonny had said to her. "Wow, Sonny. I'm sorry."

They met eyes, and something clicked. A new camaraderie had been forged. Both of them smiled when Sonny said, "You did nothing wrong."

"Yes, I know. But your mother invited me here—she almost kidnapped me, Sonny—at the last minute. I think she brought me so I would interfere with your intimate time with her. I don't think that was very nice. So maybe I did nothing wrong." One well-defined eyebrow rose. "But you let me know if I should."

Fourteen

Teresa stormed along the boardwalk at a speed incongruous to everyone else around her.

She couldn't care less if she stood out. It was doubtful any of these people had just faced an intervention on this lovely Sunday morning. Somehow she wasn't up to casual strolling or window-shopping or smoothie-sipping.

Although she was thirsty, actually. She had likely lost all of her excess bodily hydration in the cold sweat she broke into as soon as she saw Melanie. She stopped at the first drink stand she came to.

"Let me have a large lemonade, please." She realized she was hungry too. But she told Sonny they would all get breakfast together. Of course "all" suddenly carried more weight. Now "all" would probably have to include Melanie. Twenty-five years of separation and then, "Let's do breakfast!" It was like inviting a ghost to join you or something. Like entering the witness protection program, only to join your old nemesis for tea twenty-five years later. How was Teresa going to get herself out of this strange mess?

"That's two fifty, please," the girl behind the counter said, pushing the tall, striped cup across to Teresa.

It dawned on Teresa that she had walked out without her purse. She blew out her breath as if someone else were responsible for her situation. "Ugh. I've forgotten my purse."

A second's worth of frown crossed over the girl's face before she regained her smile. "That's okay." But she pulled the cup back toward herself.

"But, you've already poured it. Couldn't I—"

"I'm sorry, but I can't give it to you, ma'am."

Ma'am? On top of everything, she was being called *ma'am*? She was only forty-six, for crying out loud. She felt her crow's feet multiplying as she stood there, baking under the morning sun.

A beautiful hand, with long dark fingers, placed a five-dollar bill on the counter. "I've got that, sister, and why don't you pour another for me?"

Teresa turned around to see the African-American fellow from the beach yesterday.

"Oh. It's you." She took her lemonade from the counter. "Thank you, uh, I'm sorry, I've forgotten—"

"Zeke."

"Zeke, yes. I'm sorry."

"Not to worry. I have the same problem. I call everyone sister or brother. Maybe you noticed."

Teresa chuckled. She couldn't imagine resorting to that and getting away with it, but it certainly fit this guy's persona.

"Since you called me sister, I'll go ahead and remind you. My name's Teresa."

"I appreciate the reminder. And where are the two young ladies this morning?"

She smiled at him crookedly. "Sonny and Irina."

"Those are the very ladies I mean." He pointed at her before he removed the cover from his lemonade and took a long drink.

"They're, um, back at the house."

"Didn't want to take a power walk with you today, I guess."

She frowned. "Power walk?"

"I saw you before you stopped for lemonade. You looked like a woman with a purpose. Very fast. Very forceful."

Great. Was he making a point? Asking for information? She didn't want to have this conversation. If she had just brought her purse with her, this wouldn't be happening right now.

In the midst of her silence, he spoke again. "But maybe you weren't planning on company. I should leave you." He gently patted her on the arm. "Have a blessed Sunday, sister." He gave her that brilliant smile and turned away, not a care in the world.

Which made her feel like total dirt.

"I'm sorry, uh, Zeke." She blurted it out, as if she wanted very much for him to stay. What was she doing? "I don't want to be alone."

She meant to say she didn't *need* to be alone. Now she sounded as needy as all get out. How did that happen?

"You have troubled eyes this morning, sister." He tilted his head, gave her a gentle smile, and somehow made her feel as if he were a wide-open place for her to fill with everything that bothered her.

She sighed and raised her arm in the direction of the beach house. "I have to go back. And I don't want to."

He simply nodded, waiting for more.

"My sister's there now."

"You don't get along with her?"

Teresa shrugged and tsked. "Hard to say. We haven't spoken for more than twenty years."

"Oh." He held that word for a full second, as if it were far more than two letters. "That's a great loss."

And it wasn't until he said it that she felt it. At once she fought against tears filling her eyes.

"Did she avoid you, Teresa?"

She couldn't look at him. She simply looked down and shook her head.

"You avoided her?"

How had he managed to make her voice so small? She had the strongest voice in the Oakland Symphony Chorus, but she spoke as if she had the timidity of a child. "Yes."

"Mmm. That would make it difficult to go back."

He completely understood. She could tell. Yet she didn't feel an iota of judgment on his part. He spoke again. So gently.

"Do you think it might get easier to face her, given time?"

She laughed sardonically. "Absolutely not. It will only get worse."

He said nothing.

That dog.

This time her sigh was a rueful, strongly vocal sound, delivered with half-lowered lids. "Okay, I get your point."

He grinned, but his grin pulled her in. This was a joke they shared, not a joke at her expense.

"I think, Teresa, you might be uncomfortable with my need to pray. But I wonder if you would indulge me. Just for a moment?"

Because of his comment, she actually felt free to say, "Oh, whatever. Let 'er rip." She knew there was always the chance he would go into some showy street preacher rant, but he seemed to sense how uneasy that would make her. He actually prayed quietly, almost as if he were speaking to her.

"Father, give my sister Teresa peace. And courage. And hope. Thank You, Lord."

And that was it.

"Well," she said, "that was painless."

His smile was radiant. "Nothing painful about praying, sister. Anytime. Anywhere. In your own style. It's a gift like no other."

She didn't know what to say to that.

"I'll say goodbye to you, Teresa." Zeke lifted his cup as a salute and ambled away.

"Bye." As an afterthought, she called out to him. "I would have thought you'd be in church this morning."

He faced her and smiled, with a slight lift of his hands and a quick glance around. "I *am* in church."

She watched him for a moment after he left. Odd man. But nice enough.

Then she turned back toward the beach house. Might as well get this over with.

In a complete elimination of melodrama, she realized she needed to go to the bathroom. Doggoned lemonade. She might be a minor celebrity in Oakland, but here in Mission Beach she was plain old Teresa Miller, with the same basic needs as everyone else. She might as well start humbling herself before she got back to that peculiar little house on Oceanfront Walk.

Fifteen

Sonny spotted her mother before her mother spotted her. Teresa wasn't stomping or walking in that frankly aggressive way she did when she was angry or deprived of her own way. That could be a good sign.

Sonny had asked Irina and Melanie if they would mind taking a walk or waiting in the house so she could sit on the porch and try to talk privately with her mother when she returned.

"I need to shower anyway," Irina said.

Melanie poured a cup of coffee and headed toward her room. "Sure, that's fine. I'll check in with my husband. And I'll finish unpacking, if you think there's a point."

"Absolutely there's a point," Sonny said, crossing her arms over her chest. "This week is happening." Then her voice lessened. "Even if Mom decides not to stay."

Now she watched as her mother looked up and met her eyes. Impossible to read. No smoke coming out of her ears, but certainly no humor or openness in her facial expression.

Should Sonny talk first? Yes. She was an adult. She should take control. What would a good counselor say? Nothing defensive, that's for sure.

"Mom, I had no choice."

Man. That right there? That was defensive.

"I mean, I think we should talk before going inside, don't you?"

Her mother stepped onto the porch. She smoothed her hand down the back of her hair, a gesture Sonny recognized as a nervous one. The motion always allowed her mother to break eye contact.

So Sonny stood her ground and waited. Her mother would have to look back eventually.

When she did, her expression was prim and pursed. "I have to say, I'm disappointed in you, Sonny. I think you've shown me a great disrespect in luring me down here under false pretenses."

Really? Sonny tried to let the remark flow past her without feeling rattled. But the non-rattling didn't quite make it to her mouth.

"I could say the same—showing disrespect, I mean—about your bringing Irina down here, uninvited."

Now there was a brief stomp. "I had a perfectly good reason to bring her here. She needed some special tutoring for her solos—"

"Right now. Immediately. This week." Sonny crossed her arms over her chest again.

"Yes, and the girl's skittish as a colt. She needed to relax."

"How's that working out so far, do you think?"

"And who's fault is that? I think you, Irina, and I were getting along pretty well until this morning's arrival."

Sonny almost started crying, her sigh brimmed so full of emotion. "Mom, this week was supposed to be your graduation gift to me."

Her mother pointed toward the house, stiff-armed, as if she were the doom-portending Ghost of Christmas Future. "Not that! *That* was not part of my gift!"

Sonny mimicked the gesture. "*That* is your sister. Your twin! And twenty-five years is long enough to hold a grudge, don't you think? What are you afraid of? Are either of you homicidal? I really don't think so. And I'm sick to death of—"

She was about to mention her desire to know her family history. But she suddenly knew that asking for anything beyond reconciliation would be asking for too much. For now, anyway.

"I'm sick of not knowing her. And I'm sick of your refusal to acknowledge her."

More lip pursing. But Sonny felt she was wearing her down.

"Mom, she came here knowing you'd be here."

"Oh, so you gave *her* enough information to make a choice."

"Mom! Listen to what I'm telling you. She did make the choice. *You* were the draw for Aunt Melanie. Not me. Not so much, anyway." She flopped into one of the wrought iron chairs, feeling drained.

Her mother drew in, and released, a big breath. "Well. I'd be a fool to just leave and let her tell you her side of the story, unfettered."

Sonny carefully raised her eyebrows and was certain she looked like a sad hound dog. "That's a start, anyway." The story! They were going to tell her the story! She forced herself to remain seated.

Her mother regarded her with a what-am-I-going-to-do-with-you expression that made Sonny smile. With caution.

"So, can we go in and start over?" Sonny stood and reached for the doorknob.

"Start over." With a tsk, her mother nodded once before she tugged her shirt straight, a gesture apparently necessary before squaring off with Melanie. "All right. I suppose we can try."

Sonny opened the door, so excited she wanted to jump up and down. For just a moment she remembered the scene in *The Wizard of Oz* when Judy Garland survived the tornado and opened the door to a fantastic world of Technicolor and amazing events.

She shook off her next thought, that there were a few wicked witches and creepy monkey creatures to deal with there, as well.

Sixteen

Back in her room, Melanie had run out of ways to kill time. She simply couldn't straighten her clothing in the dresser any longer. Her shorts and shirts were so tidy she felt like an obsessive-compulsive boot camp private.

She had already chatted with Bailey to the point he clearly wanted her to hang up so he could get back to his man-cave activities.

"It's all going to work out just fine," he told her. "This is your strong suit, honey. You have the most calming attitude of anyone I know." And then he yawned so loudly she was able to picture him as if he were right in front of her.

"Bailey Hines, you do not tell a woman she's 'calming' and then yawn as if you're about to give Rip Van Winkle a run for his money. I feel like the most boring woman on earth right now."

He chuckled. "Micah and I had Italian for lunch after you left. I just need a pasta nap, that's all. You come on home and I'll show you how boring I think you are."

She grinned. "I *am* tempted. You sound like much more fun than what I'm facing here."

"That's what a husband likes to hear." And then he yawned again.

"Okay, Casanova, I'm going to hang up before my ego gets ruffled."

"Hurry home, sweetheart. I miss you."

She ended the call and looked around her little bedroom for the millionth time.

She couldn't study the seashell pictures another minute. It was time to venture back into the living room. She shouldn't make this a bigger deal than it was. Yes, so far the beach house was as comfy as a gathering of Hollywood ex-wives. But if she was honestly considering her church's job offer to head women's ministries, she needed to be the outgoing one. And probably the forgiving one.

She found Irina on the couch, chewing her thumbnail.

"Would you mind some company?" Melanie asked.

Irina looked up and labored to relax her frown.

"Please." She presented the other side of the couch with her upraised palm. She was rather regal, actually. A lovely girl, even though she was a little on the thin side.

It wasn't until Melanie sat down that she realized she could hear some of the conversation going on between Sonny and Teresa, out on the porch. She'd have to stand at the window to see anything, but she did hear Teresa's voice rise as she said something like, "*That* was not part of my—" something, followed by Sonny's raised voice. "*That* is your sister!"

Melanie grimaced and looked at Irina.

Irina nodded. "Don't feel too bad. They were talking about me before."

"Oh, this is awful." Melanie stood. "We don't want to hear this." She went into the kitchen and turned on the water full blast. She started looking in the cabinets, letting the doors close loudly.

"Ah!" She pulled out the coffee grinder. "I think it would be a good idea to grind some coffee beans right now." More searching. "If I can just find some coffee beans. Or maybe I could grind something else. Maybe…" She cast her gaze around the kitchen and living room. "Seashells?"

Irina smiled. "Or we could just turn on the CD player."

"Well, there you go. Beautiful *and* a genius."

Irina flipped through some CDs in a small case near the player. "Which one should we play?"

"The loud one." Melanie hurried over to help, but then the front door opened.

Sonny and Teresa walked in, and all four women froze, facing each other, for the longest second in time.

Sonny shut the door behind Teresa. "Um…we're going to give this another try, guys. Okay?"

One-syllable responses tripped all over each other, and then the room fell cavernously still, save the rush of water, still running full blast in the kitchen sink.

Sonny went over to the sink to turn it off. "We can just take this slowly," she said. "We don't need this week to be a melodrama or some massive pain fest, okay? No Jerry Springer stuff."

Melanie liked the sound of that. She wondered if she should attempt to hug Teresa, but it just didn't feel like the right thing to do at the moment. They would be like a couple of tin soldiers. From opposite sides of the war.

Then her stomach growled, and she embraced the inspiration. "How about we go get some brunch?"

Sonny and Irina talked at once.

"I'm starving!"

"Yes, definitely!"

Everyone turned to Teresa, who still seemed to be outside looking in.

She cocked her head toward the bedroom hall. "I need to use the facilities before we go."

It may have been Melanie's imagination, but she was certain she heard a collective sigh of relief the moment the bathroom door closed.

⌒

They didn't exactly look like the Four Musketeers as they walked down the boardwalk—no All-for-One-and-One-for-All joviality to their steps. But the fact that they were walking side by side enabled them to talk without looking directly at each other. In Melanie's opinion, the lack of eye contact helped.

She couldn't bring herself to say anything to Teresa directly. The few words they shared when they first saw each other this morning felt as if they happened long ago. The hesitation wasn't a refusal on Melanie's part; she simply felt awkward after all these years. So she asked questions of the young ones, instead, and hoped a full-group conversation would naturally ensue after a while, like slow water seeping over the edge of a dam.

"What brings you to the beach house this week, Irina? Are you a college friend of Sonny's?"

Teresa said something then—it was so swift, it might not have been an entire word—and then she closed her mouth and glanced at Irina, as if turning the floor over to her.

"No, I'm a…a friend, I suppose, of Teresa's. Or, not a friend so much—"

"You're a friend." Teresa announced it so abruptly that it sounded as if she didn't want Irina to give any more information than that. Irina must have gotten the same sense, because she sputtered slightly before falling silent.

Sonny looked from Irina to Teresa before explaining to Melanie. "Mom's giving Irina some help preparing for her solos, which is coming up in a month or so."

"Solos?" Melanie looked at Irina, willing her to speak again. They couldn't *all* lean on Sonny to carry the day. "So you sing?"

"Yes. Soprano. With the Oakland Symphony Chorus." The girl shot a glance at Teresa before speaking in a tense whisper. "But I don't want to sing right now, if you don't mind."

"Who, me?" Melanie wasn't actually certain to whom Irina spoke, but the poor girl acted like a kicked cat. "That's fine with me, sweetie. I wouldn't dream of asking you to just burst out in song like that—"

Sonny caught her eye and subtly ran her hand across her throat in a "cut" gesture, her eyes wide.

Uh-oh. Might have stepped on a little mine there.

"But, uh, I think it's wonderful you're gifted enough to be singing solos already at your age. What are you, about nineteen?"

She saw alarm in Irina's eyes. "I'm twenty-three!"

Melanie erupted in a nervous laugh. She was the prime example of charm here this morning, wasn't she? She vividly remembered those days when you wanted to look your age or older. But Irina was so coltish, it didn't occur to Melanie that she—oh, whatever.

"I'm sorry, Irina. Of course you're older than nineteen. You're just so, um, you have such perfect skin, and—"

Sonny spoke quickly. "I heard her sing yesterday for the first time. She has a gorgeous voice." She pointed as they neared a corner. "Hey, I saw a bistro down this street when I drove to the house yesterday. Called the Boardwalk Bistro. Looks nice, serves breakfast, and they have tables outside. Everyone game for the extended walk?"

At this point Melanie was game for anything that would keep her feet busy and out of her mouth.

Teresa spoke, a smile emerging. "That sounds perfect, baby."

Oh, sure, now she speaks. Now she smiles. Now that Melanie's knocked herself down a few pegs. Despite herself, Melanie felt old competitive feelings arise. Mercy, she hadn't experienced that for twenty-five years.

⌒

Melanie found herself impressed with Sonny during their meal. Of course, she wasn't sure how much of Sonny's confidence was based on reality, and how much on youthful idealism, but it was nice to have someone else talking.

"I'm just going to spill this right out," Sonny said. She didn't exclude Irina, but it was clear she addressed Melanie and Teresa. "This is obviously a difficult way to start a week together. After all, we're trying to undo more than two decades of silence."

"Are we?" Teresa's voice dripped with condescension.

Melanie struggled with more long-past emotions. She actually moved her water glass out of the way, as if she might lose control over her hand any minute and toss the cold water at her snarky sister.

But Sonny simply looked at Teresa and spoke with a gentle, pleading tone. "Well, I hope so, anyway. And I'm hoping you'll indulge me and let me try some of the counseling techniques I've been taught so far."

Even Melanie had to keep from groaning at that. How adept could Sonny be at this early stage in her studies?

Plus, through her volunteering in the church office, Melanie had seen some of the people who had come and gone for counseling sessions with the staff. She had noticed her share of couples obviously composed of one spouse hoping for progress and the other manipulating sessions into nothing more than pointless debates. She could see it in their expressions when they left the office—disappointment in one face, smug victory in the other. She knew healing could be achieved, but both parties had to be willing to grow.

Sonny spoke again. "You know, you'd both be helping me too. I mean, it would be great if I could start grad school with some practical experience under my belt."

As if they had both heard a starter gun, Melanie and Teresa spoke at once and rapidly. Melanie wasn't sure what Teresa said, but it had to be similar to Melanie's intent.

"I'd be happy to help."

Sonny smiled. "Thanks."

At least *one* of the musketeers had found something to smile about.

Seventeen

"Man, when I'm a licensed counselor, I'm going to have to see if I can always work under these conditions." Sonny sat back comfortably in her beach chair and adjusted her sunglasses before giving Melanie a grin. The heat had ratcheted up, but the waves drove a soothing breeze over them. This was definitely less stressful than brunch had been.

Melanie returned Sonny's smile. "Yeah, I guess if I have to undergo counseling, this is the way to go." She took a drink from her water bottle and stretched her legs out in front of her.

"I'm not saying you need counseling, Aunt Melanie—"

"You know, you can just call me Melanie, if you like, Sonny. You're old enough."

"I know. But I'm not sure I *want* to drop the title. It's not as if I've addressed anyone as 'Aunt Someone' in the past. Ever."

"All right, then, we'll leave that up to you. Didn't mean to interrupt you. I think you were about to tell me how glaringly sane I seem."

"Let's not get carried away, now," Sonny said, chuckling. "It's just that I think everyone can get some good out of a little guided self-reflection once in a while. And I just thought a few exercises to help you and Mom… loosen up? I thought that might be a good idea."

She sensed a moment of hesitation on Melanie's part.

"Are you all right, Aunt Melanie?"

"Sure, sure." Melanie looked at her toes, pushing them into the sand. "But I do think I should make one thing a little clearer."

"Okay." Sonny lifted her yellow note pad from her lap. She could feel the sunblock on her legs melting onto the pad's cardboard backing. She saw the care with which Melanie chose her next words.

"Sonny, I don't think I told you yet that I'm a Christian."

Sonny felt a lift in her face. "I thought so! Me too!"

"Yes?" Melanie studied her, as if seeking more information.

"Yeah! Some of the friends I made at college were involved with Campus Crusade for Christ."

She saw an instant relaxation in Melanie's expression. Those must have been the words she needed to hear.

"Ah. Good. I was a little concerned when you said we were going to do a guided whatever it was you said—"

"Guided self-reflection."

"Yes, that's it. I have nothing against self-reflection, don't get me wrong. I just wanted to make sure we weren't going to go into the lotus pose and start channeling Shirley MacLaine or something."

Sonny laughed. "No." She stopped and frowned. "Wait. Shirley *who*?"

Melanie tilted back her head. "Oh, Sonny, you make your aunt feel old."

"Sorry." Sonny smiled. "But, you're not old at all!" She saw the twinkle in Melanie's eye when she looked at her. She loved this lady. Already loved her.

"That's another thing," Melanie said. "It's not just that I don't want to do the New Age religion thing. There's no way my legs will go anywhere *near* the lotus position. I'll break something for sure."

"I think you're safe with me, then." Sonny took a drink from her water bottle. "I am going to ask you to visualize something, but it's a simple psychological exercise. This is all focused on you, not some altered state. I'm not about that stuff either." She wiped the sweat from her forehead. "But you know what? I'd love to take a quick jump in the water first. I'm getting a little toasty."

"Race you down." Melanie was already up and running before Sonny set her writing pad down and followed. She chuckled. Her aunt was anything but old.

They ran far enough into the water to dive in. Sonny flipped onto her back and floated for a moment. She loved the beach and the way the waves momentarily washed away her worries. The unique, undulating motion always triggered enjoyable memories from past beach trips. Her mother hadn't brought her to the beach very often when she was a child, so her memories of the ocean were usually about other people. Not that the memories involving her mom weren't good, but—

"Don't float away, young lady!" Melanie called out to her before heading back to their chairs.

Sonny joined her. She needed to get this psychological exercise done, especially if her mom watched them from the beach house. She had acted annoyed that Melanie would have time alone with Sonny before she did. But Sonny had privately assured her she wasn't going to ask Melanie anything about the past just yet. Irina had helped by requesting that Teresa work with her on her solos, which brought the conflict to a close.

Still, Sonny wasn't sure what to expect from her mother this week. And she didn't want Irina to have to run interference any more than absolutely necessary. Irina obviously didn't do well with stress. Sonny was almost certain she heard her losing her lunch in the bathroom after they returned from the bistro.

Melanie handed Sonny's towel to her when she approached. "That was an excellent idea, Sonny. I feel completely refreshed and ready to bare my every secret to you. Now's your big chance."

Sonny patted her legs dry and took up her notepad. "No confessions today." She sat next to Melanie. "This will probably be easier for you if you close your eyes. I don't want you distracted by any studly beach hunks or frisky schools of dolphins."

Melanie closed her eyes and chuckled. "Feel free to let the beach hunks stroll by, but I expect you to alert me to any dolphins, frisky or otherwise. There are some things I'm simply not willing to give up even for the sake of science."

"Got it. I just want you to relax and picture yourself strolling down a road. No road in particular."

"Give me a second. Okay. Got my road."

"Now, as you walk, you come upon a house. Take a look at the outside of it as you get closer. What do you notice? Give me some details, starting at the front and working your way around."

Melanie paused, took a deep breath and released it. "All right. It's a well-tended place. There are lovely flower beds in front, a manicured lawn, and a pretty little white picket fence."

"How about the house itself?"

"It's not terribly fancy, more smallish and cozy, like a cottage. Painted brick—a creamy color—with a honey brown shingled roof. And a chimney."

"Any windows?"

"Um, yes, one on either side of the front door. With shutters the same color as the roof."

Sonny wrote quickly. She was loving this. She took a quick glance at the paperwork she brought with her. She had never actually done this exercise with anyone before.

"Is that all?" Melanie spoke into the silence.

"No, hang on a second. Don't peek."

"This isn't some elaborate joke, is it? You're not slowly burying me in the sand while you distract me, right? Promise me, if I doze off, you won't stick anything up my nose."

"Get back to the house, Aunt Melanie!"

"Oh, sorry!" Melanie snorted with laughter.

Sonny couldn't help smiling. Had she really just met this woman this morning? Whoa. How comfortable was *she* to be around? "Okay, now walk around the house and tell me what you see."

Melanie shrugged. "More of the same, really. Nothing different on the sides, just windows. Maybe a door down to a basement. But still, there are lots of colorful flowers and landscaping. And the back has a good-sized yard—"

"Still fenced, or no?"

"Fenced...yes. And there's a paved patio with plenty of seating for friends, a grill, and, instead of a sliding glass door, pretty French doors."

"Uh-huh. Let's go back to the front of the house and go in. You said there was a front door, right?"

"Well, sure."

"What does the door look like? Wood? Glass? What color?"

"Solid wood. Stained brown—you know, like oak—to match the roof and shutters."

"Go on in and tell me what you see."

Melanie rested her hands together in her lap. "It's lived in but tidy. Soft colors on the walls. The furniture is along antique lines. Pretty rugs on hardwood floors—"

Sonny watched her closely. "Oh, you just found a secret door."

"I did?"

"Yep. To a secret room. Open the door. Don't think too hard. Just tell me what you see."

Melanie frowned. "Hmm."

"What? What's in there?"

"Well, I know this sounds odd, but the first thing I saw…it's mostly empty, and dark, of course, but there's a…a vase in there. A flower vase. And it's broken."

Sonny jotted notes. "Shattered?"

"No, just broken. Into a few big pieces."

Sonny hoped she would be able to read her handwriting later. "Let's leave that room, walk back to the main part of the house, and then go out the door. Go back onto the road, walk away, and stop to glance back for one last look at the house."

Melanie nodded with each of Sonny's last instructions.

"Okay," Sonny said. "We're done."

Melanie seemed sleepy when she looked at Sonny. She blinked a few times and opened her eyes wide, as if she were stretching them. "Well, you said I might relax a little. I could have dozed off without much trouble." She turned to Sonny with more attentiveness. "So. What's the verdict? Do I need my oil changed? Tires rotated?"

"I don't know yet." Sonny shrugged and laughed softly. "I haven't actually done this before. It didn't come up in my undergrad work. I need to check some of the materials I brought with me, and then I'll get back to you."

She glanced back toward the beach house, which caused Melanie to do the same. "I should get together with Mom now."

Melanie stood. "Maybe Irina and I can take a little exploratory walk up the boardwalk."

"That would be nice. I think she feels like she's intruding."

They folded their chairs and started back.

"We'll have to remedy that." Melanie gave Sonny a smile. "When you think of it, other than you and your mom, I doubt any of us feels they know the others very well."

Sonny nodded but found the comment interesting. Was Melanie unaware of how little her sister had shared with her niece? She didn't know her mom well at all. Not really.

She saw her mother at the front window for a moment and suppressed a sigh. Her relaxation ebbed slightly to make room for a familiar hint of tension.

It remained to be seen if this week would result in meaningful knowledge between Sonny and her mom. But, tense or not, Sonny was about to take the next step in that direction.

Eighteen

Oh, shoot. They were coming back. Teresa turned quickly from the window.

"Irina, I'm going to run out for some groceries. We don't even have milk for our coffee, and we need breakfast stuff, and maybe some fruit and a few munchies."

Irina had just walked out from putting her music back in her bedroom. "Do you want me to come?"

"No, no, I'll be fine on my own. You be here for them whenever they come back." Teresa dashed back to her room for her purse.

"Are you in a hurry?" Irina called to her from the living room. "Maybe we should wait for Sonny and—"

"Not necessary." Teresa rushed back out. "I saw a little market not too far away. We can always go back for more if anyone needs something else." She grabbed her keys from her purse and headed for the side door as Irina walked to the front window.

"Teresa, I see them coming, actually, so—"

But Teresa didn't hear what else Irina said, because she had already closed the door behind her. She practically ran to the car and pulled out.

She knew she was a coward, but she just couldn't do this right now. When she spied them from the front window, she saw how relaxed and happy Sonny seemed with Melanie. So, obviously, Melanie hadn't told her anything about their past. But whatever she did tell her had warmed Sonny up to her even more than she was before.

How could she compete with that?

She had no idea where she was driving. Just away. She pulled her cell phone from her purse and leaned over to open her glove compartment. She mumbled aloud. "Please be in there. Please be in there." And yes, she found her earpiece. She had already received one traffic ticket for using her phone while driving. She needed to take the time to plug the stupid earpiece in from now on.

She pressed speed dial to get her manager on the phone and sighed in relief when he picked up.

"Hey, Teresa girl, what's up? You enjoying your vay-cay?"

She would have to play this carefully. "Anton, it's great. You were right. I needed to take a few days off and bond with Sonny while she still wanted me to."

"Did I not guarantee you'd be glad you went? Am I not the greatest manager in the known free world? I look out for my girl."

Teresa rolled her eyes. "Right. You're the best. So, how are things going there?"

"Fantastic. A group of us caught a performance last night by that adorable little Korean girl who plays the dickens out of Chopin. The one who looks like a prettier version of Woody Allen's daughter-slash-wife? She was totally socks-knock-offable, Teresa. Great time."

"Uh-huh, that's good. Any crises?"

"It's Sunday, honey lamb. No crises allowed on Sunday unless we're performing, which we're not. You know that."

"Right. I'm on beach time. Forgot what day it was." Had it only been two days? How was she supposed to survive an entire week like this?

"Oh, but you know what's odd, Teresa?"

Her heartbeat picked up. An escape route, perhaps? "What? You need something?"

"I can't find Irina. She's not answering her cell or her home phone. You know how nervous she is about her solos coming up. I'm a little concerned."

Teresa pulled into the parking lot of a Denny's restaurant. If she continued to drive around at random, she would get herself lost. She needed to focus.

"I...um...actually, Irina is with me."

"What? At the beach? On your getaway with Sonny?"

She sighed. She did *not* need a lecture from her foppish, busybody manager. "I didn't have a choice, Anton. She seemed desperate to go with me. I think she sees me as a mother figure."

"You are shameless. You know who sees you as a mother figure? Your *daughter.* My mother would sacrifice her favorite manicurist for a week alone with me. Do you have any appreciation for how magnanimous a gesture it was for your twenty-two-year-old—"

"Twenty-four."

"What*ever.* For your grown daughter to offer to spend this primo quality time with you?"

"But that's just it, Anton. The quality of the time isn't as *primo* as you think. She invited my sister to come too, without warning me."

Dead silence.

"Anton?"

"Why don't I know you have a sister, Teresa? How long have we known each other?"

"Come on, now."

"Is that how little you trust me after all these years? This was no over-sight. All the soul-baring I've done with you, pouring my guts right out there, trusting you with my emotional *everything,* and you kept an entire sister secret?"

"But—"

"I even told you about my Botox injections, Teresa."

As if that hadn't been obvious. The weeks immediately after had been the only time she hadn't had to endure his superciliously arched eye-brows.

"Anton, I—"

"Big sister or little sister?"

Uh-oh, this was going to get ugly. And Anton had always been her staunchest defender. "Um, we're...twins." She readied herself for a verbal onslaught.

He spoke quietly, as if he were trying to keep a lid over what boiled within. "Twins. You've got this entire *As the World Turns* side to you, and you never saw fit to confide in me."

"It's not like that, Anton."

"I'm undone, Teresa. Positively undone."

"For crying out loud, Anton. This isn't about you."

A theatrical sigh steamed from the earpiece before Anton spoke crisply. "No. You're right. This is all about you. You need to leather up, lady, and get back to your family. I'm going to hang up now."

"But…"

"Yes?"

"Well, does this mean you can't think of a good reason for me to head home early? Like tonight?"

She wasn't sure whether he hung up in the middle of that sentence or at the end. But she was clearly on her own again. If Anton wouldn't help her get out of this week's trials, no one would. This completely stunk.

She started the car, and the engine's roar was only slightly more dramatic than her own.

Nineteen

Melanie extended no effort to love her niece. She didn't need to. She instantly and easily fell into a comfort zone with Sonny that felt as if it had been there for years. She couldn't wait to get to know her better and to catch up on the events of Sonny's life.

Now, Irina was a different story. Not that Melanie didn't consider her lovable, but that sense of ease wasn't there. Rather, Irina worked Melanie's emotions by the very way she walked, indecisively and slightly cowered. By the natural darkness around her beautiful but perpetually hesitant eyes. By the tone of her voice, which conveyed a belief that whatever she said was a mere interruption of more important conversation.

Melanie and Irina left the beach house and walked toward the boardwalk shops. They weren't far from the house before Irina's concern for Sonny struck a painful chord of pity in Melanie's heart.

"Are you sure it was a good idea to leave Sonny alone there, waiting for her mother to come back? What if Teresa is gone? Left for the whole week? Sonny will be so hurt."

Of course, if Teresa had ditched Sonny, she had ditched Irina too, with no ride back to Oakland. Didn't Irina feel worthy of that second thought?

Melanie nodded. "She'd be hurt, yes, but I don't think that'll happen. Despite Teresa's reluctance to let this week play out, I remember my sister as a curious person. And she's at least as big a control freak as I am. Now that Sonny has poked a hole in Teresa's bag of goodies, Teresa's going to want to moderate what falls out and who catches it."

"Bag of goodies?" Irina stopped at a rack of sunglasses, and slowly turned it. "What goodies might fall out?"

Melanie decided not to go there with Irina. She probably wouldn't even go there with Sonny. Most of the secrets in Sonny's life were under her mother's control. Melanie shrugged and joined Irina in trying on sunglasses.

"I'm not sure what Sonny will learn this week, if anything. I have a few questions of my own for Teresa, to tell you the truth."

Irina removed a pair of sunglasses from the rack and faced Melanie. "You have a strange family, I think. You're all so careful."

"Careful," Melanie repeated. She gave Irina a lopsided smile. "That's one way of looking at it. Your family is more candid, I take it?"

"Yes." They walked toward the T-shirt shop next door. "My parents have always spoken openly with my brother and me. That's partly because they're Christians and feel we should all try to be as honest as possible. But I also think they've spoken frankly with us because of our being adopted."

Well, that was quite an informative comment. "I didn't realize you were adopted."

Irina nodded and flipped through the T-shirts.

Melanie joined her and absently looked for something she might bring back for Micah. "How old were you when your parents told you about the adoption?"

"I knew right away. I was ten when they adopted me."

"Ah."

"My brother was eleven. We were in a Russian orphanage. We lived there five years after my mother died."

From her volunteer work at church, Melanie knew most of the Eastern European orphanages were underfunded and overcrowded. Her heart ached yet again for this girl.

"And are you a Christian too, Irina?"

Irina turned her penetrating eyes on Melanie. "Yes. But I...I still..."

Melanie waited.

"I still make a lot of mistakes."

"Oh, honey." A sigh escaped when Melanie smiled. "Don't we all?"

"You think so? Sometimes I feel that my parents, even my brother, are doing everything right. Making all the right decisions. Saying all the right words. I come across so many people who seem more…I don't know… more grown-up than I am, if that makes any sense."

Melanie couldn't help but wonder exactly how open this young woman's parents were if she thought they never made mistakes. And did Irina mean mistakes in general, or was she talking about sin? Melanie decided she could lump "sin" in with "mistakes" and probably cover whatever Irina meant.

"Listen, Irina. I don't know your parents or your brother, and I should probably only speak for myself, but I think you can safely assume that every single person you know or meet, regardless of how good or successful or confident they seem, has made mistakes and will keep doing so until the day they die. Lots of people make fewer mistakes with experience, but experience is often the result of the mistakes we've made."

"Yes," Irina said. She looked intently at Melanie. "That makes sense to me."

Melanie pulled out an aqua blue T-shirt with a sketch of a pelican on the front. "What do you think? For my son?"

Irina frowned. "Didn't you say your son was seventeen?"

"Mm-hmm." Melanie held the shirt up, imagining Micah inside it. Big enough?

For the first time today, Melanie heard Irina laugh.

"That? Right there?" Irina pointed at the pelican. "That's a mistake."

Melanie puckered her brow and tried to act as if she disagreed. But when she examined the pelican again, it looked like the very last thing Micah would be willing to wear. She laughed at herself. She was such a mom.

"See? It even happens to me. I know I seem perfect in every way, but even I get it wrong sometimes."

"Yes, you certainly do." Irina chuckled.

Melanie returned the shirt to the rack. "You have a great laugh."

The shy smile returned. "My brother tells me I don't laugh enough."

"Few people do, in my opinion."

They ventured into several souvenir shops and clothing stores. Irina bought a pair of dangling seashell earrings, and Melanie found a simple, royal blue, pelican-free T-shirt for Micah, with the words "Mission Beach" over the chest.

"Much better." Irina lifted her chin toward the shirt. "I approve."

Melanie paid for the shirt and smiled at the obvious relaxation in Irina's demeanor.

Only one thing troubled her as they left the shops and headed back toward the beach house. Irina put on her sunglasses, and Melanie was struck by how flattering they were to her high cheekbones.

Melanie hesitated to say anything. She didn't trust her memory, but she could almost swear Irina didn't have sunglasses with her when they left the house.

Twenty

Teresa struggled to keep her eyes shut while Sonny did her little house-visualization exercise with her. She felt she needed to go along with this drill because Melanie had already been so doggoned amenable.

"Well, it's a mansion, of course." She leaned back in the wrought iron chair on the front porch. "If I'm going to imagine, it might as well be big, classy, and well situated."

She had never had counseling in her life, but she had always tried to be understanding of Sonny's attraction to this sort of thing. Still, she didn't put much store in these exercises. She pictured everything Sonny described and answered all of her questions. She had been to Beverly Hills often enough to know what she liked in a dream house.

But then Sonny hit her with that weird offshoot question.

Teresa frowned. "What do you mean, secret room?"

"Don't think too hard, Mom. Just open the door and tell me what's in there."

This suddenly felt like a trick. Walk innocently through a beautiful home and then—pow!—tell me your secrets.

"I...I don't know what's in there. It's dark."

"So, turn on the light."

"There's no light switch."

"Come on, Mom. Fine. I just shined a big ol' spotlight in there."

Teresa opened her eyes. She turned to Sonny, who sat next to her, a pen poised over her notepad.

"What are you doing, walking into my house with a spotlight? Did you go into Melanie's house?"

"This isn't a competition between you and Aunt Melanie."

"Did you go into her house?"

"No, Mom! I didn't have to. She didn't try to keep me out!"

Fine. Now Sonny was going to lose it. What good was this doing? "Sonny—"

"Mom, this is ridiculous. You have to stop running away from me."

"Running away? What ever are you talking about?"

"All my life, as soon as we get past the thinnest layer of your veneer, you bolt, like you did when I came back to the house with Melanie today."

"I did no such thing! I went for groceries. Irina was supposed to let you know about that. It's not my fault if she didn't—"

"Mm-hmm, right. And where are they?"

"Where are what?"

Sonny cocked her head toward the house. "The groceries."

Nuts. "Okay, look, Sonny. If I had a room with some dirty secret in it, why would I take you in there? Why?"

She watched Sonny try to breathe her way to calmness. Sonny paused and closed her eyes. Then she looked at Teresa and spoke quietly.

"Mom, I didn't say the secret was either dirty or yours."

For some reason this comment brought Teresa a modicum of comfort.

"Oh. I thought this was my house."

"Not necessarily. It's just a house you came upon while walking."

Teresa sat back in her chair. "In that case, maybe I saw a different house."

"Did you?" Sonny tapped her pen against her pad of paper until Teresa stared at it, her eyebrow arched.

She closed her eyes again. She waited.

"No. It's the same."

Sonny didn't say anything. Teresa knew she was waiting for that secret room thing. Well, it wasn't Teresa's secret, was it? She could describe anything.

"Okay, then, I turn on the light and see what's in the room."

"Don't think too hard. What is it?"

Anything. She'd just say anything.

"It's…a doll." She waved her hand as if flicking away an insect.

"A doll. What does it look like?"

"Oh, I don't know." But suddenly she had a picture in her mind. "Pretty. Blond hair. Not like a Barbie, you know, more like one of those antique bisque porcelain dolls. The classy, collector's type."

"Anything else about it?"

She saw it pretty clearly at this point. "It's…huh." She frowned. "I think, yeah, it's broken." She opened her eyes. "Isn't that weird?"

Sonny didn't respond. As a matter of fact, Sonny had stopped writing and looked at Teresa as if the secret was not only dirty, but as if it was decidedly Teresa's, whether she wanted it to be or not.

Had she been tricked? Had Sonny just manipulated her with some psych-student "gotcha"?

There was no way now Teresa would tell Sonny the final part of the doll situation. She didn't know what it meant, but the moment Teresa visualized that stupid doll, she knew one thing for sure. And it didn't matter that this was all pretend.

Not only was the doll broken. She had been the one who broke it.

Twenty-One

Sonny tucked away her notes and determined to address them later. Within the hour she gathered the other three women and herded them all to Nick's at the Beach for dinner. She knew she needed to keep the week from plunging into constant group counseling seriousness. She had to adopt a fun approach to the evening.

"We've almost made it through an entire day without any of us withering away in dismay, do you all realize that?" She made the announcement as soon as the server gave them menus and left.

Melanie's smile was encouraging, Irina's polite, and Teresa's was similar to your average dental patient's.

"And now it looks as if we'll have a delicious dinner." Melanie read from her menu. "Sesame crusted ahi, nutty salmon. There are some great seafood choices here."

Sonny nodded and attempted to draw her mother in with a smile. "Yeah, someone left a menu for this place back at the beach house. I figured between the pasta dishes and the seafood, we'd all manage to find something yummy."

"I hope no one minds if I just get a salad." Irina studied the menu. Her comment finally prodded a reaction out of Teresa.

"Sweetie, you're a singer, not a dancer. You can afford to put some meat on your bones. We don't want you getting sick before your debut."

Melanie lowered her menu. "How long before that happens, Irina?"

"My getting sick?"

"No, your debut. When is that? I'd love to come hear you."

Both Sonny and Irina immediately looked at Teresa, as if her permission were necessary before Melanie could make such plans.

Teresa seemed taken aback. "What are you two looking at me for? Irina can speak for herself."

Hmm. Sonny wondered if this was progress. She wasn't sure, but that sounded as if Aunt Melanie could show up at the performance without Teresa having her forcibly removed by a couple of concert hall thugs. Sonny snorted at the image and then realized it looked as if she doubted Irina could speak for herself.

"I wasn't laughing at you, Irina."

Teresa raised her eyebrows. "You were laughing at me, then?"

"No, I was thinking of something unrelated. I mean, it was related but it wasn't about either of you." For some reason Sonny thought she sounded insincere. Why did she feel obligated to explain further? That's what she wondered, even as she started to explain further.

"See, I pictured two gorilla types in tuxedos at the concert hall, and they were...dragging Aunt Melanie...out of..." No, this wasn't the diplomatic conversation she envisioned for tonight. Her voice faded into the awkward silence.

But when her eyes met Melanie's, she relaxed at the outright amusement she saw. Melanie gave her a quick wink before she addressed Irina again.

"So what do you say, Irina? Are you going to let me come hear you? I'll bring my husband and son too."

Irina smiled. "That's very kind. I'm scheduled to sing next month. The tenth. It's an off-season performance, actually. Not a very big deal."

Teresa and Melanie spoke simultaneously.

"It *is* a big deal," Teresa said.

"It will be a big deal to us," Melanie said.

The two of them looked directly at each other before grabbing their menus and becoming swiftly intrigued by their dinner choices. With perfect timing, the server arrived to take their orders.

As soon as he left, Sonny spoke to Melanie. "So I have a cousin, huh?"

With an eager grin, Melanie grabbed her purse and pulled out her wallet. She placed a picture on the table.

Sonny and Irina leaned in to see. Teresa sat between them, and Sonny turned and caught her glancing at the picture too.

It showed Melanie with a man on either side. One, middle aged, with gentle, smiling blue eyes and chocolate brown hair. The other, a dark-haired young man taller than his parents and comfortable in front of the camera.

"Very cute." Irina tapped her fingernail on the teen's face.

"That's my Micah." Melanie grinned and touched the other man's face. "And Bailey, my husband of seventeen years. He's a realtor." She put the picture away. "Micah is hoping to go to Berkeley next year, to major in economics."

"Cool!" Sonny said. "I'll be at Berkeley—" She caught herself, glanced at her mother, and started again. "I mean, I'm sure I'll take a few of my graduate classes at Berkeley. Maybe Micah and I will meet."

"We can arrange that, regardless of whether or not he goes to Berkeley," Melanie said, giving Sonny a pat on the hand.

"He's seventeen?" That was Teresa, addressing Melanie directly.

Melanie looked momentarily shocked. "Uh, yes. He's a rising senior at his high school."

Teresa clearly worked to hide a thin smile.

It was a smile Sonny didn't like. Mean. And then she saw Melanie shrink almost imperceptibly.

What was that all about?

Irina spoke and provided a welcome distraction. "What do you do, Melanie? I think you don't sing like Teresa, yes?"

"Yes. I mean, no. I'm not a singer." Melanie gave a soft, self-deprecating chuckle. "Not even a shower-worthy singer, I'm afraid. I used to do human resources work, but when I had Micah, I stayed at home with him. I'm just now looking into going back to work. I've been offered a job as director of women's ministries at my church."

"So you're a people person, like I am," Sonny said, grinning. "You must be where I got that from."

"Well, *I'm* a people person too, Sonny," Teresa said crisply. "You might have gotten that from your own mother, don't you think?"

Even Irina stared silently at Teresa.

Sonny's smile froze, and she nodded once. "Uh-huh. That could be too." But inwardly she marveled that her mother actually saw herself as a people person. Sonny had come to think of her mom as a Teresa person.

Despite her financial generosity in Sonny's life, she hadn't been quite as generous with her heart. She acted as though she was impervious to the need or desire to develop relationships that required anything beyond acquaintance and basic formality.

And as much as Sonny loved her mother and knew there were hidden reasons for her reticence, Teresa didn't seem to trust or even like anyone.

Especially not Melanie. It wasn't until they were nearly finished with dinner—after plowing through one stilted conversation after another—that Sonny figured out why her mother had smiled so smugly when Melanie showed the picture of her family. Micah was seventeen years old, and so was Melanie's marriage. It sounded as if Micah had prompted Aunt Melanie's marriage to Uncle Bailey.

And yes, perhaps that was a sad—but not fatal—footnote for the future director of women's ministries. Maybe that part of Melanie's life factored into the story about her journey of faith. And Sonny considered her own beginnings. She didn't know the facts for certain yet because her mom was so secretive, but Sonny had come to believe her father was never her mother's husband.

If that was the case, how could her mom sit in amused judgment toward Melanie as she had? Did she simply derive pleasure in knowing Melanie had made mistakes in her past? Sonny hated to think it, but that *did* sound like her mom.

Sonny studied Teresa for a moment and saw the heavy-lidded condescension in her expression when she regarded others. Sonny wanted so much to bring lightness to those weighty, disappointed eyes. Her mom didn't know what she was missing.

Sonny let a sigh escape and forced herself to look away. Her messed-up, cautious mom. A people person indeed.

Twenty-Two

Melanie muttered her first waking thought the next morning. "Have I only been here one day?"

A homebody, she usually craved the familiarity of her own bed within several days of traveling elsewhere. But within twenty-four hours? This was a first. Of course, much of that had to do with missing Bailey and Micah. The few times she traveled, they tended to travel with her.

But, as she showered and dressed, she reflected on her mood and knew exactly what was up. This trip was stressful. Keeping quiet about things she could tell Sonny? Stressful. Teresa? The queen of stressful. Even poor Irina brought stress to the environment.

So Melanie was glad everyone else was still asleep by the time she made a cup of coffee and stepped onto the front porch. She looked out at the peaceful waves, the deserted beach, and allowed herself a softly spoken "Ahhhh."

"I'll second that."

She started at the unexpected voice. The next-door neighbor was on his front porch as well, and his words carried over on the morning breeze. He lifted his cup in a salute.

"Didn't mean to startle you. It seems we're destined to have our morning coffee together this week."

Melanie didn't know what to say to that. He seemed harmless and had a wonderful Scottish accent. But destiny? What was he talking about?

He walked toward her, and Melanie's hand tensed around her coffee mug. He didn't look like a weirdo, but his instant familiarity startled her. She would bean him if she had to.

"I owe you an apology," he said. He stepped onto the porch. "I didn't forget I invited you and the girls to go boogie boarding yesterday, but a few emergency matters arose at church while I was there, and I didn't make it home 'til late."

Finally Melanie understood. She hadn't thought as an identical twin for decades. She was sorely out of practice.

"Oh, now I get it. You must have talked with my twin yesterday. I'm Melanie."

He straightened and studied her. "Seriously?"

"Scouts' honor." She held up her hand in the Girl Scout salute she'd never forgotten.

He smiled and put out his hand. "Amazing resemblance." He lifted his chin at her. "You do have curlier hair than your sister, don't you? That should have tipped me off. I'm Julian. Your next-door neighbor. Teresa didn't mention you'd be here."

Melanie grimaced before she knew what she was doing. "Yeah, she wouldn't have come if...I mean, she didn't know I was coming. Her daughter—"

"Sonny?"

"Right. Sonny invited me as a surprise."

He nodded and looked out at the ocean before speaking again. "Ah. A surprise."

He turned back to her, a flicker of amusement in his eyes. "And how is that going?"

Melanie took a long drink of her coffee. She looked over her shoulder at the beach house before answering. "Stinks, actually."

They both laughed softly. Melanie couldn't believe she divulged something that personal so readily with this guy. But, despite her initial concern about him, he seemed comfortable and safe to be around. Not only did he look casual, in his T-shirt and cutoffs, but his open and nonthreatening conversation style simply relaxed her.

"Family strife." He rubbed the back of his neck. "Sometimes the people closest to us are the hardest ones to embrace."

"You said it. There hasn't been much closeness or embracing between Teresa and me for quite a while."

"Thus, Sonny's surprise, eh?"

"Yeah. And a little, uh, surprise counseling too." She gave him a rueful smile.

"Counseling. I see."

Melanie appreciated the fond expression he adopted before speaking again. Fatherly.

"Yes," he said. "I helped Sonny carry her luggage in. Rather heavy. She said she had some of her textbooks with her." He smiled at Melanie. "Obviously she has great hope. You have to admire that."

She sighed. "Mm-hmm. But it's already been a pretty rough week, and I've only been here—" She lifted her watch. "Twenty hours and forty-five minutes."

His eyes crinkled. "Not that you're counting."

"No."

Melanie liked him. He was attractive. After a quick glance at his ring finger, she wondered if Teresa would agree, and then she smiled that she even considered Teresa's romantic life that way—with optimism. That had to be progress of a sort.

Julian interrupted her reverie. "Well, I'd like to extend the same offer to you that I made to Teresa yesterday." His expectant expression and her thoughts of romance caused her to blush.

"Offer?" She automatically raised her left hand and flicked her bangs, as if he needed to see her wedding ring. Oh, heavens. How obvious was *she*?

"Boogie boarding." He pointed his cup toward the back of the house. "Faith stocked the storage shed with a good supply of boards."

"Faith?"

He smiled and regarded the beach house. "She was the original owner of this home. Lovely woman. Quite a character. And a real lifesaver to me, personally."

The front door opened quickly, and Irina greeted them with a joyful face that quickly sank in disappointment when she looked at Julian.

"Oh, I thought..."

Melanie waited a moment for the rest of the sentence, and then she smiled. "And good morning to you too, young lady. Are you feeling better today?"

"Better? Yes, I feel fine."

"I thought I heard you, um, being sick after dinner last night. No?"

The poor girl visibly shrank into herself. Was the stress of this four-some affecting her so strongly she was throwing up?

Melanie made a snap decision.

"Never mind, Irina. Our good man Julian here has just the activity we need today. As long as you're feeling fine, we're going to put our cares on hold and make like dolphins in the surf."

"We are?" Irina looked from Melanie to Julian.

Julian smiled. "We are. How about we meet back here in an hour or so? I'll help you carry your boards and chairs down after you ladies have breakfast."

Irina hesitated in joining their upbeat moods. "But, do you think Teresa will—"

"She'll love it." Melanie wouldn't let all that angst dominate the day. "Teresa was an avid boogie boarder when we were teens. If she hasn't done it lately, no problem. It'll come back to her. We could all use some loosening up."

A sleepy-eyed Sonny appeared in the doorway behind Irina, dressed in baggy lounge pants and an oversized T-shirt. "What? Who's loosening up?"

She gasped when she saw Julian and tried to hide behind Irina.

Melanie laughed. Not only was Sonny adorably disheveled and dressed as modestly as possible, the idea of anyone hiding behind the svelte Irina was hilarious.

Julian spoke over his shoulder as he left. "I'll meet you ladies in an hour."

Sonny stepped out from behind Irina. "But, Aunt Melanie, I thought I'd do another counseling exercise with you and Mom today."

Melanie took Sonny's lovely young face in her hands and planted a kiss on her forehead.

"Plenty of time for that later." She lowered her voice. "Sometimes the best therapy is just letting go and acting like a kid again." She looked from Sonny to Irina and wondered aloud. "You girls *do* remember that, don't you? Acting like kids?"

Twenty-Three

Sonny didn't know when she'd been this happy. Her mom had taken a while to "loosen up," as Melanie called it, but it was just about impossible to boogie board with a scowl on one's face.

"All together now, ladies," Julian insisted they paddle out as a group, and that simple act of camaraderie seemed to help.

Sonny floated next to him before they rode the first wave in. "Boy, am I glad you came along, Julian. Have you had training in counseling, by any chance?"

"Can't say I have, no."

"Working with children?"

He laughed. "I've simply learned that boogie boarding can break the ice with an apprehensive group."

And he was right. Once they rode the first wave in together, screaming and laughing, all kinds of formal facades fell. Well, Teresa's facade fell, even if momentarily. But hers was the Berlin Wall of tension within this group, so Sonny considered this substantial progress.

Even Irina had cast off her shyness—along with her swimsuit cover-up—and dove in. That seemed like a breakthrough in itself.

"I hate my body," Irina said to Sonny when they first headed toward the water.

"No! You're nuts, Irina. I'd kill to be even half as thin as you are."

Irina frowned. "Thin? You think I'm thin?"

But their conversation got no further as the group pulled together and waded into the water en masse.

Now Sonny stood on the beach and watched the others take a wave. Melanie and Irina nearly crashed into each other, laughing like children.

Whoa. How could Irina not realize she was thin? Maybe she had an eating disorder. Nevertheless, Sonny admired Irina's exotic beauty. And there was still something about her dramatic eyes that touched a buried memory for Sonny. It niggled at her when she stopped long enough to consider it.

But she didn't have time to stop and ponder right now. She had only left the group to tighten the halter knot on her swimsuit. The knot had an annoying habit of coming undone in the waves. She didn't want her top floating off and away. She would have worn her Speedo one-piece, but she seemed to have forgotten to pack it.

"Sonny, come on!" Melanie and Irina waved at her before running back into the waves, boogie boards in hand. Julian and Teresa were already paddling out.

She grabbed her board and ran back into the water. The group took several more waves together before Sonny realized Irina was no longer with them. Sonny stayed out on the water and scanned the beach. Finally she spotted her.

Irina was running away from them. Or rather, she was running *to* something. Someone. A guy. Near the seawall in front of the beach house. He was taller than Irina, and from where Sonny floated, he looked cover-model handsome. Irina actually jumped into his arms. Sonny was so surprised she let her boogie board slip out from under her.

She righted herself and looked again. The guy had his back to the beach now, and Sonny couldn't tell if Irina was happy or upset. She was clearly animated, though.

Julian and the twins paddled in her direction. She didn't want to call attention to Irina and possibly embarrass her, but her curiosity got the better of her. She called out to her mom.

"I'm going up to the house for a quick drink. I'll bring some water bottles out."

Before she got too far away, she heard Melanie's voice. "Hey, where'd Irina go?"

Sonny's last ride in was less than stellar. She didn't have her mind focused, and she wiped out before reaching the sand. She rolled sideways, sputtering and coughing like a chain-smoker. When she looked up she met eyes with three chubby little boys, tan and sandy, who had apparently watched her graceless arrival with rapt interest. One of them pointed at her and grinned, prompting the others to giggle as if she had performed specifically for them.

Once she was able to speak, she muttered, "Thank You, Lord." She wasn't thrilled about her crash landing, but if she had come in face first, she'd be a bloody mess by now.

She headed toward Irina and the knockout, all the while attempting to right her hair. She could tell it was tousled and sandy, but she couldn't seem to get it to fall back into place. It felt as if she had just ridden in a convertible. In a sandstorm. During monsoon season.

Irina's eye widened when she saw Sonny. "What happened? Are you all right?"

Sonny tried to shake her hair back into place before the guy turned around. When she looked back up at him, she gasped and started coughing again.

Irina rushed to her side and slapped her on the back.

Sonny shook her head and put her hand up to stop her. "No, that's okay. I just breathed in some seawater back there."

She looked at the guy again, pulled her sandy hair away from her face, and saw recognition dawn in his dark-rimmed, blue eyes.

Irina's voice had a new lightness to it. "Sonny. I know you're going to think I'm a terrible baby, but I called my brother and asked him to come keep me company this week."

Sonny whipped her head toward Irina. "Your brother?"

Irina grinned. "Yes." She put one hand on Sonny's shoulder and the other on her brother's. "Sonny, I'd like you to meet—"

"Grig," Sonny said.

"Grigori Banks. My—" Irina frowned. "Did you just say 'Grig'?"

The knockout spoke. "Yes, she did." He looked only at Sonny, and when he spoke again he blew her away. "Irina, this is Sonny. Sonata. The one I always talked about. She's the girl from Sunset Beach."

Twenty-Four

Sonny was glad Irina seemed shocked too. That way no one stood out in their dazed trio.

"Wow. You're kidding," Irina said.

Sonny looked away from Grig and into Irina's increasingly amused eyes.

Irina seemed more upbeat than Sonny had ever seen her. She broke into a full-blown grin. "Sonny, *you're* the Sunset Beach girl?"

"You make me sound like an ad for tanning lotion." But Sonny knew exactly what they were talking about. And looking at Grig brought back that month on Sunset Beach as if it had just happened. Four years gone in an instant. She had kissed him only yesterday, hadn't she?

The thought made her glance at his mouth, and that brought heat up her neck. She prayed the sun was too bright for any blushing to show.

Irina drew her hands together at her chest and talked with more energy than Sonny had yet seen in her. "I *remember*. It was the first time Grigori talked to me about anyone. Any girl, I mean. We were both at Jessup. You know, up near Sacramento? Both music majors. And he came back—junior year, right? Yes, junior year. He came back to school so sad. He was…he was…what's the word, Grigori?"

Now Sonny knew the sun didn't blot out all facial redness, because Grig blushed openly. He was adorable.

"I'm sure I don't know, Irina," he said, his voice deadpan. Sonny almost laughed.

"Smitten!" Irina raised her finger, Eureka fashion. "*So* smitten.

And that was over *you!*" She gave Sonny's arm a little squeeze. "I love this!"

Sonny tried to smile. As warm as she was from the sun, she could tell she was perspiring extra, simply standing in front of Grig. She was embarrassed for herself. Embarrassed for him. She dabbed at the moisture on her forehead with the back of her hand and realized her face was still covered with sand from her wipeout on the beach. Then she remembered her hair had felt all cockeyed as she approached Irina and Grig.

"Oh, I must look horrible." She cocked her thumb over her shoulder at the ocean. "I got kind of trashed by the waves—"

"You look even better than I remember," Grig said abruptly, looking surprised by himself, and then he gave her a genuine smile.

Okay. That did it. Smacked square in the face by the infatuation fairy. She smiled and had to fight against an eruption of a girlish giggle.

"Thanks."

Irina started toward the beach house. "Hey, I'm going to get some bottles of water for everyone."

"Oh, but..." Sonny wanted her to stay. But she wanted her to go too.

"I'll be right back," Irina said. She ran off.

Sonny tilted her head at Grig. "Um, you two have different last names. I'm sure my mother didn't say Irina Banks when she introduced her the other day. I would have thought of you."

He smiled. "Well, that's nice. I'm flattered."

Which embarrassed Sonny. She lacked that hard-to-get chip other girls had.

"She probably used Petrova. Right?"

"Yes, that sounds right. She seems so much more Russian than you. You don't seem Russian at all."

He shrugged. "I think I worked harder at losing that than Irina did. And her legal last name is Banks too. She uses our former surname professionally. Partially out of homage, I think. Partially because it sounds more..."

"Exotic."

"Yeah."

He hadn't changed a bit. Still immediately comfortable. The years had only made him more manly. More handsome.

He grimaced. "I'm sorry to interrupt your girls' week."

Sonny waved that off, and he kept talking.

"Irina can be easily rattled sometimes. She called me yesterday and asked me to come down. I hope this doesn't ruin your trip."

Considering the trip had just become as exciting as winning the Publishers Clearing House Sweepstakes, Sonny figured nothing had been ruined at all. "No. It's good you came. I mean, if she needs you, she needs you. And as much as I've enjoyed Irina's being here, I hadn't originally expected her here. My main reason for putting the trip together really, was...um..."

For the life of her, she couldn't remember what it was she came here for.

He helped. "Irina said she came down with Teresa."

Oh, right. That was it. "Yeah. They work together."

"Uh-huh. They both work with me, kind of."

Sonny raised her eyebrows. "You work with my mom?" This was too weird. "She never told me she knew you."

"But, how would she know? I mean, about our connection. I'm in the orchestra—the Oakland East Bay Symphony—but I didn't know Teresa was your mom. Miller is a pretty common last name. And I'm sure she didn't know I was your—"

Her eyes wide, Sonny waited for his next words. Old summer crush? Fantasy romance? Future husband? She couldn't help it. A crooked smile started, and he kept talking.

"I mean, I thought Irina was the only thing Teresa and I had in common. And the music thing, of course."

She tried to brush her hair back and cringed at how heavy and sandy it felt. And was that...oh, please. She pulled a small tube of seaweed out of the mess. She must look awful. He was so sweet to act as if she didn't. She attempted nonchalance when she dropped the seaweed to the ground. "So, what do you play in the symphony?"

"Violin."

"Whoa. That's so, I don't know, brainy sounding."

He laughed. "Our parents immersed both of us in music as soon as they brought us to the States. And apparently that was a good thing for both of us."

"But you never told me that, Grig. You said you were going to school for religious studies. I remember that."

"Yeah. Well, I was. But my major was the violin. I just didn't tell a lot of people about it."

"Why not?"

"I didn't want to call attention to that." He shrugged. "Just a habit I developed—keeping it quiet, I mean. When I came to the States, back when I was...what, eleven? I was already different enough. Couldn't speak English. Skinny as a post. Now, electric guitar? That might have given me some cred. But the violin?" He smiled. "Kind of geeky."

Sonny didn't catch herself before she glanced at his arms. Not so skinny anymore. And he had never seemed geeky to her at all.

She shook her head. "I'm kind of embarrassed about how little I learned about you four years ago. I didn't even know you were adopted. Or Russian. Didn't know you played the violin. I think I know more about Irina after two days than I knew about you after an entire month."

He smiled.

Whoa, she remembered how that smile affected her four years ago. It affected her the same way now. She hoped her pulse didn't make veins throb in her neck or anything.

"I wasn't very open about myself with you, Sonny."

"And maybe with Irina I'm a little less distracted by, um, other things."

Had she actually said that? There was almost no filtering in that comment. They stared at each other and Sonny started sweating again. This was both wonderful and horrible at the same time.

"Grig! What are you doing here?"

Sonny turned to see her mom approaching.

"Good to see you, Teresa." Grig's demeanor was very adult. He put his hand out to shake Teresa's. "Irina called me last night and asked if I'd come down to visit. I'm sure that's fine with you."

Goodness. Sonny looked at him and just about wanted to marry him right then and there. He wasn't the slightest bit intimidated by her mother, and that was one big fat check in the plus column.

She, however, didn't have that check in her own personal tally. She met eyes with her mom, who looked from Sonny to Grig and back again.

Teresa pointed at them and drew an imaginary line of connection in the empty space their bodies bordered. Without the slightest regard for decorum, Teresa demonstrated her ability to peg situations in that annoyingly sharp way of hers.

"Okay. What's going on here?"

Twenty-Five

Irina ran up to the group, embracing an armload of water bottles. Her eyes were filled with excitement.

"Isn't this cool, Teresa?"

Somehow Teresa knew Irina's enthusiasm was about something other than bottled water. "Isn't *what* cool?"

Irina passed bottles to everyone as if they were all about to launch a ship. "Didn't they tell you? Sonny was Grig's Sunset Beach girl!"

Teresa narrowed her eyes. "His Sunset Beach girl. Sonny, is this some urban vernacular I haven't yet learned?"

Sonny answered with her nervous laugh, the one Teresa associated with memories of Sonny's teen escapades.

"Mom, I met Grig four years ago. You remember when I spent that month at the beach with Pam Allendale's family? Right before I left for college?"

"Mm-hmm."

Sonny cocked her head toward Grig. "I met Grig there. At Sunset Beach."

"Where you were his girl?" Teresa lifted an eyebrow. "Do I have that correct?"

Sonny colored noticeably.

Teresa was surprised by the nervous flutter she felt inside. She wasn't sure what that was about. This apparent romance was water under the bridge—four years ago. Whatever happened hadn't led to any long-term results.

But maybe that was where the flutter came from. Teresa, of all people, knew something long term *could* have resulted quite easily. And she had been ignorant of Sonny's circumstances during that month. What else was she ignorant of? What was she ignorant about right now?

"We had plenty of supervision, Mom." Sonny rolled her eyes at Teresa. "And I was twenty. Not exactly a middle schooler."

Grig smiled at Teresa as if they were contemporaries. "Teresa, I think you know me pretty well. I haven't changed much in four years. Sonny was safe with me."

"Still is," Irina said. She smiled at Grig. "My brother's a total gentleman."

Teresa looked from Sonny to Grig. "Well, you have a point there. But, Sonny, obviously you weren't very forthcoming about what you were up to that summer. I had no idea you had a little summer romance going on."

She watched Sonny form a lopsided smile. "I can't imagine where I learned such guarded behavior."

Grig's eyes widened at something beyond Teresa. She turned around to see Julian and Melanie approaching.

"Oh." She stepped aside to include them in the group. "You're not hallucinating, Grig. Melanie is my twin sister. And this is Julian. He lives next door, in that gorgeous home over there."

Irina said, "This is my brother, Grigori. Grig. He works with Teresa and me. Plays violin." Irina's demeanor had changed so much, Teresa felt a twinge of guilt for whisking her away as she had. She hadn't noticed how much the girl had emotionally shriveled these past two days. Was she that dependent on Grig's presence? That couldn't be healthy.

Grig shook hands with Melanie. "You're completely identical, aren't you? Teresa's never mentioned she had a twin."

Melanie nodded, an amused, mock-innocent expression in her eyes. "Yes, I get that a lot."

Oh, yeah. That was the Melanie Teresa remembered. Smarty-pants.

Julian shook Grig's hand too. "Do you need a place to stay while you're here?"

"Yeah, I guess I do." Grig looked back at the houses along the boardwalk. "Do you know of anything decent nearby?"

"I do, indeed. I have a full apartment upstairs at my home. Separate entrance, kitchen, bedroom, the works. You're free to use that. It's available for the rest of the week."

"Or you could just stay on the couch at our place," Irina said.

"No!" Teresa spoke impulsively, not considering her rudeness until the word escaped. But then she realized both Sonny and Grig had said the same thing, just as passionately.

The three of them all looked at each other. The rest of the group exchanged glances as well. The two-second moment felt like thirty.

"Settled, then. Yes?" Julian smiled at Grig. "Come on. I'll show you the place."

Irina looped her arm in Grig's and spoke over her shoulder to the other three women. "We'll be right back." Her smile beamed.

Once they were out of range, Melanie spoke. "What a cutie-pie. Seems like a really nice guy too." With a sparkle in her eyes, she grinned at Sonny. "What do you think, Sonny?"

"He's, um, I think you're right. He's…actually, I kind of…"

"They had a fling four years ago," Teresa said.

"Mom! It was not a fling, Aunt Melanie. It was a harmless summer romance. That's all."

Teresa saw the look in Melanie's eyes that she used to get when they watched romantic films together. She thrived on this kind of thing.

"Well, isn't that something!" Melanie said. "And you didn't know 'til now he was Irina's brother?"

"Nope."

"Oh, my heavens, Sonny!" Melanie looked like she wanted to jump up and down, she was so wound up over this coincidence. "Hey, you know what else? Irina told me her parents were Christians."

Oh, brother. Not the Christian thing again.

"Yeah." Sonny darted a glance at Teresa. "Grig's a Christian. At least he was four years ago. I'm assuming he's still a believer. Isn't he, Mom?"

Teresa shrugged and raised her palms. "How would I know? We don't get into theological discussions at rehearsal. He doesn't wear a big fat 'Look at me. I'm a Christian' sign that I've ever seen."

They chose to ignore her sarcasm.

Melanie put her arm around Sonny. "Well, this just gets more and more interesting. I don't know about you, but I'm not a big believer in coincidences."

Sonny grinned, obviously enjoying Melanie's enthusiasm. But then she looked at Teresa and her grin straightened. "What, Mom? Why do you keep giving me the fish eye?"

What was Teresa going to say? She was outnumbered at the moment. And if she really thought about it, she didn't mind so much if Sonny developed an interest in Grig. He was a nice kid, and Sonny would be more likely to come to Oakland and visit if she were involved with someone who lived nearby. The fact that neither of them wanted Grig sleeping at the beach house—that said a lot.

Still, it was hard to jump on Melanie's little Christian-romance bandwagon. So she crossed her arms and raised an eyebrow before delivering her response.

"Sonny, you have a big wad of seaweed in your hair."

Twenty-Six

Melanie nudged Sonny as they walked up the boardwalk. The four women and Grig had followed Julian's advice and were on their way to Kono's for lunch.

"Best burritos on the beach," he said, before they parted ways. "Especially if you like breakfast burritos."

Now that the day was in full swing, the boardwalk was crowded. It was actually a paved road for pedestrians rather than a walk made of boards. The beach house group wove past bikers, skaters, joggers, and an array of beach lovers who would entertain the most demanding of people watchers.

Melanie and Sonny had eased ahead of the musical faction, and Melanie enjoyed the private moment with her niece. "I'm fascinated by the shifting dynamic of our little group."

"What do you mean?" Sonny asked, glancing behind herself at the others.

"Well, obviously Teresa brought Irina with her this week to put the kibosh on your plans. To dissuade you from forcing any intimate conversations."

"Yep, that's what I figured."

Melanie nodded. "And you invited me to force just the opposite environment."

"Well..."

"Come on, we both know what you're hoping for, young lady."

"Okay," Sonny said, "so why don't *you* just fill me in? Tell me my history. *Your* history. Why not just get this over with?"

"No, ma'am." Melanie shook her head. "For one thing, I don't know your history. I know some of your mom's history, but there wasn't that much going on—I mean not a lot of drama—before Teresa severed ties with me and our parents."

Sonny gripped Melanie's arm. "My grandparents. Please at least tell me they're still alive."

Melanie's heart broke. "Oh, honey. Of course they are. I thought you knew *that*, at least."

"She doesn't tell me anything, Aunt Melanie. And I've never heard a word about them or from them."

"They would have found you if…I mean, they don't even know about…"

"They don't even know about me." Sonny spoke the words to the ground, with a flat, defeated voice.

Melanie placed her hand over Sonny's. "I promise you right now that you're going to meet them. No matter what happens this week. Okay? Right away. They live in San Clemente, and they're going to be thrilled to meet you." She saw tears glisten in Sonny's eyes.

Sonny nodded. Within seconds her lips spread into a smile. "Cool."

"And with regard to what your mom has withheld, I'm really hopeful she'll talk with you. I'd like to give her that chance. And I think it would do you two a lot of good if you heard everything from her. If she bared her soul to you."

Sonny tilted her head. "I guess. Yeah, of course it would. I know that."

Melanie sensed that Sonny's sadness had almost passed, so she grinned and returned to her original subject. "But what I find especially absorbing is how our fragile little Irina has shifted the focus of the week without even realizing it."

She glanced back, and Sonny followed her gaze. The other group was a short distance behind, but Grig was the only one looking ahead. He smiled and gave them a casual wave, which they both returned.

When they faced forward, Melanie studied Sonny's flushed face and laughed softly. "See? A shift in focus. Tell me I'm wrong."

Sonny affected an expression that rivaled the primmest schoolmarm ever. "You would be wrong there, definitely."

"Oh, really? You have seemed a tad distracted since this morning."

She tapped a finger against her chin. "I'm just wondering what might be distracting you."

Sonny pointed ahead of them. "Ah! There's Kono's."

Melanie laughed again.

Sonny spoke quickly. "Help me! For some reason I'm embarrassed around him. It's like I'm a thirteen-year-old at a Jonas Brothers concert."

"What's a Jonas brother?"

"Shhh. Never mind."

Teresa, Irina, and Grig joined them in the long line outside Kono's.

Teresa looked at her watch. "Julian wasn't kidding about the line."

"But he also said it moves quickly," Grig said. "Good thing too. I headed to the airport this morning with nothing but a couple of granola bars and a big cup of coffee. I'm starved."

Irina put a hand on his shoulder. "You're such a terrific brother. Thank you so much for coming."

"Not a problem."

Melanie watched him drape a protective arm around Irina's shoulders. The girl clearly depended on him, but he didn't act as if she were weak or pitiful. Melanie liked that. Respectful and supportive.

She was struck again by how physically beautiful the two of them were. To look at them now, you'd never guess they started life under such difficult circumstances. Grig seemed to have overcome the past. But Irina? Melanie meant it when she called her fragile.

She looked away and made a mental note she had often made in the past—never assume anything about a person based on her outward appearance or public persona. There were so many hurting people living in pretense.

⌇

They ate their lunch in the brilliant sunshine at a table outside.

"Well, Julian certainly didn't steer us wrong," Melanie said, piling a few empty paper plates on top of one another. "That was a great lunch."

"Yeah. And I love watching all the people walking by." Sonny sat back in her chair. "It's one of my favorite things to do, especially in a place like this. The beach attracts such a colorful variety."

"I remember that about you, the people watching." Grig smiled at her for just a moment before popping a few fries in his mouth.

Melanie watched Sonny color again and chuckled to herself. Sonny was right—she worked herself up too much about Grig. Yes, he had dramatic blue eyes and could probably model if he wanted to. But he was just a guy, and he wasn't being particularly flirtatious, as far as Melanie could tell.

At precisely that moment Grig belched, loudly. He slapped his hand to his mouth, his eyes wide. "Oh, man. Excuse me. I'm so sorry." He shook his head and scanned the women. "Aren't you glad to have a gentleman in your midst?"

Teresa quickly looked over her shoulder. "Where?"

They all laughed. Melanie didn't know why, but she was thrilled by the fact that Teresa actually made a joke. She hadn't seen that side of her sister in forever.

"Mom," Sonny said, "are you sure you won't take a little money for lunch? I don't want you thinking you have to pay like that."

"I don't think that. I just felt like treating everyone."

"But—"

"Really, sweetie. It was my pleasure."

Sonny shrugged. "It's just that you looked a little surprised when they told you how much it was."

Teresa frowned. "I did?"

Melanie saw genuine confusion in Teresa's expression. She hadn't noticed Teresa react as Sonny described when she paid the bill.

"Oh," Teresa said. "Hang on. I think you're talking about when I took my keys out of my purse to get my wallet. It's just that I was sure I had my hair clip attached to my keys, but it wasn't there. Remind me to look for that when we get back to the house. It doesn't look like much, but it was a gift from someone special. And he bought it at Tiffany's. I don't want to forget it here."

Sonny nodded, not particularly fazed by her mother's comment.

But Melanie noticed a sudden stillness in Grig. He looked far less comfortable than he had moments earlier. Teresa, Sonny, and Irina all looked out at the passersby, complete contentment on their faces.

So Melanie was the only one who noticed when Grig shot a look of concern at his beautiful, fragile sister seated by his side.

Twenty-Seven

"So, explain to me what 'free association' is all about." Teresa had agreed to undergo yet another psychological exercise with Sonny when they returned to the house. The others wanted to linger along the shops on the boardwalk, so mother and daughter were all alone.

Teresa had done a quick search through her room without turning up the missing hair clip, but then she decided to stop and give her attention to Sonny before looking elsewhere.

"And I'd really like to hear the results of the first exercise—the house thing—before doing more of this stuff, Sonny."

They both sat on the couch. "I haven't had time to look at that one yet, Mom. I'll look at that one and this one tonight, okay? And then you and Melanie and I can have a little chat."

Teresa arched an eyebrow. "We'll see." She lifted her chin at Sonny's empty notepad. "What's this one about?"

"Okay, well, it's very cool the way this works. I'm going to say a word to you and you just spit out the very first word that comes to mind. No thinking about it, no censoring, no wondering why in the world you thought of that word, nothing."

"And what are we aiming for here?"

"I'll be listening for a kind of overall picture. We're not necessarily going to arrive at any magic word that reveals anything. But I've been on the other end—your end—before, and it was fun. And interesting."

"Hmm. Maybe a dentist thinks getting a root canal is fun and interesting. This psycho stuff is your bag, not mine."

Sonny scowled.

"Oh, all right." Teresa nestled back and sipped a glass of iced tea. "At least it will just be between the two of us. If Melanie is anything like she used to be, they'll be shopping for at least an hour out there."

"Good. Let's just try one of these to give you a feel for it." Sonny picked up her notepad and sat up, pert and businesslike.

"Yeah, okay." Teresa readied herself.

Sonny breathed deeply and then said, "Water."

"Hmm. Water. For that, I would say—"

"No, Mom. Don't stop and think. Just blurt it out."

"But—"

"Go! Water!"

"Well, wait. Which is it? 'Go' or 'water'?"

Sonny dropped her pad and pen down to her lap with a sigh. "Water. All right? Can we try again?"

Teresa nodded. "Ready."

Again, Sonny picked up her pad and pen. "Beach."

"Beach? What happened to 'water'?"

"Mom!"

"But I was all ready for 'water,' and—"

"Beach!" Sonny practically yelled the word.

"Okay! Sand!"

"Sand," Sonny said.

"Right, sand," Teresa said, and Sonny shook her head.

"No, Mom. I'm saying 'sand' now. I want you respond to 'sand.'"

"But I just said that."

Sonny gently lowered her pad. "Yes, I know. That's how I'm doing this one, just echoing the words back at you. Don't think so much."

"But…oh, all right. Go ahead."

And then the words flew like bullets.

Sonny repeated, "Sand."

Teresa: "Volleyball."

Sonny: "Volleyball."

Teresa: "Sport."

Sonny: "Sport."

Teresa: "Running."

Sonny: "Running."

Teresa: "Hiding."

Sonny: "Hiding."

Teresa: "Secret."

Sonny: "Secret."

Teresa: "Shame."

Teresa's mouth dropped open as if someone else had said the word. As if she had cursed in the middle of a funeral.

"Whoa," Sonny said. "You're really good at this."

Teresa looked at her in horror. "Good? You think that was a *good* string of words?"

Sonny snorted. "You bet it was. Pretty revealing, wouldn't you say?"

"I don't think I want to do this, Sonny."

Sonny groaned and flopped back on the couch, arms and legs splayed, as if she had been knocked there by a giant flyswatter. "Man! What are you afraid of, Mom? So you said a few words you didn't know you were thinking."

"That's just it. I didn't think those words until you put them in my head. I don't want to think that way."

Sonny turned her head in Teresa's direction. "The only word I put in your head was 'beach.'" She sat up. "But I *do* have a word to put in your head. How about 'denial'?"

"Oh, brother. That psychobabble nonsense doesn't impress me."

"Maybe not, but it obviously scares you."

"Scares me? Sonny, as a woman who's overcome plenty of frightening situations, there is no way I'm going to let anyone, not even you, call me scared."

"Fine. So let's do another word association."

"Bring it on, sister."

Sonny laughed, and Teresa almost did too. The smile that eked past her attempted composure only pulled at one side of her mouth.

"Okay." Sonny sat back up and readied her paper and pen. "Just react to the words I say."

Teresa nodded.

Sonny jotted something on her notepad before she said, "College."

"Daughter." Teresa smiled, pleased with that one.

"Father," Sonny said.

"Father? You were supposed to say 'daughter.'"

Sonny looked up from her notes. "We're doing this one differently."

Teresa sighed. She had to hand it to Sonny. She knew how to keep a person on her toes. But two could play at that game. "Okay. Father? Mother."

"Yours."

Hers? Her mother? Teresa answered with silence. How could one word—and such a simple one—suggest so many others, and so quickly? She scrambled to regain her poise and looked beyond Sonny's searching eyes. She grasped for a word.

"Book," Teresa said.

She saw Sonny straighten and knew that answer had been unexpected. Ah, now Teresa knew what to do.

"Story," Sonny said.

"Clock."

Sonny's brows furrowed. "Time."

"Mountain."

"Mountain?" Sonny stopped taking notes.

Teresa tilted her head. "Oh, are we going back to your repeating me?"

Sonny still frowned, but Teresa watched her return to her notes. She felt a pang of guilt for deliberately flummoxing her daughter.

"Um, okay," Sonny said. "Valley."

Teresa hadn't been quite ready for another word. "Uh, doily."

Sonny slammed her pen and paper onto the couch. "I knew it!" She whipped a glance behind herself. "You're just naming things in the room and in the paintings and stuff."

Shoot. "Oh, all right. Busted. I'm sorry, Sonny. I simply can't warm up to all this emotional delving, especially when it's so one-sided."

"Hey, let's turn the tables. I'm ready to dump all kinds of emotional baggage. I've got nothing to hide."

Teresa hesitated and then allowed herself a mischievous smile. "Really?" She crossed her legs and relaxed into the couch. "All right, I've got an association for you. Ready?"

"Yep." Sonny's expression was downright cocky.

"Sunset Beach."

Teresa watched Sonny battle against flustering. "Uh, well, that's two words."

The front door opened, and Melanie poked her head inside. "Okay to come in?"

"Sure!" Sonny said.

Teresa laughed. "I think we're done. But you're back early. Where are the Russians?"

"The Russians? Oh. Hmm. They needed some time to talk. They're still walking on the boardwalk. We had a little incident."

"Uh-oh. What happened?" Sonny went to the kitchen counter and poured a glass of tea for Melanie, who sat in the chair next to the couch.

"We stopped at this one store, and I found a pretty little necklace I decided to buy. Nothing pricey, but when I went to pay for it, I realized all of my cash was missing."

"Ohhhh, no." Teresa said it with very little passion, as if she weren't terribly surprised.

"What do you mean?" Sonny looked from Teresa to Melanie. "You were robbed?"

Melanie shrugged. "Sort of. It was only about forty dollars. But I knew I had it before Grig arrived, because—"

"Aunt Melanie! You don't think Grig took it? He's not like that, I swear!"

Teresa put her hand on Sonny's knee. "Relax, sweetie. It's Irina."

Sonny gasped. "Irina?"

"You knew?" Melanie asked Teresa.

"I suspected." Teresa took a quick drink. "She might have my missing hair clip. I don't know for sure, but I've noticed items missing around Irina before."

"But you didn't say anything about that today," Sonny said.

"I feel sorry for her." Teresa studied her fingernails. "I think maybe this happens when she gets especially stressed. I'm not sure why. My guess is that Grig knows about it."

Melanie nodded. "He definitely knows about it. The minute I mentioned my missing money, he looked at Irina with the saddest face I've ever seen, poor guy. And then he asked me if I would mind giving them some privacy. He said they needed to talk and they'd return shortly."

"Poor Irina," Sonny said. "I feel bad if we've stressed her that much. Do you think it was us stressing her?"

Teresa glanced at Melanie, who simultaneously looked at her.

Sonny grimaced. "Do you think they'll leave?"

Teresa heard the anticipation of disappointment in Sonny's voice. It reminded her of a teenaged Sonny, once stood up by a date. Teresa smiled at her transparent daughter. "We'll do our best to keep that from happening."

"Right." Melanie gave a quick, emphatic nod. "We'll make sure Irina doesn't get any more stressed."

"Yeah, okay," Sonny said. "We'll make sure she's having a great time. We'll do things to distract her. Grig too."

That last comment caught Teresa's attention. "Grig too? What exactly did you have in mind?"

Twenty-Eight

Of course, Sonny never considered herself a temptress by any means, and her mom knew it. So Sonny assumed Teresa's concern was a tease. Still, shortly after Grig and Irina returned, Sonny felt her spirits lifted by Grig's first comment to her.

"I don't suppose you'd like to go for a walk on the beach?"

"Sure." She looked to the other women. "Okay with you guys?"

Teresa stood. "As a matter of fact, I thought I'd run to the store for those groceries I meant to pick up yesterday."

"Good idea," Melanie said. "Let's go with her, Irina. Maybe we can find something to grill for dinner."

When Grig and Irina first returned from their talk, she had looked especially embarrassed. But now, with everyone acting so casual, she seemed to relax. "All right. I'd like that."

⁓

Sonny didn't have to wait long before Grig got right to the point. They hadn't even reached the wet sand before he broached the subject.

"I guess Melanie said something to you and Teresa when she came back without us, huh?"

"A little. She wasn't completely sure about what happened, but she knew you were troubled by the fact that her money was gone."

He nodded. "It goes hand in hand with the bulimia, I'm afraid."

"What does? Wait, did you say bulimia? Irina is bulimic?"

119

He smiled. "I thought you figured that out already. She told me she threw up several times already this week, and she was pretty sure you all knew."

Sonny massaged the side of her neck. "The thought crossed my mind when I saw how thin she was. I heard someone being sick in the bathroom yesterday, and I thought it was Irina. I thought she was maybe sick with stress. But I didn't think she *made* herself vomit. And I would have thought she was anorexic, if anything. I thought bulimics were, you know, bigger eaters. Bigger *people,* even. Irina is ultra thin."

"I think there are a lot of similarities between the two disorders," Grig said. "And Irina used to be a bigger eater. And heavier, although never overweight. But she works hard against the urge to binge now, hoping it will keep her from wanting to purge. She's done really well, but she has relapses sometimes."

"We stressed her into this relapse, didn't we?"

Grig shrugged. "I don't know. She was already wound up pretty tightly over her solos. But the obvious tension between Melanie and Teresa could have pushed her over the edge."

"Whoa. If you think the tension between Mom and Melanie is obvious now, you should have seen them when Melanie arrived yesterday morning. They barely spoke to each other. At least now they're talking, driving together, even willing to breathe the same air."

He smiled. "Progress."

She studied his profile. She loved that little scar on his cheekbone. He already had that four years ago, and she remembered softly kissing him there, as if she could make it go away. Now she appreciated its presence and the little thrill she felt, remembering the past.

"What?" He stopped and faced her, his smile softer.

"Nothing." She shook her head and starting walking again. "Just thinking about random stuff."

He joined her and she returned to their topic. "So, you said the stealing goes hand in hand with the bulimia. I didn't even know that."

"Kleptomania? Yeah."

"Oh, is that what it is? Does Irina know she's doing it?"

"Usually. Not always, though. She gets all pent up inside, apparently, and the impulsive thrill of stealing something helps her release the stress.

But taking Melanie's money wasn't typical. She normally takes items that aren't worth much. She said she took Teresa's hair clip too, but she didn't know it came from Tiffany's. I think she has a few other things to return. We'll straighten all of that out today."

"Poor Irina. As if it's not bad enough to struggle with bulimia."

"Yeah. I thought maybe I should take her home."

Sonny gasped. "Oh, please don't leave!" She burnt with a sudden flush up her neck and couldn't speak for a moment. What in the world was the matter with her? Talk about fighting impulses. Could she maybe fight the impulse to shackle this poor guy to the beach house hose bib?

Grig looked at her, surprised, but there was no mistaking the pleasure he got, knowing she wanted so much for him to stay.

She tried to regain her dignity. "I mean, we could try to keep the environment stress free, and she seems pretty relaxed now that you're here. Melanie and I don't even know her that well yet. We'd be so sorry to see her go."

As if she hadn't said any of that, he leaned down and softly said, "I'm happy to see you again too, Sonny."

She swallowed and wondered for a second where she might find a set of shackles.

They walked a short distance in silence before he spoke again.

"If it will ease everyone's mind, I could always have her stay with me at Julian's. There's a comfortable couch there I could sleep on and give her the bedroom. That way she could come stay there if she starts to feel anxious."

"Yeah, if she feels the need. But I know Mom and Melanie will agree with me that we'd love to have her stay in the beach house with us if she wants to. It will do her good to spend time with a bunch of women. Oh, but, maybe the problems between Mom and me have added to her discomfort. I hadn't thought of that."

Grig chuckled.

"What?" Sonny smiled, even though she didn't know what was funny.

"I'm just thinking about the common denominator in the areas of conflict there at the house."

Sonny laughed. "You mean Mom? Yeah. I think she tries to be an equal opportunity troublemaker."

"Everywhere she goes."

"She's like that at work too? I'll bet she's the classic diva, huh?"

He tilted his head. "She does know what she wants."

Sonny snorted softly. "Yeah. That's easy enough to figure out if you don't care what anyone else wants, I guess." She stopped and replayed that comment in her mind. "I'm sorry. That sounded pretty mean, didn't it?"

He slowed down, and the two of them faced the horizon. Sonny heard someone's radio playing an oldies' station, and a baby's tired cry faded as it was carried home. The sun was setting, and the pale blue sky had given way to a dramatic lavender-and-amber tableau.

"We watched a lot of sunsets like this four years ago," Grig said. "Remember?"

"Mm-hmm." She loved that he wanted to talk about that time.

"Sonny, I like the fact you're starting to stand up to your mother now."

She looked up at him. "That was kind of random."

He gave her another fond smile. "Not really. You just censored yourself after you said that about your mom's selfishness. It reminded me that you did that all the time that summer."

"I did?"

He nodded. "It's great you're so kind and forgiving, but I remember your not knowing much about your personal history four years ago, and I remember the pain it caused you. Do you know more now than you did then?"

Just hearing her situation put that way really ticked her off. "No. You know...no, I still hardly know anything about my past."

"Is that what's causing the conflict between you and Teresa?"

She nodded.

"Well," he said, "I didn't come down here to stir up trouble between you two. I mean, I didn't even know about you. That was a bonus."

He had her smiling again, and he continued.

"But you don't have to apologize to me if you express frustration with Teresa. I think it's time for her to stop worrying about her image and start caring about the truth. At least as far as it concerns you."

"Well, thanks. That honestly does help. That's what this week was supposed to be about, really, but we've gotten a little waylaid."

"Because of Irina?"

"No! Well, yes, sort of, but not just because of Irina."

"Because of me?"

She gave him a light push on the shoulder. "Oh, please. Well, yes, sort of, but I'm especially happy about that particular interruption."

He laughed.

"Really. That stuff you just said? It's like you're a modern-day knight in shining armor. Fully supportive but confident I can fight the dragon all by myself."

"Uh-huh."

She was mesmerized by the sudden twinkle in his eye and the half smile left over from laughing.

"Not that Mom is a dragon. I didn't mean that."

He shook his head and feigned a serious expression. "Not a dragon."

She laughed. "But maybe you'd better let Irina know she can escape to your place at Julian's if the fur starts to fly at the beach house."

"Fur? I thought dragons had scales. Who's got the fur?" He leaned back and looked at her shoulders, a grimace on his face. "It's not on your back is it?"

She smacked him on the arm and laughed. "Shut up!"

With a grin, he turned as if they were going to walk back toward the beach house. He squinted, trying to read his watch.

"Yeah," Sonny said. "We should get back."

"Uh-huh, but that's not what I'm checking. It took…about six hours."

"What did?"

"Six hours to feel as comfortable with each other as we were four years ago. I knew we'd get here as soon as I saw you on the beach today."

Definite goose bump material. Sonny smiled and rubbed her arms as they started back to the house.

He was right. He had managed to chase away that teenybopper infatuation she struggled with earlier. But they weren't in exactly the same situation as they were four years ago. They weren't involved in a summer romance. Or a romance of any kind.

Yet.

Twenty-Nine

Melanie yawned the next morning. "I hope it's not too early for me to do you any good, Sonny. You might be bright and chipper after your morning jog, but I'm still kind of sleepy."

The two of them sat alone in beach chairs on the sand. The morning air still held the coolness of the night before, so they both had afghans wrapped around themselves. They each held a steaming mug of coffee.

"You'll probably be all the more transparent for being too sleepy to keep your guard up," Sonny said, grinning.

Melanie glanced back at Julian's house. "I figured we needed to come down here to do this. Julian apparently comes outside each morning to drink his coffee. I think he's terrific, but I knew you wanted privacy for this word association thing."

"Oh, I don't know. We could always throw Julian into the mix. I'll bet we'd get some interesting associations from him."

Melanie laughed. "No doubt. I haven't had a chance to talk much with him, but he does seem to be the master of the loaded comment. Still, adding him to this morning's exercise won't get you closer to your goals for this trip, will it?"

She watched Sonny lose herself in thought for a moment.

"You know, Melanie, I'm carrying on with what I planned for this trip, but I also think I need to be open to God's tweaks."

"Tweaks?" Melanie couldn't help but smile at the image of God making minor adjustments to Sonny's tidy little machine.

"Yeah. Each day so far He's surprised me somehow, and I've had to adjust. This week isn't working out exactly as I planned it. At first it bothered me. You know, like when Mom showed up with Irina."

"Or my showing up as an identical twin."

They both smiled.

"Yeah, that was a little shocker too." Sonny cupped her hands around her coffee mug and breathed in its comforting richness. "But your being Mom's twin has deepened my interest in the family story. And I think Irina's presence has enriched this week."

"Did you notice the enrichment even before Grig showed up?"

Sonny opened her mouth in a silent gasp. "Aunt Melanie! Give me a little credit."

"Okay," Melanie said. But a smile remained, even as she brought her coffee to her lips.

"Really! Irina has proven to be an ally. And now I'm especially drawn to her because of the whole bulimia thing. I mean, it makes me want to hug her up and make it all better. And I want to know more about what she feels. All of that was there before Grig showed up, except I didn't know about the eating disorder."

"All right. You've sold me. But he is awfully cute, isn't he?" Melanie nudged Sonny's toes with her own.

Sonny had barely swallowed a sip of coffee before she answered. "One of God's better tweaks."

Melanie laughed out loud.

"So are you ready for this exercise?" Sonny pressed her mug into the sand. "You know what it's all about?"

"I assume you say a word and I give you a one-word response. Right?"

"Exactly. Try not to think. Just blurt it right out. Don't give yourself time to consider whether it makes sense or not."

"Got it. I'm ready."

"Okay." Sonny picked up her pad and pen and faced Melanie. "Beach."

Melanie said, "Trip."

"Trip," Sonny said.

"Oh! Same word. Um, sorry. Vacation."

Sonny: "Vacation."

Melanie: "Relax."

Sonny: "Relax."

Melanie: "Laugh."
Sonny: "Laugh."
Melanie: "Family."
Sonny: "Family."
Melanie: "Kids."
Sonny: "Kids."
Melanie: "Joy."

"Okay, so that gives you an idea of how it works." Sonny leaned back in her chair. "Sometimes I'll repeat your word back at you, and sometimes I'll feed you a new word."

"That's kind of fun. Do another one."

Sonny raised her index finger. "There is one thing, though. I think maybe for you we shouldn't do the echo approach. I think you might have picked an image with the first word and then you stayed there."

Melanie nodded. "Yeah, I guess I did. Is that wrong?"

"Not wrong, no. But this is more effective if you zero in on each word as it's given to you. What you just did was paint a pretty picture."

"We don't want pretty?"

Sonny laughed. "Pretty is fine, but we want to get under the picture. You'll see. Let's try again, and I'll give you a new word each time. Don't think about the words as you say them or after you say them."

Melanie sipped her coffee and stared at the sand in front of her, trying to block out anything but what her niece said.

"All right." She patted Sonny's arm. "Let's try again."

Sonny said, "College."

Melanie: "Learn."

Sonny: "Truth."

Melanie said, "Lies" and couldn't help trying to think about what she was saying. But Sonny was too fast for her.

Sonny: "Discovery."

Melanie: "Confession."

Sonny: "Sins."

Melanie: "Forgiven." Good Christian answer. Melanie liked it.

Sonny: "Sister."

Melanie: "Lost."

And the moment the word left her lips, Melanie caught her breath.

Yes, that was her sister, as Melanie saw her. She looked at Sonny, who studied her notepad, a frown marring her lovely face.

"Why did you stop, Sonny?"

Sonny looked up, a slight redness rimming her eyes. "That's it. That's the word. Lost."

"We can pray for her, you know."

"I'm not even talking about Mom, to tell you the truth. Not directly. Lost is how *I* feel, Aunt Melanie."

Tears welled up, and she quickly wiped them away.

"I'm twenty-four years old. That might not sound like a lot to some people, but it's all the life I've known, and I've spent it with a constant, fuzzy cloud of questions following behind me. I'm tired of not knowing who my father was, if my parents ever loved each other, who my grandparents are. I don't know what's shameful or sinister about my origin or birth or background, but my mom wants that part of me buried, and I want it unearthed."

Melanie struggled with sadness for Sonny and anger toward Teresa. She couldn't imagine putting her son through this kind of sorrow. She took Sonny's hand.

"Look. I'm going to tell you all about your grandparents. You're an adult and so am I, and you're entitled to know whatever I can share with you about them, as far as I'm concerned. I won't step on your mother's toes, but we can pray about all of this."

And she immediately asked for God's guidance and peace before she stood up.

"Come on. Let's take a walk."

Sonny almost looked frightened.

Melanie smiled and put out her hand. "It's all good stuff. Come on."

Sonny tucked her notepad under her chair. She stood and walked with Melanie, their blankets wrapped around themselves haphazardly, like woolen togas.

Melanie put her arm across Sonny's shoulders. "Your grandma, Barbara Hobbes, is seventy-one. She married your grandpa, Jack Miller, when she was…twenty, I think. I have a picture of them in my purse back at the house. I'll show you."

"Do you have pictures of when they were younger?"

"Yep." Melanie smiled at her. "But not with me. Looks as if we're going to have to get you over to the house. Not only do you need to meet your Uncle Bailey and Micah, you need to see some photo albums."

Sonny's grateful smile broke Melanie's heart.

"Thanks, Aunt Melanie."

"My pleasure. Your grandpa was a civil engineer. He's retired now, of course. After they married, he brought Grandma to the San Francisco Bay area, where he was involved in building bridges. Grandma taught high school English until your mother and I came along."

In this manner Melanie filled in a small part of Sonny's puzzle, and she had no doubt she was doing the right thing.

It wasn't until the two women had walked and chatted for some time that something Sonny said earlier triggered an alarm in Melanie's mind.

The realization hit her so hard, she spoke before she considered what she might be revealing.

"Hang on a second, Sonny. When you were speaking back there after our word association thing, I think I missed something. Am I remembering wrong, or did you say you were twenty-four?"

Thirty

"Here, now." Teresa passed a small condiment bowl to Irina. Dishes, pans, and various ingredients cluttered the kitchen counters. "Melt the butter in the microwave. We'll add it to the pancake mixture once I've finished combining everything else together."

Irina did as instructed and glanced over her shoulder at Teresa. "Somehow I never pictured you this way."

"What way?"

"Cooking pancakes. Or cooking anything, actually."

Teresa put a hand on her hip and shook her hair away from her face. "I'm not completely dependent upon restaurant delivery people, Irina. I'm just not a big fan of cooking. It's messy, boring, and frankly, I'm a little clumsy. Without fail I manage to cut my fingers or burn myself on the edge of a pan, a burner that's still hot, whatever."

"So why are we doing this?"

"To have fun!" Teresa used her mixing spoon to gesture, splattering batter against the wall. "Oh, perfect."

Irina laughed.

"You see?" Teresa grabbed a sponge and wiped at the batter. "Not my forte."

"But fun."

Teresa looked back at Irina and had to stop to identify the feeling that washed over her. It was pleasure. Over someone else's enjoyment. Well. She had experienced that before. Plenty of times. She was sure of it.

"Where did Melanie and Sonny go?" Irina walked over to one of the front windows. "They're joining us for breakfast, aren't they?"

"Yeah. They're out there doing one of Sonny's psycho things. They'll be back soon."

"Does Sonny call them psycho things?"

Teresa stopped wiping. She sighed. "No. I guess I say that to tease her. Not the most supportive mother, am I?"

"I don't know. Sonny said you were completely supportive about her college work."

"Did she?" Teresa smiled. "Huh."

Irina wordlessly walked into her bedroom.

Teresa wondered if she had said something wrong. "Irina?"

"Yeah." Irina walked back out, Teresa's hair clip in her hands. She brought it into the kitchen and held it out to Teresa.

"Oh. Hang on. My hands are all sloppy." She dashed them under the water and dried them, but then she stopped short of putting her hand out. "Hey, you know what? Why don't you keep that? I just didn't want to lose it. Now that I know it's not lost, I'd like you to have it."

Irina shook her head. "No. Thank you, though. That's so kind of you. But it would always remind me of something I did wrong. Anyway, I didn't really take it because I wanted it."

"Why did you take it?" Teresa asked, reaching for it. "Why do you take things when you take them?"

With a deep breath, Irina leaned against the kitchen counter. "I don't know if I can explain it. Sometimes I don't even know why I'm feeling anxious, but I am. And sometimes when that happens I see something that isn't mine. I get this urge, such a strong urge, as if the anxiety is going to make me scream. And if I take the thing I see, it's as if I got to scream without actually screaming."

Teresa didn't say anything at first. She suddenly realized how difficult the profession was that Sonny pursued. What do you say to something like that?

Irina said, "I guess you don't get anxious like that."

Teresa shrugged. "Maybe I do. I do plenty of screaming, as you may have noticed at rehearsals."

They both chuckled.

Irina went to the cupboard and pulled out plates and coffee mugs. "My therapist would probably say your reaction is much healthier."

"You see a therapist about this?" Teresa put her hair clip in her pocket, poured the butter into her bowl, and then finished mixing the batter.

"Yes, about this and the bulimia."

"Bulimia? Good grief, Irina. What happened to you to cause all of this crazy stuff?"

Irina didn't speak. She stood at the counter, plates and cups stacked in front of her, staring at Teresa with caution in her eyes.

"Oh! Ugh." Teresa smacked the heel of her hand against her head. "Stupid. I'm sorry. Not crazy. I don't mean crazy as in *you're crazy*. I just meant…oh, never mind. Let's make pancakes. I shouldn't be trying to talk with you about this."

"I think it's my mother."

"Sorry?"

Irina sighed. "My birth mother. It bothers me that I don't remember her face. It makes me sad that her life was so awful. I remember feeling as if she left me when I was little and in the orphanage. I know it wasn't her fault. She was too sick. But sometimes that's how I felt. And then when Mom and Dad—my adoptive parents—when they brought Grigori and me here, I felt as if we had deserted her. My mother."

"But, um, I thought your mother—"

"Yes, she died. But I still…sometimes I still feel as if we left her there. With the awful life she had. And we came here. To so much."

Teresa was at a loss. She should hug the girl, maybe. She was terrible at the hugging thing. But just the same she stepped around the counter and approached Irina.

Irina seemed to feel as uncomfortable with the hug as Teresa was. She was taller than Teresa, so she spoke over Teresa's shoulder.

"If my mother had lived, no matter what happened to us, she would have been able to tell me more about my early life. About *her* life and how Grigori and I came into it. It's difficult to go through life ignorant about where you came from. Who your parents were. What they meant to each other. What you meant to them. Even if it's bad, I think it would help me understand myself. I know my father went to prison. He was a thief. Sometimes I wonder if he was a thief like me."

Teresa could see through the front window. She saw Melanie and Sonny approaching. She experienced such mixed feelings. She felt outgunned in talking about these matters with Irina, so she was hopeful Sonny knew enough about her field to step in. But she wasn't blind to the parallels between Irina's laments and her own daughter's.

Was this the kind of emotional mess she forced upon Sonny? Certainly Irina's childhood was rife with turmoil far beyond anything Sonny had experienced. But that hunger for knowledge about the past—both young women shared that. It was too late for Irina. But Sonny's answers were all right here.

Teresa just had to share them. And risk losing the one thing in life that made everything worthwhile.

Thirty-One

Sonny broke out in a sweat.

She sat in her room, books and notes spread across her bed.

This wasn't good. This was right up there with that dream you have of showing up for a test completely unprepared. And naked.

Here she was, administering tests to her mom and aunt as if she knew what she was doing. It didn't matter at first that the tests were from textbooks and reference materials used for graduate studies. At least it didn't matter when it came to administering the tests. She totally understood how to administer them, and she knew she had done all right in that.

But deciphering the results? There wasn't a single instruction in these books about that. Why hadn't she checked that out before prancing around as if she knew what she was doing?

Did she dare fake it? Act as if she understood the answers Melanie and her mother had given, and hope she was right in her interpretation?

As soon as that thought emerged, so did conviction. What hope did she have of becoming an ethical therapist if she already contemplated winging it with the results?

There was nothing to do but interpret the results through her own bachelor's-degree level of competence and deliver them as such. She'd have to confess to Melanie and her mom that her interpretations might be completely wrong.

So, after giving everything a good review, she took a deep breath and left her bedroom, notes in hand.

Everyone was gone. She stepped out onto the front porch and saw them down on the beach, sitting in chairs, possibly asleep.

Well, that had been a heavy breakfast. How cool that her mom and Irina had prepared it together. And Irina had actually eaten. As far as Sonny could tell, everything had stayed put. One thing she *had* learned was that conflicts tended to be easier to handle when they were in the open, as Irina's bulimia now seemed to be.

Sonny noticed there were extra chairs in the cluster down there on the beach, and they were filled. She shaded her eyes and squinted. Melanie, Irina, Teresa, and whom? Grig—she recognized those well-toned legs and that beautiful, light-brown hair. Her pulse picked up. She couldn't wait to spend more time with him. But how about the other chair? Dark legs. Dark hair. Ah, dreadlocks.

Zeke.

Sonny smiled. He was one cool guy.

With a catch in her throat, Sonny realized that her mom was the only one in the entire group this week—Melanie, Grig, Irina, Julian, Zeke, and Sonny herself—who didn't know the Lord. Until now that hadn't dawned on her. She had never considered this trip about her mom's spirituality. Maybe it wasn't, but that had to be a pretty fantastic coincidence.

She prayed aloud. "I'm going to leave that issue with You, Lord. I'm rattling Mom's cage enough this week as it is."

She stepped off the porch, retrieved a beach chair, and walked down to join the others.

Zeke saw her coming first. "Ah, the counselor arrives." His smile filled Sonny with encouragement. But then she realized she had never said anything to Zeke about wanting to be a counselor. With dismay she understood Melanie and her mom had probably told him about her exercises with them. They were expecting a substantive psychological evaluation, and she was about to deliver nothing but guesswork.

Everyone turned to greet her. Grig got up, took her chair, and set it up for her.

"Thanks."

Zeke stood. "Here, you should take my chair. I didn't plan to stay."

"Oh, no. Please stay for a while, Zeke." Sonny had such a sense of peace around this guy, and right now that was what she needed.

She sank into the chair and let her shoulders droop. "I have a confession to make." She dropped her forehead into one of her hands. "This is so embarrassing."

No one said anything at first. Then Irina spoke. The fact that her voice sounded so innocent only made her words more amusing.

"Is it more embarrassing than admitting you force yourself to throw up all the time after getting caught stealing things from your roommates?"

They all laughed, rather cautiously, and Teresa reached over to give Irina a pat on the shoulder.

Sonny looked at Irina and smiled. She couldn't believe Irina had said that so openly. Then Sonny gasped before she could stop herself.

"What is it?" Irina looked down at herself. "What's the matter?"

"Nothing." Sonny shook her head and took up her notes as if to discuss them.

"Sonny, tell me, please." Irina lifted her eyebrows, and Sonny wanted to crawl away rather than answer her.

"I can take it."

They were all looking at Sonny, expectation and concern in their faces. Sonny put her notes down and now covered her face with both her hands. "Oh, man, I would *not* have said anything if I had thought quicker. But, Irina, I think you're wearing my missing swimsuit."

All eyes turned to Irina, who looked down at herself again. Sonny uncovered her face and saw several of the others look at each other and grimace.

Without looking back up, Irina spoke, almost as if she were speaking to the swimsuit. "I *wondered* where this came from!"

She met eyes with Sonny, and Sonny couldn't help it. She laughed. "I'm sorry," she said. "I shouldn't laugh. I know this is serious stuff."

But Irina laughed too, which seemed to relax everyone else.

Teresa frowned. "But you're a foot taller than Sonny. How can her suit possibly fit you?"

"It's stretchy," Sonny said. "And I'm not *that* much shorter—"

Irina stood. "I'll go back to change—"

"No way." Sonny put her hand up like a traffic cop. "I have plenty of suits with me. I'm just glad to know I wasn't imagining things. I was *sure* I packed it."

"Speaking of imagining things," Melanie said, "when do you want to get together with Teresa and me to discuss the exercises you did with us?"

Sonny sighed. "Well, that's the embarrassing confession I have to make. I don't want you guys to lose faith in my capabilities, but I think I administered tests to you I'm not necessarily qualified to decipher."

Teresa waved the comment aside. "Not a problem. I'd be just fine with dropping the whole thing."

"Oh, that doesn't seem right." Irina spoke and immediately looked as if she surprised even herself. "I mean, you could at least give it a try, Sonny, couldn't you?"

"I agree," Melanie said. "I'm interested in what you *think* you learned. We didn't do that much in the way of testing, anyway. We could just use your notes as a beginning point. For a discussion." She looked directly at Teresa. "Between the three of us."

Sonny took note of a subtle change in Melanie's attitude. She was more assertive about talking with her sister. Maybe this wasn't a lost case after all if Melanie was going to help her press her mother for more openness.

Teresa stood. "I'm just going to take a quick dip to cool off. I'll be right back."

Grig said, "I'll walk down with you. Come on, Irina." He looked at Sonny. "We're going to go for a swim. Irina and I will hang out in the water when Teresa comes back. That will give you three ladies some privacy." With a pointed glance in Teresa's direction, he extended a hand to help Irina out of her chair.

"I must go too." Zeke stood, but not before giving Sonny a subtle tilt of the head to signal her to join him.

She acted as if she were just being polite, standing to say goodbye. "You should stop back later if you're around, Zeke."

He spoke softly to her as they stepped away. "I'm curious, sister. If you don't mind my asking, what was your motive when you gave those tests to your mother and aunt?"

She glanced at their chairs. Everyone but Melanie was gone, and Melanie looked engrossed in watching the others walk to the water's edge.

"I just wanted to get them thinking about themselves and this family. We have a lot of, um, unresolved issues, and all of the secrets have closed us off from each other. I'm trying to encourage some openness, you know?"

He nodded. "Honesty, yes. Good motive. You have to be honest if you want more than a how-ya-doing-just-fine relationship. It can hurt sometimes, though. Are you ready for that?"

"I hope so."

"Have you prayed about all of this?"

"Lots."

His grin was brilliant and infectious. "Then you'll be excellent. I'll remember all three of you today. Blessings, sister."

"You too, Zeke."

She watched him walk away and took a quick moment to pray one more request for guidance before turning back to her aunt. Melanie waited, comfortably stretched out on her chair. Farther out, near the waves, Grig appeared to encourage Teresa to return.

Sonny smiled. Between Zeke, Grig, and Irina, she had plenty of allies in her efforts. Melanie could probably be added to that list too.

The one exception to the list, the one roadblock in her journey, looked less than thrilled as she slowly walked back to Sonny, kicking sand all the way.

Thirty-Two

Melanie's heart ached for Sonny. She didn't know when she had seen anyone so tense while sitting in a comfy beach chair. By the ocean. On a gorgeous afternoon.

"Stop stressing about this, Sonny. Do the best you can. Remember that you know more about this kind of thing than either your mom or I do."

"That's right." Teresa pulled her wet hair back into a ponytail. "You graduated with highest honors, for crying out loud. We'll keep in mind that your interpretations might not be accurate, but I'm sure we're both willing to hear what you have to say."

Melanie studied Teresa. That comment didn't sound wholly supportive.

"Um, okay." Sonny picked up her notes. "I'll tell you what I *think* your house exercises indicated. See, when you visualize the house and describe the things I ask about, a lot of what you're saying actually reflects what you think of yourself."

Melanie saw Teresa squint in thought. She was probably trying to remember and relate the responses she gave Sonny earlier. Melanie was tempted to do the same.

Sonny continued. "I thought it would be good for each of you to hear what the other said, because I imagine you've lost track of that kind of thing over the years apart. I mean, you've probably lost track of how the other feels about herself. Assuming you ever knew."

Melanie smiled. She noticed Sonny didn't ask their permission to share their responses with the other. Smart girl. Maybe not entirely ethical, but the girl knew her mama.

"Okay. Melanie, your house was unassuming but well-tended. Cosmetically the house was pretty on the outside, manicured, windows perfectly symmetrical on either side of the door, with the face of the house painted to match nicely with the honey brown roof."

Teresa and Sonny stared at her. Melanie laughed and pushed her honey-colored hair away from her face.

"Wow, when you know you're talking about yourself, it sounds pretty obvious, doesn't it? I guess I do try to keep up appearances. Except when I'm at the beach."

"One really nice thing you mentioned," Sonny said, "was that your house had room for plenty of friends. Your house was surrounded by a white picket fence, so you have boundaries—probably a healthy thing. But there was an overall welcoming sound to your description. I think that sounds like you. You seem to like people."

Teresa finally commented. "Well, who doesn't like people?"

After too long a silence, Melanie said, "Um, sure."

"Okay, so let's talk about how you see the inside, Melanie." Sonny waited for them to look back at her before continuing.

Melanie didn't want this to turn into a competition with Teresa. She had more important things to bring up with her when the time was right. "Go ahead, Sonny."

"You mention tidiness, but a lived-in feel, and soft colors. I'm guessing, but I would think that could mean you're not struggling with a lot of confusion in life these days, that you feel pretty comfortable with how things are working out."

"Mm-hmm, that feels right." Melanie thought of how much she missed the comfort of home with Bailey and Micah. The thought triggered another, and she gasped. "Oh! Heavens, what day is it?"

"Tuesday," Teresa said. "Why? What's wrong? Aren't you comfy with how things are working out right now?"

Melanie rolled her eyes at Teresa. "Nothing's wrong. I just lost track of the day. Go on, Sonny. When we're done, remind me to tell you all about Thursday, okay?"

"Uh-huh. Thursday. But for now, there was one thing I saw that you might want to think about, Aunt Melanie."

"Is this the secret room thing?" Teresa leaned forward.

"No, not yet. It's just that you mentioned antique furniture and pretty rugs on hardwood floors. And that might mean there are old issues and maybe hard things—things that are difficult for you to think about—that you prefer to cover up and ignore."

Melanie shot a glance at Teresa. Sonny was better at this than she realized.

"And then, yes, there's the secret room. You saw a flower vase—a vessel used to hold beautiful things."

"Right. And it was broken." Melanie said it without thinking. She had remembered the image so vividly she forgot to let Sonny talk. She was struck by Teresa's immediate gasp, and then she could tell from Sonny's expression she hadn't meant for Teresa to hear that bit of information yet.

"I'm sorry, Sonny. I didn't mean to jump the gun on you."

"That's okay." Sonny put a hand on Teresa's arm. "Mom, don't read too much into this. Let's just keep going. Let's look at your house description."

Teresa stood. "I don't think this makes sense, Sonny. Why are we doing this when you admit you're grossly unqualified to—"

"Mom, I'm not *grossly* unqualified—"

"She's pegged me pretty well so far," Melanie said.

"Oh, sure," Teresa said. "Your pretty little house with a tiny hidden antique here and there. Wait 'til she gets a hold of my mess."

Sonny laughed. "Mom, it's not that bad. Come on, sit down."

Teresa sighed and sat down heavily. "Fine. Go ahead."

"Okay, so you described your house as a mansion. 'Big, classy, and well situated.'"

"I didn't realize we were talking about ourselves. I wouldn't have sounded so puffed up if I had actually been talking about myself."

Melanie said, "There's nothing wrong with being classy and well situated. You *are* both of those things."

"Hey, who's doing the therapizing here?" Teresa said, but then she finished with, "Thank you."

"Therapizing?" Sonny regarded Teresa, one eyebrow raised.

"Whatever. Go on."

"All right. Melanie's correct, I think. You seem to have a firm handle on your standing in life. You know you're a success and you're unapologetic about it. That's fine. You described the items inside your mansion as expensive and delicate. That could mean you feel protective of your feelings and you don't want anyone to be able to hurt them."

Melanie watched Teresa, who said nothing but stared at the ground, pursing her lips.

"And then there was the doll in your secret room."

Teresa shot her head back up. She looked from Sonny to Melanie.

Sonny said, "The doll was broken, which I have to say could be absolutely divine revelation here, considering you both had broken items in your secret rooms. I'm like you, Melanie. I don't believe in coincidence."

Melanie couldn't speak. She didn't know if Teresa remembered the nicknames their father had for them when they were young, but she suspected she remembered now. Teresa was his little songbird. Melanie was his little doll.

"So, um, Melanie," Sonny continued, looking from Melanie to Teresa, "since a vase tends to hold pretty things—maybe we could stretch that to *precious* things—I would think maybe you feel brokenhearted about something?"

"Maybe." Melanie couldn't look at Teresa.

"And Mom—"

Teresa stood. "This is giving me a splitting headache, Sonny. I need to take a break."

Melanie said, "Wait. Sonny, how about the word associations—did you get anything from those?"

Sonny shrugged, but she spoke quickly, as if trying to get it out before Teresa ran. "I didn't do much of that with either of you." She flipped forward in her notes. "But what little I got was that you, Mom, feel, well…"

Melanie couldn't believe Teresa was still here. But her expression wasn't terribly friendly.

"What, Sonny? Please tell us how I feel."

"Um, maybe a little ashamed?"

"Oh, for crying out loud. Just because I said the *word* 'shame' doesn't mean I *feel* shame. I said 'running' too, if you'll remember. Maybe I wish I could have been a marathon runner."

"Do you?" Sonny asked.

"Ugh. Never mind. I've got to go find some aspirin." Teresa left everything behind and ran for the beach house.

Melanie watched her for a moment before giving Sonny a smile. She hoped it was more encouraging than it felt.

Sonny sighed, but she carried on. "Can't say that reaction was a big surprise." She looked back at her notes. "Anyway, Aunt Melanie, your word association suggested that you love family, but—"

"But I feel like I lost my sister?"

Sonny looked at her as if their loss was mutual. Then she gazed in Teresa's direction. "Exactly."

Thirty-Three

If she learned nothing else on this trip, Sonny had learned that her family could pretend with the best of them. Matters kept boiling just shy of the surface between her mom, Melanie, and herself, yet they could still get together for an outing like this one as if the waters were cool and calm.

Along with Irina and Grig, they strolled through Old Town San Diego as if they were happy-go-lucky tourists like everyone else. The idea made Sonny wonder how many of the groups around them were on the verge of eruption and yet not showing it.

Grig made a point of steering her away from the rest of the women. She was relieved by his efforts.

"How did the counseling session go?"

His kind eyes expressed so much understanding that she almost felt as if she didn't need to answer.

She gave him a rueful look. "Well, this is certainly good training for the real thing. I would imagine actual sessions with dysfunctional families—which probably means all families—tend to go the same way. It would be nice if the therapist could easily uncover painful issues and lead everyone to hugs and loving restoration, but I think that kind of outcome is slow in coming, if it comes at all."

"You still think this is what you want to do with your life?"

"Oh, yeah. I think this week is particularly dicey because this is *my* family. I wouldn't try to counsel Mom and Melanie for real. This is probably like being your own attorney."

"You have fools for clients?"

Sonny looked ahead at her mom and Melanie, who were perusing a Southwestern pottery stall with Irina. She smiled. "No, I wouldn't call them fools. Foolish, maybe, just as I am."

"How so?"

"We're all so frightened by the truth. But that verse from John is right: 'The truth will set you free.' I don't know why it's so scary to plow through it to get to the other side."

He grinned at her. "When did you start quoting from the Bible?"

She grinned right back at him. "What? Did you think you were the only person reading the Bible? There are others of us, you know."

He stopped walking, so she did too. The way he studied her eyes made her short of breath. He spoke quietly.

"Sonny, did you…are you…"

"What?"

"Are you a believer now?"

She laughed. "Of course I am. I told you that." Then she frowned. "Didn't I?"

He shook his head, but that grin came back.

"You mean, you couldn't tell?" She put a hand on her hip.

He chuckled. "We haven't really talked that much, you know."

"Well, didn't Irina say something?"

"She's talked a lot about you, but she didn't say anything about your being a Christian. Did you make that decision at school?"

"Mm-hmm. Remember encouraging me to look into one of the campus groups?"

"And you did it. I'm so impressed."

"And persuasive." She smiled.

He laughed. "This is so awesome! I just want to pick you up in a big ol' bear hug."

"Don't let me stop you—"

Before she could finish her sentence, he did exactly that, right in front of everyone. A tiny shriek of surprise escaped from her, and then she laughed with him. She hadn't even had time to move her arms from her sides, so the hug was definitely one-sided.

Not that she was complaining.

When he put her down, he was slow to fully release her. He loosened his grip, but his arms lingered around her for a few seconds.

Whoa. Was he going to kiss her? Her thoughts rushed. He'd only been here one day. Was it too soon to kiss him? They had a history. Did that make it all right? But they were both good Christians and needed to be wiser than that. And what did she mean, 'too soon'? Had she already decided that was where this was going?

But while she mentally spazzed and stared all sparkly eyed at him, he got a grip. Or, rather, released it. Released her.

"Sonny, I, um…"

Um, what? She wasn't going to help him on this one.

"I'm just so happy for you. This is the answer to my prayers from way back."

Was that all? Not that she wasn't thrilled that God answered Grig's prayers, and not that it wasn't completely great he prayed for her, but he had looked a little moon-eyed for a moment there too. He didn't have to do anything about it, but she kind of hoped he would at least *say* something about it.

He turned to resume walking, but then he halted. Sonny followed his gaze and saw Irina, Melanie, and Teresa all watching them. Apparently they considered the bear hug incident a performance for their viewing pleasure. All three women still held various pieces of pottery, as if the seas of Atlantis had enveloped and frozen them, midmotion. Not a single one of them had the good manners to jerk to alertness and look away, once Sonny and Grig caught them spying. Irina and Melanie had silly grins on their faces, and Teresa had a single eyebrow raised, as if this turn of events was something she had predicted.

Sonny muttered to Grig. "Man. Thanks for not kissing me."

He laughed out loud and gently knocked shoulders with her. "My pleasure."

She gave him a playful frown, but the smoldering look that passed over his face convinced her there was more there than one Christian happy to know about another. They shared a smile and headed toward the women.

He lightly placed his hand against the small of her back as he leaned down. He spoke as if they were alone, rather than surrounded by hundreds of tourists.

"I realize this week isn't about us. But I think Irina made it pretty obvious that the month at Sunset Beach meant more to me than you might have realized. I know we both had good reasons for not pursuing the relationship further, but I'd really like to spend a little time with you before we have to part ways again."

Those comments both thrilled and dismayed her. "I'd like that too." She loved the idea of spending time with him. She remembered vividly how quickly they had drawn close to each other four years ago. And it hadn't been a mere physical attraction.

But he sounded resigned to parting ways in a few days. What was the point, really, of spending time together, only to face another tearful goodbye at the end of the week? She'd rather not get too close. It would hurt less.

The other women had moved on to a restaurant farther ahead. It looked as if they were studying the menu. Grig and Sonny slowed at the ceramics stall where the others had stopped before. Grig picked up a smiling yellow sun that had a blue crescent moon face superimposed over its left half. The result was a two-faced sculpture, colorful but extremely busy.

He held it up and spoke to Sonny in his Russian accent. "What is your diagnosis, Doctor? Would you say multiple personality disorder?"

"That's pretty good." She took the sun in her hands. "Actually they call it dissociative identity disorder now."

"Have you ever met anyone with it?"

She shook her head. "No. To tell you the truth, chances are I never will. I'll do some clinical work for my master's, but when I go into practice I'll probably do family counseling or something like that. I think that's about as much sadness as I can take on a regular basis, you know?"

He nodded. "Teresa mentioned you were going back to La Jolla for grad school. When do you—"

"Oh, right. Well, listen. Don't mention this to Mom yet, because I don't want her freaking out and making elaborate plans for my time. I don't expect to *have* much time, frankly, but I'm actually not going to La Jolla. I'm going to Berkeley."

"Berkeley?" She heard a lift in his voice.

"Yeah, and—"

"How have you kept that from her?" Yes, he fought a grin.

"Well, I'm footing the bill this time, so she hasn't been in the loop at all. And I want to keep it that way for a while. If she knows how close I'm going to be to her—"

"And to me."

She stopped and stared at him. He was right, of course. He must live close to Oakland if he played for the symphony there. "You, um, you live in Oakland too?"

"Mm-hmm." He wiggled his eyebrows when he said it, which made her laugh. Now *that* was more like it.

She put the dysfunctional sun back on its peg. She heard her name and saw Irina waving them over to the restaurant.

"They're waiting for us," Sonny said. "Dinnertime already, I guess."

They walked toward the restaurant, and Grig simply said, "Berkeley, huh?"

"Yeah, but remember, not a word to Mom."

Grig nodded, and Sonny suppressed a girlish grin. She wasn't completely certain, but she thought the spring in Grig's step had less to do with keeping a secret than it had to do with the possibilities that secret held.

Thirty-Four

The next morning Melanie sat in the passenger seat opposite Grig in his rented SUV.

"I still can't believe you managed to get us all up and at it today." She glanced back at Sonny, who was flanked by Irina and Teresa in the backseat. Their lively conversation had something to do with *Carmina Burana,* which apparently was related to Irina's upcoming solos. Sonny was either listening intently or forming an evaluation of the psychological dynamic between the two sopranos.

Grig brought Melanie's attention back to him. "It wasn't my managing this morning; it was you ladies agreeing. One thing I've learned from Irina and my mother is that most women are naturally accommodating. They just want the respect of a fair warning. You can't always do that, but in this case, I guess I got the idea early enough. I'm glad you were all flexible. I've never been to Catalina."

"Oh, it's lovely. My husband, Bailey, and I celebrated our tenth wedding anniversary there."

The drive to Long Beach took two hours, and they were almost there.

"I chatted last night with an old friend of mine, Jason. He runs a helicopter shuttle from Long Beach to Catalina Island. He offered to fly us to the island to spend the day. Jason's a good guy, and I think he'd do this for us anyway." Grig looked back at Irina before continuing. "But he's always had a soft spot for Irina. I think he wanted to date her back when we were all at Jessup together."

"She wasn't interested?"

Grig shrugged. "To tell you the truth, she hasn't dated much. Plenty of guys are interested, but she's been cautious. I guess it's better for her to feel more confident in other areas before she gets too involved with anyone romantically."

Jason's continued interest in Irina was obvious, but tempered, during the short time he spent with the group. She sat up front in the helicopter seat next to his. They made an attractive couple. Her long, pale-brown hair and dramatic blue eyes beautifully offset his classically handsome dark coloring. The copter was surprisingly soundproof, but their conversation was inaudible from the middle seat, where Melanie and Teresa sat. Still, it looked to Melanie as if Irina and Jason enjoyed catching up during the fifteen-minute flight.

Melanie smiled, the eternal romantic. Irina was young, but not too young to become more independent than she was. She could beat the psychological battles she fought. And maybe she could move to the San Diego area. The San Diego Master Chorale would probably love to include her in their ranks.

Although Melanie and Teresa sat together, they faced away from each other in order to watch as they approached the island. Probably for the best, Melanie decided. Like a sore throat, their relationship on this trip seemed the least comfortable early in the morning and late at night.

Sonny and Grig sat behind them. Again, Melanie was unable to hear their conversation, but she thought the mood between them already seemed as if they were a couple. She noticed that development last night at the restaurant. Something had happened to bring them to a new level. She wasn't sure what that was, but she was pleased to see it. This was a tense week for Sonny, and the unexpected addition of Grig to the group blessed the atmosphere with promise.

And with variety! If Grig hadn't arranged this day's journey, they'd probably sit on the beach all day getting testy with one another. More specifically, getting testy with Teresa, and vice versa. Instead, they would get testy with each other while enjoying the horseback rides and snorkeling Grig planned.

Irina swung around to address the others. "There's Catalina. Look at how pretty it is! The boats all look like little jewels."

She was right. Most of the boats were still docked near the beach at Avalon. There was a symmetry to the way they dotted the shallower waters in orderly chains.

As the helicopter neared the landing pad, Melanie spotted some early morning parasailors flying behind speedboats. She turned to Grig.

"You weren't expecting any of us to do that, were you?"

Grig followed where she pointed and laughed. "I haven't even done that."

"Oh, I have!" Sonny said to him. "You'll have to try it sometime. Melanie, you'd love it too. I'll bet Micah would think you were the coolest mom ever."

Melanie patted her hair. "And what makes you think he doesn't already consider me that?"

Suddenly, the mention of Micah made her gasp.

"Rats! Sonny, I keep forgetting to tell you. I have to drive back home to Spring Valley for dinner tomorrow night."

"Oh, no," Sonny said. "You're going to come back, aren't you?"

"Sure. Micah just needs Bailey and me to join him and his new girl-friend's family for an interview dinner."

Teresa finally acknowledged that she was listening to the conversation. "Interview dinner?"

Melanie lifted her hands, palms up. "They're apparently very careful about whom they'll let their daughter date. They want to make sure Micah is from a wholesome environment."

Teresa rolled her eyes. "Positively puritanical."

"I don't think that's so bad," Sonny said.

"No?" Teresa turned to address her. "How would you react if I told you I didn't think Grig here was wholesome enough for you?"

Well, now. That just sounded like an announcement about Grig and Sonny's relationship. Or maybe it was a challenge.

Sonny reddened but sounded confident when she responded. "I'd say thanks for your concern, but I'm twenty-four, not seventeen. Whom I date is my responsibility."

Instantly the muted whir of the helicopter blades became the only sound heard for what felt like an interminable period of time.

Thirty-Five

July 1
Catalina Island, California

When they landed in Catalina, Jason seemed reluctant to let them leave.

"We have a lot planned today," Grig said, shaking Jason's hand and giving him an understanding grin.

"You should spend the Fourth of July here." Jason spoke to Irina first, but then he took them all in with his hopeful expression.

Irina's eyes widened. "Oh, I like that idea. I'll bet it's beautiful. The Fourth is when? Saturday?"

"We check out of the beach house on Saturday," Teresa said.

Jason smiled, especially at Irina. "Sounds like a plan, then."

"I...I mean, I'd want to go if the rest of you wanted to." Irina looked at the others.

"Why don't we talk about it today?" Grig shot a quick wink at Melanie. "We should let everyone have a chance to think about it."

Melanie smiled back. Smart fellow, that one. He really had learned the value of showing respect to accommodating women.

"We'll get back to you, Jase. See you in several hours. Thanks again, man." With a pat on Jason's back, Grig led the group toward the taxis.

"I'm still not sure about horses." Teresa had hung back while trail arrangements were made, and she held back now, while the Catalina Stables staff helped everyone mount.

"Come on, Mom. You'll do great." Sonny put on a riding helmet and nimbly mounted her horse.

"Sure, easy for you to say." Teresa stooped to retie her shoes. "I sent you to all of those horse camps when you were a Girl Scout. I haven't been on a horse for years."

"It's just a one-hour ride, Teresa." Grig spoke in a soothing tone. "Nothing faster than a walk. You'll love it. And the stables may not be here the next time you visit, from what Jason tells me. We should enjoy it while we can."

The staff members left them for a moment. Grig handed Teresa a helmet. "Here, I'll help you up."

Irina and Melanie were already on their horses. Melanie thought it best that she not say anything, but Irina tried to encourage Teresa.

"You can do it, Teresa. You've done much more intimidating things than this."

Teresa seemed to put her mind to it abruptly. In one swift move, she jammed on her helmet and raised her foot into the stirrup. "Help me then, Grig. Don't let me fall."

So Grig stood right behind her as she lifted herself up, but she was on the left side of her horse, and she had her right foot firmly in the stirrup.

"Well, what in the world—" She leaned back against Grig while hanging on to the saddle horn.

Grig grunted just a little and tried to discreetly support her with his hands. "No, Teresa. I think you've got the wrong foot in there."

"Mom." Sonny barely stifled her laughter. "You're going to be sitting on the horse backwards if you follow that through."

"Well, hold on to me, then, Grig, so I can switch."

Grig's voice became muffled as Teresa released the saddle horn and allowed her back to rest against his face. "Teresa, maybe you should just get down and start—"

"No, I've got it." Teresa grumbled something as she struggled. Something about her foot being stuck. And maybe a swear word.

Her horse chose this precise moment to stroll up for a visit with Melanie's horse.

"He's going!" Teresa stated the obvious with a touch of panic.
"He's—"

"Yep," Grig muttered and still supported Teresa's back with his face, his
hands ineffectively pressed against her shoulders. He sashayed sideways
to keep pace with the horse. "Teresa, why don't you—" and the rest was
all a muffled grunt.

Melanie couldn't hold back anymore. They were like a really horrible
circus act. She tried to say something heartening, but all she could get
out was a burst of laughter.

Irina and Sonny followed suit, just as Teresa managed to loosen her
foot and Grig gave one superhuman lift to help her plop on to her horse
correctly. She grabbed the horse around the neck until she could slip her
feet into the stirrups and sit up. Her antics gave the other women a chance
to get their laughter under control.

Teresa finally looked at Grig, which prompted the others to do the
same.

His hair was wet and plastered against his sweaty forehead. He looked
as if he had carried a woman far heavier than Teresa far longer than he
had.

Even Teresa laughed when he casually rested his knuckles against his
waist and tried to blow his hair out of his face.

"Thank you, Grig," she said. "You can't say I didn't warn you."

Despite the happy results of Grig and Teresa's labors, Melanie had to
wonder if they were being given some kind of divine warning when their
guide walked out of the office. He spoke behind himself to someone at
the registration desk.

"Larkspur, right?"

And then he walked directly to Teresa's horse. The man was a rugged
fellow. Fiftyish. Oblivious to the heroic efforts that led to Teresa's seemingly confident position atop Larkspur, he smiled at her. "We're going
to have to ask you to mount a different horse, little lady. This one's not
working today."

Thirty-Six

Teresa hated to admit it, but she completely loved the horse ride. The replacement horse they gave her behaved as if it were given the perfect dose of Valium, or whatever the horse pill equivalent was called. Not too skittish, not too lazy, but *just* right. And her second attempt at mounting a horse was far smoother, especially with that big hunk of a guide helping her. Ken. The man was all dark-eyed cowboy, and he took complete command of what part of her needed to be where, no questions asked. Grig was a sweetheart, but he hadn't known quite where to put his hands.

She liked that in a possible boyfriend for her daughter.

"Look, Teresa!" Irina took a particular liking to Teresa on the ride, most likely because she was also fairly inexperienced with horses. The two of them stuck close to Ken, each for her own reasons. Melanie, Sonny, and Grig lagged comfortably behind.

"See the buffalo down there in the field?" The wonder in Irina's eyes was catching.

"Well, look at that," Teresa said. "That must be a mother and her two cubs. Or, no, it's not cubs—"

"Calves," Ken said, smiling at her over his shoulder.

She smiled right back. "Of course, calves." With her heels she encouraged Zippy, as she had dubbed her horse, to shuffle on up closer to the cowboy.

"They're rather charming," she said. "And unexpected. How in the world did buffalo get over here to the island?"

She wasn't about to guess, not after the "cub" comment. But she knew there was no way they swam all the way from the mainland, and she couldn't imagine why anyone would go to the trouble of shipping them or airlifting them here.

"Someone made a silent movie here back in the twenties. A Western called *The Vanishing American*. It was about the cavalry and Native Americans. They shipped a handful of the buffalo out here and then left them behind. There are about four hundred of them now. You might even see some down on the beach while you're here."

"Can we go closer?" Irina sidled up to Teresa.

Ken shook his head. "That mama isn't going to take kindly to that, no."

So they followed him through tall, silver-gray grasses and palm trees, past an old stone wall, and then up into the hills to capture a stunning view of the shops, hotels, and restaurants that cascaded toward the sea in Avalon Bay, where the helicopter had landed earlier.

Ken pointed at one sight in particular. "That huge round building down there is the casino. You should check that out, if you haven't already. No gambling, just a theater and a ballroom. But it's really something inside. Built in 1929."

"From here the view reminds me a little of Greece or the Italian Riviera," Teresa said.

"You've been to those countries?" Ken regarded her with appreciation.

"Mm-hmm." She looked back at the view. "Really stunning places."

"Never been to Europe, myself."

She gave him a friendly, mildly flirtatious smile. "You haven't been hanging around with the right people."

He chuckled, and they headed back to the stables.

~

It wasn't until the group sat at Armstrong's Seafood Restaurant, enjoying shellfish, the sun, and the view, that Grig pulled a business card from his wallet.

"Oh, Teresa. I nearly forgot about this. Our guide handed it to me when I settled the bill for the horse ride. He asked me to give it to you."

She took the card, the front of which had contact information for the stables. She flipped it over and saw another phone number, handwritten. Beneath that was the name, Ken Wiley, and words that made her grin.

Just in case you're the "right people."

Thirty-Seven

Sonny had to laugh. Grig had certainly put some life into the party.

She hadn't lost sight of her serious motives in drawing her mom and Melanie to the beach house, but just as child therapists often use toys and puppets to help their little patients relax and communicate, she could see the merits in helping her mom and Melanie relax for the day.

It was only Wednesday. If she didn't get definite information from her mom by Friday, she would probably drop all pretense at civility and diplomacy. She would likely set aside the counseling measures and just have a full-on temper tantrum until she got her answers.

With that in mind, she figured a day of helicopter flying, horseback riding, and now, snorkeling was the perfect interruption. And Grig had thoroughly impressed everyone by picking up the sizable tab for all of these activities.

"Snorkeling?" She laughed when he mentioned it at lunch. All of them laughed, except Irina, who looked frightened by the idea. "Grig," Sonny said, "you really know how to pack a day full of activity, don't you?"

"What activity? All we've done is ride horses and have lunch. Why do you think I asked you all to bring your swimsuits?" He handed his credit card to the server. "Okay, ladies, I'm sorry. I should have mentioned the snorkeling before."

Melanie raised her hand. "He should get credit for mentioning it to me. I knew this was coming."

Grig said, "I've been trying to give you plenty of time to consider my plans," he looked at his watch, "but, it's only one o'clock in the afternoon, and I'll be the one driving us home." He grinned at all of them. "You can nap all the way back to the beach house, but how often do you have a chance to snorkel at Catalina? Really, it would be insane not to."

Teresa surprised Sonny by her somewhat agreeable comment. "I do feel pretty salty and sweaty from the horse ride. It would be nice to splash around a little."

"Well, I'm game." Melanie drank the last of her iced tea and set down her empty glass like a gavel. "I'm already dozy. This will wake me up. And I love snorkeling. How about it, Irina?"

"Grigori, you know I've never done that before. I don't know how."

Grig leaned over, put his arm across her shoulder and gave her a kiss on the cheek. "It's just like floating on top of the pool. Simple and safe. And we can hire a guide so we'll be sure to snorkel at the best sites."

Sonny nudged Teresa. "Mom! A guide! Get out your dance card."

Her eyes heavy lidded, Teresa gave Sonny a lopsided smile. "Thank you for your concern, young lady. But I'm forty-six, not seventeen. Whom I date is my responsibility."

Sonny laughed. "Touché."

In fact, their guide, Gayle, was an athletic, extremely tanned woman about Teresa and Melanie's age. And she brought them to excellent snorkeling spots.

Sonny was so proud of Irina, who had to fight a wave of panic when they first waded into the water at Lover's Cove.

"We don't have to go far, Irina," Sonny said, hoping to quell her fears.

"It's not the water that scares me. I'm fine in the ocean, remember?"

"Oh, that's right. Boogie boarding didn't bother you at all. So what's the problem?"

"Jellyfish, mostly." Irina rubbed at her arm as if she had just been stung. "When our parents first took us to one of the beach coves after we moved here from Russia, I swam into a group of them. I'm sure I'm remembering it worse than it was, but I can't help the fear."

"Oh, you poor thing. That would scare me too." Sonny looked over at the guide and said, "Hey, Gayle, what are the chances of our running into jellyfish around here?"

Her question caused both Melanie and Teresa to pop their heads out of the water. Sonny laughed. They looked like identical bookends, with ridiculous, protruding lips over their mouthpieces.

Gayle shook her head. "Not likely in these shallow waters. The divers are more likely to come across jellyfish than we are."

Grig swam over. "I'll keep my eye out, Irina. I didn't realize that's what you were worried about. But the water's so clear here. We'll be able to see if there are jellyfish anywhere around."

Irina still looked doubtful, but she gamely donned her mask and snorkel to join the group.

They threw food across the water as Gayle instructed, to attract the fish. "Now we just wait a little while." The water soon became a frenzied scene, but once the activity slowed, they were treated to their own personal view of some of God's finest work.

"The bright orange ones are our famous Garibaldi," Gayle told them. "Their young are the spotted ones." She surfaced often to describe what they saw.

Sonny couldn't keep track of which was which, especially since the juveniles looked different from the adults, but Gayle pointed out kelp bass, sheephead, and something called a rock wrasse. And a senorita, which wasn't as pretty as it sounded like it would be.

Sonny was intent upon watching one of the small fish apparently nibbling leftovers off of a larger fish when she heard a water-muffled shout. By the time she jerked her head out of the water, she heard Irina more clearly.

"Ow!" Irina had yanked her mouthpiece out and raised a hand to the side of her head.

Sonny swam to her, but Teresa was already there. As a matter of fact, Teresa was the problem.

"Teresa, you kicked me in the head!" Irina acted more shocked and indignant than physically hurt.

Teresa pulled her snorkel away from her mouth. "For crying out loud, Irina! You got me all paranoid about those stupid jellyfish. I thought I felt one on my leg."

Gayle looked as if she were trying not to smile. "I think Irina's hair might have floated near your leg, Teresa. Really, I don't think you have to worry about jellyfish."

Sonny laughed. "Yeah, but now we have to worry about Mom kicking us in the head."

She could tell her mom tried to raise a critical eyebrow at her, but her snorkel mask prevented it.

Their time with Gayle was about up, anyway, so they explored just a short while longer before returning their gear.

Sonny thought Irina looked disappointed that Jason wasn't their pilot for the return flight to Long Beach. An older man was on the job, and Grig sat next to him up front.

"Did I sense some sparks between you and Jason?" Sonny sat next to Irina in the back of the helicopter and was able to speak to her without others hearing.

"Maybe." Irina shrugged. "He was interested in me back at college, but I had too much to focus on with my vocal training and...and just life."

Sonny nodded. From what she had seen, Irina still needed some guidance with "just life." She hoped she had an effective counselor back home. "Well, I think he's still interested. And he's a cutie. Grig says he's a good guy. Maybe God has something in store for you there at some point in the future. You never know."

Directly in front of her, Melanie answered her cell phone. Sonny wasn't able to hear the conversation, but she could tell her mom was eavesdropping. When Melanie hung up, she turned to speak to all three women.

"All right, I can't remember if I told you all this. I need to drive back home tomorrow night for a dinner date with my husband and son."

"Yeah, you mentioned that," Sonny said.

"Your interview with the Puritans," Teresa said.

Melanie gave her a lopsided smile. "Right." She looked back at Sonny and Irina. "But I plan to drive back to you all directly from dinner. The restaurant is only about twenty minutes from here. I mean, from the beach house."

"Thanks, Aunt Melanie," Sonny said, grinning. "I'm so glad you aren't cutting your trip short. We still have—"

She almost said "a lot of work to do," but edited for sales value.

"We still have almost three days of fun ahead of us."

"Ah, good." Teresa said. "So we're finally done with the counseling."

Thirty-Eight

July 1
Mission Beach
San Diego, California

Teresa didn't know what the big deal was. So she said she was sick of the whole counseling thing. Weren't they all? Sonny was obviously uncomfortable with it. Melanie tiptoed on eggshells about it.

And Teresa would have given anything if the uncomfortable choices of the past several decades could be undone. But since they couldn't be, she hoped they could be ignored. Gotten over.

Couldn't they all move on?

But no.

Sonny was the dearest person in her life. Teresa wasn't all gung ho on the whole God thing, but she was no idiot. She knew Sonny was a gift in her life. A shining star, rather than what looked like a catastrophe twenty-five years ago when she learned she was pregnant.

Still. This insistence on hammering out the nasty stuff. It was too much. How had Sonny turned out this way? Certainly Teresa had never encouraged this touchy-feely, let's-talk-it-all-out nonsense. She said as much to Sonny this evening when Sonny complained that Teresa avoided reality.

"No, Mom," Sonny said. "Frankly, we're not done with the counseling."

Teresa knew her daughter well enough to know her feelings were hurt. She had that angry little quiver in her voice she got when she sensed injustice of any kind.

"Come *on*, Mom. I mean, counseling is going to be my life, and this is my life we're talking about this week."

Sonny made the comment while they flew back to Long Beach, and both Teresa and Melanie tried to keep the conversation from escalating while they flew over the Pacific. And while they drove back to Mission Beach.

But eventually it happened. Melanie spoke in Sonny's defense, which irked Teresa, and the tension pulled at all of them until everyone leaked annoyance. They quietly snarled out their comments in the back of Grig's SUV all the way home. Grig kept his eyes on the road. Irina dozed or pretended to. But the three Miller women huddled in the backseat like *Macbeth's* hags. They grumbled out an argument destined to explode once they were free from the confines of the Ford Explorer that hurtled toward Mission Beach.

By the time they reached the beach house, Irina had awakened and asked if anyone would mind her staying at Julian's place with Grig. Grig didn't even wait for a response. He simply took her bag and led her away. He called to the others over his shoulder. "See you all tomorrow."

That left the three of them to duke it out. And Teresa could see Melanie had reached the end of her sugar-sweet, forgiving church-lady rope.

"All right, Teresa," Melanie said. She dropped her tote bag on the floor as soon as they walked into the house. She turned on several lights. "I think it's time we got it all out into the open. Sonny needs this. I need this. And, although you obviously don't agree, I think *you* need this."

"Don't you think that's like picking up a hatchet and saying, 'Just bend your head forward, Teresa. It's time we made everything better'?"

"Mom! Why the melodrama?" Sonny looked as if she might cry, and that drew at something deep in Teresa's heart. "I mean, I'm not going anywhere. Think about it. Is there something I could tell *you* about *me* that would make you walk out of my life? Is there?"

That stopped Teresa. Maybe she was tired, but she honestly had to think about that. "I don't know, Sonny."

Sonny couldn't have registered more shock if Teresa had slapped her. "Mom." And it seemed someone pulled the very core of Sonny away, as if it were a miracle she even stood upright. Tears came to her eyes so quickly Teresa almost cried out. If she could only take back that moment's hesitation.

"Sonny. No. I'm sorry, no. There's nothing that would make me shut myself off from you."

Sonny sank onto the couch and cried. "But don't you see, Mom, how you've always shut yourself off from me? I've always wanted to know you. I want to know how I came into your life. Was it such a horrible event? Even if it was horrible, was it so bad you couldn't tell me, at least honor me enough to let me be a part of it?"

It wasn't until that moment Teresa remembered that Melanie was in the room. She was crying too. She sat next to Sonny, put her arm around her, and looked Teresa in the eye. It was obvious she could barely speak.

"Tell her his name, Teresa, or I will."

Teresa gasped, and the air felt too voluminous for her to bear. Melanie knew?

Shocked, Teresa spoke. "*What?*"

Melanie wiped her sleeve across her face. "I figured it out yesterday. Sonny told me she was twenty-four. I had assumed she was twenty-two, since she just graduated from college. I thought all along that you conceived Sonny years after you broke away from me."

Sonny looked up, collecting herself. "No," she told Melanie. "I traveled a little before I went to school. I didn't go to UCSD 'til I was twenty."

Silence.

"Why?" Sonny asked. "What does that mean?"

Teresa simply couldn't bring herself to say it. It killed her to let Melanie be the one. But that was how it began.

"His name," Melanie told Sonny, "is David Sommerhill."

Teresa dropped into the chair next to the couch, mute.

"He was my college sweetheart," Melanie said. "I made a lot of mistakes by the time I fell in love with him, but I didn't make a mistake with him."

Sonny frowned. "*Your* sweetheart? And what do you mean, you didn't make a mistake with him? You didn't…sleep with him?"

"Right. I wasn't a Christian then. Not yet. I had lived some pretty wild times. Survived some horrible decisions. And by the time I met David, I knew there had to be something more important than living for the day. It took a while, but years later I understood it was infinitely more fulfilling to live for Christ."

Sonny just nodded and looked at Teresa, who still couldn't bring herself to speak.

So Melanie did. "But David couldn't understand my refusal to become intimate. He thought I was antiquated. Out of touch. Still, he accepted that I wouldn't take that step until we were married. And then one day, right after we graduated, he simply disappeared. At first, I didn't know why."

Teresa looked at her lap, and despite her anger with Melanie, she felt warm tears drop onto her hands.

Melanie said, "I was devastated. And so confused. But a couple of months later, your mom came to me." She stopped and took a breath. "Teresa? Do you want to say anything?"

Teresa couldn't look up. Her world was so heavy she couldn't lift her head enough to look her dear, innocent daughter in the eye.

"Your mom told me that she and David had slept together. So then I knew why he left. He didn't have the courage to tell me. He left that task for your mother."

Teresa nodded. But she still didn't look up. She knew more was coming.

Melanie continued. "But it wasn't until you told me your age yesterday that I understood why your mother bothered to tell me she slept with David."

"No!" Teresa looked up at Melanie. "That's not why I told you."

Melanie spoke with an anger Teresa hadn't seen since they were very young.

"Yes, that's exactly why, Teresa. That's why you waited almost two months after he left me. For two months you let me cry on your shoulder, knowing full well why he left. It wasn't until you realized you were pregnant that you told me. The two of you betrayed me together."

Teresa stood, barely able to speak around her tears. "And you were so unforgiving. I couldn't tell you the rest. Couldn't tell you about the pregnancy. And I knew you'd tell Mom and Dad. I knew you'd all hate me for what I did. For what happened. I was sure you'd hate my child.

There was no way I could go to any of you with the rest of the story. That's why I left. I knew I was alone." She broke down, sobbing.

"You weren't alone." Melanie almost shouted at her through her tears. "You were ashamed. You never gave anyone a chance to forgive you. You were too full of pride to admit you needed anyone."

Sonny jumped up from the couch. She put her hands up, as if to stop all conversation. She kept her head down, and her words came out choked. "Okay. That's enough." She sighed deeply. "That's…" She took a deep breath and said it again. "That's enough for now." She turned and went back to her bedroom. She quietly closed the door.

Teresa looked at Melanie and nodded. She bit her lip and wiped tears from her face, and then she turned and walked quietly to her room.

This was supposed to draw them all closer? Teresa couldn't imagine waking tomorrow and ever finding life the same.

Thirty-Nine

The house was dark and silent, save for the hint of moonlight slanting through the windows and the muted break of the lonely waves outside. Melanie knew it wasn't as late as it seemed. She picked up a slip of paper and walked out to the kitchen.

She heard a door open and prayed it wasn't Teresa. Relief washed over her when she saw Sonny walk out of her bedroom. Sonny's eyes were puffy, and she looked as if she hadn't come anywhere near to falling asleep. She held what appeared to be a Bible in her hands.

Melanie spoke softly. She felt guilty. Not just for her anger before, but for all of the information she and Teresa had dumped on Sonny so swiftly. She sighed and mustered a humble smile. "Hi, sweetie."

"Hi."

Melanie poured a couple of glasses of water. She joined Sonny on the couch.

"I'm sorry, Sonny."

"For?"

Melanie shrugged. "For the lack of civility in how all of that information came out."

"Civility." Sonny's chuckle was rueful. "Perhaps some place exists where news like that can be shared civilly. At least you and Mom have real blood running through your veins. I can't imagine anyone spilling that kind of information without a degree of passion. Not in a world without cyborgs."

Melanie smiled and touched her niece's cheek. "I love you, Sonny."

Sonny's eyes teared up again, and she only mouthed her words. "I love you too."

Melanie looked at Sonny's Bible. "Did you come out here to read your Bible? I'm going back to my room, so you'll have privacy."

"Actually, I thought I'd sit on the porch for a few minutes." Sonny took an afghan from the couch and pulled it over her shoulders. "I think the fresh air will do me good."

Melanie nodded. She stood to leave, but she presented the slip of paper to Sonny before she left.

"What's this?" Sonny took the paper. She raised her eyebrows when she read it.

"He's a psychiatrist here in San Diego." Melanie wiped at her eyes and smiled. "You'd think I would have seen the connection, huh? Psychiatry, psychology. Obviously, it's in your genes."

Sonny looked at her. "Have you stayed in touch with him?"

Melanie shook her head. "Not for years. We crossed paths at our college reunion. About twelve years ago." She looked down the hall and back again. "Your mom didn't go. He told me then that he practiced in San Diego. I just looked him up. That's where he's currently listed. Just in case you want to call him."

Sonny looked at the paper and then tucked it in the pocket of her shorts. "Thanks."

Melanie sighed and gave her a hug. She pulled away and looked her in the eye. "I don't think he knows, Sonny. I don't think he knows about you."

Forty

Sonny lit a candle and set it on the front porch table. She opened her Bible and pulled out the small devotional magazine she tucked inside before the trip to the beach house. She curled up in one of the chairs and closed her eyes to pray.

I don't even know what to say, Lord. I feel like such a failure. This was a large piece of the puzzle tonight. And I know I've prayed for answers for a long time. But that was some pretty tough stuff to hear, and I feel like I should have handled it better. I've done nothing but bug them to unload. Then I pretty much told them to shut up. It's just that…well, I guess I already figured I came from something shameful—

Distant voices interrupted her prayer. She lifted her head and saw Julian and Zeke sitting on the seawall in front of Julian's home. The boardwalk streetlamp lit them from behind.

Despite her plan to spend this time alone with God, Sonny found herself wondering if Julian and Zeke would mind her interrupting them.

At that moment Julian laughed about something Zeke said, and then he did a double take in Sonny's direction. He said something to Zeke and then waved at her.

She waved back and stood, which prompted him to beckon her over.

Sonny pulled the afghan tighter around herself and padded across the boardwalk to join them.

"Alone tonight, sister?" Zeke welcomed her with his signature smile.

"Seems that way." She clenched her jaw to try not to tear up, but she teared up anyway. She wasn't sure if they could tell.

170

Julian gestured to the empty space next to Zeke. "Come sit with us. We're just closing out the day before I drive Zeke back home."

"Kind of late, huh?" Sonny settled down onto the wall.

Zeke checked his watch. "Nine, but my wife took our little one to visit Grandma and Grandpa this week, so I'm being the wild man and staying out past my bedtime."

Sonny smiled. "I thought it was later."

Neither of them said anything, but their faces were so kind. So welcoming.

"I've never met my grandparents before." She blurted that out without thought. And still she struggled not to cry. She didn't want to sink into self-pity. Not here, at least, in front of these men who seemed so strong in the Lord. What kind of Christian was she going to seem, all wrapped up in herself?

But Zeke's voice and eyes pulled on her emotions as if they were magnetic. "Ah, what a tragedy. Are they no longer alive?"

"Oh, they're alive." Sonny tried to smile, but her mouth wobbled. "My mother...um, she's been estranged from them all my life."

Julian nodded. "Your aunt said something about that, I think. Or maybe she just said the two of them—the sisters—were estranged."

"Yeah. That too."

"Your aunt also mentioned you were trying out a bit of counseling this week—"

Sonny burst into tears and saw both men start in surprise. "I'm a miserable counselor. I've made a mess of everything."

"Ah, no. I'm sure it's not as bad as that, sister," Zeke said, patting her on the shoulder.

Even though Julian and Zeke had the tiniest of smiles in their expressions, she didn't take offense. She actually felt a sense of relief, knowing they saw enough promise in her situation to keep from grimacing in despair. They seemed like fond uncles, so she was more comfortable talking to them.

Before she knew what she was doing, she told them everything—about the betrayal during the twins' college years, Teresa's determined separation from family, Sonny's quest to know the truth, and tonight's unveiling of her father's identity.

"And I've just stomped all over the concept of counselor-client privilege by telling you all that, so it's a good thing I don't have a license to lose."

Julian whistled softly when she finally stopped talking. "Yes, that's quite a bit of information for one night."

"I'm sorry," Sonny said, cringing. "I didn't mean to go on—"

Julian laughed. "No, dear. I meant for you. Quite a bit for you to learn in one sitting. You're certainly not imposing on me. On us. I'd love to be able to offer advice, or at least a sense of comfort." He reached into his back pocket and handed her a handkerchief. "What I don't understand is why you feel *you've* made a mess of everything."

"Did I say that?" Sonny wiped her tears and her nose.

Zeke nodded. "You did."

"Oh. Well, I guess I just think a *real* counselor could have guided everyone to open up without it all being so...angry."

"Sonny," Julian said. He looked out at the waves for a moment. "Eons ago, when my wife wanted me to see a counselor, I didn't go along. And when my misplaced priorities caused me to lose everything that mattered to me, I still fought against getting guidance from a counselor. I thank God I was eventually blessed with the wise counsel of my old neighbor, Faith, and this fine gentleman beside me." He looked at her. "What I'm saying is that I do see the value and importance of a good counselor."

She nodded.

"But in this particular case, don't you think it would be best if you stopped assessing yourself as a counselor and started addressing your situation as a daughter? As a niece? As a granddaughter?"

"What do you mean?"

Zeke said, "Of everyone involved in tonight's 'mess,' as you called it, you're the youngest person involved, the one who's had the least control. Your mother chose to run from her family all these years. Whether or not she stops running now is her choice. Your aunt has to decide for herself, after all this time, if she can find forgiveness in her heart. Your father, if he ever comes into the picture, has to make his own decisions too. But, sister, you were given no choice before tonight. You don't need to counsel your family. You need to be loved by them. Give them that opportunity."

Julian nodded.

"But how do I do that?"

"Just let them know you're available, Sonny," Julian said, smiling at her. "A simple 'I love you' to your mom and aunt should be enough. But it sounds as if you might have to take a few extra steps to reach your grandparents."

"And my father." She pulled the slip of paper from her pocket.

"Ah, is that him?" Zeke's eyes widened.

"Mm-hmm. Melanie looked him up for me. He's local."

"You bet he's loco," Zeke said, "if he doesn't jump at the chance to meet a fine daughter like you."

Sonny laughed. "I said local." She got up from the seawall and pulled the blanket back around herself. She cocked her head toward the beach house. "You know, I had just started to pray over there when I heard you two. I think God wanted me to come talk with you. You've made me feel better. More certain of what to do. Thanks."

They both smiled. Julian gave her a jaunty salute. "Always a pleasure to be in His service."

Forty-One

The house remained still when Sonny returned. She only stepped in as far as the kitchen, where her purse sat on the counter. She retrieved her cell phone, walked back outside, and quietly pulled the front door closed behind her.

This time, when she bent her head to pray, she knew exactly what she wanted to say.

Thank You, Lord, for Zeke and Julian. Thank You for using them to get my focus straight. I may not be an effective counselor yet, but I'm a good daughter. Help me to be a better daughter, Lord. A more loving one. A forgiving and understanding one. Please help me to be a loving niece to Aunt Melanie. And to Uncle Bailey. And a good cousin. And granddaughter.

And right now, Lord, I ask that You help me to communicate well, so I might be a good daughter to my father too. Help me to not be bad news.

And then, before she could talk herself out of it, she dialed the number Melanie had given her. She knew it would be his office phone, but she wanted to at least try before she went to bed tonight.

As expected, she got the answering machine. From his recording, Sonny learned that he handled his own messages, that he was *Dr.* Sommerhill, and, since this wasn't an emergency, she would hear back from him tomorrow.

Well, maybe. She'd see how he reacted to this message.

"Um, yes. My name is Sonata Miller, and I very much would like to hear back from you, Dr. Sommerhill. My mother is Teresa Miller, an old acquaintance of yours from your days at UC Berkeley. And my aunt is

Melanie Miller-Hines. I'm twenty-four years old, Dr. Sommerhill. Twenty-four. I know you were never told about me, and I only learned about you today. I'm in San Diego for two more days and would very much like to talk with you before I leave. That's all. Just a chance to say hello."

She left her number and ended the call. It wasn't until she closed her phone that she noticed her hands were shaking. She took a deep breath, blew out the candle on the table, and walked back inside.

When she got into bed, she remembered how hard it used to be to fall asleep the night before Christmas. She always struggled to calm herself down from the anticipation of the gifts that would await her the next morning.

Tonight was similar with respect to anticipation. And because she had prayed, she was determined to consider tomorrow's outcome a gift from God.

Even if it didn't feel that way.

Forty-Two

Melanie was ninety-nine percent sure she was doing the right thing by sneaking out and heading home. She had prayed like mad about it because the decision didn't sit completely well with her. Her plan felt like the very behavior she had accused Teresa of these past twenty-five years.

But she was certain the time had come to do something other than pretend nothing had happened. If she did that with Bailey, with Micah, with anyone other than Teresa, her life would be utter chaos and confusion.

Yet every time she stopped to pray about what to do next, she didn't feel comfortable with hashing out more fully the screaming match they had when they arrived home from Catalina. Not even calmly. She told God she was willing to forgive, to ask for forgiveness, and to accept that Teresa might want to go right back to her separation from the rest of the family.

Was leaving really what God wanted her to do?

After three hours of sleep, she awoke and reached her decision. She packed her bags, and then she stopped to pray about it again, hoping to feel more certain. She wasn't blessed with any more assurance, but time was short at this point. She had to act.

She wrote the note.

It was only five in the morning when she quietly stepped out of her room. She carried her bag and the note.

She tiptoed across the darkened living room and set the paper in a prominent place on the kitchen counter.

She felt the cool morning air and quickly closed the door behind herself to avoid letting the dampness or early morning sounds sneak into the silent house.

She placed her bag in the car and hunted for her keys.

With a glance at Julian's upstairs apartment, Melanie uttered a hushed, "Thank You, Lord." With Irina sleeping over there, instead of her usual room at this end of the beach house, she wouldn't hear Melanie's car door or the turn of her engine.

Melanie rested her head against the steering wheel before she pulled out.

"I'm leaning on You, Lord. At least I *think* I am." She frowned and heaved a resigned sigh.

She gave the adorable little beach house a final once-over, took a deep breath, and drove away.

Forty-Three

Teresa closed her eyes and pressed her palms against them. She was still so tired.

Certainly coffee would help. After all, she hadn't been drinking the night before. She had merely been crying. And depressed. And full of anger, fear, and she didn't know what else. All bad stuff. So of course she felt horrible this morning.

She dressed and tucked her cell phone into her pocket. She would check in with Anton. Yes, he had hung up on her last time they talked, but she had endured quite a lot in the last few days. Surely he would find a good excuse for her to leave when she explained Melanie's tirade against her last night.

She didn't hear anyone else moving about when she opened her bedroom door. Good. She wasn't quite sure how to handle anyone. Of course, it would have to be done. They would all have to face each other today. She couldn't just sneak away. With her history, she would never hear the end of it.

But coffee first. She walked toward the kitchen.

At least Grig and Irina had been spared. They would be on the look-out for the Miller women this morning, no doubt. But at least the Miller women wouldn't have to extend considerable apologies to them. Yes, they had nitpicked in the back of Grig's SUV, but Grig had *no* idea how bad it got afterward, and that was just fine.

She saw an open note propped up on the kitchen counter. She glanced at the signature.

Melanie.

Teresa looked behind herself, and then she stepped back to the bedrooms. Melanie's door was open, and there was no sign of her. Not even an item of clothing, a brush, or a flip-flop.

She hurried back into the kitchen and read the note.

To the beach house ladies:

I promise you, I'm writing this note after much prayer. I want you all to know I haven't made this decision emotionally or quickly.

I think it's best that I head home today. I was going to leave anyway for Micah's "puritanical dinner," as I believe Teresa called it. And I think it's best for me to just go and to stay in Spring Valley afterward. I wanted to leave early this morning to avoid anyone trying to talk me out of this.

Sonny, I think this is a good time for you and your mom to spend together. We unveiled some significant revelations last night, and I think my purpose—as somewhat of a catalyst—has been served. If I'm gone, I think you'll be more likely to talk with each other these last few days. After that, I'm only a phone call away, and hopefully we'll have more time together during the summer and during your graduate work at La Jolla. I love you and am so happy you found me and some of the other answers you sought.

Teresa, I must admit this is easier to say in a note. I'm sorry for the anger I threw your way last night. I should probably have talked with you as soon as I figured out about David the other day.

But I was angry then too. I'm sorry for sounding so harsh twenty-five years ago and yesterday. You were right. I was unforgiving when I heard the news back in college, and I was unforgiving yesterday. But I'm forgiving today, and I hope you feel the same way. When Sonny contacted me about coming to the beach house, I was eager to meet her. But I was eager to see you, as well. I hoped the empty years would fall away as soon as we saw each other. Maybe next time.

Irina, I meant it when I said I wanted to come hear you when you solo. Please be sure to contact me and give me the details. My number is below. You're a lovely girl, and I hope to get to know you and your gent of a brother better.

Much love to all of you,
Melanie

Melanie was gone. Teresa's initial relief vanished in the wake of sudden panic. Sonny would blame her for this, without a doubt. If she hadn't kept her secrets bottled up for so long, the whole explosion yesterday wouldn't have happened. And Melanie wouldn't have run for the hills. Or, in this case, for the valley. Whatever, Teresa was dog meat. She was sure of it.

Never mind the coffee, Teresa was abruptly filled with the desire for a brisk morning walk on the beach. She didn't even sneak back to her room for her sandals. She would barefoot it out of here and try to figure out her defense.

She had almost shut the front door behind herself when she dashed back in and grabbed the note. She thought she heard movement coming from the bedroom area, so she ran out and quietly shut the door. If Sonny didn't read the note until Teresa returned, that would give Teresa more time to prepare a plan to elicit Sonny's sympathy.

There weren't many people out yet, and the air was nice and cool. Teresa actually wouldn't have minded having her cotton pullover with her. Ah, well, she'd just walk harder and work up more body heat. She needed to cover some distance quickly, anyway.

When the beach house was well out of sight, she slowed, and her mind relaxed too.

Anton. She'd get his advice. She pulled him up on speed dial.

"Well, you're up bright and early." His voice shook, as if he were in quick motion.

"I'm taking a walk on the beach, Anton. I need to talk with you."

"And I'm taking a walk to my spin class. Aren't we the healthy ones? My class starts in a couple of minutes. What's up? More drama, I assume?"

"Well, we sure aren't sitting around crocheting doilies. My sister and I had it out last night, and this morning she ran off."

"So you're out looking for her?"

"Good grief, no. She drove home. Back to…I don't know, not far from here. But she's blown off the rest of the week."

"What did you do to her?"

Teresa gasped and slowed down. "Thanks so much for the support! Believe me, she gave as good as she got."

"Fine. So why are you calling me? I'll tell you you're in the right if you cough up some details, but give me the abridged version. I had Chinese last night and the sodium bloat is the worst. I've got a little Jabba the Hut thing going on around the eyelids. I can't afford to miss this class."

"Okay. We kind of opened up a twenty-five-year-old conflict."

"Twenty-five years? Honey, that must have been like getting a peek at Dorian Gray's ugly mug. Lots of anger and bitterness built up, I'll bet."

"Well, on her side, yeah."

"Which tells me you were the one who stomped all over her, lo these many years ago. Am I right?"

She sighed. "Why did I call you?"

"Because I know you *and* love you, Teresa. Look, my class is about to start. Where do you and sissy stand right now?"

"Hello? Didn't I call you because she ran off? My daughter's going to—"

She stopped walking. "Wait a minute. What am I doing?"

"Saying goodbye to your manager?"

"Why do I always assume it's my fault, Anton? I didn't tell Melanie to run away, did I?"

"I'm going to trust that you didn't."

"Doggone right. Sonny had better not blame me for this one. I'm willing to accept the blame for the other stuff, the awful things I did twenty-five years ago. Even the one detail that hasn't come out yet. But I'm not about to take the hit for Melanie's cowardice."

"Well, there you go. Glad I was able to help. Especially considering I don't have a clue about what's going on—" His gasp and exasperated sigh caught Teresa's attention. "Now there isn't a bike for me! Teresa Miller, you've sentenced me to days of puffer fish face, do you realize that?"

"I'm sorry, sweetie."

He sighed. "No, I'll just wait for the next class. Okay. So now I have half an hour to kill. Tell me everything."

She stopped walking. She spotted a good-sized form up ahead. It looked as if something had washed up on the beach overnight.

And then she saw it move.

"Oh, my."

"Oh my what? Talk to me, Teresa."

"I'll call you back, Anton." She ended the call even though she heard a tinny version of his voice trying to keep her from doing so.

She looked around and saw no one else out. She almost turned away, but then she heard it. A pain-filled bleating sound.

She looked back again and walked closer. "Oh, no." She sighed. "It's a little seal."

She took a few more steps, but she knew nothing about wildlife. She didn't know if the thing would be so crazy with pain that it would attack her if she got too close. And was that really pain she heard? Maybe it was just scared—

But when she got close enough, she saw blood—stripes of it—beneath its flipper thingy and around. It was cut on its back and possibly its underside.

She actually spoke out to it, making a helpless grimace. "I…I don't know what to do." She looked back toward the beach house. "I can't help you—"

And it cried out that awful, lonely sound again.

Teresa released a heavy sigh. "Well, that's it." She couldn't just stand there while the poor thing suffered. She looked at the houses off the beach. They were a ways back, but they were the closest people in sight. She started over the dry sand, putting her hand out toward the seal, as if it would understand.

"Just…don't move. I'll…oh, what am I saying? I'm talking to a seal, for crying out loud."

She tried to run, which she hated doing, even on ground that *didn't* fall away underneath her. In no time she was sweating like a farmhand. So much for needing that cotton pullover.

The distance felt like miles, but she finally got to the nearest house. She knocked on the front door, and a kind-faced Latino-looking man answered. A curly-haired toddler with a pink pacifier in her mouth stood at his side, hugging his knee.

Teresa tried to smile. "I'm sorry to bother you so early—"

"Are you okay?"

She didn't know why, but tears came to her eyes when she spoke. "There's a helpless, injured seal down there on the beach. I don't know what to do for it."

He looked past her, squinting. He drew in his breath. "*Si, claro.*" He nodded to Teresa. "You're right. Hang on, I'll get my phone and come with you." He turned toward the kitchen. "Heddy, come get the baby. I need to help someone with a seal out on the beach."

His announcement prompted his entire family to come to the door, and they all spilled out of the house past Teresa. Seven or eight of them, easily. They headed toward the beach, everyone talking at once, some in English, some in Spanish.

Teresa felt responsible for the seal since she was the one who found it. "Don't touch it, okay? Don't go too near it. It's hurt."

The father called out to everyone. "Yeah, no touching. It might bite." Then he yelled at them very quickly and passionately in Spanish, but Teresa seemed to be the only one riveted by him.

"Don't worry," he said, smiling at her. "The police will know what to do." He walked out with her, his cell phone to his ear.

"They won't shoot it, will they?"

He looked at her as if she were joking. He chuckled in a comforting way.

"It's not a racehorse, lady. It's a seal. They'll do everything they can to help it, I'm sure.

She took comfort in his assuming control.

By the time they reached the beach, a few more people had gathered around.

Teresa couldn't fight the need to protect the little thing. "Stay back from it. We don't want to scare it. The police are sending help."

She heard snippets of conversation around her.

"Looks like it got tangled on some fishing line."

"But why would the mother leave it behind like that?"

"Maybe they got separated before it got hurt."

The Latino man told the group, "You know, I heard that sometimes, if a group of seals are sunning on the beach and they get startled, they panic and hurry to the water. And sometimes the babies get lost from their mothers like that."

Teresa didn't want to speculate with the rest of them. She stepped back from them but watched intently to make sure no one came too close to the injured pup. She figured they could look out for themselves, but she was worried about the seal. Poor thing. No mother. Hurting. So confused and alone.

Warm tears fell down her cheeks, and her throat tightened. Why did she feel so protective of this little creature? She wasn't even that much of an animal person.

But she felt as though this pup was her own. And…and…

It hit her, and she sighed.

Sonny would *love* this. The psychological symbolism was glaring.

This wasn't about the seal at all.

Forty-Four

Sonny sighed, flopped down onto the couch in the living room, and glanced around. She muttered under her breath. "Was it something I said?"

They were all gone. But maybe that was a good sign. She knew she didn't need to be concerned about Irina. She and Grig were probably at Julian's having a calm, cozy breakfast. Maybe she should go over there.

And there was always the chance that her mom and Melanie had gone for a beach walk together. Maybe even breakfast. It was weird, though, that they hadn't left any word of their whereabouts. Possibly too wrapped up in making amends? Fighting some more?

She got up and looked out the front window. It was too late in the morning for dueling at dawn.

Sonny hadn't forgotten her plan. Whatever she awoke to, she was determined to see God's loving hand in it.

Irina walked into her view from the front window just before she opened the door and peeked in.

"Anyone up?" Irina said, and then she saw Sonny. "Ah! Are you the first up?"

Sonny shook her head. "The last. Melanie and Mom are out. I'm not sure where."

"So come have breakfast with us. Grig ran out to get some bacon and eggs and stuff."

"Do I have time for a quick shower?"

"Super quick. No getting pretty after. Grig likes you natural, anyway. He told me so." Irina grinned and left.

Sonny smiled on her way back to the shower. That little tidbit was definitely like a gift on Christmas morning.

⁓

Grig, in a faded blue T-shirt and knee-length cutoffs, stood next to the small table in the apartment's breakfast nook. He held a sauté pan and a large serving spoon. Sonny took in his stunning features and thought he looked like a fetching commercial for stick-free cookware. Or the egg industry. Or hearty breakfasts in general. California. Romance novels. Anything.

He served her with a smile, and Irina brought plates of toast and bacon to the table. Sonny was pleased to see Irina looking comfortable with a relatively full breakfast plate. Maybe a night away from the Miller women had done her good.

That made Sonny a little sad, but she was *not* going to wallow today.

After they prayed and started eating, Grig broached the subject.

"Was it bad last night? Things sounded pretty heated by the time we left you."

"Sorry about that, Sonny," Irina said, "the leaving you thing. I just couldn't—"

Sonny put up her hand. "No apology needed. Not at all. If any of us could have escaped last night, I'm sure we would have tried." She snorted softly. "That was what my mom did for the past twenty-five years, to tell the truth. But hers was a faulty plan. Last night was just something we had to hash out. I mean, that clash was what I set this week up for."

Irina's eyes twinkled. "So you found out all you wanted to? Did Teresa tell you everything?"

"Um, well, between the two of them, I heard most of it, anyway."

She told them what she learned through Melanie and Teresa's angry exchange.

Grig studied her face. "How do you feel this morning?"

"I feel some relief, obviously, because I know so much more. But I just hope they're together right now, making amends. There was a lot of pent-up hurt being expressed last night from both of them."

"And your father, wow!" Irina leaned forward. "Are you going to try to find him?"

Sonny knew her smile was sly, but she couldn't help it. "I've already called him."

Grig and Irina looked at each other and laughed.

"I love that about you, Sonny." Grig leaned back in his chair and rested his chin on his knuckles. He grinned. "You do *not* mess around."

"I don't know that I'll hear back from him, but at least I'm doing what I can. This won't be easy for him to learn about, after all these years." She shrugged. "I would have contacted him sooner if I had known about him. I guess I always thought my father knew about me and just wasn't interested. That could turn out to be the case now too."

A pounding knock at the door startled them all.

"Grig! Irina!"

It sounded like Teresa.

Grig stood quickly to answer the door, and the girls followed him.

Teresa spoke to Grig the moment he opened the door. She looked frightened. Or maybe distressed.

"Have you heard from Sonny this morning? I can't—"

Grig had already opened the door and stepped back so Teresa could see Sonny.

"Mom? What's wrong? Is it Melanie?"

Teresa walked forcefully toward Sonny and threw her arms around her. The moist heat from her body suggested a nervous, rapid walk before she arrived here. She simultaneously burst into tears and talked into Sonny's hair. Sonny could tell the tone was confessional—or maybe needy—but her mom was so upset, she sounded as if her mouth were stuffed with Jell-O. Sonny couldn't make out a word she said. When she heard what sounded like "seal pup," she knew there was no hope of understanding her mom until she calmed down.

Sonny pulled away and looked her in the eyes. "Mom. Take some deep breaths. I can't understand you."

Grig put his hand on Teresa's shoulder. "You want to sit down, Teresa?"

Sonny watched him guide her mother to the couch, and she could have just hugged him. She knew how her mom could be toward coworkers, and

Grig had playfully hinted at her divalike behavior on the job. But right now he was protective and nurturing.

Teresa wiped at her eyes, and Irina brought a box of tissues to her. Teresa looked up at Sonny and patted the couch beside herself. As soon as Sonny sat down, Teresa turned and put her arms around her again. It looked like they were simply going to replay the Jell-O scene all over again, just from a seated position.

"Mom, what happened?"

Teresa released Sonny and heaved a sigh that traveled right down to her shoulders.

"I left you on your own, Sonny. For twenty-four years. You were alone."

"What?" Sonny shook her head. "Mom, that isn't true."

Teresa waved her off. "I know I was present. I provided for you. I showed up for your school events. I supported you financially—"

"And emotionally," Sonny said.

Teresa shrugged one shoulder. "Sort of. But I knew you were confused. You told me so a million times. Even the kids from divorced families knew their parents, you said. You used to ask me what to tell people when they asked about your father. About the rest of your family. I remember telling you to say it was none of their business. What kind of a thing was that for a schoolchild to have to say?"

"I didn't say that, Mom. I just said I didn't know. Or I said you wouldn't talk about it."

Teresa laughed ruefully. "Yes, I'm sure that depicted you as a kid from a good background. Your own mother was ashamed to tell her daughter about her family."

Sonny almost argued for her mother's sake, but she did remember some of the embarrassment she felt as a child. The absence of family members wasn't the issue. The ignorance about them was. Or, rather, the obvious secrecy.

"Sonny, I don't know why I didn't realize it fully until this morning, but all of the secrets, all of the silence, was for *my* sake. No one else's. Certainly not yours. I hung you out to dry, sweetie. I was the one person you turned to for protection. For enlightenment about your father and family. But I refused you. I left you alone on the beach, injured, crying, and confused while people gathered around, staring."

Her compassion brought tears to Sonny's eyes. But then Sonny frowned. "On the beach? Staring? Who stared? I never noticed that."

Teresa seemed to snap out of a reverie. "What? Oh, no, that was a seal pup I found this morning. But it made me think of you. I'll tell you later."

"Wow," Irina said. "So I'm *not* imagining things. I thought I heard you mention a seal in there somewhere."

They all looked at Irina, whose face suddenly registered awkwardness. "Sorry."

Sonny smiled. "No, I heard seal pup too."

Teresa looked at Grig, who raised his right hand as if he were taking an oath.

"Wounded seal pup, yep."

Teresa laughed. Sonny didn't know if she had ever seen her mom laugh so comfortably, even though her face was covered with tears.

So she was struck by how abruptly Teresa's laughter ended when Sonny asked her next question.

"Where's Melanie?"

Forty-Five

Teresa pulled the crumpled note from the pocket of her shorts. She didn't have to look Sonny in the eye, because Sonny was busy looking at the note.

She opened it, and Teresa saw her eyes immediately scan down to the bottom. She looked up at Teresa.

"Where was this? I didn't see it when I got up."

"Uh, well, that's because I took it with me. To read on my walk. And Melanie's fine, so don't worry in that regard."

Sonny's eyebrows barely moved.

Yet Teresa felt the conviction. "Oh, all right, I didn't want you to see it before I had a chance to think about it. But I had no intention of keeping it from you long term."

Sonny smiled and shook her head. She sighed. "Mom."

Teresa laughed a little. "Hey, old dog, new tricks, and all that. This was before the new leaf turned out there on the beach. With the seal pup."

Grig sat across from them and propped his feet on an ottoman, his hands behind his head. "That must have been *some* seal pup. Like an oracle or something."

Sonny laughed. "I do want to hear that story, Mom. But let me read this first. It's addressed to 'the beach house ladies,' so do you guys mind if I read it in front of our resident male?"

They all said no, including Grig. Irina swatted his feet and sat on the edge of the ottoman.

When Sonny finished reading, she lowered the note to her lap. "Well, shoot. She was supposed to take me to San Clemente to—"

She shot a look at Teresa.

Ah. So that's where they had retired. Teresa nodded. "To meet your grandparents."

"Yeah. Sorry, Mom. That was insensitive. But you could come too, you know. I mean, whenever we actually *do* go there. It sounds like Melanie may have forgotten."

"No, I don't think so," Irina said. She leaned forward and pointed to the note. "There, she says to call her 'After that,' meaning after these last few days at the beach house. I think she's expecting you to call her, like, this weekend, after we all leave."

Irina picked up the note. "But did you catch this? She thinks you'll still be local, in La Jolla, for grad school. Grig said you were going to Berkeley."

Grig sat up abruptly at the same time Sonny nabbed the note from Irina's hand, as if either action could erase what Irina had just said in front of Teresa.

But Teresa heard her perfectly well. "Berkeley? Sweetie, what's she talking about?"

Sonny looked sheepish, and now so did Grig and Irina.

"I'm sorry, Sonny," Irina said. "I forgot you didn't want to tell—"

Sonny put her hand up and shook her head at Irina.

"Sonata Miller." Teresa stood, hands on hips. "Are you telling me you'll be right around the corner from me in Oakland for the next three years? And you weren't going to let me know?"

She watched Sonny roll her eyes and grimace, expecting a rant. Instead Teresa fell onto the couch next to her and gathered her up in another hug, delighted. Her smile belied her words. "You bad thing, to keep that from me. Are you afraid I'm going to be a control-freak if you're that close?" She squeezed Sonny and released her. "Give me *some* credit, baby. And believe me, you wouldn't have kept that secret from me much longer. I'm the queen of secrets, and I can tell you, *that* one would have been tough to keep."

"I planned to tell you during the summer, Mom, after I solidified my living arrangements and stuff. I just hadn't gotten to it yet."

"Well, watch out for plans like that. Secrets have a way of dragging on and getting big, I'm here to tell you."

"Yes, ma'am."

"So what do you want to do about Melanie?" Teresa asked Sonny.

Sonny shifted to look at her more directly. "What do you mean?"

Teresa shrugged. "I just assumed you'd want to call her and convince her to come back tonight after her dinner with the dating police."

Irina nodded. "That's what I thought too."

Sonny looked at both women and then at Grig.

Teresa saw he didn't feel the need to volunteer an opinion. She gained more respect for this guy every day.

"Why is this my decision?" Sonny said.

Teresa chuckled. "Sonny, you're the grand marshal of this week's festivities. What do you want to do?"

After a moment Sonny said, "I guess we shouldn't ask her to come back."

Teresa was surprised by how much that plan bothered her. Hadn't her first reaction been relief when she learned Melanie was gone? "But, um, why?" She scratched her head.

Sonny seemed to enjoy Teresa's reaction. Well, fine. She could take Sonny's amused scrutiny.

Sonny said, "Melanie said she prayed about this. She says she thinks God wanted her to go home."

Teresa crossed her legs and considered that. Then she pointed her finger as she thought out loud. "Okay, but maybe that was what God wanted *her* to do. Maybe He wants *us* to call her back."

Sonny smiled. "Mom, do you feel God is telling you to call her back?"

"Don't be so smug. So I don't know what God wants. But do you think He can't talk through me just because I'm not all churchy like you and Melanie?"

Irina stood and cleared the cold breakfast from the table. "Hey, I remember a story in the Bible where God spoke through a donkey. So He probably *could* speak through you, Teresa."

Teresa stared at Irina. Sometimes the girl just shut her right up. When she looked at Grig and Sonny, she could see they were thoroughly enjoying this exchange.

"Mom, I don't doubt God's ability to speak through you. It's just that I think Melanie made her decision after considerable prayer. And we do want to try to honor His will here. So have you…prayed about this at all?"

Teresa was *not* going to lie about something like that, but after a moment she looked at Irina. "Did the donkey pray?"

Grig laughed out loud. He joined Irina in the kitchen and grabbed a few pieces of toast. "How about we give it a little time this morning? We can pray—"

"You mean, silently," Teresa said. "I'm fine with you guys praying, but I don't want to sit around having a church service over this."

Grig extended his hand and nodded. "Whatever, that's fine. We can pray in our own ways. And we can listen, and then around lunchtime you ladies can decide."

"I like it," Sonny said. "Sometimes the answer becomes pretty clear all by itself when you do that."

A light knocking caught their attention. Teresa opened the door to Julian. He wore his swimming trunks.

"Ah, good, I hoped you ladies were here. Good morning."

A chorus of greetings followed.

Julian said, "I promised Melanie one more day of boogie boarding before the week was out. I was about to hit the waves and wondered if you'd all like to join me this morning before lunch." He frowned and glanced around the room. "Where *is* Melanie?"

Forty-Six

Sonny stood next to Irina's beach chair and grabbed a towel. She shook the water from her hair and adjusted the back of her swimsuit. "I don't know, it just doesn't feel right."

"Got sand in your suit?"

Sonny laughed. "No. *I* feel fine. The day is fine. The water's great, the sky is gorgeous."

"Yeah."

"But spending the day without Melanie as part of the group? It feels like we're betraying her." She sat in the chair next to Irina's.

Irina tapped her knee against Sonny's. "Hey, where's that desire to be in God's will you told Teresa about?"

"Yeah, I know. But there's definitely a hole in the beach house atmosphere. Don't you sense that?"

Irina bent forward in her chair, stretching like a cat. "Our own little environmental crisis. I miss her too."

Grig walked toward them from the waves. He moved slowly and comfortably, so his healthy, nutty-brown tan was right there for Sonny to appreciate. She was reminded of that day at Sunset Beach when he ran back to her from the water one last time before they parted. He had only improved in the four years since then. More confident, more responsible, more mature, even more kind. She respected him, and she found that exciting. And with all due respect, she thought he was totally hot. With a thrill she considered the fact that she and Grig might actually have a chance of developing a long-term relationship. At their age, that meant more than simply dating. It meant commitment and promise.

She was amazed she even had room in her thoughts for Melanie. But she did.

"You really like him," Irina announced.

Sonny hadn't realized she'd been staring. Embarrassed, she smiled but looked down. She nodded. "So much." When she looked back at Irina, she casually rested her index finger against her lips. "But, shhhhh."

"What's that about?" Grig had run toward them when Sonny wasn't looking. He gained enough ground to catch her gesture, but she knew she could trust Irina to be discreet.

Irina said, "She doesn't want me to tell you that she likes you soooooo much."

Sonny gasped. "You're terrible!"

Both Grig and Irina chuckled. Irina fended off the little smack Sonny pretended to give her, and Grig sat on Sonny's other side.

"Hey," Irina said, "I've learned a lot, watching all the trouble Teresa's secrets caused between you guys. I'm becoming a firm believer in spilling my guts."

Sonny frowned.

"Not spilling my guts like I did earlier this week," Irina said, rolling her eyes. "Not literally. But I've decided to be as honest as I can be."

"Yeah, well, I'm all for honesty," Sonny said, "but you and I need to have a little chat about filtering your inner monologue, girlfriend."

Irina laughed and got up. "I'm getting kind of hungry. I'm going to go see if Teresa and Julian want to quit for lunch."

She ran off. Sonny was left alone with Grig and Irina's "honesty" dangling in the air between them. She sighed. "I'm busted."

Grig chuckled. "Oh, come on, I'm sure she's 'spilled her guts' just as much with you, telling you everything I've said about you this week."

"Not necessarily. Why don't you tell me what you told her, and I'll let you know if she spilled that one or not."

She loved the way his eyes twinkled at that. He leaned back in his chair, breathing in deeply, as if he had much to say.

"Let's see. I told her I liked your natural look. Your beach look."

Sonny nodded. "Yes, indeed. That has been duly reported."

"And I know she told you I raved about you at school after we spent that summer together at Sunset Beach."

"Mm-hmm."

"That I came back to school smitten."

Sonny nodded, her lips prim. "That was the word used, if I do recall correctly."

"And that this week our years apart have done as Melanie described in her note. They've fallen away. And I find I'm still smitten."

Sonny stopped playing. Grig had spoken the words in the same, light voice, so it took a moment for her to grasp what he said. She shook her head. "Irina didn't tell me about that last part."

He held up his index finger. "Ah. That's because I didn't say it to her." His clear blue eyes were suddenly serious as he said, "I'm saying it to you."

Sonny was dumbstruck. She was absolutely at a loss for a response that wasn't babbling.

He sat up and leaned closer to her. He spoke quietly. "What do you think?"

"Sonny!"

No! No interruptions right now! She wouldn't even look toward Irina's voice.

"Sonny, Teresa has an idea!" Her voice was closer.

Sonny sighed and blinked slowly.

Grig smiled. "We'll talk later."

The two of them faced Irina, who had almost reached them. Teresa and Julian walked up from behind. They carried their boogie boards and looked ready to quit.

Irina pulled her towel off her chair and patted her face dry. "Teresa came up with something we can discuss over lunch."

Teresa and Julian reached the group. "It wasn't my idea, really. Julian is the one who figured it out."

"I'd say it was a joint effort," Julian said, smiling at Teresa. "We watched a child in the water who was having too much fun to come in for lunch."

Teresa laughed. Sonny didn't know when she had ever seen her mom as relaxed as she had become. She hoped that was more about the seal pup than Melanie's absence.

"Yeah," Teresa said. "His mother was calling him in, and he wouldn't budge. He was beyond the point where the waves break, simply floating on his board. And he deliberately wouldn't surf back in, probably because he knew he'd have to stop if he did."

Julian continued. "So, rather than getting angry with him, his mother simply swam out to him, bringing a board for herself."

"She joined him, just for a while." Teresa looked to Julian for confirmation. He nodded. "And they ended up riding in together, laughing all the way. Completely relaxed. It was a wonderful little thing to see."

Irina looked at Sonny and Grig, excitement splashed across her face. "Isn't that a great idea?"

Sonny looked at Grig, who appeared equally confused. "Isn't *what* a great idea?" she asked. "Mom, what are you suggesting?"

"We're—"

Irina jumped in. "We're going to go out to the dinner interview tonight and coax Melanie back to the beach!"

Forty-Seven

Teresa could see Sonny was uncomfortable with this idea. She wasn't all that sure of its wisdom herself.

"I don't know, Mom," Sonny said. She passed chopsticks around for everyone.

They all sat on the front porch of the beach house, enjoying Peking dumplings and bikini shrimp salad from Chang's. The warm breeze from the ocean was mild enough that they didn't have to weigh down their paper plates or napkins.

They had talked Julian into staying with them for lunch.

"We need your advice on this," Sonny told him.

He smiled. "I'm not exactly a visionary in family matters, but I'll try to help."

"I can't say I'm sure about this plan either, sweetie." Teresa set her chopsticks aside and picked up a fork. She never had caught the hang of those things. "It was just a thought that came to me. Or maybe it came to Julian." She looked at him. "We were kind of bouncing ideas back and forth when we got caught up in watching that kid in the water."

Sonny spoke as she scooped salad onto her plate. "You know, we could end up ruining Micah's…"

"Interview dinner?" Irina said.

"Yeah." Sonny nodded. "And Melanie said he really likes this girl."

"I don't know if this will help at all," Julian said, "but I *did* pray for guidance after you explained the situation. The boy in the water might have been coincidence, and maybe Teresa and I are reaching, but—"

198

"No," Teresa interrupted. "I…uh, want to say something about that." She looked at Sonny, and she struggled to have to admit this. She wasn't sure why. "I prayed too."

Sonny just looked back at her, her eyes wide, as if they were waiting to take in more than they could see at the moment.

"I'm not saying I've turned some great corner, sweetie, so don't get all churchy on me, but there's something about this place." She gestured with her arms to indicate the beach house. "Or maybe it's you people. But something makes me feel as if there's a point in trying to communicate on a number of different levels. So I prayed this morning. Didn't have a clue what I was doing. Maybe the thing with the kid and this plan of crashing the interview dinner had something to do with that, I don't know."

She looked at Irina. "I'm still counting on your donkey theory, young lady."

Irina smiled, and then she looked at the rest of the group. "We're not bumbling cavemen. Couldn't we go to the restaurant without embarrassing Melanie and Micah? We wouldn't be sitting *with* them, right? I'm probably the most messed-up person in the group, but I think I could manage to make it through dinner without burning the place down."

Grig said, "What, exactly, would we be trying to accomplish in going to the restaurant?"

Teresa came to life. "Think about it. Well, maybe this won't be exciting for you and Irina, Grig, but for Sonny and me, it wouldn't just be a chance to surprise Melanie and show her the effort we made to bring her back to the beach house. It would also be a chance for us to meet Bailey and Micah before having to head back home. I have to get back to Oakland once this week is over. I can't hang out here, waiting for my brother-in-law and nephew to show themselves."

From the way they all stared at her, one would think she had spoken in Mandarin. All but Julian, who smiled at her as if he had just watched her graduate from an arduous academic curriculum. With honors.

"What?" She popped a dumpling in her mouth and labored to close her mouth around it enough to chew.

"Whoa, Mom," Sonny said. "That was quite a leaf you turned this morning."

They all laughed.

Teresa shrugged and pointed at her lips, as if she would give an explanation for herself if only she didn't have a face full of dumpling. The corners of her mouth were barely able to turn up.

Grig ran his hand through his hair, a grimace on his face. "I think you might have missed a pretty important detail for this caper. You don't know where the dinner is. And if you call Melanie to find out, your surprise is blown."

Irina moaned. "You're right."

"Shoot," Sonny said. "Just when I was warming up to the idea. Maybe we should go ahead and call her."

Teresa finally swallowed enough to speak. She waved her finger. "Not necessary." She dabbed at her mouth with a napkin. "I know where they're meeting. Brigantine's. In La Mesa. At seven o'clock."

Irina reached into her beach bag for something.

Sonny said, "Mom, how in the world did you figure that out?"

Teresa smiled. "I have eavesdropping down to an art, baby. I heard her talking with Micah on her phone when we were in the helicopter."

Irina held up her iPhone. "Mapquest says Brigantine's is less than twenty minutes from here. I can call for reservations right now if we want to commit."

They looked from one to the other. Teresa thought they all looked sold on the idea but were waiting for someone to make the decision.

"Julian? Would you like to join us?"

"I'm afraid I already have plans this evening. But I'd love to hear a full report in the morning."

Teresa smiled with confidence. "We'll have Melanie come over and tell you all about it."

Forty-Eight

The group took on a new vitality. Irina called Brigantine's and asked if seating for four was still available for seven o'clock that evening. Teresa took the phone and chatted with the woman taking reservations.

"What was your name, dear? Candice? Candice, my name is Teresa. We're hoping to surprise some friends there this evening. I believe their reservations will be for six people at seven also, and possibly in the name of..." She looked to Sonny. "Do you know Melanie's married name?"

"Hines."

"Hines," Teresa said into the phone.

After a pause, Teresa grinned and gave Irina and Sonny a thumbs-up. "Hines–Vincent, yes that's got to be them. Excellent. Now, if you could possibly seat us so that the party can't see us right away—is that possible?" Pause. "Oh, Candice, you're my hero. Thank you so much. We'll see you tonight."

Once Teresa hung up, they made plans.

Grig said, "You ladies just let me know what you need me to do or not do. I'm clueless about anything requiring finesse."

"Grig, you and I need to go get something decent to wear," Irina said. "I know I didn't bring anything other than beach gear, and I'm sure you didn't either."

Teresa grabbed her purse. "I'm in the same boat. Should we all go? Sonny?"

"Actually, I have a dress I hoped to wear this week. This will be the perfect occasion."

Sonny thought she heard her cell phone ring, back in her bedroom. She dashed to answer it, but she didn't recognize the number.

"Hello?"

"Uh, yes, hello. Is this Sonata? Sonata Miller?"

Sonny pulled in a great breath and froze. It was him. Her heart suddenly ached. She couldn't speak.

"Hello? Sonata? This, uh, this is Dr. Sommerhill. David Sommerhill?"

"Yes." She simply couldn't get her words out.

Irina came to the door, all breathless and upbeat. "So, Sonny, do you want to come shopping with us even though—" She stopped when she saw Sonny's face.

Sonny raised her index finger. "Excuse me just a moment, Dr. Sommerhill."

She pulled the phone from her ear, pointed to it frantically, and mouthed to Irina, "My father!"

Irina's mouth dropped open, and Sonny managed to speak calmly to her.

"Why don't you all go on without me. I'll see you when you get back."

Irina nodded and started to walk out. But then she ran back in and gave Sonny a quick, awkward hug. She pressed her head against Sonny's for a moment, and then she ran out. Sonny heard her whispering excitedly to the group.

She sat on the edge of her bed and spoke into the phone again. "I'm sorry, Doctor—"

"I think you could call me David. That would be all right with me. If you don't mind, that is."

She nodded, but she didn't say anything else. He had a kind voice. Warm and clear.

Teresa suddenly appeared at the door, looking at Sonny with great concern.

Sonny waved her off because he spoke again, and she couldn't concentrate on everything at once. Teresa retreated.

"Sonata," he said, "I, um, you were right. Your call was a complete shock to me. And your age. I understand. I understand the significance."

Sonny still didn't know what to say, so she waited until he spoke again.

"I would be happy to meet you before you leave. Did you want to come to my office? I'm right here in the city, at State and West A Streets. Four zero two West A. I could give you directions."

"I'll find it."

"Ah, good. All right. Will you be—"

"When?" She wished she didn't sound so stupid, but she was completely overwhelmed. "When would I come?"

"Tomorrow, Friday? Afternoon? Say, one o'clock?"

"Yeah, okay."

He hesitated.

"Okay, bye," she said. She ended the call. She dropped her phone onto the bed and waited for her heart to calm down. Then she replayed her monosyllabic prattle in her head. She grimaced and smacked her palm against her forehead.

He probably wondered how *his* child could have turned out with a ten-word vocabulary. She would have to get a grip before tomorrow.

Nothing like having one chance, possibly a half-hour chance, to make an impression that normally required twenty-four years of interaction. She shouldn't care so much what he thought of her. But the fact that he cared enough to call made her care enough to impress.

She stood, turned around, and went down on her knees.

This called for a calming she couldn't muster all by herself.

Forty-Nine

July 2
La Mesa, California

Melanie couldn't shake the feeling. She had decided that leaving the beach house was what God wanted her to do. So why did she feel as if she had run away?

On top of that, she knew she shouldn't have expected anyone from the beach house to call her today to try to convince her to come back. But there was no denying it. Her feelings were hurt.

How silly she was being. She had told them in her note that she prayed about this. She went to some length to impress upon them that this was what she felt led to do. Did she expect them to argue with that? The only one who might argue with God's will was Teresa, and she was probably dancing on the beach with relief.

"You all right, honey?" Bailey asked as he opened the door to the restaurant. The concern in his eyes chased away some of her bruised feelings. "You've been a little down ever since you got home. You sure you don't want to head back to the beach house after dinner?"

They entered Brigantine's, and the inviting atmosphere immediately soothed Melanie. A gentle adagio played from speakers in the ceiling. Melanie loved the warmth of the goldenrod walls. And the oak-and-leather furniture and rich tapestry carpeting made her feel as if she had entered someone's cozy living room.

She sighed. "Don't mind me, Bailey. I'm happy to be back home. I'm just being a baby. I want them to want me back, that's all."

He put his arm around her. "I'm sure they do. I know I did the whole time you were away."

Micah stepped up to her other side. "Mom, you're not going to be all depressed and, you know, sad at dinner, are you? That's not like you. I want them to meet the real you."

She patted his cheek. "Don't worry, honey. We're all going to do fine. We'll impress the socks off of Chelsea's parents." She straightened her little black dress and patted the back of her hair. She had pulled it into a simple updo for the evening, something she didn't have occasion to do as often as she liked.

Bailey spoke to the maître d'. "We're half of the Hines–Vincent party of six."

"Yes, sir. The rest of your party is already seated. Right this way."

Melanie felt a slight dip in her gut when they approached the table. The first thing she noticed was Mr. Vincent, the father, checking his watch, a slight purse in his lips. They were only five minutes late, for goodness' sake.

Good old Bailey took command right away. He smiled broadly and put out his hand.

"Bailey Hines. How you doin'? You must be George."

Mr. Vincent stood and shook hands with Bailey. But he didn't smile. He didn't actually have a negative expression on his face. He didn't have *any* expression on his face.

"Yes. George Vincent."

He sat back down. He didn't introduce his wife or daughter, so Bailey stepped in again.

"And you must be Doris. Great to meet you. This is my lovely wife, Melanie."

Melanie got the same, blank reaction from the mother. "Hi, Doris. And this must be Chelsea."

The daughter was a different story altogether. In a fascinating genetic anomaly, Chelsea seemed to have been born with a cheerleader's disposition. She was up and pumping Melanie's arm, and then Bailey's, as soon as it was timely for her to do so.

"I'm so happy to finally meet you, Mr. and Mrs. Hines. Micah talks about you two all the time."

Melanie met eyes with Bailey for a smile, and then she spied Micah. He studied Chelsea as she spoke, and his eyes reflected something Melanie had never seen in his expression toward a girl before. It wasn't infatuation, or shyness, or any of those young-love kinds of gazes. He looked proud of her. Melanie saw respect, and that made her want to hug her son right in front of all of them. But she knew enough about what was cool and what wasn't. She would hug him later.

Bailey said, "We're even, then, Chelsea, because we hear about you all the time too."

"Good to see you again, Mr. and Mrs. Vincent." Micah shook hands with Chelsea's father before they all took their seats. "I hope, uh, I hope that..."

Melanie smiled. Her poor baby. He hoped that these very careful parents would give him their stamp of approval. He was doing so well, considering how nervous he was. She spoke up to help him out. "We'd love to help you feel comfortable about Micah and Chelsea attending the lacrosse awards dinner together this Saturday. Bailey and I will be there, as well."

She thought she saw a hint of a polite smile cross Doris' lips. Maybe the Vincents were just shy or slow to warm up.

If they didn't warm up enough to contribute to the conversation pretty soon, though, this would become awkward. Wasn't this dinner arranged so the parents could get to know each other? How was that going to happen unless they *all* spoke? This really might end up being an interview.

Melanie thought of Teresa's "puritanical" comment and looked at the staid, pallid couple sitting across from her. Actually, if you threw a barn and a pitchfork into the picture, *American Gothic* would be sitting right there across from her, ready to have a nice dinner at Brigantine's.

The dear, dear server showed up and gave them something to do. In a clipped tone, George Vincent asked questions about the walnut-crusted rack of lamb and the calamari relleno as if the server were trying to get away with something. Melanie thought about her Micah possibly having this man for a father-in-law, and the shrouded figure of the Grim Reaper suddenly flashed through her mind.

While the server took orders from George and Doris, Melanie spoke softly to Micah. "What looks good to you, honey?"

He looked at her and they had an unspoken moment, with quick glances toward Chelsea's parents and slight crinkling at the corners of their eyes.

"Okay with you and Dad if I get the New York steak?"

"I think that's a great choice."

They heard Chelsea's bright voice as she placed her order. "I'll have the New York steak, medium rare, please."

Micah laughed. "That's what I'm getting. Exactly!"

Chelsea laughed back. "Great minds, right?"

Oh, she was a sweet girl. And she and Micah simply seemed like a couple of kids who enjoyed each other's company. If George and Doris Vincent wanted to squash a perfectly innocent relationship, shame on them.

"So, George." Bailey spoke in his usual, upbeat tone, which seemed extra jovial in contrast with his counterpart. "What is it you do for a living?"

George frowned for an unknown reason. "I'm in demolition."

Melanie had to keep from nodding.

Maybe so. But not tonight, Georgie boy. Not if she could help it.

Fifty

Teresa patted Sonny's hand as Grig pulled into the restaurant parking lot. "Don't worry, baby. We're only ten minutes late."

Sonny sighed. "I'm not so much worried about our being late. I'm worried about our being caught."

"Well, aren't we planning on showing ourselves at *some* point?" Grig turned off the car, got out, and opened the door behind his for Sonny. "I mean, our initial reason for coming out here was to convince Melanie to come back with us, right? You weren't planning on jumping her from behind and throwing a bag over her head, were you?"

Sonny laughed. "Only if she turns us down. No, I just want us to be extra careful not to mess things up for Micah. Agreed? We'll do whatever it takes to not give a bad family impression."

"I guess that leaves Grig and me in the clear, then," Irina said. "We can get creative. We're not family."

Sonny just pointed at her and gave her a stern teacher look.

Irina laughed. "We'll be good."

Teresa observed the group. These young ones exuded such a sense of fun and adventure. She hadn't been like that in years.

They entered Brigantine's and quickly scanned the tables visible from the entrance.

"I don't see Melanie anywhere," Sonny said. Her eyes darted at the neckline of Teresa's little black dress. Again.

"What?" Teresa said. "You won't find Melanie there, either. Why do you keep eyeballing my neckline?"

Sonny shook her head. "Nothing. I'm just being overly protective."

"Of what? My chest?"

"Shhh! Mom! No, of Micah. Your dress is just a little…sexy, that's all."

Teresa snorted. "You think you have to protect Micah from my sexiness? I'm his aunt, for crying out loud."

"No, I'm…oh, never mind. It's just that the girl's parents sound very conservative, and you're kind of…hot looking tonight."

Teresa patted her updo and smiled, just to tease Sonny. "Well, thank you very much. I do try."

Sonny gave her mother a heavy-lidded look, but a smile crept into her expression.

"If you'll follow me, please." The maître d' led them to their table.

Teresa gave Sonny a quick, one-armed squeeze. "Relax, sweetie. If we have anything at all to do with the girl's parents, it will be in passing. And if it comes to that, I'll squat demurely behind a potted plant."

Grig laughed. Until then Teresa hadn't realized he was listening.

They reached their table in a cozy corner of the restaurant. Teresa looked around to make sure they weren't exposed to Melanie's group.

"All three of you ladies look stunning." Grig pulled out Sonny's chair for her, while the maître d' did the same for Teresa and Irina. "The parents would have to be dolts to find you anything but charming."

"Right," Irina said. "We're a classy bunch. So where are they? And what's our game plan for crashing their dinner?"

Teresa chuckled. "Hopefully *this*—our attendance here—is all the crashing we're going to do. We don't want to interrupt their evening. We're just going to wait for a good time to casually run into them. Melanie will know why we're here within moments after that. Simple and, as you said, Irina, classy."

Sonny gasped. "I think that's Micah sitting over there, the tall, dark-haired guy, see? At the far end?" She looked at Irina. "Doesn't that look like the picture Melanie showed us?"

Irina grinned. "I think you're right. Cute. Yes, and I *kind* of remember what the dad looked like. That *might* be him—"

"There's Melanie!" Grig whispered.

Teresa saw her taking a seat between Micah and his father. She must have gone to the ladies' room. "Good grief, will you look how she's dressed?"

Sonny laughed, almost loudly, before stifling herself with her hand. "Oh, my goodness, Mom. You two are like some science experiment."

Teresa had to admit Sonny was right. Melanie's dress wasn't as, well, *hot* as hers—the neckline was more demure—but it was black, sleeveless, and eerily similar.

"And the hair!" Teresa said. All this past week Melanie had worn her blond hair loose and curly, while Teresa had worn hers straight.

"Wow," Irina said. "What are the chances you'd both put it up tonight? Sonny and I didn't put ours up, but you and Melanie both did. That's just weird."

Teresa stood abruptly. "I agree. I'm going to run down to the ladies' room and comb mine out. I've had too many years of living apart. I'm not ready for this twin stuff."

Grig said, "Would you like us to order something for you? An appetizer, maybe?"

"Always the gent." Sonny said, smiling.

He returned her smile. "I'm starving."

Teresa waved her hand at him and turned to leave. "A Caesar salad." She glanced back over at Melanie's table before she left. "That's probably what my sister is having, as we speak."

Teresa bent over and finger-combed her hair loose as soon as she entered the ladies' room and removed her hair clip. She was glad she hadn't done any dramatic styling to it this evening. She should be able to get it to lie down without much trouble.

She stood upright and ran her hands through her hair again. Yes, that was much better. She felt less clonelike.

Another woman walked in, gave Teresa a polite nod, and then jerked to such a stop Teresa gave her a second look.

Anxious-looking little thing, rather pale. Clutching her purse with both hands and holding it to her chest exactly as a mouse would do with its cheese. But upon facing Teresa, she lowered her hands, and her shoulders followed.

"I'm so sorry." She said that as if Teresa would know what she meant.

"Uh, that's…all right. I was just fussing with my hair. The stall is free—"

"No, I meant I'm sorry about my husband."

As were many women, Teresa was sure, but what had that to do with her? "Excuse me?"

The woman put up her hand. "I don't mean to complain. I have the utmost respect for George, but I just wanted you to know he doesn't normally behave as he is tonight. He's actually very personable and kind." She laughed softly. "Chelsea takes after him in that regard."

Teresa wondered how Sonny, the future psychologist, would handle this lady. Just let her talk?

"He was laid off today. A complete shock to us, you see. And I'm afraid I didn't take the news all that well. We had a horrible argument just before we got here. We're both feeling awfully tense."

Well. Stranger or not, Teresa wasn't heartless. "Oh, that's horrible. I'm very sorry."

The lady widened her eyes. "But please don't mention it to Chelsea."

No problem there, since she didn't have a clue who Chelsea was and wouldn't know her if she walked out of the bathroom stall at this very moment.

"She drove separately from us to get here," the woman said. "She came directly from drama practice. She doesn't know yet about her daddy's job."

Okay. Time for Teresa to back away from this lady, who was perhaps a little disturbed. "You can count on my discretion. Truly."

The woman's eyes suddenly darted to Teresa's neckline before she stepped toward the stall. An expression crossed her face. Not disdain or disapproval. It was…confusion.

What was with the preoccupation about her chest? Her dress wasn't cut *that* low.

The lady spoke one last time before entering the stall. "And I suppose it would be best not to mention this to Micah, either. Not until we've had a chance to talk with Chelsea, and we'd like to wait until George has a chance to look for another position before we talk with her about it."

But Teresa didn't listen clearly to anything the woman said after she uttered Micah's name. Of course. This had to be Mrs. Puritan. The dinner must be going poorly. And now this lady would think Melanie knew why. If the laid-off husband was being offensive, Melanie was probably about to—

No, Melanie wasn't likely to speak to George as rudely as Teresa probably would under the same circumstances. But Teresa knew her sister. Sarcasm might creep in there, and wouldn't that be a mess if George picked up on it?

Teresa spoke quickly to the closed stall before leaving. "Please don't worry about a thing. My family is…your family."

She frowned as she walked out. What was *that* supposed to mean?

She couldn't worry about that right now. The lady would think Melanie was the one who said that, anyway.

She took the stairs to the dining area two at a time, which was the least feminine thing she'd done in years. She dashed to her table.

Irina smiled. "That looks good, your hair—"

"Yeah, yeah, never mind that." Teresa sat unceremoniously in her chair. "We have a problem."

Sonny looked over toward Melanie's table and back. "Mom, you were only supposed to go to the ladies' room. What happened?"

"George got laid off today, so he's upset—I mean, he and his wife had a horrible fight on the way here, and she was all confused about me, and George is being a…a jerk, apparently, only he's not normally like that, and he's making a horrible impression, and there's a good chance his nasty attitude will ruin everything if we don't get to Melanie right away, before she decides she doesn't want Micah associating with mean old whack job George. She might start getting snarky with him, you know? And believe me, she can get pretty curt."

The server placed her Caesar salad before her.

"Thanks." She popped a crouton into her mouth and realized she was short of breath.

Grig, Irina, and Sonny spoke at once, but they all said exactly the same thing.

"Who's *George*?"

Fifty-One

Melanie took a deep breath to keep her cool. She caught herself drumming the table with her fingers, which was probably almost as annoying as George's behavior. The man was amazingly testy. She had already excused herself from the table once to get away from him, so she was stuck now for the duration.

Poor Chelsea had finally succumbed, to some extent. Her bubbly personality held a few less bubbles. Melanie wondered how often this happened to the poor girl, with a sourpuss of a father like George.

But Bailey hung in there, and Melanie couldn't have been prouder of him.

"So, George, Micah tells us you have a budding actor here in Chelsea. You must be so proud—I understand she's quite a talent." He smiled at Chelsea, and she perked back up.

"Yes, we're proud of her. I just hope she has more in mind for her future than acting. These days, if you're not a doctor or a lawyer, you're vulnerable to any little swing in the economy. Acting is a gamble even in the best of times."

Chelsea's smile dropped, but Melanie watched her fight to hide her disappointment. George's comments seemed to surprise his daughter a little, which Melanie supposed was a good thing. If she hadn't heard much of this negative attitude before, maybe there was something else going on here tonight. You'd think, though, that the man could carry on more politely for a lousy two-hour dinner.

"Chelsea's also the smartest student in our AP calculus class," Micah said. He and Chelsea exchanged a united front kind of smile. "I know she's going to succeed, no matter what she decides to do."

Bailey nodded. "Sure she will. You both will. You're smart kids. And just about every profession has its pluses and minuses. My business—real estate—has been quite a bit tighter this year, but you have to plan ahead for times like we're having, right, honey?" He looked at Melanie.

Before she could answer, Doris returned. The moment she sat down, she looked Melanie directly in the eyes. She appeared suddenly more eager to communicate, even if nonverbally. Then she glimpsed Melanie's hair. She frowned and glanced away, as if collecting scattered thoughts.

Melanie couldn't resist reaching up to make sure her updo was still in place. It felt fine. Doris' frown must have been about something unrelated.

Odd. Even more strangely, Doris did a double take at Melanie's chest, followed by a perplexed expression so graphic, Melanie glanced down at herself without thinking. Had she spilled something on her dress? She saw nothing and was about to ask Doris if everything was all right.

"Yes," George said, "it's wise to plan ahead. To set aside for a rainy day. That's wise, but not always easy."

Goodness. Melanie forgot about Doris and focused on George again. Really, his pessimism was so draining. But Melanie knew most men loved talking about their businesses. Maybe she could turn his mood.

"So, George! Demolition! You know, Micah was so fascinated by demolition and construction when he was a child, I was certain he'd go into some facet of the industry as an adult. What do you think of your profession? Do you enjoy your job?"

Rather than yammering about himself, George fell as silent as a mortician. Everyone turned to hear his answer, but he just stared, speechless, at the lamb chops on his dinner plate.

Melanie turned to seek input from Doris. Doris waited for her, her eyes filled with horror. She looked a little like Janet Leigh in *Psycho*.

This had to be the strangest couple Melanie had ever met. *How* had Chelsea turned out so normally?

Over Doris' shoulder, beyond the dining area, Melanie's eyes caught movement. She focused, and there, in an area that appeared reserved for the servers to use, stood her mirror image. But no. Of course that was no mirror image.

That was Teresa.

"Good *night!*" Melanie caught herself too late. She looked at the others and started coughing, as if that would explain anything. Their server stopped at the table to check on their dinners, mercifully taking the attention off of Melanie. She looked for Teresa again.

There she was, dolled up, wearing a dress strikingly similar to Melanie's, but with her hair down. Teresa waved her arms around as if she were trying to guide a landing airplane. She actually elbowed a waiter in the head before she lowered her arms and apparently apologized. The waiter spoke to her for a moment, probably commenting on her being in that area. Teresa nodded to him. Then she looked back at Melanie and ran her hand across her throat in a cutting gesture. She pointed to the other side of the restaurant and cocked her head in the same direction.

Everyone at the table looked at Melanie again. Apparently their waiter had asked if her dinner was all right.

"Oh, yes, wonderful." She stood. "But I'm afraid you'll all have to excuse me again. I'll be just a moment."

Micah and Bailey both looked at her with questions in their eyes.

"I'm fine. I'll be right back."

She walked in the direction of the stairs to the restrooms, but she scanned the room for Teresa.

Teresa came at her from the side, startling her again. "Melanie! This way."

"What are you up to, Teresa? I don't want trouble. Please. This night is important for Micah and…why aren't you with Sonny and the Russians?"

"I am!" Teresa pointed to the other end of the room, and Sonny, Grig, and Irina all waved at her, frantic but wearing big, cheesy grins.

"What in the world?" Melanie went with Teresa to the table.

The girls and Grig stood to give her hugs, but Teresa immediately starting coaching her.

"Now, whatever you do, don't talk about George's job when you go back to the table."

Melanie frowned. "What are you talking about? You know George? Isn't he a horrid little man? I mean, no, I don't mean that. But he's—"

Sonny said, "Aunt Melanie, he got laid off today. And he and Doris had a big fight on the way to the restaurant. So you have to cut them some slack."

Melanie's hands went to her face. "Laid off? Oh, no. Oh, my stars, I've hurt him. I've said exactly the wrong things to him." She gasped. "No wonder Doris looked at me like I—"

She stopped and looked at Sonny. "Wait a second. You know them too, Sonny?"

Irina spoke up. "Teresa just learned about them when Doris went to the ladies' room at the same time she did. Doris thought Teresa was you, and she told her all about George's job. And she asked her to not say anything to Chelsea or Micah."

"I tried to get your attention right away," Teresa said. "But then Doris got back to the table, so I was afraid she'd see me, and then it took a while for me to get you to—"

Melanie lowered her head. "Oh, this is awful. She thinks she asked me to be discreet, and the first thing I did was ask him about his job."

They all groaned softly at that.

A waiter arrived to serve their dinners. Melanie recognized him as the fellow Teresa nailed in the head with her elbow. He looked at Melanie, and then he jerked his head like a chicken to look at Teresa.

"Hey, twins!"

Clearly annoyed by the distraction, Teresa half smiled and said, "Yeah, but not now, okay?"

He set down the plates he carried and scurried away, rubbing the area where Teresa had hit him earlier.

Oblivious, Teresa put her hands to her hips. "I'm going to have to talk with Doris, that's all. Tell her what happened. And she'll know how to make George feel better."

"No." Melanie shook her head. "I'm the one who was offensive. I should talk with Doris and apologize."

Grig said, "Why don't you both talk with her?"

Melanie nodded. "Yeah. That's probably a good idea. But we don't want to embarrass George by discussing this in front of everyone. How can we get Doris away from the table without the rest of the group getting suspicious? I've already left twice. Unless I insinuate I have some pretty bad digestive issues, I don't know how to—"

"I don't think that will be a problem," Grig said, smiling gently and looking just beyond Melanie and Teresa.

They turned around to see an angry Doris approach them both. When she saw them side by side, she stopped dead, a victim of total confusion.

Fifty-Two

Melanie found it interesting to work in tandem with Teresa. They seated Doris and clustered around her at Teresa's corner table to explain themselves. They comforted her about their intentions. Melanie experienced shades of high school and tag teaming with Teresa to convince their parents of some privilege or another.

She didn't know what had happened to the Teresa she left back at the beach house—angry, defensive, and unrepentant. Could Melanie's note have affected her so much that she would come out here to…why *had* she come out here?

"I didn't try to make you think I was Melanie," Teresa told Doris. "That just happened, and I didn't realize it until it was too late. And then I couldn't get to Melanie until she had already slammed George's ego to the ground."

Melanie scowled. "Thank you, Teresa. Look, Doris, I need to apologize to George. I would never have put him on the spot about his job deliberately."

Sonny took a bite of her dinner. Melanie noticed they had all resorted to nibbling in the midst of the hubbub, poor hungry things. "But, Aunt Melanie, if you talk with George about this mix-up, he's going to know Doris told you—well, told Mom—about his getting laid off."

Doris nodded. "That's true. George tries not to be a proud man, but what man would want such personal news announced so blithely? And because we fought about it, he's going to be particularly sensitive about this." She looked at the group. "Especially if he finds out you *all* know about it. I hadn't intended that at all."

"That's my fault, Doris," Teresa said, sighing. "I didn't think it through before blabbing your private business to everyone. I just panicked, since you thought you told Melanie, and I wanted to warn her before she—"

"—right, yes," Melanie said. "Before the foot-in-mouth incident." Melanie sought to avoid another "slamming" comment. "Too late. I'm sorry, again, Doris."

Doris stood. "Really, I understand. And eventually George will too." She looked at Melanie. "But I think we'd both better get back there before they send a search party after us."

"Certainly." Melanie stood. She looked at the group and hesitated. "Thanks for coming out here, everyone. Don't leave without coming over to—"

"Oh, we're not done with you," Teresa said.

Sonny grinned. "Yeah. Don't *you* leave without coming over *here*."

"Right," Irina said. "As you can see, we know how to track you down."

Melanie laughed.

They all looked at Grig for *his* clever comment, as if they were each required to make one. Grig obviously had been listening, because he was smiling. But he was focused on cutting a filet mignon until he apparently felt their eyes on him. He looked up. "Oh. Don't mind me. I'm just here to be the pretty face in the crowd."

Doris spoke softly and made them all laugh. "Well, you certainly are that."

When Melanie and Doris approached the table, only Micah and Chelsea were there. Micah had moved to sit in George's seat, next to Chelsea. She laughed at something he said. A sweet mandolin melody played in the background.

Doris sighed. "They look more relaxed than they have all evening."

"Of course. All of the uptight adults are gone."

Chelsea was the first to see them. "There you are. Dad and Mr. Hines went outside for a little walk."

Uh-oh. "Everything all right?" Melanie looked at Micah, who didn't seem upset by anything. A good sign.

"I think so, Mom," he said. "Mr. Vincent asked Dad if they could speak privately for a minute, and they excused themselves and said they'd be right back."

Melanie heard a subtle groan from Doris.

But Bailey's unmistakable laugh turned her head. He and George walked back toward them, and, although George still seemed fairly serious, he didn't look as cross as he did before. He actually had a faint smile on his lips.

"Time for dessert?" Bailey asked everyone. Micah returned to his seat so George could sit by Chelsea.

Melanie and Doris had barely eaten dinner. But that was fine. Melanie was just glad to see they had made some progress. Now she simply needed to apologize.

"George, I wanted to tell you—"

Doris caught her eye from across the table. The almost imperceptible shake of her head signaled Melanie to avoid the subject altogether.

"I wanted to tell you I'm so glad you and Doris had the idea of the six of us meeting for dinner. I hope we'll have other chances to get to know each other better."

"I have a feeling we will, Melanie." George actually spoke pleasantly and looked kindly at each member of the Hines family. Melanie hadn't realized until then how much she wanted to hear that tone from him. She grinned back at him, relieved.

⌒

They walked with the Vincents to the door of the restaurant, and Doris spoke softly to Melanie.

"I didn't mean to cut you off, Melanie, but I saw no point in your apologizing. George and I showed poor manners right from the start. And Bailey seems to have boosted George's spirits somehow, so I thought it was best not to remind him of his troubles."

"All right." Melanie gave Doris a light hug. "Until later, then. I hope you don't mind if we don't walk out with you? I want to drag my men over to my sister's table."

Melanie stopped Bailey and Micah from leaving when the Vincents did. Doris smiled at her and corralled her husband and daughter out to the parking lot. She gave Melanie a small, friendly wave before turning to take George by the hand.

"What's up, Mom?" Through the glass doors, Micah watched Chelsea get into her car.

"Bit of a surprise. It was a surprise for me too." Melanie placed herself between Bailey and Micah, and then she guided them to Teresa's crew.

Fifty-Three

Sonny hadn't expected to be as moved meeting Uncle Bailey and Micah as she had been when she met Aunt Melanie. Maybe the joy was ramped up tonight because they were the first male family members she had ever met. Maybe watching her small family expand by two was the source of delight.

Melanie brought them toward the table without warning them, from what Sonny could see. But the moment Bailey saw Sonny, he stopped in his tracks.

"You're Sonny!"

His grin was wide and only grew wider when she stood and he laughed out loud. He gave her a hug that lifted her off the ground. He quickly lowered her back down when heads turned and diners' voices rose around them.

"How did you know she was Sonny?" Melanie asked with tears in her eyes.

Micah chuckled. "Dad already put the picture she sent in a frame on the mantelpiece."

"I'd have known anyway," Bailey said to Melanie. "She looks just like you."

Sonny heard the pointed clearing of a throat behind her. They all turned to face Teresa, who slowly stood from the table.

Without a moment's hesitation, Bailey stepped forward and lifted Teresa into a hug only slightly less dramatic than Sonny's. He glanced over his shoulder at Melanie. "*She* looks just like you too!"

Even Teresa laughed at that.

Sonny followed Bailey's cue when Micah introduced himself. Rather than shaking his hand, she put her arms around him and gave him a hug. He was a good six inches taller than she was, so he bent to give her a gangly hug in return.

"Whoa." Sonny looked up at him when they released each other. "I guess I expected you to be shorter since you're seven years younger."

Suddenly shy, Micah simply smiled and said, "Yeah."

Melanie put her hand on his shoulder. "I love how big he's gotten." She looked up at him. "Well, honey, what do you think of your mom's identical twin?"

He looked at Teresa and back at Melanie. He shook his head and said, "That's freaky."

Teresa said, "Well, freaky or not, come give me a hug, good looking."

Their waiter arrived. He looked uncomfortable. "Do you think we could move your party to a larger table?"

Teresa said, "We're all about to leave, I think." She smiled at the diners nearby, and a touch of the performer blossomed about her. "Family reunion. So sorry. We'll be out of your way in a minute."

That seemed to be enough to keep the other diners happy.

Sonny put her hand on Bailey's arm. "Bailey, Micah, this is my friend Grig." She looked around. "Where's Irina?"

Grig's smile didn't look quite genuine to Sonny. "Ladies' room. She'll be out soon." He stood to meet the men, and then the group started toward the front of the restaurant.

Sonny said, "You guys go ahead. I'll wait for the check and for Irina."

"Check's done, baby," Teresa said. She gave Sonny a wink and then turned to Bailey and Micah. "Now, there's something we beach house people wanted to discuss with you boys and Melanie."

Grig held back and stood beside Sonny. "This is what you came for, Sonny. You go on. I'll wait here for Irina."

He was right. Sonny didn't want to miss anything with her newfound relatives. "But I have a funny feeling about Irina. Do you think I should go back to the ladies' room and make sure she's not—"

"I thought of that too. I'm not sure when her mood changed, but she seemed completely fine until Melanie and the guys showed up. Then she got kind of emotional and left quickly."

"Are you sure she went to the ladies' room? She wouldn't leave the restaurant, would she?"

He shook his head. "I think she's all right. You go on. We'll be right behind you. Thanks for caring about her." And then he crooked his arm behind her, bent toward her, and pressed a soft kiss against her temple.

Well, great. Now she didn't *want* to leave.

But she did. The group stood under the pale light outside the entrance to Brigantine's, and Teresa had already begun the discussion.

"I don't know," Melanie said. "I already unpacked my bags at home. And we're only talking one more day."

Sonny said, "But there's a lot to do in that day, Aunt Melanie."

Melanie turned to face her. "You had things planned already?"

Now Sonny had to drop the bomb, and she hoped it would encourage Melanie, rather than drive her away. She hoped the same about her mom.

"I arranged to meet my father."

Micah was the only one of them who didn't suddenly look uncomfortable. He appeared to notice that fact. He looked at the others, and then Sonny heard him whisper to Melanie. "What's up with that? Who are we talking about? Darth Vader?"

Teresa said, "Sonny, I'm fine with your meeting your father, but you certainly weren't expecting any of us to come with you, were you?"

"Yes, I have to agree." Melanie glanced at Bailey and back at Sonny. "It would be inappropriate, honey."

Sonny put up her hands. "No, I didn't expect either of you to come into his office with me. But I *did* have an idea about the rest of the day, and Melanie, we'd need you to pull it off."

"I'm listening."

"My father's office is in the city. I thought we could all drive in, and maybe you guys would like to kill an hour or so, while I'm visiting. I know there's plenty to do. And then I hoped we might drive about an hour north. To San Clemente."

Melanie slowly smiled and then turned to Teresa. "Now *that* is an interesting idea. If they're available and you'll go along, Teresa, I will definitely repack my bags."

"What are you guys talking about, Sonny?" Micah scratched his head.

She grinned at him. "I want to meet our grandparents."

"That's a fantastic idea," Bailey said. He took Melanie's hand. "I think Micah and I can hold down the fort for another day or so, honey."

"Awesome plan," Micah said. "Grandma and Grandpa Miller are great. That's who you meant, right? Mom's parents?"

"And Teresa's," Melanie said. "What do you say, Teresa? Do we have a deal?"

"What deal are you wild and crazy twins cooking up now?"

Everyone turned to see Grig, sporting a teasing smile.

Sonny loved Grig's smile, but she could tell he worked at this one. She thought maybe he hoped to attract some attention away from Irina, around whom he draped a protective, brotherly arm.

His ploy worked to some extent, although Irina had to make it through introductions. But then Sonny filled the two of them in on her proposal for tomorrow, and everyone seemed to have something to contribute to the conversation.

So they didn't notice what Sonny noticed—that Irina, although lovely and gracious, had cried most of her makeup away.

Fifty-Four

The drive home was quiet compared to the bustle of the restaurant. Sonny knew part of the silence was due to relief. Mission accomplished!

She turned toward Teresa and Irina, who were in the backseat. "Melanie told me she wouldn't take long to grab a few items and head right out. I gave one of the beach house keys back to her, in case she gets there and we're asleep or out for a boardwalk stroll."

Teresa sounded relaxed in the back of Grig's SUV. She practically purred. "No stroll for me tonight. Unless one of you has immediate plans for the tub, I plan to take a nice soak and read a romance novel some other tenant left behind."

"The one with the pirate on the cover?" Irina asked, her voice soft.

"I think he's a swashbuckler." Teresa sighed, as if she were already easing down into that tub. "Not that it matters, really. We're not exactly talking Dante." She sat up slightly to address Irina. "You weren't already reading, it, were you? I could find something else if—"

"No. Really. Help yourself."

In the front passenger seat, Sonny glanced over at Grig and frowned. He kept his eyes on the road, but she could tell he was preoccupied. What had Irina told him when she came out of the ladies' room at the restaurant? Both Grig and Irina had been so upbeat before dinner. Now Irina was more like the shy, self-conscious waif who arrived at the beach house six days ago. And Grig looked as concerned as the father of a teenager on her first date.

After they pulled up at Julian's house, Grig took his time parting ways

226

from the women. Sonny assumed he wanted to leave open the option for Irina to stay at Julian's if necessary. But she didn't need that, apparently.

"Night, Grigori. Love you. See you in the morning." She gave him a hug and followed Teresa in.

That left Grig and Sonny alone, and an awareness overwhelmed her. She didn't want to leave him. This seemed totally inappropriate to the mood of the moment, but she wanted to *kiss* him. Where did that come from so randomly? Just because they were alone in the dark? Because he was such a loving brother to Irina? Because four years ago she would have ended a night like this doing exactly that, kissing him?

But he jingled his keys and looked as if he were about to climb the stairs to the apartment.

"Are you okay, Grig?" She slowly walked toward the beach house as she spoke, in case she sensed the slightest bit of dismissal in his response.

"Uh, yeah." He took two steps toward the stairs before he stopped. "But, hey, you want to take that stroll on the boardwalk you mentioned?"

She stopped walking and came just shy of doing a fist pump. Instead, she made a graceful turn and faced him. "Sure. Let me just tell Mom and Irina where I'll be."

Neither woman was in the house's common area when Sonny walked in. Irina's bedroom door was closed, and so was the door to the bathroom. Sonny walked back toward her bedroom and heard water running in the tub.

She grabbed a hoodie from her closet, in case she grew chilled, and took a pen and some paper from her room to leave a note on the kitchen counter: *Going for a walk with Grig.* She left her slingbacks and purse behind and slipped back out of the house, barefoot.

Grig walked back down the stairs as Sonny approached Julian's house. The outdoor light shone on him as he descended, coloring his hair a pale shade of winter wheat. His bangs fell forward as he watched his step.

"Ah, barefoot," he said when he saw her. "Good idea." He opened the door to his car and rested a foot against the front seat. He slowly untied his shoes and removed his socks. He wiggled his eyebrows at Sonny, as if he were doing something provocative, and she cracked up. Still, his look—crisp, lavender dress shirt, collar undone, and sharp, dark slacks over tan, naked feet—was even more attractive than when he was tidy and buttoned up in the restaurant.

They headed toward the boardwalk, under the streetlamps and misty air. Sonny put on her hoodie over her filmy green dress, as Grig courteously held up one sleeve to make it easier for her.

He smiled and assessed her.

"What?" she asked. She looked down at herself.

"I like the sweatshirt with the dinner dress."

She laughed shyly.

"No," he said. "I really do. I like touches like that, making the formal casual. I'd love to show up at one of my concerts in my full formal wear, but barefoot." He lifted a foot, as if he needed to demonstrate.

"I love that picture." She smiled. "Actually, I *would* love a picture of you like that. Do you have a camera back home?"

"Nope. Looks like you're going to have to come take a picture yourself, if you want it."

"I just might do that. I mean, I'll definitely be there for Irina's solos, and you'll be playing then, right?"

"Mm-hmm." A few steps more. He didn't look at her when he spoke next. "Or you could come sooner than that."

She tried to keep from appearing too giddy when she smiled, but she knew her eyes would give her away if he looked into them. "Maybe I will."

He nodded once and spoke softly. "All right, then."

She had gone through four years of college dating several guys without having to keep her infatuation in check. No one clicked with her the way Grig did.

He casually vaulted over the seawall to stand in the sand. He put his hands up to help Sonny join him, and she loved how easily he bore her weight when she stepped off the wall. They walked in silence for a short time.

"Are you a good violinist, Grig? I still have such a hard time imagining you that way." But every time she did, picturing him in a passionate, physical performance of Brahms or Beethoven, she thought he was just about the most romantic man she had ever met.

But the romantic man simply shrugged. "I'm okay, I guess. It's nice to be able to earn a living doing something I love so much."

"Do you think Irina feels the same way about her singing?"

"I think she will. She just doesn't have her feet firmly planted yet, but she'll get there. And she has a beautiful voice."

"Yeah, amazing. The first day she was here, Mom strong-armed her into singing, right out in public, on the beach. The two of them together. I have to admit it was a wonderful experience for everyone around, even if maybe it wasn't so comfortable for Irina. I get chills just remembering how lovely they sounded."

He shook his head and looked at the ground. "Teresa. What a character."

"Yeah, sorry about that."

The sand was soft under her feet this far from the waves. They walked more slowly than they had on the paved boardwalk.

"But what a gift from God," Sonny said, "that Irina's able to sing like that. Mom tried to interest me in singing when I was younger, but it was definitely not my talent."

"You have other gifts." They smiled at each other.

"So, was it more nature or nurture for you and Irina?"

"Hmm?"

"Were your *biological* parents musical, giving you musical genes? Or did your *adoptive* parents simply expose you to music all your lives?"

He grinned and nudged her shoulder with his. "Sorry, Dr. Miller. It was both. I think both of my biological parents were musically gifted, but complications in their lives kept them from doing anything about it. Mom and Dad—our adoptive parents—always loved music. They asked us which instruments we wanted to try, and we experimented around until we found what we liked. Both Irina and I play a little piano, but Irina discovered her voice early on. Same for me with the violin."

Sonny looked out on the horizon and saw the light of a distant ship. She sighed. "This turned out to be a pretty interesting night."

He chuckled softly. "And it's not over yet."

There were those chills again. She said nothing. Goodness, Grig managed to either send a heated blush up her neck or chilly goose bumps down her arms, like an emotional thermostat gone wild.

"So, was everyone all right in there?" he asked. "Back at the beach house?"

"When I went in to tell them we were walking? I guess so. It looked as if they both made themselves pretty scarce as soon as they walked in. Mom was already running her bath, and Irina was already in her bedroom. I didn't knock on either door. I just left a note."

He nodded. She waited a moment for him to speak again, but he didn't appear to be in a hurry.

"Do you mind coming along tomorrow?" she asked. "To meet my grandparents, I mean? *I* don't know them any more than *you* do, but obviously I have more at stake in meeting them. Will you be bored? Would you rather do something else?"

"No, not at all. I'm looking forward to meeting them. It, uh, it makes sense to me for a number of reasons. And I think we'll have fun. Meeting your family members at the same time you do is pretty trippy."

Sonny laughed. "I hadn't thought of that."

"Yeah. It's kind of like one of those afternoon shows Irina likes, where the host brings out the long-lost brother or the biological mother. And everyone cries and hugs all over the place. But with you, it's live."

"I'm very happy to provide you with such stimulating entertainment."

With a quirk of a smile, he said, "Stimulating. Yes."

Grig had always been able to make her blush during their time at Sunset Beach, and this was no different. Something about his confidence and the way he could look her straight in the eye when he paid her a compliment or told her how he felt evoked a reaction from her. It was strange that his sister didn't have the assurance he seemed to have.

"Grig, is Irina all right?"

"You mean tonight? Or in general?"

"I meant tonight. But I guess I mean in general too."

He looked at her without speaking. Then he sighed. "I *think* she's all right. Her therapist is helpful, but she's been on maternity leave for two months. Irina struggles mostly with her thoughts about our biological parents. That, and the years in the orphanage. She's just a little unsure of herself sometimes. And something obviously triggered her emotions tonight, but I don't know what."

"She didn't talk with you about it when you waited for her outside the ladies' room?"

"No. I think she didn't want to give in to it, completely, so she said she didn't want to discuss it yet. That's good to a degree, I think. She needs to be able to cope in public when she gets upset."

"I feel kind of responsible." Sonny hoped Grig didn't agree with her.

"She seemed fine until Melanie brought Bailey and Micah over, isn't that what you said? I don't know why that would make her sad, but she definitely seemed to be having fun before then."

He put his hand on her shoulder as they walked. "Now, why would any of that make Irina's mood your responsibility?"

She laughed at herself. "I guess that does sound a little egocentric. I just mean anything connected with all of this family reunion stuff, you know? All of that has been thrown in Irina's face because Mom practically forced her into coming here. And that's what seemed to set her off earlier this week, the family friction. Since I'm the one who engineered this get-together, I guess I feel responsible."

He removed his hand, and Sonny's shoulder felt naked. Abandoned. Come back, Grig's hand!

"In that case," he said, "it's Teresa's fault." He smiled at her. "If it hadn't been for Teresa, Irina wouldn't be here."

"And neither would you."

"True."

That was that. She wouldn't say anything else that would sound even slightly flirtatious. She didn't trust herself. She might say too much if she let the floodgates open.

"Unless…" he said.

"Unless?"

"I might have ended up here anyway if God had that in mind."

Why did her heart pick up its pace at that?

"Is that, um, what you think? God wanted you to be here this week?"

He stopped walking and faced her. His eyes were beautiful and serious. "Man, I sure hope so, Sonny."

She stood very still and whispered, "Why?"

He leaned forward and slipped his hand under her hair, cupping the back of her head. He looked into her eyes with an almost pained expression. "Because I'm so happy to see you again. This *has* to be a blessing."

She shivered and stepped into his warm arms as he kissed her lips, her eyes, her forehead. She rested her head against his chest and smiled.

Without a doubt. A total blessing.

Fifty-Five

Fragrant steam wafted around Teresa. She read deep into her romance novel. As soon as the tub water started to cool, she drained enough so she could refill it with hot. But eventually she dragged herself out, her fingers and toes white and pruny. After slathering body lotion all over and slipping into her favorite pajamas, she padded out to the kitchen.

She retrieved a box of fudge she bought on the boardwalk this afternoon when they shopped for clothes. With all the running around at the restaurant tonight, she hadn't eaten enough dinner, and she skipped dessert altogether. This would take the edge off.

Sonny's brief note sat on the counter. Teresa read it and smiled. She did love her girl, despite their repeated clashes over family secrets. And Grig seemed like such a kind person. She had thought so before this week, although she didn't pay him much attention at work. But now, seeing how he cared for his sister and obviously cared for Sonny, he had grown on her. The idea of a blossoming relationship between Sonny and him brought Teresa nothing but warmth.

What didn't bring her great warmth were thoughts about what tomorrow might be like. For her and for Sonny. She didn't know how David would behave with his daughter, but she didn't feel she had any control over that anymore. All these years she thought she could protect Sonny from any rejection he might throw her way. Of course, she kept quiet for her own sake too. She knew David felt nothing but shame and resentment toward her.

And the idea of facing her own parents was daunting. Not only because she betrayed her sister and they probably knew that. But her deliberate severance from the family must have hurt them as much as her affair with David—and her pregnancy—would have. Probably more. Twenty-five years was a long time.

With a sigh, she brought her book to the couch and snuggled into one of Faith Fontaine's colorful afghans. She honestly hated the idea of tomorrow and feared she couldn't endure it. But she would have said the same about that blowup with Melanie last night too. And she had survived. Sonny hadn't left her, as Teresa had left her own mother. And, if anything, she and Melanie were closer than they had been before her confession that awful day twenty-five years ago. They weren't bosom buddies, of course. But years of ice had melted away in their heated argument yesterday.

Still. She had yet to apologize to Melanie. And to Sonny, for that matter. She couldn't help but feel she might as well wait until Sonny met with David. She had a hunch she would owe yet another apology after David told Sonny his side of the story.

The side door opened, and Melanie stepped in, a tote bag slung over her shoulder. "Hi."

"Hi." Certainly less dramatic than Melanie's original arrival here, but not a great deal more comfortable. Now that it was just the two of them, Teresa felt more of the twenty-five-year-old stiffness between them.

"Are you here alone?" Melanie stepped in and set her bag down. She didn't seem in a great hurry to reclaim her bedroom.

Teresa sat up and adopted a less-relaxed posture. "Sonny and Grig are on a walk." She looked at Irina's closed door and spoke softly. "I'm taking it for granted Irina's gone to bed. She was awfully quiet on the drive home. She and I haven't practiced her solos for days. Maybe she's starting to worry again, now that the week is almost over."

Melanie lifted her eyebrows. "Hmm. Maybe."

Teresa waited until Melanie was almost back to her room before she spoke again.

"I'm wondering…"

Melanie stopped and turned. "Yes?"

Teresa played with a small hole in the afghan. "I just wondered if it might be best for Irina and me to stay here tomorrow while you all go into the city and on to San Clemente. It would give us a chance to work on her solos. While the house is empty, I mean." She gave Melanie a casual glance.

Melanie smiled as if she had caught Teresa skipping school. She set her bag on the floor outside her bedroom and walked calmly back to the living room.

"Teresa, I came back here tonight because I promised Sonny I would. I promised I would, in part, because *you* promised to come with us to San Clemente tomorrow to see Mom and Dad."

"Yes, I—"

"You are a forty-six-year-old woman. No one is going to force you to do something you refuse to do."

"It's not that I refuse—"

"But you have an opportunity to repair a number of relationships tomorrow. You also have an opportunity to destroy them further. I'm not going to debate right and wrong with you tonight."

Teresa huffed and pushed the blanket away from herself. The closed romance novel fell to the floor, face up. Both she and Melanie looked at the open-shirted beefcake poised on the cover. Teresa cringed. Nothing like showing her silly, shallow side while being chastised for being irresponsible. "Well, no one's asking you to debate anything, Melanie."

Melanie talked as if she weren't listening to a word Teresa said.

"It's time you stopped using Irina to avoid your own responsibilities. She's been a delightful addition to the group this week, but she's not your personal shield to pull out whenever you want to deflect difficult situations. The girl has her own problems to deal with. Leave her alone."

Teresa clenched her jaw and stood to face Melanie. She glanced at Irina's door and tried to speak quietly, but it was difficult to be angry and polite at the same time. "Since when did you become Irina's guardian? You always were the bossy one, Melanie."

"And you were always the selfish one."

Teresa gasped. "Me? The selfish one? All right, that does it. You are *not* going to force me to dance to your tune. I'm staying here tomorrow, whether Irina chooses to go or not."

Melanie's eyes narrowed and her lips pursed. "So now you're using me as your excuse rather than Irina. Well, you can give that news to Sonny yourself, do you understand? I will *not* be the one to deliver your bad news to that poor girl." She walked back to her room.

Teresa lobbed her response in a kind of whispered shout. "Yeah, well, just remember. That poor girl is *my daughter.*"

Without a word, Melanie made Teresa flush with shame. She simply looked Teresa in the eyes and nodded in agreement, the indictment more harsh than anything she could have said.

Fifty-Six

Melanie was so miffed she pulled out her cell phone and called her mother as soon as she closed her bedroom door. It was like college days all over again, with Teresa being a complete villain and Melanie seeking solace from her greatest source of comfort.

Before her mother answered the phone, Melanie realized what she was doing. Her sources of comfort had changed since her college days. She was a believer now. She was a wife. But she hadn't turned to God for comfort. She hadn't called Bailey. She called her mother, but not for comfort. She called to rat on Teresa. There was no denying it.

She couldn't stand it when God did that to her.

"Hello?"

Drat. "Oh, Mom. Hi, it's Melanie."

Barbara Miller's melodic voice belied the late hour and any fatigue she might possibly feel. "Melanie! Honey, I'm so glad you called. I thought of you this week. Hadn't heard from you, and your father and I went out to a movie the other day which bored him to tears, but you and I would have had a great time watching it together. The one about the woman from South Dakota inheriting a fancy Swiss hotel, you know that one?"

Melanie smiled and let her mother explain the movie's plotline in detail. She kicked her sandals off and relaxed back onto the bed. She didn't mind the one-sidedness of these conversations. Her mother was a fantastic storyteller, which must have been one reason she was such a popular high school English teacher. Within minutes, she had Melanie laughing and far more at ease than when she called.

So she received comfort, after all. She loved it when God did that to her.

"But I've been babbling," her mother said. "You should stop me, Melanie."

"Not a chance. I enjoyed every minute of that. Thanks for not telling me the ending. We'll go see it together."

"Will we? You'd better hurry on up, then. It probably won't be in the theaters much longer."

"How about tomorrow? Do you think it will still be showing tomorrow?"

"You're coming up tomorrow? Honestly? Oh, honey, that's great! Your father and I are driving each other insane. Bring Bailey and Micah up here so your dad can go do some outdoorsy stuff and get it out of his system for a while. So he can get out of my hair."

Melanie chuckled. "Um, actually, Bailey and Micah..." No, if she said Bailey and Micah weren't coming, one thing would lead to another, and her mom would get the whole story out of her. She didn't know exactly *whom* she would bring up there. She didn't want to get her mom's hopes up about Teresa. She shouldn't have called so impulsively. "I'm not—"

"You're not coming?"

"Yes, I'll be there. In the afternoon, probably around three. But, Mom, don't tell Dad yet. I...I'm bringing a little surprise." That was true. She would definitely bring Sonny, which would floor them. She hadn't alerted them to Sonny's letter. They didn't even know she existed. Maybe that would take the sting out of their stubborn songbird's continued refusal to see them.

"A surprise? For your father? Or for both of us?"

Melanie chuckled. Her mother would do it, anyway. She would figure it out. Melanie knew this woman. If the conversation went any further, she'd figure out Teresa's part in the story.

"I don't want to tell you any more information, Mom. Just you guys be home around three, okay?"

Melanie ended the call and sighed. She knew Sonny would be like a gift from heaven for her parents, and Sonny couldn't ask for better grandparents.

But, despite Melanie's comment to Teresa—that *she* would have to break the bad news to Sonny if she refused to accompany them—she still dreaded her own responsibility if Teresa refused. If only two of the three Miller women showed up in San Clemente tomorrow, someone would have to explain about Teresa.

There was no way that task should fall in Sonny's lap. So it would be Melanie's job to break her parents' hearts all over again.

Fifty-Seven

Sonny and Grig were almost back at the beach house when he brought up practical matters. Practical matters Sonny was thrilled to discuss with him.

"If you're doing your graduate work at Berkeley, you need to move up there soon, right?"

"Yeah, end of August. I planned to look for something this month. The people in the counseling office said they could help me find a place."

He draped his arm over her shoulders and spoke close to her ear. "I have a few connections in the area, you know. I might be able to help." He sounded as if he were trafficking in sensitive state secrets.

"Connections, huh? I appreciate that."

"My understanding," he said, "is that the prime area for psychology graduate students is within a one-mile radius of College Street, in Oakland."

She turned her head just a little and was within an inch of his face. "That's your street, I assume?"

He stood more erectly but kept his arm around her. She loved the protective feel of the gesture.

"That would be correct, yes."

When they reached the beach house, they sat for a while on the seawall. They positioned themselves close together, but the arm was down and their faces a decent distance apart.

There was little sound around them, save the breaking waves, as constant and steady as a sleeper's breath.

"So," Sonny said.

Grig smiled. "So."

"What are we talking about here?" Sonny rested her hands on either side of herself. The flat top of the wall was dry and sandy.

"Between us?"

She nodded. "Yeah. I mean, I know they're going to have me hopping while I work on this degree. And I hear your social life can get totally squeezed when you go for your master's."

He bobbed his head. "I could use some squeezing."

She gently banged up against his side. "Come on, talk to me, goober."

He laughed out loud, which made her laugh too.

"Okay," he said. "Here's what I propose. I'm already up there in Oakland, fifteen minutes away from Berkeley, firmly ensconced. My sister lives there, my parents live there, my job is there. The fact that you're about to engage in three years of study at Berkeley and everything worked out so that you and I would meet again, *here,* four years after Sunset Beach, site of the most remarkable…" He lifted his hand and shook his head, at a loss for the word he wanted.

Sonny was certain he didn't notice incorporating the words "propose" and "engage" in what he had just said. She certainly didn't expect such a thing for a long time, from Grig or anyone else. But wouldn't old Dr. Freud have gotten a kick out of that?

"…well, it was the most remarkable month of my adult life, how about that?" He looked at her.

She gave him a broad smile. "Yeah, how about that?"

"Anyway," he said, a lopsided smile on his face. Then he raised his eyebrows and pointed at her. "Oh, and your mother lives there too. More family, that's another thing. And you're a believer now." He laughed. "I mean, Sonny, for me, this is too amazing to shrug off. So when you move to Oakland or Berkeley, I'd really like us to spend as much time as we can 'squeeze' out, as you say, to get to know each other as well as we can."

He turned halfway and straddled the wall so he could face her better. He leaned toward her as he spoke, his voice throaty and an earnest crease between his brows. "I don't know what God has in store for either of us. But I've been praying for you for four years, Sonny, ever since I met you. And I've been praying for my future spouse for even longer. I honestly didn't expect to ever see you again, so I never thought of the two people as possibly the same person. And maybe they're not. But maybe they *are*."

Sonny's heart raced, and she had to breathe deeply in order to feel she breathed at all. But Grig's frankness was the most refreshing experience she had ever had. After years of evasive communication with her mother, this was like fresh air blowing her away. She swallowed. All she could say at first was a very small, "Whoa."

Grig stared at her for a moment. Then he affected a hugely nerdy posture and expression and spoke nasally, his eyebrows crumpled and fearful. "Too much?"

She laughed until she cried, and she could tell he thoroughly loved having made her react that way. She turned enough to put her arms around him, and he reached out to hug her back.

When they pulled apart, she was able to speak more clearly. "I love the plan, I love the way you said it, and I love that God brought you to Mission Beach to find me again." She put out her hand, businesslike. "I agree to your terms. Henceforth, we shall date."

He shook her hand. "Yeah, henceforth. Glad you see things my way." His grip was strong and warm.

They heard soft walking behind them and turned to see Julian approach. He smiled at them. "Good evening. You two conducting business out here, then?"

They both laughed. "Sort of," Sonny said.

He sat on her other side. "I was about to turn in for the night, but when I saw you two I wanted to make sure to say hello. Your week is quickly drawing to an end, isn't it?"

Sonny nodded. "Yeah, just tomorrow and Saturday morning. Oh! But, Julian, I'm meeting my grandparents tomorrow!"

His face lit up with a grin. "Ah, Sonny, what excellent news. Are they coming here?"

"No, we're all driving there. To San Clemente."

"Lovely place, San Clemente."

Grig nudged her foot with his. "Tell Julian who else you're meeting."

Julian raised his eyebrows in anticipation.

"I'm supposed to meet my father before we go to San Clemente."

"Well, now." He searched her eyes, as if he were trying to gauge something. "How do you feel about that?"

"I'm a little freaked out, to tell you the truth."

Julian smiled. "I think you're going to do just fine. My own children, well, they knew me a bit, of course. But when their mother and I divorced, they were very young. There was quite a period of time when we didn't see one another. And that first meeting when they were young adults was, I think, frightening for all of us. But you just pray about it, Sonny. You'll do well. If he's worth anything, he'll recognize you for the gem you are."

He glanced at Grig and grinned. "And I don't think he'll be alone in recognizing you as such."

Sonny looked at Grig, who nodded, a twinkle in his eyes.

Julian stood and dusted off the back of his shorts. "So I suppose we've boogie boarded our last together—"

"Unless we get a quick run in before we check out Saturday," Sonny said.

He spoke as he walked toward his home. "I'll be here. You just let me know. Blessings with your family reunions tomorrow."

After he left, Sonny stood from the wall. "I guess I'd better get to sleep. Assuming I *can* sleep, that is."

Grig stood and walked her to the front door of the beach house. He adopted the businesslike attitude they had playfully assumed before. "I appreciate your taking the time to meet with me. This has been a fruitful meeting, our immediate goals having been met."

She smiled up at him. "Well, almost." She stood on her tiptoes and rested her hands on his shoulders. She leaned in and gave him a soft kiss on the lips, which he gently returned.

He took her hand, kissed it, and gave it a light squeeze. "Night."

He walked half the distance between the houses. He glanced at her over his shoulder and stopped.

She tilted her head, puzzled, as he faced her again.

He stared at her for a moment, heaved a sigh full of emotion, and jogged back to her. He wrapped his arms around her and gave her a kiss far more reminiscent of their month at Sunset Beach. She weaved her hands into his hair and found herself breathless.

Grig broke away and jogged away from her just as quickly, tossing her a smile and a wave as he went.

For a few seconds she watched him, and then she stepped inside. She leaned against the door, knowing her expression had to be a silly, dreamy one.

She whispered to the dark. "Whoa."

The house was silent, so she assumed everyone had a head start on her, sleepwise. She smiled and silently lifted up a quiet prayer of thanks to God.

Yes, there was something going on with Irina, and they would work on that in the time remaining. But other than that, this week had been, to use Grig's word, fruitful. Tomorrow she would meet her father, after twenty-four years of seeing that role empty. And she would surprise her grandparents, who probably didn't even know there was an entire person in the family they hadn't yet met.

She walked back toward her room and looked at the closed doors, behind which her mom and aunt slept. Another grin. They were reconciled, to some extent, and things could only get better from here on out.

Fifty-Eight

Melanie sipped her coffee the next morning and watched the beach from the window. The morning looked beautiful, as always. She would have liked to sit on the front porch, but she simply wasn't up to running into Julian, should he decide to join her. He was such a lovely man, but she…well, there was no getting around it. She was in a snit. And how could one get away with a snit around that man? Between Zeke and him, it was as bad as walking into the fellowship hall of a church and growling.

She knew the solution to that dilemma was in her hands. And she had every intention of eventually thinking and behaving like the mature woman of God she was supposed to be. Especially if she thought she might serve as director of women's ministries at her church.

She clenched her jaw. Oh, if the church staff could see her heart right now. They would run screaming. But they couldn't see her heart right now, so she would just nurse this grudge for a while.

Irina's sweet voice interrupted her bitter little party.

"Are you up for a walk down to Kono's for breakfast, Melanie?"

Melanie turned and put on her happy face. "Sure. I'd love that."

"I'm going to run over to Grig's and see if he wants to come too."

Melanie nodded, and Irina left. Melanie noticed Irina had dark circles under her pretty blue eyes. Hmm. She had gone to bed rather early, so Melanie wouldn't have thought she would look so tired today. Maybe she really was stressed again about her solos, as Teresa suggested.

No. That had been an excuse. Teresa was her usual self last night—evasive, cowardly, and not the slightest bit concerned about Irina's needs.

Or anyone else's. How could she let Sonny down like this? How could she continue avoiding her own parents?

"Morning, Aunt Melanie." Sonny walked out of her room as perky as Tweety Bird, still in her pajamas. "You're up bright and early." She headed straight for the coffee pot and poured herself a cupful.

Melanie snorted a sharp laugh. "I'm up early, anyway." She saw Sonny hesitate.

"You're not feeling well?"

Now it was Melanie's turn to hesitate. Did she want to tell Sonny anything about last night?

But Sonny jumped back in before Melanie could speak. "Oh, Melanie, I'm sorry. Was I completely selfish last night, asking you to come back? There you were, all comfy and back home with Uncle Bailey and Micah—"

"No, Sonny." Melanie put up a hand to stop her. "You weren't selfish, honey. You just want a little time with your family. What aunt wouldn't feel flattered? What father? What grandparents?" She tried not to purse her lips. "What mother?"

Sonny was too upbeat to notice the sarcasm, apparently.

"Oh, good. I'm relieved you see it that way." She came up and gave Melanie a strong hug. "I so appreciate having you in my life. Really. I love you."

Melanie hugged her back. "I love you too, honey." All right. That was it for the obsession about Teresa. This week was about Sonny and building a relationship too long denied.

Thanks to Teresa.

Melanie tried to force away such thoughts. Grow *up*, woman. *Help me, Lord!*

Irina walked back into the house, and Sonny pulled away from her hug.

"Good morning," Irina said before she dashed into her room.

Sonny called out to her. "Morning. You haven't already been out on the beach, have you?"

Irina emerged with a change of clothes. "No, I just went over and asked Grig if he wanted to come to Kono's with us for breakfast."

Melanie saw Sonny brighten even further before she spoke.

"Oh, yum. And is he going?"

Irina nodded and headed toward the bathroom. "Yep. You too, right? I just want to jump in the shower quickly."

"Yeah, I'll go. I was going for a quick run, but I'd rather go with you guys. I need to shower too, though."

Irina closed the door, and Melanie studied Sonny's happy expression.

"Oh, yum," Melanie said, repeating Sonny's words. "Were you talking about breakfast or Grig?"

Sonny laughed and put her hand to her mouth. "Aunt Melanie!"

Melanie chuckled. God bless her niece. She made up for all of the disappointments of this trip.

Sonny looked toward the bathroom door and her smile vanished before she softly spoke again. "I'm a little concerned about Irina."

"You know, I noticed dark circles under her eyes this morning." Melanie took a drink of her coffee. "What's wrong?"

Sonny shook her head. "Grig and I talked about that after dinner last night. She was awfully quiet on the ride home from the restaurant."

"Do you think it has anything to do with her upcoming solos?"

Melanie was embarrassed by the smugness she felt when Sonny answered.

"I doubt it. She was fine almost all the way through dinner. But by the time we finished up, she had retreated to the ladies' room and came out upset."

"Oh, no." Melanie's heart broke. "I was so wrapped up in my own little world, I barely even noticed her last night."

"It's going to be all right." Sonny put her hand on Melanie's arm. "One of us will get a chance to be there for her when she feels up to talking. Maybe she'll be in the mood after breakfast, or even during." She smiled. "Nothing's going to mess up our two meetings today, right?"

Melanie sighed. "Right, honey." Blasted Teresa.

"I'm going to go see if Mom wants to come to breakfast." Sonny put her coffee cup on the counter.

Of course, Teresa was too tired to go. Sonny came back completely unaware of what lay ahead.

"She didn't sleep well, she says." Sonny washed out her cup in the kitchen. "So she'll catch up with us when we get back."

Melanie simply nodded and avoided letting Sonny look too closely into her eyes. She'd be surprised if Teresa was even here when they got back.

She heard the jingle of keys and looked up to see Sonny placing Teresa's car keys into her own purse. Melanie looked at Sonny, a question in her expression.

Sonny grinned. "I'm no dummy. I've been with your sister for twenty-four years. She's not going anywhere."

Fifty-Nine

Melanie ate the last of her breakfast burrito and laughed with everyone else during Grig's self-deprecating account of his first professional violin solo. There were even a couple of teenaged girls listening surreptitiously from the table next to theirs. Melanie wondered if they would have paid as much attention to Grig had he looked less like a musician and more like a computer geek.

"I broke my E string at a critical point in the piece," he said. "I was sure everyone in the entire hall would boo and throw rotten fruit at me—"

"Something every serious music patron brings to the symphony," Sonny said. She sipped her orange juice, a smile wrapped around her straw.

Grig nodded in accord. "Of course. But it didn't go that way at all. In fact, everyone waited until I made a stupid face before they even laughed. And it gave me an opportunity to feel and look like one of the gang. Really took the pressure off."

"But, how did you finish the solo?" Sonny asked.

He shrugged one shoulder. "I compensated. I played the right notes, just at different positions. You know, on the remaining strings. And we moved right along. I got loads of compliments on that performance. People can be really forgiving in situations like that."

He clearly hoped to calm any fears Irina might have, in case her solos were the reason for her stress. It looked as if he had a positive effect on her. She had an appetite and looked perfectly happy, albeit a little tired.

There was a good chance Sonny would soon be the one in need of cheering up. Melanie held true to her promise to Teresa. She wouldn't be the one to bear the bad news about Teresa's decision not to accompany them today.

However, judging from Sonny's savvy move in taking Teresa's car keys, perhaps this turn of events wouldn't floor Sonny the way Melanie feared it would. But no doubt it would still disappoint her.

And Melanie had to admit that she would be disappointed too. She loved the idea of walking into her parents' home, their long-lost daughter and granddaughter in tow. If she was honest with herself, she knew she looked forward to the approval her parents would feel toward *her* for encouraging Teresa to come home. But that was nothing compared to the joyful surprise she wished for her parents.

She was diverted from her thoughts when she saw Irina putting on lipstick. Sonny and Grig were engrossed in a story about another concert snafu, and Irina was obviously listening. She laughed when Grig or Sonny said something humorous.

But Melanie couldn't take her eyes off of Irina's small, pink-jeweled lipstick case—so gaudy it was cute. It was only large enough for a tube of lipstick, with a hinged top and a tiny mirror inside. It was flashy and unusual. And that's why Melanie knew she had seen it before. But she felt certain the last time she saw it, it didn't belong to Irina.

"Let's take a walk on the Crystal Pier before heading back!" Irina hooked her arm through Grig's as they walked away from Kono's.

Sonny did the same with Melanie.

Once Irina and Grig walked far enough ahead, Melanie spoke softly to Sonny. "I don't suppose you own a little pink lipstick case, do you?" She put her finger to her lips and raised her eyes in Irina's direction, trying to signal the need for discretion.

Sonny shook her head. "I'm a lip gloss girl, myself. Why? What's up?"

"Do you think maybe your mom has such a thing?"

"The pink case? Doubtful. But I could check when we get back."

Melanie sighed. "I'm afraid we might have another light-fingered episode going on."

"Light-fingered?" Sonny followed the jut of Melanie's chin toward Irina. She whispered, her voice falling sadly. "Oh, no."

"Maybe not. I could be wrong. But—" Melanie gasped. "Sonny. I just realized where I saw the case before." She lowered her head and pressed her fingertips against her forehead. "Oh, poor Micah will have a fit if I don't handle this well. I wonder if we can just leave the whole matter alone."

"Micah?" Sonny looked as if she might laugh. "How does a seventeen-year-old boy end up connected with a lipstick case?"

Melanie sighed. "It belongs to Doris. His girlfriend's mother."

"No!" Sonny stage-whispered her reaction.

"Yes. The woman we're supposed to impress with how straight-arrow our family is," Melanie said, moaning.

Sonny still looked as if she could laugh. "I'm sorry, Aunt Melanie. I know this is bad. But first of all, I love Irina, but she's not a member of Micah's family. Anyway, somehow I can't picture that Doris lady with *any* lipstick case, let alone a pink-jeweled one. Are you sure about this?"

"I saw her put it back in her purse when she returned from the ladies' room. You know, the trip where she met Teresa?" She frowned. "I just can't imagine how Irina got it. She wasn't really around Doris last night that I'm aware of. I'm telling you, Sonny, the girl's like the Artful Dodger. I don't think she even realizes she stole it."

Sonny sighed. "What I wonder is whether the theft is why she was upset last night or if the theft was because she was upset. About something else, I mean. It's kind of a psychological chicken-before-the-egg situation. Either way, something's stressing her again."

Melanie knew it couldn't be the clash she had with Teresa. Sonny said Irina was upset driving home, and that was before she and Teresa had their quiet screaming match outside Irina's bedroom door.

Grig and Irina doubled back to join them as they approached the end of the pier, so the conversation stopped. But not before Sonny muttered to Melanie, "Let me talk with Grig about it. He would want to know, anyway."

Melanie nodded. Going back to the beach house would be interesting. If Irina was stressed now, imagine how she would react to the scene between Sonny and her mother when Teresa announced she wouldn't go to San Clemente today.

Sixty

"Sonny?" Irina sidled up as they walked the boardwalk on their way back to the beach house. At that point, Sonny happened to be alone, heading toward a rack of beach hats. "Do you think before we head out today that we could make a trip to the market for bottled water and maybe something to munch on for our drive to San Clemente?"

"Sure." Sonny looked back at Melanie and Grig, who had stopped at a postcard carousel. "Hey, anyone else want to—"

"No." Irina put her hand on Sonny's arm. "Just the two of us."

Sonny looked into her eyes, which were especially dark rimmed today. "Oh. All right." She glanced back at Melanie and Grig, who had stopped to listen to her. "Anybody, uh, want anything from Trader Joe's? Irina and I are taking a drive."

"Chips?" Grig asked. "For later?"

"Nothing for me, thanks." Melanie returned to picking out postcards.

"Okay, we're going on ahead of you, then. See you when we get back." Sonny turned to Irina. "Come on. Let's not bother going into the house. I'll pick something up for Mom in case she's hungry. I don't want to give her a chance to ask for her car keys."

"You have her car keys?" Irina was unable to suppress a tiny smile. "You're holding her hostage or something?"

Sonny smiled. "Maybe not. She might not even realize I have them. But in case she woke up feeling impulsive and ready to run, I figured I'd help her take some time to think things through."

"Hmm. I think you're like her just a little sometimes." Irina half smiled.

"Impulsive? Or manipulative?"

"Yes."

Sonny laughed. They reached her car and pulled away from the house a moment later.

They drove in silence for a short distance. Sonny almost asked Irina a question to get her talking. But the "manipulative" comment gave her pause. She didn't *always* have to be in counselor mode. Irina would talk when and if she was ready.

That time came as they pulled into the Trader Joe's parking lot. Sonny put up the car windows and turned off the ignition.

"Wait a minute, can you?" Irina asked. "Could we talk a moment before going in?"

Sonny nodded. "Sure." She turned the key enough to lower the windows again. She faced Irina and rested against the car door, giving Irina as open an expression as possible.

Irina looked at her lap and toyed with the frayed hem of her cut-offs. "Grig told me you two were talking about me last night."

"Oh. Yeah, a little. You were so quiet—"

"I stole something again, Sonny!" Irina blurted the comment, and immediately had tears in her eyes. She reached for her purse and opened it up.

Here it came. The pink lipstick case. Sonny almost said those words but stopped herself again when she saw what Irina pulled out.

Reading glasses. A slim, plaid case from which Irina removed the half-lensed glasses most often seen on women at least Teresa and Melanie's age.

"And I don't even wear glasses," Irina said, sighing. She put the glasses back in the case and set it carefully on the dashboard.

Sonny's brow furrowed. "Do those belong to Doris too?"

Irina turned to Sonny, her eyes wide. "*Too?* What do you mean, 'too'?"

"Oh. I, um…" Sonny sighed. "The lipstick case? Pink? It belongs to Doris, too."

Absolute confusion crossed Irina's expression. She opened her purse again, rummaged for a moment, and then withdrew the case. She frowned at it, as if this were the first time she had seen it.

"I don't remember taking this." A tear fell down her cheek, and Sonny saw her clench her jaw before another tear fell.

Sonny leaned forward and put her hand on Irina's shoulder. "Irina, what's troubling you? Obviously something's stressing you out. And it must have happened at the restaurant."

The moment Irina tried to talk, her words mingled with tears. "Sonny, I'm embarrassed to tell you this, but I guess you're the one I need to say this to."

"Then go ahead. Please don't be embarrassed. It's just us here, and I love you like a sister." She opened the console between the seats and pulled out a minipacket of tissues. "Here. Have at it, sis."

Irina smiled through her tears. "I'm jealous, I think. That's what's wrong."

"Jealous? Of what? Or, of whom?"

"You." Irina looked back down at her lap.

"But, why? You're amazingly beautiful and talented. You have a bright career ahead of you—"

Irina shook her head. "No, not those things. It's your family."

Sonny almost laughed, but she knew how inappropriate that would be. She spoke calmly.

"Really? Irina, don't get me wrong. I totally love the family members I've discovered so far. But consider the facts." She ticked the items off on her fingers. "I had to hire a detective agency in order to find my aunt and, ultimately, my uncle and cousin. I had to trick my mom into seeing the sister she betrayed and deserted twenty-five years ago. I have my mother's car keys in my purse, for goodness' sake, to keep her from running away rather than meeting her parents. Those parents are my grandparents, who don't even know I exist. And today I hope to finally meet with the father who did his small part in creating me before disappearing from my life for twenty-five years. I mean, there are plenty of players here, but the game is seriously being played with a warped set of rules."

"Yes, all of that's true," Irina said. "But look at how much is coming together for you. Look at what you're discovering this week. I envy that."

"But you *have* a family, Irina. A great family, from what I've heard. I know you have an amazing brother who loves you—"

"Yes, and my parents are the best in the world. My family is wonderful. That's why this feeling upsets me so much."

"I guess I don't understand what that feeling is." Sonny scratched her head. "I mean, I understand what envy is. Or jealousy, as you said. I just don't understand what you think I have that you don't have."

"Identity." Irina said it and nodded. "That's it. You're learning more about who you are because you're identifying where and whom you came from. I love my parents, but—"

"Oh, it's the biological parent loss you're feeling."

"I'll never get any of that back, Sonny. They're gone. If it wasn't for them, I wouldn't be alive, but I hardly know anything about them. I feel empty when I try to imagine them. You're just beginning to learn. I see how excited you are. And I'm sorry, but I get jealous. And then, last night, when Melanie brought your uncle and Micah over, and they were so happy, and they hugged you, I don't know, I just wanted to cry."

Sonny saw the moment from Irina's eyes, and the image made her cry too.

She always thought she wouldn't feel so driven to learn about her family—the one her mother hid from her—if another family had formed through the years. If her mother had eventually married, for instance, and people had come along to fill in for her missing father, her grandparents, and her other relatives. But considering what Irina felt, despite her circumstances, that wasn't necessarily the case.

She didn't want to feel guilty about the way her family had grown this week. But she would love to be able to help Irina feel better. She wished she were better equipped for this kind of thing.

Irina said, "What I wouldn't give for someone to bring my birth mother and father to me for a hug, just for a minute."

Well, Sonny was at least equipped enough to give her a hug. So that's what she did. She leaned forward and embraced Irina.

"I'm so sorry, Irina. I'm sorry this is all I can give you. Just a hug from me. And a promise that I'll pray for you to be at peace about the family you have."

Irina nodded. "Prayer helps. And I do love my parents."

"You know, you might be going through a grieving process, sort of."

"You think?"

"Yeah. Even though you lost your parents when you were really young, maybe you didn't allow yourself to grieve until you were older. Maybe once you felt secure in your adoptive family, you felt you could afford to grieve your birth mother and father. And I think the sense of loss never goes away. It just loses some of its power over time."

Irina stared out the windshield, but she didn't appear to focus on anything. "You could be right. Everything started to get a little strange for me when I hit puberty. The stress, the eating disorder, the stealing. My counselor thought it was all because of body changes and hormones. Things like that. But that *was* just two years after Grig and I were adopted. Maybe—"

"Well, let's not take my ideas for anything other than speculation. One thing I've learned this week is that I have a lot of learning to do before I can counsel as anything but a friend."

Irina smiled, and this time she didn't look as if she had to work at it. "I'm happy to hear your counsel, friend." She picked up the two cases she took from Doris. "What will we do about these?"

"We'll give them to Melanie. She'll work something out."

"Wow, what a mess." Irina rooted through her purse. "I hope I don't have anything else I shouldn't have."

They got out of the car and walked into the store.

"Ah, here we go," Irina whispered to Sonny. "At least I know I didn't steal this."

Sonny looked over. Irina held her driver's license next to her face. "This is the one thing in my purse I'm certain is mine."

"Oh, stop." Sonny pulled Irina's arm down and laughed. She was glad she would see a lot of Irina after moving to Berkeley. Not just because Irina might need the friendship, but because Sonny had plenty of room in her heart for a friend. Or maybe even a sister.

Sixty-One

Teresa set the romance novel on the couch beside her and blew out a breath of exasperation. Novels like this were supposed to offer pure escapism, weren't they? That's why she was reading it this morning, rather than facing her daughter and all she hoped to achieve today.

In one of the book's story threads, Garreth, the swashbuckling hero from the front cover, found the long-lost son who was taken from him ten years ago. Even though he'd been a ladies' man and a rake through the entire story, he completely changed tacks when his former love came back with their son. Garreth was a new man, due to the deep love he felt for his boy. He swept him into his arms and nearly cried into his dark locks. He forgave and embraced the boy's mother, with whom he had always been in passionate love. Of course, their fiery, furious love had torn them apart, time and again, only to draw them back together.

This particular part of the book was a little too close to home for Teresa's liking. Yes, the circumstances were different. David Sommerhill never looked remotely like the hunk in this book, and she was no passionate, raven-haired vixen with a figure that never quit. Her figure wasn't the worst, but it certainly *did* quit. And love had never been a factor between David and her, fiery or otherwise.

Still, despite the differences, she and David had a child in common. Teresa scanned the novel's reunion scene again and sighed. She knew there'd be no such scene this afternoon when Sonny showed up at her father's office. David hadn't sought Sonny. He hadn't even known about her before this week. Rather than sweeping her into his arms, there was every chance he would try to convince her to lose his number.

When Teresa pictured that outcome, she knew there was no way she could stay here at the beach house or head back to Oakland and leave Sonny to risk that rejection without her.

Teresa shook her head. She didn't know if Irina was right about the ways God used to get one's attention, but she had to laugh. First, Irina's talking donkey, then the seal pup on the beach, and now a trashy novel. Not exactly the fire and brimstone she always pictured as God's communication tools.

Melanie walked into the house, locked eyes with Teresa, and looked away again. She muttered as she scuttled back to her room. "Morning."

"Where are Sonny and Irina?" Teresa called back.

"The grocery store." Melanie walked back into the living room. "To get snacks for the drive today."

"It's not a terribly long trip," Teresa said. She thought she saw a subtle roll of the eyes before Melanie responded.

"I think Irina wanted to chat privately with Sonny, that's all."

"Ah." Teresa nodded. "And when are we leaving?"

"We?" Melanie frowned. "Have you changed your mind?"

"Well, I hadn't completely decided not to go in the first place." She was prepared to argue that point. Yes, she had said she wouldn't go, but she felt Melanie had pounced too quickly on her inkling about not joining them today. Teresa wouldn't have said she was staying behind if Melanie had been more gracious.

But no argument ensued. Melanie just dropped it. "We're leaving when Irina and Sonny return. Excuse me a minute. I want to freshen up." And she went back toward her bedroom.

Teresa couldn't help but feel childish for her own behavior. Why was it so difficult to behave as an adult when it came to interacting with Melanie? Sometimes she felt like the kid she was when she and Melanie shared a room, fighting like grizzly bears one moment and skipping arm in arm the next.

When Sonny and Irina walked through the front door a short while later, they behaved very much as Teresa and Melanie had in their better times.

Sonny laughed at something Irina said before they entered. "Well, I consider this challenge good training for Aunt Melanie. After all, she's going to have to be diplomatic as the director of women's ministries." She saw Teresa in the living room. "Oh, hey, Mom. You ready to go?"

Teresa stood. "More or less. What training were you talking about for Melanie?"

Sonny looked at Irina, as if she needed her approval to tell Teresa. That hurt a little, knowing she obviously planned to tell Melanie.

Irina grimaced when she looked at Teresa. "I, uh, had a little setback when we were in the restaurant last night."

"I noticed you were quiet on the drive home. What was the setback?" Sonny placed two items on the coffee table.

"Those belong to Doris," Irina said. The amusement had left her eyes.

Teresa picked up the reading glasses in their case. "Uh, no. These are mine." At once Teresa realized why Sonny would have thought to tell Melanie. If she thought both of these items belonged to Doris, Melanie would be the logical bearer of returned items. Teresa felt some relief in that, and less exclusion.

Irina gasped. "Teresa, please forgive me. I don't know why—"

"Sweetie, you were obviously upset. And you didn't even know these were mine. How can I make a fuss as if you meant something personal by it? And I had another pair in my luggage, anyway. I'm forever losing my glasses."

Both Sonny and Irina looked at her with that same weird, I-can't-believe-you-have-a-heart expression. She was a little tired of seeing that. Had they forgotten so quickly about her seal pup epiphany?

"What are you upset about, Irina?" Teresa asked. "Is it your solos? Because we can stay here today and—"

Both Sonny and Irina crossed their arms over their chests and regarded her with similar, chastising expressions. Words weren't necessary. Teresa nodded.

"A united front, I see."

Sonny pulled something from her purse. Teresa's keys.

Teresa frowned at them. "What? Are you starting to pinch things too?"

"No. I took them in case you needed a reason to stick around while we were at breakfast."

"Sonny Miller! Did you actually think I would have left you here to face your father alone?" That girl knew her mother too well, and her mother did *not* like it.

"You mean you even want to come with me into his office?" Sonny gave her a sly smile.

"Well, no. I simply meant I'd be waiting for you when you came out."

Sonny placed Teresa's keys on the coffee table. "All right. I appreciate your coming, Mom."

"I mean, you don't actually *want* me to go up with you, do you? Your father and I have no reason to see each other. But if you need me to..."

"Why don't we play that by ear? Let's see how we both feel when we get there."

The very idea that she might have to face David, to be there when he gave Sonny his side of the story? It was so daunting Teresa began to perspire. Wasn't it enough that she was going to face her parents after deserting them so long ago? She suddenly felt queasy and empathized more than ever with Irina.

"If you don't mind," she said, "I'm going to go splash a little cool water on my face." She headed back to the bathroom.

She had been in situations tenser than this. She knew a face full of cold water helped. So did looking in the mirror and giving herself a quiet talk of encouragement. But this time she thought maybe she would give that prayer thing a go as well.

Sixty-Two

July 3
Downtown San Diego, California

Sonny expected a receptionist when she opened the door bearing a plaque reading "David Sommerhill, PhD." But she found a small, sage green room awaiting her, with several brown leather chairs and a glass table topped with magazines. She smelled coffee but didn't see a pot anywhere. The far wall held two closed doors, and Sonny heard nothing beyond them.

The left door opened, and a man emerged and smiled quickly at Sonny. His white, short-sleeved shirt and black tie and pants made him look like a computer repair man. He couldn't have been taller than five foot four, and Sonny was certain she weighed more than he did. His dark-rimmed reading glasses sat near the tip of his nose, and he sported an especially unfortunate comb-over.

"Dr. Sommerhill?" Sonny felt awful about her first thought, but she simply couldn't picture her mom and aunt feuding over this guy. And her second thought wasn't any better. She'd never imagined her father as someone she could easily pin in a wrestling match.

Before he could answer, the other door opened.

Sonny's hopes rose. *This* had to be him.

The small man said, "No, I'm his assistant. This is Dr. Sommerhill, dear."

"Thank you." She smiled at the little man and then looked at her father for the first time in her life.

Yes, he was taller, as she imagined him. And he looked a lot like Tom Hanks, she thought. Same wavy, dark hair and high forehead. But his nose was sharper and his eyes were a vivid blue. When he spoke she recognized the warm, clear voice from the phone.

"You must be Sonny." He stepped confidently toward her and took her hand with both of his. "How nice to meet you."

Well, good. At least he wasn't freaked out by her.

"Yeah. It's a little weird, I guess."

He smiled. "Weird. Yes. Here, we can talk in my office." He looked at the comb-over man. "Thanks, Charles. You'll let me know when Mrs. Arbogast arrives for her one thirty?"

"Sure will, Dr. Sommerhill." Charles retreated to his office but left his door open.

A one thirty appointment. Only half an hour away.

David shut his office door. Rather than sitting behind his desk, he took a seat on one of several lush, upholstered chairs next to a couch. He motioned for her to sit. "Did you find your way easily enough?"

"Here? Yes. I'm with my mom, aunt, and a couple of friends."

He looked slightly shaken. "Your mom and aunt? Were they planning to join us?"

"No, we decided against that."

If she weren't so overwhelmed by the moment, she would have found his obvious relief amusing.

"So you're just visiting San Diego, is that it? And where do you live?"

"Just north of here. I live in La Jolla right now. I got my bachelor's from UCSD this past month. In psychology. I'm doing my grad work at Berkeley."

He smiled. "Psychology? Hmm, that's a fascinating coincidence."

"Yeah." Sonny grinned. "I was surprised when Aunt Melanie told me you were a psychiatrist. I mean, Mom never told me anything about you, so I just found out about you this week."

"Your aunt kept quiet about me all these years too, then?"

"Uh, I guess. But I just met Aunt Melanie this week too."

He sat back in his chair and steepled his fingers. "Please tell me if you'd rather not answer this, but why didn't you meet your aunt earlier?"

Sonny studied his blue eyes. She could see what an effective therapist he must be. He appeared so open and caring.

"Oh, that's right. You don't know about any of this. My, uh, my mom, when she found out she was pregnant back then...well, she ran away from her family."

He frowned. Sonny thought she heard conviction in his sigh. "No, I didn't know that. I ran into your aunt years ago, at one of our college reunions—"

"Yeah, she mentioned that."

"But she didn't tell me Teresa had run off. She downplayed the fact that Teresa wasn't there." He sighed. "I suppose she thought that the best stance to take, out of respect for Teresa."

Sonny wondered. Maybe Melanie didn't think David had the right to know anything else about Teresa.

"Anyway, that's all changing," Sonny said. "I'm meeting you now, and I'm meeting my grandparents after we leave here."

He scowled. "You've never met your grandparents, either?"

"Not yet."

"Twenty-four years with no family contact. And this is all because—"

"Because of how I...because of the circumstances of my...conception."

He steepled his fingers again and bent his head slightly forward to rest his fingertips against his lips. Sonny watched him clench his jaw and then swallow. When he looked back up, she was sure his eyes were misty. She was a sucker for things like that, and if he acted too kindly toward her, she knew she would cry.

He sighed. "Sonny, I'm so sorry. I would have helped out if I had known. At least I think I would have. People make a lot of bad decisions when they're young. Some people do, anyway. I did. When I realized it was your mother I was with, I just made matters worse. I shouldn't have run, but I—"

Sonny frowned and put up her hand. "Wait a second. Back up there. What do you mean, when you realized it was my mother you were with? How could you not know who—" Her stomach tightened. "Are you saying you thought you were with Melanie?"

He hesitated.

"Dr. Sommer—"

"David. Please."

"David." Sonny started again. She leaned forward. "Are you saying my mother tricked you into being with her? She pretended she was Melanie in order to be with you?"

He looked down and sighed. "Sonny, we're talking about something that happened when your mother was—when we were *all* very young."

Sonny couldn't help grimacing about this new piece of information. Her mother wasn't a monster, was she? But this was horrible. She didn't just betray her sister. She lured this man by offering what he obviously thought was Melanie's demonstration of love. None of the scenario was morally acceptable, but this part was downright evil.

"I realize you were all young." Sonny struggled to keep tears from developing. She thought it might help to look away from him when she talked, so she spoke to the corner of the office. She saw the coffeepot she smelled earlier and focused on that.

"But it's hard to think my mother was that conniving. No wonder she ran away from everyone. She was probably afraid you'd tell them how she fooled you. And no wonder *you* ran."

"Wait, Sonny, maybe I can make this less awful for you. I want to be fair to your mother, at least. Look at me. Please."

It hadn't really helped, looking away. She had tears in her eyes when she met his gaze.

His smile was kind.

She said, "This will break Aunt Melanie's heart." And that thought spilled a few tears over the edge.

He leaned forward in his chair. "Your aunt already knows, Sonny. I explained everything to her when we spoke at our college reunion."

Whoa. Aunt Melanie was an awfully strong woman to forgive something like that. Even when she lost her temper the other night and told Sonny about the past, she didn't mention this part.

"And to be absolutely fair," David said, "your mother fooled me, but only up to a certain point."

"What do you mean?"

He took a deep breath. "Does your mother still sing?"

"Yeah. She sings professionally. In Oakland."

He nodded. "She sang back in college, of course. And she sang when we were together. Just an absentminded tune, something that came on the radio. But I knew that wasn't Melanie's voice." He smiled fondly. "Melanie had many talents, but singing wasn't one of them."

"So, did you confront my mom for what she was doing? Did you tell her you knew she was Teresa?"

He stared into her eyes and seemed to gauge whether to tell her the next part or not.

"I didn't confront her, no. And we hadn't yet…done anything."

She stared back at him. "But you went through with it anyway. That's what you're saying, right? You were just as guilty as she was."

"I was." He nodded. "As I said, we were young and we made a bad decision."

She shook her head. "And how is this supposed to make me feel less awful?"

"I suppose it doesn't, but I didn't want you to think your mother was solely responsible for what happened." He leaned back in his chair. "It might even have been a good decision for her to keep me from knowing about the pregnancy. I was radically pro-choice back then. My mistakes might have hurt you even more than they already have."

Sonny nodded and looked at her hands. That was good information to have. Even in the messed-up way she came about, God took care of her.

She looked back at David. "Do you have any other kids?"

He raised his eyebrows in surprise, as if he hadn't yet thought about the fact that he had a kid. "Uh, no. But my wife is in her early thirties, and she wants to have a child."

In her early thirties? He had to be around forty-six, like her mom.

"So you waited a while to get married after all of this happened at college?"

He squirmed just a fraction. "Not exactly."

"Oh. This is your second marriage?"

"Third."

She gave a little laugh of surprise before she could stop herself.

He nodded. "I imagine I've toppled off any pedestal you might have set me on over the past twenty-four years."

"No, I didn't have you on any pedestal." But she did. She realized it the moment she spoke. That's why it was so important for her to meet him.

She was a part of him. He was part of her identity. Of course she wanted him up there, dressed in shiny armor.

A tap on the door brought David to his feet.

"Mrs. Arbogast is here," Charles said, when David opened the door. He peeked at Sonny and gave her a kind smile.

"Thanks, Charles." David looked outside the office. "Hello, Edna. Just give me a minute, and I'll be right with you." He closed the door and leaned against it. "I'm sorry to have left so little time for you, Sonny. It was all I had while you were still in town."

She stood. "No, that's fine. Maybe we can meet some other time."

He walked to his desk and got a business card, which he gave her. "Maybe before you move to Berkeley, you could give me another call. I'd like to hear more about your plans for the future. Here." He took the card back and wrote something on it. "Here's my cell phone number."

"Right."

"I'd also like—"

He stopped abruptly, and his lips tensed. He swallowed before going on. "I'd like to hear about your childhood. I'd like to know what I missed."

Sonny simply nodded. She completely identified. She'd wondered that very thing all her life.

Sixty-Three

Melanie's heart went out to Sonny when she rejoined them. The group reached the vast, modern art-filled lobby of David's building as she walked out of the elevator. She looked as if someone had smacked her in the face and she was trying to act as if nothing had happened. Melanie didn't know what that expression of hers signified, and perhaps Sonny didn't even know how she felt just yet.

They all seemed to fear asking her the wrong thing at first. All but Irina, that is.

"So, what did you think of him? Does he look like you? Are you going to visit him again? Did he—"

Grig put his hand on Irina's arm for a moment. "Take it easy, Irina. Give her some air." Then he tilted his head and gently placed his arm across Sonny's shoulders. "You okay?"

Sonny nodded. "I think so. I hate how overused that word 'surreal' is, but that's how it felt, meeting my father after all this time. Twenty-four years of nothing, and then half an hour of..."

She glanced at Teresa, who wouldn't look Sonny in the eye for long.

"Half an hour of info dumping, I guess you could call it," Sonny said.

They walked outside into the constant sunshine and headed toward Grig's SUV. Melanie watched the interaction—or lack of interaction—between Teresa and Sonny. What might that be about? She had witnessed such an ebb and flow of ease between the two of them this week. One moment of comfortable joking was often followed by an episode of deliberate avoidance. This moment was surely a bout of ebbing. Why?

She reviewed the past and wondered what David could have told Sonny that Melanie and Teresa hadn't already said. Melanie had been so angry the other evening, she wasn't completely certain of what she blurted out.

But Teresa practically cowered right now. She obviously expected Sonny to be newly upset with her.

Melanie couldn't figure it out.

And then it hit her. Of course. The part David told Melanie at their college reunion. Teresa had tried to fool David by acting as if she were Melanie. How had Melanie forgotten that? Her blood heated up again just thinking of it. That was why she had prayed about forgiving and forgetting, wasn't it? Because she hated how she felt when she thought too much about Teresa's calculated betrayal.

She sent out another quick prayer about the memory. It was no longer her issue. She would leave that for Teresa and Sonny. And for God.

She opened the passenger door of Grig's car. "Are you still up to the San Clemente trip, Sonny? Or is this just too much for—"

"Absolutely!" Sonny immediately brightened up. "I am *so* up to the San Clemente trip. It can only be an improvement."

Oh, no. So the meeting with David hadn't gone well, after all. With an inner sigh, Melanie determined to make this part of the day as enjoyable as possible. If Sonny needed to discuss anything about David, she would be available. But frankly, she would just as soon forget about David Sommerhill for the rest of her life.

Sixty-Four

July 3
San Clemente, California

"That's it, right there," Melanie told Grig. "The cream-colored stucco with the green-framed windows."

Sonny leaned forward in her seat. "Oh, I love it. I like the Spanish-tile roof."

Melanie turned to look at her. "Yeah, Mom always said she wanted to retire in a house with a Spanish-tile roof. Remember that, Teresa?"

"Uh-huh."

Poor Teresa looked nearly catatonic. Melanie couldn't even begin to imagine the fear she must be feeling. Their parents were wonderful, lovely people, but it would be scary facing anyone after blatantly avoiding them for twenty-five years.

"The plants in front are so pretty. Tropical looking." Irina spoke to Sonny. "I think your grandparents like gardening."

Melanie said, "That's Mom's hobby. Helps her relax."

Grig pulled up to the house. "Is this okay, parking in the driveway?"

Melanie nodded. "I'm sure their car is in the garage. They knew to be home." She faced the back again and smiled at all three women. "They know there's a surprise coming. They just don't know what it is."

Grig turned off the car. "How do you want to do this? Should Irina and I stay out here until you've all blown each other's minds at the front door?"

The women laughed. Even Teresa, whose eyes seemed frozen open, emitted an odd, nearly maniacal sound that was probably as close to laughter as she could get.

"Please don't stay out here, Grig," Sonny said. She spoke to Melanie and Teresa. "Do you two mind if Grig and Irina come with us?" With one glance she included them in the group. "I'd love for you to be a part of this."

"I like the idea," Melanie said.

Everyone looked at Teresa, who had yet to blink, as far as Melanie could tell.

"Uh, yeah." She gave a quick nod.

"Yes!" Grig looked as excited as Sonny about meeting the grandparents. He was the first one out of the car.

They walked up the brick pathway huddled together like the Keystone Cops. Melanie felt a case of the giggles coming on and knew she was more wound up about this than she had expected to be. On a whim, she hooked her arm through Teresa's and pulled her up next to her.

She whispered to Teresa, "We'll do this together."

Teresa looked into Melanie's eyes. Her expression altered visibly, as if she had just taken a very warm, comforting drink. Her eyes teared up, and then she watched Melanie's hand as she pushed the doorbell.

They all looked at one another, grinning, as they heard voices inside.

The door swung open. Melanie's mother, Barbara, wore a navy blue tracksuit and her polite smile. Her husband, Jack, strolled up behind her. They both looked at Melanie and Teresa. Teresa and Melanie.

Then Jack merely whispered one word. "Teresa."

As if she stood strong all these years, waiting for the relief this moment would bring, Barbara Miller let out a soft cry and crumpled softly to the floor.

Sixty-Five

Sonny had never seen her mother move so quickly.

Teresa dropped to her knees beside Barbara within seconds after she fainted.

"Mom!" She slipped her hand under her mother's head, and Barbara's bewildered blue eyes fluttered open.

"Oh, goodness." Barbara spoke weakly at first and looked around herself. "What happened?"

Jack Miller bent to help her up. He was obviously still as fit and strong as a younger man, despite his thinning gray hair. "Your daughter scared the wits out of you, that's what happened. I would have caught you, dear, but I almost passed out myself. My response time was off."

They stood and got their bearings, as did Teresa. Then Jack and Barbara repeated what they did immediately after they opened the door. They stared at their twin daughters, shock on their faces.

Only a few seconds passed before Melanie finally said, "Well?"

"Well, come here," their father said. He stepped forward to hug Teresa, but Barbara got to her first, grasping her with a passion. She was a few inches shorter than Teresa and significantly more petite, so Teresa's arms enveloped her.

Sonny grinned, mesmerized by the moment. And then she heard her grandmother crying, her head tucked into Teresa's embrace.

Sonny only understood "my baby," as her grandmother's choked words emptied onto Teresa's chest. Her cry was full of relief and pain, and suddenly no one there was able to avoid tears, including both of the men.

Jack wiped at his eyes and put his arms around both Barbara and Teresa.

"I'm so sorry, Mom and Dad," Teresa said, her voice broken. "I'm… I'm just so sorry. I don't know why I was so scared to come home. Such a waste. A stupid waste."

"You don't need to talk about that right now," Jack said. He squeezed Teresa harder and kissed the top of her head. "You're home now." He looked at Melanie, his eyes still wet. "Thank you, honey."

Melanie shook her head, contentment in her smile. "Nope, it wasn't my doing."

Teresa gasped. She pulled back from her parents' embrace. "Oh! Yes. This—" She turned to pull Sonny toward them. "This is your grand-daughter."

Barbara repeated the word with a voice full of wonder, as if Teresa had presented them with a unicorn. "Granddaughter!"

Sonny didn't know what to say. It seemed so odd to call a total stranger Grandma. So she simply smiled and said, "Hi."

Teresa spoke more formally, but her grin was wide. "Jack and Barbara Miller, this is my daughter, Sonata Miller. Sonny."

"Sonata." Barbara took both of Sonny's hands and studied her. Then she grabbed Sonny with the same passion she had shown toward Teresa and threw her arms around her. But now laughter mingled with her tears. "Trust our little songbird to give her child a musical name." She released Sonny and took hold of her face. "Sonny. And look at the tears in those lovely brown eyes. You have your Grandpa's eyes."

Teresa chuckled. "I thought she had my eyes."

"I thought she had *mine*," Melanie said, dabbing at tears with the back of her hand.

Jack managed to squeeze past Barbara so he could get his arms around Sonny. She loved that he talked to her with the familiarity of someone she had known for years. "You see what your grandma and grandpa had to live with, Sonny, having these two around? Always arguing about *something*."

Sonny didn't want to speak. She might have met her real father a couple of hours ago, but *this* was what she imagined a father's hug felt like. She closed her eyes, nestled in, and never wanted to leave.

She heard her grandmother speak. "And are these beautiful young people ours as well?"

Oh! Sonny had actually forgotten about Grig and Irina for a moment. She forced herself to leave her grandfather's embrace with the intention of introducing them.

But Melanie beat her to the task. She stood between the tall, gorgeous siblings, an arm around each of them.

"Mom, Dad, these are our good friends Grig and Irina Banks."

Grig shook Jack's hand, but Irina jumped right into a hug from Barbara and then moved swiftly over to embrace Jack, which made everyone laugh.

"Sorry!" Irina said, smiling shyly about her affectionate behavior. "I already told Sonny I was jealous about all of her family. I couldn't resist."

She and Sonny shared a smile.

"That's all right, dear." Barbara looked from Irina to Teresa. "Jack and I have been holding on to a lot of love for the past couple of decades. We have plenty to go around."

Sonny listened while Teresa confessed everything to her parents. The only thing left out of the tearful confession was the fact that Teresa pretended to be Melanie in order to seduce David. Sonny said nothing, but she knew she wanted to talk with her mom about that issue later.

She got the distinct feeling that Melanie's presence made Teresa's revelations easier for her grandparents to accept. If Melanie accepted Teresa after such disloyalty, who wouldn't? So the pain of more than two decades was set aside, at least momentarily. Jack and Barbara kept their hearts open to everything Teresa chose to share.

Still, there was clearly no way the Miller family would be able to catch up on twenty-five years of family history during this one visit.

"That just means we'll have to do a lot of visiting with one another," Barbara said, smiling at Sonny. "Your grandpa and I are retired now, and frankly, sometimes we get bored with each other. We'd love to come visit you in La Jolla." She looked at Teresa. "And you in Oakland."

Teresa lifted her chin toward Sonny. "Actually, Mom, Sonny will be moving up in my direction for grad school in the fall. You'll probably be able to see us both whenever you come up."

"And us too, maybe," Irina said.

Sonny laughed. "Girl, are you trying to steal my grandparents?"

"We'll be your honorary grandma and grandpa, how about that, Irina?" Barbara said, smiling at both girls.

Grig said, "We actually have grandparents—adoptive ones. But one set lives on the East Coast, so we don't see them much. And the others live in Ireland. We've never even met them." He smiled. "So honorary Grandma and Grandpa sounds good."

Sonny wasn't sure if her grandparents heard Grig's mention of adoption. They didn't react at all. She figured that was a conversation for another day.

Teresa's smile was sly. "Consider yourselves complimented, Mom and Dad. Irina and Grig *never* asked me to be their honorary mother." She crossed her arms over her chest and arched a brow. "Why is that, I wonder? Should I feel slighted?"

Before they could answer, Jack spoke to Grig. "How do you and Irina know this band of troublemakers, anyway?"

Teresa put her hand on Irina's arm. "Irina is my protégée at the symphony chorus. She has a stunning voice."

"Amazing voice," Sonny said.

Grig added, "She'll be performing her first solos soon."

"Maybe we can sing a little for them before we go, you think?" Irina looked at Teresa for approval.

The entire beach house crowd gawked at her.

She shrugged. "My honorary grandpa and grandma make me feel confident. What can I say?"

Jack's eyes crinkled at the corners. He looked at Grig. "You're just along for the ride, Grig?"

Irina said, "Grig came down to the beach house for me. I…I was missing him, I guess."

With a swift glance at Sonny, Jack said, "I see. I thought maybe there was another reason Grig was with the group."

Sonny nearly gasped. Were they that obvious?

"Are we that obvious?" Grig asked, and Sonny laughed out loud.

Jack sat back in his chair. "I'm getting a little more observant about such things as I get older. I don't know if it's the result of life experience or the aftermath of watching too many daytime soap operas."

"Oh, Jack, stop." Barbara laughed and headed out of the living room. "He does no such thing. I'm going to throw something together for dinner. Teresa? Melanie? You want to help out?"

They both got up and followed her. Melanie affected a younger, whiny voice. "Okay, but it's Teresa's turn to do the dishes tonight."

"Is not," Teresa whined back.

"So." Jack addressed Grig again. "You're Sonny's young man?"

Sonny felt her face flush, and she saw the same reaction in Grig.

He spoke to Jack, but he looked at Sonny. "We're discussing that, actually. I, uh, I know I'd love to be a part of her future." He flashed a grin at Jack. "If there's any influence you might have in that regard, I'd really appreciate it."

Sonny basked in her grandpa's warm smile. He also watched her as he spoke to Grig. "Funny, I was going to say the same thing to you."

Sixty-Six

Teresa did, in fact, take it upon herself to do the dinner dishes. When her parents protested, she insisted.

"There aren't many there. Anyway, I haven't done the family dishes for twenty-five years. I'd like to do my small part in making that up to everyone." She smiled primly at Sonny. "It will be *therapeutic* for me."

A few minutes later Sonny joined her.

"What are you doing, sweetie? Get back in there and visit."

"I will in a second." Sonny glanced at the doorway. "There's something I need to tell you, Mom."

Teresa abruptly stopped rinsing. Sonny's expression was seriously troubled.

"Uh-oh. It's not Grig is it? Baby, you and Grig haven't already—"

"Mom!" Sonny looked shocked. Even a little insulted. "No, it is *so* not about that. Grig and I aren't even officially dating yet. And I already told you I was committed to purity."

Teresa tilted her head. "Yes, I know what you said, Sonny. I just thought that, you know, once you were tempted—"

Sonny snorted. "You think I've never been tempted? Really?"

Teresa stared at Sonny and then placed the plates she held in the dishwasher.

"You, my darling daughter, are certainly a different creature than I was at your age. In this case, that difference is just fine. I don't want you in the boat I was in twenty-five years ago."

Sonny's wave of the hand signaled a dismissal of their topic. "Anyway, that wasn't what I wanted to tell you." She glanced at the door again.

Teresa said, "Who are you looking out for? No wonder I jumped to the conclusion I did. You look positively guilty."

"Mom, it's about David Sommerhill."

Teresa's heart sank. Not this. When Sonny didn't say anything upon leaving David's office, Teresa got her hopes up. But she had a pretty good idea what Sonny wanted to tell her. Oh, couldn't she be admitting to cheating on her college exams instead? Gunrunning? Interfering with efforts to balance the global economy? Anything but what Teresa thought she was about to say.

Sonny continued when Teresa failed to respond. "Today he said something about that time...um, the time you two were together. He said he thought *you* were—"

"Yes, yes, I know what you're talking about, Sonny." Teresa gritted her teeth. So he had told her. "He thought I was Melanie. Now you know how horrible your mother can be, not only scheming behind Melanie's back, but duping David as well. So your father was innocent—well, not innocent, but at least he thought he was faithful to Melanie."

Teresa saw mild surprise in Sonny's eyes. Maybe she hadn't expected her mother to come clean, even now. Sonny hadn't behaved angrily in the first place, but now Teresa watched an edge soften in Sonny's expression.

"No," Sony said. "He wasn't innocent."

"Well, not in your purity-focused mind, I guess. You probably think he sinned just by being intimate with someone he wasn't married to. But compared to me, I'll bet you even consider him blameless. He would never have behaved that way—not with me, anyway. Not if he had known it was me."

She couldn't keep looking at Sonny, so she spoke to the sink. She was determined not to cry tears of self-pity.

"That was the one thing I really hoped you'd never hear, sweetie. And I knew David would tell you. At least, I assumed he would. *I* would, in his position."

The tears came anyway.

"I think this particular shame has been the heaviest, Sonny. Please don't tell your grandparents about my fooling him. Hurting Melanie was bad enough."

Teresa heard Sonny's sigh and felt a warm hand on her shoulder.

"Mom, it's not like you think."

Teresa faced her. "What do you mean?"

"He did tell me he thought you were Melanie."

Ugh. Teresa couldn't hold eye contact with her daughter.

"But he was as much at fault as you were," Sonny said.

Teresa shrugged. "He didn't exactly know what he was doing. I made sure of that."

"You sang, Mom."

"What?" Teresa jerked her head up. "I sang? What are you talking about?"

"At some point you sang. Some song on the radio or something."

Teresa shook her head. "I don't remember that. But even if I did, what difference does that make?"

"He said Aunt Melanie couldn't sing."

"Well, that's true. She couldn't carry a tune with both arms and a knapsack."

"So when *you* sang, he figured out it was you."

"He did?" Teresa's eyes widened. "He realized I was the one who seduced him before I even told him?"

"Before you two even *did* anything."

"Before we—" Teresa put a hand on her hip. "Before we *did* anything? You mean, he did that *knowing* he was doing it with me?"

Sonny nodded. "He did. So you were both equally—"

"Well, that dirty dog." Teresa tightened her lips and narrowed her eyes. She slapped the sponge dramatically into the sink. "He took advantage of me!"

Sonny laughed softly. "Okay, let's not get carried away. You kind of set yourself up for what happened. Right? You *do* see that."

"But that skunk! He pretended—"

Sonny laughed again, with affection. "Whoa there, Mama. Grab on to that pendulum while it's in midswing."

"What?"

"I think you could say you were both in the wrong, Mom. Both. Equally. In the wrong."

Teresa took a deep breath and tried to unpurse her lips. Then she cocked her head to the side. "Yeah, whatever. I guess this is good to know."

"And God still used your bad decision for something fabulous."

Teresa looked at her, a question in her expression.

"You got me!" Sonny raised her hands and seemed just shy of saying "ta-da!"

Teresa gave her a lopsided grin. "Yes, I did." She stepped toward Sonny and kissed her on the cheek. "So you could actually accept your mom, knowing her darkest secrets?"

"I'm not saying it was easy to hear, Mom, but there's something about knowing what there is to accept that makes the decision feel more…significant."

"And you're okay with all of that? My scheming, your father's complicity? Those are some sneaky genes you've inherited."

Sonny returned the grin. "You will recall how I managed to engineer this past week? Maybe we both have to work on being more upfront."

Teresa chuckled. She picked up the sponge from the sink and nodded toward the doorway with her head.

"Now take your fabulous self in there and visit with your grandparents. I'll be right behind you."

Sonny nodded. She gave Teresa a hug. "You always have been, Mom. Don't think I don't know it."

Sixty-Seven

Melanie got dozy early into their drive back to the beach house. The smell of her mother's roast clung to their clothes, so the coziness of her parents' home seemed to ride along with them.

She looked at Irina and Teresa sitting next to her in the backseat. They had both dropped off to sleep. Teresa rested her head on Irina's shoulder, and Irina leaned against Teresa, as well. They looked like a couple of kids.

Melanie smiled. She didn't know for sure what kind of friendship—if any—Teresa and Irina had before this trip, but something told her they wouldn't have snuggled so comfortably with each other last week.

Up front Sonny and Grig carried on a conversation Melanie couldn't hear. All she saw of Grig was the back of his head. It was even too dark to see him in the rearview mirror. But Sonny was so focused on him, she was in nearly constant profile. She looked utterly happy. Again, theirs was a relationship that had flourished beautifully this week. Melanie felt as if she knew these two young people far better than she could possibly know people after less than a week.

What was it about that beach house? It was like a relationship incubator. Melanie liked it. Maybe she, Bailey, and Micah should take a week down there before the summer was out.

As if her thought had been miraculously dispatched, her cell phone rang. It was Micah.

Sonny glanced back casually, but both Irina and Teresa jumped when the phone rang. They glanced at each other and looked slightly embarrassed.

279

"Hi, honey," Melanie said into the phone. "What are you doing still up?"

"Hi, Mom. Am I calling too late? Dad and I just finished watching an old war movie. I figured you'd have your phone turned off if you were asleep."

"Yeah, I would have. But we're all together in Grig's car. We left Grandma and Grandpa's a while ago, and we're driving back to Mission Beach."

"Cool. So did they freak out when they saw Sonny and Aunt Teresa?"

"They did, indeed. Grandma fainted."

"She *fainted*? *Awesome*! Man, I wish I could have seen that!" He spoke off to the side. "Dad! Grandma *fainted* when she saw Teresa!" Then he returned to his call with Melanie. "So, did she like, splat right out on the—"

"Micah, I think you're getting far too much enjoyment out of your poor grandma's circumstances. And no, she fell very gracefully. She didn't *splat* anywhere."

A soft snort came from Irina's general direction.

"Okay," Micah said. "Anyway, Mom, I'm calling because I messed up on the awards banquet date."

"How so?"

"It's not tomorrow night. I don't know what I was thinking. It's not 'til *next* Saturday. Tomorrow is July Fourth."

"Ah. Right." She remembered that Grig's friend Jason had asked if they would come back to Catalina for the fireworks. Of course, they all knew he would be perfectly pleased if only Irina returned.

"Yeah," Micah said. "I wanted you to know so you didn't think you had to hurry back in the morning."

Although she liked knowing she could sleep in tomorrow—it was nearly midnight, after all—Melanie would have liked Micah to be a little less comfortable with her being away any longer.

"The only thing, Mom…"

"Yes? Let me guess." She spoke through her teasing smile. "You've run out of clean underwear? You need your allowance so you can meet your friends at the movies?"

She heard Micah chuckle. "Yes and yes. But that's not the only thing I wanted to mention."

"Okay, what's the other thing?"

He was quiet for a second. She could almost hear him shrug. "Well, you know. Just...I miss you."

She broke out in a huge grin. She sighed in contentment. What a kid she had. "I miss you too, honey. I won't be late coming home. Did you make any plans with your friends for tomorrow night?"

"Can you believe Chelsea's parents are going to let her go with me to the fireworks at the community center?"

"So we passed the test, huh? Even after they saw our wacky family?"

"Yeah, well, Dad and Mr. Vincent talked today about some kinda work stuff. I think Dad knows someone who might have a job for Mr. Vincent."

"How great! That can't hurt your standing with the man, I suppose."

"Yep. Dad rocks."

Melanie laughed. "Yes, Dad rocks."

Another snort from Irina. Or was that Teresa?

"Let me talk with him for a minute, will you? And I'll see you tomorrow."

"Okay. I love you, Mom."

"Love you too, honey."

She didn't really have much to say to Bailey. The call from Micah was a shot of pleasure, and all she needed now was to listen to her husband's comfortable voice saying good night to her.

"Hey, sweetheart," Bailey said. "What's up?"

She made both Irina and Teresa chuckle with her response. "Bailey Hines, you rock."

Sixty-Eight

July 3
Mission Beach
San Diego, California

As Grig drove them all home to the beach house, he and Sonny had an animated discussion about how great Sonny's grandparents were. While he talked, Sonny watched him with a bittersweet plucking at her heartstrings. Yes, there was the promise of time together in the near future—albeit time stolen between grad school and concerts. But there would probably be a considerable time gap between tomorrow and whenever Sonny managed to move herself up to Berkeley. After seeing Grig almost every day this week, the distance would be acutely felt.

They pulled into the driveway at Julian's home, and the other women said their good nights and headed directly to the beach house.

Grig walked around to Sonny's side of the car as she stepped out and into the glow of the outdoor lamp. He had worn a lightweight, chocolate brown shirt and blue jeans that day, and his deep blue eyes had never looked so smoldering. Sonny exercised extreme verbal discipline in front of the other women, but now she felt less need for censorship. "You looked like something out of a magazine today."

He immediately struck a corny model pose, one hand to his waist, the other pointing at something in the distance. He fixed his expression into that of the clichéd man-about-town. "*Popular Mechanics,* perhaps?"

She laughed. "Not exactly. But you fell into that pose awfully easily there, mister."

"Well, you know how it is. Practice makes perfect. I need to be constantly on alert. The paparazzi are relentless." He took her hand and smiled at her laughter. "Are you too tired to sit on the stairs and talk for a while?"

"Nope. But do you mind if we sit on the seawall instead? I'm going to miss the waves after we leave tomorrow."

He put his arm around her, and they walked the short distance across the boardwalk. "I'm going to miss a lot too." He gave her shoulder a gentle squeeze.

They sat snugly together on the seawall. Sonny shut her eyes for a moment and listened to the waves. She breathed the salty air in and let contentment wash over her when she exhaled.

She said, "What happens after you and Irina leave tomorrow? What are your plans? Driving? Flying?" She turned to him. "Actually, I just assumed Irina would go with you and not my mom. Is that right?"

He raised an eyebrow. "Right. But, actually, that was something I wanted to talk with you about. Remember my friend Jason?"

"The helicopter guy with the crush on Irina."

"Right. He called me this morning and asked if there was any interest in his earlier offer about flying over to Catalina for the fireworks tomorrow. I wondered if you had to get right back home or if we might extend the fun one more day."

"We?"

He shrugged. "You, me, Irina, and anyone else who wants to come."

"Have you asked Irina about this yet?"

"No. I figured she'd go along with the idea. She seemed up to it when Jason mentioned it before."

Sonny tsked at him before she laughed. "Why, Grigori Banks. I do believe that's the most stereotypical guy thing you've ever done around me."

"Something tells me that's not good."

She gave his shoulder a little shove. "Not in this case, no! I agree, Irina did seem kind of interested in Jason. But I don't care how interested she *seemed*. You can't make plans for her without making sure she wants to see him tomorrow."

"Oh, shoot. I *have* been trying to be more considerate lately. Guess I fell from grace a little there." He grimaced. "Oops."

Sonny gave him a sideways glance. "Oops?"

She saw humor in his eyes, despite the discomfort in the rest of his expression.

"Um, *you* were really the only part I didn't confirm with Jason yet. I already confirmed for Irina and myself."

Sonny couldn't help but laugh. "Well, you have to let Irina know first thing tomorrow in case she doesn't want to go. You never know. She may have been acting positive about going back for the Fourth just to be polite. She hasn't mentioned him *once* since then."

He nodded but didn't respond. He stared out at the waves for a moment and then put his arm around Sonny again. "Did you mention me much after we met?"

She smiled at him. "Remember my friend Pam? The one whose family I was with at Sunset Beach?"

"Vaguely, yeah."

"She was a real sweetie. She let me babble on about you all month. She listened to it all—or faked listening really well." She sighed. "My college roommate was a little less tolerant."

"Oh?"

"Yeah, well, I guess I was more mopey about you by then. You were gone." She smiled at him. "Gone forever, I thought."

She loved what she saw in his eyes that moment.

He took a deep breath. "I told you this whole week was a blessing." Then he leaned over and planted a playful kiss on her earlobe. She was amazed at how she reacted to that. Just for a moment she identified with women from Jane Austin's time, getting all flustered over holding hands while dancing a quadrille.

A flush ran all the way up her face and past her ears, where he still *was*. She pulled back to speak. "Did, uh, did you? I mean, did you talk about me much after we met?"

He chuckled softly. He removed his arm from her shoulder and took her hand in his. His voice was almost a whisper. "Don't you remember what Irina called you?" He absently kissed her fingers, one by one. He was oblivious to the fact that she was captivated by what he was doing. "She dubbed you my Sunset Beach girl." Kiss. "She was an avid listener." Kiss. "She told me—" Kiss. "Our story was the perfect romance." Kiss.

Sonny pulled her hand away. "I need to go inside."

He seemed to shake out of a dream. "Oh, okay." He looked confused. "Did I say something wrong?"

"Good grief, no." Sonny stood and dusted herself off.

Grig did the same. "Okay, well—"

She reached up, grabbed either side of his head, and pulled him down for a long, strong kiss before she released him abruptly.

He looked bleary eyed for a moment, and then he gave her a slightly foolish smile.

She nodded once, almost businesslike. "All right, then. I'll see you tomorrow." She dashed to the side door of the beach house, peeking out one last time to give him a wave.

She stopped at the kitchen sink and splashed some cold water on her face.

The more she got to know Grig, the more attractive she found him. By the time they were living in close proximity, things could get mighty heated.

She would have to make a crowd of chaperoning friends, right off the bat.

Sixty-Nine

Teresa would have liked to sleep late the next morning, but once she awoke, it didn't matter that it was still dark outside. She was *awake*. She tried to arrange herself in every conceivable position in bed, but the problem was in her mind. It wouldn't stop.

Her relationship with Sonny had greatly improved this week. They still had far to go, but what strides they had made! She had Sonny to thank for that. The girl would make a good counselor. Probably an annoying one, because she was like a rabid fox at the ankles when she thought she knew what was best for you. But she had been effective.

Ditto with Teresa's relationship with her parents. Good grief, to go from *nothing* to hugging, kissing, confessing, and forgiving? There were undoubtedly plenty of bumpy areas and hurt feelings to work through, but still. Teresa was overwhelmed. She had been an idiot. She would never make that mistake again. From now on she would take every opportunity to visit her parents or bring them up to Oakland.

Even her relationship with Irina and Grig had changed drastically. Although clearly a nice young man, Grig had always been simply another musician, standing out only by dint of his being Irina's brother. And Irina had been a mere protégée. Now Teresa felt like their surrogate mother, to tell the truth. She had to admit she felt a protective kind of love for Irina. And if Irina thought she could fall back into that whole binge-and-purge, klepto-my-stress-away thought process, well…Teresa would do whatever Irina needed her to do to keep that from happening.

When Teresa thought about her relationship with Melanie, however, something was still off. They had obviously come far this week, but Teresa knew that this was the relationship that had her mind spinning this morning.

She swung out of bed and took a shower. By the time she emerged, the sun had risen. She would take an early morning stroll down the boardwalk. She liked the fact that few people were out this early. She could be alone with her thoughts and let the breeze from the ocean bring her some clarity.

She walked as far as the lemonade stand where she ran into their Jamaican-looking friend, Zeke, before she stopped. And she stopped because she saw none other than the man himself, stepping onto the boardwalk from a side street. He didn't see her.

She smiled and called out to him. "I think I owe you a lemonade."

The way his smile lit up upon seeing her was truly flattering. Of course, one could never get fatheaded around Zeke, because it was obvious he couldn't remember her name. "Well, hello, sister. You must be near the end of your stay with us, yeah?"

She laughed. "I'm not leaving until you tell me my name."

He pulled at his chin, head tilted, and studied her for the longest time. Finally, he said, "Rumpelstiltskin?"

Teresa threw back her head and reveled in the most freeing laugh she had experienced all week. "Teresa."

He chuckled. "Yes, that would have been my second guess."

Teresa ordered two lemonades and handed one to Zeke.

"I thank you, Teresa. And I have to say, the beach house has agreed with you. I would guess you unloaded some worries this week. Is that right?"

She nodded. "Yeah. Quite a lot, really. Improved every relationship I could. My daughter, my parents, my coworkers, even my sister."

"But?" He tilted his head at her again. "I can hear that there's something still not settled. Yes?"

Teresa sat on a bench near the lemonade stand, and Zeke followed her lead. They faced the waves and let the clear morning air refresh them.

"I don't know what's bothering me still. Melanie and I were apart for twenty-five years thanks to my boneheaded fear and shame." She looked at him. "I, um, I can't remember. Did I ever tell you what happened between us?"

His smile was absolutely full of acceptance. "I know what happened."

She sipped her lemonade and then gazed out at the waves. "The words 'shame' and 'guilt' have been slung around a few times this week by my sister, my daughter, and even myself."

"All with regard to you?"

She nodded at him. "Yeah. So maybe that's what lingers still. You know, Sonny did these psych tests with Melanie and me this week. For one of them she had us imagine a house, and eventually we looked at something hidden in a secret room in that house. She tested us separately, but she told us some of the answers when we were all together. I was a little shocked that both Melanie and I had broken things in our secret rooms. But Sonny said Melanie's meant her heart was broken, while mine meant I felt shame."

Zeke was quiet for a moment. "Does that seem accurate to you? Do you feel shame?"

"Well, yeah. I feel like I'm responsible for both of the broken things. Like I broke Melanie's heart, and that's where my shame comes from."

"Maybe what *you* feel is actually a broken heart."

She looked at him and shrugged. "No one's broken *my* heart. I've made sure to never put myself in that position."

"But *you* could have broken your heart." His dark eyes softened toward her. "Did you ever think of that?"

She snorted. "No. I don't even *get* that."

"The Lord loves a 'broken and contrite heart.' Have you heard that before?"

"I guess that's from the Bible, huh?"

"Mm-hmm. Those words are used in the Psalms."

"So God definitely loves Melanie, since I broke her heart. And, come to think of it, I probably broke Sonny's heart by keeping her from her family. And there are my parents—"

"Wait a minute." Zeke chuckled. "This is a different kind of broken heart. The kind I think you have."

"Which is?"

"Teresa, I think you're sad because of the choices you made. I think you wish you had never hurt your sister. Or your daughter. Or your parents."

She nodded. She didn't know why his saying that choked her up, but her throat tightened uncomfortably.

"*That's* your broken heart. You're brokenhearted by the things *you* did. Does that sound right?"

Again she nodded. "Mm-hmm."

"So, the real question is, do you have a *contrite* heart? Are you sorry?"

"Well, sure I'm sorry. Isn't that what I've been saying?"

Zeke took a long drink of his lemonade. "Maybe. Do you remember telling Sonny you were sorry?"

She didn't have to ponder long before remembering the whole seal pup incident. "Yes. I definitely told her I was sorry."

"Good. And did you tell your parents you were sorry?"

"Yep. I did that as soon as I saw them."

"Excellent."

He said nothing for a moment. Then he looked at her, as if he didn't even need to ask the next question.

She gasped. "Melanie. I never told her I was sorry for betraying her."

Zeke tilted his head and looked at her. "Did you just feel an aha kind of moment, sister?"

She took a long breath. "I *did*, Zeke. But it doesn't really make sense. I mean, Melanie left me a note the day after we fought with each other this week. She pretty much said she forgave me for everything. I don't think she expects me to apologize, to tell you the truth."

"Mmm." He nodded. "Or maybe she forgave you because the Lord tells us to forgive others even when they don't ask us to."

Teresa stood up from the bench. She dusted the sand from her shorts. "So maybe that's why I still feel off. Okay. I'm going to take your advice. But…"

Zeke lifted his eyebrows as he stood.

Teresa said, "It feels like it's going to be hard, just saying sorry. I know that's awful, but I can feel that."

"When you get to the words and feel whatever it is that makes you unable to say them," he said, "just tell yourself, 'God loves my heart.' Because He does. A broken and contrite heart. You're already halfway there."

She nodded, and a surge of determination filled her. "All right. I'm going to do that right away. Melanie's probably up by now, so I'm going."

She gave him a light hug. "Thanks, Zeke. This is probably it for us. We're all leaving today."

"It's been a pleasure, sister. I hope to see you and your family again some time."

"The Rumpelstiltskin family?"

He pointed at her before walking away. "That's it."

She smiled as she turned away. This was the most emotionally purposeful she had felt in a long time. She wanted to hurry and do this thing before her resolve faltered. Zeke had convinced her of her need to finish the other half of the broken-and-contrite-heart thing. It wasn't until she was nearly back at the beach house that something amazing dawned on her.

When had it become so important to her that God love her?

Seventy

Melanie placed the last few items in her overnight bag and zipped it up. She got down on all fours to look under the bed and the dresser, just in case she dropped anything during the week. She had left so quickly the first time, she skipped this step.

"Are you all right?"

Melanie popped her head up to see Teresa at her door. "What? Oh, yeah, thanks. I'm fine. I'm just making sure I have everything." She took one last peek under the dresser.

Teresa said, "Hmm. I usually keep everything *in* the dresser when I travel."

Melanie stood, smiled crookedly, and rolled her eyes at Teresa. Before she could say anything, Teresa started again, the playful attitude gone.

"Hey, I, um…"

Melanie was surprised when Teresa suddenly grabbed her by the hand.

"Come here. I need to talk with you before I…before anything stops me."

Melanie heard her mumble something about God loving her heart. She followed her to the living room just as Sonny walked in the front door.

"Irina and Grig want to get a bite of breakfast—"

"Yeah, okay, but give us a minute, will you, baby?" Teresa plopped onto the couch and motioned for Melanie to sit.

Sonny raised her eyebrows. "Oh. All right. I'll just wait over at Grig's with them." She stepped back outside.

"Uh-huh. Thanks, sweetie." Teresa looked up at Melanie. "Sit, sit."

Melanie sat but was startled when Teresa changed course again.

"No, Sonny, wait!" Teresa jumped up from the couch.

Sonny had barely closed the door. She opened it again and peeked in. "Did you call me, Mom?"

"Yeah, I'm sorry. Come back in here. I may as well talk with both of you at the same time."

Sonny glanced toward Grig's apartment and hesitated.

"Come on, Sonny," Teresa said. "Come sit."

Sonny pulled her phone out and rapidly typed a text message as she approached them. She snapped it closed and smiled.

"There. I asked Grig to wait a few minutes for us."

"Okay," Teresa said. She looked from Melanie to Sonny. "Look, I figured out something this morning, thanks to Zeke."

Melanie smiled. "You saw Zeke already today? Where did—"

Teresa waved the interruption away. "We were both walking on the boardwalk at the same time. I got an early start, and I guess he did too."

"Hmm," Sonny said. "I kind of wanted to say goodbye to him. Did he say how long he'd be—"

Teresa put her hand up. "Not relevant right now, Sonny, okay?"

Sonny snapped her mouth shut like a marionette and gave her mom a quick nod.

Melanie almost laughed, but clearly Teresa wasn't in a humorous mood.

"Sorry," Teresa said. "Listen, I've been feeling a little, I don't know, a little weird about everything that's happened this week. I'm sure you're both somewhat overwhelmed too. Especially you, Sonny."

"Yeah." Her voice was soft.

"That's what I talked with Zeke about this morning. I told him about your house test."

"My house test? Oh, the psych test. But, Mom, I told you not to put too much store in how I deciphered any of those answers."

"Yeah, I know. But something stuck with me and bothered me, so I mentioned it to him."

Melanie suddenly knew. "The broken items."

On a sharp intake of breath, Teresa said, "You too?"

"Mm-hmm." But Melanie wanted to hear what Teresa had to say first, especially if she had discussed it with Zeke. There was something sure about Zeke's insights.

"What about the broken items?" Sonny addressed her mother, specifically.

"It bothered me, to tell you the truth, that Melanie's item got her a brokenhearted prognosis, while mine got me guilt and shame."

A hushed cry of exasperation escaped from Sonny. "Oh, Mom, really. I should never have tried to play counselor—"

"You were right, Sonny."

"I was?" Sonny brightened but quickly adjusted her expression to reflect a more serious attitude.

"Yeah," Teresa said. "Shame and guilt. That's exactly what I've carried around with me for years. Wouldn't *you* have?"

Melanie decided to treat that as a rhetorical question.

But Sonny cocked her head and raised her eyebrows as if she were about to respond. Then she obviously caught herself and said nothing.

Teresa didn't seem to notice. "And, despite whatever barriers we might have broken down this week, a big chunk of that feeling is still in here."

Teresa's voice shook almost imperceptibly as put her hand to her heart.

"I don't like it. I never realized how much I didn't like it until I started chipping away at it the last few days. It's odd. You know how sometimes you don't realize you're hungry or thirsty until you take a bite or a drink, and then you suddenly realize you have a ravenous hunger or a debilitating thirst going on?"

They both simply nodded.

"That's how this was. I relieved part of my shame, and I suddenly became so aware of how much of it there was inside me. After the seal pup incident, Sonny, when I realized how much I had hurt you—"

Melanie *had* to interrupt. "Wait. What's a seal pump?"

Sonny put her hand on Melanie's arm. "Seal pup. We can tell you later."

Teresa nodded. "Right. After I apologized to you, Sonny, I think that might have been the first chunk that chipped away."

Sonny smiled at her mom with such warmth. Melanie thought that had to help Teresa carry on with her explanation. Teresa looked at Melanie next.

"And then, with Mom and Dad, it just burst out of me without my even having to think about it. Apologizing to them broke a huge chunk away. It was like having a cancerous growth surgically removed or something. It was amazing."

Melanie smiled. "I have to say that was the most like the old Teresa I've seen you all week." She was surprised that her eyes suddenly stung. "I missed joking around with you like that."

The way Teresa caught her breath, she sounded midsob. "Which…" She swallowed. "Which brings me to the last chunk. And they're not chunks, really. They're broken pieces. Zeke helped me understand. My heart was broken too." She started to cry. "It's just that I'm the one who broke it." She gazed levelly into Melanie's eyes, and tears escaped.

"Melanie, I read your note Thursday morning, when you left. I accepted the apology you wrote in there for me. I knew you had forgiven me. And I thought that's all I needed."

Melanie wiped her hand across her cheeks. Sonny jumped up from the couch and grabbed a box of tissues from the kitchen counter, pulling a few for herself.

"But I'll never get this last jagged piece out of my heart if I don't ask you…" Teresa's voice broke. "…to please forgive me. What I did to you was horrible. So horrible. It was mean and vicious, and the idea came from the very worst part of me."

She talked around the tissues she dabbed across her eyes and cheeks. "All through college I focused on nothing but my singing. I didn't have time to pursue many relationships, especially not romantic ones. When you found David…well, I saw how happy you were. I know I should have been delighted for you, but I wasn't. I felt as if I had missed my chance to find what you found with him. I was so steeped in envy, I refused to consider the consequences of what I did. If I had the power to undo my actions, Melanie, the only reason I wouldn't is because the most wonderful thing in my life came about as a result."

She reached over and squeezed Sonny's knee. Sonny covered Teresa's hand with both of her own and let her tears fall unhindered.

Teresa looked back at Melanie. "So will you? Will you please forgive me?"

Melanie smiled at her through her tears. "Yes. Absolutely I will." She leaned forward to give Teresa a hug, prompting Teresa to do the same.

Because they were just far enough from each other to have to lean out of their seats, Teresa moved from sitting to kneeling, rather than taking the time to stand. Melanie laughed through her tears and did the same. So they hugged each other on their knees. It was strangely like something they would have done as children, quite a long time ago.

Seventy-One

"Sonny! Are you all right?"

Irina's concern when she opened Grig's door reminded Sonny she had probably cried all of her makeup off and had blotchy redness around her eyes and nose.

"Oh, shoot." Sonny remained outside the apartment. "Do I look that bad? Maybe I should go freshen up. I was just crying, that's all."

"But why? What's happened?"

Grig came to the door, and Sonny cringed.

"Is something wrong, Sonny? Can I help somehow?"

"Ugh. Yes, you can help. Don't look at me." She put her hands in front of her face and tried to arrange her fingers so she could still look at Grig and Irina without their being able to see her face. All three of them laughed at how ridiculous she looked, standing outside their door, peeking through her fingers at them.

Grig gently pulled her hands from her face and brought her inside. "Come in here, you little weirdo." He kissed her on the top of her head, and she had to fight to keep from throwing her arms around him right in front of Irina. Despite the progress of her relationship with Grig, it was only a few days old. It seemed strange to show too much public affection yet.

As it was, Irina smiled and wiggled her eyebrows at Sonny over the kiss.

Grig walked into the kitchen and held up a coffee mug, to which Sonny said, "Yes, please."

"Why were you crying?" Irina asked. She walked toward the kitchen. Sonny followed her and sat at the small table in the dining nook.

"Whoa, it was really something over there. Mom had a talk with Zeke this morning—"

"He was over there?" Irina asked. "I wanted to say goodbye to him."

Sonny chuckled. "That's exactly what I said. But no, they saw each other farther down the boardwalk, when Mom took a walk. And he helped her to realize she would feel a lot better if she apologized to Melanie. You know, about their past."

Grig brought Sonny's coffee to her. "And she was open to that, after all these years?" He went back into the kitchen and emptied items out of the refrigerator as they spoke.

"Yeah, isn't that something? She said other things that happened this week led her in that direction. I think the talk with Zeke was just the thing to tip the scales. Her running into him couldn't have been timed better." She sighed. "It was really beautiful to see the two of them hugging. On their *knees,* of all things."

Irina said, "Wow, I wouldn't have thought either Teresa or Zeke would hug each other at all, let alone on their knees."

Grig laughed. "I think she means Teresa and Melanie hugged, Irina. That's great, though, Sonny. So your tears were happy ones, I take it?"

She grinned. "Yeah. Really happy. What a great week." She continued looking at him after she spoke, and he caught her gaze and held it. Those dark rimmed eyes of his! She said it again. "Really happy."

She saw a slight flare to his nostrils when he took a deep breath, still looking at her. "Me too."

Irina cleared her throat, and they broke eye contact to look at her, mildly embarrassed.

"Just wanted to remind you I was here," Irina said.

Grig looked at the items he placed on the counter. "Looks like we don't have quite enough here for a meal."

"What are you doing? I thought you guys wanted to go out for breakfast." Sonny stood and examined what he placed on the counter.

He shrugged. "I got the idea that maybe instead we could throw breakfast together with the stuff we didn't finish this week."

Sonny held up a half jar of Greek olives and a Styrofoam container that smelled suspiciously of fried food. "Seriously?"

"No, not that stuff." Grig chuckled. "I'm a bachelor, but not *that* much of a bachelor. We have about four eggs here and just under a half pound of bacon."

Irina looked in the cabinet. "And you still have plenty of bread. I'll bet we have enough next door to make it a full meal." She widened her eyes at Sonny and smiled. "We could have a nice breakfast on the front porch for our last morning here."

⌒

And so they did. Sonny marveled—during their breakfast prayer and during their meal—at how far this group had come in one week's time.

"This funky little house turned out to be the perfect place for us. I kind of hate to leave."

Irina perked up in her chair. "Why don't we plan to do it again next year?"

"You want to plan for an entire year from now?" Teresa's dubious tone failed to dampen Irina's enthusiasm.

"Why not?" she said. "Our concerts get planned that far in advance. Why can't we do the same with our vacation plans?"

Teresa looked from Sonny to Grig. "Situations could...um, change by then, Irina—"

"I'm game," Grig said. He smiled at Sonny and winked. He turned to Melanie. "And if Micah isn't too caught up with his friends to break away, he could stay at Julian's with me."

"Yeah," Sonny said. "And Uncle Bailey could stay with you, Aunt Melanie."

Melanie laughed. "Bailey? In this house? With us four females? For a week?"

Irina drew her hands together. "And the grandparents!"

They all laughed. Teresa made a great show of pulling her cell phone from her pocket. "Hang on for a minute. I want to call my manager Anton and ask him if he wants to join us. Oh, and Ken!"

The laughter petered out and was replaced by expressions of confusion.

Melanie spoke for them all. "Who's Ken?"

Sonny couldn't remember if she had ever seen her mother blush before.

"You know. Ken. From the Catalina Stables."

Sonny grinned. "The guide? You remembered his name?"

Teresa slowly closed her eyes and pursed her lips. "I happen to have spoken with him a time or two since Wednesday." She held up her phone. "Even have him on speed dial."

"Well, Mom, you sly thing." Sonny nudged Teresa with her shoulder. "I had no idea."

"I'm aware of that." Teresa nodded. "The whole secretive thing is a little hard to shake. But I'll take a big step and tell you all now that I have plans to watch the Catalina fireworks with him tonight."

"But that's great!" Irina put her hand on Teresa's shoulder. "Grig and I talked about that too. And Sonny, right?"

"I'm in." Sonny looked at Melanie. "What do you say, Melanie? You think Bailey and Micah would be interested?"

Melanie leaned back in her chair. "I'm afraid not, folks. I love you all to death, but I need some alone time with my hubby. And Micah has his first date with Chelsea tonight. I want to be home for that."

They all nodded.

"Next year, then," Sonny said.

Melanie smiled fondly at her niece. "Next year." She stood and started clearing plates away.

Sonny followed. "Wait for me to help you with this stuff, Melanie. I just want to place a quick call to my...to David. Just wish him a happy Fourth."

She didn't want to be a nuisance to her father, but that half hour simply hadn't been enough. She wanted one more chat before leaving the area. One never knew. Maybe he wanted to see her again.

Seventy-Two

Sonny went back to her bedroom and rifled through her purse until she found David's business card. She called the cell number he had jotted down for her. Regardless of the positive end to their meeting, she couldn't calm the increasing beat of her heart as she waited for him to answer.

The phone rang a number of times, and she was certain she was going to have to leave a message. She hadn't prepared for that. She almost ended the call, and then he answered.

"Yes? Hello? Blast, I missed it."

"Uh, David?"

"Yes, who's there? I'm sorry, I was mowing the lawn and didn't hear the phone. Who's calling?"

"It's me. Sonny."

No response.

"It's Sonny Miller. Hello? Are you there?"

"Ah, yes. Yes, Sonny. How, um, yes, how are you?"

"I just wanted to wish you a happy Fourth of July."

"Could you hold on a second?" Without waiting for her answer, he apparently covered the mouthpiece. Sonny heard his muffled voice calling out to someone. Or possibly yelling at someone. When he spoke again, he sounded even less focused than he had before.

"What did you say you were calling about, Sonny?"

"I just called to say happy Independence Day. And I wanted to say hi one more time before I head home. I'm going with some friends to Catalina today, and then—"

"Right. Right. Well, I should probably fill you in a little better here about things."

"Things?" She didn't like the way her stomach felt.

"Yes. Well, you see…I mean, I told you about my wife, Allison, I think."

"I didn't know her name, but yes, you told me you were married."

"Uh-huh. And she's actually a very good woman. But she wasn't very pleased…that is, she hasn't taken the news very well about my having a grown daughter. Especially one I didn't tell her about before."

Sonny sank to her bed. "But you didn't know before this week. How could you have told her?"

"Exactly. You understand. And I'm sure she will eventually too. As I said, she's really a good woman."

Yes, she sounded absolutely lovely. Somehow Sonny didn't think she would be invited to visit again before leaving the area. Or ever, maybe.

"Are you still there, Sonny?"

"Yes. I'm here." And she felt as if she had to apologize for being here. "So, are you saying—" She stopped and took a long breath. "Are you saying I shouldn't call you anymore?"

"No, no. That's not it at all. I meant it when I said I wanted to hear more about you. That I wanted to hear about your childhood. I simply need to ask you to hold off for a little while. Just to give Allison a chance to get used to the idea. You think we can do that?"

We? It sounded as though he would be able to do that just fine. Sonny nodded. She would have liked to sound peppier when she spoke, but she couldn't help but come across disappointed. "Sure. I can do that. I'll hold off calling. You have my cell number now, so you can call me when she's all right with your talking to me."

"Sonny—"

"Bye." She ended the call. She looked at her phone as if it had been the thing that hurt her. She jumped when it rang right back. It was him.

"Don't hang up, Sonny."

She didn't say anything.

"Look, you don't know anything about me. At least I don't think you do. But I told you I didn't belong on any pedestal."

"And I told you I didn't have you on one. But you're right. I don't know you."

"So let me remind you," he said gently, "that this is round three for me, marriage wise. And I might know how to counsel others in marital relationships, but that doesn't mean I'm all that great at it myself."

"How can that be?" She was flabbergasted by this concept.

"It can be, Sonny, because I'm a weak man in some respects. I've learned and I've improved, but I don't want to fail again. So I'm trying extra hard this time. Can you understand that? I need to give my wife some time to absorb this news and adjust to it. That's all."

As much as it hurt to think she was someone's bad news, Sonny felt some sympathy for him. She sighed.

"I understand."

"Really?"

"Mm-hmm."

"Look, you could call me at the office number on the card I gave you. I could talk with you while I'm at the office."

She shook her head. "No, I won't be doing that. You just let me know when—if—your wife is willing to accept me. I'm not going to sneak calls to you at your office. I have nothing to hide."

He was quiet for a while, and Sonny didn't feel like helping him. Finally he said, "You're right. And I'm not hiding you, either, okay? Allison knows about you, and she and I need to make this right between us. I honestly look forward to her getting to meet you."

"Right. Well, I'm going to hang up now."

"Goodbye, Sonny."

She hung up without saying goodbye. Her phone slipped from her hand, and when she kneeled down to pick it up, she decided to stay down there for a few moments. She didn't pray on her knees that often, but this seemed as good a time as any.

Lord, help me be adult about this. I know lots of people have fathers they never see. Like Irina and Grig, with their birth father. I don't want to be selfish about this week. You gave me so many blessings. If my father is a part of my identity that I'll never really know, I ask that You'll help me to accept that. I'm just going to trust You in that, Lord. Amen.

She walked back into the common area of the house to join Melanie in cleaning up. She wished she hadn't announced she was calling David. If anyone asked, she would do her best to pretend his presence in her life was of no great concern. After all these years, she should be pretty good at that.

Seventy-Three

Melanie rinsed off the last of the dishes and smiled at Sonny, who emerged from her room. "How did the call go? Oh, no. What happened?"

Sonny shook her head and sighed. "Well, so much for *not* wearing my heart on my sleeve." She glanced out the front window. "Where did everyone go?" She walked into the kitchen, grabbed a towel, and started drying the pans Melanie had washed.

"Teresa took her phone and went for a walk on the beach. Said she needed to check in with her manager."

"Anton."

"Right. And Grig went to the apartment to pack, and I think Irina's in her room. I didn't pay much attention, but her door's closed, and she said she needed to pack. She made some crack about needing us to give her suitcase a quick once over, in case any of our stuff was in there."

Sonny smiled at Irina's door as if it were Irina herself. "I know I'm not missing anything." Then she looked back at Melanie. "Well, other than a father."

"What happened, honey?" Melanie closed the dishwasher door.

"I guess I'm a little embarrassed that I called him again already, and he had to ask me not to." She grimaced.

"Are you kidding me? What's the matter with him? Did he tell you why?"

Sonny nodded. "He said he wanted to get to know me better, but his wife was upset when she learned about me. He said she needs time to get used to the idea."

"Oh." Melanie dried her hands on a dishtowel and looked as though she were trying to work math sums in her head.

"What are you thinking?" Sonny said.

"I'm trying to put myself in her shoes. I can't, completely. But didn't you say this is wife number three?"

"Yeah."

Melanie nodded. "Right. Then, as much as I think he should be welcoming you with open arms, try not to take his stalling too personally. From the conversation he and I had way back at our college reunion, my guess is that David's made a lot of mistakes in his marital behavior. I don't think his infidelity toward me was his only misstep, not by a long shot. If he's trying to ease you into his life while struggling to hold together his marriage, he's probably scared stiff he's going to blow it again. Give him time."

"I don't have much choice about that, but I'll try to understand. I sure wouldn't want to be the cause of a failed marriage. Maybe we shouldn't mention this to Mom, though."

Melanie tilted her head at Sonny. "Why not?"

"I know she kept David secret because she was ashamed, but I think she also wanted to protect me, you know? To keep me from being hurt in case he didn't want to have anything to do with me. If she hears about this, she might never be up front with me about anything difficult again."

Melanie chuckled softly.

Sonny smiled at her. "What's funny?"

"You're telling me that, in order to keep your mom from withholding information from you, you want to keep information from her?"

Sonny gazed at the pan in her hands and frowned. "Oh. Yeah." She looked at Melanie. "That's stupid, isn't it?"

They both laughed.

Melanie said, "I think the best thing you can do is be honest with your mom and show her you can survive the truth. You've done a good job of that this week. When people know the truth won't crush you, they're more likely to trust you with it."

"Okay." Sonny sighed. "Can I trust you with a bit of truth right now, Aunt Melanie?"

"Sure you can."

Sonny frowned, as if disappointed in herself. "It really did hurt, that phone call with my father."

Melanie set down her dish towel and hugged Sonny to herself. "I know, honey." She ran her hand down Sonny's straight blond hair. "Family members are bound to let us down at times. Even my parents…" She hesitated. Was this something she wanted to share?

Sonny pulled back and tilted her head at Melanie. "Grandma and Grandpa? How did they let you down?"

"I don't know if I should even call it that." Melanie shook her head. "I'm not sure if you did the math, as Teresa obviously did, when she asked me how long I'd been married and how old Micah was."

"Oh. That." Sonny glanced down for a moment. "Yeah. I only noticed, really, because Mom did."

Melanie nodded. "Right. Well, consider what it was like for Grandma and Grandpa. One of their daughters had simply chosen to shut them out of her life. They didn't know why, exactly, and they had to suffer with that loss. They ended up pinning much of that unrequited affection on me, which had both good and bad sides to it. They had great expectations for me."

"Sounds like a lot of pressure." Sonny grimaced.

Melanie shrugged. "Bailey and I dated a year, and we both came to the Lord while we were together. But we didn't clean up our relationship, not right away. We would have married eventually, but we did things out of order."

"And your parents freaked out when you told them you were pregnant?"

"It was so hard for them to hear that news. I had never seen your grandfather that angry and upset. Not before then, and not after. He wouldn't speak to me for quite a while. If I hadn't had a loving, supportive church family, if I hadn't had God, I don't know what I would have done."

"Whoa." Sonny sighed. "I can't picture Grandpa that way."

Melanie's smile was sad. "You know what? I think your mom was able to picture him that way. I think that contributed to her running away from the family, rather than facing him with her news."

"You think Grandpa knows that?"

"I think so, yes. I think that was one of the reasons he drew me back to him. He didn't want to chase off another daughter."

Melanie smiled. "And he's a wonderful man. A better man than he was before." She took one of Sonny's hands. "I'm telling you this, Sonny, because I believe your father's failings will probably hurt you less if you focus on your heavenly Father's love." She pulled back and looked into Sonny's eyes. "He *always* welcomes you and listens when you call, right?"

Sonny gently smiled. "Yeah. I actually gave Him a call right after talking with David. I probably should have placed those calls the other way around."

Seventy-Four

Within the hour Sonny carried her luggage outside and saw her mother already closing the trunk of her car. Teresa dusted her hands off and looked up at Sonny.

"Come give me a hug, sweetie. I want to get going."

They walked toward each other.

Sonny said, "You're not going to drive along with us, caravan style? We could stop together for lunch, if you want."

"No, you kids go on together. I have a hotel room booked in Catalina. I want to get there early enough to freshen up before Ken picks me up for the evening. Did you want to stay over? I think the room's a double. You and Irina could—"

"No, actually, Jason—you know, the helicopter guy? A coworker of his is going to put us up for the night. She lives near Jason. Should we try to meet up in Catalina, though? Is that insane? I don't know how crowded the place will be."

"We can give it a try. Let's try to meet at that casino where nobody gambles. The big round theater building. Keep your cell phone on, and we'll call each other." She took Sonny's face in her hands. "But just in case it doesn't work out…" She kissed Sonny on the forehead and gave her a firm hug.

Sonny hugged her back and breathed in the clean scent of Estée Lauder's White Linen. "Thanks, Mom, for this week. It was exactly what I wanted for a graduation gift."

Teresa pulled back. "It was an eye-opener, wasn't it?"

Grig called over to Sonny. "You want me to load your bags in your car, Sonny?"

"Oh, thanks, Grig, yeah."

He lifted the bag that carried all of her psychology textbooks. "Wow. Are you making off with the silver or something?"

Sonny laughed.

"Go help him out, baby," Teresa said. She gave Sonny's shoulders a little squeeze. "I'm going to go." She called out, "Bye, Grig. See you tonight. Or Monday."

Grig put Sonny's bags in her car and jogged over to Teresa. He gave her a hug. "Maybe we'll cross paths tonight."

"You take good care of my girl."

"That's the plan." He and Sonny exchanged smiles.

Irina and Melanie hurried out of the house, and Irina waved her thin arms.

"Don't leave without a hug, Teresa."

Teresa smiled, obviously flattered by Irina's enthusiasm. She gave her a brief hug and said, "I might see you young ones in Catalina tonight."

"Well, you won't see this old one," Melanie said. "Probably not until the night of Irina's solos." The sisters embraced earnestly.

Teresa whispered something in Melanie's ear, and Melanie nodded. Sonny was awash in curiosity, but she doubted she would ever know what her mother said. She shook her head and smiled. Twins. This was an entirely new side of her mother to which Sonny would have to adapt. She liked the idea of that—learning about the childhood her mother had kept secret before now. Filling in the empty vision of her mother as a young girl, as a teen, as a new coed. Sonny had heard snippets, but they were always shared cautiously, as if the exposed details were selected with care from the full picture.

Teresa surprised Sonny by taking her hand and pulling her, alone, toward the car. The others went back to loading their luggage.

"Sweetie, I just wanted to tell you that I think you're going to be a good counselor."

"You do?"

"I most certainly do. I know your motives this week had a lot to do with your own needs, but you seemed to know about my needs too. And

Melanie's. You were a little sneaky about how you went about getting me here, but you risked the wrath of your diva mama to bring about something long overdue. That was gutsy. And you'll probably have to risk being disliked at times if you want to be an effective counselor."

Sonny simply raised her eyebrows and nodded.

Teresa said, "You did the right thing arranging this week."

Sonny hadn't recognized the sheepish weight she carried on her shoulders for having fooled her mother into the reunion with Melanie. But as the guilt lifted, she was able to identify that it had been there.

Teresa took hold of Sonny's shoulders again. "Do you realize I might have spent the rest of my life fighting with you about your...your heritage? I suppose that's what you could call it. And I would have gone to my grave with a massive hole in my life, even if I refused to acknowledge it. My sister, my parents. Sonny, you gave them back to me. Thank you."

Her mom had never spoken to her like this before. She was encouraging and supportive, but never grateful. Sonny had always felt like the taker. Never the giver. She was blown away.

"Oh, Mom." Her throat tightened.

Teresa cupped Sonny's cheek. "Now don't you get weepy on me. I don't want puffy eyes when cowboy Ken shows up later today."

Sonny's laugh kept her from getting any more emotional than she already was. "Cowboy Ken. You think there's any future there?"

Teresa shrugged. "Who knows? We've had a couple of enjoyable phone calls. He sounds like a good man. And if you'll recall, he saw me mount that horse as if I were the grand prize winner of one of those funny home video shows, yet he still wants to go out with me. That has to say something for the man."

"Yes. I hope to be able to make a fool of myself in front of the man I love."

Teresa nodded once. "Exactly." She gave Sonny a quick kiss on the cheek and got in her car. "Call me later, sweetie. I love you."

"I love you too, Mom."

As Teresa drove away, she honked once and waved to everyone.

It wasn't until she was gone that Sonny realized she hadn't yet told her what David said about his being radically pro-choice back when Teresa was pregnant. There would be time for that later. But Sonny imagined being alone and pregnant at this age. As devious as her mom had been during that time of betrayal, she had chosen to carry and raise her child.

Sonny may have given Melanie and her grandparents back to her mom, but her mom had given her something she could never repay. Sonny may have forced Teresa to give her back her heritage. But Teresa had chosen to give her daughter life.

Seventy-Five

Melanie leaned down to talk to Sonny and Irina, who were ready to drive away. "You girls are making Grig drive on his own, then?"

Sonny said, "Only as far as La Jolla. We're dropping my car off at my place."

Irina leaned over to join in. "Anyway, I think maybe Grig wants the time alone. He's had enough female company to last him for weeks."

Sonny chuckled and glanced back at the beach house. "Aunt Melanie, are you sure you don't mind locking up?"

"Not at all. My drive is short, and I'll be leaving right behind you."

They had hugged and kissed among themselves already, and Melanie wanted to let them get on their way.

"Just remember to call me, Sonny, so we can have you over to the house at least once before you move to Berkeley."

"Definitely. I'm dying to see those photo albums of Grandma and Grandpa. And I want to see you and Mom when you were kids. Give my love to Uncle Bailey and Micah."

Irina said, "And tell Micah we'll pray for a good first date. And, um, tell Doris I'm sorry about the lipstick case." She grimaced.

Melanie smiled. "Right. Don't you worry about that. Love you guys. Go on, now."

She waved to Grig, who waved back and drove out, followed by Sonny.

Irina leaned out her window. "Next year, Melanie! Put it on the calendar!"

Melanie gave the beach house one last check. They had left it in good shape, no worse for wear. She smiled. But the house had left them in far better shape than when they arrived, that was certain. A reunion visit next year would probably be a very good idea.

She stepped outside and locked the door. She saw Julian on the board-walk, and when he approached his front door, he caught sight of her. He waved and walked over.

"I thought you'd all left by now. I knew I was too late for that last bit of boogie boarding Sonny and I considered."

"Afraid so. I'm the last." Melanie jingled her car keys. "It's been quite a week, Julian."

"Quite a good week? Quite a tough week?"

She spoke in a world-weary voice. "Absolutely, honey."

They both laughed.

"Did you and Teresa make amends? Or get any closer to that? Teresa promised me a full report after they surprised you at the restaurant. And she said *you* would deliver it."

"Did she, now?"

"She did. But the fact that you came back to the beach house is prob-ably report enough."

She nodded. "Actually, we had a wonderful breakthrough. I think Zeke played a role in that."

"That sounds like Zeke."

"Yeah, he and Teresa had a chat this morning—"

"Oh, this just happened this morning?"

"Right. Somehow he motivated her to come apologize to me. Julian, it was one of the most liberating experiences I've ever had. I still haven't had a chance, really, to talk with Teresa about it as much as I'd like."

"You needed that apology, did you?"

She shook her head. "No, it wasn't that, really. See, Sonny did these psychological exercises with us—"

"Yes, she mentioned those to Zeke and me. She felt she'd made a dog's dinner of them, if I remember correctly."

"Sorry? A dog's dinner?"

He chuckled. "She told us she'd messed up. Said she was a horrible counselor."

Melanie tilted her head. "On the contrary. I think she's got some pretty good instincts. She might even give Zeke a run for his money." She smiled at Julian.

They walked to Melanie's car.

"Anyway," Melanie said, "I didn't realize until Teresa talked with me this morning—after her talk with Zeke—that I hadn't truly forgiven her for the things that happened between us in the past. I thought I had. I *said* I had. But one thing Sonny suggested when she gave us those tests was that I secretly felt brokenhearted. I just took that in stride. Sure, I was brokenhearted. My sister and my boyfriend had betrayed me."

She opened her car door and tossed her purse on the passenger seat.

"But if I still hung on to my broken heart, how much forgiving had I really done? And when our conflicts finally came out this week, the first thing I did was run back home. I thought I was listening to divine guidance, but I think I was being kind of a chicken."

Julian smiled.

Melanie said, "I've been carrying around this hidden feeling of entitlement I wasn't even aware of. Here I am, thinking of going into women's ministry, and I haven't quite grasped the concept of forgiving others as I've been forgiven."

"Ah, that's a tough one. Not quite possible on our own, sometimes."

"Amen to that, Julian." She put out her hand. "It's been a pleasure. This place is special."

He nodded and shook her hand. "It is that, Melanie. I can't tell you how often I see God's hand at work here. Just lifts me up, over and over."

She got in her car and said, "Give my best to Zeke, will you? Maybe we'll see him next year."

"Next year?"

She smiled. "Surely we wouldn't be the only visitors who made a repeat visit?"

He returned her smile. "No, you wouldn't be. And I have to tell you, Melanie. There are times I think of that verse from Hebrews about entertaining angels without knowing it. I have experienced some truly angelic personalities, thanks to the beach house."

When Melanie drove away, moments later, she looked at Julian in her rearview mirror and thought the very same thing.

Seventy-Six

July 4
La Jolla, California

Sonny gave Grig and Irina a quick tour of her apartment before they headed out to Long Beach to meet Jason and fly over to Catalina for the evening. One of Sonny's idiosyncrasies had always been to clean her home before going on a trip. She simply enjoyed coming back to tidiness rather than clutter. With this unexpected visit by Grig and Irina, she had a new justification for her quirky habit. The various cleanser smells had diminished, but there was a freshness in the air to accompany the white wicker furniture and pastel colors on her walls.

Irina made note of the fact that Sonny had few family photos displayed in her apartment. "But imagine how many pictures you'll have soon. So many relatives—"

"And, of course, Irina and me," Grig said.

Sonny chuckled. "Of course. But you two are so gorgeous, people will think yours are the photos that came with the picture frames."

Both Irina and Grig looked at her, surprised.

"You really think that?" Irina asked.

"Good grief, are you two really that unaware?" Sonny's eyes widened. "I can't be the first to mention that. And you *do* have mirrors and a general grasp of the overall appreciation of the viewing public, right?"

Grig laughed. "Thanks, Sonny. It's just that Mom and Dad always played down the importance of a person's outer beauty. But the compliment is nice." He wandered toward the hallway. "The bathroom was down here, right? I want to make a quick stop before we leave."

Sonny gave him a knowing smile. "Want to take a look in the mirror, now that you know you're a hottie?"

"Definitely. And there was a breeze when we walked from the car to the apartment. I thought I felt a hair fall out of place."

July 4
Catalina Island, California

They arrived in Catalina near the tail end of the Fourth of July parade down Crescent Avenue.

"I love this!" Sonny said, laughing as the slow parade of golf carts wove its way past them and hundreds of other onlookers. "It's a home-town parade!"

"Yeah," Grig said, "but with palm trees and tropical music."

A ragtag band in shorts, Hawaiian shirts, and straw hats followed a golf cart with a speaker mounted on its roof. Sonny recognized their song, a cover of a Jimmy Buffet tune, with the lyrics changed to honor "Catalinaville."

Jason spoke loudly over the music. "And we can head over to the Casino Ballroom afterward for barbecue, if you guys want to. The USC marching band will be playing, and it's a good spot for watching the fireworks over the bay. It'll be crowded, but if we head over right after this, we should be able to find a good spot for an evening picnic."

Sonny opened her cell phone and spoke to Grig. "That's where I told Mom we'd try to meet up with her. Let me see if I can track her down." She sent a text to Teresa.

But Teresa's response, which came within minutes, put an end to that plan.

> sorry, baby. on the water.
> ken owns beautiful boat.
> think has $$$$.
> who knew? love u. ttyl.

So the young foursome bought barbecue from the casino buffet and found the perfect spot outside to relax and await the fireworks. The entire area was packed with people, but everyone was in a festive mood. Sonny loved the sense of community, especially considering the fact that most of the people were probably visitors, as she was.

Jason brought his binoculars, and they had fun trying to find Teresa and Ken by scoping out the numerous boats on the water. Their lack of success didn't dampen the enjoyment of the search.

At one point during their picnic, Sonny told them about the disappointing phone call with her father. "It's probably just a setback, not the end of the road. Aunt Melanie thinks it's just a matter of time before his wife is open to my talking with him."

Irina sighed. "That has to be hard, though, knowing he's there, knowing he's interested, but having to remain quiet for his wife, who isn't even family."

Grig said, "But she's *his* family. That has to be respected." He put his hand on Sonny's shoulder. "I'm sorry, though."

He chuckled when he removed his hand. "Oops." He wiped her shoulder with a napkin. "Barbecue sauce."

Jason said, "So that was what you were aiming for on this trip, huh? You wanted to get to know the family you didn't know?"

"Yeah." Sonny took a sip of her drink. "It's been a life-changing week for me."

Irina smiled. "And now you've found your identity, like we talked about before. You know your history. Or part of it, anyway. And the rest should come soon." She counted off on her fingers. "This week you discovered your aunt, uncle, cousin, grandparents, even your father." She sighed. "What I wouldn't give—" She looked at Grig. "What I wouldn't give to know more about our mother and father in Russia."

She glanced at Jason before saying the next part, speaking so softly he might not have even heard. "I wonder about our father. I'd like to know what I inherited from him."

Grig's warm, protective smile made him seem so much older than Irina. "Maybe someday we'll go back and see what we can discover."

Sonny said, "Yeah, that's a great idea. But it wasn't really finding my family members that was so life-changing this week."

She looked down and gathered her thoughts. "I loved learning about my heritage, as Mom called it. But Melanie said something to me when my father told me not to call. She said the pain wouldn't be so bad if I focused on my heavenly Father's love." She looked at Irina. "That made a lot of sense."

"What do you mean?" Irina asked.

Sonny shrugged. "I mean no matter what happens with my relatives, I know who I am."

Irina said nothing. She simply gazed into Sonny's eyes as she digested that thought. Eventually, a sweet smile spread across her face. "I know who I am." Although she parroted Sonny's words, the sentiment seemed to be her own.

Then, as if timed specifically for them, the first burst of celebration filled the evening sky.

Seventy-Seven

Before the fireworks were over, Sonny had settled against Grig as if he were her favorite comfy chair. They watched the display with their heads close together, and she tried not to think about the time they would spend apart, starting tomorrow. They had spent four years between their last encounter and this one. Surely one month would be easy.

Naturally, Irina and Jason were less demonstrative, but it was clear they enjoyed each other's company. When they all walked to his coworker's home, Jason said good night to Irina at the door. She accepted a quick peck on the cheek from him before going inside.

"I'll be right there, Irina," Sonny said.

Irina smiled at her before she closed the door. "Take your time."

"You go on ahead, Jase." Grig gave him a pat on the shoulder. "I'll be there in a minute."

Jason nodded at both of them. "Right, I'm going to hit the sack. Door's unlocked. The couch has sheets and blankets on it. See you tomorrow. I'm not working, but I can fly you back to Long Beach whenever you're ready. Just give me a little notice."

Grig took Sonny's hand and walked her to the front steps. They sat together quietly for several moments, and then he put his arm around her. "I don't want to go."

She laughed softly and rested her head against his shoulder. "No. Me either. And tomorrow morning will be that much harder."

She felt his kiss against her head.

He said, "We can do this. We're grown-ups."

They both chuckled.

"I really do have a friend in real estate back home," Grig said. "I'll put you in touch with him as soon as I get back. We've got to find a good reason for you to come up and check out the area."

She lifted her head and gave him a half smile. "I think I've found a pretty good reason already."

She leaned into his kiss and snuggled into his embrace. They sighed simultaneously when they parted, touching their foreheads together. She could smell his aftershave or shampoo. Something warm and woodsy.

"You always smell so good," she said.

He pulled back and smiled. "Huh. I actually told Irina the other day that I love the way you smell."

"Well, this is good news. It would be a shame to fall for someone stinky."

He laughed, and Sonny rested her head against his shoulder again.

"So," he said. "Is that what's happening? You're falling for me?"

She didn't budge. "I meant you. It would be a shame for *you* to fall for someone stinky."

She jumped at the little poke he gave her in the side. He nuzzled her neck and she laughed.

"I like what you told Irina earlier," he said. "About your identity in Christ. I feel as if I always knew that, but sometimes you don't even think about things like that until someone points them out."

"Yeah. I mean, if I want to learn about my heritage, I should really be reading my Bible more diligently."

"Mmm, right." He swayed gently with her in his arms. "We could become accountability partners on that. What do you think?"

"I love that idea."

They said nothing for a while, and then Sonny said, "But you know, I'm glad I didn't figure out what I told Irina—or I'm glad God waited before showing me—until this morning. I do feel the contentment of knowing I'm His, but I'm also glad I was driven to find the rest of my family." She cocked her head. "For that matter, I only found one half of my family. Someday it would be nice to meet my paternal grandparents, if they're alive. And any other uncles or aunts or cousins I might have on my dad's side."

She felt him nod beside her.

Still resting against him, she reached her hand up to touch his face. "Thank you, Grig."

He pulled away to look at her. "For what?"

"For how you treated me four years ago at Sunset Beach."

He smiled. "Like I was crazy about you, you mean?"

"That too." She grinned briefly. "But I was clueless about a lot of things. I could have made some pretty bad choices if you hadn't kept your head." She raised her eyebrows. "I meant it when I said you were picture-frame gorgeous."

He didn't say anything. He glanced down for a moment, and she was captivated by those thick, dark lashes of his. She felt that same emotional stirring she felt four years ago, when she wanted to use the word "love" with him. But thick eyelashes had nothing to do with love, and she knew it.

She said, "You remember the other day, when I said it was good my mom dragged Irina down to the beach house, because otherwise you wouldn't have come down?"

He smiled. "I don't remember your saying it was good, but I like your version of the memory better."

"And then you said God would have gotten you down there anyway, if it was His will that you went?"

"I remember."

"I think that's what happened at Sunset Beach."

He shook his head. "I don't follow."

"Grig, before that month we spent together, I honestly thought so little about God, I don't know when I would ever have gotten around to Him. I definitely never considered who Jesus was. And even though I didn't know Him by the time I left Sunset Beach, I sought Him out because of you. Because of what you said and, more importantly, how you behaved."

She saw such pleasure in his eyes.

"Wow. I don't think I've ever been told I played a role in someone's salvation. You always hope, right? But I always wished I could know for sure."

"Well, now you know. You played a huge role for me. I think it was no accident, our meeting at Sunset Beach."

Grig smiled. "Sonny, meeting you was like a dream. A blessing. Maybe even a miracle, but one thing I've always known is that meeting you was no accident."

He leaned in slowly and kissed her. He stopped, and she opened her eyes. His were already open, waiting for her to look at him. The twinkle of happiness was unmistakable and contagious. Wrapping her arms around him, she tilted her head to kiss him again.

She couldn't have dreamed up a better end to this week. In a mere seven days, her relationship with her mom blossomed. She discovered an aunt who was already an invaluable confidante. Two loving grandparents embraced her as if they had known her forever. And she made friends with a sweet, sensitive woman with an angelic voice.

God brought all of those things to pass. But He didn't wait until this week before answering her prayers. Because He knew she needed Him, God provided a lovely young man to set her on her way four years ago. Sonny kissed Grig again and knew.

God gave her a gift at Sunset Beach.

Epilogue

July 4. One year later.
The Beach House, Mission Beach
San Diego, California

Sonny was late. There were too many cars parked at the house for her to get a spot, so she parked farther down the road. She saw Julian crossing from his house to the beach house.

"Julian!" She turned to walk toward him.

He greeted her with a broad smile and open arms. "I remember this beautiful young lady. Welcome back, Sonny."

They shared a light hug and she gave the beach house the once-over. "Hasn't changed much, has it? Still standing."

He appraised the house too. "You're right. Still Faith Fontaine's funny little house. Most of the changing goes on inside."

She grinned. "You mean the inhabitants, not the house, right?"

He pointed at her. "That's right. You're the insightful one, aren't you? You were working on your counseling degree, I think. Yeah?"

She exhaled. "Yep. That's why I'm a little late. Had some summer course work to turn in before I could head down from Berkeley. Otherwise I would have come with Irina and Grig." She cocked her head toward the house. "I assume they're all here?"

Julian shook his head. "I couldn't tell you. I haven't been home. We'll check it out together." He glanced at his watch. "Your Aunt Melanie was fairly laid back about what time festivities would begin."

"I guess she'd have to be with this crowd."

The first people Sonny saw when she walked through the front door were her mother and Ken. They had their backs to her, and they were apparently laughing about something Uncle Bailey had said.

Every time Sonny saw Ken, she liked him even more. Just as he did today, he typically kept a comfortable, affectionate arm around her mother's back. This past year, as Teresa worked to rebuild her relationship with her parents, Ken had been an excellent sounding board and a supportive friend. Sonny never realized how much joy she would experience, seeing her mother loved the way Ken clearly loved her. Sonny smiled to remember Ken and Teresa's first meeting, when Ken literally swept Teresa off her feet and onto a compliant horse at the Catalina Stables.

Bailey caught Sonny's eye and let out a welcoming cheer. "Sonny! Finally!"

Teresa and Ken turned. "Oh, sweetie," Teresa said. She went to Sonny and hugged her up. "I missed you."

"Me too, Mom. Welcome back." Sonny looked from her mother to Ken. "Well, I have to say Europe agrees with you two. Or is it marriage?"

They gave each other the slyest grins before Teresa said, "Europe was definitely the icing on the cake. But the cake is to die for." She reached up and gently stroked the back of Ken's neck. His grin turned into a shy smile. Adorable, Sonny thought, on such a rugged man.

Someone grabbed Sonny into a hug from behind. She'd know those arms anywhere. The moment Grig released his hold, she turned and gave him a kiss. Then she stood beside him and gestured toward the newlyweds. "What do you think of these two, Grig?"

He smiled. "I already told them I thought they were a terrific ad for wedded bliss."

Teresa leaned forward. "How's Irina doing? Should we refrain from being too celebratory around her?"

Grig exchanged a look with Sonny before he answered. "To tell you the truth, Teresa, she and Jason are..."

"In talks again," Sonny said. She smiled. "Irina's not interested in anyone other than Jason. But since making such great progress with her counselor, she's mostly focused on building her career—"

"As I was at her age," Teresa said.

Sonny nodded. "And long-distance romances can be difficult."

Ken snorted. "Tell us about it."

"Yeah, you two know what that's like." Sonny looked around the living room and finally spotted Irina, who looked perfectly happy, chatting with Zeke and his wife.

Teresa spoke to Ken. "And poor Jason can't afford to fly back and forth all the time like you did, Ken. Maybe we could help him out a little there?"

Sonny wiggled her eyebrows at Grig about that. Ken had turned out to be humble, wealthy, and graciously generous. His guide work at the stables was simply something he loved to do.

Grig smiled and put his arm around Sonny. "Since you were a little late in getting here, Melanie asked me to hurry you around the room to say your hellos. She wants to toast the lovebirds—" He cocked his head toward Teresa and Ken, "and she said you'll be distracted if you see anyone you haven't already greeted."

Teresa chuckled. "My sister knows her stuff. Go ahead, Sonny. We'll all talk later."

So Sonny and Grig moved on and wove through the chattering crowd, tightly packed into Faith's sunflower yellow living room. Sonny got a chance to hug her grandparents—

"Has anyone given you two the tour of this funky little place?" she asked them. "I'll have to show you the themed bedrooms. So cute."

She had a brief girly moment with Irina—

"We have to talk. I think Mom is cooking up a plan for you."

She made Zeke's lovely wife laugh out loud—

"So Zeke really does shuttle off home at night, huh? I always pictured him just sitting on a cloud somewhere, bathed in heavenly light."

She spent a few minutes with Micah—

"Yeah," Micah said, "Chelsea and I are still going strong. She's going to Berkeley in the fall too. Theater major. Maybe we can all get together up there sometime."

She got a cuddle from Uncle Bailey and Aunt Melanie—

"We miss you, pumpkin," Bailey said. "Spend a few days at the house with us before you head home."

"Definitely," Melanie said. "And plan a few more visits between now and Christmas. We're going to be empty nesters. We won't know what to do with ourselves."

"What are you talking about?" Sonny said. "Your women's ministries job sounds like it keeps you plenty busy."

Melanie waved off the comment. "Naw. Piece of cake." She glanced around the room. "Okay, have you said all of your hellos?"

Sonny laughed. "Yes, I think so. But you honestly didn't have to wait for me. I could have behaved myself through a simple honeymoon toast to Mom and Ken."

Melanie nodded as if she weren't really listening. She walked away from Sonny and Bailey and positioned herself near the front door of the house. Sonny watched her try to call for attention, but the various conversations drowned her out. Then Melanie spotted Grig and called out to him.

"Grig, come help me out."

He excused himself from his conversation with Julian and stepped up next to Melanie. His voice was much stronger than hers had been.

"Listen up, everyone!"

The conversations died down quickly, and they all gave Melanie their attention.

Melanie heaved a contented sigh and looked at Teresa and Ken before talking to everyone.

"As you all know, exactly one year ago today, on the Fourth of July, a group of us finished a rather, ahem, intense week—"

Several members of the group chuckled.

"—which was organized by my clever niece, Sonny. The week involved the unveiling of a number of family secrets. It also involved the beginnings of some wonderful new friendships."

Sonny and several others looked around the room. She spotted Irina and smiled. She did the same with Julian and Zeke.

"And a few family members met for the first time. Those relationships have grown this year. Some slowly—"

Sonny thought of the two times she and her father met this past year.

"—and some very quickly."

Melanie and Sonny met eyes and grinned.

"Finally," Melanie said, "a few romances also blossomed that week."

Melanie looked at Teresa and all eyes followed suit. "My dear twin found the love of her life in Ken Wiley. We want to congratulate Teresa and Ken, and we pray they enjoy a long, happy life together."

It dawned on Sonny that she had nothing with which to toast the newlyweds. Had Melanie forgotten that detail? Her eyes darted around the crowd. Other than a glass of soda here or there, *no* one had anything to drink for the toast.

She looked up at Melanie and tried to warn her. She raised her empty hand as if she held a glass that Melanie had forgotten to supply. She pretended to sip from that forgotten glass.

Melanie looked right at her, unperturbed, but then she said, "Grig, help me out here," just as she had done at the beginning of her toast. Grig stepped in for her and she walked toward the kitchen.

Finally. Maybe Sonny should help pass out beverages to ward off an awkward wait. Before she moved toward the kitchen, she glanced at her mom, to see if she looked uncomfortable by the snafu. Her mom looked right at her.

So did Ken.

Sonny frowned.

Then she realized her grandparents, who stood near Teresa and Ken, were looking at her too.

She didn't know why, but she looked behind herself. People had backed away from her.

And every eye was on her. Smiles broke out.

Goose bumps ran up her arms, and she nearly shook her head to settle her thoughts.

When she turned back, she was startled. Grig had quietly come closer and waited for her.

She felt his hands shaking when he reached for hers. He smiled at her as if he had caught her at something.

"Now, we talked about this, Sonny."

"Oh, Grig." He was going to—

"And I racked my brain to try to think of how to surprise you."

Her eyes prickled with the onset of tears.

"So I thought what better way than to get everyone together? The people in this room are here because of the steps you took last summer.

I know you wanted to do away with your family secrets, but I thought you might be able to handle just this one. Just one more."

He reached up and wiped a tear from her cheek.

"This reunion wasn't organized because of Teresa and Ken's wedding."

Sonny glanced at her mother, who had her hands drawn under her chin in anticipation. Sonny looked back at Grig.

"We're here for you, Sonny."

He opened his hand, revealing a diamond ring. When had that gotten there?

"*I'm* here for you," he said. "Will you have me?"

She drew breath in with a sob. She probably would have said yes even that summer at Sunset Beach. "It broke my heart to say goodbye to you five years ago, Grig."

He nodded. "Mine too. Let's never do that again."

She laughed and threw her arms around him. "Never again. Yes, I'll marry you."

Sonny barely got the last word out before the room erupted in cheers and applause. But she barely noticed. She focused on the softness of Grig's lips, the strength of his arms, the tears in his eyes, and the promise of his love.

Questions for Discussion

1. *Sunset Beach* addresses the concept of self-identity. Why did Sonny feel unsure of her identity? What was her idea for uncovering the truth?

2. Have you ever felt shaken in your sense of who you are as a result of your circumstances? Discuss.

3. Why do you think Teresa felt the need to bring Irina with her to the beach house? Why do you think Irina came?

4. Do you sense any jealousy in Sonny toward Irina? Why do you think she is/isn't jealous?

5. Sonny knew Melanie's arrival would surprise her mother. But what surprised Sonny upon Melanie's arrival? What kind of surprises have you experienced through family members?

6. What is it about Irina's past that enables her to identify with Sonny's quest? Do you identify with either of these young women? How?

7. Was Sonny fair in her various confrontations with her mother? Why or why not? Assuming you had been put off for twenty-four years, would you have approached the problem differently?

8. Irina clearly leans on her brother for strength and moral support. Do you have such a figure in your life? Whom?

9. Should Melanie have been more forthcoming with Sonny regarding the family details she knew? Or was she right to leave those revelations up to Teresa?

10. Was Melanie's leaving the beach house similar in any way to Teresa's running away twenty-five years earlier? How was it different?

11. What causes Teresa to finally empathize with Sonny's pain and apologize to her? Have you ever had an unrelated incident bring you to an awareness like that? Discuss.

12. How might Melanie's dinner with Chelsea's parents have turned out had Teresa not run into Doris in the ladies' room? Can you think of a time someone's behavior impressed you negatively until you learned what colored that person's mood?

13. Sonny learned much about her family during her week at the beach house. But who was the most important family relation she unveiled in the process? How did her discovery relate to Irina? How does it relate to you?

Meet Trish Perry

Trish Perry is the award-winning author of *The Guy I'm Not Dating, Too Good to Be True,* and *Beach Dreams.* She serves on the board of the Capital Christian Writers organization in the Washington, DC, area and edited its newsletter, *Ink and the Spirit,* for seven years. She has published numerous short stories, essays, devotionals, and poetry in Christian and general-market media, and she is a member of American Christian Fiction Writers and Romance Writers of America.

Says Trish:

"I live in Northern Virginia with my brilliantly funny son, whom I love and can embarrass with one hand tied behind my back. I have a gorgeous adult daughter who has become my most intuitive friend, and an amazing grandson who sweetly calls me MayMay instead of…the G word."

Trish loves to hear from her readers. Please feel free to contact her via mail at:

Trish Perry
c/o Harvest House Publishers
990 Owen Loop North
Eugene, OR 97402

or

via her website at:
www.trishperry.com

or

via e-mail at:
trish@trishperry.com

Have you read Beach Dreams *yet?*

Here's a preview...

One

March 11, Northern Virginia

Tiffany lugged her suitcase up the three steps of the airport shuttle bus. If she hadn't packed the case herself, she'd be suspicious of its contents. It felt as if it were full of cinder blocks.

The March air hung colder here in Northern Virginia than it had in South Carolina. Yet Tiffany perspired with the effort to carve out a spot for herself and her luggage in the shuttle. Every spot was filled, jammed with people eager to get to their cars. Evening rush hour at Dulles Airport—never one of Tiffany's favorite situations.

She lurched backward and might have fallen when the bus took off, but there was nowhere to fall. Everyone on board groaned when the bus crawled to a stop for even more passengers in front of the American Airlines exit.

Oh, man. They were all getting on through the back door, where she stood sandwiched between a woman with an over zealous fondness for perfume and a man wearing too little deodorant.

The new passengers entered with a cold whoosh. There were only three of them, but three too many as far as Tiffany was concerned. She looked down to make sure no one stepped on her Moschino slingbacks. Why did she do stupid things like this? Why didn't she wear sneakers when she flew, like normal people?

She closed her eyes briefly. She was doing it again. Complaining about her circumstances, which really weren't all that bad. For the past six months—ever since she came to Christ—she kept catching herself like this. With an exhale she determined to upgrade her attitude starting now. *Appreciate, girl, appreciate.*

When she lifted her eyes, they fell on the most attractive man she'd ever seen, especially this close. The cramped quarters forced him to stand within kissing distance of her.

Thank You, Lord!

He and Tiffany looked directly into each other's eyes—there was really nowhere else to look at the moment. He topped her in height by a few inches, despite her heels. The bus took off, and the quick forward movement shoved them against each other. They each grabbed at the hand rail and offered one-word apologies to the other.

Oh, mercy, did she hear an English accent? Maybe. And she was a sucker for an accent. There was something familiar about him. What was it? Had they met? Or was it just because he looked like Jude Law? Or Jude Law's even cuter brother.

Dear Lord, is it okay for me to talk with You about stuff like this? My goodness, he's so close I can tell he has really excellent skin. And the perfect amount of five-o'clock shadow. Is that bad of me to notice? Am I a horrible Christian for absolutely loving this moment?

She tried to sneak a casual peek at his ring hand, but the handrail obscured her view. Oh, wait, now, that was the wrong hand. But his ring hand was blocked by other people.

She glanced back up and saw him studying her with his crystal blue eyes. He looked quickly away, but then he playfully looked back at her, sideways.

She laughed, maybe a little too loudly. Embarrassed and reluctant to look at him again, she trained her eyes on his warm brown sports jacket. And his white shirt appeared freshly starched, even this late in the day. Six months ago, she would have made an unabashed comment to get things rolling with this guy. Where was the old Tiffany?

Me again, Lord. I cannot believe I'm getting shy. Me. The biggest flirt ever. This is Your doing, isn't it?

The man next to him asked the time. Mr. Gorgeous looked up at the handrail to read his watch. Hmm. A watch on his right wrist? That usually signaled a left-hander. Maybe he was creative. An artist. An actor.

Would you look at those eyelashes? And yes, he said the time—six thirty—in a distinctly British accent.

Wow, it really was hot in there.

The shuttle stopped at the first parking lot. Ah good, the cool air would help. And now people would get off and she could check out his ring finger.

As he rolled his luggage out of the way, she saw. Single. She smiled.

He smiled back. Friendly; not particularly flirtatious. He smelled like soap and spice.

And then he stepped off the bus.

He stepped off the bus!

She knew her disappointment was obvious, but she couldn't help it. She realized she had already mapped out some wonderful plans for the two of them. She'd accompany him to his next gallery opening. To his opening night performance. Anywhere!

He turned to face the shuttle before it pulled away. She saw him look for her. When their eyes met, he smiled again, but with a hint of sadness. It was a smile that said, "What a pity." Then he nodded once in her direction, as if he were saying goodbye.

She actually raised her hand in a resigned wave.

Okay, Lord, that was not fun. You and I both know I decided to trust in You about everything, especially men. And I'm going to try to be good. But that one right there? I'm going to need a whole lot of help, if You're going to parade many more like that in front of me.

She sighed and watched for her stop. She was home. It was time to focus on getting her life back in order.

Two

Three days later, Tiffany stood outside Ledo's Pizza, a hungry grumble in her stomach and a hint of dusk in the sky. In one swift moment, she kicked her flat tire, broke her stiletto heel, and gave voice to the thought floating through her mind.

"Maybe coming back here wasn't such a great idea, after all."

But she immediately regretted her negative words. No, that wasn't the attitude she wanted to adopt, was it?

She had made it this far. She had moved back into her condo and restarted all of her services and utilities. She had put in a call about her old job at the gym. Tomorrow she would touch base with some of the people she left behind when Mama's cancer got so bad.

During those five sad months, she had noticed it: South Carolina didn't feel like home anymore. Even with Daddy still there.

This was home. Northern Virginia was home, and Tiffany had missed living here. She was surprised at how much she missed her...friends?

Yeah. Friends. Kara and Ren had sent flowers and the sweetest condolence cards to Daddy and her while she was away. They would even have come for Mama's service if Kara's wedding wasn't the same week and Ren's pregnancy wasn't so far along. Considering they had barely met Mama, their intentions said "friends" to Tiffany.

She smiled at that and sallied forth, hobbling like a peg-legged pirate on her broken Biba pump. She walked into Ledo's, where the lights were dimmed for the dinner crowd. That unmistakable aroma—bread, garlic, oregano, and burnt cheese—made her stomach growl again. She had planned to grab dinner, even before the tire blew. Maybe someone here would help her change the flat.

She reached the front counter and stopped in her tracks. Wasn't *he* just the one for the job? The guy behind the counter focused on the cash register, his pale brown hair soft against his forehead. He looked more than friendly; he was one red-hot pizza man. Tiffany didn't even have to try to smile at him; he brought her mood up several notches just standing there.

When he turned his attention to her, she saw a visible lift in his mood as well.

Then it seemed to hit them both at once.

Mr. Gorgeous from the shuttle bus. The Jude Law look-alike. He worked in a pizza joint? She would never have placed him in this environment. He *had* smelled spicy, but not garlic and basil. So much for galleries and stage performances.

He seemed slightly embarrassed, but he quickly recovered. "Fancy a pizza, love?"

Were they not going to mention the shuttle-bus incident?

Seeing him for a second time triggered something else in Tiffany's mind. She felt like she had met him—actually been introduced to him—somewhere before the shuttle bus. The gears in her rewind machine worked quickly. Had they dated? No, no way. She'd never dated a pizza man. Plus, she would definitely have recognized him on the bus if they had dated in the past. But her stomach tightened, and the pieces of her memory fell into place.

"Miss?" He had a polite question in his expression.

Shoot, she'd just been staring at him, glassy-eyed. She ordered the first thing she saw on the menu behind him. "I'll have the Hawaiian pizza, small. Please."

"Righto." He jotted her order down, and she felt minor frustration with him. Wasn't he going to say anything about the other evening?

"Hawaiian pizza." He looked up at her and smiled. "I always thought that was an odd combination."

"What?" Tiffany frowned and focused for a moment on what she ordered. Hawaiian pizza. Yeesh. She hated ham. "Oh, hold the ham, okay?"

He gave her a nod and jotted again. Fantastic forearms. "Right, then.

So…hmm." He glanced up, looking confused. "I have to say that sounds rather more odd than the original. You just want a pineapple-and-cheese pizza, is that it?"

"Ew. No. Hold the pineapple too." She grimaced. She was an idiot.

"Ah…" He altered the order form again. "You want a Hawaiian pizza, hold the ham, hold the pineapple. The cheese, apparently, stands alone. Do I have it, now?"

She would have found him annoying, but that accent was so charming, and he had the slightest grin on his face. She was reminded of his sideways glance in the bus. She couldn't help but laugh. "Just a plain pizza, okay?"

His eyes crinkled, and Tiffany's stomach did a little flip. Too, too cute. She paid him and saw him considering her. He cocked his head before he spoke.

"I think you were on the Dulles shuttle the other night, yeah?"

Finally! "Yeah. I wasn't sure if you recognized me or not."

He retrieved her change from the register and spoke without looking up. "You have rather unforgettably blue eyes."

A blush ran all the way up to her ears, especially when he gave her the change and she felt the warmth of his hand.

She was blushing? What had the good Lord done to her?

"Wow, what a nice thing to say. Thanks. But, um, I feel like we were introduced sometime in the past. I'm not sure when—"

A woman's tired voice interrupted them.

"Hey, Jeremy, could you please come help me carry this tray of pasta dishes when you have a second?"

Tiffany turned her head, blinked once slowly, and opened her eyes and mouth in shock. "Ren!"

The immensely pregnant woman looked just as amazed as Tiffany when she turned in answer to her name.

"Tiffany?" Then her expression brightened, and she came as close to hugging Tiffany as she could, considering the size of her belly. She smelled like a pizza oven. "Are you back home now, or just visiting? And, oh, I'm so sorry about your mom. Did you get our card? The flowers? Oh, don't answer that; we were just so sorry everything happened over the Christmas break and during Kara's wedding. We—Hey, what's with your shoe?"

Tiffany glanced down. She'd already gotten used to favoring her right side and had nearly forgotten. "Broke it. Kicking my flat tire. Outside."

Ren heaved a commiserating sigh. "Not your day, is it?" She glanced into the dining area, which seemed full of an inordinate number of kids with their parents.

The guy from the shuttle bus—Jeremy—had quietly gone after that tray for Ren. Tiffany heard his voice above the din of all those families clamoring for their orders.

Ren adjusted the short green apron over her belly. "Let me go help Jeremy with those entrees and I'll be right back. Sit!" She gestured toward some chairs for waiting patrons and took off.

Tiffany obeyed, but she was totally confused. Now she knew why that adorable Jeremy looked familiar. He worked with Ren; she had heard Ren and Kara talking about him in the past. But Ren and Jeremy were schoolteachers. Tiffany was sure of that. She felt like she inhabited some alternate universe, watching them serve pizza and pasta to the masses, especially with the once-svelte Ren waddling like an emperor penguin in baggy drawers.

Then the *other* memory hit her. A slow seep of acid started in her stomach. She had met Jeremy when she worked at the gym. He was a member. Just as she had done on the bus the other night, she immediately saw a big neon "Gorgeous!" sign over his head the moment she met him. But something she said back then turned him off. She remembered seeing it in his eyes—from appreciation to disdain in a few easy words. And she hadn't crossed paths with him since.

Here he came back again. Tiffany sat up and tried to look like someone who wouldn't *think* of saying anything mean or stupid.

But it was too late. He must have remembered too.

"Right, I'll see how your order's doing." He passed her. A kind smile on his face, but he appeared determined to avoid her eyes. Wow. What a difference one little memory made.

Now he was very polite. But very *not* interested. Whatever she had done or said before, it had oozed into his mind as the acid had her stomach.

"So, how are you holding up, Tiffany?" Ren eased herself down in the seat next to her and drew her attention away from the kitchen and Jeremy. Sympathy was clear in Ren's small smile. "Everything happened so quickly with your mom, didn't it?" She placed a hand on Tiffany's knee.

Despite all the kindness shown to Tiffany and her dad over the past several months, she still found it difficult to be comfortable with most physical gestures of affection. She didn't like that about herself. She willed her knee not to tense up under Ren's hand.

"I still can't talk about Mama very well." She stared at her lap.

After a quick pat Ren moved her hand away. "That's okay. Don't talk about her if it hurts too much. I can't imagine your pain. But…I never got the chance to tell you something."

Tiffany looked at her and saw respect in her eyes.

"Your leaving here to spend those last few months with your mom? So loving, Tiffany." And then Ren must have sensed that Tiffany couldn't talk without crying, because she swiftly changed the subject. "So has your health been all right through all of this?"

"The diabetes?" Tiffany shrugged. "Pretty much the same. No better, no worse. It's just a way of life, and as long as I get my shots on time, I'm fine."

Ren tucked a long stray lock of her dark hair back into her ponytail. "I'll bet you never expected to see Jeremy and me working at Ledo's, huh?"

Tiffany gave her a weak smile. "Yeah, what's up with that?"

"School fundraiser. Most of the people working tonight are teachers from our school. We're working for free, and Ledo's is contributing fifty percent of the night's profits to the school. A bunch of the clientele tonight is from our school."

Tiffany's eyes wandered to Ren's massive stomach. "I can't believe they're letting you work here like that!"

"Why not?" Ren laughed and gently rested her hand on top of her tummy. "I'm pregnant, not radioactive."

"But you're huge!"

Ren looked down and smiled at her abdomen. "Twin girls."

Tiffany's cell phone rang, and she looked at the ID. "Oh, good. It's the gym about my job."

"You mind if I stay here awhile?" Ren pressed her hands against the small of her back.

"No, stay. This shouldn't take long." She answered the call. "Hi, Mickey. Thanks for calling back so soon."

But as he began to speak and she heard the frown in Mickey's voice, her own spirits fell.

"But I left to care for my dying mother, Mickey!" Tiffany said. "Do they know why I left?" *Don't cry. Do not cry.*

Tiffany glanced at Ren but had to look away. Those kind eyes were going to break her down right in the middle of this restaurant. She finished the call with Mickey and stared at the wine-colored carpet, willing her heart to slow down.

A couple of waiters passed by on their way to the kitchen. Ren broke the silence. "How can I help, Tiffany?"

Tiffany looked at her. "They replaced me. I don't have a job."

Ren sighed. "Oh, Tiffany. That's not right." After a pause, she began again. "Listen, Tru and I don't have much, but we could help you out financially for a while—"

"Oh, no, that's not really a problem." Tiffany couldn't help the little rush of appreciation she felt. "Thanks, though. Mama left me a little money." She frowned. "I took the job for granted, that's all. I'm a little disoriented."

"But there are other gyms, right?"

Tiffany nodded. "Sure, sure. I just need to get my thoughts together. I've been so distracted by my mom and then making sure Daddy was going to be okay when I left. He's been so lonely. I've just had a lot on my mind and wasn't expecting my circumstances here to change. And I do have my mortgage on the condo, so I—"

As if given an electric shock, Ren sat upright and gasped. "Tiffany! I know what you should do!"

Her enthusiasm made Tiffany chuckle. "You do, huh?"

"Absolutely!" Ren put her hand on Tiffany's arm, and this time the gesture didn't bother Tiffany. "You should take a couple of weeks at the beach house."

"The what? What's the beach house?"

Ren sighed and looked up with a dreamy expression. "Mission Beach. In San Diego. Tru and I spent a fantastic week there a couple of months ago, and I've been raving about it ever since."

"Fancy, is it?"

Ren snorted in laughter. "Not exactly. Compared to the houses around it, it's the ugly-but-lovable child in the group."

"Then what's the big deal?"

"Did I mention it's in *San Diego?* Come on! Gorgeous weather every day.

The locals are cool. The guy who lives next door is this charming Scot—you'll love him—and the house is right on the beach, and—" She stopped to take and expel an ecstatic breath. "You've just got to go, Tiffany."

Tiffany raised her eyebrows and cocked her head.

"To get your thoughts together, like you said."

Tiffany laughed. "What, are you on commission with the rental company or something?"

She was suddenly aware of someone behind the counter.

Jeremy patted the top of the pizza box he held. "One plain pizza, ready to go." His behavior was still friendly but distant. Yes, he had obviously recalled their brief meeting in the gym all those months ago.

"Hey, Jeremy," Ren said. "Tiffany's got a flat tire waiting for her out there. Do you think you could be a gent and change it for her?"

Tiffany looked quickly from Ren to Jeremy. Man, nothing like putting him on the spot.

He hesitated for only a second or two. He untied the chef's apron from his waist. "Righto." He picked up Tiffany's pizza, came out from behind the counter, and gestured for Tiffany to leave ahead of him. "After you."

Tiffany harrumphed inwardly. He *might* have been after her, had he not remembered who she was. Everything had seemed so romantic for those few minutes on the bus. Now she had to suffer the consequences of her own bad behavior of the past. And what should it matter, anyway? She needed to focus on getting a job, not a boyfriend.

She stepped in front of him, and her heel finally fell completely off her shoe. With the sudden, four-inch drop to the floor, she nearly lost her balance. The spastic jerk she did with her other leg and both her arms kept her upright but thoroughly goofy looking. As an added bonus, she punched Jeremy in the chest with her elbow when she jerked her arm back.

"Oh, I'm so sorry!" She turned to catch him grimacing, teeth clenched. He rubbed the center of his chest.

He quickly regained his composure. "Not a problem. Really."

Ren said, "You'd better get those shoes off, Tiffany, before you hurt yourself."

"Yeah." Tiffany bent down abruptly, which Jeremy obviously hadn't expected. He only took one step forward, but that was enough to bang into Tiffany's backside and send her further off balance and falling forward.

Jeremy cried out something that *may* have been a British swear word.

When he lunged to catch her, he put his entire body into it and simply furthered her momentum. The two of them sailed forward in graceless symmetry, like two geese coming in for a landing. They finally stopped by crashing, face first and momentarily entangled, against the opposite wall. It was as if a tightly strung catapult had launched them as one. Neither was significantly hurt, because Tiffany's upended pizza box formed a cushion between them and the wall.

"Blasted twit!" Jeremy straightened up and unsuccessfully tried to catch the pizza box. It fell, half-opened, to the floor.

"Well, I don't think I'm *totally* to blame for this!" Tiffany yanked off her shoes. She nearly started crying, so she charged out of the restaurant. Before the door closed, she heard a sputtering attempt at communication from Jeremy, along with Ren's admonition to him.

She tiptoed gingerly across the cool asphalt, trying to avoid anything that might hurt her feet. She had been through enough today.

Jeremy ran out behind her. "Tiff!"

She quickly dabbed away a few tears, stiffening her posture in the process.

"I didn't mean *you* were the twit," he called.

She turned to face him.

Jeremy rubbed the back of his neck. It was almost too dark to tell, but Tiffany thought he might be blushing.

"I was talking about myself. I should have watched where I was going." After a resigned sigh, he put his hand out to her. "Truce?"

Accepting apologies was not something Tiff had much experience with. But she was working on that—along with what seemed like a thousand other things. She took his warm hand and shook it. "Truce." She opened her car, threw her broken shoes inside, and retrieved her gym sneakers. Great. She would be elegance personified, wearing these with her little black pencil skirt.

He smiled. "I believe I owe you a Hawaiian pizza, hold the ham and pineapple. Why don't you go back in and order another, my treat. I'll get this tire changed while you wait. And tell Ren we've kissed and made up. She's worried."

Tiffany refrained from making a bold comment about the kissing and making up—yet another thing she was working on. And God seemed to be lending a hand in that area, too, with all the doggone blushing and shyness she kept experiencing.

"Thanks." She gave him her keys and turned to tiptoe back to Ledo's, her sneakers dangling from her hand. She suddenly felt happy. Hopeful. And far more confident. She might be unemployed, but coming home may have been a blessing after all.

She looked over her shoulder and couldn't help but exercise her most innocently flirtatious eyelash flutter. "You need a ride home after slaving away here? I'd love to return the favor."

He opened the trunk of her Corolla, matched her smile, and brought her mood swiftly back to earth.

"No worries. I've got it covered. My girlfriend's due here any moment."

The Beach House Series

(based on an original concept by Sally John)

THE BEACH HOUSE—*Sally John*

Jo, Andie, Char, and Molly—friends since they were nine years old—reunite to celebrate their fortieth birthdays at a Southern California beach house. As they recall the past and reconnect in the present, the women find hope and faith for their futures.

CASTLES IN THE SAND—*Sally John*

The wife of a well-known and popular pastor, Susan Starr feels torn apart by her unmarried daughter's surprise pregnancy and her husband's reaction to it. In the weeks that follow, the Starr family discovers God's amazing mercy and love even as their foundations begin to crumble.

BEACH DREAMS—*Trish Perry*

Tiffany seeks rest for her body and soul at a cozy beach house in San Diego. The warm sun and good-looking boy-next-door help her find comfort for her heart and hope for her future.

SUNSET BEACH—*Trish Perry*

In the popular Beach House series, a worn and comfortable coastal home in San Diego intersects with charming, contemporary stories. Trish Perry returns to the beloved backdrop for a story of family secrets, gifts of forgiveness and faith, and the amazing things that happen when women gather.

Other Books by Trish Perry

The Guy I'm Not Dating

Kara Richardson vows to stop dating until God leads her—and *then* she meets handsome Gabe Paolino. Is it perfect or tragic timing? This funny tale explores the adventure of living and loving by faith.

Too Good to Be True

Brokenhearted Rennie Young meets Truman "Tru" Sayers after fainting at a super store. Despite their unromantic start, true love could be in the future. But can Ren trust her heart and God again?

…from a sliver of brass

Book One
THE LAND OLD, UNTOUCHED

ADVENT
OF THE ROAR

a folk tale by BENJAMIN M PIETY

Approsh.

First Printing, 2018

ISBN 978-1984136091

An introduction to the

ADVENT OF THE ROAR

I met Bernard Babek in the strangest of ways, but despite the unusual circumstance, he welcomed me with generosity, kindness, and a compassionate smile. He was one of the bravest persons I ever had the pleasure of knowing.

He was a good man.

When we encountered each other all those years ago, Bernard's heart was heavy as an uncertain decision pressed on his thoughts. One that would have grave and lasting consequences, for him and all of those he loved. But our meeting is, perhaps, a story for another time.

This tale instead begins in the peaceful and lush green state of Radiba where Bernard lived a simple life as a night gardener. A tale set in a Land with a language and governance all its own filled with adventure in places far from home.

A tale that opens in the thick of a hunt and the brewing of a storm.

Enjoyments,

CONTENTS

FOR NINA
with whom there was coffee, giant pancakes, & courage

BERNARD

Chapter One
THE NEOX

*B*ernard ignores the first raindrop that hits the large frontz leaf next to his ear, and instead aims a worn, modified rifle between the shoulder blades of a neox standing only six strides in front of him. Scavenging alone in the Radiba Forest, the five-foot-tall four-legged frek rummages with a long, headless neck into a blue brackleberry bush, pressing its snout between the leaves and folding a circular mouth around a trio of seeded fruits. This peaceful major breaks when the clouds that had throughout the afternoon rumbled with distant thunder, and now hide on the upper side of a thickly branched canopy, cool and condense into a substantial rain.

As droplets hit the sizable neox's matted brown hair, it bolts. *Don't run, you little frek*, Bernard thinks. Within minors, the storm strengthens, and the rain proliferates into the crash and smash of a torrential downpour, masking the neox's silent crosscut through trees and bramble. Bernard lifts his brown leather hood, streaming a thin rivulet of water across his face, before stepping over to the brackleberry bush, pushing it aside, and discovering a set of triangular hoofprints pressed into the fresh mud.

Hunting neox is laborious work, as not only are they quick as snips but they're also engineered with keen senses of smell and hearing. To double, their fragile anatomy requires that their pursuer sends them left with a single round of ammunition—a single shot after hours if not days of tracking and patiently waiting for precise timing. Missing the neox means the timid frek will run thirty sometimes forty miles in a single effort; and because they're scavengers, they don't return to a shelter or cave or nest where a hunter could set traps. And this isn't the worst of things; neox also never sleep and instead exist in a constant state of panicked paranoia brought on by the gentle snap of a twig, the crunch of dry leaves, or the innocence of rain. All these factors culminate into a hunt that extends beyond rational judgment, beyond a normal friend's exhaustion, and a hunt that often ends in painful futility.

Setting hardships through dense landscape and time aside, the neox, unlike other dangerous freks, exudes a placid temperament, minimizing the probability of a counterattack. Adding a reward of delectable and easily stored provisions, nearly a month's worth, makes the difficult chase perhaps a touch more appealing. For centuries, many have attempted neox husbandry, but attempts to tame and domesticate these fickle beasts failed within a single generation. These elements combine to draw out even the most cynical of hunters' desire for pride and power and braggart's rights. And the rare appearance of these headless freks, especially for a Radibian like Bernard, is thought to bring great luck or great misfortune, hinging on the outcome of the hunt. *So don't give up now...*

As night approaches, the rain continues to thump with the sound of a thick-barreled drum pounding on the overgrown canopy. This shift and hug of dark clouds fade the natural emerald forest into a sodden gloom, creating unknown figures in the surrounding trees. The howl of the storm amplifies the pressure to find the hidden neox, as Bernard believes it won't be long before the frek steals away forever. He attempts to follow the hoofprints, but the trail begins to slosh together in the relentless pitter-patter. His instinct at this point is to light a frontz torch to illuminate the forest, but he knows this will only frighten the fearful neox even further. Instead, he waits for his eyes to adjust to the increasing darkness, relying on hope and some of that foretold neox luck.

After eighteen hours, the bit of granola Bernard had shoved in his pockets as he'd run after the neox is long gone, and his stomach rumbles in hunger. And then, with a set of prints untouched by the rain ahead, he is back on the neox's trail. He pushes through the leaves, through the vociferous storm, beginning to wonder what in Lincoln he's doing here.

Bernard thinks of Jame back at their haynest and of the likely ringing of incessant whines through the halls as Jame lies upright and alone in their master, waiting for Bernard to answer. Waiting for Bernard to come to his aid only to entreat for a mug of water or peck of food. When Bernard first caught sight of the neox the night before, without a minor's hesitation, he stood, ran inside, grabbed a rifle and a once packed rucksack for a trip south they never took, and yelled out to Jame that he would return in a major.

He didn't wait for an answer.

Even with a pinge of guilt for Jame, coupled with the creak and groan of an aging body without proper rest, it was surprising to Bernard that the whole of the hunt had been unexpectedly moving. For some time, Bernard's life has been an endless routine: waking up; making mornmeal; taking quiet solo treks through the forest; returning haynest to a mindless novit or tabletop game of Raising Jarjers with Jame, a game he's notoriously terrible at; then falling asleep. Boredom and small living have become a constant companion of their—

Bernard halts.

Ahead in the forest, standing between two dark trees, the neox, its attention riveted on Bernard, its headless neck aiming in his direction. The neox waits motionlessly as if attempting to catch the slightest sound or faint scent of its pursuer.

Bernard remains still, unable to cope with an eighteen-hour loss should the neox decide to take off again. He peeks to his west and finds a nearby tree to take cover behind. The *thump thump thump* of rain plops against some of the bigger leaves above, marking the rhythm of his heartbeat.

The neox, uncharacteristically, steps toward Bernard. In turn, Bernard raises his gun, knowing it's unwise to shoot the neox in its neck or one of its legs. Shooting a neox anywhere other than between its shoulder blades ruins a significant portion of the meat, which, after these endless hours, is not an acceptable outcome. *If only it would pass me; I could take it out with my knife.* Bernard counter steps the neox as it continues pressing forward, creating a slow motion and unintended dance through the brush while the neox's bobbing neck remains fixed in the center of his rifle's crosshair. Fog rolls in around them as the neox stops only under four strides away.

Bernard sinks into the wet dirt, and as he lifts his leg, his mud-covered foot produces a loud *slurp*. This sudden sound catches the neox's attention, its neck craning to follow it. *Why aren't you running, little frek?* Lightning illuminates the dark russet trunks around them, followed by distant reverberations of thunder, signs of a strengthening storm. The neox continues to plod closer, and as it does, the end of its neck opens, exposing a slick, salivating mouth and rows of gnarled flat teeth. Another lightning strike exposes the inside of the neox's black throat and two piercing red eyes staring back at Bernard. The flash of this horrific absurdist sight gone as the forest reverts to darkness.

The neox pounces.

Bernard stumbles backward in shock, his arms bracing for the massive frek's impact. It knocks him to the ground, causing him to minarily lose his breath. After a brief stagger, the neox curves its long neck toward Bernard, attempting to bite him. Bernard struggles a minor to free his hands from beneath the heavy frek and instinctively grabs for its thick, wet neck, holding the neox back as it *snaps snaps* at him, hot spittle dripping onto his face.

The rain continues descending on them, making it difficult to breathe without water running up his nose and into his mouth. Thunder claps. He wrestles the massive neox that fights with doubled ferociousness with each passing minor. Its behavior is erratic with an unruly, almost zealous need to devour.

The neox shifts and Bernard edges from underneath it, gaining an advantage. He reaches for his fallen rifle, which is made more difficult with the relentless snapping and the deluge dulling his senses. His heart beats wildly. *This can't be the end, not by a neox. I want to see Jame again.* One hand continues to hold the neox's chomping mouth away while the other barely fingers the rifle.

Lightning strikes.

Snap snap.

Closer.

The gun tips away.

Shnite! The neox thrusts itself forward, throwing off Bernard's hold. He rolls the neox toward the rifle, finally wrapping his hand around the weapon. The neox stands and shakes itself in the rain, bending its neck to attack. It opens its mouth, emitting a silent roar, as it is unable to produce sounds. The minor, guided by hateful rain, turns surreal.

Bernard faces the neox, and in a flash of lightning, its red glowering eyes become visible once more down inside its throat. With the butt of his rifle and one sharp motion, he bats the neox across its neck. The frek slams against a nearby tree, dropping noiselessly to the ground. The intensity of the fight draws still as the rains continue around them. Bernard takes deep exhausted breaths as he reaches for a knife carried in his waist belt and, without hesitation, stabs the unconscious neox between its shoulder blades.

❖ ❖ ❖

It takes over an hour to find a nearby station at which to rest, as the dragging of the neox and the constant miserable rain slow his pace considerably. Ahead, Bernard encounters a small cave carved out long ago from a lesser hillside in the forest. Inside, he plops the muddy neox down before starting a fire from some hideaway flint and steel.

Now a bed to sleep in. He scans the small cave, hoping for one already assembled by other passing travelers, but the cave lies vacant and undiscovered. Instead, he'll need to gather large frontz leaves fallen from the upper canopy and fold them into a makeshift sleeping pad. The raging storm outside will make this quite the chore, and Bernard considers just sleeping on the hard surface. After stomping the dirt, however, he thinks better of it. He's wet already, and a good night's rest far outweighs a reluctance to face the rain. And so, he sets out.

Many majors later, he returns with a few dozen wet frontz leaves, most for the bed, but a few he'll use for torches to explore deeper into the cave and for a bit of wrapping for the neox once he finishes dressing it. He sits cross-legged and begins folding the leaves vertically, laying each, almost six feet long, on the cavern floor before slicing them across the middle to their centerfold. He takes another and repeats the process, placing this new doubled leaf between the first. With every third or fourth layer, Bernard fastens first the top, then the bottom halves together. In this way, he continues, back and forth and back and forth, folding and cutting until he's fashioned a woven bed, thirty layers thick. He sets the tied frontz leaf pile close to the fire to desiccate while he continues his other tasks.

The soft crackle of flames serves as a nice respite, coaxing Bernard's eyes to sag with fatigue as cold water drips from his black jeans and brown leather jacket. He reaches up to squeeze the rain from his long hair but abruptly remembers it's no longer there. Jame had insisted on giving him a haircut only a few days before he'd taken off after the neox, commenting that his long tail of hair would get caught on something or send him left in some terrible way. *He's as nervous as a neox.* His cropped scalp feels queer in his hand, like a young boy's, though a quick glance at his wrinkled skin contrasts the thought.

Across the fire, the stiff corpse of the neox waits. Bernard knows it won't be long before its sent stench draws in decomps, a swarm of little clicking, clumping black festatars, that even a raging storm cannot prevent from arriving.

Taking a few more frontz leaves and wrapping them around a thick handheld branch, Bernard lights a makeshift torch, turning to the inner cave and exposing a small tunnel. He steps over to it, the walls glittering in the golden-yellow torchlight, and as he continues through, the path grades downward ever so slightly, and the sound of the storm fades. After he walks a few hundred strides, the route opens into a large, round chamber.

The light of his torch flickers across the room, and upon closer examination the walls exhibit a rough natural stone with hints of faded crystalline rock. A few thick stalactites hang above him, and one looks to be a perfect hanging post for the neox. Bernard points the torch down a pair of outlier paths on the other side of the room, revealing nothing but long tunnels of darkness.

Innate curiosity charges him to explore each of them, but he knows that the distraction will only cost him the neox. Grudgingly, he returns through the narrow tunnel to his modest fire flickering in the night. He checks on the bed, almost dry from the heat of the flames. Sleep becomes a hungry frek. Rain spills along the upper mouth of the cave like an erratic waterfall as he drags the neox on the long trudge back to the inner room.

Endless majors later, sweating, tired, and half asleep, he drops the neox and sets his torch on the ground, lighting the cave. He pulls a silver anchor from his waist belt and attaches it to the tip of his rifle. With careful aim, the crosshair focused on his chosen stalactite, he pulls the trigger, hearing a sharp *thunk* as the anchor penetrates the stone. He pulls out a silk rope, already looped with a small metal stub, and tosses it into the air near the secured anchor. It misses at first, but after another try, it catches on a magnetic attraction with a crisp *shink*. He flicks the line in his hand until the metal stub falls through a tiny hole in the anchor. It sinks, and he takes the fallen end, yanking back on each side as hard as he's able to test its hold. It does.

Bernard digs through his bag, pulls out a small peg, and then hammers it into the dirt with the butt of his rifle. He then drags the neox over, tying the hanging rope around its neck like a noose. The knot here will need to be extra secure, as there's no head to catch the loop if it starts to slide. Confident the neox is ready, he pulls on the rope, grunting and cursing as he lifts the massive and cumbersome frek.

He proceeds to raise it farther, inch by inch. At times, it slips in his hand. He curses again. Once the neox is a foot above the ground, he wrangles and ties the pulled end of the rope to the hammered peg and lets the whole pulley system go. As he tenses in anticipation of the hanger failing, the neox swings in the dim light, its shadow cast tall across the cavern walls. He wipes his brow and catches his breath.

With a penknife in hand, Bernard steadies the neox's swing and then measures with his fingers, starting from where its neck begins, about eight fingers down. He sticks the knife into its fur, and as he slices downward, thick red blood oozes out, and its organs and intestines spill into the shadowy darkness, plopping onto the dirt in wet clumps. The stench of the neox fills the air, burning the hair of his nostrils.

As scavengers, neox eat a range of food, from any number of brackleberries to rotten vegetation, and if they ever find a patch of fungi, they'll eat the entire growth, which is evident in the sour smell emitting from this one's innards. Bernard continues to pierce deeper past the neox's duodenum, cutting and sawing away nearby bone. At one point, he accidentally punctures its bladder, and a putrid urine sprays over him. He steps back, coughing and holding back vomit, elbow to mouth. *Marked by a sent frek.*

Something scurries past the corner of his eye. He turns to the empty room, the torch flickering and casting new shadows across the walls. The emptiness feels ominous as he turns the knife in his hand for defense, scanning the chamber for movement. He steps over to the two tunnels he found earlier and screams into one, attempting to scare away whatever might be hiding down in the darkness.

Nothing stirs.

He turns back to the neox and catches a small red frek digging into the pile of innards beneath it. Bernard calls out, "Heyo!" He stomps over, shooing the frek off. It runs a few strides and then turns, standing on its tiny hind legs, no more than a foot tall. *Must be a creshwillow.*

With someone to talk to, Bernard speaks to the tiny frek. "I'll give you what remains when I finish. Bargain?"

The creshwillow tilts its head, standing in wait. Bernard returns to the neox and starts to cut back into it, and as he does, the creshwillow becomes more daring, stepping closer to him and the neox. At first, Bernard attempts to scare him away, stamping his foot at the small frek, forcing it to run back two strides before stopping and standing back on its hind legs. After a time, the persistence of the creshwillow begins to grind Bernard down until he's too tired to care. So as he skins the neox, below him the creshwillow gleefully chews and eats at its bowels, particularly a long pile of small intestines.

The dressing continues for the next hour until Bernard sets aside enough meat to make the whole affair worth it. The creshwillow is curled up asleep on the other side of the room, and Bernard, needing to gather a few more frontz leaves to wrap the last bits of meat, attempts to leave the cavern without waking it.

At the cave's entrance, a cold sunrise peeks through the foggy, storming forest. The rainstorm has let up some but still pours with a constant, unwavering persistence. Bernard leaves the cave and gathers more leaves.

It takes another half hour before he returns. At the entrance of the narrow tunnel, he finds the creshwillow standing on its hind legs in wait. It turns its head as Bernard approaches.

"Did you take any of my meat, Brute?"

It tilts its head without answer. He walks past it and makes his way back down the cavern path, creshwillow in tow. In the cavern room, over a dozen more creshwillows, each varying in size, wander about. Some are small, some are fat, others extra furry.

"You brought friends?"

He turns to the creshwillow following him, who reacts by bouncing and jumping into the room full of scampering, hairy freks that fill it with a cacophony of whimpering noises. None, *approshed,* seem interested in the neox muscle he's piled nearby. He watches a few gritting over the neox's bloody carcass and leftover innards that are scattered across the cavern floor. Gently pushing the soft, fuzzy creshwillows aside, he begins to wrap the ignored portions of meat in his gathered leaves. One of the creshwillows hops onto his back to get to a higher ledge. It fails and flops to the ground, shaking its head. Bernard ignores them, annoyed more than angry.

"All right, friends, the rest is yours."

They all stop and stare at him, confused and curious. He shakes his head, waves them off, and gathers the large stack of wrapped meat, heading for the exit. As he steps out of the room, one of the creshwillows behind him hollers, startling him. He turns, catching the other freks padding away from the whimpering creshwillow. Below it, a small object reflects the light. Bernard sets the meat down and walks over, picking up the dropped item. He dusts away a bit of dirt and finds a sliver of metal, which he turns over in his hand. It's roughly a thumb's length with sharp, chipped ends, blood from the neox or creshwillow coating it. For no reason, he pockets the sliver and turns back, taking the meat and leaving the pack of creshwillows behind. After a minor, he hears them return to their feast, the whole affair forgotten.

Finished, Bernard seeks his long-awaited night's rest, ignoring the sunlight beginning to light the cave. He starts a new fire, warms his hands, and sprawls out along the warm, soft bed. It crunches beneath him as it wraps around his body. Before dozing off, he pulls the sliver of metal from his pocket. It flickers in the fire and sunlight pouring in from outside the cave. The sliver appears to be made of brass. *I wonder if this was in that neox?* He puts it away.

It may be due to the fact that it's been over two days since he's last closed his eyes, but he compliments himself on the softest bed he's ever made and falls fast to sleep.

Chapter Two
A PROTNUK'S RIDDLE

A hooded figure dressed in green slips out into the rain as Bernard opens his eyes. With strained effort, he catches the figure disappear out of sight to the east. Body sore, he props himself up on an elbow and scans the room. Remnants of the night's fire emit a thin trail of smoke while rain, pattering across the mouth of the cave, breaks up midmorn rays reaching through a thin fog rolling between the trees. But the sight that calms him after this sudden awakening is the neox meat still piled neatly at the foot of his sunken frontz-leaf bed.

Bernard sits up, rubbing his old hands, stretching the muscles of his face, cracking his neck, and turning his head in a circle. *You're getting too old for these young-man travels,* he imagines Jame stating when he ultimately returns haynest, a sentiment, though true, that's worn tiresome.

For as long as he can recall, Bernard has stood by Jame, and because of this, only in the rarest of circumstances has he been able to explore the greater Land around him. The routine paths that circle their simple haynest have long since lost their original luster, and his half-day treks have grown stale with predictability. The thought that the last thirty-six hours have been the most exciting thing that's chanced him in the past few decades carries with it an unexpected agitation and disappointment.

With the neox meat packed after a small slice is cut off to curb his morning hunger and his rucksack slung across his back,

Bernard walks to the edge of the cave, placing a hand on its roof. He surveys the surrounding forest, with rain and fog eddying among the trees. In the mud below, a pair of wet boot prints have been pressed in by the green-hooded figure. Curiosity creeps in as he wonders who might have been in the cave while he slept, though the temporary enigmit breaks as he concludes it was likely only a friend taking shelter from the rain. Since they left his well-earned neox meat alone, thinking too much about their presence seems superfluous. Even so, with Radiba's state population being fewer than a thousand, the sight of another in these far-flung forests is worth noting.

The fleeting thought of the hooded friend shifts to the two dark tunnels in the large chamber behind him. Perhaps whatever conundra they hold is what first led the green-hooded one to the cave, and this thought—investigating the tunnels himself—takes actual hold.

Though never a full-fledged explorer, Bernard considers himself to be a spontaneous Radibian, a trait that at times has gotten him into bits of trouble, specifically when he was younger. He once traversed beyond the Radiba state line and into Carvinga, coming face to face with a tenfooter. A mistake he's long regretted after narrowly escaping the tall friend and hobbling home with a busted hand and broken leg. On long, cold winter nights, his hand aches in remembrance.

Ignoring Jame's position on the matter, he decides heading out into the storm seems the less-advisable of two options, and so Bernard turns around with a pinge of guilt, knowing he's following desire over duty. He pulls a couple of frontz leaves from the homemade bed and wraps them around his torch, lighting it once more for the dark cave ahead.

❖ ❖ ❖

Bernard moves through the narrow tunnel as he attempts to defend his unusual behavior. With his routine upended, the further he withdraws from it, the more unwilling he is to return to what became the usual, even at the cost of Jame's wrath. His imaginings of Jame have transformed from a partner who's merely curious about his goings-on to a partner who requires a full-on explanation of this adolescent attitude. Why did he wander for over two days chasing some frek through the wilderness? And why is he now traversing some unexplored cavern when he should be heading haynest?

This internal debate slows his walk for a minor as he questions the impulse to investigate the twofold tunnels. Another roll of thunder echoes through the cave, causing his indecisiveness to worsen as the ceaseless rain, rolling fog, and cracks of lightning suggest not the passing of a thunderstorm but rather an approaching tormisand.

Unlike a storm that lasts for an afternoon or evening, tormisands tend to persist for longer periods of time, upward of weeks, months, or sometimes years, and the first real sign of a thunderstorm evolving into a tormisand is the fog that rolls in. A tormisand marks its territory by sitting atop its prey, hammering the Land until there's hardly anything left. And after these weeks of rain and storm and fog, on some arbitrary major, the tormisand will escalate into a row of considerable squalls, testing the foundations of its target's architecture, which is already softened by the previous rains. This constant barrage forces most friends to build haynests inside rooted, unmovable hills and large trees.

The prolonged, tortuous tormisands are a relatively recent phenomenon, and their first appearance happened only three hundred years ago. Before they arrived, Radibians lived peacefully along the state's shoreline and out on the small Radiba Isles, a region once considered one of the most tranquil paradimos of the Land. But after the first few tormisands ruined haynests and livelihoods, a migration into the uncharted Highlands transpired, where, unlike on the flat shores and open isles, the torrents and winds were diminished in the thick forests and stony mountains. Since this migration, no one risks living anywhere other than in the Highlands.

Following days of destructive squalls proceeds what Radibians have come to call the Peace Hours. A period the naive might assume marks the end of the tormisand, when in truth it only marks its first half. This stillness, where rain and fog and wind completely disappear, where the sky is blue and clear and calm, will last twenty or thirty hours. Then the Peace Hours end, and like clockwork, the second half of the tormisand persists as the first, only in reverse: first the squalls; then the lightning and thunder; and gradually the rain, which fades to less and less in its waning hours.

Because the winds following the Peace Hours arrive so suddenly, Radibians designed a warning system that's installed outside haynests and along many of the trails throughout the Highlands that alerts passersby of the precipitous approach of the tormisand's second half. Hearing these warning whistles across the forest demands immediate shelter.

Shaking off the fear of a tormisand, Bernard finds the cavern room now quieter than it was the previous night. In the dim and shadowed light of his torch, he regards the hanging neox: slaughtered and skinned, picked bone dry by the drum of creshwillows, now gone. Walking to the other side of the room, he aims his torch down each of the two tunnels, finding shadow and equivalent marks of time and age in both, giving no reason to choose one over the other. He decides to take the west tunnel, based only on the fact that it's somewhat larger than the other.

The walls here are similar in texture to the chamber's, with spotted crystallinity glittering against his torchlight. The path winds in on itself, curving downward and to the west, and soon forms tiny steps. He focuses the light toward the ground and discovers the steps are carved into a rough staircase. This puts a smile on his face. *What could possibly be down here?*

As Bernard continues downward along the now full-fledged and winding staircase, a small draft brushes against his skin, rippling the flame of his torch. The stairs straighten, and around fifty strides ahead, he sees hints of light coming from an archway. The sight quickens his steps, making him eager to see what's on the other side. The wind strengthens as he steps closer to the entrance, and soon he catches the first glimpse of a considerable vista.

Through the arch, a grand stone bridge spans thirty strides wide, crossing a chasm that looks to be a hundred measures deep and two or three hundred across. Looking up and to the east, Bernard sees where a narrow opening in the cave ceiling permits a shaft of light, fragmented by incoming rain, to illuminate the enormous expanse. To the west, a formidable waterfall pours in from an unseen stream a hundred measures above and the whole of the room echoes its wallop into the darkness and rocks below. Across the bridge, another archway leads into a darkened turnaway.

Bernard strolls across the bridge, taking in the beautiful, remarkable exhibition, and upon reaching the other side, he finds the archway here is marked by long scratches in the stone, which don't appear to have been made by conventional tools or machinery. Rubbing his fingers along them, he discovers they dig deep into the rock.

Bernard continues through the arch, which leads into a long and narrow hallway. At first, the turnaway appears to be the same in design, with stone floors and crystalline walls, but occasionally along the ground, skeletal remains lie in small piles. Bones and skulls. Light from the waterfall and bridge room is faded here, and he yields to the limit of his torchlight flickering no more than ten strides in front of him.

The hallway continues, stone after stone, a uniformity that is broken only by the occasional stack of bones. Ahead, a tiny squeal that resembles the sound of a creshwillow seizes Bernard's attention. *Must be a nesting ground, which explains the piles of bones.* He pushes a pile over with his foot. Dust clouds around it. *Been here a long time.* Though the creshwillows act friendly enough, the sight and sound of little hidden freks slow his travel. From early readings, he's sure that creshwillows don't attack the living, but he's not certain how they will react when someone invades their nesting ground; and after what was supposed to be a peaceful neox attacking him the night before, he's not too confident he can rely on the suppositions of frek behavior.

The hallway stops and opens into a sizable square room with each wall carved in ornate reliefs. The scenes depicted are worn with time and difficult to discern in the low torchlight. A few look as if smaller-shaped friends cower before much larger ones. The light picks up half a hundred creshwillows in various states of sleep, some of which squeal and scratch in kiptales. Though a few rest on top of each other, most are scattered about the room alone.

Across from him, on the other side of the chamber and at the edge of his light, he sees a black throne. It looks to be made of polished and sculpted onyx. An odd double to the room, which appears more comfortable in stonework and natural formations. He decides to push his luck with the peaceful creshwillows and investigate the throne closer. As he walks, he catches a glimpse of the ceiling and a series of starscapes engineered from mined and purposely set crystalline rocks.

Drawing closer, Bernard finds that unlike the whole of this cave and the hallways and staircases leading up to it, the throne is in near-perfect condition, without a scratch or mark to show its age. Moving his torch up and down the slick black stone, he notes that the throne appears almost entirely unused, and, what he finds most peculiar, it emits heat.

He reaches out, and just as he touches it, he hears a polite cough behind him. He spins and finds standing before him a short, stout man dressed in uniform purple, with wild gray hair. His eyes are pure white without a hint of pupils. The little man smirks before speaking in a soft and friendly voice.

"Looking for something important?"

Unsure where the man appeared from, Bernard takes a small step backward as a few of the creshwillows wake up around them, stretching and yawning. One hops up, sits on the short man's shoulder, and picks through his hair.

The man in purple steps closer, his eyes unsettling. "What color do you see?"

"Apory?"

"The throne. What color do you see?"

Bernard turns back to the throne, wondering if there is some trick, if it would not be there. It sits in wait. In silence.

Turning back, he answers, "Black?"

"Black?"

The small man's eyes widen as he steps closer still. Bernard counters the movement, preparing to exit quickly should the need arise. More of the creshwillows wake and watch the two friends chat.

"How delightful that you see black." The man starts forward and sits on the throne. "To me, it's constructed in stone. Dulled by age like the walls around us. You don't see all this green moss?" As he speaks, the man pinches near one of the throne's arms (that isn't there), extracts a strand of moss (that isn't there), and fiddles with it in his fingers before dropping the invisible plant to the floor. "Back to my original question, looking for something important?"

Humbly, Bernard answers, "I was just delaying going back out into the tormisand. I'm not looking forward to wading in the rain again."

"Ah, a bit of an explorer then?"

"I wouldn't say that." He smiles politely, creeping backward toward the exit of the chamber and putting more distance between himself and the small man on the throne.

"It's nice to meet you after so many years. Do you live near?"

"So many years?" Bernard questions before continuing, "I do not. I live south of the Lothatin." His eyes dart to either side of the room as the creshwillows look on in curiosity and hunger. "I again appize to have intruded on your haynest. It was wrong of me."

"What's your curam, young man?"

"Young man? That's kind. My curam is Bernard."

"Zabjed here."

Bernard nods, stepping closer still to the exit.

"Don't you want to know why you see a black throne when all we see is a stone one?" Zabjed questions. Bernard, untrusting, fears the man in purple may be something more malevolent than he's let on. "It's all a riddle you know. What a man sees. The one who sees this throne as black is a valor. A Dark Valor." Zabjed says this as he stands up and on the throne. He grins widely.

"Sounds grim."

"Oh, it doesn't have to be. I could help you see more. Help you understand why . . ."

"While I am approshed of your kindness, I think it would be best if I'm on my way."

"Come now, Bernard, aren't we all friends in Radiba? And you so graciously fed my little creshwillows. How happy they were when they came to me this morn."

"Of no worries. There's no reason to let neox go to waste."

"That's the Radiba spirit. Fully engage our nature." Zabjed flops back down onto the throne, his legs slung over its side and resting on invisible arms. "Before you say anything. You should know it was not the exarmadasis." He pauses, as if . . . *sad.*

For Bernard, the words are lost against the curiosities of the unseen throne. *It's not safe here.* Bernard turns to leave, attempting to gesture goodbye and feign careful respect. "A fateful sun moon then."

At this parting remark, Zabjed's attitude changes and his casual tone lifts. He stands and creeps forward, waving both of his hands at Bernard. He holds up seven disparate fingers and, as he speaks, counts down on them.

"Seven questions of war, answered by seven foretales among a half-dozen natives as mottled as the spectrum." With this, he points to Bernard with one hand while his other remains palm out. "Their bonds to you, however, can be tallied on a solitary hand." Four fingers. "Four objects conceal themselves, while three spheres have a purpose unknown." Two fingers. "When a pair of plots come into debate and execution of each is at a hand, there shall be another single resolution to everything you pursue and how everything shall end."

At this, Bernard has no doubt that Zabjed is a protnuk, a shapeshifter who speaks in nonsense riddles to drive victims mad. Bernard ignores the midfrek's riddle and weighs whether he should run or attempt to leave the protnuk's nest more calmly. The scratches in the stone are the protnuk's. He was correct to think that no tool or machinery could have made those marks, as they were created by the protnuk's purest form: an enormous and fearsome midfrek. The sort of creature more intelligent than your normal frek, but not quite as human. And they're often infused with tricks of word, of logic, and of the Land's known physics. Zabjed grins, bearing previously unseen and sharpened teeth.

"While I've enjoyed this friendly talk, I think it's time I leave. Believe that we are unheard, unseen, my friend." Bernard walks backward, afraid of turning on the protnuk. The creshwillows become restless, the protnuk appearing to draw out their aggression.

The time comes. Bernard runs.

Behind him, he hears the boom and roar of the protnuk transforming, he imagines, into something monstrous. He continues down the long hall, catching sight of the light and bridge ahead. In his fearful run, he kicks piles of bone, some of which knock into his shins and cut through his black jeans. A bass growl builds behind as dust and rubble tumble around him. The protnuk is in pursuit, and if there was any doubt about what it is, it *roars* out.

Jame knew I'd die one day poking my head where it doesn't belong, and here I am with death heaving behind me. Bernard tries to run faster, begging his legs to give him inches more. Finally, he exits through the first archway and arrives at the bridge. The echo of his heartbeat is unmatched by the waterfall and the thumping, rumbling of the midfrek only minors behind him, unseen in the darkness.

He races across the bridge, reaching for his dagger in some useless thought he might be able to use it against what is sure to be a colossal beast. It's then he catches sight of a figure ahead, a handsome woman with dark hair and a crossbow loaded with a flaming bolt aimed at him. No—aimed across the bridge and toward the archway.

He turns around to catch a flash of the protnuk as it abruptly leaps into the air. Its large head is doubled in size by an oversized mouth with multiple rows of teeth the size of fists. Its two pale eyes are as angry and chilling as death. Its abdomen is covered in thick, curling purple fur, and six crooked, thrashing limbs sprout in a patternless arrangement, each bearing piercing claws.

Bernard stumbles back as the protnuk takes a sudden flaming bolt to its abdomen. It falls backward with a loud *thump*, collapsing a segment of the stone bridge. It cries out in fear and anger, attempting to use its half-dozen limbs to climb back upward. Bernard stands, his footing shaken by the crumbling bridge, and uses this minary advantage to deftly draw and aim his rifle. Within minors, he cocks and unloads a double shot between the carnivorous protnuk's eyes, slamming it backward. It loses its hold and tumbles into the darkness below. A major later, the splash of its body hits water and a distant echo crashes up the walls.

"Come on. It won't be down there long."

Bernard turns to see the woman holstering her crossbow as she waves for him to follow. Shaken, but certain she's right, he heads toward her. Together they take the stairs, double steps, toward the exit of the tunnel. As they enter the neox chamber, Bernard stops to catch his breath and bends over with hands on knees.

"Apory, just need a second."

The woman waits, watching the tunnel, her hand ready at her crossbow. "It's wisnok. Catch your breath, old man."

He stands up and smiles. "You saved my life."

"What sort of flam body goes into a protnuk's nest alone?"

Bernard nods his head in agreement. *How would I have known a protnuk was down there?* And then he thinks. The meaningless bridge to nowhere. The odd hallway. The scratch marks. An incongruous throne. *I should have known there was nothing worthwhile traveling down there for. Jame will be happy to hear that. Perhaps the routine is best for me. This kiptale of living an explorer's life is only that: a kiptale.* This thought lies reserved and withdrawn, Bernard unsure he's ready to face its reality.

In a minor, he mumbles, "A bored one, it seems."

She smirks and heads onward while Bernard quietly follows her through the narrow tunnel to the cave entrance and what remains of his frontz bed and the fire pit. The sunshine and rain outside look almost pleasant in comparison to the horrors behind them. Once again, Bernard's explorations have gotten him in trouble and nearly sent left. With a heavy heart, he's learned his lesson, and for the first time in over two days, he is ready to return to Jame.

The woman pulls her hair up into a bun and lifts her green hood. "Good thing you didn't have long hair, that protnuk would have seized it. And you're welcome for the save." She holds out her hand.

"My curam is Sanet."

Chapter Three
WINDS, CALMS, & FIRES

*T*he hike toward Lothatin Bridge, toward home, toward Jame, a hike that distances Bernard from protnuks and exhaustive hunting, manifests itself with ephemeral bliss, softened only by the constant, constant, constant rain. Using the familiar landscapes of the northern Radiba Forest, such as guide marks left on old trees and distinct growths of red and green brackleberry patches, Bernard estimates they are no more than eight hours from his haynest.

Sanet, Bernard finds, is quiet. Her features are young yet studied, and her eyes dart from east to west with curiosity and a permanent suspicion of her surroundings. The idea of something unusual here in the tranquil forest amuses Bernard, who's spent his entire life wandering the wood.

"How long did you say you've been hunting that neox?" Bernard inquires.

Sanet speaks without looking to him. "Off and on for a few months. I would lose it, then spend the larger part of three or four days retracing its tracks before finding it again. I'll say it was no joy to find you sent it left so quickly."

Bernard laughs, rubbing the palm of his hand. *Eighteen hours is hardly quick.* "If it's any consolation, that was the third one I've sent over the years, so I do know what a feat it can be to surmount. Your tenacity is admirable."

"It wasn't tenacity. If it were any other frek, I would have given up long ago, but this one swallowed something I've been after."

"Is that why I found you leaving the cave this morn?"

"Yes. I went looking for it in its corpse after you went to sleep. Went down in that protnuk's nest believing, hoping, perhaps those creshwillows had taken it."

"Oh, so you're not flam for going in there." He watches Sanet smile to herself.

"Well, like you, I didn't know what was down there."

Bernard hums. "We all do things we're unproud to claim. In any case, did they take it?"

"No. It was a sliver of brass. So small, I'm not sure how I'm supposed to find it. And in truth, after all this, I'm just tired."

Bernard flushes, and a broad smile sweeps across his face. "Well, thumb to fingers, Sanet." He picks through his pocket and pulls the small brass piece out, presenting it to her between his fingers.

"Lincoln, you did find it."

"Well, one of those fur traps did and made a huge ruckus after I dressed the neox."

"May I?"

Bernard doesn't hesitate and hands her the small brass sliver. She takes it acquisitively. "I don't know why I kept it. I was likely to throw it out."

"Glad you didn't."

Bernard watches her happily turn it in her hand. A look of relief mingled with exhaustion spills over her. They remain quiet for a time before he breaks the silence. "You're not going to say what it's for?"

"Oh, well, I'm not too certain. It's part of a larger object, and I know there are other pieces out there, bigger ones. My employer has spent considerable time and coin looking for these, so I can only assume they're quite valuable." She studies and flips the sliver in the light before returning it to a small pouch attached to her belt. "I'm glad I didn't have to send you left for it."

Bernard coughs. "If that was the alternative, I'm glad as well."

Sanet smiles to herself again as their hike returns to silence, save for the incessant rain.

⋄⋄⋄

The constancy of fog and rain give no sign of relief, a sentiment compounded by erratic periods of thunder and lightning. Bernard breaks their silence once again. "Is that why you returned to the cave? For the brass?"

She answers plainly, if not carefully. "Yes. And no. The protnuk was disguised as a young girl when I went down there and she recited to me a riddle, stating that the man who sleeps above is the Dark Valor."

Bernard laughs. "Grave bent on selling that foretale, isn't he? Did he also say it was because you saw that black throne?"

"Black throne?" Sanet questions.

"You didn't see a throne down there?"

"There was a chair, but it was made of stone, covered in green moss or something."

"I see," he states. *Perhaps, I'm in tiddles.*

"I'm not too well versed in Radiba freks, but I do know that protnuk riddles are only meant to send you mad," Sanet doubles.

"I've read the same. That they confuse you just enough that you'll wander back to their nest, where they attack and feast on you in your weakened state. Supposedly, they find the blood that flows through your veins flavors the meat if it's panic filled. That said, this protnuk didn't seem to have much patience for me to leave and return. I've heard they're fearsome, but never seen one change form like that."

"I've only read about them. Haven't gotten to see much, if you're wondering." She smiles, pulling out a handful of blue brackleberries. "What did she say to you? Anything worth remembering?"

Bernard thinks back. "It was a countdown of sorts, I assume to lull me into trance. Let me think, there were seven foretales, four mysterious things . . . two plans, a single answer? Nothing worth remembering if—"

Sanet stops him, holding her hand out against his chest. "Speaking of."

Bernard looks around. " . . . of what?"

She nods to him, her eyes aiming above. *Is that a creshwillow following us? But I thought they didn't like the rain.* He watches as she slouches, her eyes fixed on the rain-thumped canopy. She holds a finger to her lips. Bernard stands in wait, instinctively reaching for his dagger, half expecting the little frek to pounce down on them. The trees and leaves sway in the breeze as the droplets of rain and the rolling fog limit their visibility to a dozen strides.

Nothing happens.

After a major, Sanet gives up her watch and looks to Bernard. "I guess it knows we're watching. Luckily they only pursue the sent." She stands straight again, shaking off a bit of rain pooled on her green hood's crown. "We should find a spot to rest for the night. The sun's almost at crest." Though they were close to his haynest, she was right. *No reason to trek through the forest at night.*

"I think there's a shelter tree we could rest in ahead."

She nods and they carry on. After another half mile, they find a carved-out tree trunk large enough for four friends to sleep in. Shelter trees like this one were engineered as final-ditch safety points should tormisand squalls arise while anyone traversed the Radiba Forest, though the rhythm of a tormisand is well enough known these days that they're likely used only to aid weary travelers or a passing hunter.

Pushing aside a bit of false brush, they step inside. Here, a pair of prefabricated frontz beds hangs in a corner that, for their single night's rest, should suffice. As Bernard assembles them, Sanet ignites a small fire in a pit formed at the center of the trunk. The tree has been hollowed out ten measures above with ventilation holes cut near the top to allow smoke from the fire to escape.

Finishing and placing the beds, Bernard takes a couple of slices of neox from a larger chunk and sets them on a metal round he unpacks from his rucksack, then places the round atop the fire. He sprinkles a bit of seasoning from a small tin and lets the meat fry in its own juice, filling the room with a delightful aroma. "Have you had neox before?"

Sanet shakes her head. "I've not had the pleasure. And if it's the one I've been after, I'm sure it'll taste all the better."

"You're in for a treat; there's nothing like it." He watches the meat, flipping it after a few majors as it makes a distinctive and appetizing sizzle. It's then that the creshwillow, the same as the one that followed Bernard around on his first night in the cave, appears. It stands wet and pitiful at the small opening in the trunk, and although creshwillows by nature are skittish freks, this one acts determined to intrude. At the sight, Sanet reaches for a small dagger on her waist.

"Hold on, Sanet. It's hungry." Bernard looks down at the creshwillow, who's motionless at the opening, rain pattering down behind him. "Come on, Brute."

"Brute?"

"He doesn't look like a brute to you?" Bernard smiles.

The creshwillow doesn't hesitate and hops its way toward the fire, staying closer to Bernard than to Sanet, who sits back with judging eyes resting on the creshwillow. After gaining a bit of confidence, it snuggles in close to Bernard.

When the meat finishes cooking, Bernard cuts the steak for the two of them, handing over a third, smaller portion to the little creshwillow. Sanet speaks up, "I've read they multiply in the hundreds. You bring one into your haynest, and you're soon to be overwhelmed by them."

Bernard looks down at the creshwillow, who doesn't seem particularly interested in a fully cooked slice of meat. It taps it with its paws, tearing it apart and slurping a bit of the rare blood remaining inside. "He seems wisnok. Are you, Brute?" The creshwillow looks up, responding to its new curam. "I think it wants raw meat." Bernard leans back to his rucksack and takes out a bit more of the neox, slices a small portion, a fattier, bloodier piece, and tosses it to Brute, who instantly digs in. "There you go."

"I'll never understand Radibians."

"Us nature folk? No reason not to enjoy and use the Land around you. Where are you from?"

"Yikshir Sands." Sanet takes her first bite. "Lincoln, this is good." She quickly takes another. And then a third.

Bernard beams. "Yikshir? You don't look like you're from the desert, though I've never actually been to Yikshir. Never had a reason to leave the state myself, and the one time I did, I ended up toe to toe with a tenfooter."

"And lived?"

"Just." He grins.

Sanet asks with a mouthful of food, "Do you find yourself always on the edge of being sent?" A bit of food falls out of her mouth, and she catches it with the back of her hand. "Apory. Hungry."

"I guess curiosity has always been my weakness. I can't turn away from a path I haven't visited before. Or at least I think that's the way of it."

"I can say I'm full of curiosity but was told not to turn down darkened paths unless I'm looking to be sent."

"A young lady without the Land of wonder to her?"

She laughs. "You say 'young lady' as if you know how old I am."

"I would guess you're at least . . . a triple decade younger than me."

"If only. I'm thirty-three if you're asking. At least that's what I'm told."

"Well, you could still be my daughter, so I'm happy to call you a young lady." Bernard smiles, taking a large bite for himself.

❖ ❖ ❖

Finished eating, Brute curls close to Bernard and closes his eyes, his wet fur warming in the fire. "You've made yourself a little friend," Sanet says.

Looking down at the quiet frek, Bernard shakes his head. "Jame will not be happy."

"Do you bring freks home often?"

"On the few treks I've been allowed, I've brought back a frek or two. The last one was a drum of bomwigs, which Jame refused to take care of until they became sick. Then he was insufferable. Our lives for two whole months were nothing but taking care of those slimy little festatars. You'll find that I'm the one who starts things, but Jame's the one who finishes them." Guilt courses through Bernard, who imagines how lonely and frightened Jame must be alone in their haynest, no one to answer his call. *I don't even know if Jame knows where I've been . . .*

"Have you two been together long?"

Bernard looks up, out of sorts. He takes a deep breath. "Apory. Twenty-three years. I found Jame while I was hunting. He was caught in an emorteen trap, and his legs were mangled. I brought him home and nursed him back to health, though he's not been able to walk properly since. Some wounds never heal, as much as oilments act as cure-all these days. We have bad days, as any relationship, but he's *the* great joy of my life." For a minor,

Bernard loses his thoughts to Jame but shakes out of it. *I'll be haynest soon, the whole affair behind us.* "So, you've found your sliver of brass. Are you returning to Yikshir then?"

"There's another one I need to find before heading back. In the Tunnels."

"How many are there?"

"Not exactly sure. But not very many. Maybe a dozen? There are very few, I'm told." She pats her bag where the brass is kept.

"Sounds like quite the trek for such an enigmit thing." Sanet nods in polite agreement. "I can't believe you're not the slightest bit curious about what it's for," he doubles.

"There are a few things I wonder about, but fragments of brass are not one of them." She takes a deep breath, lying back on the bed.

"May I see it again? For a minor?"

Sanet hesitates, then pulls it from her small pouch and hands it to Bernard. He turns it over in his hand. Innocuous in shape and form, it has an odd smooth and faintly bowed back.

He looks back to Sanet. "The neox attacked me last night while I was hunting it. They've never done that before. In fact, it had a pretty good chance of escaping me. I was tired, ready to go haynest. And when the storm started, I knew the hunt was over. So when it turned on me, when it came at me, it was alarming." He studies the sliver more closely. "I guess it must have had this little shard jabbing in its gut. Maybe it made the frek more aggressive?"

"Perhaps."

"Lincoln, a sliver of brass nearly sends me left, and the next day, it saves me." Bernard tosses the brass across the fire to Sanet, who returns it to her pouch.

"Well, Sur Bernard, I think it's time we retired. Approsh for the delicious duskmeal and warm company."

He nods as Sanet turns over on her bed. Lost in the flickers of the fire, he scratches under Brute's chin as it sleeps. "Don't mind me if I stay up a while. Too eager to see Jame."

❖❖❖

Hours later, the winds wake them.

Inside the trunk, ash and remains of the fire swirl in a miniature whirlwind. Brute huddles close to Bernard, shaking in fear. Sanet covers her face as she attempts to repack her rucksack. Some of her possessions, a pad, clothing, and a small letter, spill across the trunk and whip across the room. Bernard helps to gather her things and she shoves them hurriedly back inside the bag.

An ear-splitting howl, the noise deafening, whistles across the small opening of the trunk. Bernard screams over the noise to Sanet, "We need to get out of here! We'll go deaf if we don't."

Screaming back, she asks, "Is it safe to go out there?"

"If we stay low to the ground, we can find somewhere safer."

"You're mad."

"I'm not going to lose my hearing over a little windstorm." Bernard smirks and grabs his rucksack. He pushes toward the opening, covering his face.

Sanet looks around, repeating, "You're mad."

He turns. "You've said that. Let's go."

As they exit, they're met with slamming horizontal rain that cuts at their faces like tiny razors. Bernard turns to Sanet, speaking as loudly as he can and gesturing with his hands. "Stay. Low."

She nods. They start to crawl along the ground, mud and water pummeling their heads and necks.

They crawl inch by inch away from the trunk. Bernard attempts to gauge his surroundings and recollect a nearby shelter. He looks around. "Where's Brute?"

Sanet looks around, too, and finds nothing.

"Is he still in the tree?" Bernard glances at their abandoned shelter. *That mangy frek.* He turns back.

"Where are you going?" Sanet screams out.

"I can't leave him behind."

"Are you mad?"

"Look, we can grit about my madness later."

She rolls her eyes, turning back as well.

When they reach the shelter tree once more, their ears are assaulted as the whistling grows louder with the strengthening winds. Brute huddles near the edge of the tree's opening, immobile from fright.

"Come on, Brute. You need to get out of there. We're leaving." The creshwillow tarries, watching Bernard with concern and confusion. With a booming voice and broad gestures, Bernard attempts to coax the creshwillow into moving. "We can't stay here. You have to come with me, or you're going to be all alone in there."

Brute refuses to move.

Bernard becomes furious, slamming the ground with a palm. "You move your shnite right now." Brute jumps and then creeps forward. "Come on now."

Sanet yells from behind him, "The wind's getting stronger. We'll be flying soon."

Brute inches his way closer.

"Come on . . . come on." And then, finally, Brute's within reach, and Bernard grabs the creshwillow by its scruff. He turns to Sanet. "We should go."

"Where to?"

"I think there's an old house east of here. Out of the way, but close."

"Wisnok, lead the way, madman," she calls out, letting Bernard pass.

He scrabbles his way along, holding Brute to his chest as he crawls. The journey to the old house is tumultuous. The longer they're in the storm, the fiercer the squalls become, causing a struggle with every stride gained. Brute digs into Bernard's chest, which he's sure will leave lasting marks. And then, a branch crashes into and knocks Sanet to her side.

Bernard turns, exposing Brute to the winds, and the frek clamps down even harder. "All running well?"

She groans, her noise masked by the howling wind; then grimacing, her face injured, she nods and motions to continue. Bernard acknowledges and resumes moving in the direction of the house, only a few hundred strides away. The rain cuts and thunder booms.

"We're almost there."

Behind him, she curses, "Approsh Lincoln."

Within a short distance, the front door of the wooden house swings violently, slamming and banging in the wind. Its windows have long since shattered.

Bernard catches the door as it pivots open and struggles to hold on to it as Sanet passes. He sees she's battered more than he first thought, with blood dripping from her hair, tangled in mud and rain. Inside, she collapses to the ground.

There's no warmth in the house nor shelter from the rain, which pours in and on them in buckets; but as a barrier and being a few decibels quieter, it'll do for the major while the echoes of wind still ring in their ears. Brute releases Bernard and finds a dark corner to cower in.

"Well, that was unexpected," he says.

"I thought there were warning whistles for tormisands?"

"There are, but not this deep in the forest." Bernard pauses. "This storm is terribly short. It only rained for two days before the squalls started. Hopefully, that means we should get some Peace Hours soon. We can walk back in that and wait out the second half of the storm in the warmth of a haynest and bed."

"I'll take it." Sanet rubs her head.

"I should probably look at that." He walks over to her, rain pattering on his back. "May I?"

She nods and he grasps her head, moving her hair aside to find the cut. She winces as he touches close to her wound.

"Not the worst head injury I've seen. I can't do much with it until we're haynest, but I can patch you up temporarily until then."

"Approsh, Bernard."

"Brute, you mind handing me my bandages?" He looks over to the creshwillow, who shivers in fear in the corner. "He's going to need training," Bernard jokes.

Sanet smiles back meekly. "You are a madman, an old and reckless madman."

"Should have left me to the protnuk."

❖ ❖ ❖

To Bernard's surprise, the winds cease after an hour. Sanet is bandaged and resting her eyes. Brute has begun to warm up to the haynest and grows more energetic as the sound of the wind fades to a whimper. Bernard looks out into the forest and watches as the fog retreats. Everything is exceptionally still during Peace Hours, and excessively green. Sounds are reduced to a mild, wet drip of water from leaf to leaf, leaf to mud.

"We should go soon. This is one of the shortest storms I've ever encountered, which means I don't imagine it'll be long before the squalls return."

Sanet opens her eyes and lifts herself up. Bernard reaches out to help, but she waves him off, grunting as she stands.

"You might have a broken bone there."

"Pretty sure I have more than one broken bone." She smirks, lifting her rucksack.

"Jame will make you a neox soup that'll cure all wounds."

"I look forward to it." She pats him on the shoulder and steps outside. Bernard motions for Brute to follow. The little frek hesitates but obeys.

Everything outside feels better. Rays of sunlight reach through the leaves and create a lush green paradimo around them. They walk with haste, though Sanet needs an extra step for every one of Bernard's.

As she takes in the surroundings, she comments, "Now this is the Radiba Highlands I've read about. I mean, I knew about the tormisands, but they say there's nothing to compare to the green of the forest, a real envy for us in the desert."

"I've seen some incredible paintings of those Redrocks."

"They're nice, but they're also dull." Her response drips with hesitation, her quiet nature returning.

Bernard continues to lead, knowing they're only hours away. Above them, Brute hops from tree to tree, shaking leaves and drops of water in his wake.

❖ ❖ ❖

The smoke first looks like a return of fog, but its blue tint hints at something different. Soon, the smell of burned wood, charred meat, and vegetation fills the air. The smoke begins to billow around them. This alarms Bernard.

"Is that fire?" Sanet says aloud what Bernard is reasoning.

"I'm going to run ahead."

Before Sanet can answer, he takes off, running into the smoke and leaving her and Brute behind. The farther he runs, the thicker it becomes. In minors, the first hint of heat touches him. His eyes burn from the miasma, and ahead there are tiny hints of yellow, orange, and red.

Please don't be . . .

He fights his way through the smoke before coming face to face with the fire. It licks and spits and crackles around him. His haynest, his Land, is burning.

"Jame!" he screams, the blue smoke disorienting. It masks the warmth and bright flames coming from all directions. He covers his nose and mouth with his arm as he attempts to locate the front door. *How is there a fire after so much rain?* Finding the short gray wall that surrounds his haynest, he hops over it and lands in a patch of green-orange vegetables. There's a small shovel in the dirt. The one he dropped when the neox passed the yard. *Planting vegetables as an old man, to run off a little boy.* He runs toward the haynest drenched in horrific flames.

"Jame!" he screams again and pounds at the door. Through a small glass frame in the door, Bernard glimpses inside. Everything is on fire. He pulls his sleeve over his hand to grab hold of the homemade door handle. Seven years ago, he'd melted a dozen silver arrowheads that he'd gathered in the surrounding Land and carved them into an intricate knob that he'd given Jame on their sixteenth anniversary.

Opening the door, he's met by a backdraft of flame. Shielding himself, he falls to the ground.

"Jame!" He stands and rushes inside. "Jame!"

The main room is still a mess. Jame used his lack of "easy mobility" as an excuse to leave his dirty rounds and half-drunk mugs of tea around the haynest. A pile of clothing sits in the corner, an unwelcome bonfire.

"Jame!" Fighting down his hallway, Bernard sees their portrait frames have fallen and shattered on the ground. Jame's terrible paintings of the two of them. Mostly crude drawings he'd spent hours on. The ones where he painted himself with the bigger cock. *You wish, Jame.* He cracks a glass frame with his boot as he runs forward, continuing to shield himself from unexpected bursts of fire.

"Jame!" The door to the master is burned almost off, only half hanging on its hinge. Jame is always so shy, needing to close the door even when they're alone in the haynest. Even though there are no neighbors for miles around. In the middle of their peaceful haynest, amid the quiet forest, they could never slip together without the doors locked. *And Lincoln forbid we go outdoors.* Jame is a private man. He is a handsome man. He is a loving man. He is sometimes a real proshing shnite. He is finicky. And persistent. He is kind. He is sometimes so wrong that Bernard wants to strangle him in his sleep. And then sometimes he is right. Like about Bernard's haircut.

"Jame!"

Bernard catches the first and last glimpse of him. Burned in their bed, half hanging over its side and reaching for the door. In horror, Bernard screams. He attempts to get closer, but smoke and fire and heat prevent him. He wants to touch him one last time.

"Jame!"

And then everything goes black.

Chapter Four

HE WHO MISSES NINE
BUT ONE MORE

tanding in a new and empty vacuum, Bernard is alone. Above him are thousands of pinpoint holes creating a star-filled dome with light from an unknown source pouring in as far as he can see. Around him, the vacancy holds naught but absolute black. Walking, one foot in front of the other, his steps echo outward as he moves what he believes is forward even as at the major, he finds himself ostensibly nowhere.

And then, ahead, a frontz torch is lit, and a friend begins walking toward him, his steps matched to Bernard's. Partly afraid and wanting to escape the intense isolation that drips around him, Bernard runs toward the stranger, who in turn, with perfect symmetry, runs at him. They continue toward each other until Bernard stops, which halts the mysterious figure.

"Jame?" Bernard calls out, but the figure does not answer. Instead he stands inert, without emotion, without fear or sadness or happiness. "Jame, are you there?" The shadow of what looks like Jame turns and begins walking away, and this action sends Bernard to his knees.

For Jame walks.

And continues to, leaving Bernard behind. Bernard stands and, jogging closer, attempts to keep in step at Jame's side. "Where are we?"

Jame doesn't answer, his expression stoic and forward. After a long silence, Jame stops just before a small bed. Bernard's attention focuses on its sudden appearance just as it alights with fire. He shields himself from the heat and flames, turning away, and just as sudden as it was there, everything dims to dark again.

"The sixth and second foretales will come after and before you send the burned man left," Jame says in a calm and steady voice.

"But I didn't send you left . . ." Bernard murmurs. Jame walks without reacting, without answering. Bernard follows, heart sunk. "Jame, please, what's going on?"

Ahead, a huge orange protnuk with its six monstrous limbs stalks the darkness. It crouches as if ready to attack, growling at the two as they approach.

"The seventh shall be translated . . ." But the protnuk's roar overpowers them, and Bernard is unable to hear the last of Jame's sentence.

"Translated by who?"

Jame doesn't answer and turns to where the protnuk stood and where absence has taken its place.

"Jame, stop." He does not and they continue forward. "Apory," Bernard's face contorts with uncontrolled emotion. With sadness. "Apory crept in a millenary sword. Apory that I wasn't there when . . ." Before he's able to finish, a looming figure stands before them, its palm held face up, and inches above it floats a small silver orb.

Jame speaks again. "The fifth shall come by enemy whose path you choose to cross." The looming figure dissipates into fog as Jame continues, Bernard left to silently follow.

Ahead, a small house built on long wooden legs rises from the floor, which ripples like black water. The haynest is half their size, as if designed for a child's play. "The third and the fourth arrive by handwritten note from a friend long left." The haynest looks familiar, as if he had been there many years ago, years before Jame. Bernard steps closer, and just as he sees a woman in the window pulling its curtains shut, a black wave surges from the floor and engulfs the miniature house, returning the space to darkness.

Jame stops just before a final object, a towering and mirrored wall reflecting the image of Bernard, but not of Jame. "The first foretale comes from you, emerging from the past and the future. All seven foretales will guide you on your final venture. And return you to me." At this Jame's expression shifts, as if emerging from a kiptale. "Bernard?"

Bernard's heart lifts at his curam and he embraces Jame. They spin and squeeze each other with the smells of burned wood and fresh dew emanating off Jame's clothes. Bernard grabs him by the head, running his fingers through his long hair.

"Jame, Jame. Forgive me."

"Forgive you for what?"

Bernard pulls back, holding Jame by the shoulders, and smiles, looking him over, pressing his rough and aged hands to Jame's face. "You look so young."

"You're only two years older than me." Jame rolls his eyes. They don't speak for a minor. The darkness around them ignored. The pinpoint stars above them ignored. Jame wipes his mouth. "I'm really thirsty. You have any water?"

Bernard nods and grabs Jame by the hand. "Are you angry?"

"Should I be?"

Just as Bernard is about to answer, a heavy weight presses against his legs, and it feels as if he can't adjust them, as if some dense lump rests on the blanket near his feet, holding them down.

Jame.

His eyes flutter open. Light replaces dark. Cold air. He turns from facing the wall onto his back. He's shirtless with marks of Brute's claws still freshly dug across his chest, and he finds himself lying in an unfamiliar bed. His hands, wrapped in thick bandages, pulse with pain.

Everything is quiet in the room. Dark wood walls. Modest, customary furnishings. A three-drawer dresser. A circular nightstand with a mug of water and a small vial. A lamp and a bowl of cold, untouched soup. Brute sleeps, warm and curled up, at the foot of the bed. Bernard rubs the little frek with his feet from under the soft blanket. It stretches and rolls onto its back, returning to its nap. A sound of faint ticking from an unseen clock. A quiet breeze wafting through an open window, its curtain dancing with a soft elegance. The sun shines affectionately against the forest outside.

No rain. No smoke. No fire.

Jame. His heart skips. He blocks the image, too dreadful to stomach. The sight of the body covered in flames. Of the penetrating heat. Bernard's hands burn and throb with his heartbeat. *Bury the thoughts or they'll send you.*

Footsteps.

He sits up just as the door opens, revealing a handsome Radiba man curamed Logan Hunst, who was once Bernard's neighbor, or as close to a neighbor as one gets in the sparsely populated Highlands. As he recalls, Logan is a traveler and often away on extended treks west. The sight of him suggests that Bernard is in the haynest of Logan's mother, who was sent left only a year ago.

"Sur Babek, good morn," Logan starts.

Bernard attempts to say hello back, as is only proper, though the words never form.

"You took quite the burn to your hands. Nearly lost them both."

They throb. "Are we at Edith's?" he manages to gasp.

Logan walks over and sits close, reaching for Bernard's hands. "Yes. Though it's my haynest now, I suppose. I never sent my approsh for coming to her arrangements last year." While he speaks, he delicately unwraps Bernard's bandages. "Sanet pulled you from the fire. You were lost in there. I found the both of you after following that smoke across the Lothatin."

"Do you know what happened?"

"No, but every haynest south of Lothatin Bridge was on fire. Down the chasm a near mile. And if you ask me, it looked on purpose, but I'm not sure why. By luck, most of the forest was damp from the tormisand, which I think prevented the fire from spreading."

Bernard winces as the bandages pull against his tender skin. "By luck?"

Logan looks up. "Apory, Sur Babek."

"You said more haynests burned?"

"Every one I could see. Crentak's. Travis's. Dotted reds against a line of green and stone. Frightful sight."

"Lincoln," Bernard whispers in disbelief. "Any others sent?"

"Couldn't say, but I can't imagine not . . ."

As Logan trails off, Bernard can't speak. In the silence, Logan peels off the last layer of the bandage. Bernard's hands are mangled. Unrecognizable. The skin flaked and rippled, only a single finger left uninjured: the little one on his west hand. The rest are charred away or missing entirely. A sight that's grotesque and disturbing. "What did I do?"

"Sanet says you grabbed Jame's body. He was . . . on fire."

Bernard looks to Logan and holds back his tears. He moves to cover his face with his deformed hands and winces, every curl and touch bringing him tremendous pain. "Who could do such a thing?"

Logan shakes his head without an answer. Behind him, from the doorway, with a bandage wrapped around her head, Sanet watches. Once noticed, she moves inside. "Are you wisnok, Bernard?"

"He should be," Logan answers in Bernard's silence. He reaches toward the nightstand and dips his fingers into the vial.

He draws from it a thick, white oilment and rubs it into his palms. "This will hurt, but you'll feel much better afterward, I cross."

"Will I get my fingers back?"

Logan shakes his head. "Appize, but there's no oilment in the hundred thirty-three that regenerates limbs." Bernard knew. He and Jame spent many years attempting to find a cure for Jame's legs. Oilments had come far, able to repair most any injury. Broken bones. Burns. But nothing worked on Jame, and they came to the conclusion that the offending trap must have been coated in an incurable slick, preventing its victim from fully healing. A clever tool for hunting wily emorteens, but a terrible fate for an absent-minded traveler. They once thought to purchase a pair of walking legs from the Misipit Valley but found they wouldn't work unless Jame lost his legs entirely. A decision he refused to make. But for Jame, he led a life he loved: being at home, being away from an uncaring wilderness, and being alone with Bernard.

Logan presses his oiled hands to Bernard's and begins to massage them. Soft at first, then with more vigor. Bernard groans. Sanet steps in closer and sets her hand on his shoulder while Brute wakes to catch what's going on. It pads across the bed closer to the action.

And then Bernard feels a thousand needles prick his hands as if he has plunged them into freezing waters. He starts to breathe deeper while Logan continues to massage them, each stroke pressing harder into the muscle. Bernard grits his teeth, taking deep and studied breaths.

"Almost done, Sur Babek."

The pain intensifies, agonizing. He's ready to pull away . . . until . . . his hands feel cold and then nothing at all. His breathing calms, and Sanet squeezes his shoulder.

Finished, Logan asserts, "That should do for now." He stands and holds his oiled hands to his side. "When you've rested a bit, I thought we could find a smith to help with your hands. Perhaps engineer a pair of mitts?"

Bernard's hands glisten, crinkled and worn, with the single finger standing oddly alone. "I should lose the little one. I look absurd."

Sanet laughs. Logan follows. Bernard huffs through his nose, holding back the *thoughts*. He swallows. "Approsh, Logan. Approsh, Sanet."

Their laughter shifts to soft smiles.

"You should rest. We'll bring you a duskmeal later," Sanet assures him, standing with Logan.

They leave and Bernard lies down, taking stock of his new-formed hands. *If that's what I can call them.* Brute, awake and wandering the room, sniffs along the windowsill before hopping down and out of sight. The room fades to quiet again. The ticking clock. The faint, weak whip of the curtain. *Who would set a man's house on fire? A community of haynests? It had to be coordinated. It had to be planned.*

These were sendlefts.

The understanding of who they are, of why they undertook such an act against friends, slithers in and out of his mind. His focus remains on these thoughts as he attempts to avoid others. It would be important now to seek these festatars out. To find them, to bring them to justice. A fitful wish for brutal revenge washes over him.

❖ ❖ ❖

At Logan's mornmeal table, Sanet feeds Bernard a bit of noodle, some of which falls down his chin. Bernard rolls his eyes. "Have you never fed your children, Sanet?"

Scooping bits from Bernard's scruffy and unshaven face, she answers definitively, "There's no day on this Land I'll have children despite what others say."

Bernard grins, but Sanet is absolute in her statement. "I'm sure you'd make an excellent mother."

"It's just not my bargain, plus wanting to travel across states, I can't be tied to a haynest and whining baby."

Logan enters, washed and toweled. "I'll have to double on Sanet. Traveling is no life for kids, though I wouldn't mind bringing a little one haynest." At this statement, Sanet bites her lip and spoons Bernard another mouthful of noodles.

Bernard talks through the hot food. "I always wanted children. We thought about heading to a children's square someday, but there wasn't one close enough for . . ." He trails off.

Sitting across from the others, Logan reaches for a bread roll and changes the subject. "You're welcome to stay here as long as you like, Bernard, though I'm headed back to Organsia in a few days. I'm already late as it is. Though I'm still willing to escort you to that smith before I leave, if you'd like. Perhaps once this tormisand is over?"

Bernard nods. "This is still the Peace Hours?" He studies the outside through a nearby window. *What strange pacing for a tormisand.* "Approsh, Logan, but I'll need to perform arrangements . . ." He pauses, not wanting to say the curam aloud or have the *thoughts*. "I don't think I can stay either."

"Are you going to travel?" Sanet asks, feeding him another bite.

He considers the thought. *Where would I go? Where is my haynest without Jame?* It has been thirty years since he'd first made one in the Radiba Highlands. His parents were long left, living the last years of their lives near the foothills closer to the shoreline. He could relocate to where he grew up, to the west, near the Guloren border. That's where his first haynest was, carved out of a large stone boulder and enveloped by trees, though he'd long since abandoned it after tormisand squalls nearly destroyed it. Marking two haynests he's lost.

The thought creeps in unwelcomed. He was young then and didn't bother rebuilding the first house, believing at the time that the Land didn't wish him to remain there. Radibians live on the Flow—obligated to subsist off the Land and accept nature's rhythm. Landscapes are their emblems, caves and outsized trees their shelters, and tormisands are the reason they stay indoors with others. *Perhaps I could live somewhere else?*

In his studies, Bernard read that most other states are almost inhospitable in comparison, as they're each in a condition of solitude, governing themselves in an anomalous isolation. When friends cross borders—through a legal act bestowed by the Law of Passage—doing so without a semblance of recognition of that state's culture and position is usually met with enmity if not one's permanent removal.

North of Radiba is the state of Carvinga where the tenfooters dwell, a state particularly unwelcoming to outsiders. Just under six hundred years ago, the tenfooters excavated a vast network of tunnels that allow roamers and travelers passage underneath their state. An act meant to circumvent the Law and remove any intrusion into their hedonistic, barbarous lifestyle. Once they finished building the tunnels, the tenfooters soon deserted them, making them one of the wildest and most illicit areas in the hundred thirty-three.

Then, north of Carvinga, Yikshir Sands stands as an assemblage of redrock cities, each acting as sovereign over its own sect of religions. Collectively, the Councils of Yikshir convene to delegate and regulate high-held state laws.

Bernard has a harder time recalling the geography to the west. He remembers a bit of Organsia, through Logan's exploits, where great lakes and rivers feed a massive neon city and flow into a dull-green sea. Before Organsia, there's a state blanketed in ash from a chain of active volcaks . . .

As he ponders the Land around him, a sudden conflict of emotions develops, the cropping up of his desire to explore. A desire that's resided in him since he was a small boy, a desire to discover the diverse Land around him and to indulge in infantility and recklessness. It is an unclaimed desire. These sorts of feelings are what sent Jame left. Had he left for haynest earlier that morn, had he not wasted his time engaging with protnuks, he would have returned hours before. *Before the fires were set.* In truth, had he let the neox pass unfollowed in the first place, none of this would have chanced at all. The neox did not bring him tremendous luck. They were not in need of food. There was no need to chase and hunt wild freks, bad omen or not. A careful reaction could have prevented Jame's sending, and there was great horror in the *thoughts.*

"Wisnok, Sur Babek?" Logan reaches out in comfort.

"Apory, I don't know what I need right now." He stands, readying to leave the room. Sanet and Logan stand as well. "I just need a major." They don't respond, but nod in quiet acceptance.

Outside, the air is crisp. The yard lies overrun, forgotten by its peripatetic owner. Since Edith's sending, it had become a place built for rest between feats and grand travels. He smiles at the thought of exploration. *I shouldn't smile.* He walks down a narrow path deeper into the forest.

He finds a tiny pond and in it a drum of bomwigs, slimy little freks that slither and squirm, feeding on the mud and muck beneath. Bernard reaches in to hold one but remembers too quickly he has no means to grasp them. *How useless is a man without fingers?*

He stands and looks around. The picturesque wood rests, lush and green. Wet. The remains of a *drip drip drip* of rain fading. But the absence of the jarjer's song still signals the tormisand's looming second half.

What was he to do? Where was he to live, to stay, to be? It had been so long living with a partner who never wanted to leave their haynest. Bernard once made Jame crutches, but he never used them. They now lay in ash, burnt and forgotten. Jame wasn't a fighter. He carried with him no sense of adventure or passion. Instead, he was sensible and kind. Welcoming when it came to matters of coupling, yet cautious and dire when anyone was leaving. Jame never was the one to go and, if it were up to Jame, Bernard would stay. Rebuild their haynest. But that's not what Bernard wants. In some ways, Jame's sending was . . . liberating. *I can't think like that.*

There is nothing to keep him here in Radiba, as wonderful and lovely as this place might be. He couldn't stay. He can't stay. *Jame wouldn't approve, but one can't live their life in service of the left.* The thoughts are there. As the thoughts will always be. There would be no hiding from them. But the decision to leave drives him to his knees.

Agony flows through the forest.

❖ ❖ ❖

Returning to Logan's a few hours later, Bernard looks tired, covered in dirt and grim. Sanet greets him in the main room. "All well, Bernard?"

"I am, approsh, my friend." He smiles and sits.

Logan enters a minor later with sliced neox and blue brackleberries. "Can I get you some steamed tea?"

"That would be lovely."

Logan nods and exits.

After a minor, Bernard looks to Sanet. "I wouldn't want to impose, but would you mind a friend in tow on your return to Yikshir?"

"Are you sure you're able, old man?" she replies in jest.

With a faint smile, he responds, "I think these bones can handle it."

"Well, I'm not going there directly. Not sure how long the trek will be, since I've another fragment of brass to find before I return."

"Well, all the Land sits before me, and I ignored its grand adventure first by listening to careful, warning parents, then by listening to a careful warning husband. I think it's time I let *my* soul have its way."

Sanet remains silent in acknowledgment, then answers, "Well, it would be an honor to share the Land with you."

She raises her mug. Bernard lifts his little finger. At this, they laugh. Logan enters shortly after with tea for each.

"So, you're off to travel with the handsome lady?"

"Once I get some usability back, I hope."

Logan sets the mug on the table in front of Bernard, who takes it with the palms of his hands. "I think this smith can fashion you a set of mitts. Though he'll require a steel bargain," Logan says and takes a seat between them.

Bernard lifts his mug. "Whatever the bargain set before me, my trek is north."

Chapter Five
SMITH TUNSTON

*A*s the night approaches, the friends decide to play dice and drink fruin until their bodies call for bed. Bernard wins almost invariably and on occasion purposely rolls the dice off the table to change the pips in the others' favor. His two-palm, fingerless rolls are blamed for their misfortunes, and Sanet states that his gaming skills will come useful on the road.

Later, alone in his room anticipating the end of the Peace Hours, Bernard sleeps in fits, with the white-moonlit forest glowing outside. Eager. Excited. Horrified. Nightmares and sadness blend with the lifting of his spirit, and his boyish elation struggles to free itself from a looming guilt. He rises the next morn just before the sun hits crest. Brute returns, hopping in the window and looking a tad rounder if not entirely satisfied. The quiet mornlight is odd as the Peace Hours evolve into Peace Days, which leads Bernard to hope that the whistles and sudden bursts of wind won't hinder them from leaving. He can't wait any longer.

Discussion of the peculiar tormisand's pattern takes over the mornmeal table. Logan and Sanet work together to plan several protections along their trip north should squalls develop. Bernard watches them as they address each other; Logan's eyes expose a spring affinity toward Sanet, who blushes at any waggish story or compliment he delivers her way. *That boy has great landmine charm.*

And so, with plans in hand and rucksacks packed, they set out.

Fresh air meets them. Logan shuts the door behind him, and they start up the narrow path leading into the larger wood. Brute runs ahead, scurrying into the trees and disappearing. Their adventure begins.

Before they travel too far from Logan's haynest, Sanet steps close to Bernard. "I didn't ask, in earnest too shy to, but did you want to perform an arrangement for Jame?"

Bernard turns in soft gesture. "I did on the yester."

"You went back?"

"He would have been nimed to be seen as he was. And it was only proper."

With that, Sanet nods and squeezes Bernard's arm. "You make a good man, Bernard Babek."

They walk wordlessly, taking in the sweet, crisp air and emerald-olive foliage. For a time, their way twists along winding trails, cut between narrow and worn paths, and they stride over large trunks and lesser stone bridges.

Many majors pass before Logan interrupts their quiet trek. "The smith's shop should be down here, but we'll need to cut this way."

Following Logan, they turn off the trail into a bit of denser undergrowth he clears from their way with a small blade. Sanet walks ahead of Bernard, pushing aside larger malleable branches for him, and as they pass, the brush springs immediately back, causing the trail to fade behind them.

The lives and histories of smiths have been kept private for over a millennium, and the fact that one resides so close to Bernard's old haynest, about a day's trek north, surprises him. Leading hermetic lifestyles, smiths wait unseen unless sought, and going into a bargain with them tends to be a precarious matter even though what they offer, from exotic weapons and armor to tools and machines that operate in unknowable and unimaginable ways, gives its bearer an advantage unmatched against enemies.

"Here we are."

In a small clearing, the shop comes into view. Its presence is almost unnoticeable, with its walls built in a distorted and arched style among what might have once been a massive tree. A staircase hewn from overgrown roots leads to a complexly engraved door ten measures above. Around them, sunlight, mostly blocked by the dense bramble, reaches in in narrow streaks.

Sanet drops her rucksack and pulls a handful of granola from it. "I'll wait for you here. Don't give away too much."

Brute pads into the area and hops onto Bernard's shoulder. Logan holds Bernard's bandaged and fingerless hand as they step up the precarious staircase, which narrows as it rises toward the upper landing and closed door.

Closer, the smell of burned leather and a surge of heat emanate from inside the shop, a *clank clank clanking* carried with them.

"You sure we're not intruding?" Bernard worries.

"You're always intruding on a smith, which is why their bargains cost so much. But you have real purpose for asking, and he'll see you're a true Radibian, not some festatar seeking treasure."

They read a plate on the door engraved plainly:

Tunston

They knock, and after a major, the clanking stops. Bernard takes a small step backward, and the ground near the edge loosens. Logan catches him before he recovers.

"Approsh."

"Don't be nervous. He'll say either yes or no. In either case, we'll have a pair of mitts from him or another."

Bernard nods, listening as muted footsteps draw closer to the door.

A minor passes, and the door opens. At it, Tunston stands before them. A tall and hulking friend, three sizes wider than either Logan or Bernard. His arms and forearms are round and thick, and each hand has four long, extended fingers at the top and two bent thumbs on either side of his lower palm, for a count of twelve digits in total. On the smallest finger of both hands grow sharp nails, unnaturally orange in color. His face is black with scars and marks, though bright blue eyes, buried deep within, pierce through. Overall, the smith appears swollen and puffy and wears a black leather cloth around his neck that is wrapped five times over, down, and across his muscular and naked figure.

"Whats am I helps yees for?" The smith speaks with an odd, uneducated accent.

Bernard steps forward. "Good friend, I hope I have not disturbed you, but I'm seeking a pair of mitts, as you can see." With this, he raises and displays his mangled hands.

The smith narrows his crystal-blue eyes and bends over for a closer inspection. "Yous have thees wee one fram whats?" He points to Bernard's lone little finger.

"I was unfortunate not to lose them all, I guess."

"Unfortunites, yees."

"Can you help me?" Bernard asks again.

"And whats it to me and yous that yous bring for bargain?"

"I am willing to bargain what is fair. I can offer fresh neox meat perhaps?"

The smith sniffs the air. "A start, friend. Yous bring me neox and yous may enter, but thas fur stamp stees outseed." The smith turns back into his shop, leaving the door open.

Logan and Bernard look at each other and shrug. Below them, Sanet is unpacking a tent from her rucksack. She looks up to Logan, who holds up his hand, thumb to fingers, relaying their success. She returns the gesture.

Bernard grabs the creshwillow and sets its down. "You're staying out here, Brute."

It looks at him with a twisted neck but remains. Logan and Bernard step inside.

After they close the door behind them, the air rolls warm and dry. Yellow, orange, and a flickering red replace the daylight and greenery of outside. Wall to wall, inlays of flaming coals light the shop and, from where they stand, lead to a long and looming hallway. Winding through, displays of the smith's past work showcase the precision and grandeur of his efforts. Behind glass windows are blades of many colors and material, some green with jade, others shining with sharp serrations. There are crossbows with double lines and gauntlets made of what resembles flexible gold. A small onyx orb floats in one of the displays, and every item shines with an air of handcraft and sophistication.

At the end of the hall, Logan and Bernard find the smith working at a forge. They step into a larger room many times hotter, which triggers both to sweat.

"Bring thees meats, friend."

Bernard pulls a few chunks of the neox from his sack and walks over, handing them to the large smith. Tunston takes the meat in hand, drawing a long whiff of it before setting it aside.

"Its bargain has begun buts yous must geeve more fram mitts."

It's unclear what the smith seeks. Tunston walks over to a stone oven and pulls an unfamiliar object from an iron pot before returning to the forge. He begins his work again, clanging the item against the anvil to shape it. Bernard stands motionlessly, his mind reaching for some intelligent thing to say or approach to employ the smith.

Logan steps in. "I have my father's blade to bargain."

"Logan, you don't—"

The smith looks up from his work and then takes the blade in his hand. "Thees blade fram Organsia. Yous father fram thees?"

"He was from Organsia, and his wife, my mother, was from Radiba. It is forged from their respective homes in water and land." He brushes his fingers across swirled indentions engraved in the blade and draws the smith's attention to the hilt formed of an ash-colored petrified wood. "It's been in my family's line for over three hundred years."

The smith ponders. "Thees is good fram bargain, buts only one mitt. Thees needs more bargain fram two."

Bernard rolls his eyes at the absurdity. "Maybe we should go elsewhere?"

Ignoring Bernard, Logan continues, "The creshwillow will stay, as will the woman outside."

Bernard moves to interject, but Logan holds him back.

At the prospect of two new companions, the smith's eyes widen a bit, and he looks at them fully for the first time since they entered. "No fur stamp. Yous wilst instead."

"For the work of Smith Tunston, it would be an honor." Logan's flattery comes off a touch insincere, and Tunston's eyes narrow.

"Yous lie and yous die."

Logan nods. "No lies."

Tunston steps toward them. He looks Bernard over closely. "Yous a good man?"

Bernard gulps. *I sent Jame left.*

"I try to be."

"Try ees no good. Yous mus be good to bargain fram mitts."

"I am a good man, Tunston. A friend. A fellow Radibian."

"Thees Land not cares who yous fram. It needs good. I provide only toos good."

Bernard has no answer. He wants to be a good man, but now the thought of leaving Jame buried under a rock six strides from his haynest makes him question it.

Tunston stares and, before Bernard answers, turns. "Thees bargain set. Return on thees morrow." He waves them away.

Logan nods and turns, grabbing Bernard by the jacket. Bernard remains quiet and follows.

Exiting the shop, they find Sanet has set camp, with a tent and little fire. At the major, she's writing in a small notesbook. Brute finds Bernard and hops onto him.

"Easy there, Brute."

Logan leads Bernard down the rooted staircase and they join Sanet near the fire. Though the sun won't set for a few hours, the clearing is already dark, lit by the few hints of fires burning inside the smith's shop and against their modest camp.

"So, what did you bargain for?"

Logan smiles. "It took some neox meat, my blade and . . . us."

"You two?" Sanet inquires.

Bernard interjects, "Not me. You two. And it wasn't my bargain. I'm not sure what happened in there. And I didn't have a minor—"

"There was nothing you were willing to part with that he would have accepted. You have to give him anything he asks for and then . . . renegotiate the bargain once the item's made."

Sanet is unconvinced. "Have you renegotiated with a smith before?"

"I've heard it can be done," Logan replies with unwarranted confidence.

Bernard looks at his single-fingered hand, shaking his head. *I'm going to be mostly fingerless forever.*

"What we must do is convince him that the things he's bargained for are not worth keeping, but only after he's made the mitts."

"And if he's not convinced?"

"Let's cross that Lothatin when we have to."

❖ ❖ ❖

The next morn, Bernard wakes to a shaking tent. *The tormisand. Shnite.* And then, the growl of the smith. "Yous get up. Mitts finish."

Sanet and Logan wake, her having slept on Logan's bare chest.

In a scratchy, half-awake voice, Logan answers, "One minor, Tunston."

He pulls a shirt over his head as Sanet sits up. She gathers her tangled hair back into a bun and shoots Bernard a knowing grin. Logan climbs over them and leaves the tent half-dressed. Brute lifts his eyelids lazily before going back to sleep. From inside, Bernard listens to the conversation between Tunston and Logan.

"Whys yous sleep so late?"

"Apory, the light here is so dark, hard to know when the sun rose."

"Yous make excuses."

"Never. You said you have finished already?"

"Yees. Mitts are esee. Where ees old one?"

Bernard's eyes widen. He looks to Sanet, who's buttoning her shirt, and mouths, *I told you.* She rolls her eyes in response.

"He's asleep," Logan says.

At this, Bernard crawls out of the tent, using his stumpy hands, and comes face to face with an entirely naked Tunston. Bernard quickly shields his eyes from its double low-hanging crotch.

"I'm here. I'm here." He stands with assistance from Logan and attempts to wipe the dirt from the stubs of his hands. A thin and damp fog floats quietly through the brush.

"Yous lie," the smith snarls, narrowing his eyes.

Logan shrugs, "Was it?" Silence sits between them.

"Follows me." Tunston makes for the shop, and with his turn bares a large, hairy rear topped with the stub of a tail. Bernard and Logan each hold back a cough. They follow at a distance.

Sanet pokes her head from the tent and whispers, "Should I follow?" to Bernard, who nods. At that, she pops back into the tent and exits a minor later, setting a dagger into her belt and quickly catching up.

At the top of the staircase, Tunston grabs his leather apron hanging from the door and wraps it around himself as he walks down the long hall. The three follow behind and find the shop in the same state it was before: hot and lit by coals.

At the forge, Tunston reaches for a box and turns to the three as they enter. He presents it to them and then opens the box with minute fanfare. Inside lay a pair of ordinary dark-brown leather mitts. Both mitts are filled in at the fingertips with an unknown material and the rest lays flat and unusually thin. With silent permission, Logan takes the east mitt and places it on Bernard's hand.

At first, it feels like a fresh leather glove, but then an odd sensation passes over Bernard's hand. It's cool to start, as if dipped in a polar sea, and then unexpected pressure squeezes against his skin, similar to when Logan massaged oilment into his hands. Its heavy touch develops into a hypnotic and soothing sensation. A constant, repetitive rhythm. After a major, Bernard closes his hand into a fist as the fingers of the mitt, filled with what he imagines are carved stones, move with his thoughts. He opens his hand and then closes it again before a grin forms on his face. "Lincoln, it feels like my own."

"Of course, ees yous own."

"Apory for my old friend," Logan interrupts. Bernard quiets. Logan reaches for the second mitt, but Tunston stops him.

"Yous mas loose thees wee one."

"What?"

"Thees mitts not works weeth fingers."

Bernard looks the smith in the eye. "Well, you didn't say that was part of the bargain."

"Yous not wants mitts?"

"No, I mean, I want the mitt, I just don't want to break off my last finger. It's my last finger!" Bernard's breath forms thick.

"Yous loose finger. Ice break it." The smith moves toward Bernard, who steps back.

"Please, we can—" Before Logan can finish, Tunston reaches out and skillfully grabs Bernard's hand. Without hesitation, Tunston's double thumbs pinch and snap, cracking Bernard's little finger. Bernard drops to his knees in pain.

Sanet, responding without thought, grabs her dagger and swings toward the smith. Logan tries to stop her, but she outmaneuvers him. In the same minor, Tunston snaps Bernard's little finger a second time, dislocating it from its socket. With his other arm, as if controlled by a different mind, Tunston grabs Sanet by the throat, lifting her off the ground. The swift tactic causes Sanet to drop her dagger as she instinctively grabs his forearm, struggling to release herself from the smith's choke.

Logan holds out his hands. "Everyone, please calm down."

Bernard screams out as Tunston rips the little finger from his hand and in the same motion throws Sanet to the ground. Bernard grabs his fingerless hand with his gloved one, attempting to stay the blood that pours out.

Tunston tosses Bernard the other mitt. With struggled effort, Bernard bears his bleeding finger and slides the mitt on, with increasing agony and a bitten lip. The sensations return. The cooling and massaging over his skin, the stones tumbling into order. He looks over his new hands, closing and opening them both. For the minor, he's lost in their power and the tight brown leather against his skin. As he watches, his west little finger begins to bleed through the mitt, turning it a dark and sour red. He stands, time returning as his pain subsides. Sanet sits up, holding a hand to her bleeding head.

In the minary silence, Logan presses his luck. "This is no way to treat your new friends. I think we must go."

Tunston's face contorts with sudden fury. "Yous lie?"

"You hurt my friends. You did not say that was part of the bargain. You lied."

"Ice no lie." The smith stomps one of his feet, causing the shop to rumble and bits of dirt to shower from the ceiling. "Yous lie!"

"Bernard, Sanet, it's time we left."

Bernard steps carefully over to Sanet to help her up. When he takes her by the hand, he finds that his grip feels remarkably firm, as if he could easily crush anything. Once standing, the two of them turn back toward the smith, who appears confused and angry. Logan attempts to calm Tunston down. "You have the blade and the meat. We offered the creshwillow, but you were not interested. And now I do not think it's safe for the two of us."

The smith stomps his foot again. "Yous lie, yous die!"

Tunston holds his hand up, and in the same instant a longblade flies from one of the glass cases, slinging glass shards across the room. The blade lands in Tunston's hand, and he immediately swings it at Logan. To Tunston's surprise, Logan dodges the swing and slides into the smith's knee, kicking him before rolling away. Tunston hops with awkward pain and then swings the blade again on the ground inches from where Logan rolled. Sanet pushes Bernard aside and reaches for her fallen dagger. With one swift motion, she pitches it across the room into the swollen smith's face. He stumbles backward, losing his footing.

"I think renegotiations are over." Logan leaps up and runs toward the exit, Bernard and Sanet following. As they scramble,

Logan calls over his shoulder, "We'll need to grab our things quickly."

They exit the tree, and Logan jumps straight forward, landing with a dexterous roll. Brute, perched on its hind legs, eyes them while Bernard and Sanet, not as daring or unafraid as Logan, stumble down the curved staircase and jump the last few steps.

As they hit the ground, Tunston emerges from his shop with fits and screams. "Yous lie, yous die!"

Without stopping, Logan gathers the tent in a handful, Bernard and Sanet grab the remains of their camp. They thrash back through the thick brush, regrown since their yester trek inward. Adrenaline forces them to stagger into the bramble, which cuts their clothes and skin.

"Shnite!"

Fearing the smith is close, they turn to see Brute charging directly at him, skipping the stairs and scaling the tree.

"Brute, what are you doing!" Bernard calls back.

Marking the rushing creshwillow, Tunston unexpectedly changes emotion from a furious rage to a puerile scream. He retreats into the shop, slamming the large wooden door as Brute launches toward it, scratching and making a noiseless whimper. The scene prompts the three to hold their run, with little control over their breathing. Between heaving breaths, Bernard speaks. "I think this draws Brute and I straight."

Chapter Six

AN UNWELCOME
DRUM AT BOMWIGS

omwigs Ale is the last tavern before the northern Radiba and southern Carvinga border, and it's around here that the forest canopy begins to open, allowing the cloudless pale-blue sky to make its first appearance. On the full day's trek north from Smith Tunston's shop, the three friends hike down from the mountain on rocks and large boulders that act as a natural staircase out of the Highlands.

Eventually, they come to an overlook. Below on the valley floor, the large entrance to the Carvinga Tunnels can be seen where faraway figures and friends mingle within and without. Ahead waits Bomwigs, built hundreds of years ago with simple sticks and stones and mud. Smoke rises from its chimney, and a flamboyant commotion pours out from its dirty windows. After the day's trek, the only thing the three friends can talk of is a refreshing pint and a soft bed to rest in.

They enter through a wooden door mantled in little carvings of bomwigs, so many that they make more a knotted pattern than an accurate depiction of the little freks. Warmth, humor, and an uncouth behavior permeate the guests of Bomwigs, which is usually populated by friends from all over the Highlands. Regulars and travelers alike descend upon the little tavern for nights of drinking and, in the sleeping rooms below, a bit of debauchery.

Bernard leads the three to an empty table near the hearth. As they sit, a barman walks up to them, scrawny, unshowered, and stains of ale covering his shirt. "What is it then?"

"Four Bomwigs Ales, of course, and some fried jellies as well." Logan points to Bernard and Sanet to see if they'd like to double anything. They shake their heads. The barman scribbles on a small pad and walks away.

Bernard takes in his hands again, noting a disconnected feeling in them. Though he can see his fingers, move them, when he concentrates on how they feel, there's only a cold press of stone from tips to knuckles.

Overheard conversations revolve mainly around the extended Peace Hours. Numerous bets on when the storm will pick up again are placed between a pair of rough-looking Radibians, while a sweet made couple seems to think that in fact it will be the last tormisand to pass through Radiba.

Bernard rolls his eyes and turns to the others. "Tormisands have no calendar. No watch, no schedule. Soon enough it'll return and probably be as fierce as ever."

"I'm sure of it," Logan doubles.

In a distant corner sits a family consisting of a father and mother along with their young son; their demeanor, when compared with the rest of the room, morose. The father's head is dressed in a bandage, which Bernard assumes is a result of the fires from nearly three days ago. *Jame has been gone three days.* He closes off the thoughts as the barman returns with four ales, dark and muddy in color, and a bowl of square fried jellies that he plops down before them. Brute hops onto the table and sniffs at the bowl before sneezing and turning away back under the table, curling in Bernard's lap.

"Four?" Bernard asks.

Logan replies, "For Jame. He won't mind if we drink for him, you suppose?"

Bernard presses his lips into a smile. He then grabs the first jelly and pops it into his mouth—*red brackleberry*—while overhearing some merry chanting behind him.

"The advent of the Roar. The advent of the Roar. The fires here we celebrate, the advent of the Roar."

Bernard turns and sees a group of men dressed in crimson and each with a small cape. One of them, the one with his back to Bernard, has a cape much longer than the others. Around them, patrons watch in annoyance. Though friends alike, they seem out of place here, as is their slurring, jarent celebration chant. Another barwoman walks past them, and they grab at her.

"Another round, sur."

"I think we've had enough, don't you?"

"Another! And another for the whole proshing place!"

At this liberality, the tavern erupts into its own gleeful cheer. Bernard turns back around. "Well, jarent friends can always be counted on serving too many." Logan and Sanet raise their mugs and drink to the adage as the tavern returns to its normal clamor.

"How's the hand, friend?" Logan asks later.

Bernard lifts his west hand for display, rotating and squeezing it in the hearth's light. "They're not my old fingers, but they'll do."

"Do you feel as strong?" Sanet asks.

He takes the mug into his hand and squeezes without effort. It immediately shatters, surprising everyone. The Bomwig Ale sprays across their faces and shirts.

"Lincoln," declares Sanet.

They laugh as onlookers shuffle slightly away.

After a few more rounds, the day's events seem weeks away. They laugh again at the image of the charging creswillow and raise an earnest toast to the lonely smith.

" . . . And his doubled cock."

The full moon approaches as the tavern gradually empties. Logan and Sanet plan to sleep in a single room while Bernard keeps to his own. After an exchange of coin for their room and board, the crimson friends begin their chant again: "The advent of the Roar. The advent of the Roar. The fires here we celebrate, the advent of the Roar." The chant, on and off for the past few hours, has grown tiresome among the patrons. On this recent round, the father of the corner family stands up, having worked up what appears to be jarent courage from a few pints of ale.

"Your celebrations are unwelcome here, friend. Friend and family died in those fires, and it was a nasty tragedy. Not a celebration for some new found Roar." He remains standing, if not wavering.

The din quiets against his anger, leaving only the crackle of the hearth. A major passes, then one of the crimson men stands. A man with dark, unkempt hair. Because his back was turned throughout the night, when he turns to Bernard's view, Bernard sees a surprising set of deep scorch marks that jacket his older face, nearly the same age as his. The jovial nature of his chant washes away. Replaced now by vehemence.

"Your witlessness is what saves you, friend," the man hisses in a slight lisp. "I assume your *words* have come from the bottom of that pint you've drunk."

The father swallows, gathering his wits. "You're monsters. Shnite inconsiderable monsters."

Silence.

Waiting.

And then the burned man replies without melody, his eyes never losing the father's, "The advent of the Roar. The advent of the Roar. The fires here we celebrate, the advent of the Roar."

He swallows as he finishes. The others he sits with smirk and huff, each licking their lips with hinted-at bloodlust. When the burned man speaks again, he walks closer and closer to the father, while still addressing the others of the room. "The Roar . . ." the burned man sermonizes, "the advent of the Roar is upon us. Found three days the yester. His coming will bring the union to these divided states. It is the will of the Land. Seven from the advent of the Roar." His last sentence is said inches from the father's face.

In response, the others at the man's table call out, "Seven from the advent of the Roar."

And a few others in the tavern now call out, "The advent of the Roar."

The father, either valiant or senseless, replies, "You sent my daughter left." His words are stilted with anguish.

His wife reaches for his arm. "Henrick, don't."

The burned man turns to the tavern. "Your lives do not matter. You've lived generations and generations apart from the union. You are all festatars upon us. We set the fires to show the Land that the war is coming. That soon the plague of being priced, of separation, shall come to an end."

These friends sent Jame left. Bernard grips the side of the table, barely holding his composure. It cracks.

The father punches the burned man in the back of the head. The man tumbles across a table, spilling mugs and ale.

Henrick's wife holds him back. "Please, Henrick. Stop."

Bernard and Sanet stand as the burned man recovers, wiping blood from his nose. "You're pushing tragedy, friend."

"Please, Henrick, let's go."

The father takes deep and uncontrollable breaths, his fist bloodied and closed, but ultimately, he gives in to his wife's request. She leads them out of the tavern, their son in tears in tow. The bar lies in a quiet major as the burned man returns to his table, ruffling his crimson cape across the back of his chair.

Bernard and Sanet sit down again, Sanet placing a calming hand on Bernard's mitt. The little finger on his west mitt dampens with blood.

Logan drinks, then says, "There's no reason to pick fights. Especially with union proselytizers."

Bernard is incensed. He chugs the last sip of his ale and slams the mug down. "I need rest. Come, Brute." He heads to the staircase leading to the sleeping rooms below. Brute hops after him.

"I think we all do," Sanet says, following his lead.

❖ ❖ ❖

Bernard doesn't sleep. Brute has long since slipped out into the night, and he lies alone on his bed. Jame's absence pulls over him. He turns to his side, hugging one of the pillows, in lucks to have it hold a hint of Jame's smell. When he performed the final arrangement for Jame, a painful and awkward affair without fingers, he also attempted to find a keepsake of their haynest. Something he might use to hold as memory, yet everything was burned. Nothing smelled the same. Nothing looked the same. It was no longer their haynest.

A creak in the hallway. Bernard rises to his elbow, listening. The footsteps are faint, as if not to be heard. Above him, the tavern has calmed. Bernard tosses off the blanket and grabs a hanging shirt. He creeps over to the door and slowly inches it open.

There, Henrick ambles. Hunched over with a small dagger in hand. *What are you doing, friend?* Bernard slips out of the room and follows Henrick as he turns a corner. He steps along and peers down the hallway.

Henrick extends his hand to a knob, looking both ways before touching it. Bernard leans back out of sight. He counts in his head before looking back down the hall. Empty. *Shnite, that man is going to send him left.*

Though no laws in Radiba prohibit sendlefts, the proper morality of Radibians has kept the state civil, that and the guilt of sending someone is taught to be worse than being sent.

Reaching the same door, Bernard finds it cracked open. He presses forward into the room and finds Henrick on his knees before him. Bernard looks ahead at the burned man sound asleep. *Still alive, approsh Lincoln.* Henrick turns to Bernard and silently gasps. Bernard hushes him, four fingers to mouth. He then motions for Henrick to leave with him. For a minor, Henrick looks as if he'll entertain his act of bloodlust, but instead he follows Bernard.

Returning to his room, Bernard pulls a few green brackleberries from his rucksack and hands them to Henrick.

"Green berry?"

"For calming. I usually smoke them but haven't had a chance to grind and roll." Bernard pops a few for himself and sits on the bed. "You would have regretted that, Henrick."

"I know. They were so callous. They're monsters." Henrick takes a seat on a chair near the door.

"I don't disagree. They," he hesitates to bring it back up, "they sent my husband left as well."

"Then they should pay. Shouldn't they?"

Bernard contemplates for a major. *Maybe they should.* At this, Tunston's question, "Are yous a good man?" crawls through his mind. "But bloodlust is no way to enact justice," he says, settling the debate.

"There is no justice in Radiba. This lawlessness only works if you're civil and kind. These aren't friends. They acted in selfishness. With—without empathy." Henrick stands, heated, chewing a few more berries.

Bernard finds it hard to answer. "Were you taught about the tallingstones?" he asks after a minor.

Henrick shakes his head and returns to his seat.

Bernard continues, "The tallingstones were a passive drum of freks who lived contentedly in the forest. Each tallingstone, as you know, subsists off the nutrients from a single mineral. Some eat stone, some wood, some leaf, and some subsist on water. And as a drum, tallingstones dwelled happily, living peaceful lives. And even though they shared that single forest, they lived off it as individuals. And it came one day that the wood tallingstone took a sip of water. And it found that water to be the most delicious thing it'd ever had. And so, it began to drink it every day. It drank and drank and drank. And this made the water tallingstone grow angry, for what was once only for itself was now being violated by another. In retaliation, the water tallingstone attempted to eat wood but found it to be completely inedible. So, they began to rival with each other, drinking more than they needed each day. When one saw the other drinking, it drank as well. This went on and on and on until all the water was gone. The streams and ponds dried. In the meantime, the wood around them grew thick. And it made the area the dirt tallingstones lived on uninhabitable. The leaf tallingstones could no longer climb the wood to reach the canopies. The entire drum was in disarray.

"With no water left, the wood tallingstone returned to eating wood and soon things were as they had been, except for the water tallingstone. It searched the forest for more water that it might drink, but the water never returned, and eventually the water tallingstone died. Over time, the other tallingstones asked the wood tallingstone why it had drunk all the water when it could easily have had its own abundance of wood. It replied that in truth, after only a few sips, it had had enough. But when the water tallingstone reacted so feverishly, it was afraid that it might not ever be able to taste water again. It only continued to drink because the other tallingstone wouldn't stop drinking. It told them that had the water tallingstone let it have those few sips every now and again, it would have quickly tired of the water and gone back on its own."

Henrick sits quietly for a major before asking, "Are you're telling me I should accept my daughter's sending?"

"I'm only saying that escalation leads to ruin. You sending that man left would mean that the others would send the rest of your family. And perhaps you. And then they'll go off and continue with their fanaticism, and what will have come to you?"

Henrick is quiet. He holds back emotion and then can't. He cries in his hands. Bernard leans over and hugs the friend, who easily returns the embrace.

The sound of whistles come, breaking the hug.

"Lincoln, the winds are back." *I hope Brute will be wisnok.* Bernard looks outside and sees the valley trees still.

Henrick stands, wiping his eyes. "I need to shelter my family. Approsh, friend. I don't know if you're correct, but hopefully, in the end, justice commands its way."

Bernard nods. The howls of wind draw his eyes to the window. He watches as squalls rip through trees, branches, and leaves, pulling horizontally, and then bring rain.

Henrick has left the room. Bernard hesitates to close the window in case Brute makes his way back. The rain splatters inside, and so he takes the blanket from the bed and rests himself in the chair, curling up as the storm gathers in size, the squalls squealing in pitch and the walls of the tavern grumbling at its rule.

A knock comes at the door before Sanet enters. "Your storm is back." Bernard looks back to her. "And your window's open." She points.

"Waiting for Brute."

"Aren't you always?"

Bernard huffs.

Sanet grins. "Well, grats moon."

"Good morrow."

Sanet closes the door. Bernard looks back to the window, the wind whistling in the open crack before a flash of lightning and boom of thunder. Six days ago, he was in this storm hunting the neox, the biggest venture he's had in years, and now he sits on the border of Carvinga embarking on a trek to Lands he's only kiptaled of. In search of . . . what? *A young man's adventure.*

Brute hops in. Wet and angry. He shakes himself on the bed and buries himself under a blanket.

"Good frek," Bernard says, standing to close the window.

He returns to the bed, consciously tired but unable to sleep. The story he told Henrick replays in his head, a parable for children to teach them of placidity. To show that slights of the Land are not worth a futile reaction. *Jame was sent left by that man.* Bernard's desire to stop Henrick was in proper morality; he had a family, and any retaliation against these crimson men was sure to be amplified with interminable wrath.

But I have no family.

The thought sticks. He lies in bed for a major. Then doesn't.

Bernard digs through his rucksack and pulls free a dagger before leaving his sleeping room. In the hall, he looks in both directions. Quiet. The staircase to the east sits in the soundless dark. He creeps forward, walking to the west, turning the corner, and stepping up to the burned man's room, where he places his ear to the door. Quiet.

He turns the knob gently, watching the hall, and then slips in silently.

The man remains asleep, this time on his side with a pillow over his head. Outside, the winds wail, this side of the tavern taking the brunt of the storm. Occasionally, twigs and tiny leaves slam with diminutive *thunks* into the glass. Bernard edges softly to the side of the bed. The burned man stirs and Bernard holds his breath and stops. The burned man shifts, causing his blanket to reveal intricate tattoos imprinted across his entire nude back. Tattoos of flames and barwolves, words and sentences from an old language. All his tattoos appear older than his more recent burn scars. The burned man stirs again, flipping onto his back and revealing a tattooed chest. One catches Bernard's eye: a black throne.

Bernard reaches out, the dagger in his east hand, the other at the burned man's neck. His heart beats wild. Like skinning a neox. *Are yous a good man?*

Bernard chokes him.

The burned man immediately reacts and pulls against Bernard. Scratching his forearm, his eyes begging for release. The pain is evident as he kicks and struggles with Bernard. *What am I doing?* And then he thinks of Jame. Burning in the house alone. Unable to escape. Bernard squeezes his mitt, and the burned man's eyes begin to bleed. His entire face goes purple. The man squirms hopelessly in Bernard's potent grip.

Bernard then stabs him in the side; the man's mouth opens to scream, able only to gasp. Bernard stabs again, a tear in his eye. He leans in close to the man inches from being sent left.

"Your war will never start. Your fire's unlit."

The man is left.

Motionless. Bernard stands in horror. *What have I done?*

Without hesitation, he turns and pulls a stick and pad. He writes a note and sticks it to the blood of the man's body, which gradually soaks through it. Bernard opens the door. The hall is still empty. He leaves and returns to his room.

Are yous a good man?

Chapter Seven

SANET'S CONFESSION

*I*f it wasn't the scream of panic and anger that awoke the sleepers of Bomwigs Ale, it was the banging on everyone's door. "Get up. Get up!" Bernard, already awake, stands at the door, waiting for the crimson men to reach his. He keeps his ear to the wood. Two doors. One door. *Bang bang bang*.

"Get up."

Bernard leans back and pulls the door open, holding his foot at the base to keep it firm in case the men attempt to barge in. He holds his dagger at the ready. Down and up the hall, other patrons peek their heads out, confused and out of sorts.

Logan pokes his head out. "What's all this ruckus? It's barely morn."

"Someone calling themselves Stone Fingers sent Franz, whose being torn apart by proshing decomps. And this sendleft wrote a note like a shnite vigilante."

Others in the hall begin to murmur. Logan doesn't answer. His eyes dart to Bernard, who nods. Logan attempts to hide his surprise, but not before the man sees the exchange. He turns back to Bernard.

"Do you know something about this 'Stone Fingers,' friend?"

"That man was asking for it from a dozen eyes."

"Yes, but he wasn't asking to get sent." The man narrows his gaze, peering closer at Bernard's visible hand. "Why are you wearing those leather mitts, old man?"

Logan calls out from behind, "Heyo." The crimson man turns straight into the butt of Logan's pistol. He falls unconscious to the ground. Another of the crimson men, who at the time is interrogating another friend down the hall, turns. Logan looks to Bernard. "Time to go then?"

Without waiting a minor, Bernard grabs his already packed rucksack as the crimson man shouts to anyone who'll listen, "Stop them!" Sanet steps from her sleeping room and aims her crossbow down the hall and shoots the man in his leg. He pauses in a stupor before falling to the ground.

Barely dressed, Sanet and Logan take a major to grab their rucksacks and then head for the stairs. The rest of the patrons, still waking, remain motionless, unsure of who to trust or what to do.

Rain pours as the door to Bomwigs bursts open, the three friends tumbling from the tavern. Catching step, Logan points to the road leading down into the valley and toward the Carvinga Tunnel entrance. "This way."

As they run, they fling their rucksacks over their backs. Brute comes jogging from the forest edge around the backside of the tavern. Faster than them, the creshwillow leaps and claws onto Bernard's rucksack.

Behind them, eruptions of gunfire. "Get back here, sendlefts!"

They continue to run, the road having turned into slick mud.

Sanet shouts through the heavy rain, "We should steer from the road."

In agreement, the three shift from the main path and onto what transforms into a sudden drop. Bernard halts before the others and grabs a tree. Ahead of them, lightning flashes, followed by thunder.

"It will be tricky getting down there quickly."

"Don't think you've given us a choice, Stone Fingers," Logan replies with fury in his eyes.

"Apory. They sent Jame left." Bernard's heart feels a sudden tightening. *What have I done? Why did I have act in such malice?* He feels sick. And vomits.

"We can grit about this later; let's first get to the Tunnels. They won't shoot us once we're around all the other bodies," Sanet yells, pulling Bernard, who wipes his mouth.

She leads them through a hazardous descent. Slick rock covered in moss and rain and towering trees and branches make every step a careful choice. Above them, the shouts of the pair of crimson men echo across the valley, though their pursuit loses steam after a few early stumbles on the rocks.

"You can't run, Stone Fingers. We know who you are, you shnite beast." After a few missed shots blasting the branches and trunks above the three, they halt their pursuit.

Continuing down the rocks takes the better of two hours and with a few nicks and bruises on their arms and legs, they make the valley floor with the Carvinga Tunnels entrance only a few hundred strides away.

Sanet turns to them. "It'll be good to put the tormisand behind us, right, friends?"

Bernard is the last to drop to the level ground, where Brute is waiting for him. He hops onto his shoulder. "I'll need a minor please."

"There's a killhung once we're inside, Bernard. We should rest there." Bernard, kneeled over, takes a deep breath and waves them off.

"It's you who put us in this rush, Bernard," Logan calls back.

Bernard knows. Perhaps he wasn't ready to move on. Perhaps he forced this adventure. But it's too late to turn back. He takes a deep breath. "I know. I'm coming."

The entrance to the Carvinga Tunnels is grand, standing two hundred measures high, five hundred strides wide, and noticeably busier than the forest Highlands behind them. Friends march in and out, making their way along a main road, which leads to the sea to the far east and the Guloren border to the west. The walls of the entrance cut sharp and straight, vertical to horizontal.

Pacing closer, Bernard glances up at strings of yellow neon illuminating the tunnel, solid strips of light as far as he can see. Stepping in, he notes the way the rain behind them creates a curtain of water from the top of the Tunnels and splashes down into mud-drenched puddles below. Children play against the waterfall, splashing each other, jumping into the water, and laughing uncontrollably. Older friends move with purpose and direction, while others, like Bernard, stand in awe of the impressive sight.

Ahead, among other shops and stores carved into the Tunnel, a killhung serving food and drink curamed Radiba Lasts stands, bustling with friends. The neon throughout this building fades from green to red. Friends sit and eat an assortment of odd delicacies. As Bernard passes one breathless-looking friend, he sees little bomwigs wiggling about a plate as the man stabs at them with his prong and then slurps them down, with an indulgent gulp. Sanet and Logan, unmoved by the alien Land, find a booth inside the killhung. Bernard sits, setting the rucksack to his side. Brute pads back and forth along the back of the seat, observing his surroundings.

"Stone Fingers?"

"Apory."

Logan speaks plainly. "You could have sent us left."

"I didn't go into the dusk to send a man left. I couldn't sleep. And I heard footsteps. And Henrick had returned."

A thick waitress comes up to them. "What can I get you?"

"Waters, please," Sanet answers.

"Some coffee sticks to start. And eggs under," Logan orders.

"Over for me," Sanet doubles.

"Nothing for me," Bernard says, still sick in his stomach.

The waitress writes the order on her pad and walks away. Bernard looks to the two of them, who sit in silence, watching him with confusion and judgment.

"Henrick went to that burned man's sleeping room to send him, and I gritted him out of it. When Henrick left, I couldn't sleep. The thought of Jame—" Bernard looks to his hands. His little finger is bleeding.

The waitress returns with three glasses of water. "Your sticks and eggs will be out in a minor." She leaves.

Logan fiddles with his thumbs before responding. "Were you not taught that retaliation is no way to uncover justice? It's one of the most basic Radiba tenets. It's how we live in this peace. That was an act of a tenfooter. And those men won't stop—"

"I know, Logan. I know. But it's not the way I chose to act, nor what I think was right. It was just what came over me."

"Why did you leave a note?" Sanet asks.

"If I didn't write anything, they would have believed it was that family. I would have sent them left for what I did." The burned man's purple face flashes before him. The stab of the dagger. His hatred.

"Bernard," Sanet starts, "I have to tell you something, and this may counter Logan's belief; but when I spoke to that protnuk, she said something about you."

"The Dark Valor . . . you've mentioned."

"Yes, that. But she also said that you would 'miss the nine but one more.'" Bernard looks up. "When you went into that fire, when you lost your fingers, all but one? I thought it was a coincidence. And then I thought the one more was Jame."

Logan interrupts. "Protnuks? How is that relevant?"

"Miss the nine but one more?" Sanet looks to Bernard, staid. "She also said the Dark Valor, the sleeping man, you . . . would be the one who reunites these pieces." She pulls from her pouch the sliver of brass. "That you were the one who would stop the war."

Logan's eyes narrow in confusion. "Brass? What is that?"

"Me?" Bernard asks.

"I know. As I said, I dismissed it. Even with the coincidence of your fingers."

"Why do I have to reunite the brass? What does that even mean?"

"Do you know what a Dark Valor is?" Sanet asks. Bernard shakes his head. "He or she comes from humble beginnings and is met with great tragedy before the Land calls upon them. They are not heroes. Nor villains. They act only as arbiters for the Land. To protect it."

"Are you saying sending that man left was what the Land wanted?" Bernard scoffs.

"I'm saying the fury you felt inside you is from forces larger than your own."

"If it weren't me, it would have been Henrick. And my fury was from that man setting fire to my haynest. It was their act of selfishness and it was my act of retaliation."

"And that's what I'm saying a Dark Valor is . . ."

The waitress returns with the eggs, setting a plate in front of Sanet and Logan with the bowl of coffee sticks between them. "Enjoyments."

"I'm going to double with Bernard, I find these religions of Yikshir to be a bit flam."

"I'm not saying this to convince you that some protnuk in a random cave foretold the coming of a Dark Valor. I'm telling you what she said, and what that means to me."

Logan takes a few bites of his eggs. "Look, Bernard, I do hope you can approsh that I understand what you did. I think it was the wrong thing, but I also know we cannot undo our past. A truth I struggle with. And I know it won't be easy dealing with what you did."

"They sent him. That proshing beast sent him left." Bernard starts to cry.

Sanet reaches over the booth to comfort him. "You have nothing to concern yourself with. The Land chooses the path."

Bernard takes Logan's and Sanet's hands and squeezes them. They both wince.

"Careful there," Logan yelps.

Bernard retracts his mitts. "Apory."

Logan smiles. "With a grip like that, you better find someone else to jumble your jolly, or you may end up hurting yourself." Sanet and Bernard grin slightly. "I know you're a good man, Bernard." Logan squeezes his shoulder.

After their mornmeal, they each take a bit of coin to purchase appropriate clothes, for the trek into the Tunnels would get considerably hotter the deeper they delved. Sanet bargains for a new dagger, as does Logan, though his new blade is duller and simpler than the one he gave away to the smith, and ammunition for his pistol.

As Logan sheathes the knife, Bernard calls out to him, "I cross to reclaim that blade for you."

"If you're going to be some Dark Valor, that'll be good enough, Stone Fingers."

Bernard grins and shakes with Logan on the terms.

Part Two

LOGAN

Chapter Eight
FIRES ACROSS THE LOTHATIN

*P*erhaps it's because he's feeling tipst from a doubled pour of Bomwigs Ale, but when Logan sees the handsome woman in a green hood tracking carefully through the forest, he elects to tail her. Her efforts between the trees and across the boulders of the Radiba Highlands is smooth, precise, and hypnotic. He wonders who or what she might be tracking, and as the full sun passes toward dusk, Logan's patience wears. He becomes bolder. And decides to approach.

She stoops behind a large rock and raises a crossbow hung from her side, aiming it into the deeper forest. Logan scans its trajectory and discovers a frek he hasn't seen since he was a boy: a large headless neox. Returning to her aim, Logan projects that she's likely shooting the neox square, but the bolt would hit the frek in the best parts of its meat. *Probably flam, but—*

"Ma'am. Psst. Pssst." The bolt releases. And misses.

Still crouched and with a single and unflinching reaction, the woman reloads, then aims her crossbow toward Logan, who responds by lifting his hands to his head.

"Ma'am, I appize the missed shot, but you were going to ruin a good portion of the meat there." He points his finger to an absent neox.

She stands upright, her crossbow fixed straight and paces closer. "Are you jarent?"

Logan grins, taking a step backward. "A pinge."

"I've been tracking that beast for months."

"Tracking? One neox? For months? Are you that afraid of omens?"

She presses the crossbow closer to his face. "Is this how you bargain for your life?"

"No, apory. May I put my hands down? I cross I'm not your enemy." Carefully, Logan draws a small *X* on the east side of his chest. The woman aims only a minor longer before dropping her crossbow in frustration. Relieved, he lowers his other arm.

The woman looks back to the empty forest. "Your timing is shnite."

Unable to disagree, Logan doesn't answer. After a minor, he says, "I can only give appize once. Curam's Logan." Without turning back, she gives her own.

"Sanet." Looking at the elegant woman further, Logan has a sudden rush of guilt. *Something about her—*

And then she turns back, her face both anxious and—*is it shock?* "You said your curam is Logan?" He nods as she bites her lip and narrows her eyes.

In this minor reflection, Logan presses further, "If that neox is headed south toward the Lothatin Bridge, any number of friends on the other side are sure to . . . find it. Its parting path now is likely but a . . . fiddle and tease."

In a deep breath, Sanet replies, "I'm just tired. I should be after it, but I need sleep." She leans against a tree, closing her eyes.

Logan steps over. "You seem so familiar to me. Like I've seen you in a kiptale."

Sanet opens a single eye. "You say that to all your lyns?"

"Did it work?"

She shrugs as she leaves the tree, adjusting her rucksack and holstering her crossbow.

Logan continues, "I should at least cook you a duskmeal. As I said, that frek's long gone and will be likely hunted by a dozen friends. If you need further sums, my home's a day-and-a-half's hike in the same direction." She doesn't answer. Still pressing, he goes on, "You're heading there anyway, so let me walk with you."

Sanet eyes him slightly before giving a resigned huff. "A hot meal does sound good."

"A bargain then."

He pops out his hand in wait. Sanet presses her lips together, and they shake.

❖❖❖

As they set off through the forest, Sanet undoes her long black hair, letting it tumble past her shoulders. "I say this with no intention to frighten you, but I followed you mainly because you're tremendously handsome." A sudden flush of embarrassment washes over Logan. "That and I was feeling a little bold after some Bomwigs Ale."

"I've not had the pleasure of Bomwigs.'"

"Well, I can't refuse terrible ale. Bomwigs is the first taste of home after the Tunnels, regardless of where the sun's living."

"You're from here in Radiba?"

"I am. Parents took me in when I was very young. My mother's from here. My father from out west in Organsia."

"I've yet to travel west. Is that where you came?"

"Yep. Where I go every year. Four months there, four months back. Though, I decided that this will probably be my last trek haynest. Only staying for a few days."

"A four-month trek for only a few days haynest? You sound as flam as me." Sanet steps across a puddle. Logan attempts to help her, but she quietly refuses.

"In truth, I wasn't planning on coming back but didn't want to leave a few things behind. And to double, Radiba's a handsome sight this time of year, isn't it?" The air sits brisk and light while songs of jarjers soaring above fill the lush green forest with a familiar and welcoming sound.

"One last look couldn't hurt." He continues on as he helps Sanet atop a sizable boulder. She smiles polite, both knowing she doesn't need the assist. "So, how does one track neox for months?"

"Mostly through Carvinga. Slowly through Carvinga. Very. Very slow."

"Tracking through tenfooter land?" Logan is incredulous.

"It did keep me focused. When I lost the neox in the blades, it made for some . . . precarious nights. As I'm sure you're aware, the grasses are difficult to navigate. Fear of losing that neox outweighed any fear of tenfooters."

"I'd surmise you're Yikshir if you're that frightened of a neox's omen."

"I do come from Yikshir, but it's not omens that push me. It's what the neox has inside it. And why shooting it square, losing some useless meat, was the last of my concerns."

"You know any trash that neox ate would have passed?"

"What I'm looking for didn't pass . . . I checked." Sanet frowns as Logan laughs but, on seeing the reaction, propers himself.

"You're quite the florelle." She doesn't answer as the conversation draws quiet to the simple sound of their paired footsteps traveling in and out of sync.

Time passes before it's late enough for them to set up camp. They sleep in separate tents. Logan is unable to fall asleep. Almost giddy in his instant attraction. *To have a quick snuggle with her. To be worthy of her.*

The next day brings with it a long trek upward as the two continue to discuss their travels and the plenitude of dangers they have faced. By the time the sun hits crest, they're nearly great friends with an ease between them that Logan can't help but latch on to just as his haynest comes to view.

A narrow path leads to his front door, which is faded underneath a crinkled weed that Logan brushes and kicks away in a sudden burst of humiliation. He reaches the door and holds it for Sanet, nodding with approsh as she steps inside.

"You're welcome to take my old room. I've moved over to the master."

"This isn't yours?"

"It is. But it was my parents' haynest until they moved to the shoreline, against my suggestion. Tormisands and all. But hard to break that custom with old Radibians. In any case, when my father was sent left, my mother returned here and took back her old room."

"And where is she now?"

"Sent left, last year."

"Oh. My sympathies."

"Approsh. She was happy to the end, which is what matters." He pauses. "In other ways, you can unpack there and settle in. I have a few slices of meat left over from the Tunnels I had planned to grill tonight."

"Sounds delightful."

Sanet leaves the room, and Logan enters the kitchen. With a quick glance at piles of filth and used dishes, he panics and rushes to straighten up. Leaving the house in such a state became suddenly disconcerting with a handsome woman around. *Mom would be ashamed.* After a quick and surface clean, he begins to grill.

It's not long before Sanet enters, fresh as flowers. "I took a shower. I hope that was wisnok." She's handsome cleaned up. Though she was beautiful with layers of dirt and tangled hair, freshly showered, she carries the air of a royal family's Mane.

Logan attempts to say something, perhaps a compliment of her looks or smile or presence, but instead he remains in a silent stupor, responding only in a flamboy nod. Sanet flashes him a smile and leaves him sure they'll be single souls.

Engorged with unstinting drinks and a splendid duskmeal, the two friends laugh and talk past full moon. Sanet continues to present herself as generous, intelligent, and well traveled. Causing Logan to take note of the minor. A recollection of his lost happiness. And of what has filled it.

The things he broods on.

The fulfillment of his unhappiness.

Of the debts he owes to the Victors and the troubles awaiting him on his return to Organsia. And for this passing major, Logan thinks he could remain here, in the peace of Radiba with the company of a handsome, beaming woman.

But the Victors would find me. There was no hiding from them. And with the excessive debts that Logan owes, there will be no forgiveness. To double, he is confident that if they had to make a four-month trek east to track him down, his life would not end in smiles. For now, however, his apprehension is measures away, replaced by the leer and curves of Sanet.

She continues talking, " . . . are you tipst again? Are you always so flushed?"

"What was that?"

She laughs. "A perfect answer."

Logan smirks. "Apory. It seems yes. Always."

Sanet stands and, without warning or circumstance, kisses Logan, taking his face in her hands. In turn, Logan reaches around and grabs her from behind.

Sanet backs off, biting her own lip. "I've heard good things about Radiba men."

"You'll find us friends incredibly generous."

They kiss again and make their way into the master.

❖ ❖ ❖

Bare in his bed, Sanet sleeps soundly against his chest, her hand intertwined in his. Rough skin, from hard labor. *She's of the*

Land. Logan massages her fingers with his thumb while a midmorn shaft of sun carries small specs of dust across the room.

Sanet opens her eyes and, looking toward the window, props herself on her elbows. "I haven't slept that well in months." She kisses Logan on the cheek. "Grats."

As she sits all the way up, her lack of modesty draws out a rise in Logan. He reaches from under her, cupping her breast before peppering her back with soft kisses. He rubs his nose against her skin, breathing in a natural sweet scent.

She giggles at his touch and spins back onto him. "Another slip, my friend?"

He nods, eyes wide like a child.

The two wander the haynest bare through the full sun, stopping between meals to slip in and out of each other. They stretch in the sunlight and roll on the front lawn, then shower and wash and sit outside. Dusk comes. Sanet curls into Logan's shirt. Logan wraps in a towel. At the major, Logan is shining his parents' blade. A gift to him when they'd moved to the shoreline. The sky bears a swirled shade of pink and orange and red.

"Looks like a storm's looming."

At this, Sanet's mood changes. "You think?"

"Sky like that's somewhat telling. May not be a tormisand. Could just be a little thunderstorm." He sits back, holding the hilt of the blade between his legs. And then, as if coming out of a daze, Sanet stands.

"I should go."

"Go? Where?"

"If this is a tormisand, it'll make tracking that frek impossible."

"The neox?"

"Despite what some may want, I didn't trek all this way to just slip with a boy."

"First, approsh for the soft compliment. Second, I'm sure you can hold that frek as a loss."

"Unfortunately, it's not something that can be lost."

She retreats inside, stripping herself of Logan's shirt and tossing it to the floor. *A fling, I suppose. Better than none.* Logan takes the shirt and follows her into the master as she dresses.

"You're a handsome slip, Logan. I wish it were better timing."

"If you find your frek, will you come back?"

"I'd have to go back to Yikshir then."

"I won't be here long, perhaps we could travel north together?"

"I'm sure we'll meet again. Maybe at the Crossroads in a year's time, something like that?"

Logan frowns. *I'll never see her again.* "Going all the way to the Crossroads? I usually take the Rail, just after Barwolves Pit."

"Well, that's my only bargain . . . I should go." She walks over, dressed and with her rucksack over her shoulder. She reaches around Logan's neck, pulling him in for a kiss one last time. "Approsh, Logan. You've given me the energy to make things right. And to let myself . . . give in a bit."

"It was my pleasure."

As she leaves, she kisses two fingers and rests them a minor against the top of the doorframe before stepping outside, where the first drops of rain hit her face. Logan watches her disappear into the wood before stepping inside.

Alone again.

❖ ❖ ❖

The next day, he packs the few items he returned home for and sets them in a rucksack by the door. He wanders the house, shutting the windows and doors and cleaning the mess from both his extended absence and the twenty-four-hour tryst. While picking up, he finds a forgotten shirt left by Sanet—*on purpose I hope*—and stuffs it into his rucksack. The rain outside doesn't look to be too troublesome at the major, and he hopes that by morn it'll clear up. He falls back onto the master bed, restless with endless thoughts of Sanet, while rain patters rhythmically and unbroken against the windows. One more night, before he returns . . .

❖ ❖ ❖

Squalls already? Logan wakes to the master window hurling open and closed. He hurries over, slamming it shut and attempting to lock it. The window struggles against his strength. *Proshing bells.* He turns the latch at the sill, but it snaps off its hinge, which permits a torrential rain to teem inside. "Forget it."

Leaving the window flapping and a small growing puddle on the floorboards, he walks down the hall into the kitchen to make himself an early mornmeal, an under of eggs and granola. The broken master window becomes another sign that his trek here was the wrong idea. The haynest sitting alone in his absence, abandoned and forgotten since his mother was sent, fits the current state of things.

Wanted thoughts of the handsome Sanet, wandering through the halls naked under a borrowed shirt, grow further away as the threat of the Victors skulks back in, riding atop the regret he holds in hiring them. His incautious attempt to discover a purpose for his father's sending ignored warnings from friends that "only the flam enter into a bargain with the Victors." *But who sent my father left?* These thoughts bring an unwanted memory of his father's sent corpse twisted in that inhuman form—

Logan has long thought about what he might do when or if he ever found out who sent his father. Immoral thoughts consume him, a desire for what he knows would be an unsatisfying retaliation. A hollow vengeance. *The tallingstone's tale may be shnite pacifism*, but it does earn itself one truth, that the only friend damaged in retaliation is the retaliator. His Radibian upbringing of gentleness and pacifism is why he eventually called off the Victors' investigation. He realized he shouldn't know who did it, and he also didn't want to face a decision to "let it go." That was when the Victors tripled what he owed, an unfounded and unfair turn of events. *But no one says no to the Victors.*

Outside, the winds die down after only an hour. *An oddly timed tormisand if it is one.* He stands and looks around for the last time, knowing this would be as good a time as any to leave. He lifts his rucksack and flings it over his shoulder—breaking and spilling his belongings across the foyer and into the front yard.

"What in proshing bells is going on today."

Remnants of rain drip from the roof onto his exposed clothes and rations. Logan curses as he retrieves his belongings, returning everything to the house in a slopped mess.

It takes hours before he's repacked, retooled, and ready to return to the trail. As he shuts his door and begins down the narrow path, a glimpse of smoke to the south catches his eye. The dark plumes appear to originate from a fire. *After so much rain?* He conceives that lightning must have caused a spark or perhaps a small brackle fire but believes it won't last long in the rain-drenched forest, *except frontz leaves don't burn out in water.*

His curiosity draws him closer and he wonders if he might get a better glimpse of the fire from across the Lothatin Bridge. He sets off along the trail, making his way through the forest, losing sight of the smoke as the canopy above thickens. *You're delaying yourself again.*

After a half mile or so, the colossal Lothatin Bridge, one of the key landmarks of the northern Radiba Highlands, comes into view. Its foundation was erected in timber, then reinforced with high stone columns carved with figures and scenes of a distant past that detail the fabled tale of the Last War, two and half thousand years ago when the North fought the South. A war protracted and expanded through the whole of the Land. A war that left humanity with no more than a hundred thousand friends. These final men, women, and children made a Great Migration to what is now the state of Niance, a city built over a city built over a city until the entire state itself became one of the tallest manmade peaks in the Land. There, debates took place over many decades that eventually led to the formation of the first borders of the hundred and thirty-three states. Each state chose to govern itself in isolation without fear of intervention from its neighbors, regardless of politics or moralities, a predilection that was one of the leading causes of the Last War. It was important that the states had total independence of each other. Once formed, the remaining hundred thousand returned to their new and individual states, leaving some with a return of only a few hundred friends. After the Last War, most of the Land, once populated with large numbers of friends, lay sparse and unclaimed.

The smoke across the Lothatin Bridge is not of a single forest fire but of many smaller fires, each originating from a distant haynest along the Highland ridge. *Lincoln, what chanced here?* Logan hurries across the bridge, wondering if anyone might need help. As he approaches, he sees the old Babek house aflame and then . . . a fleeting impression of Sanet, running in her green hood, screaming for his neighbor Bernard.

Chapter Nine
SOUTH FREKS WORTH IT

*T*raveling deeper into the dimly lit Tunnels, the gang finds the endless strip of yellow neon isn't the only thing that's distinctive from Radiba. The Tunnels also breathe in a despotic heat, without a cool breeze carrying through; an air that presents itself stale and listless, gluing sweat to skin. Friends, colloquially known as "denizens," often amble about bare chested and when the heat at times rises to temperatures too unbearable, they quite literally strip to their unders. Around them, lone window shops sell an assortment of odds and ends. Foods. Weapons. Sex and ales. Bernard, who at the minor is ogling the air of sexuality floating through the Tunnels, amuses Logan. *The innocent kid.*

The friends here are rougher. Meaner. And more primal. Witnessing an all-out brawl in the road or an outright sendleft is commonplace. Passersby sometimes wear busted noses or spit blood as reward for escalating trivial slights. The lawlessness of the Tunnels operates in near opposition to the lawlessness of Radiba. There, there's a moral center, respect for friends and the Land. Here, the Tunnels are populated with travelers from across the Merigen states, with clashing cultures and moral truths creating a constant unspoken tension.

This is doubled by an abnormal perverseness hiding in the Tunnels. A knowing that anyone can victimize with anything, where judgments are kept to one's self. Flings and behaviors travelers avoid elsewhere are encouraged, if not desired, here. When the tenfooters built and soon after abandoned the Tunnels, they made the prodigious assertion that these Tunnels would devolve into the sewers of the Land. And it would be difficult to find anyone who doesn't agree.

A trio of hardened men shrouded in dull-yellow hoods pass by, seated on giant krakes. They leer down at the three friends from the towering and plodding freks, a standard mount of the Tunnels. Krakes were first discovered in small scattered-about nests during the tenfooters' excavation beneath the Carvinga surface; though most krakes are domesticated these days, these first exposed drums reacted with extreme violence, causing many horrific casualties among the Carvingians.

It took nearly ten generations to domesticate these slow freks wandering about the tunnels, made so as they subsist on tiny parcels of meat and excessive amounts of sleeping. Known by many as the "scaled sleepwalkers," krakes can trudge along, step by step, while they're resting, which, without the careful guidance of their riders, leads many parties into hidden, sometimes undiscovered expanses. When not sleeping, the sightless krakes lick the air to orient themselves. In total, they make better-suited and quicker mounts than getwishes, the more traditional riding frek over the hundred and thirty-three states. As they plod along, their glinting scales rattle about as if attached to loose strings and cause a soft and distinctive *klink klink klinking* echo, another hallmark of the underland sewers.

"I feel like a kid seeing the Land for the first time," Bernard states as the strange trio on krakes passes.

Logan grins. "Had I known you'd enjoy a good trek, I would have invited you on a trip west." As solo treks across Merigen are often coupled with gloomy isolation, warm company offers a welcome respite. These thoughts drift toward Logan's impending goodbye, as the turnaway toward the Rail is only a few hours away. *Perhaps I could continue north with them and then break away at the Crossroads?* The Victors, however, would know. *They know everything.*

"As much as I love that idea, I couldn't leave Jame by himself that long."

Logan swallows. *Of course.* "I'm appize. It still doesn't seem real."

"Doubled."

"In any case, you both should grab your own krakes for the venture north," Logan continues. "Though, I'd keep that creshwillow of yours safe, Bernard. They could mistake him for a mood cog."

"Brute is no cog," Bernard says, offended. "And why aren't you heading north with us?"

"After Barwolves Pit, I'll be taking the Rail. Easiest way west. If I don't, I'll have to make my way all the way through Misipit Valley on foot."

Sanet speaks up, "I, for one, am no gully for that state."

"It's not the most pleasant in Merigen."

Bernard speaks to them both. "How have I missed so much in life?"

A few hours pass before they arrive at a large hollow in the Tunnels. Here, the floor and walls and ceiling open into a massive chamber. "And there it is, Barwolves Pit," Logan presents.

Along an endless circular wall, storefronts are stacked on top of storefronts, each carved into the stone. Glass and neon signs flash, each competing for attention. Sex and weapons shops, bookstores and killhungs. Denizens stand outside begging passers to partake in their wares. They insult and jab, compliment and whistle. The center of the pit is populated by hundreds walking in all directions, with no order to the chaos. Barwolves is a choking point in the southern Tunnels, a hub of grand- and low-man activities. Logan takes Bernard by his mitt, leading him through the crowd. Brute acts enamored by the noise, hopping purposelessly between Bernard's shoulders.

"Careful there," Bernard warns as he helps balance the frek.

Behind them, Sanet walks with purpose, indifferent to the denizens and their hostile energy. "The sooner we can get a mount, the better."

"Not a friend of Tunnelers, are you?" Logan jabs.

Before she's able to answer, a muscled, well-oiled denizen approaches, tapping her on the shoulder. "You looking for slip?"

Sanet turns to Logan in response. "Not for me, but I'm sure this one is."

She jerks her thumb at Logan. The large denizen scans him a minor. He approves, lifting his head to repeat the offer.

Perhaps with Sanet in play, Logan thinks before answering, "Not today."

"Fine. You then, old man?" The denizen nods to Bernard, which puts him in a twisted state. Logan squeezes him by the hand and edges him away from the decision. And so they continue through the crowd as the man behind them calls out to any passing ear, "Looking for slip?"

On the other side of Barwolves, the neon-yellow light continues its trail northward, while a bright-green neon strip turns west, denoting the route to the Rail. *Where I say goodbye, it seems.* As they continue closer and closer to the turnoff, Logan's heart skips with anticipation.

"Why don't you come with us to pick out krakes, Logan?" Sanet suggests. Her voice soothes him.

"We get to pick our own beasts?" Bernard says, excited.

"I should head west . . ." Logan states without conviction.

Sanet grabs him by the hand and pulls him forward. "Don't break up the gang. Plus, neither Bernard nor I have ever ridden a krake." Her argument is flimsy at best, as krakes are the easiest of all the Land's mounts, but her eager eyes and sensual smile coax him to stay.

"I guess I could take a small detour."

"That's my boy," Sanet says, squeezing his hand before letting go. She hurries forward, wrapping her arm around Bernard.

She's hard to read. *Why drag me along?* But in the end, it doesn't matter. It is further from the inevitable.

❖ ❖ ❖

With the green neon turnoff far behind them, the three friends approach a desolate store curamed South Freks Worth It. It carries a quiet, humble façade where a broken neon sign, with only the *W* flashing in blue, hangs off an outstretched roof. Fluorescent lights pour out of the store's interior as they approach the front glass door. Logan holds it for the others.

The inside reeks of death, feces, and urine. Logan passes and leads them to a counter where a portly man with bright-red hair bites his nails. They wait, as this strange friend either doesn't see Logan or is ignoring him.

"Afternoon, my friend. We're here to bargain for a few krakes," Logan states.

Silence. An earnest-looking woman, no more than twenty and with short blonde hair, walks through a back room holding a sickly-looking cog. It's green, fuzzy, and ostensibly without a face. *A small obnoxious puff ball.* The cog sneezes, tossing thin green hairs into the air that change into a myriad of colors ending in black.

The woman looks up from petting the cog, bored. "Welcome, travelers, can I help you?"

Logan turns. "Yes, we were hoping to bargain for a couple of krakes?"

"Oh, then I can help with that. And don't mind Earls; he's half-deaf and expressly hates Radibians."

Logan turns back to Earls, who spits a fingernail to the ground.

"It's your woodsy smell. I, luckily, don't care for any one state over the other. Follow me." She turns with a spin in her step and leaves through the back door. They follow.

Cages of multicolored cogs and other smaller freks line the walls of the back room. They stride through before exiting through another door leading to the back of the building. Brute acts unimpressed by the tens of useless cogs potentially staring back at them. *Small obnoxious puff balls.*

Outside, the woman continues across the darkened dirt yard to a large pen where a drum of krakes sleep or wander about. As they approach, the green cog begins to whimper, and its coat turns a bright shade of yellow. "I'm not feeding you today, Lady Floon." Cogs, innately one of the most submissive of all freks and chiefly dependent on their human protectors, are often curamed after weighty or ironic leadership titles. "How many did you say?"

"Two should be enough. Unless you have one that can handle both riders?"

"You're not traveling with them?"

"Not this time."

Logan peeks over at Sanet, who's at the minor scanning the perimeter of the fence considering the sluggish freks. Looking himself, he's sure this drum of beasts is supplied by concession breeders from deeper in the Tunnels. He catches sight of one that has large chunks of scales missing from its side and another who is dull with age. *It looks nearly sent.*

Confidently, the young woman speaks: "I would imagine most of them could handle the trip north. Assuming you're headed to Yikshir?"

Sanet nods.

Bernard steps up and onto the fence, inspecting the roaming freks. "Where do they go once we're done with them?"

"They eventually make their way back here. Most of the time," she answers.

"How much?" Logan asks.

"For two? Two hundred, though you'll need to supply their food."

"Shouldn't be an issue." Logan begins to dip into his pockets, pulling out some coin, then turns to Bernard. "You have any spare?"

Bernard quickly fishes out the remaining total.

"This one looks wisnok." Sanet points out a particularly bright gold one.

Logan agrees. "All right, the gold one there, and . . . Bernard?"

"Me? Choose? Oh, I don't know."

"Pick the youngest one you see," Logan encourages. Bernard's eyes widen, taking to the task with the utmost care, his childlike wonderment infectious.

Shuffling the nervous yellow cog to her other arm, the woman stands on one of the fence rails and points to a small purple krake in the far back. "That one's our youngest."

Bernard shifts his focus past the others. "I don't see him."

"Right there, past that older—has he been sent left?"

As she questions the old krake's health, Logan takes notice of the young woman's arm. Welts and bruises cover it from wrist to shoulder. "Krake bites?" Logan asks, pointing to her arm.

At this, the woman quickly hides it with the yellow cog and steps off the fence. "Oh, it's nothing. Tunnels can be a rough bargain sometimes. Can I get you the purple one? I call him George. Been training him myself."

Bernard nods approval.

Unimpressed by the answer about her arm, Logan drops the issue for a major. "It's a bargain then," he says.

The woman smiles. "Wonderful. If you will just meet me out front, I can have them ready for you in just a few majors."

Bernard nods. "Approsh, friend." Before hopping the fence, she sets the yellow cog on the ground, which scurries off into a deeper part of the Tunnel. As Logan and the others head back to the store, Logan's mood heats. The girl's demeanor comes off as jovial, but something about her feels hurt. *That disgusting man inside, Earls, is an abuser.*

Stepping into the main store, they find Earls still seated and oblivious. The only change from his earlier position is that he's chewing on his other hand's fingers. Walking a few strides faster than Bernard and Sanet, Logan steps up to the counter, reaches over, and grabs Earls by his black suspenders. Before he can react, Logan has him on the ground and starts to punch him in the face. Sanet runs over and attempts to hold Logan off, and after a few more hits, Logan stands, giving Earls one last kick while huffing from his adrenaline.

Earls curls on his side, bleeding from mouth and nose. Through the blood, he spits, "Are you proshing flam, boy?" Before he finishes, Earls flips himself and trips Logan to the ground while pulling a dagger from his waist. He stops himself when Sanet and Bernard draw their own weapons.

"Why doesn't everyone calm down!" Sanet calls out.

"What happened to peaceful actions, Sur Tallingstone?" Bernard jabs.

Logan narrows his eyes. *Not the time, Bernard.*

The young woman hurries in through the front door. "What is going on?" After seeing Earls with a dagger held midair, she calls out, "Earls, what are you doing?"

"This shnite Radibian attacked me."

Logan stands, brushing himself off as he attempts to explain. "Apory. I don't like seeing people abused. And I thought—"

"Abused?" Earls's face is fractious.

Suddenly flushed, the young woman steps to Earls to help him up. "He's not an abuser."

"There's no reason to defend him."

"You can prosh off, friend." Earls spits out the term.

The woman interrupts. "While I appize the gesture, Earls is harmless."

Earls wipes the blood from his nose before it drips into his mouth. "I should break your face." And then to himself, "Harmless . . ."

Logan holds back. "Apory. I made a judgment."

Earls says, "You some vigilante?"

"No. I only assumed." *Emotions held prisoner by fears will manifest in the queerest of ways.* The Victors' encroachment as his wants remain unanswered. The sight of his sent father's body, cracked open in two, bloodstained. Sent left, then alone. His mother oblivious in her haynest. Never knowing the truth. *There is no truth.*

Resigned, the woman states, "Earls isn't my only employer."

Sanet steps in and addresses the two shopkeepers. "Logan here gives his sincere appize. Seems he's a desperate single-souls sort. Here's another hundred for your troubles." Earls takes the coin. Sanet turns. "We have clearly overstayed our welcome here."

Logan's demeanor turns sheepish as the gang exits, followed by the young woman.

Outside, the gold and purple krakes stand ready near a post. The young woman assists them on, starting with Bernard. She then says to Logan, "I am approshed of the gesture. Logan, is it?"

He nods. "And apory for my temper. I can't say it's the first time I've gotten myself into trouble with it. Setting a bad example for my friend." He eyes Bernard.

The young woman smiles and helps Sanet onto the krake. "It doesn't go unnoticed. In truth . . ." She pauses as she supervises Sanet into the saddle. "If I were to tell you who my other employer is—"

Logan stops her. "No friend should bear those marks without their enjoyments."

The woman rubs her arm, smiling a little. "I know, Logan. I know."

"I want you to know, you can tell me."

She looks back to the shop. "Could you meet me at Greren and Tapsters, tonight? You can take a room in the Co-Ed Hall and I'll find you there. I would understand if you . . ."

Logan interrupts. "We'll be there."

"And my curam is Iahel." She nods quietly before dismissing herself and hurrying back into the shop. Logan turns back to the krakes and unhooks them.

Sanet eyes him as he does. "Greren and Tapsters? It's obvious who she is, Logan. Those marks are part of her job."

"Not if she's receiving them without consent," Logan grits.

"There's no law down here that keeps her there. She's welcome to leave whenever she likes."

Logan thinks of the Victors. Of the pressures of debt. Of consequences. There's never true lawlessness, regardless of any Radibian or Carvingian attempts. There's always a way of things. An order between friends. A ranking of classes. "We don't know the whole story." He mounts the gold krake behind Sanet and thrusts his hips to guide it down the Tunnels, north of Barwolves Pit.

Bernard, having mounting experience with getwishes, follows behind on George. "I assume, then, you're not going back to the Rail?"

"Those ventures will wait for tomorrow's rise."

"You're quite the hero, aren't you?" Sanet responds, pushing her hips back into his.

❖ ❖ ❖

A mile and a half north of South Freks Worth It, they take a western turn off the main thoroughfare and into a red-neon tunnel where the imposing façade of Greren and Tapsters waits in rest. Down the red path, the climate is mired in a wet, thick stickiness as denizens crawl in the shadows. Reverberations of soft moans and angry grunts emanate from unseen balconies overhead. With her still seated in front of him, Logan whispers softly in Sanet's ear, "If anything, since we'll have a room . . ." She almost immediately ribs him in the stomach. Reeling back with a grunt, Logan laughs. "Just a silsong suggestion."

"I think you know my answer to every question of this affair. We're in full tiddles to help this girl, especially here. A girl who might be luring us into a trap."

Logan finds her suspicions dampening. "I've known friends who enjoy suffering marks like hers. She's not one of them."

No response. Unable to see Sanet's reaction, Logan wonders what's causing her hesitation to help the young girl. Even if she is right, he couldn't allow Iahel to continue potentially to suffer, especially when she asked him so explicitly.

Logan directs the krakes toward the grand entrance of Greren and Tapsters, the curam flashing in tall, dark-red letters across the tunnel's back wall. Across from them, on the purple krake George, Bernard is lost in the hypnotic view of the building.

Forty-four steps lead to the double-door entrance that stands twenty measures high and glistens in the bright neon light. Each side of the staircase flows with a looping fountain of black water cascading down along ornately curved steps, while two statues, carved on either side of the doors, loom over them. The west figure embodies an idealized male body, and the east, a voluptuous woman. Both are nude, with flawless exaggerated features.

"Erotic," Sanet says sarcastically.

Denizens enter and exit through the doors, some with shame, others with unabashed hubris. Before going inside, Logan ties the two krakes to a post near the east wall and Bernard feeds them torn pieces of neox. They eat happily, licking Bernard in approsh.

Inside, a massive foyer greets them. Large, wide staircases lead in three directions: to the west, east, and rear of the room. In its center, a thin, bored-looking man wearing a red leather jacket with nothing underneath welcomes them from behind an embellished circular desk. "Looking?"

Logan approaches. "For a single room only."

Eyeing the three, he says, "The Co-Ed Halls are straight back. Thirty coins each." Sanet steps up and places a hundred on the counter. He takes it. "We don't give change here, denizen."

"Of course you don't."

The man smiles without baring teeth. He turns to a drawer and pulls out a small box. "Your room key." And then, as if routine: "A fateful moon sun to each of you."

Sanet seizes the box, and the three walk around the desk toward the staircase in the back of the foyer. From the west staircase, the sounds of men howling and kissing each other carry through the foyer, while to their east, two women, barely halfway up the stairs, slip naked.

"Never have I ever," Bernard titters.

Climbing the back staircase, they find a warren of hallways and doors. Men and women alike laugh and run, kiss and intertwine. Some are dressed in top-line garments, while others wear ripped clothes or nothing at all. As they pass different rooms, moans of pleasure, screams of pain, and other sounds not as distinguishable float about.

"I think I've seen more tits in the last five minutes than I've seen my entire life," Bernard declares after a gaggle of naked girls race past down the hall.

"Everyone here's high on green," Logan suggests.

"Pretty sure it's not green they're on." Sanet stops at one of the doors, opens the box, and pulls out a small, flat chrome key. She presses it into a slot, which quickly swallows it. The door pops open, and she holds it as Logan and Bernard enter.

The room is modest, with a single three-person bed and a simple wooden dresser its only furnishings. The relief room is as large as the room itself and has a spacious glass shower at its center, lit overhead by a dim neon strip bent in a cartoonish phallic shape.

Sanet flops onto the bed and props herself on her elbows. "Now what, Dread Copla?"

Logan walks across the room and looks out a window that overlooks the main foyer and back side of the circular desk. The thin man in red leather wisecracks over the counter, giggling with a pair of jarent women. He scratches his bare ass.

"I'm sure if she asks, it won't be hard to find us," Logan says, looking back at the others.

Bernard sits on the bed next to Sanet. "What an odd Land this is."

"Well, in truth, this isn't a part of the Land to compare. This is just the sewers." As Sanet speaks, a muted cackle of mirth slams against the room's door, followed by a high-pitched woman's voice: "You going to slip me, Sur Taron? Is Sur Taron going to show me how he slips?" After looking at each other a minor, the three friends burst into a fit of muffled laughter, trying to keep each other quiet. They fail.

❖❖❖

Hours drip by. Bernard lies fast asleep in the bed, and to a dim and yellow light, Sanet writes in secret in her pad. Logan stands at the window, observing the denizens as they leave and arrive below. From the silence, a knock at the door. Sanet looks up from her writing as Logan steps across the room. He pauses for Sanet to place herself around the corner, hand on her dagger, before reaching for the knob. The noises of the hall have not waned in the subsequent hours, and as Logan opens the door, bits of arguing and curses carry through the air. It's then Logan catches sight of the short blonde girl standing before him. Iahel barges inside and shuts the door behind her.

"I didn't see you come in," Logan says, surprised.

Iahel is dressed in a white button-up shirt, unbuttoned to reveal modest cleavage, and black leather pants with black zippers in odd and strategically arranged points. "I don't come in through the client's entrance."

Logan follows as Iahel eyes Sanet, who continues her routine scrutiny of the girl.

Iahel continues, "I was thinking about all this, and I think, actually, this probably isn't the right way to go about this."

Logan's heart skips. *But I don't want to go back to the Victors.* He steps forward. "You can tell us. I've bargained with these types of friends before," he says, trying to comfort her.

Iahel hesitates, biting her lip and looking at the two. Bernard is still asleep behind them. "This isn't just for me. There are others."

"Others?" Sanet asks.

"Yes, the demvirst has more than a hundred in its employ."

At this answer, Sanet sits down, staggered.

Logan is dumbfounded. "A demvirst?"

"Yes. What else do you think runs a place like this?"

Silence follows this answer.

After a minor, Sanet stands, packs her writings, and closes her rucksack. "Logan, this is not the sort of rescue we're prepared for. There's no reason to deal with midireks like that. We at least had a reason to bargain with Tunston." She reaches over to shake Bernard, who wakes in a bit of confusion. "You don't bargain with a demvirst for its victims."

Iahel corrects her. "They're not all victims. Some of them come here willingly. Some of them want to be here. Some of them . . . like it, for one reason or another. But they're not enough to satiate its hunger."

Bernard, half listening, sits up and rubs his eyes and the back of his neck. "Are you guys talking about a demvirst? Here?" Sanet nods. Bernard's eyes widen. "Here? Lincoln." He looks among the three, then promptly hops from the bed, scattered in thought, and searches for his own rucksack. "Doubled with Sanet, demvirsts are not looking to bargain."

Logan stops them both. "We can't abandon these friends. Not if they want to leave and can't."

Not listening, Sanet tosses Logan his rucksack, who catches it as she says, "Your hero charm is wearing thin, Logan."

How can she be so cold? He is no hero. The Victors are what's driving him. Delaying his return to Organsia. Delaying the inevitable servitude waiting for him. And knowing someone else is in similar straits drives him.

Logan watches as Iahel reacts to the tension in the room. "It's not a simple ask, I know. But we're desperate. It sent my single soul. It's taken too much. It's become too . . . lustful."

"Why don't you run?" Logan asks.

"Some have, but they are slaughtered on the road. A demvirst has many eyes. Many denizens addicted to the lusts it provides, and it makes them desperate to maintain it, willing to do its bidding. It's not a relationship that one . . . leaves. People will do anything for it."

Sanet finishes packing. "The tenfooters were right to abandon these Tunnels. Without laws, the Land devolves into the worst of us."

"There are no laws in Radiba," Bernard reminds her.

"And you sent a man left, did you not?" Sanet reminds him in return.

Bernard quiets, and Logan takes a deep breath before sticking up for him. "If you're not willing to help, if you think we're flam, you're welcome to leave."

Sanet looks around; all eyes are on her. "You're not flam for wanting to help. I understand it feels right to help. But in a state without laws, this is what happens. Maybe some can live in peace, states with good people, but when bodies are allowed any whim or indulgence, it breeds this type of violence. It attracts these kinds of midfreks. And the solution is not to take on egregious monsters; it's to bring a semblance of order."

Logan counters, "So, you're in agreement with those crimson men? The ones who slaughtered families? That sent Jame?"

Bernard doubles, "You don't believe what those crimson men said? That we should unionize the Land?" As he speaks, Bernard looks almost guilty for doubling on Sanet, who stands defiantly among the four of them.

She defends herself. "No. I don't agree with fanaticism, of course, but in some ways, there are merits to a union. We could prevent bodies from being priced. From being abused. How can you not agree with that? To prevent the worst in us."

It's hard to disagree. The Victors, rulers of Organsia, prey on the weaknesses of others. As does this demvirst. But then there's always Radiba, existing true in peace without laws.

"This might have been wrong to ask." Iahel moves to leave.

Logan stops her. "Where can I find it?"

Iahel hesitates in her answer, looking to Sanet and then Bernard, both of whom stand quietly. She lowers her head. "When it takes us, it's hard to know where we are, but I've heard rumors that it's on the upper floor." She looks up. "It's up there. Waiting. Breathing in the heat and elation of this place. It will never be satisfied. It will never stop."

She presses for the door before turning to the others. "If you find me, you'll forgive me, won't you?"

Logan, confused, nods as she leaves the room. The door closes behind her just as a jarent naked man pulls her away and she emits a false giggle. Turning on an act.

Logan turns to Bernard and Sanet. "We have to help them."

Bernard steps forward. "I know this is what's right, Logan, but I don't think this is the right way."

"Not sure there is a right way," he responds.

Sanet watches Logan and takes a major before speaking. "Well, we can't let you do it alone."

"You don't need to do me any favors."

"If you're sent left saving some stranger, I don't think I'd feel right about that."

"Neither would I," Bernard doubles.

Logan smiles softly. "We're doing good. We're being good friends. And just because there's no law to stop this frek from preying on the weak, there's also no law to say that we can't send it permanently left."

Chapter Ten

LUST OF THE DEMVIRST

*"O*n *the first day of the year, Marcus Greren dragged his bargains partner, Lindsay Tapsters, to the newly christened Tunnels beneath the state of Carvinga, which had recently opened seven months prior. It was a project rumored to have taken more than three centuries to complete, with wild tales of unseen freks and buried architectures from citizens past emerging from the excavation. It was a place of mystery, of opportunity, and for Marcus, a place to escape.*

"Rail Station Six, the last eastern station in Misipit, used to be a destination reserved for quick treks south to the states of Guloren and Radiba, as further east would lead citizens to the contentious state of Carvinga. And although Carvinga did not outright ban passersby—in accordance with the Law of Passage—there was . . . much discouragement. Upon the formal opening of the Tunnels, Carvinga's surface trails were closed, leaving what goes on within the tall-bladed grasses to absolute secrecy.

"After their three-month journey, as Marcus and Lindsay left Station Six with rucksacks over their shoulders and the fresh-dug Tunnels ahead, a feeling of sheer excitement that anything was possible bubbled between them. Though it took Lindsay about half the Rail journey to feel the chance of opportunity Marcus did, by the time they entered the Tunnels' entrance, it was undeniable.

"The subsequent years after the Tunnels opened were some of the most violent and arguably most extreme living the Land has held since the Last War, with citizens and bodies alike sent within its labyrinthine paths.

There were turnaways that many learned not to tread down in fear of having their lives sent, and the Tunnels swelled with a general gathering of the Land's most unsavory citizenry. For Marcus and Lindsay, however, it was everything they hoped it would be.

"Within months, they set up a breathing parlor in a large opening of the Tunnels that later was curamed Barwolves Pit, a shop that soon became the place for rest and relaxation in the southern parts of the Tunnels. With early and rapid success, their business was able to bargain for a larger structure just under two miles north of it.

"The building, on its purchasing date, was dilapidated and entirely unlivable. How or why the building existed in the first place is likely the Tunnels' greatest enigmit. It took Marcus and Lindsay and many others over two decades to set the place to their liking. But it was to become a grewst unlike any other. A place not just where one got a good night's rest, but where one could visit and escape. They curamed the place Greren and Tapsters and opened it one late summer after a severe heat wave passed through the Tunnels. It was an instant success and, as was the way for them in the Tunnels, everything they could hope for. But this luck and contentment devolved over time, when their grewst become known as the place for sexual depravity.

"When the garish and flamboyant grewst saw its first customers after that terribly hot summer, the Tunnels were already beginning to attract the horrid masses of the Land. Early attempts at putting together a Tunnel Council quickly fell apart after citizens of the Tunnels decided that instead of drafting meaningless and unenforceable statutes, they would mimic the lawless code of Radiba to their south, as at the time it was an admired neighbor. Though Radiba remained technologically behind, its people remained closer, and therefore more desirable, to the ancestors of the old ways. To double, the lawless Tunnels did not attract the kind and morally upright Radibian sort, but instead those who sought escape from other states, especially from the strict religions of Yikshir or the unbearable debts of the Victors in Organsia. The high and mighty politics of Quemon and the unwavering cross and dots of Niance also brought many to seek refuge in the new, unclaimed Tunnels.

"Marcus's hopes for a better future continued to fade as guest after guest at Greren and Tapsters repeatedly defamed the place. Lindsay, with another coin, saw the potential profits and spent more and more time renovating its rooms and areas to reflect the clientele that came, not the clientele they desired. It caused a great rift between them, and there were many nights when the yells of their arguments carried through the upper floor down into the grewst below.

"And then, one day, Marcus left, storming from the lobby and disappearing into the Tunnels beyond. Lindsay chased him as far as the entrance doors but warned him that if he left, he would never be allowed back. Marcus turned and stated with no uncertainty, 'What we've built is a place without love. A space to devolve into a beast of no curam. And what are we but beasts without love? What will separate us from the freks?' At the close of his words, he disappeared into the darkness and was never heard from again. Lindsay, unable to express his true feelings for Marcus, was hurt by his departure more than he ever admitted publicly. And instead of closing the doors of Greren and Tapsters, reuniting himself with whom he was in single souls, he turned back into the work and growth of their grewst.

"The Land has a way of evolving to the needs and desires of the people, and it wasn't long before an air of heat and sensuality poured from the walls. Lindsay became a shut-in, even as the profits and circulation of people increased. No one is sure when or how Lindsay Tapsters sent. There was never a body found, though finding the left lying in rooms after nights of unspeakable debasement was commonplace. Greren and Tapsters became the central site of sexual release in the Tunnels. It is the landmark by which citizens describe the 'sewers of the Land.' It is both a place to loathe and a place to covet.

"Over the next half millennium, the people of the Tunnels continued along the path of Lindsay Tapsters, reveling in the title of 'denizen' and hating being called 'friend.' To stay at Greren and Tapsters meant you needed a good slip, not a good friend."

Logan closes the small pamphlet titled the "Untold History of Greren and Tapsters" and returns it to a side drawer next to the bed. Alone in the room, he wonders what Bernard and Sanet found in the other areas of the grewst. The clock strikes past full moon, denoting Logan's time to begin his exploration of the Co-Ed Halls.

Pushing into the early morn, he notes that the hall has calmed since they first arrived. The moans and grunts of the denizens still carry through closed doors as Logan passes them. He turns corners and attempts to keep track of where he is in relation to the room he shares with Sanet and Bernard and the entrance staircases. Turning west, then east, then west, then east, then west grows almost spellbinding. Each turn he hopes to see a new sight, a new area, but instead finds more doors and more halls. After the tenth corner, he spots a door unlike the others at the end of the corridor. He quickens his pace, opens it, and steps through.

On the other side, he locates a spiraling staircase lit by a narrow, unending strip of red neon that goes all the way up and all the way down the west wall. In such dim light, Logan is unable to see more than a few flights up or down. He tiptoes up the stairs, attempting to soften the echo of his footsteps.

After a few flights up, Logan hears a door open floors below him. He stops and presses up against the wall, closing his eyes to listen to where the footsteps head. One after the other, each step softens, fading away. And then another sound of a door opening, this time, quieter. He opens his eyes and takes a deep breath.

Logan climbs another six flights before reaching the top floor. Here, a single door, dull and silent, waits.

He presses his ear to the wooden door, listening for sounds or movement. Any indication of what might be on the other side. Nothing. Wanting to open it, he feels his curiosity piqued. *I should stick to the plan.* Reluctant, he turns and creeps back down the staircase, recounting the flights to the door he entered.

When he walks back into the hallway, he's minarily blinded by the light. After adjusting, he sees a thin woman leaning against a cracked-open door. She smokes a cig of green and eyes Logan, who attempts to pass her.

She holds out her hand. "Where are you going, boy?"

"Tired. Just went for a walk before bed."

"Who said you were allowed in that stairwell?"

Logan looks back at the door he entered from and back to the woman. "Doesn't say it's off limits. Thought there were no rules here?"

"There are the rules I set, boy."

"My appize to you then." Logan nods and starts to step away when the woman reaches for his black leather jacket and grabs him with surprising force.

"Ted. Ted, we got a hot one."

The strength with which she takes his arm, and the fact that she sets her foot just behind his ankle, causes Logan to fall backward to the ground. As if following a choreographed dance, a man, apparently Ted, takes him by the shoulders and drags him into the room. The woman, with cig stuck to her lip, stomps after him, slamming the door behind her.

The room here is larger than their own, with a bed made for six unsavory denizens and shaped without corners. A circle. At the major, it is stripped of any sheets or blankets, and instead leather shackles sit in wait. Being that Ted is twice the size of Logan, he effortlessly tosses him onto the bed, where three women grab his limbs and click him into shackles.

"Friends, I know this is the kind of place for this sort of fun, and in truth, on another night, I might be into this kind of enjoyments, but I'm really not up for—"

Before he's able to finish, Ted covers his mouth with a slimy rubber ball that is wrapped in stretched leather and ties it to the back of Logan's head. Logan squirms to escape but finds the effort hopeless. The woman from the hall kneels over Logan's stomach, lifting off her sheer top and revealing a pair of modest round breasts. She leans over him, placing her chest on his, and licks his face before staring at him inches from his eyes. "You ready for a night to remember?"

Unseen, but felt, Ted and other women begin to rip and tear off the remaining clothes of the woman sitting atop Logan, who squeals and grins with a sexual ease and hunger. She gently nibbles on Logan's nose. It's not long before Logan can feel the hard, wet hands of Ted reaching for his belt, the others giggling and clapping.

"What kind of happiness are you packing today, boy?"

On the road, Logan liked to get into trouble. Usually, on the long, monotonous Rail through Misipit and Renant before entering Organsia, there would be a lady or more he would have a fling with. One year, it seemed there might be something more, but this certain brunette disappeared late one chilly night, and Logan remembered that he never caught her curam. Lying tied to the bed with a woman hanging over him is not the sort of scene he hasn't been in or slipped solo about at times—but it is telling at this minor that his thoughts go straight to Sanet. He is drawn to her for an unknown reason. Drawn to her like mud on white. Something about her feels right. There are hints of maternity in her. Signs of a family. As much as she is handsome and a good slip, she is also . . . strong. And protective. What she feels, what she wants, are important.

"You must be ready to move, boy."

The woman grins as he feels the grip of Ted's hand over his swollen cock, guiding it into the woman. As they meet, she leans back and calls out in a long, hoarse moan. Logan closes his own eyes, yanking on the leather strips holding him tight to the bed. The other women in the room rub and massage his legs and arms as the entire scene evolves into sensory overload.

"Strop poleeth," Logan says through the gag, his eyes closed. The leather straps press into his flesh, their edges like knives cutting into his skin.

"Oh, boy, you're perfect. This is perfect," the woman continues to call out as she rocks herself atop Logan, who tries to tug against her, but only makes the rhythm worse and his cock harder.

And then a scream causes Logan to open his eyes and witness a dark ooze sliding down from a long and slender grate in the ceiling. The inky black slime drips like a thin tentacle before wrapping around the waist of the woman. The others in the room stand back, hands to mouths, eyes wide with shock and fear. The woman is still lost in Logan's struggling thrusts, unaware of the black ooze coiling around her breasts and neck. In fact, judging by her reaction, the whole affair seems to lure her even more out of control. Her moans rise in passion, and her momentum becomes erratic to the point that Logan can't hold back. His head tilts, and his hips lift her up. At the minor of climax, he winces in pain, but the woman only closes her legs, squeezing him, at which Logan screams out, both with total pleasure and absolute pain. The woman's eyes open, and she reaches out to his gag, taking it in her hand.

The slime yanks the woman, jerking her off Logan and dragging her to the ceiling. The gag rips from his face, but the unknowable sight silences the room. The woman realizes what's happening and screams out, reaching for Ted and the others. Her eyes catch Logan, who's nearly faint from the uproar. When she's pressed against the ceiling, the ooze doubles in size, covering her entire body and creeping down her throat. It glistens in the soft neon light of the room and flows back and forth in a peculiar, ruthless action. The woman's head lurches backward as she finds herself in another state of unfelt pleasures while the smell of burning flesh fills the room. Before long, she passes out, and her body is carried up through the broken grate and disappears, leaving Logan and the others alone, as if the woman was never there.

For an extended major, no one moves. Logan squirms, still trying to loosen the leathers. Ted grabs two of the women and drags them from the room as Logan calls, barely audibly, after them, "Heyo, don't leave me here." Ted turns back but ignores him. The last woman in the room is still motionless, tears streaming down her face. Logan cocks his head to her. "Please, sur, I know this was all in fun, but you have to let me loose before that frek returns."

She looks at him, her eyes flush with fear; she shakes her head as if she doesn't understand him.

"Please. I don't care what you and your friends were doing. Just let me go. Please—" He shakes violently in protest.

The woman nods meekly and then fumbles forward, her dainty hands attempting to manipulate one tangled strap's lock.

"It's wisnok, just take a deep breath. You have it."

She nods again, shaking her hands and taking a deep breath. Behind her, the black slime starts to ooze back toward them. Logan turns back to the woman, who's nearly finished with the first lock. He attempts to hide his panic, but she notices his glancing eyes and turns her face upward, screaming.

She stands. "Apory, little boy," she says and runs off without looking back. The ooze drips downward toward Logan.

He shakes the hand the woman was working on; it's loose enough to slide through the cuff. *Free.* He rolls to his side and quickly begins to fiddle with the other strap, every few minors catching a quick glimpse of the black tar falling toward him. As it's about to touch, he sets his second hand free and rolls off the bed, slamming to the floor. He stands, lifting his pants, watching the black slime thud onto the space where he was just held before slinking toward him.

He runs from the room, slamming the door behind him, and finds himself back in the hall with the stairwell door behind him. Disoriented, he tries to retrace his steps: east, west, east, west, east, west—until he returns past the room and back down the steps of the entrance stairs.

As he steps down, he sees Sanet pacing calmly in the foyer. She nods politely to various men and women who show her signs of affection or attraction. He walks up to her, and they step out of others' hearing.

Sanet starts. "Find anything?"

"More than I cared to. I found a staircase that rises eleven stories up. You?"

"Same."

Logan looks around. "Let's wait for Bernard, but I think we should go in through our co-ed hall." He rubs his neck. The thought of the black ooze wrapping around him feels both horrifying and strangely . . . desirable.

"Agreed. Do you think the top floor is all connected?" Sanet inquires.

"I would imagine." Looking up, Logan sees the windows of rooms that overlook the entrance. He tries to find theirs but can't discern one from another. In some, couples are slipping each other, their parts pressed against the glass. Farther up, the windows stop. He counts the floors. A shiver shoots over his skin. The image of the woman on the ceiling being pulled into the darkness. Something touches his forearm. He jumps.

"Hey, is everything wisnok?" Sanet asks, recoiling her hand.

"Yes. Apory. This place isn't what I thought it was." Focusing, he continues, "It looks like thirteen floors. Ours, then eleven more. Counting these, there's only twelve. So that thing's room should be overhead." He points straight up. Sanet looks. "I told you this was a flam plan. Where do you think Bernard is?" he asks. Knowing the sort of danger he was in, Logan's heart skips at the thought of what Bernard may be facing.

"He did take a major to ready Brute and the krakes outside; perhaps that's why he's taking so long."

Logan nods without an answer. *A boy can hope.*

They wait.

And wait.

And wait.

"You don't think they caught him?" Sanet asks.

Logan observes the west staircase occupied by any number of men, hoping to see his old friend. *Come on, Bernard. Please be safe.*

"Should we go after him?"

"Maybe. I can go looking . . ."

"If anything chances to that man, I'll never forgive you," Sanet states.

I'd never forgive myself. Prosh, I should have just let Bernard and Sanet continue north, instead of dragging them into this nest of hazards.

Endless majors later, Logan catches Bernard zipping up his leather jacket and adjusting his pants as he jogs down the staircase. "There he is." The two attempt to hide their relief from others watching as Bernard meets them.

He looks disheveled. "If the threat of some monstrous frek weren't looming and I wasn't still coupled . . ."

"Don't say it, Bernard." Sanet presses her finger to his lips.

If Bernard only knew what waits for us. "Come on, let's go. I don't want to be here any longer than we have to."

Logan leads them back up the Co-Ed Hall's staircase and through the maze of rooms to the back door, edging slightly away from the room where the black ooze is kept. Ahead, they wait for a young woman leading a parade of half-dressed men into another room before they enter the dark staircase.

"Red? My staircase was green," Bernard notes.

"Yellow for me."

At the top floor, Logan presses his ear against the door again. Still nothing. "Shall we?"

They nod. Logan turns the metal knob and pushes the door open far enough to peer through. Another hall. This one lit in the same manner as the staircase, with green and yellow and red neon lining the walls. They enter.

As they walk, they come to an intersection. Looking down both ways, they infer that the dark staircases from each hall must all lead here. Ahead, the path widens enough to present double doors standing ten feet high.

"This is odd, right? I mean, any jarent friend could stumble up here," Bernard says as he grabs for his rifle.

"I don't think whatever's behind those doors would mind," Sanet replies as she, too, loads her weapon.

Whatever is behind that door isn't just there. It's in the entire grewst, Logan imagines.

They sneak toward the doors.

With each step closer, sounds begin to emit from behind the door. At first only the usual sounds of moaning. Then piggish grunts. These sounds are more primal. And then there are squeals. The shouts of men and women. Noises of pleasure and pain. Heavy breathing. Panting. Curses. Yells to stop. Faster. More.

As Logan paces nearer, he feels himself getting warmer. Flushed. Unexpectedly, he wants to turn and rip off Sanet's clothes. He wants her to be on top of him like the thin woman with the cig. The fear he felt, the shock and terror, fades into a hunger for pleasure. He wants to expose Sanet. He swallows, turning back to her, and finds that her eyes are filled with their own lustfulness.

He asks, "You feel that?"

Sanet can barely answer; she nods and squeezes Logan's forearm. Her touch makes his pants tighten. He turns to Bernard, whose arms sweat and biceps pulse. His short hass and pestler hair brings a masculinity to him that Logan hadn't noticed before. Though he's been with men, it's usually with another woman to break the monotony of travel. Bernard is something more. *Maybe I could experiment a little with the old man.* Turning back to Sanet, he watches her chest move up and down. A drop of sweat trickles down into her cleavage. *To taste that drop's destination.* He licks and bites his lip.

Around him, the hall begins to spin. The colors of the neon breathe. Logan feels jarent. Lightheaded. He turns back to the door. "We need to go through there—"

Bernard nods, unable to break eye contact with him.

Logan reaches for the handle; it's soft and warm. He opens the door and is met by a blast of hot air that pulses through him. There's breathing in the darkness. Moans and whimpers. Logan drops to his knees. His clothes feel suffocating. He rips off his shirt and tosses his jacket aside. As his eyes adjust to the darkness, a silhouette appears ahead of him. It oozes in a humanoid form. Logan wants to feel it. To cool his warm flesh against it. The moans of the room pulse with his breath. Louder when he breathes in, softer when he breathes out. His mind slows. The room retards.

This is your nature. You are meant to breed. Logan closes his eyes, attempting to remember why he ever came in here. The form ahead beckons him to crawl toward it. *Be my boy, Logan,* it calls to him. Then a woman's screams. He struggles to tilt his head upward and finds Iahel tied upright and spread-eagle while another man whips her with a stick topped by leather straps. She screams again. *There's no pleasure in those screams.* Logan closes his eyes. Fighting against the heat. The desires to touch and feel and breed. He forces himself to stand and then to draw his pistol and, with every ounce of his will, to pull the trigger.

He can't.

"No!" voices scream out around him. Shadows reach for him. From the corner of his eye, he sees Bernard step forward with purpose, cocking his gun and blasting at the oozing shadow. With each shot, Logan jumps. The air feels thinner. Cooler. His breathing regains a semblance of control. The air around lightens. Quickens.

And then, from his east, a swift flaming arrow shoots past him and into the ooze, illuminating a melting figure, its facial features deformed. The oozing demvirst has four black eyes leaching from their sockets. It moans and dissolves onto the floor, losing its shape. It reaches out with its dark, dripping limbs, and with newfound confidence, Logan fires his own gun. The flaming bolt is extinguished, returning the room to darkness. The other denizens around them fall to their knees. Their pleasuring, painful moans subside as the demvirst continues to melt into an ever-expanding pool of black liquid. From what was its form, a waning hiss issues.

Logan's normal temperament returns as he gains more awareness of the room, brightening with each breath. Naked men and women come to, as if from a long sleep. They hold their heads and squint. The black oozing corpse of the demvirst seeps into the floorboards through to what Logan presumes is the large foyer below. He holsters his pistol, hurries over to Iahel, and unlatches her wrist and ankle straps. She embraces him, in full tears, her voice soft and trembling with gratitude. Bernard and Sanet pace the room, untying ropes and knots from bound men and women, each of them professing their deepest approsh.

"I think it's time to leave," Logan states. As they do, he picks up his jacket and wraps it around Iahel. The rest of the denizens are in different states of awareness.

They return down the dark staircases and through the halls. They seem quieter, though the sounds of slipping are still prevalent. On occasion, denizens hurry past them mumbling about the collapse of a beast. Iahel limps as they walk, and seeing so, Logan picks her up and carries her.

The entrance foyer is in total chaos. The demvirst's ooze drips down in giant globs onto the center desk, having smothered and sent left the man in red leather. A few other denizens are covered in the black tar, which burns and eats at their skin. They scream, falling to their knees and reaching out for help. No one does. The screams of panic in the crowd make for a simple escape, with Bernard running ahead, pushing and yelling for everyone else to move aside.

Outside, Sanet and Bernard untie the krakes as Logan lifts Iahel onto the bigger gold krake. He hops onto it behind her. With Sanet's assistance, Bernard leaps onto George. Brute eagerly dances around, excited that Bernard has returned. It makes quiet whimpers and clawing motions at him. Sanet leads the two krakes away from the red-neon building as even more denizens run out in various states of bewilderment and horror.

Logan holds a shaking Iahel. *You're no hero, Logan. You nearly lost yourself up there.* He shoots a last look back at the entrance to Greren and Tapsters. The male statue's head has for some reason fallen and landed in the waterfall staircase, cracking the stone and causing the black waters to stream out onto the ground below.

Sanet leads them along the road to the main thoroughfare. Before deciding which direction to take, Sanet asks Iahel, "Do you want us to bring you back to Earls?"

Iahel shakes her head. "I want to leave these Tunnels forever."

With that, Sanet gives her a giant smile. "That's the first thing you've said I double on."

Chapter Eleven

TREASURES & RETALIATIONS

*A*s he holds a shaken and quiet Iahel after the unsettling events at Greren and Tapsters, Logan decides not to turn back south toward the Rails. Instead, he'll continue north with Sanet and Bernard until they reach the Crossroads. The thought is wrong. The plan . . . is wrong. But Iahel is too frightened to let go and, perhaps, so is he. From the Crossroads, he'll have to take the longer trek through the fogs of the Misipit Valley and eventually catch the Rail in Renant. Under the weight of the events back at the grewst, no one questions or comments on his decision.

Along the way, Bernard and Sanet switch off riding George, which can handle only a single rider at a time, while Iahel and Logan ride in tandem on the gold krake, still uncuramed, though Logan half thinks Carl or Whistlers would make solid choices. Iahel's behavior is quieter than when they first met at South Freks Worth It. *Embarrassment or shame,* Logan imagines. A flam mood to feel. There's no shame in being sucked into an addiction. No shame in finding your path or choosing a path that dead ends. That drops you into the unexpected. But there's no convincing the lost they're not.

One of the first stops they make after a few hour's trek is at a small shop that sells clothing and simple weapons. Inside they bargain for supplies and a hideaway dagger for Iahel to carry during the dull yet often dangerous trip north.

They continue.

As the days pass, and the events of the grewst decay into a withdrawn and kiptaled memory, the moods of the others warm—others, save for Iahel, who were not the recipients of an unexpected assault. Logan overhears Sanet and Bernard snigger as they attempt to out-describe the other's visualization of "Sur Taron." Electing to ignore them, Logan attempts a bit of innocuous dialogue with Iahel, asking her about the long, unbroken neon light overhead. It's a sight he's often seen but never spent much thought on, being that most trips into the Tunnels ended just under a day's trek in.

She answers courteously, with an air of obligation over eagerness. "Earls used to contend there were factories on the surface that generated the energy down here. That they were run by hundreds of priced denizens."

So many friends in chains; so many in service across the Land. Hypocrisy leaches through every state as they justify their own priced while in the same breath condemn others for the same transgressions.

After a while, they find a quiet tavern to sleep off the night. Sanet and Bernard sleep in a bed together, while Iahel sleeps wrapped around Logan, who doesn't sleep at all. Thoughts of the demvirst stay with him. How easily he fell to its lust. How easily it snatched that woman.

He watches Sanet sleep. Quiet. Her appeal still clawing for him. She is unknown, yet entirely familiar. As he closes his eyes, his mind wishes that the next few weeks in the Tunnels could continue forever. His considerations of the impending conflict with the Victors in Organsia and leaving Sanet and Bernard behind turn his stomach. For a fleeting minor, Logan imagines continuing north with Sanet, into the Yikshir Sands, avoiding and hiding from the Victors altogether. *But they'd find me. That would put her in danger.* The thought speeds away as quickly as the demvirst stole the thin woman. He opens his eyes again, watching Sanet sleep in peace while he can only sleep in fits.

Over the next few days, Iahel's mood softens. She details her youth in a children's square in the state of Niance and how she was orphaned and faced, by state law, being sent left at the age of five. However, she was given a respite after a massive explosion in South Province opened its population numbers. Iahel was one of only ten children in Niance who met the requirements to continue living, solely because of the fact that she and the others were the youngest of the population. At fifteen, she stowed away on a kleep and traveled across the sea, landing many months later in Yikshir. After a year or so, she migrated south and into the Tunnels, where she met Earls, who hired her to act as an exhibitionist for him at Greren and Tapsters. Since Iahel refused to slip with any man, and Earls, a recent widow, enjoyed only watching women, they found themselves in a mutually beneficial relationship that grew over the next two and half years. Eventually, she offered to help run his store.

She remarks how she felt a pinge of guilt for leaving Earls and makes it clear to herself and the others that she must send him a note of approsh once they arrive at the Crossroads. Their arrangement, she maintains, was always temporary and she often warned him that she had a wandering soul. Even as she justifies not saying goodbye to Earls, there is melancholy in her voice.

Nine days pass. Most nights, the gang sleeps in a crowded tent in small alcoves in the Tunnels. On occasion, a forgotten tavern or grewst would call to them like light sticks in the fog. A welcome reprieve. These became the most prized nights. They would laugh and pass the time with off-color jokes and stories of past exploits, competing with the farthest places they've been, their unhappiest times. Their loneliest.

To be a traveler of the Land is to lead a solitary life. When the states were formed, three laws were agreed upon. The first, the Law of Isolation. All states would govern themselves, and none other shall interfere. The second, the Law of Population, declares that no state is allowed more than ten thousand friends at any given time. Some states live far below this allowed population number, such as Radiba. Others, like Yikshir and Niance, push dangerously close to the limit. Whenever it does, a solution is prepared that results in what Logan has read as "state-sponsored cleansings" of the lower classes. The last of the three laws is the Law of Passage. Each state is to provide a safe and peaceful passage through its territory. Carvinga, wanting nothing to do with the other states, created the Tunnels. In the far northeast, the Long Bridge spans a thousand miles over the state of Aska which connects the bordering states of Aripa and Jussin, allowing the Askan folk a privacy they intently seek.

The Three Laws: Isolation, Population, and Passage, are all that bind the Land together. The Laws' purpose is to prevent any conflict that could escalate into the total annihilation of friends, a war like the Last War. Letting cultures be, keeping the Land sparsely populated, and preventing border confrontations have kept the past two and a half millennia peaceful. Of course, man-to-man violence and ill moralities are still prevalent in the Land; but the need for power, the desire to spread and conquer have been seemingly tamed. Though there is not an overriding government for the states, their compliance to the Three Laws is the mutual fear of war. A fear of ending everything, and because so, the Laws are as common and absolute as the rising and setting of the sun.

Without catastrophic war or friends overpopulating the Land, freks of all types, of all backgrounds, have appeared. They are ever-changing beasts, evolving faster than during any time before, and ultimately the friends of the Land are no longer the dominant species; they are not the predators of yester but have become more often prey. A simple piece of the Land. And so, Radibians, like Logan, believe everything resides within the Flow of the Land, an attitude that grows ever-more necessary as the remnants of the older era continue to erode. In his travels, especially off thoroughfares and central arteries, where the Land stands empty of anyone but him, Logan wonders about his own place. About where one belongs in the Land old, untouched.

As they travel north, Iahel grows eager to reach the Carvinga Treasures, a monument she last encountered over two years ago. Sanet titters at the label and refuses to let Bernard in on its irony. Watching Bernard discover the Land, commenting on things no one has bothered with in a long time, makes the trek more pleasurable than usual. He sees the grand things that Logan has forgotten. Having taken the trip a half-dozen times before, Logan's grown to view the sights as dull, though admittedly he's only traveled through the northern bits of the Tunnels a few times before. Once with his father and on a couple of occasions when chasing a girl. *Like now, Logan?*

His thoughts of the lone trip west, after the Crossroads, are interrupted when Iahel hints that she may be interested in heading there with him. Concerns over the Victors notwithstanding, the idea of having company fills him with a temporary comfort.

Ahead, illuminated by the strip of pale-yellow neon, are mounds and endless mounds of trash. Over the past few miles, the ceiling has risen a hundred measures higher. When the first hint of the Treasures is seen, the smell confirms their proximity. Rotten, foul, and sour stenches mix in the air. *A decomp's kiptale.* The *click click click* of the decomps digging and scurrying through the piles of old furniture, rotten food, and waste amplifies as they continue toward the mounds. When Brute catches its first glimpse, he leaps from the back of the krake and runs off toward them, disappearing around one of the initial heaps. Above the enormous trash piles, large holes populate the vast ceiling. Where they lead is anyone's guess, but most assume the Carvinga Treasures are the dumping grounds for the state above them. *The sewers of the Land.*

As they reach the Carvinga Treasures, the stench becomes so intense they can taste it.

"Lincoln, this place reeks," Bernard notes.

"You don't like treasure?" Iahel jests.

Bernard rolls his eyes, finally in on the enigmit. Iahel hops down off Whistlers and begins to wander and rummage through the piles. If one can forget the stench and the blatant waste strewn over a ten-mile stretch, the site is one to behold. Some of the knolls are stacked all the way up, plugging the hole in the ceiling. Others are fresher, no more than ten or twenty feet high.

Bernard strolls through, lifting a cloth to cover his nose and mouth. Sanet and Logan, the veterans of the group, ride the krakes and watch the children play. Iahel digs into a pile, this one crammed not by waste and food but instead by old furnishings and tools.

She pulls out a small timple. "Dustian, in perfect shape."

She digs a bit farther and finds the corpse of the timple's owner, long left, his skeletal remains buried among the trash. The tenfooters aren't known for their interest in art and music and likely threw the old denizen away with his instrument.

Iahel begins to pluck a few notes on the timple. "An old Canerio body I met on the kleep to Yikshir had one of these. She taught me to play it. Said it was the instrument of the sea."

They roam through the mounds over the next few hours, growing accustomed to the smell. Logan watches as the little black decomps move like a shiny, slick black pool. They react in concert when a heap adjusts or settles. Other decomp hordes slide with ease toward a freshly fallen pile. This one a hulking muddle of food waste. *Fast little festatars. Like that ooze.*

Nearing the end of the Carvinga Treasures, Sanet leaves George and steps up to an unusually tall hill that almost touches the ceiling. She climbs onto it, stepping carefully as little bits and boxes shift under her weight.

"Careful up there," Bernard shouts.

Sanet looks focused, determined.

"See something?" Logan asks.

"I chased the neox here. There's a little opening there that leads to the surface."

"Leads to Carvinga, you mean?" Logan reminds her.

"Yes, I'm not going all the way up again, lyn lyn. I just need to check something."

The three others watch as she steps from object to object. Graceful and bold. At the top, Sanet reaches for the opening and then disappears.

Still on Whistlers, Logan thrusts his hips, causing the krake to move closer. "Sanet?"

No answer.

"Where is she going?" Iahel wonders aloud and shoulders the timple.

"That woman is written with mystery," Bernard suggests.

"Or foolishness."

They wait for a major longer before Sanet returns from the hole. Logan sighs with relief. She carries something in her fist, pocketing it before stepping back down.

"Careful there."

"You've made your point, Logan."

She finds her footing along a narrow path and steps down from the mound. It shifts. The three below step forward.

"Sanet. The pile's moving."

"Please."

They quiet. The area takes on new stresses. Around them, everything stills, save for the *click click click* of decomps raiding a nearby mound and the occasional crash of newly dropped garbage. When she is halfway down, the heap shifts again. Logan hops from the krake and heads for the foot of the pile.

"Do not come up here," Sanet warns. "You'll only make it worse."

"I'm not. I'm here, though. If you fall."

"I'll be wisnok. Just one foot before another." She steps onto a desk jutting out from the rubble. Testing her weight, she pulls herself onto it.

"There's the next step there." Logan points.

Iahel steps up and pulls Logan's arm back, whispering to him, "Let her concentrate."

Sanet steps onto the next piece of trash, and as she settles on it, it shakes, and she loses her balance. For only a minor.

Prosh this woman. Logan continues to hold his breath with every step she takes, his confidence growing the closer she gets to the ground. When she does, she bows her head, both hands gesturing thumb to fingers.

Iahel presses her lips in a grin of admiration. Sanet and Logan then lock eyes, his judgment palpable in the silence.

Ignoring his look, Sanet turns to the others. "Shall we move on from this terrible-smelling place?"

Bernard nods, giving up his spot atop George.

"Approsh."

"You're a brave woman, Sanet," Bernard states.

She rubs Bernard's growing hair. "Only as brave as your friends let you." She turns to Logan as she says this.

Is she trying to hurt me?

They leave the Carvinga Treasures, excited to note they're halfway through the Tunnels.

❖❖❖

Over the next few days, Logan feels isolated from the gang. Since Sanet's flam venture atop the garbage mound back at the Carvinga Treasures, Iahel has warmed to her considerably. They act like giggling sisters, though Iahel's flirting suggests she's looking for more than a close friend. Over duskmeals and fires, the girls use inside jokes and silent hand gestures that only they understand.

Bernard is friendly enough, answering questions and engaging in small talk, but he too has drawn distant. Logan wakes up on some morns to find Bernard having walked away. And on one occasion, he finds Bernard crying near a tunnel river. He turns to Logan as he approaches and proceeds to explain that his wet face and red eyes are from a reaction to the river. The smith's mitts are placed carefully to the side, and Bernard's mangled fingers drip with water.

The heat becomes oppressive in the Tunnels. At first, there was a pleasantness to it, but as they near a month of traversing the endless halls, it begins to make the friends more irritable, and the initial awe of the thin yellow neon line starts to feel mocking as if it were a torture device. *Never-ending. Never-ending. Never-ending.*

When footsteps of other friends arrive in the middle of the night, they come as a welcome reprieve. The last friends the gang ran into over a week ago were a boring lot who wasted no more than two words between them. The krakes they rode had bigger personalities.

Logan sits up, having decided on this night to sleep on an old bed set into an alcove that was left by travelers. The tent, across the tunnel thoroughfare, had begun to feel too crowded. It took him longer every night to fall asleep due to the agitation of their constant giggling and snickering grating in his ears. The immersion of the nineteen-year-old Iahel seemed to have lowered the maturity of the others. *You're a fifty-year-old man, Bernard,* Logan would think whenever he laughed uncontrollably with the other giggle-fest girls. Logan also had difficulties being touched by Sanet, who on nights would reach out to slip with him. But the thoughts of the demvirst, of the thin woman mounting him like some primitive beast, only made him push her touch away.

On this night, he is trying to fall asleep when he hears the approach of the friends in the dark. As he squints in the faint light, he sees that they are wearing what look like red capes. His heart skips. *Crimson men. Have they followed us all the way from Bomwigs?*

Logan pushes himself back into the darker side of the alcove and watches as they creep up to the tent. He reaches for his pistol and loads it as quietly as possible. The crimson men, three in total, surround the tent, gesturing to each other to at once be quiet and on the ready. One of them peeks into an opening at the back of the tent. Logan aims the gun at this one, who he infers is the leader based on the length of his cape. The man looks back to the others after peering inside and raises three fingers. This puts the other two on alert. *They know I'm not in there.* The two others step away, craning their necks and scanning the tunnel, they seem not to notice the dark alcove where he's hiding.

Feeling safe for the minor, Logan continues to keep his eye on the leader. His gun is trained and ready for the man to make a move. A loud blast comes from inside the tent and blows the man backward, slamming him into the wall. *Shnite.* At the sudden attack, the other two turn, pulling their own weapons. Logan aims squarely and shoots, taking one of them down. He then rolls out from his spot and directs the gun for a second shot.

"Hold there, friend." The man's hand is around his weapon as if ready to draw, but looking to the other two, he changes his mind. He places his hands to head.

As Logan steps closer, the flaps of the tent unzip, and Sanet steps out in a loose shirt, holding Bernard's rifle. She's shaking. Behind him Bernard and Iahel exit, half asleep. Looking impressive and imposing, Sanet steps up to the last crimson man and places the hot rifle tip to his chest. The man recoils, but dares not move.

"What are you doing here?" Sanet asks.

"Looking for a place to sleep."

"Not what I saw, friend," Logan states and steps forward.

The crimson man turns to him, narrowing his eyes. His attention returns to Sanet, then he eyes Bernard. "You're the one who killed Franz. In the squalls of a tormisand. In his sleep."

"And he sent a dozen people with those fires." Bernard's remorse for sending a man left has shown over the past weeks, but here he hides it behind vengeance and excuses. He's hardened. Perhaps from the heat, but he isn't himself. He isn't the simple Radibian who spent his time night gardening.

Sanet stands firmly, unflinching.

"You can't stop him. The Roar is already here, and the war is coming."

Sanet steps up. "There's no such thing as war." She switches from Bernard's rifle to her own crossbow and without hesitation—*shunk*—bolts the man through the skull. He slumps to the ground.

Bernard turns, holding his mouth. "Sanet, why?"

"These men were here to send us left because they're after this." And with that, she fishes from her pocket a small, flat chrome key. "They're after the brass."

Chapter Twelve

BENEATH THE STONETIN

*T*he gang drag the three men's corpses into the alcove where Logan had attempted to sleep. They don't speak of the incident until they are packed and back on the road. Looking back, Logan feels an air of anxiety and paranoia in the darkness. *Who else has been watching us? Who really is Sanet? How could she send that man left when his hands were on his head? Would she have pulled the trigger on me when we first met?* Her mystery and purpose have become more dangerous than intriguing.

Logan and Iahel ride Whistlers, while Bernard, riding George and with Brute lounging on his shoulder, speaks first. "Was that key what you recovered at the Treasures?"

"It is. I lost it there chasing the neox and didn't know it until I was already in the grasslands."

"What does it open?" Iahel asks.

"There's a stonetin a few miles south of the North Tunnels entrance that holds one of the two pieces of brass I was asked to locate and return. I was given this key by my employer's acolyte."

"If the brass is found in stonetins, what was a neox doing with one?" Logan asks, as if interrogating her.

For a major, Sanet doesn't answer, walking on and leading George by its scaled scruff. "That sliver of brass was stolen from me by a crimson man after I left Misipit. I was sleeping in a tent, and he sneaked up on me like they did tonight. I saw him just as he was getting away. But he was fast. I had to track him across the valley fogs and through parts of Yikshir, far north of the Crossroads. When I did find him, he had been sent, and a neox was feeding off him. I scared it away and searched the body, but the brass was gone. Knowing how valuable the brass is and that there wasn't anywhere the man could have hidden it between there and where he took it, my only guess remaining was that the neox had swallowed it.

"I then had to spend the next few months tracking it. Through these Tunnels, even past here. All the way to the Carvinga Treasures, where that frek climbed up a mound to the surface. I was determined. I had to. I had to get it back. So, I chased it up and through there, into the grassland. Which is when I realized I'd lost the key. I hoped it might have fallen out somewhere in that small turnaway back there. And, luck has me, I was right." She pats her pocket.

"Seems like a remarkable venture for a piece of metal," Iahel comments.

"My employer insists that it's for the better of the Land. But also, that it's valuable. I assume others want it because they can sell it for considerable coin. To fund their supposed war, or whatever they're rattling about."

"And that key there is to find another one?" Iahel asks, intrigued.

"Supposedly. And the other one is larger."

"Dustian. You think you could sell it? How much do you think they're worth?"

"Well, being that my employer is insistent that as few bodies as possible know about it and that these other men seem to be unspent on finding it, I imagine they're worth a lot."

"I'm in." Bernard grins, his eagerness for venture whetted by the prospect of real treasure.

Logan doesn't speak. *A side trip only delays my return.*

Sanet falls quiet as well and then speaks without prompt. "If you want a bit of truth, I was told how much they're worth." She whispers this last part as if she isn't allowed to admit it but can't help herself.

"Yes, please," Bernard and Iahel ask with eager curiosity.

"Ten thousand an ounce," Sanet says coolly.

Calm. *Lincoln, what are we getting into?*

"Ten thousand coin?! No wonder those men were trying to snip it. I just may have to lift that piece myself," Iahel jests.

"Lincoln, what do you do with all that?" Bernard asks.

I'd pay off the Victors, Logan thinks. *I could be happy.*

"I don't know. I figure it could give me a bit of independence. Perhaps I could use it to learn a little more about my past—"

"Freedom, you mean?" Logan corrects.

"That's what I said."

"No, you said independence. You'd still be tied to the coin. And all the friends who beg you because you're heavy. You'd be free, yes. But you wouldn't be independent."

"I'm not finding Acolyte Logan that attractive either," Sanet jokes.

Iahel turns to him. "Don't piss on the joys, Logan. It's exciting. It's a treasure hunt. Where's your sense of adventure?"

And now the world shifts. Before, they stood against Sanet. Now, they stand against me. Why am I so angry?

Over the years, Logan struggled to settle in a relationship, each one falling apart for any number of reasons. His traveling. Their jealousy. Their infidelity. His infidelity. And recently, the distractions of his father's sendleft and the fear of the Victors' punishments. What drives him to anger now is that in a few weeks' time he will have to leave them. And he is tired of moving on. He is the one who wants independence. And he longs to be in single souls. Sanet makes his stomach flutter, yet she treats him so callously. If only she understood him. But the closer they are to parting, the more he finds himself distancing from them— to ensure that when he does, they won't stop him.

Sanet continues, "If Grumps over here doesn't mind, in two weeks' time, we'll be near the stonetin entrance, and even better, only a few miles from leaving these Tunnels forever."

"And then Yikshir?" Bernard asks.

"Yep. Haynest. Finally."

"Do you have any family there?"

"I'm not sure. A ranpart found me seven years ago, and I don't remember much before that . . ." She trails off.

"A ranpart, what is that? Is that your employer?" Bernard asks.

"Yes. And no. He actually doesn't know I'm still looking for them. But, how do you describe him? He's a researcher. He studies the Land. He travels. Full of secrets for sure. I know there are a few others like him, but I'm not sure how many. Ranparts, I guess, are the ones who keep an eye on things. They find little artifacts and secrets and study them. Sometimes for naught."

"So, his interest in this brass, you think, has something to do with that? With the Land?"

"Perhaps. I guess brass is not a very common metal. Or at least, these pieces aren't," Sanet replies.

"I hear they're ghastly," Iahel doubles. "Ranparts, I mean."

That's what I know about them, not someone to trust. And the more Sanet speaks, the more there's truth in it.

"You're brave to associate with a ranpart, from what I've read," Logan doubles.

"Bodies aren't always what they seem, as I'm learning," Sanet says in defense.

"'Bodies'? I haven't heard that term in ages." Iahel smiles.

"Yeah, though I find 'friends' to be the much more pleasing of the classes."

"Anything's better than 'denizens,' which I'm stuck on saying sometimes. Stupid Tunnels." Iahel spits on the ground.

They travel on, discussing all the various details of life in Radiba versus Yikshir versus the Tunnels. Logan attempts to join in, conflicted by the companionship he feels and the anxiety of what's to come. Unsurprisingly, it doesn't take long to begin laughing with them.

On an excursion away from the girls, Logan comments to Bernard on how well he acts in the face of his apparent internal struggles. How affable and mature he acts.

"Logan, I've done what must be done to survive. I'm Radibian."

"I guess I am too . . ."

"You are, good friend. You are." Bernard squeezes his shoulder, and Logan cowers away, the strength of the grip unnatural.

Each day of the next two weeks strains them more and more and lasts longer and longer. Bernard's childlike quality dwindles to falling asleep with the rhythmic walk of the krake, the rattling of its scales.

Shink.

Shink.

Shink.

The glow of the yellow neon entrances.

Their moods perk when they arrive at Krakes Pit, a northern version of the Barwolves Pit. Here, the friends attempt to bargain for jewelry and various items of divination and communicating with the left.

An older friend waves a string of garons at the passing crowds. "Ward off welkings. Ward off welkings with green garons!"

The gang, knowing they're close to their real destination, push through the crowd and head back into the darkness.

After leaving the Pit and going back into the lonely Tunnels, Sanet speaks. "My guess is that the passage to the stonetin is a little over three hours from here."

With shared excitement, and a desire for something new, their pace unconsciously quickens.

Around full sun, they come to a small nook. Sanet stops and leads the krakes into an enclosure to tie them off. By Sanet's suggestion, Bernard leaves Brute behind, telling the creshwillow to stay with the krakes. Brute gives him a puzzled look, craning his head. He then turns to the krakes, which are licking their lips.

"I won't leave them hungry." Bernard laughs, pulling a few pieces of neox and tossing it to the two krakes. As they eat, Brute watches them and then hops over to a corner, digging into the ground. "I'm never sure if that frek understands me or if it's only a kiptale," he says to Logan as they leave the three freks behind.

Afterward, Sanet and the others continue hiking through the tunnel thoroughfare. After a few hundred strides, they turn east at an intersection. A broken line of neon above them sets this new path into a long-forgotten darkness. Iahel and Sanet flip on neonlights to illuminate the trail ahead.

"I have to say," Bernard comments, "I don't like the glow of those neonlights. I'd much prefer my frontz torch."

"Frontz torch?" Iahel inquires.

Logan speaks up. "Radibians like to sustain from the Land. We found that frontz leaves burn best for light."

"They also provide heat and can be used as a weapon in some circumstances," Bernard doubles.

"Yes, but can they make different colors?" Iahel switches hers from blue to red to pink, then back to white.

"Lincoln, how useful," Bernard says sarcastically.

Ahead, the trail narrows. Eventually, the gang squeeze through two collapsed walls. Logan looks upward to the neon where the walls close in, crushing them and darkening the light.

"I was told an armincrok collapsed this tunnel over a hundred years ago. Sealed off this stonetin," Sanet states.

"Were friends trapped down here?" Bernard asks.

"Rumors were, there was a group of bodies sent left from starvation when they were unable to escape."

"You don't believe in welkings do you?" Iahel says with a shiver in her voice.

The others ignore the comment. Welkings are a children's tale of the left who've been reanimated into deformed freks that grow superfluous arms and legs and other heads.

"Yeah, me neither," Iahel responds sheepishly.

The gang continue to squeeze through the tunnel before coming to its end. Passing through, the four come to the start of a large, wide staircase that half-circles a large stonetin below. It stands quiet and impressive in size. Two cylindrical spires rise from either side of the large but otherwise mundane building.

Stonetins are built as places of worship, whether for religious purposes or political. Unlike taverns, or grewsts, or haynests for families and friends, stonetins are private spaces, each one built with a singular purpose. They earn their designation because the architects of a stonetin hide scraps of tin somewhere in the building's foundation, bringing prosperity to those who enter the building, whether it be for the worship of Lincoln, Dustian, or whatever other deities the Land offers or for the assembly of a council to oversee a state's law. They are often found to be quite ostentatious and bursting with mystery.

The cave itself is lit by a turquoise neon hidden in shelving across the ceiling. The light, set back and unseen, casts cool blue-green shadows. Closer to the stonetin, they find its walls covered in odd symbols and characters, presumably in a language from before everything transformed to the common Merigen. At its front, tall, cracked stone doors hang open, one half off its hinge.

They step through.

Inside, they view a massive cathedral. Engravings on the walls detail stories from one of the many Yikshir religions. Logan, a nonbeliever, is unsure which religion is detailed here. From a far west wall comes the sound of dripping.

Light fades as they walk, and the nave runs cooler than outside. The only light inside comes from the blue-green neon beaming in through slits and small windows. On the ground are the remains of both old and recent traffic, prints of freks and friends alike.

"Looks like others have come through. You sure the fragment is still down here?" Iahel wonders.

"I'm sure many have explored here over the years, but none had a key."

They continue along the rows of broken and dust-covered pews. At the back of the nave, a tablatur stands in front of a giant statue of a human-shaped frek, carved with two heads. One that smiles. One that frowns. A growl comes from a distant room. Logan steps closer to the gang, gripping his pistol.

Sanet stops. "Now, I was told there might be some freks down here," she comments offhand.

Bernard takes Iahel's hand, who yelps from his firm grip.

"Apory."

When they reach the two-headed statue, Sanet sets her neonlight on the nearby tablatur and begins to put her weight on it, attempting to push it aside. Seeing her struggle, Logan quickly steps over to help her. Together they grunt and inch the statue away from the wall. It scrapes and echoes through the cathedral. Something reacts, shuffling in the shadows. Iahel spins around, shining her light down through the other parts of the nave.

Logan and Sanet continue to push the large statue, cold and dusty to the touch, and soon uncover a small opening that is hidden behind it.

Bernard steps up. "Lincoln, who knew?"

Sanet stands, wiping her brow, and grabs her neonlight. "This way."

She squeezes between the statue and wall and slips into the opening. Logan and the rest follow. The stairway here is small, making everyone hunch over and hold on to the walls as they step downward. The air cools as they descend, a welcome change from the heat above.

"I feel like we're headed to another protnuk's nest," Bernard comments.

"No protnuks down here," Sanet assures them. "Though there might be some of those welkings Iahel cares about."

Logan stops, causing Bernard and Iahel to stop behind him. "Welkings?" he asks.

"Yes, but that's only rumor. No one believes it, right?" She looks back and smiles before continuing downward.

The other three look at each other with worried eyes, pondering the thin line between brave and flam. *Odd how she's careless now, but back at Greren and Tapsters, the plan was unwelcome.*

Sanet shines her light into a room ahead, where the bottom of the staircase opens into a chamber stacked with boxes and barrels. As Logan and the other two follow her into the room, Sanet walks around, pointing her light across the walls in search of something. "Down here there should be a dark stone. One that's different from the others."

As she investigates the chamber, the others follow suit. The room is medium in size, unlit and covered in webs and grime.

After a major, Iahel focuses her light on a brick in the wall, darker than the others around it. "I think I found it."

Sanet steps over, shining her own neonlight. "Good findings." The brick is near the ceiling, beyond her reach. "Logan, would you mind pulling that block out?"

Without question, Logan hurries over. He reaches up, finding it a bit out of reach as well. Looking around, he takes a nearby wooden crate and drags it over. Bernard helps.

As they watch Logan, a shadow steps into the room from the staircase behind them. Sanet turns first and immediately bolts it with her crossbow—*shunk*. It stumbles backward. The frek is terrifying to behold. It walks on four boney legs that carry the bare-chested torso of a human. It has a single arm and abnormally long fingers that extend into thin serrated claws. Its face is gnarled and severe, and it drools from a mouth of sharp fangs. Its eyes are blood red. *A welking.*

Bernard and Logan both lift their guns and shoot simultaneously. The boom echoes through the chamber as the welking is stopped but unscathed by the bullets.

"We have to tear its heart out!" Sanet yells at the others.

It scuttles toward them with a snarl and snap of its jaw, reaching out its arm and slashing. The gang separate into the four corners of the room, each brandishing a dagger. The welking stands in the middle of the chamber, then turns for Sanet.

Logan steps in behind it and stabs it in its back. The welking's skin is soft but thick. The creature reacts, attempting to confiscate the dagger, but its single arm is ineffective at the task. Remaining on the opposite side of the swinging arm, Logan, finding the skin hot and sweating, which causes him to slip and trip against the spinning frek, tries to pull his blade out. The dagger remains piercing the frek. As the welking stomps around, swinging and trying to remove the blade, Logan rolls out of its way, barely missing its clomping, long-nailed feet.

Bernard tries next, stepping in and slicing the welking's arm. It howls in pain as it spins toward him but misses as Bernard jolts backward. Iahel runs in at full speed, screaming and stabbing its side, the force of which knocks them both to the ground. It kicks its legs, and a hoof lacerates Iahel's stomach. She reels in pain. Sanet takes her turn, stepping on the welking's arm before it's able to stand. Bernard follows suit, attempting to grapple the frek motionless. It wriggles and howls at them. Sanet begins to knife into its chest as it attempts to escape with wild thrashes. Logan hurls himself onto the welking's body squishing and squirming underneath them. He uses his entire weight and muscle to keep it pinned. Its hot, sweating skin feels like boiled flesh. Sanet screams with each dig of her dagger, gradually cutting a ragged gully in its chest. After each cut, she attempts to jam her bare hand into the small cavity, slitting with her knife to widen it. Iahel winces as she stands up and steps toward them.

Logan, tiring, uses his whole strength to hold down the frek that, with each passing minor, becomes more hysterical. "Can't hold much longer, Sanet."

"I've got its arm for now." Bernard sweats and shakes, holding the welking's arm, its claws reaching treacherously close to his face. Bernard's effort, however, appears nearly trivial compared to the other three's.

Sanet grits her teeth, both hands digging into the welking's chest. Tugging. She holds her breath. Grunting. And then, she falls back, flinging the welking's heart into the air, and at the same minor, it collapses. Sent left.

Bernard and Logan release their holds, breathing loudly and heavily.

Iahel stumbles over to it and kicks the frek in its side. "Proshing frek."

Taking a breath, Sanet sits and recovers, her hands covered in its thick red blood. She pulls herself up, walks over to a corner of the chamber, and vomits.

Bernard wipes his brow before remarking, "I'll say, seeing the Land has been a much different spin than reading about it."

Logan smiles to himself.

Recovered, Bernard helps Iahel bandage her stomach. The welking only cut the surface. Sanet cleans her hands with a bit of cloth and spit. Logan returns to the dark brick. He positions the crate and stands on it to dig around the black block and remove bits of loose dirt with his dagger. After a major, he maneuvers the knife against the side of the block and wiggles it from its setting. Sanet watches, while Bernard and Iahel stand guard for other welkings that may wander down the staircase.

Finally, he's able to remove the brick and hands it down to Sanet. She in turn hands Logan her neonlight and the chrome key she recovered at the Carvinga Treasures.

Shining the neonlight into the empty space, Logan spots a small keyhole about an arm's length back. He reaches in, using his hand to feel around for where to insert the key. After considerable effort, the key snaps into place, and he's able to turn it. For a minor, nothing happens. And then, a soft click. He pulls his arm out and hops down from the box. "It's in." Sanet grins at him.

Taking the neonlight back, Sanet moves over to the other side of the chamber, where she presses her hands on the brick wall. Nothing. She moves a few inches to the east and presses again. Nothing. A few more inches. Then a few more. And then, a reverberation. A moan in the room around them. Dirt spills down along a thin line above as some of the bricks swing inward, revealing a slender doorway. "And here we are."

"Who would build such a place?" Iahel wonders.

Sanet steps through the new doorway. Like before, Logan and the others follow.

Chapter Thirteen
INTO THE TEMPLE OF KRAKES

*T*he door opens into a long, wide hallway where the walls and floors look like polished black rock that reflects Iahel's and Sanet's neonlights in elongated streaks. In front of them, a massive rectangular pit opens in the floor, and as they peer down into its darkness, the neonlights are unable to reach all the way to the bottom.

Ahead, every ten strides or so, a thick line marks the floor. They cross the hole by sliding carefully along a narrow ledge on the side of the pit. Though they go no more than twenty strides, it takes a few extended majors of slow and cautious footing before they find themselves safe on the other side. As they enter the black stone hall, each footstep echoes out, and to their dismay, the heat has returned. Logan examines the architecture with a mixture of fascination and fear, passing his hands over the smooth black surface. The heat emanates from it. There's something unsettling about the stillness of this darkness. The unnatural sleekness, how quietly the space waits.

Someone, or something, built this. *But who?* It wasn't the tenfooters. They are a practical friend and wouldn't spend time on such precision or careful architecture. The long and vacant hall provokes other questions. *Why would a piece of this brass be left here? What do all these pieces form?*

They continue along, cautious of their surroundings, and are quiet, anticipating a sudden click or noise—or another monstrous frek—around each corner. Though Bernard is confident there's going to be a protnuk down here, for the major, it's only vacancy and emptiness that they find.

The hall continues, wider now so that the four can walk abreast. The ceiling is designed the same as the walls, slick and black and looming ten measures above them. Ahead, the hallway curves to the west and begins to ascend.

At first, the incline is gradual, but the farther along they trek, the steeper the slope becomes. As it rises, they find themselves once again having to step sideways, gripping the wall and pressing their backs against it, shuffling their feet, half foot by half foot. They move slowly so as not to slide into that unending pit. *Which waits.*

They step sideways up the sloping hall that curves from west to east until they reach its peak, where they find a massive, placid pool of dark water sitting in the middle of a large cavern. The walls hereabouts are made of the same slick black material. A narrow path no wider than a double stride circles the pond, and on the other side, two thin lines of green neon illuminate a small doorway. Stepping up to the pool, Logan attempts to look beneath its surface while Iahel aims her neonlight into the water. Below the dark waters, dozens of enormous krakes swim about.

"Lincoln," Logan mumbles.

"I'd beg to offer that these krakes are not as friendly as George and Whistlers," Iahel says. One of the krakes, three times the size of any they've seen before, floats near the surface.

"No one up for a swim then?" Logan jokes.

Sanet sneers and walks along the path to the east, circling the pool. As they wander after her, Logan glances up toward large slits, which serve an unknown purpose, in the ceiling above them. The pool room's heat and humidity create a muggy atmosphere, making each breath a challenge. On its other side, a raised area steps up and forms a considerable floor, and on closer inspection, it appears to resemble a quaint porch from a modern house with short, uneven railings and even two small chairs canted against either side of its doorway. The entire porch, including the seats and railings, is covered in the same slick black and reflects the two vertical green neon strips lining the door.

They step up to the porch and its doorway, which is built into the back wall opposite the sloping hall from which they entered. Shining their neonlights through the open doorway, they find yet another turnaway, though smaller than any of the others. This hallway holds arched doorways every ten strides or so. They step in, and as they pass each open archway, they see chairs and beds inside small rooms, covered, like everything, in the smooth black stone. One room is arranged as a sleeping chamber, while another resembles something of a lounging area. Altogether, the rooms appear to create a single haynest, but as it's currently arranged, the space feels disconnected and isolating.

Nearing the end of the hallway, they locate a throne room. When Bernard steps in, he speaks up. "That's it. That's the same throne I saw in the protnuk's nest back in Radiba." He walks over to the high black throne and reaches a hand out. "This is unbelievable. It has that same heat."

Logan has never met a protnuk but knows that their tricks on the eye and senseless riddles cause friends to go mad. If Bernard believes this is the same throne, the protnuk's enigmit may be working.

Iahel scans the room. "Where's this brass supposed to be?"

"I don't know," Sanet answers. "I was only told it was beyond a door beneath the stonetin in the Tunnels."

Bernard is mesmerized by the throne, afraid to touch it. The throne is also of the same black rock. However, it looks to have been made of it, rather than covered in it. Logan looks around and notes more unrecognizable lumps and boxy shapes like those in the other rooms.

"Here's another hall." Sanet points to the back of the throne room to the east, toward a small and narrow corridor, nearly hidden in the black wall. She walks over and disappears around a corner. Bernard follows. Iahel and Logan take the rear.

Down this hall, barely wide enough for a single friend, another room sits on its own, this one smaller than the others, with built-in bookshelves covered in the black stone.

Inspecting the shelves, Sanet says, "I wonder if it's buried under this rock?"

"Under it?" Bernard questions.

"Doesn't it look like this whole temple is covered in black stone? It's overgrown with it, like some sort of mold."

"Do you think we should try to dig it out?" Iahel asks.

"I don't have any other ideas. This room is the only one left. Unless we're missing something."

"I'll double on that; I hope it's underneath this stone. Not sure I'm keen on learning it's lost down in that pool with all the krakes," Bernard doubles.

"Let's hope not." Sanet steps up to one of the bookshelves, unsheathes her dagger, and taps the stone. It clinks and echoes in the small room. She then throws her weight into it, attempting to chip away bits of rock. It does nothing, leaving no mark of her effort. She looks around.

Logan pulls his pistol and points it at the bookshelf. "Stand back."

The three step aside, and he pulls the trigger. The blast booms through the room, causing everyone to clasp their ears. When the sound diminishes, Logan studies the impact to find the bullet lodged in the stone as if he had merely pressed it in, but no other residual marks. "Well then."

"I wonder . . ."

Bernard removes his rucksack and pulls out a frontz-leaf torch and lights it. The room comes into full view as each of them shields their eyes from the sudden bright light. Sanet and Iahel turn off their neonlights.

"That *is* an excellent match," Iahel remarks.

Bernard tips the torch toward the bookshelf, and the stone glistens and sweats. With curiosity, he touches the stone with the fire. The black rock retreats, producing a high-pitched hissing sound.

Sanet steps over. "Lincoln, it's working." As the rock clears, the shelf's contents come into view, books on history and biology. With renewed excitement, Sanet scans the room, rubbing her fingers over pieces of furniture. "Try here."

As soon as Bernard leaves the shelf, the stone returns, closing back over the books. He walks over and tilts the torch onto a flat surface behind the desk, and the stone recedes, revealing a painting. It's a nude scene of a woman pushing away from long and fearsome arms. Bernard waves the torch around the picture to show the whole scene. The woman is being attacked by prominent friends covered in brown hair, twice her size. "Tenfooters."

"Try over here." Iahel guesses at a spot.

Bernard walks over and tries an area lower and against a side wall.

"Looks like a trophy case. Earls had one that was fashioned in the same shape."

Bernard touches the stone as the others watch. As the black oozes aside, hissing, glass replaces it, and behind, objects rest quietly on display. Small figurines posed in fighting stances. Metal coins pressed in ancient styles. And then, a large fragment of brass, shaped like a pointed wedge about the size of a fist.

"That's definitely larger than what you found, Sanet," Bernard observes.

Iahel's eyes widen. "This is exciting."

They all smile at the find. *Lucky souls, we are.*

Shink. Shink. Shink.

Logan turns. "Krake." They position themselves in anticipation. *Shink. Shink.* "Any suggestions, Iahel?"

"It's probably hungry."

"I only have a little neox left. Hopefully enough," Bernard says.

Iahel nods, her eyes showing she hopes the same. The rattle of the krake's scales grows louder. Closer. Bernard hands the torch to Logan while he rifles through his rucksack, pulling out and unwrapping the last of his neox meat. The room has grown considerably hotter since the torch has touched the walls around them, which are sweating and beginning to melt.

"We should grab that brass and get out of here," Logan says.

Shink. Shink. Shink.

Iahel turns to the others, "That krake sounds like it's in the throne room. Can it fit down the hall?"

"Logan, help me get the brass," Sanet says. "Bernard, go with Iahel and see if that neox meat keeps it occupied."

Bernard nods at her instruction and leaves the room with Iahel. Logan, meanwhile, tilts the torch back toward the trophy case and once again reveals the glass case and the brass wedge. After a large enough hole opens, Sanet smashes the glass with the hilt of her dagger. It shatters, and she reaches in, grabbing for the brass. As she pulls away, her forearm touches a bit of the heated stone, and she screams in pain, dropping the brass back into the case. She falls backward holding her arm. Logan drops the torch onto the case and turns to Sanet.

"Are you wisnok?"

Unable to speak from the pain, she shows Logan her injury. Her skin is burned away nearly to the bone.

"Prosh." She points to the case.

Logan turns and sees the walls have quickly gone up in flames, the black stone melting even faster. He grabs Sanet and pulls her away. "Get to Bernard; I'll get the brass."

She nods and hurries away, holding her arm.

He turns back. He pulls from his rucksack a leather water bag, twists its cap, and pours the contents over the fire, extinguishing it into blue smoke. Without hesitation, he holds his breath and steps into the hot steam and reaches past the shattered glass. Through eyes stinging from the smoke, he catches a glimpse of the brass wedge and pulls it out. The back of his hand scrapes a piece of black stone oozing back to form, which burns layers of his skin. In pain, he retracts his arm, tosses the brass across the room, then falls to his knees. The room has returned to darkness. He's temporarily blinded, but in a minor he sees the dim glow of Iahel's neonlight down the hall and stands, breathing through his mouth, grabs the brass, and packs it into his rucksack.

He finds Sanet and the others. They're across the throne room, sneaking toward the exit. In the middle of the room, an enormous krake is sprawled out tearing into the neox meat. Logan holds his breath as he slips along the wall. The krake looks up at him, and Logan stops. It stands and stares.

Remaining still, Logan sees in his periphery the other three at the exit hall. Bernard reaches into his bag and tosses a new piece of meat across the room opposite of Logan. The krake turns its neck to the landed meat, and as it does, Logan runs.

Once he reaches the others, they all run through the hall of doors toward the pool.

"Did you get it?"

"Yes," Logan says.

Sanet's eyes show she approves.

Anything for you.

Quickly returning to the humid pool room, they find several krakes walking along the path and others swimming around in the dark waters with a growing sense of agitation. The room has brightened considerably since they left. Upon looking up, they see the slits in the ceiling have opened into large circular vents to the surface. As they watch, a shadow appears in the light of one of the holes, followed by a scream. The screaming friend looks to have been pushed and is now falling toward them. As the shadow drops, it appears to be a tenfooter, easily identified by his large size and hair-covered body. They catch a glimpse of his arms tied behind his back just before he crashes into the water with a tremendous *crack*, producing a splash that juts up and onto the path. Krakes swim from underneath the fallen tenfooter, attacking him as he squirms and tries to swim away. The attempt to fight them off is unsuccessful.

"It's . . . an execution pit," Logan states in a skipped breath.

After a minor, another tenfooter screams, falling from above. The few krakes walking along the path slink back into the water, clearing the gang's eastern path. Behind them, the enormous krake from the throne room rattles toward them.

"Time to go."

They creep along the edge of the pool as three more tenfooters, tied together this time, splash and smash into the water and are quickly devoured by the swimming krakes. At this point, it's a feeding frenzy, and the krake from the throne room drops into the water for its own taste, ripping the head from one of the already sent tenfooters. Ahead of the gang, another krake blocks their path. Bernard, in front, yanks his rifle free as he runs, aims at it, and pulls the trigger. Its scaled head shakes off the shot, and it retreats into the pool unharmed.

"Good show, Bernard."

They hurry forth, making their way back toward the sloping hall. "Careful, friends. If we slip, there's that pit below to who knows where," Bernard warns.

Nodding in agreement, they each press against the wall, gingerly feeling along the floor, which is slick with splashed water. Behind them, they hear a cacophony of screams just as the light from above the pool darkens temporarily.

"Hold on!" Logan calls out.

Just barely out of sight, a huge ball of tenfooters roped together crashes into the pool, sending a massive wave up and over the path, down the sloping hall. The water hits them, and Sanet, still clutching her injured arm, slips. Logan reaches out to grab her but instead falls forward with her. They fumble and slide with the water. They hear Bernard and Iahel scream after them. Logan and Sanet slide down the hall, curving around the edge.

Logan screams, "Push yourself to the side! That pit only opens in the center!"

Sanet nods, turning her focus to in front of her.

I can't lose her. I won't lose her. Unable to get ahold of her, he instead takes his own advice and attempts to guide his body as close as he can to the wall. Around the final corner, they slide feet first. The path levels out as Logan calls, "Here it is!"

The pit ahead waits for them. Closer. Closer. *Closer.*

Logan and Sanet press to the wall, the sides of the pit not as wide as he remembers, but it seems safe. *Hopefully safe.* The hole approaches, and they both lean up toward the wall as their speed slows. Logan holds his breath, feeling the open air at his back as he crosses past. They slam—*ooof!*—into the wall, unharmed. Before he's able to breathe in relief, he looks back to see Bernard and Iahel, tumbling down and out of control. Logan screams, "Push yourself to the edge of the wall!" *Shnite, not Bernard.*

Bernard turns, catching Logan's eyes; he's fallen face first and straight toward the center of the pit. Logan immediately crawls to the edge, reaching his hand out. "Sanet grab me."

Sanet doesn't hesitate and reaches out with her good arm to Logan's leg. He braces himself as Bernard flies toward him. *He'll never make it.* Bernard grabs Iahel by the forearm. He reaches out his other hand toward Logan, coming in fast.

Bernard screams, "Move, Logan!"

Logan rolls to the side as Bernard flies from the water slide and across the pit, reaching out to the other side's edge. It cracks on his impact and against the strength of his grip, but somehow, he holds on, his mitt having created deep-fingered valleys in the stone.

Logan crawls back and, grabbing Bernard's arm, pulls him up. *Heavy.* Sanet wraps her arm around Logan's chest and pulls with him. Bernard assists, lifting himself and Iahel by his fingers. With an effort run purely on adrenaline, they pull everyone up, and all four collapse in exhaustion and heavy breathing. They remain this way for an extended major, calming under the release of pressure and stress. Logan closes his eyes, the pain on the back of his hand pulsing.

Iahel speaks first. "Ten thousand coin. Worth it for ten thousand an ounce."

They laugh.

After a few more majors, they sit up and assess their wounds. Sanet takes the most time. Logan pulls from his sack a bandage kit to tend to her. He clasps her arm and rests it on his knee as he slowly wraps her forearm. "We'll need to get this looked at by a nurse soon."

"Good thing we're almost at the Crossroads." Bernard stands.

"Look out." Iahel screams, pointing. And then, down the water slide, they see a krake come tumbling toward them. It snaps and twists hysterically. The gang stands away but watches as the krake, too large to pass the narrow side paths, falls into the hole. Its wail fades as it falls, but no sound of it hitting bottom reaches them.

Bernard looks up from the darkness below. "Remind me to send my deepest approsh to Smith Tunston for these mitts."

Logan, turning back to Sanet, finishes the bandage. "Are you wisnok?"

She looks at him and nods. And kisses him. "Approsh for staying back for the brass."

At first, thoughts of the demvirst, of his troubles with the woman back at Tapsters and Greren, flood back. But Sanet's touch is gentle and more maternal than that of an aggressive lover.

He blushes. "You're welcome." *I can't leave Sanet now. I'll suffer the wrath of the Victors. But we can survive them together. If she'll have me.* He smiles at the thought.

Logan reaches into his rucksack and pulls out the brass wedge, big and sharp in his hand. Sanet takes it, turning it in examination before placing it in her own rucksack. "Well, enough ventures for one day?" They all agree and gather their bags, leaving through the door into the chamber beneath the stonetin.

They ascend the staircase and squeeze back through the two headed statue into the cathedral, where dozens of welkings crawl throughout the nave, stopping their trek. Every welking is different in form. Some walk on two legs or three. Others have multiple arms or none at all. There are ones with two heads and ones with none. All deformations of freks spread before them. They're friends long sent and mutated by a foul air.

"Can we catch any luck?" Iahel whispers.

Logan looks around. "What about that way?" He points.

To their west is a closed door built along the far wall of the transept.

"I don't know where that leads," Sanet replies.

A single welking, this one four-armed, drags itself along without legs. It's the only one near the door.

"It's safer than going straight through all those other ones. We could wait them out, perhaps. Or maybe find another way?" Logan suggests.

"We shouldn't wait; it could only get worse," Bernard doubles.

Agreed, they plan and point their steps to sneak along the back wall. Slow and steady, watching their footing. All appears safe, until from above a welking peers down with its red discordant eyes. It screams, alerting the others, before falling to the ground.

Bernard is unable to contain himself and curses. "Shnite."

They run toward the closed door over thirty strides away. Logan pulls his pistol and shoots at the four-armed crawling welking that is reaching out for them. His shot strikes its hand and knocks it back. Iahel reaches the door first and tears it open. *Approsh Lincoln it wasn't locked.* At the rear, Logan steps through and turns to shut the door as one of the welkings thumps into it. He braces his body against the closed door and the thumping and scraping of a growing number of welkings attempting to come through. Bernard and Iahel find a nearby dresser to block the door while Sanet helps Logan hold it closed. The blockade is set, making the room safe for the major. The gang turns to see where they have landed.

The room is filled with papers, all written in an old language, the same as on the outside of the stonetin. In the back, a lesser spiral staircase ascends to the upper floors. Sanet leads them.

As they step up the stairs, Logan looks back at the door, now being pressed open as claws slide through and the welkings muscle their way in. "We'll need to be fast."

They double-time. At the near top of the stairs, an open walkway lines the ceiling of the cathedral. Stepping out onto this narrow path, they can see the horde of welkings gathered fifty measures below them.

"Here or farther up?" Logan asks.

"We should be going across, not up," Sanet states, stepping out onto the walkway built with a narrow beam of wood held only by metallic rods. Each step on the old and rotting wood feels precarious. Whispering to the others, she says, "I think we should stay apart, keeping as little weight on the wood as possible." She looks up at the ceiling within arm's reach. "Grab here. It might relieve some of the pressure." She reaches up and grabs ahold of a groove in the roof, moving hand over hand as she walks.

The rest follow suit. Logan watches as the welkings claw and score the door. When they are halfway out onto the wood plank, the welkings break through, bursting in and disappearing into the room below.

"It won't be long before they're behind us," Logan states. They speed up despite the creaking of the wood that threatens to snap beneath them. Soon, Sanet reaches halfway across and turns west, following the nave toward the entrance. Bernard paces behind her and Iahel behind him. Logan, at the back, turns to the spiral staircase. A two-headed welking appears. It has two arms and three legs, each protruding limb marked with exaggerated fingers and claws. It screams. *Shnite.*

Sanet picks up her pace ahead. Logan holds the ceiling above him and begins to stomp at the wood below. It cracks as the welking steps onto the wooden path. Bernard and Iahel are farther ahead and Logan continues to stomp the plank, cracking and creaking. The welking continues closer. Stomp. Another welking appears in the upper room and begins to climb out toward them. *Crack.* The wood below him breaks in two, falling to the cathedral below, echoing across the chamber. This alarms more of the welkings below, who look up, vehemence pouring from their beady red eyes. They scatter; some begin to climb the walls. *Prosh, they climb walls?* At this, Logan turns, hurrying hand over hand to catch up.

Sanet has made it to the other side and waves for Bernard and Iahel. "Come on, come on."

Logan is twenty or more strides away as some of the welkings scream, climb the walls, and then hang along the ceiling. With Logan only a stride or two from the others, Sanet turns into an upper front hall that leads to another spiral staircase. This one is set inside one of the front-facing towers they saw as they entered. The gang hurries down two sometimes three steps at a time, using the walls to keep balance and leap forward. Behind them, they hear the raging screams of the drum of angry welkings.

At the ground floor, Sanet smashes open a door only to find one of the welkings in wait. This one, a six-legged frek with two claw-tipped arms, screams at her presence. Its headless neck is reminiscent of a neox's. Without thinking, she kicks it, sending it stumbling back enough for her to pass. Bernard swings his rifle like a bat, and the welking slams into the wall, knocked prone for a major. Sufficient time to allow the gang to pass and exit.

As they run from the stonetin, they rush up the large staircase that led them down here, looking over their shoulders and watching for welkings that may follow. Halfway up, they're still alone. No welkings in pursuit or leaving from behind the stone doors. Not taking chances, they continue to the top of the staircase where they reach the narrow and crumpled tunnel. From this perspective, Logan can see piles of rubble on either side of the restricted entrance, presumably where the first explorers pressed in. They take hands as they squeeze through, scraping their skin and faces in their haste.

On the other side, they collapse once more.

"I'm done. I'm done. Done, done. No more ventures. I'm done." Bernard lies on his back. "Jame was right. It's flam to want a traveler's life."

Logan watches Bernard take deep breaths. He grins at the truth in the words, then looks to Sanet, herself out of breath. *I won't leave her. I'm in single souls.*

As they rest, a noise rustles in the shadows. They watch in anticipation. Logan, his heart barely settled, moves his hand to his pistol. "Lincoln, what next?"

From the shadow pokes Brute. He waits and stares at the frightened and exhausted gang before hopping over onto Bernard's lap, snuggling in for a nap. Bernard, followed by the rest, bursts into relieved laughter.

"You win the day, little frek," Bernard says as he pets and comforts the lazy creshwillow. "You win the day."

Chapter Fourteen

CROSSROADS

*U*pon returning to their glass-eyed and slithery-tongued krake mounts, Logan realizes how unexceptional they are compared with their grander brethren haunting the stonetin below. Waiting, mindless and slow, with their labored head bob and leaden scales long washed in travel grim, they present what once might have been a remarkable sight, but one that now falls entirely flat. *And how so less threatening these two flamboys are.* He pets Whistlers under its collar and it chortles at his touch.

Across the inlaid nook, Iahel pulls out stick and pad to finish a letter she's writing to Earls. A letter she's toiled and troubled over for the past few days. Bernard slings his rucksack to the ground and pulls out a slice of dried lyn to chew as George presses its slimy muzzle against him.

"Regrets, my friend, but your big brothers ate the last of our neox," Bernard says, pushing the hungry krake off him.

In the same instant, Brute dashes underfoot to sneak his own slice of lyn. Sanet adjusts the gold krake's halter in preparation for riding, but Iahel stands and suggests this place is as decent as any to send the two krakes back south.

"Only a few miles left to the Relights," she notes.

And so, with Iahel's note to Earls secured on the gold krake's headstall, the gang each raise their right hand, palms out and fingers spread to signify a lamenting goodbye as the two krakes mosey along south—*shink shink shink*—disappearing into the darkness.

They set off and conversation turns to the Relights, a series of rooms intended to adjust one's vision to the bright and white sunlight, which is altogether blinding after the many weeks traversing the dark and neon Tunnels. Travelers who occupy the Tunnels' neon for more than two weeks are encouraged to spend at least twenty-four hours in the sleeping chambers to reacquaint their eyes with daylight. Each room is increasingly brighter, and travelers can rest or read papers to orient themselves to Yikshir traditions and behavior.

Sanet explains, "Yikshir bodies, I've noticed, are customarily ritualistic, with an order to everything they do."

Ahead, an arched doorway greets them, and they walk inside, entering the first of the Relight rooms. Around them, other friends walk about in a muted area comparably brighter than the Tunnels themselves. In the ceiling, a semitransparent shade shields a large rounded opening to the surface. Illustrations and writings hang along the white walls, acting as a unispar invitation to the virgin-eyed Bernard, who takes each paragraph in with great fascination. He reads enthusiastic recounts of Yikshir's history, of its competing religions, and of some of the more unfortunate tragedies the Council of Yikshir caused in order to remain in stride with the Law of Population.

Logan follows behind Bernard, smiling and glancing over the small plaques of Yikshir propaganda. *Yikshir is a place of high religion, but fortunately for you, a place of many different faiths. Does one not touch your soul? Find another! Bodies are welcome to celebrate all the various religions under the hospitality and guidance of our Leader Rockshire, a woman of distinguished intellect and empathy. Make your first stop the Wishingtim Center where Leader Rockshire or any of her abled acolytes can guide you to your exceptional place among the Yikshir Sands.*

Bernard turns to Logan. "They seem to gloss over those tragedies, don't they? A nasty way to bargain with the Population Law, if you ask me."

"Doubled. I don't know the whole of the story, but I believe they did try other means to curb their overpopulation. Negotiating with other states. Deportation. But it didn't sit well with the spirit of the Law. Which is when they turned to," he pauses, "darker methods."

"Terrible."

Logan nods in agreement. Bernard returns to the welcome plaques as Brute curls around his neck, twisting its head in boredom. Logan continues to read as well, finding Yikshir to be a place of sunlit darkness. A place that welcomes friends if they practice the right religions and celebrate Yikshir in the right ways. Though they claim to endorse total religious freedom, the Linconists and Dustians clearly take precedence over the lesser-known Rainmen.

Stepping into the next room, which is considerably brighter than the first Relight room, causes Logan to squint and shield his eyes from the forceful, demanding white light. This room is a sleeping chamber with two dozen beds lined against the walls, each no more than two strides apart. Mollifying music, consisting predominantly of soft beeps and hums, floats through the air from unseen origins.

Bernard's ears perk up as he turns to the others. "Is that music?"

"Fussy noise is all that is," Iahel responds.

Music must be rather personal to her. Over their trek through the Tunnels, she often toyed with the small timple she recovered in the Carvinga Treasures, and although she lacked skill, her demeanor often grew quiet while she played. Sometimes she teared up, but she would quickly wipe the tears away, as if embarrassed.

"Probably should rest here tonight," Logan recommends. "There's a librok in the back area if you're looking to learn a bit more, Bernard, but most of it's nonsense."

He chooses a bed to sleep in, setting his rucksack at its foot. Iahel plops herself in a bed next to him while Bernard, ever the explorer, zealously heads for a room filled with facts and trivia on Yikshir. Sanet sets her things down on a bed next to Iahel and away from Logan. *Sometimes, I think she's purposely avoiding being around me.* Pushing the thought aside, Logan lies down and finds the bed to be the softest he's lain in in over a month. It wraps his body in instant warmth and comfort that within minors sets him fast asleep.

❖❖❖

The next morn, Bernard shakes Logan awake. "Time to head out."

Logan squints at the bright light, and he turns to find Sanet and Iahel giggling at something.

"You were a tree in the night there, Logan," Sanet comments, reaching out her hand to help him up.

He accepts the gesture, but not because he needs it. Packed and ready, they step into the next area, which comes after a short hall, and find that this final room is brighter still, almost unbearably so.

"Lincoln, you think the sun needed another sun here?" Bernard states, shielding his eyes.

"You'd be surprised how dark the Tunnels are. You've been staring at a little yellow neon for three and a half weeks," Sanet says.

Bernard nods slowly, as if thinking about the entire trip. This room appears to be a welcoming space for the Tunnels, detailing its unispar sights, such as the krake mounts, and its different places to visit, from Barwolves Pit to the Carvinga Treasures. The

Treasures are described coyly to keep the insider's jest. A few friends enter from the other side of the large white room, and they appear to be heading into the Tunnels. *Good luck to them.*

"I don't remember Relights when we came in from Radiba," Bernard says.

Logan grins. "I think some friends will bargain you a pair of dark glasses for a few coin, but most stay at Radiba Lasts for a day or two while they adjust to the light in their own time. And because the Highlands aren't as bright as Yikshir, most seem not to mind."

As they cross the room, they come to the exit of the Relights and, finally, catch their first glimpse of the Yikshir Sands.

Bernard's eyes widen at the staggering sight, his demeanor dumbstruck. Before them stretches a vast red desert with colossal redrock formations in every direction. On some of the distant redrocks, buildings and towers rise along with their peaks. Where the Tunnels exit, the coastline lies east of them, and smaller yet no less majestic redrocks line its shore. Farther out in the tranquil blue-green sea float a myriad of kleeps.

Directly north of them, a massive construction stands, with hundreds of friends wandering around on a multitude of floors. Roads and paths lead in and out of the structure: east, west, north, and south.

"The Crossroads," Sanet points out.

"My Lincoln, this Land is ever surprising," Bernard says in bewilderment.

At the sight of the Crossroads, Logan's heart skips a beat. The structure, standing straightforward, still, and unassuming, acts as the point where he must make his decision. *Am I leaving or am I staying?* The choice at times has been as clear and clean as a Radiba tormisand, and then it falls away, muddled in and on itself.

As the choice struggles inside him, the group sets off toward the Crossroads, walking the broad path that emerges from the Tunnels.

"Where do the Crossroads lead?" Bernard asks.

Logan answers, grateful to set his mind on something else. "Well, north there is the full state of Yikshir. And to the east, way east, across that sea," he points, "is Niance, though I believe there are a few abandoned island states along the way. And west, over there, is Misipit, which is known mostly for its winding valleys." A small trail leads from the Crossroads downward toward what looks to be a deep canyon. "And, of course, Carvinga lies behind us."

Looking behind them, they find the familiar neon lights glowing across the top of the Tunnels entrance, and with the flat desert around them, the stretch of Land above the entrance sits as an odd and peaceful grassland brushed by soft winds. What lies beyond those tall and quiet grasses is untold and frightening. *What a mysterious state, Carvinga.*

"I think we should spend one more day together, don't you?" Sanet suggests, taking Logan by the arm.

Logan smiles, surprised and without answer.

"I'd like that, Logan. Wouldn't you?" Bernard doubles.

Unsure and unwilling to commit to his final decision, Logan shrugs, impish and resigned. "One night wouldn't hurt, I guess."

Sanet squeezes his arm with a smile and rests her head on his shoulder, causing Logan to question why he'd ever leave her.

After a few majors, they reach the Crossroads' main gates, a looming archway that leads into a grand general expanse populated by those seeking to bargain. Vendors and friends call out to them for any number of sleeping rooms and offers to visit their killhungs to drink and eat or partake in a bit of uncouth amusement.

The gang pace through the carved redrock Crossroads and bargain for a set of sleeping rooms, one each for Bernard and Iahel and one for Sanet, who convinces Logan to share it with her. *Now she wants to bring me in, a fiddle and tease.*

After dropping off their belongings, the gang decides to meet at Logan's favorite killhung in the Crossroads: Radnicks. Served by handsome friends, it's a place where the younger crowd goes for a bit of relaxation and drink, where the air carries recklessness and boisterous screaming at any of the many sanctioned fights playing out on stages built throughout the enormous tavern. On this morn, a tournament of thickset women spans across the dozen or so stages, where friends of all backgrounds dress in colored patterned capes to share solidarity with their chosen champion.

"I learned that the length of those capes denotes their place within their religion. That the longer the cape, the more important the wearer is to the cause," Bernard recalls from his readings.

Sanet nods politely at his boalerboy observation. Around them, most capes stretch below a friend's shoulder, though some fall as far as the waist. An older friend has a cape draped down and along the floor, his hair just as long.

They are soon seated in a long booth and met by an exceptionally handsome server, who welcomes them to Radnicks. When Iahel catches sight of her, she looks altogether enamored while at the same time taken aback by shock. Logan decides against inquiring further. They order a couple of grilled lyn sandwiches with side orders of garon chips and double rounds of Crossroads Ale, the local brew.

When the sandwiches come, Iahel, a dedicated veggie, passes her lyn portion to Bernard, who in turn reluctantly shares half with Brute, to the laughs and amusement of the others. They all eat and drink ravenously, and soon, as dawn becomes dusk and after much coin and many more rounds, they find themselves entirely jarent. Logan hangs on Sanet's every breath, his hands unable to leave her inner thigh, and any thoughts of Victors lie buried deep inside. Iahel had long since disappeared, having run off with the server when her shift ended, and Bernard is himself in an arcane conversation with a sociable friend about the various religions that have stemmed from Lincoln and how others outright despise the old god.

The rest of the killhung has mostly emptied. With the tournament over for the day, most friends have either returned to their sleeping rooms or continued on their various journeys.

Sanet holds Logan by the collar. "Should we slip now or later?"

Having suppressed his hesitations to be moved by Sanet's warm eyes and irresistible smile, Logan replies simply, "Yes." He then kisses her, a hand behind her neck, and after a major he pulls away, staring deep into her striking brown eyes. *Shnite, she's beautiful.* As they stand to leave, Logan turns to Bernard, who's still engrossed in conversation and unaware the two of them even moved.

"He'll be wisnok," Sanet says, pulling Logan by the hand.

They giggle and stumble back to their room, and when they close the door behind them, Sanet rips Logan's shirt and fumbles with his belt. Logan stands back, hands on his head, letting her undress him clumsily, with intent and glee and sensual bites of her lower lip. His breath is heavy. Nervous. He imagines the black ooze waiting in the corners of the room. The image fades as he closes his eyes.

When he's fully undressed, he starts on her, taking his time to remove her clothes, kissing and caressing each area of skin he exposes, the room spinning endlessly around him. He gently kisses each finger, each breast, each inch of skin, and eventually his worship ends between her thighs. He pulls her into the soft bed and they roll together, slipping in and out of each other. They sweat and laugh and groan. They talk without speaking, their eyes watching each other, adjusting to the other's flinches and subtle movements. Faster when it's right. Softer when it's close.

The night moves with greater and slower speeds.

Later, Sanet falls asleep while Logan toys with her hair, moving it behind her ear and across her face. He gives her a mustache and smiles to himself. He moves to the relief room to piss and looks at himself in the mirror, sweat covering his body. He lifts his hand to see the rough blisters and bruises from the black stone. *Quite the prize for some meaningless piece of brass.*

With the brass in his thoughts, he returns and decides to search through Sanet's rucksack, pulling the small fragment out and looking it over, unable to discern how it has any significance. *A flam chunk of metal. A rock with little weight.* He turns it over and rubs a surface that's perfectly smooth, though on its other side it's jagged and chipped. He puts the fragment back and retrieves the smaller sliver that Bernard found inside the neox. A portion of its surface is also smoother than the others. He returns the sliver and comes across her pad. For a minor, he wants to read it, curious about what she writes in there at night, but decides against it. With the ale still spinning inside him, he continues to dig through the rucksack and discovers a small and folded note. *She won't mind if I read this.* He smirks to himself and takes the note in his hand, his heart beating like a child snipping from the sweets jar. He looks over his shoulder at Sanet, who sleeps, tranquil and soft, lost in a boundless kiptale. Carefully, he unfolds the note and finds, written in neat cursive handwriting, a letter addressed to Sanet.

My Dearest Sanet,

When I found you all those years ago, alone and frightened, I brought you into my life against my acolyte's wishes. And during those years, your presence in my life has been overwhelming. You have become a daughter I always wanted. In some ways, ways you may never know, it was fortuitous that we met. And so, I am sending you off with great reluctance even as I am aware it is time for you to see more of the Land. I hope I have taught you much and that you know how important it is to me that we reunite the brass. Even if we disagree with whom should recover it. I hope you trust my judgment in this matter.

However, this note is not to reiterate what I'm sure you already know, but rather to set you upon our other task. One with a purpose I know you do not understand but that you must trust is in the interest of us all. The man I spoke of last eve is curamed Logan Hunst. From my research, I've learned he is tall, with dark hair and friendly eyes. He should be near the same age as you and, according to rumor, should be traveling south through the Carvinga Tunnels around early spring. As it will be difficult to find him there, you're likelier to find him at his mother's haynest in the Radiba Highlands, the closest house north of the Lothatin Bridge. It has come to my attention that he owes an immense debt to the Victors of Organsia. You could use this information to encourage him to return to me. To us. We can alleviate that debt if required. You're also welcome to use whatever means you desire to bring him back, but as we have discussed, he is as important to our history as much as is the brass. If you should miss him altogether, we may be able to send for him after he's taken in by the Victors, but I do wish that you meet him on your own. I think you'll agree that this is the best way. If we are to fulfill our futures.

I cannot stress enough how vital this task is. The Land has called upon us to act. I should return by late summer and hopefully in time to greet you and your newfound body, Logan, in kind.

Yours in true, with luck and praise,

Ranpart Cadwellion

Logan turns back to Sanet. His face contorts in unexpected anger and utter confusion. He stands and his naked body suddenly feels vulnerable and flam. *She knew me? Was this an act to make me follow her?* His mind races, replaying all their interactions and trying to recall every way in which she might have manipulated him. His feelings for her turn his stomach. How flam was he to fall for her?

And who is this ranpart? He thinks of all the things he knows about them but can only remember how secretive they are, bargaining in the ways of the Land most friends could not understand, studying histories and the old ways. He remembers Sanet's confession that Bernard is some Dark Valor and how that should have clued him in to her devotion to a ranpart. *Such fleeting affection comes built on ulterior motives.* He remembers hearing rumors and beliefs that ranparts are, in truth, monstrous freks who disguise themselves like cave-dwelling protnuks or shrillers of the frozen south.

And then he thinks about his father. *Was this ranpart a part of that?* The Victors had refused to divulge to him what they'd uncovered in their short investigation of his father's sending until he paid them the coin they were owed. If this ranpart knew him, if this ranpart knew about the Victors, he must know about his father. This thought boils him even more, anger evolving into an outright hatred of Sanet.

Without a minor's pass, Logan quickly dresses and grabs his rucksack, leaving a few coin on the bed for his portion of the room. In the hall, he decides to get Bernard, afraid of what she might have in store for the old man. Logan knocks on his door, but no answer. He knocks again, impatient. No answer. He knocks a third time, pounding without pause. The door opens, and Bernard, half-dressed, peeks out.

"Logan? Are you mad?"

"We should leave, Bernard. Something is going on here, and I don't think it's safe for you or me." He looks up and down the hall in a bit of paranoia. *What if Sanet wakes up?* He doesn't want to face her.

Bernard looks at him perplexed and annoyed. "Come in." He opens the door farther and Logan steps inside.

"I know this sounds mad, but I read a letter in Sanet's rucksack that says she is supposed to find me. That she's to bring me back to her ranpart."

Bernard looks flustered. "What's that?"

"Sanet's a shadow self." Logan crosses his arms, his whole body shaking with anger and confusion and a growing fear that Sanet was going to know he found her out. "We should leave before she wakes and tries to talk her way out of it."

"What about Iahel?"

"I haven't gotten to her yet."

"Well, did you ask Sanet about it? Maybe she does have an explanation?"

"Ask her why she's labored to stalk me? Why some ranpart wants me? What explanation is there?"

To this, Bernard shrugs. "I don't know. I'm tipst, and all this paranoia seems unsung. I'm not sure we shouldn't take the night to cool. Perhaps we can talk about this in the morn?"

"I don't need the night. We need to leave. And I don't want you to stay."

"Logan, friend, don't go. Don't you like this girl? Maybe this is a good thing? Did it say for what purpose?"

How can he be so flippant? So careless? "Something's not right, can't you see that?" Logan pleads.

"In truth, I don't. And it's probably because I've had three too many ales." Bernard smiles and pats Logan on the shoulder. "We should talk in the morn over some coffee sticks and with clearer heads." He ushers Logan back into the hall. "Now don't think me dismissive, but I believe you're a bit tipst as well." Bernard pauses. "Grats moon, Logan."

He closes the door, leaving Logan standing alone and frightened in the hall. *Maybe I am paranoid. Maybe I should confront her? But what is she going to say that I don't already know?*

And with that last thought, Logan decides to leave.

He's sure that Iahel will give him the same speech, and if he's honest with himself, he wasn't going to stay. The Victors would be sure to find him. *Maybe it's best Bernard and Iahel are not with me when they do.* He sets off down the hall, through the various vendor booths, and leaves the Crossroads proper, heading toward the trail of the Misipit Valley. *All that time I fretted over whether to stay, and all along it was but one choice to choose.*

❖ ❖ ❖

As the dawn hits crest, Logan's eyes droop. Tired and sore, he barely plods along, with the Crossroads hours behind and the Misipit Valley, a warren of deep canyons that produce, in some, a severe and imposing depression owed to an interminable gray fog for weeks and weeks, ahead. He continues to trek down into the valley, along switchback trails a mile below, his mind drifting through a surplus of Sanet's actions and words. He questions her every minor over the past month and attempts to sort his boalerboy crush and place her betrayal square on the ranpart's door. He imagines the midfrek to be a tall and looming shadow, nestled silently behind Sanet, reaching around her with lurid claws like some unleft welking from beneath the stonetin.

The air grows colder as the fog rolls in around him. Soon he finds himself completely alone in the valley, unable to see more than twenty strides ahead, stepping in a measured pace, like the krakes of the Tunnels, his soft footsteps in the dirt the only noise for hours at a time.

Past full sun, he reaches the canyon base to find an etched wood sign pointing in three directions. Renant is six hundred thirty-two miles to the south, Quemon one hundred forty-eight to the north. The Crossroads behind him only seventeen. *She's still so close. Closer than he is to them.* He turns south for Renant.

A friendly tavern, Bluesteep Sleep, lies only a few hours ahead. If he can carry himself there, he can finally rest his eyes and settle his mind. The valley is a quiet trek, especially heading southwest toward the ashen, abandoned state of Renant.

The fog buffers the full sun overhead and limits Logan's view to irregular patches of trench-limb shrubs, and he hears only the trickles of an unseen creek. A couple of getwishes pad by. In the dense fog, the tall harmless freks are merely a pair of knobby legs that approach and pass in softly padding steps that grow louder without incident. Majors pass, and Logan's eyes continue to droop heavily, making him unsure he'll last the remaining hours to Bluesteep. After a few more strides, he decides to lie out on his rucksack to catch a few minors of rest.

Setting it down on the trail, he finally closes his eyes, which might have led to an excellent nap—if it weren't interrupted by an echo of approaching footsteps.

Part Three

IAHEL

Chapter Fifteen
LEFT WITHOUT A WAVE

*A*cross the promenade, she looks like any other. Plain. Not especially handsome, not especially disagreeable. An average heavyset woman playing a timple. The breeze carried over the sea on this particular day brushes through the woman's light-brown hair. It's romantic, if not brisk. Iahel holds herself, rubbing her hands against her arms to keep warm, as she watches and hears the distant notes of a melody she's never heard but would never forget.

When the woman stops and saunters over, edging closer and closer, Iahel isn't sure how to react. She steps backward and hits against the rail. Only fifteen years old, having stowed away on this passenger's kleep curamed *Gilraymond* and sailing from the smog-ridden state of Niance to what she heard was the picturesque expanse of the Yikshir Sands, she is sure the woman will report her to the captains in charge. Would they throw her overboard or send her below to await a trial? Are there trials on a kleep? Laws she's unaware of? Fear rises against the unimaginable conditions that await her.

Iahel steps east, making her way to the kleep's stern. Waves churn below from a recent storm, breaking on the port side. Gray clouds agitate and swirl above, while in the distance, the abnormally thick red-and-aqua-blue glow emitting from the abandoned state of Trimod catches the attention of the other citizens aboard. Iahel decides to return to the hold where she's slept and remained secret for the past week. Return to the quiet trip across the sea. *No more day trips, Iahel.*

Before she's able to reach the door to the companionway, the woman grabs her by the shoulder. "Why are you running away, girl?"

Iahel spins, taking a deep breath. Afraid. This can't be the end. She escaped being sent times before, such as when the caretakers of the children's square sat her down to say that she was being spared after the destruction in the South Province. It hadn't made much sense at the time, but as she's grown older, she's realized how significant that was. How narrowly she escaped the short life. Most children who turned five without parents, without a haynest, were sent left. The idea bothers her— that an explosion somewhere south of her, in an unknown place and where unknown citizens were sent left, gave her another chance at life. *But why?*

Up close, the woman has the most striking eyes. A dark green that pierces straight through Iahel to underneath, where no lies, no hiding are allowed. She feels naked before her. Iahel blushes.

"I was going back to my cabin."

"And who are you here with? Where are your parents?"

Iahel swallows, annoyed at being treated like a child, though being small for her age and looking no more than twelve doesn't help. Nor does having short-cropped blonde hair. So much so, that her natural position is the offense when adults treat her as if she needs someone. She has been alone her entire life, and this day is no different.

"I'm alone. And I'm old enough."

The woman laughs loudly. "Well, sur lady, my appizement."

Iahel waits quietly, unsure of what the woman wants.

She continues, "If you're old enough, then may I invite you to have a bit of fruin with duskmeal? Because, if you're not too bothered by the words, I say you look absolutely starved."

Iahel stands tall and defiant. Her stomach, however, rumbles with agreement. The woman grins.

Below, in the kleep's opulent dining hall, the woman and Iahel sit on opposite sides of a white-cloth-covered table set with utensils and rounds carved in ivory and porcelain. Iahel attempts to eat with precision and care but caves to her hunger after the first course of braised lyn is set before her.

"Carnivorous, aren't you?"

Iahel looks up, her face stuffed with bread and gravy. She smiles and nods. Her game is ruined, but it doesn't matter to either of them.

After eating, Iahel notices that the meats on the woman's round remain untouched. *How can she let them grow cold?* The woman looks to her, studious, and pushes the plate to Iahel. Without question, Iahel grabs the food.

"Manners, sur lady. You're not a frek in the wild."

Iahel drops the food. She licks her lips and then carefully uses her prong to pierce the lyn and place it on her own round. She eats using blade and prong and starts to imagine herself a decent woman, like the one she sits with.

As the duskmeal finishes, Iahel notices the woman's expressions have changed. Though elegance and sophistication still blanket the woman and pull in Iahel, who sits straighter in her chair in an attempt to meet the woman's standard, she appears . . . softer. The woman says little. Iahel starts sentences as if to state something, all mundane things, but anything to burst open the silence. Instead, she mumbles halfway through words, which hold little substance or encourage additional comments. Iahel had been nearly noiseless over the past week. Alone. She realizes at that minor that she misses those full-moon conversations with some of the other girls and boys in her children's square, and giggling until the sun rose.

The wonderment of the woman before her makes her body ache with pangs of wanting to touch her and be her and know everything about her. Instead, Iahel blurts out, "Who are you?"

A pause as the woman smiles with consideration. "My curam is Aerial. And I'm returning to Yikshir from Canerio for my mother, who was recently sent left." She speaks with confidence and calm.

"Apory."

"Nothing to appize for. My mother met triple numbers, and no one can be down about that. Now where are you from?"

"Niance."

"Obvious. And," the woman leans in, "why have you stowed away on this kleep?" She beams as if the whole affair is a bit of salacious gossip.

Iahel indulges her, leaning in too. "I've run away."

"I see. And what, sur lady, from?"

She's unsure. "From . . . Niance?"

Aerial laughs. It's a loud laugh that echoes across the dining hall. Nearby citizens turn their heads in a bit of disgust. Aerial calms and wipes under her eye. "You remind me of a dew drop."

Iahel's not sure what that means and whether to take it as a compliment or an insult. She decides the former but fears the latter.

"Why don't we return to my cabin? I'm sure where you have slept the past week can't compare, but hopefully it meets your standard."

Iahel flushes. She nods, hiding her eagerness and joy at her turn of fortune. They place their hankers on the table and leave for the cabins below.

Aerial's cabin is three times the size of any room Iahel has ever slept in. There are seats and beds, dressers and closets. "Do you have any belongings?" Aerial asks as she removes her coat.

Iahel shakes her head.

"Tragic. Perhaps when we dock in Yikshir, we could find something to dress you up with? I assume you've never been to Philsburg?"

Iahel remains quiet.

"It's a fine city. Not my first choice, but I manage to make it work." She heads into her sleeping room and closes the door, leaving Iahel alone in the lavish living room.

Iahel swings back and forth, dancing with herself while looking around. The dark wood walls are covered in ink paintings of nude men and women. Some embracing. Some sitting back to back. On closer inspection, Iahel reads the initials *A.R.* signed on the bottom east of each.

After a major, Aerial returns dressed in a nightgown and silk robe and drops onto the couch, staring intently at Iahel. From the sleeping room ambles a little pink cog. It's overweight and walks with a challenged waddle. When it reaches Aerial, it paws at her to be picked up. Aerial obliges, grabbing it between its chubby little limbs. Iahel, happier than ever, hops onto the couch and kneels beside Aerial.

"This is my cog, Lady Floon." She hands over the little fuzzy frek.

Iahel holds and squeezes it tight. Floon changes from pink to yellow.

"How sweet, she likes you."

As Iahel stares down at the cog, attempting unsuccessfully to see its face, it vibrates softly in her lap. Aerial reaches into a small drawer in a stand beside the couch and retrieves a tiny vial filled with violet powder. After unscrewing the cap, she pinches a bit of powder between her fingers and brushes it into her gums. Before it hits, she screws the cap back on and within a minor closes her eyes, moaning and leaning her head back.

Iahel has never seen anyone rub violet before. Bodies from the seedier parts of Niance would sometimes solicit her to try some, but she had always been warned against it. "A steep slope one stumbles on when rubbing gums," her caretakers would caution. Iahel's attraction wanes a little as she watches Aerial float away, unable to hear anything Iahel has to say. In the quiet, Iahel thinks about snipping the woman but finds the idea flam in the middle of the sea with nowhere to run. And the woman had been kind so far. *Why ruin this?* Instead, she continues to play with Floon, who is eager but unwilling to fetch the small object she tosses across the room.

Over the next week, Aerial and Iahel stay together. Aerial details the beauty of Canerio and speaks in awe of its green sky, which she says gave her her eye color. She comments on the dreariness of the brown Niance smog, the stacked city buildings, and "those awful Dustian crowds." Her admiration of Philsburg, where she works and lives, is limited to the magnificent sight of an entire city built atop the redrock formations. Philsburg is one of the largest cities in Yikshir.

Above all, Iahel enjoys when Aerial plays the timple. She is masterful with it, especially when high on violet. She closes her eyes and drifts as the music swims through the air. Aerial calls the timple " . . . the instrument of the sea. Music of the freks beneath the waves."

Iahel is in single souls with the woman.

Their relationship becomes so strong that Iahel thinks she might ask Aerial to, perhaps, stop taking violet. She thinks it is unhealthy. The first few times she asks, Aerial laughs off the suggestion in the same loud chortle she always makes, but it isn't long before Aerial's mood reveals a hidden rage whenever Iahel pushes too much.

On the day before they reach Yikshir, Iahel attempts to hide the vial of violet. Aerial reacts with wrath, screaming so loudly one of the captains comes to her quarters. Floon turns a bright red. The captain settles the situation by giving Aerial a pinch of his own stash. Iahel appizes, and Aerial accepts, knowing she is only acting out of care. "For Dustian's sake, you don't interfere with the makers of happiness, sur lady. Not your own, and especially not others'." The conversation ends abruptly when Iahel returns the vial, with Aerial taking it hungrily.

On the following day, standing on the main deck where they first met, Iahel waits as Yikshir's redrocks come into view from the sea and stand as a sight to behold. The towers and constructions built along their plateau rival the natural formations of the Land. After docking and unpacking, they'll ride a flat-backed horsal along the sea to Aerial's home city in Philsburg. With Iahel's trip across the sea complete, she can't imagine a better beginning.

❖ ❖ ❖

Over the next year, Iahel became Aerial's acolyte, assisting with keeping a calendar and her many assemblages but mainly acting as a sympathetic ear to the many unresolvable complaints Aerial faced. Aerial labored as one of the leaders on the Philsburg Council, which attempts to regulate and resolve conflicts between the religious sects of the city. For Philsburg, this is the Dusters and the Rainmen, a religious rule that never ended. At the end of long days, Aerial would lose herself in violet, a habit Iahel eventually gives in to as well. Though in doing so, she crosses herself never to use it because she needs it but instead to use it only when she is in the mood.

The first time Iahel rubs gums, she floats away. Or, in truth, her hands and feet float. Through her closed eyes, she rises to the ceiling, spinning in a circle, where an unknown face appears in its middle. It smiles and transforms into a peculiar blend of her old caretakers and Aerial.

On this calm summer's eve, over duskmeal, Aerial suggests to Iahel that she should leave the walls more often. Be more social. "Go out and see the Land before you lose your youth, sur lady. You're almost eighteen."

Self-reflective but in agreement, Iahel decides to venture out that night. *But what to do?*

Later, she finds the streets of Philsburg relatively clean. As with most cities in the state of Yikshir Sands, it's characteristically covered in a thin red dust, remnants of the sands below. About a mile from Aerial's haynest, an alehouse and dance bar curamed Tunnel Visions, which Iahel passed by over the last few months, looks relatively inviting. She hesitates at the entrance. She has never been one to approach others, to start conversations. She likes to be the loner. The friends she's made come from bodies who've cornered her first, usually by asking for a favor. Realizing she's been standing outside too long, she takes a deep breath to start anew. She walks inside.

Darkness greets her, along with a thin yellow neon line that circles the wall. There are four unispar bars in each corner of the alehouse, each designed to replicate well-known landmarks in the Carvinga Tunnels. One is curamed Krakes Pit, another Radiba Lasts. A shirtless bartender tends to Greren and Tapsters, and the last bar is called Fogs of Misipit. Not wanting to go near the crowd of men and women huddled around Greren's, she decides to grab a drink at the decidedly less crowded Krakes Pit. The blue neon sign above the bar resembles a large-scaled frek she's never seen before. The female bartender pours her a small mug of water, adding the slightest pinch of violet.

She sips and watches the citizens of the alehouse when a handsome young woman walks up to her. Iahel straightens up as the girl speaks. The bar is loud, so the woman leans in close and yells, "Drinking alone?"

Iahel blushes slightly. The girl wears a sweet and intoxicating perfume. "Yes. First night out," Iahel yells back into the girl's ear.

"Long week?"

"Well, first night ever."

The woman leans back and grins with a crooked, toothy smile. She pushes Iahel's shoulder. "Ever? We should celebrate then. Can I buy you another?"

"I shouldn't mind." She pauses. *Don't.* Swallows. "Iahel."

"Ruth." They shake hands and Ruth orders two more light-violet mugs of water. "I took a chance you might like a drink with a girl like me, being how you're alone and didn't sit over there with Wilson." She points to the shirtless bartender, who at the minor is tongue-in-throat with a girl across the bar.

Iahel giggles. "Not sure why, but they've never appealed to me."

"Me either." Ruth simpers and clinks her mug.

Stumbling out of the bar hours later, Ruth and Iahel are updown friends. Ruth mostly carries Iahel, a lightweight drinker, as they blunder back to Ruth's small apartment. Iahel, barely able to keep her west foot ahead of her east, peppers Ruth's cheeks and neck with kisses. It's the first time Iahel has been with anyone. Not that she's never thought about or had kiptales of when the time would come. She's barely able to contain herself, as the smell and the tenderness of Ruth envelop her. Waves of pleasure course up and down her body. When they fall into her bed, they come and rest and come and rest until the sun beams through the apartment's dirty windows. As they enfold each other, arms and legs, Iahel falls asleep, entirely, completely satisfied.

When she wakes, Iahel finds herself naked and alone and the apartment still. Cold. Wrapping the sheets around her small frame, she wanders the rooms, yawning and rubbing her hand through her hair. Photographs of a family, a man and a woman and their child at different ages, line the hallway. There's a note to pick up lyn and garons at the market. A room filled with a kid's toys. The more she looks, the more she realizes nothing in the house resembles Ruth or the presence of a young woman like

Ruth. Puzzled, she continues to tour the halls and rooms, calling out for the girl of the night. And no one answers.

She returns to the sleeping room to recover her clothes and finds them missing. Along with her purse and all the coin she had stored away. Truth sets in. "Shnite."

The sound of clicking. Someone coming home. She spins around the room, looking for an escape, and catches sight of the window, red dust piled in its corners, leading out to a second-floor rooftop. She tucks the sheet closer to her body, tight enough to hold, and opens the window, listening as a family enters through the front door on the other side of the house. She hops outside, meeting a brisk, chilly wind and bits of red dust striking her skin. She closes the window and scampers across the rooftop, hopping down from the second floor, losing the sheet in the action. Gathering it around her body again, she retreats to Aerial's. Angry, confused, and laughing. *What a tale I hold now.*

Entering the haynest, she calls out for Aerial, who doesn't answer back. *Most likely at work*, though the thought is odd bearing in mind the time of day. *Rubbing gums, then.* Iahel heads upstairs, ready to shower away her sticky, sloppy night. Eager to make herself decent again.

Once cleaned and outfitted, she decides to make Aerial an excellent duskmeal. *For giving me the courage to see the Land, even if it was just a mile away.* As she steps into the kitchen, she sees Aerial lying flat and still on the floor. Facedown. Floon, currently blue, sleeps beside her, whimpering in its sleep.

"Aerial?" She hurries over and turns the woman onto her back. Sent left with a purple face and wide, bloodshot eyes. "Aerial, no." In her hand, Aerial grips an empty vial of violet. "No. No, no."

The house sits in silence. Floon wakes and hops innocently into Iahel's lap. Iahel falls over the large woman's body. In tears. To run so far away from tragedy. To attempt escape from the horrid life. It wasn't far enough. She wipes her eyes and stands.

The house suddenly feels six times its size. Everything waiting for her to act. To move. To run. *What happens to me now?* She isn't family to Aerial. Or Yikshir. She is an alien to the state. *What do I do here?* In a town built on its own selfish views, in arguments and debates over who is the real god, she instantly feels an outsider.

I'm leaving again. With that, she deposits a hefty pouch of coin into her pocket, snipped, no, *borrowed*, from Aerial. Locking the door behind her, with an unforgotten Floon underfoot and following, Iahel heads south. To the real Tunnels. Not a kiptaled bar. And where she's once again a stowaway alone.

Chapter Sixteen
HIDDEN WITHIN THE FOG

*T*he young woman sleeping next to Iahel, the woman Iahel slipped with when she shouldn't have, the woman who shouldn't be here, is Ruth. And when she came up to the gang the previous night, Iahel thought she saw a gapsian, a remnant of the sent left. When it sank in that it was Ruth, Iahel's first reaction was to hide her face, causing Sanet, Bernard, and Logan to prod for details, which made Iahel eventually transgress on her uncomfortable past transgression.

As the night continued, it became apparent, painfully apparent, that Ruth had no recollection of snipping from and leaving Iahel over three years ago. This revelation became a competition between the gang to see if they could get her to remember without outright asking. They each started dropping diminutive hints to Ruth as she passed by or handed them another round of ales, but as the night wore on, the whispers grew less subtle, and ultimately, Ruth caught on. Her face flushed with embarrassment, and she spilled an expletive of appizement with what Iahel took as a genuine sense of regret. She had changed since then she repeated on every pass of their table.

Iahel didn't take the appize at first. Remembering that day brought back forgotten heartache. When Iahel told Ruth what happened later that morn, detailing finding Aerial's body overdone on violet, Ruth's face sank. She reached out her hand

and took Iahel's, squeezing with an unconscious compassion. At this, Iahel recoiled, remembering Jules.

"I'm truly apory, Iahel," Ruth insisted again.

Later, Ruth took Iahel aside and gave her a long, forceful hug. She told her how much of a tale Aerial's death became in Philsburg, since she was such a prominent figure on the council. "It was such a scandal. But where did you go? Why didn't you stay?"

"I couldn't. Around all those strangers. And after you left . . ." Iahel trailed off, still unsure of her feelings for Ruth. "In any case, I just needed to keep moving. Philsburg was only along a longer path."

"Where did you end up? It's been, what, three years?"

"I headed south for Radiba but ended up in the Tunnels and started working at Greren and Tapsters for a while."

"You did? I've always wanted to go there. I hear it's just wild."

"It . . . was."

"You've led such a savage life, Iahel." Ruth smiled.

"And why are you here? Why'd *you* leave Philsburg?" Iahel asked, attempting to ignore her growing attraction to the warm, alluring aura of Ruth.

"Oh, I've been all over Yikshir since you left. I went north for a bit, passed Salsman, and then strolled to a few of the smaller sand towns. Thought I might even head farther up to Porsans, but instead chased a girl south along the coast until we ended up here. But she did what I do and left without a wave, and I haven't seen her since. So, been working here, thinking one day I might head out. Maybe. Though the owner has been thinking about moving on, and since we've become good friends, I might take the lead at Radnicks when she's retired."

"You have enough experience to run a killhung?"

"I basically do it now. Only thing that changes is the coin." Ruth grinned. "But, yeah, I don't know. I've been bored, I guess."

Iahel didn't answer.

Ruth reached out her hand again, taking Iahel's, massaging the skin between her thumb and index finger. "I missed you."

Iahel gave in.

It wasn't long before they kissed and left the gang for the eve. They tipped choice fruin until they stumbled back to Iahel's sleeping room, in fits of giggles. Between breaths and slips and moans, Ruth continued to insist on how much she missed Iahel. *Such a performer.* But Iahel didn't mind. *She's handsome. And sensual. And exciting.*

On this night, however, she didn't sleep, instead watching as Ruth closed her eyes and spoke, half-unconscious. "Be still, Iahel, I'm not cruel enough to snip from you twice."

And I'm not flam enough to fall for your sweet smiles and lies twice.

❖ ❖ ❖

After the night passes, and the morn arrives, Ruth wakes with a soft yawn, catching Iahel already dressed and standing across the room applying color in the mirror. "I didn't take you for one who wears color. Where are you headed?"

Iahel doesn't answer because she doesn't know. She figures she might tag along with Logan, as secret as he is about why he is going all the way west to Organsia. Or perhaps with Bernard and Sanet, who are continuing north with the fragments of brass of which Sanet crossed to share part of the rewarded coin. But going north doesn't feel right. Going farther into Yikshir seems backward, and the thought of Aerial's left body still haunting the sands doesn't double on the choice.

Ruth stands from the bed and wraps her arms around Iahel's neck. "Why don't you stay? Come labor with me at Radnicks?"

Iahel smiles at the thought, for only a minor, because it would bring her too close to Ruth. Not because the trust between them is glass in a tormisand but because she doesn't want to get close to anyone. For her, tragedy follows intimacy.

No parents or guardians ever came to choose her, and her caretakers were around only to advise and feed and board her. They hadn't been denizens to whom she could grow close. As for the other boys and girls in the children's square, they often disappeared without notice. To tell them confidences or hold them accountable for the next day's happiness would only produce spoils because, on any given morn, she'd wake to discover they were sent left in the night or taken in by a desiring family. Learning that another girl was chosen over her prickled the most, not because they were taken but because they were selected before her.

There was Earls, who was kind to her. Perhaps the most loyal of them all; and though a shnite beast on the outside, it wouldn't surprise her to learn that he was part cog. Soft-hearted and dim. But she knew she couldn't spend a life with him. A widow who barely spoke. A man. But he held the Temporary, as she liked to call it. As the girls and boys did. Or Aerial. Or Ruth. Or Jules. Earls was just another Temporary even if she couldn't shake the throbs of guilt for abandoning him. And a happy guilt for making Earls care for the ever-needy Lady Floon, Aerial's cog. Until this minor, she had forgotten about the useless frek. *For the best, perhaps. I can't hold on to it forever.*

Over the past month, Logan had become the new Temporary. Though, like most men she meets, he is also a clueless cog inside. Tender and easy to swoon over a woman's smile. *So am I.* But he is moral. And kind. He came to her rescue. Like a valor of old, a soldier for the denizens. Chivalrous as he is slow.

Ruth stands away from her, bare chested, and sits back down. "You're not going to leave so soon? I did appize for what happened. You do believe me?"

Iahel spins to face Ruth and steps closer. "You did." She kisses her, and they slip again.

Afterward, they lie silent in the bed, with Ruth's fingers running up and down Iahel's arm, causing grenspimples. Iahel suddenly jumps, the thought of the demvirst overtaking her.

Ruth sits up. "Are you wisnok?"

Iahel nods quietly, not wanting to think on the thoughts any further. "It's not you." *Trust is not my cloth.*

A knock. Iahel sits up and pulls on a long shirt. At the door, Bernard stands sheepishly. "Apory to bother you, friend, but is Logan here?"

"Isn't he in Sanet's room?"

"They had some grit. Logan found a letter or something. I was a little jarent when he was yelling at me about it."

Iahel grins, knowing how passionate and unreasonable Logan can be.

"I'm sure he's at duskmeal. I can meet you there in a few?"

Bernard nods. "You're right." He walks away.

Letter? Boyish troubles. She finishes her color, speaking to Ruth through the mirror. "Well, the night has set and kiptale faded, sur lady."

"So, you're just going to run away again?"

No answer.

Ruth then stands to dress as both remain silent. The room drops in temperature, and after a major, Iahel leaves without a wave.

❖ ❖ ❖

At a booth, Bernard and Iahel drink steamed green tea and munch on a basket of warm coffee sticks. Sanet appears around the corner and finds them. "Have you seen Logan?" she asks, sitting down beside Bernard. They shake their heads. "Odd boy."

"I think he went," Bernard says, munching on a coffee stick.

"Went?"

"He said that, well, this is personal, but that you had some letter?" Bernard questions.

Sanet's reaction is at first one of shock, then forced confusion. "Letter?"

"In truth, I was a little tipst, but he knocked on my door this morn in a bit of a panic, wanting me to leave with him. Saying I shouldn't trust you because you were stalking him."

Sanet laughs at this and Iahel watches the two intently. Sanet's reaction to the news of Logan is the same as Aerial's would be whenever Iahel confronted her about overusing violet. *They wear a hidden agenda.*

Bernard, with his own inner cog, shrugs it off. Sanet's a wall. Guarded at all times. Their conversation continues, about Logan and how boyish he is. How sweet. How generous a partner he is when they slip. Sanet's descriptions come off like calculations of her emotions. Untrue. Unreal. Unfelt. As if it is how she is supposed to talk about him. That she is resigned to be with him, being that they were just . . . available to each other, but that he didn't mean anything and that, beyond a good slip, he was beneath her. That's at least the tale she presents, but as they speak on Logan's behaviors, it's clear she's more upset than she's likely to admit.

The letter must have been in that pad she always writes in. Her real thoughts. And Logan's little cog heart broke when he read it, and so he went. As they finish their duskmeal, they discuss the upcoming day.

"Are you still going west, Iahel?" Bernard asks.

"Since I'm not too keen to return to Yikshir, and it would be exciting to see the Land beyond, I think so. Though I do hope you keep your cross to save some of that brass reward for me."

"I would never break it," Sanet says, drawing an *X* on the east side of her chest.

At this, they drink and eat until midmorn, laughing and sharing stories. They toast a sip for Logan.

And then, they part ways.

❖ ❖ ❖

On the road west with the sun above her, Iahel is alone and traveling again. It's been three years since she was last on the road, on her own, and never this far west. She's read and heard stories of the west. Of an ashen state. One with snows. With rivers. With waterfalls. In her life, she's lived only in the smog high-rises of Niance, the red desert of Yikshir, and the dark tunnels beneath Carvinga. She is ready to see green. And water flows. Flowers. Freks of the wild beyond the endless parade of useless, domesticated cogs.

The path beyond the Crossroads descends into a canyon, and below, a thick fog creeps around her. After a few hours, she comes upon a signpost that reads Renant, six hundred and thirty-two miles to the south, and Quemon, a hundred and forty-eight to the north. Quemon is more of the same, another Yikshir governed by politics over religion. Many discussions over which state was better could be overheard in Yikshir. The thought of hearing more of that makes her skin crawl. She chooses south. Renant is a state covered in ash, abandoned a decade ago when a volcak on the border of it and Maheet exploded. The tragedy gave Yikshir and Quemon permission to expand their populations with the influx of Renant denizens, though it was written only to be a temporary expansion.

Beyond Renant and Maheet is Organsia, where Logan is returning to. From all accounts, Organsia is one of the most impressive states in the Land, populated with overflows of rivers and lakes and waterfalls. A near paradimo. It is also known to be one of the more modern states.

As her trek continues, she thinks back to Ruth. Though she said goodbye, with a kiss and a hug, she feels as if she has abandoned her. *For the better, I guess.* But something makes her question the thought. When she left Niance at fifteen, she was ready to find a family. That was her goal, and she thought she had found it with Aerial. And being with Ruth, her first, even for just a night, made it seem like the Land was finally falling into place. But in the one-two kick of that morning, without a wave goodbye, she was alone. The Tunnels never felt like haynest, even if Earls was kind. When the demvirst took Jules, it became apparent Iahel was not to fall in single souls. Was not to have a family. And here, in the fog, she is alone again.

In fact, the thought occurs that she might just stay in the mist. Find a hole in the canyon walls and live out the rest of her days away from getting close. From disappointment. Because there is always disappointment. Logan left her. Without asking. Without caring if she might want to follow him. Ruth left her once. And Aerial was too selfish to know that Iahel needed her. *Prosh that woman.* Whenever Iahel thinks too much about it, thinks too heavily, it hurts her. It hangs on her like a rucksack full of stones. She brushes off the thoughts and continues on.

Walking in the fog is its own experience, and looking over one's shoulder or to the side leads only to curiosity and anxiety. Anything could be beyond in the fogs. Perhaps only canyon walls or a family's haynest. The people of the Misipit Valley are rigorously private denizens, keeping to themselves and using its fog as cover. If one wanted to hide, this might be the place to do so.

Iahel continues along for some while. Then, ahead of her, she sees a rucksack lies overturned in the brush. Her footsteps, the only sound in the fog, lead her closer until she realizes that it looks exactly like Logan's.

She hesitates. Looking around. Standing still and listening. The air is silent. She hunches over and looks into the rucksack, and to her shock, it is Logan's. At this, she stands and grabs for her dagger.

Quiet.

Still.

She looks around. *Why would Logan leave his rucksack?* She wanders the area, pressing farther into the fog to the west and then the east. Circling the bag's position. There are too many footprints to tell which are whose.

And then she sees them.

A pair of legs covered in decomps. The little black festatars scurry and burrow into the remains of the flesh. The two legs are severed from a torso and lie in a pool of dried blood. She covers her mouth at the sight.

They're Logan's.

Chapter Seventeen

THE TWOFOOTER'S TALE

*T*he fog looms around Iahel thicker than it was minors before. Every creak and noise surrounding her gathers a newfound intensity. Her instincts kick in. She steps away from the severed legs and returns to Logan's rucksack. Digging through, she seizes his personal effects: notes and maps, coins and pictures. There's a portrait of a woman with wild red hair, her arm around a shorter bald man, and standing in front of them, a young boy no more than ten. Logan's family.

She packs the effects into her own rucksack before tossing it over her shoulder. For a major, she contemplates her direction. *Perhaps return to the Crossroads and venture back with Sanet and Bernard.* But they're presumably long gone. Maybe she could retreat north, as whatever happened to Logan had likely come from, and returned to, the south.

The dense fog reinforces each course, charging each decision with a rising threat. Whatever or whoever did this to Logan could be anywhere. The hold on her dagger tightens as she chooses, like a flamgirl, to continue south. She won't return to the Crossroads. There is nothing for her there but Ruth, and she quickly shakes the idea. Ruth had left without a wave. *I won't let her do that to me again.* As for the dangers of what waits for her ahead, no matter where she goes, dangers could loom. Rapacious freks. Violent denizens. There's ever something or someone wanting to send a denizen left, and it is the labor of self to remain alert and at the ready. So, she ventures south.

The wide trail continues straight for miles before splitting in a myriad of directions. The Misipit Valley is known for its twisted trails, and in a lot of ways, it reminds her of the Tunnels; but instead of a perpetual cavern overhead, there is a claustrophobia of enclosing gray fog. As she treks, the only markers that differ from one step to the next are the assorted dried shrubs and fallen dead branches. To look ahead or behind is to find the persistent curtain of fog.

When the sun sets, Iahel's forced to switch on her neonlight. *A frontz torch would do me well now,* she notes, thinking of Bernard. The turn of dusk paints the trail in a soggy gloom, aided in part by the dim and circular glow of her neon, which stops short in the obstinate gray.

A sign ahead reading "Bluesteep Sleep" and carved in wood breaks the monotony of her dull steps. *Approsh Dustian.* Her pace quickens. As she draws closer to the establishment, the fog clears, revealing two small lanterns hanging on either side of Bluesteep's small entrance door built into the brown canyon wall. Nailed to the door is an invitation for local folks to enter.

Relieved, tired, and ready to put the day behind her, Iahel goes in.

Everything inside is abnormally slight, even for Iahel's petite size. So much so that she must hunch over, with her head pressed nearly to the ceiling. The barroom is no larger than an average living room, with a hearth and a hallway that leads up an eastern staircase where there are likely sleeping chambers.

The tavern is empty except for a quiet female denizen, in her late ages, behind a counter who is flipping through a paper. As Iahel steps up, the denizen takes first notice and greets her with a gentle and welcoming smile. "Good dusk to you."

"Evening. I'm looking for a place to sleep."

"Got that for you folk. For one night only?" She retrieves a leather-bound book from under the counter.

"Yes."

"Splendid then. If you could sign your curam here. It's a coin for the night, another if you're looking for a meal."

"I'll definitely take the meal."

"A double splendid then. I haven't had my duskmeal either, so you've arrived just in time." The woman squeaks with enthusiasm at the prospect of having another to spend the evening with.

After exchanging coin and key, Iahel departs for the sleeping room to drop her rucksack. She finds that the hallway and the sleeping room are smaller than usual. The bed itself would make most denizen's feet hang over, but with Iahel's height, she'll sleep triple perfect. The thought brightens her mood. *A place just for me.*

A small oil lamp lights the room and the modest wardrobe where a mirror hangs. Iahel sets her rucksack at the foot of the bed before falling back onto it. At this temporary pause, she's immediately invaded by her avoided thoughts on where she'll go from here and what happened to Logan. Neither question is answerable. Though she has only known Logan for a few weeks, he is someone she quickly grew fond of. Someone she would want to know better. *A good friend,* the Radibian might say. He is different from most of the men she's met in her life, who operated on rough or aggressive or dim behaviors.

Thoughts of Logan being sent left lead to the forgotten and suppressed memories of Jules. The most handsome girl she's ever met. *Maybe not more so than Ruth . . .* She had met Jules at Greren and Tapsters after Iahel had wandered up the women-only staircase. In the private hallways, she passed by every form of girl. Young and old. Nude or elegantly dressed. Some in tuxedos, some in decadent costumes or dresses. In her ogling and aimless amble, she bumped and shouldered Jules, who fell to the floor. Jules, at the time, had been tipst, barely able to walk. Iahel attempted to lift her up, giving her appize, when she instead fell atop Jules. They kissed there, rolling to the side of the hall. Any care of another woman around them watching hadn't mattered. Jules's lips, skin, and breasts had felt precious and beautiful and endless.

The next few months passed in minors and became one of the happiest times in Iahel's life. When the coin between them ran out, Iahel and Jules grew desperate to stay at the grewst and so decided to bargain as exhibitions for paying onlookers. At first, they found other women who would watch them, but it wasn't enough to sustain all the ale and food and room they consumed. So, eventually, they ventured over to the Co-Ed Halls but found the brutishness of hungry men nearly overpowering. Many times, they had to fight off the unwanted advances of turned-on men, and whenever they discussed leaving, the coin they were receiving made staying another week, another month, worth the hardship.

After nearly six months, they met Earls, who had recently been widowed and who agreed to give them the right balance of coin and personal freedom. He'd never wanted to touch them, and the worst thing about him was the loud masturbatory sounds he'd make watching them. Over time, it became more charming than repulsive. A game emerged between them to see who could get him to groan the loudest. He fell in single souls with them, inviting them to labor together at his frek shop mainly taking care of the older and sickly krakes that travelers would bargain for to traverse the Tunnels.

As the next year passed, life in the Tunnels was perfect. Iahel, for the first time in her short life, felt at peace. She had a family. Once every few months, Jules and Iahel would take the short trek south to spend a few days in the Radiba sunlight and keep their eyes healthy. But inevitably they loved their lives at Greren and Tapsters, and with Earls.

Then the demvirst arrived. It's unclear when the unknowable frek slunk into the den, or if it had always been there, but the mood of the whole grewst changed. The lusts of everyone intensified, sometimes unbearably, and the gentle freedom the grewst provided began to feel heavy. Like an addiction. Spending more than a day away hurt. One's hands would begin to shake, and a nervous sweat would come. Jules had taken it worse than Iahel, and it wasn't long before she and Iahel "disappeared into the darkness." To experience "the greater pleasures," as denizens called it. And they had been. During the day, while Iahel labored with Earls, tending to the krakes, her mind would return to the grewst. To the demvirst. To the sharp yet erotic crack of whips.

When Jules was consumed by the demvirst, Iahel had wanted to run, as many did, but the demvirst's power, its lust, convinced its priced that it was too dominant to destroy. Too fearsome to escape. The thought of being sent left wasn't the worst of things. The worst would have been to never feel its pleasures again. Iahel and the others had all been internally captured. All she wanted was to leave. It was her natural mood. To leave that which was not her own. And nothing was ever her own. Her body had refused to listen. And she hated that frek.

Then Logan saved her. In so many ways, she owed him for that. At these recollections, Iahel begins to cry. It rolls over her, because everyone she's ever known, everyone she's ever wanted to know, is gone. Taken from her. Aerial. Jules. Logan. Why did she leave Ruth? She could have been happy. And her heart skips at the thought of Earls. How unhappy he must be now without her. How lonely. He had to know how she felt. That she couldn't stay. Not with the memory of the demvirst so close. The memories of Jules.

She lies in her bed, quiet until a soft knock comes on her door. She sits up. *Our duskmeal, I forgot.* She wipes her face, checking herself in the mirror. Red, bloodshot eyes. When she opens the door, she's surprised to find the woman is shorter than she as she stands without legs and moves around by her knuckles.

"Were you still hungry for a little duskmeal?"

Iahel nods. "Apory, it's been a long day. I'll be right there."

The short, legless woman smiles. "Take your time, dear, there's no rush. Though my soup doesn't stay hot forever." She turns and swings herself skillfully down the hall and into the barroom.

Taking a last deep breath, Iahel steps from the room, closing the door behind her.

At the table, Iahel sits with the woman, who says, "I never properly introduced myself, my curam is Gretchel."

"Iahel."

They shake and then eat quietly, Iahel's mind on Gretchel's injury. Or was she chosen this way? Is this what happened to Logan? She didn't know much about the Misipit Valley denizens, beyond their secrecy and privacy. The mood between Gretchel and her sits between peaceful and tense.

In the end, Gretchel speaks up. "I guess you're not from around here. I'm sure you wish to know about us, why they call us 'twofooters'? Dreadful curam."

"No, but you don't have to . . ."

"Oh, it's fine, dear, you seem kind enough."

Iahel smiles politely.

"You see, we're created this way. Two legs missing. At first, there were just a dozen of us. An outcast batch of children. We lived outside these canyons. In the Lands above, but others in Misipit and Carvinga were cruel. They saw us as freaks and cast us down here in the valley fogs. They called us 'knuckledraggers.' Or 'twofooters.' Carvinga folk especially hated the fact that we were what they described as deformed. They've spent generations choosing the best, choosing only the tallest and most fearsome. We were the opposite of their ideal form. So, they shunned us. Eventually, they were so disgusted by us that they closed their borders, outright denying anyone from entering their state, a clear violation of the Law of Passage, which is why they eventually fashioned those ghastly Tunnels. Their hate, their disgust of others, knows no limit."

"I've never met a tenfooter."

"You probably never shall. And, if you do, it'll probably be the last folk you'll find."

"Are you saying that all the Misipit people are . . . like you?"

"No. There are others who are like you outside the valley, but most of us live here in the fogs. Over the generations, we've become proud of our form. Even proud of the term. We have our own children's square. It's Luckers blessed. Some, like myself, enjoy our natural state. And for most others, it's made them great innovators. Twofooters all over have created machines most would never spend a kiptale on. This 'mistake' made us a strong and proud folk. We embraced who we are. And won't allow others to drag our pride down with words or insults."

Iahel wonders about Logan. Afraid to ask, but . . . curiosity takes over. "I had a friend who was traveling through here. He had only left a few hours before me, but I found . . . I found his legs on the road . . ." She trails off, not sure exactly what she's asking, what answer she's seeking. Gretchel takes another bite, letting the statement hang in the air.

"What are you asking, dear?"

"I don't want to presume anything; I don't know the customs here. And you can't fault me for setting two lands together, as wrong as I might be." Iahel remembers that she forgot her dagger in the sleeping room. Why she remembers it now, she isn't sure.

Gretchel takes another small bite and looks to be in thought. She answers calmly, her tone shifting from kind and soft to bold and stern, filling the silence with a revelation. "There is a march on hand."

"A march?"

Gretchel pauses again before speaking up. "Yes, dear, into Carvinga."

The thought is wild. "But . . . why? How?"

"It's not for me to spread. I don't know if I double or not."

"Isn't that an act of war? Isn't that illegal?"

In fact, the last major conflict Iahel remembers hearing about was one deep in the Azom state, a state in constant turmoil. Azoms are violent people, but they never take their violence into other states. The mere idea of two states going to war is outrageous. The Last War nearly eradicated everyone, and the only laws of the Land are designed specifically to avoid war. *Not to mention going to fight the tenfooters? Denizens who tower over everyone else, whom no single body has met and not been sent?*

"Forgive my forwardness, but the idea of some march going into Carvinga seems a bit wild, don't you think?"

"Wild or not, it's happening. The antipathy of our folk runs generations deep. But it's not just hatred. There are rumors about what the tenfooters are up to. What they're hiding."

"Hiding?"

"We've received letters and information that they are attempting to bring back an ardroke," Gretchel states plainly.

At this, Iahel laughs. "An ardroke?"

Gretchel grins in kind but without humor.

The thought of a giant frek, hundreds of measures high, looming over buildings and hills—it is a terror story for children. "You can't believe that's true?"

"I'm just a simple woman running a tavern, but I do believe they're up to something and that they're attempting to disrupt the natural order. Growing themselves so tall. Why are they so secretive? What are they doing that we can't go and see?"

"Why does it matter? It's been over two and a half thousand years. Every state can rule themselves how they want, right? And the Law of Passage isn't being violated since they created the Tunnels."

"The Tunnels. That wasn't the soul of the Law. The Laws were written to prevent war. To prevent conspiracy. To avoid collision." Gretchel's tone adjusts and flames, her hatred for tenfooters permeating her words.

At this, Iahel limits her outward shock and tone of accusation. "Well, I hope you're wrong. I think an act of war is unlikely; that's the whole point of the states. The Last War nearly destroyed everyone."

"And if the tenfooters bring back an ardroke?"

"Apory, but I don't believe in the stories of ardrokes."

Gretchel looks insulted. She presses her lips together and takes the bowl from which Iahel was eating and climbs down from her chair. "I'm feeling tired. Feel free to stay up longer."

After a minor, Iahel is left alone in the room. The Misipit denizens are simple to believe in such children's tales, and easily tricked into a conspiracy. Iahel sips the last drops in her mug and retires to the sleeping room. Images of giant freks, of two- and tenfooters fighting, roam her kiptales.

❖ ❖ ❖

She is awakened late in the night by new noises from the barroom; when she left for bed, she was the only guest at Bluesteep. She tosses on her clothes and then presses her ear to the door, hearing only muffled sounds and whispering, none of which she can decipher. With curiosity and impatience, she opens the door and peers down the small hallway and the stairs. The fire is still lit, and a pair of shadows hang on the back wall. A conversation continues, first with Gretchel.

"Are the rumors true?"

The second voice, a man's voice, is gruff and spotted with coughing. "Yes."

"Luckers, I can't believe it. After all these years, they're finally following through. Marching into Carvinga." There's a long pause.

Iahel's heart beats louder. *They're mad.*

"Something is in those stonetins. Something big."

"Of course, there is. They're obsessed with the ardrokes."

"If we don't stop them, a return of ardrokes would be the end of us. Of everyone."

"The other states won't join. Not until it's too late."

"They're afraid to face the tenfooters," the man adds.

There's a pause. Gretchel's shadow sips from her mug's shadow. "In all my years, I've known no greater courage than yours, Erish."

"But I am afraid." He coughs. "I'm not as young as I once was and our march is not strong enough to withstand the forces of tenfooters. Even with the crimson men."

"This war will raise awareness. This fight is important. The tenfooters will destroy us if they're given full reign. They can't be trusted."

At this, they clink mugs and drink. "I have another purpose here," Erish states after gulping down the last of his ale. "A man was on the road. A man wanted by the Victors."

"The Victors? What are they doing with a Misipit folk?"

"He was a Radiba man. Or an Organsia man, I'm not sure. The Victors are insistent on finding him. It was part of our conditions. Part of our payment to bring him in, if he traversed the valley."

"I warned you, Erish, about involving yourselves with the Victors. They bring no one any good."

"We needed the coin and the intelligence. The Victors are the ones who confirmed our suspicions about the stonetins. About the ardrokes," Erish says before coughing again.

"Well, what do you want from me?"

"He was taken by one of our regiments. They're holding him closer to the border, but I'd like to transport him back here for the exchange."

"Here? I don't want the Victors here."

"They're already on their way, and we can't drag him across the state to meet them."

"Drag him?"

"Yes, Drax cut off his legs; he's barely alive now."

At this Gretchel hushes him. She begins to whisper.

They have Logan. She knows I know. Iahel closes the door. *Shnite.* She spins and grabs her rucksack, packing it with the few items she'd removed for the night. She puts on her boots and jacket and grabs her dagger. It is time to leave.

Pressing her ear against the door again, she listens for Gretchel and Erish. They're approaching. Iahel locks the door and steps backward. Waiting. *They won't kill me, will they? They probably want to talk.* A knock on the door.

"Iahel, dear? Are you asleep? I need to ask you something." Gretchel's voice trembles slightly.

Iahel looks around the room and moves to hide in the wardrobe. Too small. She's nervous and scared. Unsure of what their motives are. Then, the sound of a key.

No time to think, Iahel. She runs to the door and holds it shut. "Hello, Gretchel. What's going on?"

The key stops. A bit of shuffling outside the door. Gretchel replies, "Iahel, I'd like to ask you something if you wouldn't mind. I know it's late, dear, but it's important."

Iahel swallows. *Why would they want to send her? If she could convince them she doesn't know anything—*

"One minor. Let me get dressed."

She sets her sack to the side and removes her coat, both within easy reach. She keeps her boots on before returning to the door.

She unlocks it and holds it slightly open, trying to look tired and giving a fake yawn. "Is everything wisnok?"

Before her stands Gretchel and another man, a twofooter himself. He's as tall as the ceiling, bigger than Iahel, and he slouches his shoulders. He wears two mechanical legs built with intricate pulleys, gears, rods, and wires. "Evening, sur. My curam is Erish."

The dagger is in her hand, behind the door.

"Would you mind coming with us back to the bar?"

Iahel waits for a major. Weighing the dangers. "I'm pretty tired, can this wait until morn?"

Gretchel and Erish exchange a look before Gretchel answers, "It's important. Please. Come with us."

"Wisnok, give me a minor."

Erish nods and turns away, as does Gretchel. When Erish spins, Iahel sees a holstered shotgun. Earlier that night, Gretchel had spoken about two exits. The main hall, where she had entered, and a cavern deeper in the canyon where Gretchel said she would take long walks when she didn't want to face the fogs.

She closes the door again. To run or stay. The behaviors of the twofooters seem one of paranoia and fear. If she were to stay, they could send her left. She puts her jacket back on and grabs her rucksack, slinging it over her shoulder.

She reaches for the door handle, swallows. When she opens it, Erish stands before her with a smile. And then, out of instinct, perhaps because nothing ever went right for her, possibly because something about Erish reminds her of the way men would look at her and Jules at Greren's, she runs from the room and pushes him against the wall. He makes a soft *ooof* when he hits it. She turns west, down the hall toward the back door and into the cavern. She isn't sure how far it goes or if it leads anywhere, but she isn't ready to be sent left tonight.

Behind her, Gretchel screams out in shock and anger. "Come back here! Why are you running?"

Iahel isn't entirely sure. She's thinks she's as mad as they are as she opens the door and disappears into the darkness beyond.

Chapter Eighteen

MARCH OF THE INGREVES

*F*or a minor, Iahel runs in complete darkness, her arms flailing in front of her, before light illuminates the cavern walls when Erish steps into the tunnel behind her. In the minary illumination, she catches a glimpse of a division in the tunnel ahead. She chooses east, where she believes she'll find the exit to the outer canyon. West is likely only deeper underground.

The footsteps behind her gain speed. "Why are you running, girl?" Erish cries out.

In the pitch-black, Iahel courses through the tunnel, her hand running against the rough rock wall, leading her along blindly. And then she feels the air lighten. *Escape.* She quickens her step as the sound of Erish fades behind her; he likely took the west tunnel. After a forty stride, moonlight beams into the tunnel. She sighs with relief as she exits into the night.

Outside, she studies both directions and chooses to run west, away from the Bluesteep entrance. The night fog strangles the sights ahead, with each gigantic footstep echoing across the canyon and foretelling her exact location. She glances over her shoulder every few steps, fearing the sight of Erish. Her side begins to burn, her breathing heavy, uncontrollable. The farther she runs, the less her adrenaline carries her. She gives in and stops, bent over with hands on her knees, taking long deep breaths and exhales that release in shakes. A major passes before she collects herself. Staring back into the fog neither gives her a break in relief nor causes her more fear. Instead of running farther, she stumbles to the side of the road and hides behind a large brackleberry bush that stretches along the canyon wall. From this perspective, the fog hides a sizable portion of the road. She tries to calm herself, to silence her breath, and since she's unable to see anything, she closes her eyes to listen.

In the distance: the din of footsteps.

She covers her mouth as panic rises again inside, in harmony with the fear of what Erish may do if he finds her. A flash of Logan's amputated legs looms in her mind. She grabs her upper thigh as if she can feel a sharp passing phantom slice. When his steps draw closer, she opens her eyes.

Ahead, silhouetted in the moonlit fog, Erish jogs past her. "Come out, girl. You're only making this worse."

She breathes in and holds the breath, her heart thumping against her chest, giving her away. A tear rolls down her cheek. But instead of turning to her, Erish continues forward, his footsteps diminishing across the valley.

As the still and quiet settle around her, her mind races. *Logan is still alive.* For a minor, feelings of relief and panic conflict. All that she knows is to run. And that running should carry her as far away as it can. Away from anyone she knows. Away from anyone who could hurt her. Anyone she could get close to. And to double on, on no green Land would she want to be near something as mad as a war. A real and violent war—not a skirmish between rival cities or a little street violence. But all-out, the-end-of-everything war.

On the other side of things, Logan is alive. *That proshing man is alive.* She's overcome by imaginings of him lying in pain, his legs torn from his body. Of how alone he is. How selfless he had been when she whispered about her hedonism with the demvirst. How could she leave him there? What person would she be if she left her rescuer to his sending?

But who are you, Iahel? You are no rescuer. You are no heroine. But when the sun rises, *prosh,* when the sun rises, she has to find him. She must. At the very least, she has to know she couldn't have done something to save him. She has to know a rescue would have been hopeless. The thought raises grenspimples.

Until the sun rises, she needs rest. Pushing herself deeper into the bush and throwing a shirt over her head, Iahel closes her eyes, knowing the day ahead inevitably brings an arduous charge. With Erish long gone, her heart finally calms. Her breathing becomes manageable. Sleep, however, is impossible.

After what feels a week's length, the sun begins to peer through the fog and brush. Jarjers sing as they pass in the sky above her. In her small travels, she's only heard the melody of the Radiba jarjers. Each of these state's flying freks carry hums and melodies that offer a spirit of the area. Radiba's swell with a hopeful, quiet tune. Whenever she and Jules would emerge from the Tunnels for a day or two, the jarjer's song carried an almost peaceful tranquility to the trees and looming Highland. Listening now, the song of the Misipit Valley jarjers offers only lonesomeness and paranoia.

Iahel stands, her body aching from the impossible position she placed herself in overnight. She rolls her neck and steps back out onto the road, her ears attuning to its noise. Quiet. Unsure of where to go or how she would even find Logan, she listens to her instinct to instead track Erish. Perhaps he'll lead her to wherever Logan is being held. *But for how long?*

She starts by heading west where Erish disappeared only a few hours ago. Since nothing much can be seen around her, she focuses on the road below and the dirt where the most recent of many boot prints have traveled. She walks with soft steps, aware that anyone could be in any place.

The morn passes without event. Iahel's only interactions with others come when a pair of getwish legs pass by, its body high above and hidden in the fog. Twofooters must hate these freks. She smiles for the first time that morn at the irony of getwishes in Misipit.

Erish's boot prints, or what she's chosen to believe are Erish's, turn off the trail and begin trudging up a west canyon wall. Hopeful she's on the right path, she follows them.

The way is winding and narrow, and if anyone were to come down, they would have to hold on to each other as they pass or risk falling from the steep ledge. As she ascends, the fog begins to clear, and after an hour's trek, out of breath and leg sore, she finds herself at the top of the canyon.

The expanse is fresh and spacious with sporadic low-lying hills slouching across an endless crisp green landscape. Impossibly large boulders and petrified trees pepper the vista along the plateau. Below, the fog flows in channeled streams deep in the canyon valley. The boot prints Iahel had carefully followed throughout the morn have disappeared now that the path beneath her feet is stone. She grabs a bit of granola from her rucksack and takes a few bites to curb the rumble in her stomach. Starting her trek along the plateau, she finds no discerning course to track and no trails or roads or paths. In the far distance rises a cloud of dust.

The midmorn all too quickly vaults to full sun before Iahel finds shade under an overhanging rock. Over the past hours, other destined landmarks turned false when she discovered the penetrating heat of the sun was generating watery mirages. Here now, in the shade, she is grateful the rock is real. Taking a few last sips from her water jug, she closes her eyes for a major, deciding that reaching the next landmark ahead will take her the rest of her day, but the cool soft breeze coaxes her into a long kiptaleless nap.

Rumbling.

The ground beneath her shakes. Iahel wakes nearly an hour later and braces herself against the back side of the rock. Around her moves a massive march of ingreves easily hundreds and hundreds deep. The ingreves stomp to her east, to her west, and some down from the rock above. Standing twenty feet high and nearly as wide, the gray-and-brown-striped ingreves plod along. Their narrow, vertical heads open, revealing mouths in the same vertical direction with a double layer of rounded teeth. On either side of these sideways mouths are inlays of a half-dozen unblinking eyes that are frequently calcified from an endless amount of debris caught in their lids. Occasionally, they release a low, booming growl that reverberates through the air.

Riding these monstrous freks are dozens of twofooters, each in elaborate harnesses. Some ride on the sides of the ingreves, while others ride on top. Adding to the march are twofooters mounted solo on tall getwishes. The getwishes' long legs, some five feet high, lead all the way up to rounded black-and-white-feathered bodies. Matching their thin double-jointed legs, long skinny necks rise to beaks, around which small bridles are used to lead them. The march is easily thousands thick. It takes nearly an hour to pass. Iahel huddles as close to the inside of the rock as possible, holding her breath once more, hoping no one turns around or notices her.

Luck to her, the march is indifferent to its surroundings. She listens in on pieces of conversations of twofooters complaining about the heat or what they ate for their mornmeal. Intermittently, Iahel hears twofooters speak of tenfooters, followed by many curses and guttural spits.

And then a cart pulled by a smaller ingreve passes. Atop it sits three large metal cages with rounded tops. In two of them are denizens Iahel has never seen, but in the middle cage sleeps Logan, his face bruised purple from a visible beating and burned red from a shadowless full sun. What's more shocking in person than imagined lies below his torso, where his legs should be. Two bandaged stumps. *Dustian, the poor cog.*

After another ten minutes, the last freks and twofooters pass, leaving behind deep indentions and tracks in the loose gravel. Iahel continues to watch from the relative safety of the rock as the march grows smaller and smaller along the crest. The day holds only a few more hours before dusk. *Now you know, Iahel.* She remains under the rock, unsure of what she's to do or how she might go about freeing the priced Logan. *Shouldn't you just run?* One twofooter is enough to scare her, let alone a thousand of them. *And is this not the march heading into Carvinga?* The thought sends grenspimples across her arms as she imagines the destruction of the Land passing her by. War is an experience reserved for only the long ago of history.

I can't allow Logan to be sent left.

Gathering her rucksack, leaving her fears behind and against her stomach's churning, she follows the march. Tracing and hiding behind one large boulder or petrified trunk after another, she draws closer and closer to the plodding march. Having no real weapons on her, Iahel shakes through many ideas of what she's going to do. She hates the idea of using guns, and her paltry dagger is little use against a single twofooter let alone an entire march. Her attempt to rescue Logan will require a unispar recipe of stealth, timing, and untold luck.

Last chance to turn away, Iahel.

With a deep, unsettled breath, she continues forth.

About an hour before dusk, the march stops and begins building a temporary camp populated with quick pop tents and tended fires. The many ingreves are gathered and fed while the forty dozen on dozens of getwishes wander free, some chasing others.

Iahel finds a safe lookout rock two hundred strides away from them. She scans the far-reaching camp for the three cages and finds them almost immediately, only to see them occupied by other priced men. The large assortment of the twofooters' cages scattered among the entire encampment makes the task of finding Logan's nearly impossible.

She hunts and watches. Scanning for another triple set of cages that hold Logan, and it's not until the sun falls below crest that she finds him asleep and lying motionless in his cage. She watches him anxiously. *He can't be sent; they would have thrown him away.* Anticipating any sign of movement, she waits. *Come on, Logan.* Near him, an irregular arrangement of twofooters, getwishes, and ingreves are led by the man from Bluesteep curamed Erish, standing on his two wood-and-metal legs. Others in the small camp among the larger march maneuver about on stout, dexterous arms and hands.

The most important part of her plan, *luck*, is in her favor, as this grouping is on the outside circle of the march. She scans the area near them and spots what might work as a hiding space relatively close.

Since Logan is without legs, she'll need to find some means to move him quickly. Her first instinct is to find a getwish they can ride. *What I wouldn't do for Whistlers right now.* Getwishes, with their high, flimsy legs and long necks, look more troublesome than they're worth. As she investigates the encompassing area for a solitary getwish wandering around, she spots a baby ingreve not fifty strides from Logan's cage. It roams in a small grass patch alongside a larger ingreve that, due to similar striped patterns and colors, Iahel assumes is the little ingreve's mother. *That could work.*

She makes her way down the overlook rock and toward the baby ingreve and its mother to prepare them for what and who might chase once Logan's released. While sneaking closer, she plots their escape. Her first notion is to head south. If they're on the same plateau Sanet had visited three months ago, there will be a lone manor there, where she'd snipped that sliver of brass. *South is too much open air. Dangerous.* Their other option would be to head east and into Carvinga, maybe a half-day's trek. *Twofooter to tenfooter.* The other directions are not an option, as they're either into or through the ingreve march. Unsure, she returns to her reconnaissance of the camp.

A still-burning fire mixed with the full moon offers Iahel enough light to find the right path but enough darkness to keep her presence covert. She treks closer and finds a quiet hiding place in the remains of an old overturned tree, fossilized over the eras. She watches as the smaller ingreve playfully pounces in the grass, hunting an unseen frek. Its eyes are bright and new, its mouth without teeth. Once every few majors, it bites down into the field but comes up empty, shaking its little head. The larger mother ingreve stands unmoving on thick, stumpy legs while her unblinking eyes make it unclear whether she's still awake or asleep.

When the moon falls past full moon, the area quiets to sleep, and the ingreves rest, still in their patch. Resolved once more, she slinks into camp. *Now or never.*

While a few whispered conversations from other parts of the march linger about the air, within the circle of tents where Logan's cage rests, the twofooters are asleep. The crackle of a paling bonfire radiates in the middle of the campsite as Iahel squeezes between two tents, each with its front door tied open. As she catches sight of a twofooter dressed in leather shifting in his sleep, her heart skips. She waits an eternity.

Iahel finds Logan is in even worse shape up close, with dirt and dried blood covering his face. She reaches a hand into his cage—*don't make a noise, Logan*—and shakes him awake, four finger to her lips. Logan shuffles and his eyes grow wide after catching a glimpse of her. He sits up, wincing in pain. His hands are bound, and he looks to his legs. He whispers, "You shouldn't be here."

"Shnite talk. You're coming with me, so we're square," she whispers back.

Logan smiles weakly and drags himself closer using his elbow, then reaches for the cage door. "I think Drax has the key. He's the one in that tent over there." He nods his head, and Iahel turns to see a tall and triangular tent. "I'm moderately sure he's alone in there."

She nods again. *Why didn't I think of needing a key?*

She spins in place, taking stock of the small camp. There are five tents of various sizes all similarly triangular. She steps toward the tent Logan pointed toward, careful to avoid various trash and sticks on the ground. As she approaches, she reaches out to grasp the tent flap only to hear a small grunt. She turns to see Logan motioning his head. *Wrong tent.* Her heart skips a beat, and she moves over one tent and confirms with Logan, who nods approval.

There are no windows in the tent, so Iahel presses her head close to it to listen for any signs of motion inside. *Still.* She lifts the tent door, a small leather flap, and reveals Drax sleeping with two other female twofooters. They're intertwined head to waist, Drax sleeping with one of the women's tiny foot-like stumps in his mouth. His hair is long and unkempt. Scanning the tent, she notices a small bag sitting against the wall to her west. She reaches in. Slow. Steady. Quiet.

One of the female twofooters wakes and stares at her. Iahel freezes. The woman looks dazed and half asleep. She smiles at Iahel before laying her head back down on Drax's body. With a quickened pace, Iahel grabs the entire bag and lifts it up and out of the tent. She swallows and takes a deep breath. The fire crackles and fades, the light around them darkening. She returns to Logan's cage and carefully rifles through the bag, keeping the noise to a minimum. Along its side, hooked on a small flap, is a set of keys. She takes them in her hand. At the sight, Logan's eyes beam with excitement.

She places the first key into the lock. It clicks and the cage door pops open. "Lucky try," Logan whispers. "Now how are we going to escape?"

"I have a plan, but it's mad."

"Can't be worse than what's happened to me today." He compresses his lips.

Logan grabs the side bars and pulls himself, likely more from a desire to escape than from a remaining strength, out of the cage and drops to the ground with a pathetic *thump*. The sight is surreal. Here is a man who once stood tall and handsome, who once was charming and a bit of a child, and who now lies mangled and physically destroyed. And he was not proud and confident, like Erish or Gretchel. He was forced into this condition.

Taken from.

After releasing Logan's hands, the two begin to move past the tents when Iahel spots Erish's legs. The wood and stone and metal machines stand in wait next to his tent. She motions to Logan, dragging behind, who nods at her before she grabs them.

Leaving the small camp, they return to Iahel's hiding tree trunk in view of the sleeping ingreves, where she left her rucksack.

"You want to take that little ingreve," Logan whispers.

"Little" wouldn't be how Iahel would describe the baby ingreve, which is easily big enough for the two of them to ride. "You have a better idea?"

"Can't I just use those?" Logan points.

Iahel looks down at Erish's legs. "I'm not sure there's an easy way to put them on without some . . . alterations."

Logan takes one of them and inspects it with his hands. "Yeah, you're right. Looks like there're pins here. Not sure I can handle any more injuries right now." He gives a wincing smile.

"Once we're on that beast, we'll get far enough away that they won't find us. We'll get you walking again."

"Maybe. They seemed pretty determined to turn me over to the Victors."

"I heard them. You'll have to tell me about that once when we're out of here—"

"Once we're safe, I'll tell anything you want."

With that, Iahel shifts her focus back to the baby ingreve.

"Wait here." She steps out of the trunk and closer to the two freks. When she's within a few strides, she begins to ruffle the grass, making a smacking sound with her lips. The little ingreve turns its head. Its eyes spark to life. It looks frightened at first. Iahel continues to play in the grass and make the smacking noise with her lips. It's not long before the ingreve hops in place and begins to circle a bit in the lawn. Standing up, it's close to four feet tall. Its pounces rumble the dirt beneath it.

Iahel draws the frek toward her as she backs away toward Logan and the trunk. It follows unknowingly, its vertical mouth opening in a soft growl. A red tongue slips out and wags eagerly. When it's away from the mother, Iahel reaches out to pet the side of the young ingreve's head. It pushes into her, licking her arm. Iahel contains a giggle. *Just like calming a krake.*

Growing confident, and knowing time is short, she motions for Logan to appear, and he crawls from the trunk. The ingreve stumbles backward a bit but is assured by Iahel, who continues to pet and smack her lips. Logan attempts his own smacking noise, but it comes out wrong, and the ingreve shows a slight agitation. Iahel hushes him. Logan nods, embarrassed.

She looks the ingreve in the eye. "We're going to get on you now, are you ready for that?" The ingreve doesn't react. Saying a quick Dustian, Iahel takes the ingreve by the neck and pulls herself up. It immediately stands straighter and starts to circle erratically as if uncomfortable with the sudden weight. Iahel, with both hands, massages either side of the ingreve's neck, calming it.

Pressing deeper with her west hand, she leads the young frek toward Logan, who pulls himself up and atop the ingreve using Iahel to support him. With both on, the ingreve grows more restless, spinning and bouncing up and down. It begins making little roars. *Don't wake mama, little frek,* she thinks with apprehension, looking toward the other impossibly large and motionless ingreve.

Iahel closes her eyes, pushing and massaging her hands deep into the ingreve's neck, calming it with more lip smacking. It slows.

"I think we're good. Let me get our stuff." She leads the ingreve over to the trunk and hops off, ensuring her hand never leaves its neck. It appears content and curious as she grabs Erish's legs and gives them to Logan. "You should start to massage its neck here. Right there where it's warm."

With one arm wrapped around the mechanical legs, Logan uses his other to rub the ingreve's neck. It reacts to the change of hands but finds the new motion comforting. Iahel hangs her rucksack over her shoulder and hops on behind Logan.

"Let's get out of here." She moves her hand around Logan and leads the ingreve. It happily plods along away from the camp and toward the moonlit grasslands ahead. Looking back, Logan stares at the other large ingreve.

"Is it going to miss its mother?"

"Hopefully not anytime soon. I think it's enjoying this for the major, but eventually it will, I don't doubt. But, with any luck, after we're long gone from the march."

Facing south, they trek along and into the night.

Chapter Nineteen
THE MAN WHO LOST HIS LEGS

*I*f the threat of vengeful twofooters chasing them wasn't looming, the moonlight radiating off the landscape of large boulders and petrified trunks would have been a calming and picturesque scene. From crest to crest, the sky marks itself with thin strips of noctilucent clouds and an untold number of dotted starscapes. Behind them, the fires of the camp fade into the distance, evolving to less and less threatening specks of light. Iahel spies a large boulder they might use as a safe space to rest out of sight.

She guides the ingreve toward the arched rock, dismounts, and helps Logan perch against the crag. The ingreve, groggy in step, promptly spins and plops to the ground, and Logan drags himself toward the rock, propping himself upright. Iahel sits next to Logan, and they wait patiently. And for an extended major, they both remain silent.

After a time, Logan breaks the quiet. "Approsh, Iahel."

"This just makes us square." She shrugs off the appreciation, her feelings for Logan shifting. In the rush to rescue, she'd buried her thoughts, but over the calm, she's come to believe her bravery was only obligation, convincing herself she was supposed to be the heroine even though all it will lead to is inevitable. Her lot in this story is loss. Departures without waves or single souls sent left. Attempts to hold stability or a foundation in her story would always and have always been uprooted and splintered into dust.

Aerial was right to believe in Dustian. Consuming life until there's nothing left. Until there's only dust.

The ingreve lifts its head, then stands. Without notice, it speeds away even as Iahel reaches out a hand to stop it. Missing her grip, she stands and turns toward its trajectory. Her heart quails at the thought of what might be on the other side of the rock. *A scouting party or twofooters on getwishes hunting the runaway long legs.* She finds instead the ingreve's shadow diminishing in the moonlight as it hurries toward the camp. *To its mother.* The instinct for haynest, for family, evades her; she's unable to comprehend the concept of having a mother or being a daughter, of having another to call her constant. To double, since she never wanted children herself, it is a relationship she would never understand. Turning back to Logan, she finds his expression begging for good news.

"Nothing to worry about. Guess it missed its mother."

Relief crosses his face. "Good to hear. If it had been twofooters, I don't think I'm up for a quick jaunt at the major."

Iahel smiles in sympathy. "We should see if these work then, you think?" Logan looks apprehensively at the two legs.

"Maybe tomorrow."

"I'm not confident we won't be running for our lives tomorrow. Or even later tonight. We should do this before it's too late. Labour through . . ." Iahel hesitates. "Through whatever pain these have in store for you. At least so you have some time to recover." She watches Logan's face as he contemplates the logic.

With a huff, he says, "Fine then."

At that, Iahel plucks the legs from the ground and lines them up with both of Logan's stumps.

"You think we have to do this raw?" he asks.

"Take off the bandage?" She looks down at each stub bleeding through.

"Shnite. You're probably right," Logan says, defeated. He reaches down and begins to unravel the bandages.

She turns and pulls an old shirt from her rucksack and aligns it under the tip of his stump, three-quarters up from where his knee might have been.

As Logan finishes, Iahel gets her first glimpse at his horror. At her expression, he offers, "They cauterized the legs as soon as they cut them."

The end of each stump is mangled and black. Iahel covers her mouth.

"I don't remember them cutting the second. I went dark as soon as they hit an iron to the first. Told me I shouldn't have run. Bragging, they said I was."

"Dustian."

"So, bring on these penetrating pins, shall we?"

Iahel looks at Logan. *Radiba cog spirit through and through.* Carefully, she helps set the first leg into place as Logan grabs and adjusts it, pulling it farther back into the stump.

He grimaces. Grits his teeth. "Apory, the pins are scraping a little."

Iahel stands back, holding hand to mouth. "I don't need the details."

"I should get the other one in place, in case this first one doesn't go well and you have to finish."

The thought terrifies her. "Let's not need to do that." She reluctantly steps closer. The smell of his wound hits her nose, and she suppresses her gag reflex, attempting not to look at his legs or his flaccid cock having spilled out after he unraveled the bandage.

"Apory again." He covers himself, slightly flushed.

"I've seen it before, just reinforces why I'm no gully for them."

Logan laughs. "Make a boy feel real special."

She shrugs. "My specialty," she says, then sets the other leg and stands back, returning to her safer distance.

Logan adjusts the second leg, breathing deep with each slight movement, pausing and then readjusting. Once both are set, he looks up. "Here's to nothing," he sighs before commencing to screw in the first leg using both hands, one to hold it in place, the other to spin the many little cranks.

At first, he seems capable of hiding the anguish, biting down and attempting to power through the screws digging, cutting into his skin. But soon, tears well as he closes his eyes, and the pain shrinks his heavy breathing into a low, managed grumble—before he gives in to an all-out scream.

At this, Iahel kneels before him, covering his mouth. "We have to stay quiet out here."

Logan continues to turn the screws, his eyes focused entirely on Iahel's. Soon he finishes the first leg, red-eyed, his face flushed and sweating.

"You did well. Halfway there." She releases her hand from his mouth. His lip bleeds from a tiny bite.

With a deep breath and eyes once more closed, Logan begins again on the second leg. This one is sure to be even more painful, knowing what pain awaits him. He's slower to finish, each turn followed by an excruciated holler. Iahel returns to holding back his scream, and her hand grows wet from the stream of tears pouring down his face. His breath steams in her hand.

You have this.

He stops and his eyes roll back before he slumps over. She catches his fall and softly lays his head to the ground. She looks at his leg. *He finished.* Blood streams from the holes made by the screws. Iahel stands and shakes the sight of the gore off, holding back vomit.

Positioning herself across from Logan, she lies in the soft grass and dirt with her hands behind her head, trying to rid herself of the horror. It has been a while since she's taken a major to watch the night sky and soft twinkle of the stars, whose movements and sparkles increase the longer you stare. When she was younger, she believed that the night sky was only a giant dome with millions of tiny holes poked through. A half dome. Like a bowl that circles the Land and rotates around the planet with the light of the stars beaming from sunlight constantly shining through. One of the caretakers had told her this child's tale, concluding that even when the Land is night, when things are at their darkest, the light remains, shining through the pinholes of the sky and reminding us that the light is ever there. Lincoln sent.

Perhaps that's what it could be. Iahel imagines the conceit, the flatness of the atmosphere, of a giant hole-filled blanket. Her mind wanders to Jules. A kiss they had once in the dark. How her lips felt bigger than her entire body. She floats away and falls asleep.

❖ ❖ ❖

The next morn, Iahel wakes up soaking wet. Her dark and undisturbed sleep in the grass left her drenched in the first morndew. Logan still sleeps, unmoving in the night. She stands and stretches and yawns, catching the sun peeking over crest, and looks behind the rock to see if twofooters are tracking them. The early morn mists hide any sight of denizens in the far distance. For the major, things are clear.

She moves to Logan and gently shakes his shoulder. He stirs, grunting slightly before opening his eyes. "Good kiptales?" she asks.

"Morn." He smiles, pushing himself up, and looks around. "I kiptaled I was back in Radiba. I spent a night with Sanet there. Before all this."

"She told me." Iahel smiles.

Logan looks back to his legs. "Think these stumps work?"

"Let's hope so, or we're in trouble."

She watches as he stares at the foot of each leg. There are no toes or discerning digits. After a minor, the west foot moves.

Logan's eyes widen and he gasps. "Lincoln, we did it."

"Try the other," Iahel insists.

Logan nods and looks to his east foot. It moves. "It moves!"

"Grats."

Logan immediately pushes himself up.

"Careful, Logan."

She stands close, but he holds her off, attempting to do it on his own. Bracing himself on the rock behind him, he slowly shifts upward. His new legs wobble underneath him. Iahel reaches out her hand again; Logan denies it.

"I think I have it."

Stepping back, she watches as he stands completely, his hand on the rock for balance. "Can you walk?"

"The feeling is only here." He points to where the artificial legs meet his stumps. "Feels like needles dotting my skin." He pushes himself off the rock and steps forward. One foot clumsy before the other. He takes a second step. This one with a bit more confidence. Another step. He grimaces.

"Are you wisnok?"

"The pins are settling." He grits his teeth but takes another step. "Shnite. It feels so . . . it feels almost natural. Like I can feel them." Logan begins to walk in a circle, each new step more accepted than the last.

"Well, I won't lie that I almost couldn't bear to watch last night."

"You don't like watching friends stab themselves with piercing pins and cutting screws?" he jokes.

Iahel swallows back the disgust. "We should move."

Logan, whose face is twisted in both elation and surprise, agrees. She grabs her rucksack, and they set off.

The day passes slowly. At times, Logan runs on his new legs. He's fast. Quicker than Iahel, who attempts to race him. "Our little twofooter friend," she jokes. He shudders.

The conversation then turns to the twofooters' march. "They seem dark bent on bringing war to the tenfooters. As if being slighted in some long way was too much to be forgiven," Logan doubles.

"But why now? How long have they been planning this?"

Recalling what he overheard, he says, "There were rumblings about that Roar. How his advent inspired them to act. I heard another group of twofooters singing that same chant the crimson men did back when we were in Radiba. The one about the advent of the Roar. 'Seven from' or something like that."

"They sound Yikshir. Believing in a bunch of superstitions."

"I'm not sure why they believe in the advent of some child, like that's possible. Or why that starts a war, but it seems more likely they're using it to justify an act they've wanted anyway. Or at least some of them. Others seem happy just to leave the valley fogs."

"I've never met a tenfooter, but I can't imagine that march is significant enough to win against them," Iahel contemplates.

"I don't know. No one knows what goes on within those grasses."

"Do you believe Bernard fought one before?"

"Maybe. Bernard was young. Maybe he just met a really tall adult."

At that, Iahel laughs. Suddenly, the thought of Sanet and Bernard sends her heart a passing pang. *I hope they're safe.*

In the distance, beyond the monotonous pattern of rock and tree, stands a grand manor. At first, it resembles any other house or farm one might encounter in the more populated states, but as they draw closer to it, its size triples, making it closer to a mansion than some pedestrian ranch. Iahel can't believe the sight. "Logan, this is the manor Sanet said she went to. Where she found that little brass sliver."

The sun is soon to crest, and both are hungry, even after their makeshift duskmeal of small roasted tallingstones Logan hunted on his new legs earlier in the day. An unnerving, surreal, and awesome sight. As they watch the manor, lights shift on and off.

"We're not too far from the Tunnels then?" Iahel asks.

"Probably a half-day from the Carvinga border. Another day to an entrance. The Crossroads are still closer."

"Sanet didn't say much about who she got the brass from. You think they're twofooters?"

"Maybe. But not all Misipiants are twofooters. Especially ones who live on the plateaus," Logan answers. He takes the last small bite of his tallingstone meat.

"I wonder if they're friendly? Should be, if Sanet met them."

"I'd imagine. But that's if Sanet's telling us the truth." There's a grimace to the comment. "She could have stolen it. And now they're not so friendly."

At Logan's hissy fit over his girl crush, Iahel rolls her eyes. "If they're not so friendly, we'll need to find somewhere else to refresh supplies," she points out.

"Now that we're so close, I'm wondering if someone should tell the tenfooters about this impending attack."

"You're not volunteering us, I hope. It's not my war. And if I never meet a tenfooter in person, I'll be wisnok with it."

"Wasn't saying you or us. But I think someone should at least warn the Carvingians," Logan states. *The rescuer returns. Barely restored to health before he's ready to save the day again.* "Seems a little cruel to let friends be taken by surprise like that," he continues. "Especially if the attacker is seeking revenge for some iniquities of a generation past."

"Yes, but assuming you're even able to have a conversation with a tenfooter without being crushed or torn apart, how would you explain that an entire march is breaking the spirit of the Laws to start a war?"

Logan shrugs without an answer.

They sit quietly for a major before he changes the subject. "You think we should investigate the manor tonight? To get an idea of who lives there?"

She looks ahead. The manor, oddly built in the middle of the plateau, waits in stillness and, at the major, lies unlit. Whoever or whatever lives inside is asleep, and the idea of sneaking up to a mad woman's haynest or into the house of another crazy twofooter or perhaps a tenfooter who crossed the border makes her stomach uneasy. With few supplies left and no other real direction, however, she decides it's their best option. "It's our only option."

Logan smiles. He's quick to be distracted, seeking any opportunity to run off to investigate. He seems purposeless. More to it, he seems afraid of his fate with whoever the Victors are. With no other objective to claim, they continue closer to the manor.

"How are the legs holding up?"

"They feel good. Almost too good. I forget they aren't my own, but now that I'm thinking about it, I don't have any soreness. I don't feel like we've been walking all day. I guess the march of twofooters can do that . . . no rest?"

"Denizens still have to eat. And the freks need rest."

Logan nods in agreement. The manor is built of marble, stone, and timber, four stories tall including its attic. Numerous gables form the roof. They approach with caution, hiding behind a waist-high and worn fence that surrounds it.

"Now what?" Iahel asks.

He shrugs and peeks over the edge of the fence. Iahel does as well. The yard is dark and still. Logan hops over.

"Are you flam?" she whispers as loudly as she's able. As he creeps closer to one of the windows and looks inside, she scans over her shoulder at the endless plateau behind them before hopping the fence herself.

As she gets closer to Logan, she slaps him across the back of his head. "I should have left you in that cage."

"Wasn't the point of coming here to investigate—"

She hushes him, covering his mouth, and points with her other hand. Inside, a denizen walks about. Not a twofooter—an older man, who appears behind one hallway and crosses into another.

"We should go."

Agreed, they turn and find themselves surrounded by a drum of cogs. Each is gray against the moonlight. They seem eager and happy to see the two. One of them hops up onto Iahel and turns yellow.

"Shnite. Cogs."

Logan taps her shoulder and points. Iahel turns back to look inside. The denizen, now walking with a smaller child, heads back through the manor and toward the front door. Aware of the impending danger, Logan leads Iahel away from the window and back toward the fence. She sets the cog down, and it joins the dozens of others, which all follow them across the yard. To Iahel's east, she catches a glimpse of a beautiful garden. Logan hops into it first, followed by Iahel. The cogs gather at the fence. From above them, a searching beam from a neonlight hits a boulder near the manor. The denizens are outside.

"Let's get farther away. Hopefully, they'll blame any intrusion on tallingstones or something."

They run, slumping as low as they can, toward a hollow tree trunk, barely big enough for either alone. Inside, they're unable to see the goings-on at the manor. So, instead, they wait, the only view the flat plateau ahead.

A commotion breaks out in the manor behind them. The trunk muffles the sound to the point that neither of them can decipher what's said. And then, a cog appears. *Proshing freks.*

Followed by another. They playfully bounce and hop into the trunk.

"Over here," a young boy's voice calls out.

Iahel grabs for her dagger.

Logan stops her. "That was the boy."

Iahel, unsure she cares, releases her hold. They wait for a major before a moonlit shadow covers the cogs, followed by the barrel of a rifle.

Logan raises hands to head. Iahel follows. They exit the trunk slowly.

"Careful, folk." A bearded man stands before them, his gun pointed at Logan but his eyes darting between them. "What brings you all the way out here tonight?"

Iahel starts, "We were traveling past. We're low on supplies and didn't know if anyone lived here."

"I've told the last of you that there's no brass here."

"We're not looking for brass, friend. Just a place to rest and some supplies, if you have it," Logan states.

The dozens of cogs, all of them pink, run freely between their legs. The man lowers his gun. "Well, if these damn cogs like you, I guess it's not worth letting the boy see me send you two left."

Iahel grins with grateful apprehension.

Chapter Twenty
AN INEVITABLE CONCLUSION

"*M*y curam is Carson. Carson Stollamite."
The older man pours two mugs of white steamed brackleberry tea and hands them to Iahel and Logan, who at the minor are seated around a quaint wood table in a nook that overlooks the manor's back garden. With approsh, they sip the clear and soothing flora and nibble on a few warmed biscons pulled fresh from a hetsonbox. Carson's haynest, constructed with dark wood walls and lit by warm, practical lighting, reminds Iahel of her time aboard the *Gilraymond* where she first met Aerial, marking the manor and Carson's friendly demeanor in stark contrast to the threats of the looming twofooter march.

"You say you were traveling past?" asks Carson. "Whereabouts are you headed?"

Logan answers, "Orga—"

"—nowhere in particular," Iahel interrupts.

Carson doesn't respond, setting the teakettle back on the hetsontop. He walks back and sits down across from them. "And you're from the valley?" he asks Logan with an eye toward the false legs.

"Well, that's a whole story, isn't it?"

And then, against Iahel's silent judgment, Logan recounts, without lies, their encounter with the twofooters' march, how he lost his legs, Iahel's brave and audacious rescue, and he ends the tale by forewarning of the imminent assault in Carvinga.

Carson listens with quiet eyes and at one point lights a green cig. As Logan finishes, Carson, taking a long drag, lets the room fall silent. "If you'd indulge me, I have something I'd like to show you."

With little pause, he stands and exits the room. Iahel and Logan exchange an apprehensive look before following the curious old man.

The house is a gallery of oddities teeming with statues cast of countless materials; multisized paintings stacked on top of each other unhung; piles of papers, a notesbook, and old tomes; globes of the hundred and thirty-three states; and maps written in the ancient languages. He continues through the lower floor to an office kept in similar disarray, then steps across the room to a glass trophy case that stands behind a large wooden desk.

"Here is where we kept a bit of brass. A sliver in size, at the most. My great-grandfather discovered it on this property almost a hundred years ago. Though it bore no marks or interesting properties other than being in an unusual place, he kept it, likely since he was a bit of a luckers. As you might guess, my family is in the collections business. With our specialty in artifacts and treasures of the old Land. Some of these things we keep around for sentimental reasons. And most of it, there's no telling why we keep it or what it does." He grins softly. "That brass sliver was no different. Sitting there. In that case. For decades without a thought. Pieces like that fade, forgotten around here. But then, three and half months ago, it was snipped."

"Stolen?" Iahel asks. Sanet had said he gave it to her . . .

"It's the only position I can determine. To tell the truth, I didn't notice it was gone until a group of men, wearing red capes, approached the house and demanded I turn it over. I thought they were tipst at first, but they pulled guns. A whole messy affair. So I led one of them, their leader I assume, here. And that's when I realized it was missing."

"Did their leader have a burned face?" Logan asks.

Carson's eyes widen. "Yes. He did. He went by the curam Franz, if I remember. After I indicated that the brass wasn't here, they tore the place apart. Then they sent one of them north, while the others, including Franz, headed south, where I overheard they had other business to attend to."

"We had a run-in with Franz over a month ago," Logan recalls.

"My appizement," Carson doubles, then continues with an air of exhilaration in his voice, "In any sorts, once they left, their interest in the brass, and the fact that it was suddenly missing, naturally ignited a bit of curiosity."

He walks with a lightened step across the room to an unadorned cabinet. *The thrill of a mystery to a bored old man.* He pulls from the cabinet a massive tome, which he promptly plops on the desk, tossing a thin whiff of dust into the air. He opens it and scans for a specific passage. "Here."

Logan and Iahel walk around the desk to view the page from a better angle. Where his finger points, there's an illustration of a large sphere. It's drawn next to a denizen slightly smaller in size.

He says, "I believe that that sliver of brass is a fragmented bit of a larger orb."

"An orb? For what?" Iahel asks.

"Ah, a mystery this all is. I asked the same question. So I started to research the purpose of orbs, and the only thing I came across," Carson spins on his heel and pulls from the same cabinet a smaller leather-bound book, which he hands to Iahel, "was this."

She reads the title aloud, *"The Unknown History of Ranparts."*

"The only folk I can find who have anything to do with orbs are ranparts. Usually, they commission a smith to craft them, or, if they already have one, they'll pass it down to their acolyte. In any sorts, ranparts use them for many reasons, such as performing ceremonies and all number of various tricks, but what is odd is that a typical ranpart's orb is usually the size of a fist." Carson makes said fist to demonstrate. "Not the size larger than you or me, as this illustration suggests."

"Are you proposing it's a ranpart trying to make an orb like that?" Logan asks.

"That's my theory. This sliver we had, I've looked it over many times throughout the years. Though it was small, it had a single smooth edge, something that didn't seem in narrows with those of a smaller sphere. Its curve was too wide, if that makes sense? I also believe that it's for a ranpart because there's not much use for brass besides in an orb. Brass is one of the many lost metals created long ago."

Logan looks to Iahel, who nods in agreement before speaking. "We were traveling with someone who was looking for pieces of brass. It's clear now that she's the one who came here before the crimson men did. She even told us about this place. Though she said you had given the brass to her." Logan eyes Iahel knowingly, who shrugs him off. "Anyway, while we were traveling, we found a second fragment hidden in this stonetin within the Tunnels."

Logan doubles, "She told us a ranpart had been looking for them, so your theory holds up. He was offering a heavy coin for their recovery."

"Which is why I think the crimson men are after it."

At the revelation, Carson smiles broadly, as if his ideas had gone too long unsubstantiated and had finally found corroboration.

"Luckers sent. Though she should have told me. She didn't have to snip it. I guess that's beyond the tale now. The real question is, for what purpose?" Carson, sitting down at his desk, strokes his beard.

They each remain quiet in thought before Logan speaks up. "This may sound flam, but this friend of ours, the woman who stole your piece, believed that reuniting the brass would end a war."

"A war?" Carson questions.

Iahel wonders aloud, "Perhaps the march happening now, between Misipit and Carvinga?"

"The crimson men did mention something about a war. They repeated this phrase, 'Seven from the advent of the Roar.'"

"Roar? That's a king, right?" Iahel questions.

"Not exactly." Carson starts. "A Roar is one of the many positions within a royal family. The Roar is the voice, the one who delivers proclamations and speeches. They're usually the leader and the one who inspires the masses. But it's not the only position. There's the Lion, who's the body of the family, the spirit. There's the Mane, who serves as the face of the royal family, usually the most amiable, acts as a diplomat of sorts. They're usually behind the tall curtains. The Tail, who's the strategist, the planner. And last is the Paw, who is the might of the march. While the Roar leads, the Paw is the strength to crush and conquer its enemy. But a royal family hasn't ruled in over . . . three hundred years? The terms are antiquated, if anything."

Logan attempts to work things out aloud. "Seven from the Roar . . . perhaps that's seven weeks? Which is almost how long it's been since they claim the advent chanced."

Iahel remembers Bernard and Logan talking about that day. The day the crimson men burned down Bernard's house, sending his partner left.

"How does a seven-week-old baby give speeches that inspire a war?" she asks, unimpressed.

Carson sits down. "Obviously they don't. There wouldn't be babies created outside of the Paseco."

"Paseco . . . I've heard that curam before, but never really understood it," Iahel states.

"Well, when the Laws were written, the remaining folk of the Last War turned over their ability to procreate. Or at least that's how the story goes. They made a bargain with something known as the Paseco, which would help control the population. As no one trusted folk would follow such an . . . unnatural way of things. What or where this Paseco is has long been lost over the millennia. Today, going to a nearby children's square to adopt a child or two is as commonplace as the sunset. Folk approsh not needing the worry of unwanted children, and prefer being able to have them when and where they choose. I'm sure it was controversial at the time, but with a war that nearly destroyed everyone in their recent memory, many accepted the Law as a necessary compromise. After two and half millennia, not many people even think about the Paseco. Especially younger generations. It's just the way of things."

"I've only heard the curam in passing while I was in Organsia. Don't the Victors have a connection with it?" Logan asks.

Carson shrugs, losing interest in the topic. "No one really knows. A secret lost in time. Nothing we can do about it."

Iahel contemplates the story. "You're right in that I never really thought about where we came from. So, if that's all true, then it *would* make sense denizens are celebrating a birth. A baby that's not created from this . . . Paseco."

"Maybe. In truth, none of this doubles up. Brass orbs. Pasecos. Wars. But if research and history tell us anything, it's that a ranpart isn't known for logic or folksy ways. A fascinating enigmit for sure." Carson leans back in his chair, lost in thought. After a major, he stands. "Well, it's well past my sleeping hours. Why don't I show you a room? You're welcome to stay here as long as you like, though I must warn, I make a shameful mornmeal."

"Approsh," Logan responds, standing himself.

Iahel's thoughts about all the various elements circle her mind, lost in the thrill and terror of what it all might mean.

Carson walks them across the manor to a small guest room on the second floor. After showing them a few of the amenities, he tips them good morrow and slips off to his master upstairs.

Logan turns down the sheets. "Question now is . . . do I take these legs off?"

"I don't think so," Iahel states, remembering how awful it was to see him put them on.

"Doubled. I'm not sure I could handle getting them back on."

With that, Logan heads into the relief room to shower. Iahel lies back, blanket pulled tight, allowing the comfort of the bed to fade the past few days into an odd and dire kiptale.

❖❖❖

A small girl stands in the doorway when Iahel yawns and opens her eyes. The room is bursting with sunlight. Iahel sits up, covering herself. "Morn."

The little girl waves meekly. After a minor, a handsome woman with short gray-and-blonde hair appears and grabs the girl in surprise, another boy in tow behind them. The girl laughs at the snatch and tickle. Once she holds the girl correctly, the woman turns to Iahel. "We're serving mornmeal if you're hungry."

"Approsh." Iahel nods.

The woman smiles and leaves, the children following. Iahel stands, dresses, and shakes Logan awake. He's sweating and in a fitful kiptale. "Logan. Logan."

He grunts and startles himself awake. "No." He looks at Iahel and shakes his head. "Apory. Malicious thoughts."

"They're serving. We should be polite."

Logan nods.

After he's dressed, they make their way to the dining area. The aromas of eggs over and under, roasted garons, and fried jellies fill the air.

"It smells incredible."

Logan and Iahel sit down. The woman sits next to the boy who was up on the previous night. The little girl sits close to Iahel, smiling at her while chewing her fingers. Carson sets the last of the mornmeal on the table.

"Enjoyments."

They eat until they're full, discussing all varieties of things: the tormisands in Radiba; how the plateau sometimes receives small remnants of them; the peculiarity of how short the last one lasted, under a week.

"Not even sure it could be called a tormisand," Logan says.

When Iahel attempts to bring up the march, she's abruptly quieted by Carson, who gestures toward his children.

Mareen, the woman, switches subjects. "If you're not in a hurry, we could use some help in the gardens today."

Logan agrees without question, and Iahel follows. "Of course."

After cleaning up, the children begin to run around outside, chasing the horde of cogs, which scurry about for a bit and then turn to pursue the children. Iahel and Logan are tasked with picking weeds as Mareen prunes various veggies and fruin plants. The morn passes with gentle ease, Iahel feeling wholly at home. She looks over at Logan, whose muscle and sweat look handsome on him. *My little Radiba boy.*

It's then that the little girl comes up to Mareen and whispers in her ear. The woman's face twists. "Carson."

He looks up, rubbing dirt from his hands. "Yes?"

She shakes her head. "You two should come as well."

Iahel's heart skips. *The march.* They make their way through the house to the front yard where the little girl points out into the distance. Iahel scans the crest and catches a large black carriage over a mile away. It looks to be parked, still and motionless. "What is that?" she asks.

"The Victors," Logan states, rubbing his hands on his jeans.

Mareen turns to Logan. "Victors? Are you in debt?"

Logan steps backward, fear sweeping across his face.

"How did they find him?" Of Logan, Iahel asks, "How did they find you?"

Logan wipes his brow, shaking his head in absolute disbelief.

Carson continues to watch them. "What are they doing way out there?"

Stepping forward, Logan answers, "They're letting me come quietly." His face is riddled with angst.

"Well, you can't go," Iahel states plainly. "Not now."

"They found me. I don't know how, but they know where I am."

Iahel turns to Carson, who quickly defends himself. "It wasn't us. We have nothing to do with them. I've never been to Organsia."

Iahel returns her gaze to the black carriage.

Waiting. Silent. Still. Ominous.

"This can't be happening. They can't just take you."

"Why are you in debt to them?" Carson asks.

"I bargained for an answer about my sent father. I didn't know how much they'd want for it."

Iahel is upset. "You little cog. Why didn't you stay with Sanet? She has all that coin coming. We could have used it to help you."

Logan looks her in the eye. "I didn't want to put her in danger. Or Bernard. Or you. Can't you see how they are? I've been here no more than a night, and they're here. Threatening us. Threatening near strangers." He gestures to the family, then steps into the yard.

"Logan, wait. Stop," Iahel yells. "Stop. There has to be another way!"

Logan, having now stepped past the fence, turns back. "Apory, Iahel. They'll never stop, and I can't stop them. This is a debt that doesn't go away. There's not another way."

Mareen steps in. "I won't let them any closer to my family. You both can solve this how you want, but we can't have them any closer."

"Fight, you shnite beast," Iahel calls out. Words that fail to matter as Logan turns to the Victors. Iahel steps into the yard and catches up to him. "You can't leave me. You can't leave me too."

He drops his head. "Iahel, this was always the way. I made my choice."

"But did you get your answer? About your father?"

Logan shakes his head. "I realized I didn't want an answer. And they asked for more."

"Why? Why do you have to suffer if you got nothing for it? It's unfair."

"It's their bargain. It's their way."

"You're a cog. You're all cogs. Useless, unreliable bastards!" She starts to run toward the Victors.

"Iahel, stop!"

She doesn't. The Victors are under a mile away. Her adrenaline carries her closer and closer. She pulls out her dagger as the black carriage draws imminent, its size rising impossibly high, towering ten measures in the air. Closer. A denizen emerges from the carriage wearing an expressionless black mask with painted white eyes and a clownish grin. He holds a rifle. Behind her, Logan screams at her to stop. She begins to slow.

The Victor raises the rifle in her direction. She stops and steps backward in fright. The Victor fires. Iahel feels the shot strike her shoulder and spins to the ground. She blacks out.

❖ ❖ ❖

Light pours into the room. Iahel wakes in the guest bed. *Logan.* She attempts to sit up, but her shoulder prevents her. She reaches over and feels a thick bandage. Her eyes slip closed, her face an expressionless mask. The rifle. Logan's scream.

She slips into darkness.

When she opens her eyes again, it's night out. The sky outside floats in bursts of color. Red, then yellow, then white, then purple. It darkens and then brightens again. Like tiny colorful explosions.

She slips into darkness.

Opening her eyes again, she finds Carson sitting beside the bed. "Morn, Iahel. How are you feeling?"

She attempts to speak but decides against it. She doesn't feel like facing the Land.

She slips into darkness.

Dusk light filters into the room where Mareen cleans around her, dusting and picking up various clothing. *Where is Logan?* Iahel thinks she says this aloud. Mareen doesn't answer.

She slips into darkness.

"Time to start walking, young lady." She's shaken by Carson, who has her by the shoulder. "Come on. Up and up." Iahel squints as the light presses on her skull. Her head feels crushed. Every joint and pressure point aches. "Come on." By the hand, she's led from the bed. There's a deep wound in her shoulder. Feels like a knife, not a bullet. She grabs for it but finds the bandage. "You're healing nicely. You'll be good in a day or so."

She looks to Carson. "Logan?"

"Apory, Iahel. The Victors have him." This stops her. "There was nothing you could have done. What was done was done."

As quiet as a snip, she whispers, "But it's unfair."

"It seems that way, but he did not have to go into a bargain with them. He should have known better."

"It was a mistake. Logan was grief-stricken. They took advantage of him."

"That may be so, but many people suffer from grief. Not everyone makes a bargain they can't afford."

Carson's lack of empathy frustrates her. His lack of understanding. Logan isn't a bad person. In some ways, he's too good. It hurts her to see someone without a chance. Without a choice. *I made my choice.*

They walk around the house a bit, the little girl dancing playfully in front of them. When they step out into the front yard, Iahel is accosted by the horde of pink cogs.

"Back now." Carson shoos them away.

"It's wisnok." Iahel starts to walk on her own. Stretching her arm and legs. She rolls her east shoulder with strain and effort and winces. "Perhaps not everything."

Carson smiles. "You should feel much better on the morrow. I, well, now that you're awake, I'd like to ask something of you."

She turns back, rolling her neck. "What is it?"

"This woman. The one working for the ranpart. Do you know where she is now?"

Iahel pauses. After the Victors, her trust in Carson, family or not, is shallow. "Why?"

"I ask only because things are . . . escalating. The tenfooters are raising their own march."

"So this whole thing about the Roar is happening? A war is coming?"

"I don't know if you were awake, but there were celebration lights a few days ago. The whole sky lit up in color."

"Days ago? How long have I been asleep?"

"You were in and out for about a week." *A week?* "Whenever a member of the royal family crossed a state border, it was tradition to send off sky colors. My assumption is the Roar, or someone folk believes is the Roar, has crossed the border into Misipit. And if he's marching with any sort of pace, he could be at the Carvinga border within the month."

"And you believe the brass orb could end it, end the war?"

"While you've been asleep, I've been communicating with a friend of mine. He believes that the orb is something more than that. He believes that it could be used to end the Land. He believes this whole affair is only a proxy war and the real purpose is to regain control of that orb and what it creates."

"The ranpart wants to end the Land?"

"Or the crimson men do. Perhaps the ranpart knows this and is trying to prevent them from reuniting the brass. In either case, whoever has the orb has the power," Carson states.

"Then how does this Roar fit in? What does it have to do with a proxy war?"

"In truth, I think the Roar is merely a symbol. A false light. Propaganda to convince the twofooters to go to war."

"Why would someone want to end the Land?"

"They don't like the system. The states. The thousands of priced folk. They don't like entities like the Victors. Or the Laws. There're any number of reasons why the Land isn't working. Why someone might want to cleanse the whole thing. There's a hundred and thirty-three states out there. They can't all be as wonderful as Radiba."

"So, what can I do?" Iahel asks. *I'm just a girl from the Tunnels. A stowaway.*

"My friend in Carvinga is willing to meet you. I'm not as well versed in the brass. And you said you found another piece in a stonetin, right? He wants to show you something. About the dangers the brass pieces hold. He wants you to warn your friend. Before everyone is sent left."

"Wait. He's in Carvinga?" Iahel says, skeptical.

Without pause or care, Carson answers, "Yes, he's a tenfooter."

"A tenfooter?" Iahel reacts: scared, shocked, nervous.

"Yes. But he's not like the children's tales. He lives on the outskirts, like my family and me. As I am not with the twos, he's not with the tens."

"This sounds mad."

"I'm sure. But if your friend has those pieces, if she's trying to reunite the orb, that may be the wrong course. If this orb is for the good of the Land or to end a war, why was it broken into all those pieces to begin with?"

Iahel stands quietly. The cogs simpering around her oblivious. She turns to the calm plateau. In the farthest distance looms a cloudy storm.

"That's the march of twofooters out there," Carson states.

The peace of the manor runs warmly against the thought of war. The last conflict between states had almost exterminated everyone.

"So you want me to meet your friend?"

"He's more studied in things like this orb than I am. Let me show you." He leads her back inside and to his office. She stands in wait as he digs through stacks of paper on his desk. "I haven't been there myself in some time. Not since we brought home Willow. Here it is."

Iahel steps over.

Carson grabs a stick and begins to mark the map. "If you cross here, it should be safe. There's a trench that runs along the border, south of where the march is headed. His house is about three miles east of there."

"And how will he know it's me?"

"I told him about you, but you should give him this." And from the desk, he pulls out a small round imprinted metal with the letters *CS* on one side and on the other *SC*.

"SC?"

"His curam is Crench. You shouldn't worry. We've been talking back and forth." He points to a small tapping device with a wire that falls to the floor.

"You have a tapper?" Iahel says.

"Not many do, but yes. We're collectors." He smiles.

Distracted by the idea of being able to talk to people across state lines, she returns to the idea of going into Carvinga. "This is mad. Why can't he just tell you to tell me?"

"He says he has to show you. That you won't understand, you won't believe him, without seeing it." Seeing her hesitate, Carson continues, "I've made the trip many times. If you stay on course and don't wander, don't get lost, you should be fine."

Iahel laughs.

He smiles back and then becomes serious. "A war is coming. There's not much time, and if these crimson folk are trying to unite that orb, they're sure to seek out your friends. They're in danger."

The sentiment hits her. She likes Sanet. She is friendly, even in her cold demeanor. And Bernard is a nice older man, but they aren't friends. She didn't let them become friends. If her history was any indication, getting close to them would only get them sent. *Do you want to send them left or do you want to leave them?* That's the Iahel life.

"We can refresh the bandage and get you any supplies you'll need before you leave."

On the road, again. It might have been nice to live here. To be a family. As foreign as the idea is to her, the small taste of a haynest life is like a hit of violet. Intoxicating. Addicting. And yet, every time she feels comfortable, it's taken away from her.

"Why do you care so much, Carson?"

"Because I want a Land to pass along to my children. Maybe I'm overreacting, but it was the apathy of generations past that allowed the Land to nearly eradicate them before."

She doesn't counter.

Iahel sits down with the family over duskmeal as a cog curls up on her lap and buzzes. The hearty meal goes down noiselessly, with her imposing duty lying heavily over the evening.

"You appear to be great with freks, Iahel," Mareen points out.

If only that were true of denizens. That night, Iahel tosses and turns. Thoughts of Logan. Of Sanet. Of the Victor's mask. Of going into Carvinga. Of Jules. *Who am I to any of them?*

The next morn, with rucksack packed and ready, she hugs the family. Willow, the little girl, gives her the biggest squeeze. "I liked having a sister."

Iahel smiles and presses the little girl's nose. "You're sweet. Take this." She slips a secret something into the little girls hand. They grin in knowing.

She stands, nods to Carson and Mareen, and sets off.

A thin trail leads her from the rear of the manor down a small hill and eventually back down into the valley fogs. Before descending once more through the switchbacks, she looks across the wide crevasse as a quiet breeze brushes the tall grasslands of Carvinga. In some ways, she understands their private nature. She understands keeping the Land, and all it carries, away. She looks to her east and watches the impending battle storms marching in the same direction.

Is this my choice?

Chapter Twenty-One
INTO CARVINGA

*R*eturning to the Misipit Valley fog amid the looming threat of twofooters on patrol, even for a short while, makes Iahel's uneasiness resume. Not to mention her heightened awareness of war and bloodlust, which makes this limited visibility even more terrifying. As the hours pass, with nothing to pursue or pay attention to, her mind wanders.

At first, it's full of thoughts of Logan. What state is he in? Is he in pain? Is he going to survive? What will they do to him? She grows angry at how flam he was to give up so easily. *Just what you do, Iahel.* The weakness of Logan leads to thoughts of the strong will and coldness of Sanet. How secretive she is amid her calmness and evenness. Her outward behavior reminds Iahel of Jules, who floated with the Land wherever it took her. She was a believer in the Flow. Which meant Jules didn't have secrets—*or, in truth, live long enough to earn them.*

The trail eventually leads back upward. Iahel looks to the map given to her by Carson and finds markings in the rock that should lead her to the tenfooter curamed Crench. A sign on the path leading upward warns denizens of entering Carvinga and in no uncertain terms that death will be immediate and without judgment upon stepping across the border. It also offers directions to a Tunnels entrance fifty miles south. *Maybe I could just turn away, head back to Earls.* But, instead, she buries the thought when Willow, Carson's small and sweet daughter, flashes through her mind. She can't let her own fear send an innocent girl. It's cruel. And selfish. With a swallow, Iahel ignores the warning sign and ascends upward, out of the canyon fog once more.

Arduous. Step after step. This trail is less traveled, most of it comprising large rocks hanging precariously over grander ones. Every hundred strides or so, the stones below her feet shift and slide, causing her to catch hold of an outstretched rock or suffer a fall.

The trail ends above the fog and with the top of the canyon wall nearly ten feet above her. She checks her map but is unable to decipher if she's still on the correct path, though she attempts to recall the switchbacks and forks leading her here.

Looking up, she can hear an implacable wind howling across the prairie. Below, a sheer drop through dense fog and jagged rocks waits. With a deep breath, she grabs on to the nearest outcropped rock, steps onto a lower one, and hoists herself upward. Another rock hangs barely in range. She stretches, her fingers nearly pulling from their sockets, and grasps. She tries to look down, but her body is so carefully, fearfully pressed against the wall, she's unable to see. So, without looking, she begins to move her free foot around slowly, attempting to find the next foothold. Her toe hits a rock. She presses on it with her foot, testing the weight. It holds. She steps up.

Halfway.

Adjusting her weight, she looks for the next handhold. This one is only a foot below the top, but about two inches from her actual reach. She'll have to jump. *What if the rock can't hold my weight?* Thinking makes it worse. She jumps. Her fingers grasp the rock and she's successful. With every grunt in her body, she pulls herself into position to grab the top of the canyon. The grass at the top is thick and hearty, and she takes hold of a large handful and pulls herself up. Her body rolls across the top, landing on her back. Iahel begins to laugh.

Now I know why Carson didn't want to go.

She recovers a major longer before rolling to her knees and then standing. The air here is gray with a storm gathering in the distance. The wind smacks across her face, thrashing little sandstones against it. Behind her, the boulder-strewn plateau looks quaint across the deep canyon valley.

She's entered Carvinga.

Looking to her east, she attempts a glimpse of the twofooter's march, but the gray and looming storm only darkens the Land. Without much else to go on, she begins her trek into the grasses, the blades of which grow thicker and taller the farther she travels in. Before long, the grass is over her head. Carson told her to use the shadow after full sun to keep in an easterly direction, so she raises her hand until her palm is fully lit and catches where the shadow falls and then follows in that direction. Crench's house is only a three-mile trek from the border, which should take her no more than an hour.

Every few hundred steps, she raises her hand again to check her direction, and she notices at some points that she's walking entirely north. Frustrated, she adjusts to an eastern trajectory. The dark-green grass in front of her needs to be continuously brushed aside, but after the strenuous climb up the canyon, her arms are weak and tired. Ready for rest, she repeats to herself that it's only an hour. *It's only an hour.*

When the hour passes, the grass around her remains as thick and as monotonous as it was when she first began. She raises her hand and notices she's once again moving north. *Shnite.* There are no landmarks or ways to get above the grass. She begins to feel a bit claustrophobic, the grass becoming a source of paranoia. The fear of running into a tenfooter grows with each passing major.

She raises her hand, finds her direction, and starts to trek again.

Another hour passes. Panic starts to set in. When she raises her hand, she's no longer able to discern any shadow. The sun is setting. The thought of being in the grasses overnight brings back a heavy breathing, each breath profound and uncontrollable. She raises her hand again. Darker again and no telling in which direction she's headed. *Do I turn around?* She looks behind her and finds it looks the same as ahead. The same as the east. The same as the west.

Without another minor's thought, she runs. Grasses thwack her in the face as she tries to brush them aside. All she wants now is to find something. Anything but the tall green grass. She continues to run, and her mind believes she's turned north again, so she corrects herself. Turning east. *Did I overcorrect?* There is no way she's going to make it to Carson's friend's house by the full moon. And at this point, she just wants out of the grass. She needs to escape the torture of the nothingness.

There is no end. The grasses grow darker and darker. The moon above her, which had been so bright the previous night, is on this night blanketed with storm clouds. She continues to run in the dark, her hands outstretched, sure she's going to run into some monstrous frek or a tenfooter. *Carson sent me left. Carson is the one who told the Victors where Logan was. I'll send that man.*

She stops to catch her breath and take a swig from her water jug, then begins again. This time walking. Resigned. She can't rest. She doesn't want to be caught sleeping here.

And then—a trunk.

She feels around and finds it's a small tree with three separate trunks interwoven together. "Approsh Dustian," she says aloud, regretting it immediately. She climbs, branch to branch. Her arms are sore from the rock climbing hours before, from brushing the grass away.

And then, for the first time in forever, she's above the grass. In every direction, in the soft translucent moonlight flows an endless sea of grass. There are no signs of houses or tenfooters or life of any sort. Off in the farthest stretch of her sight are little fires and explosions, thin white lines zooming across the night sky. And delayed thunderous, diluted booms.

The war's started.

She watches the fire show in the distance. Within it, she discerns no denizens. No telling who is a twofooter and who a ten. Only a blur of explosions and muffled blasts. An impressive, if not terrifying, sight. Iahel clasps her hands over her mouth as she realizes what she's witnessing. The first war in thousands of years. Right there. Denizens, bodies, friends, slaughtering each other. *For what purpose?* The stories her caretakers told of the Last War, how everyone was nearly sent, how war was the end of everything—on hearing those, she felt something greater than fear. Watching now, the belief the friends and denizens of old must have had that war would bring good is completely and entirely lost on her.

She begins to cry and hold herself. The storm chills the air. For all her life, she has been alone. She's chosen to be alone. She's run and disconnected; but in this minor, seeing the destruction of denizen against denizen, she wants someone to embrace.

Watching the battle throughout the night, she balances between branches, keeping her safe but not stable enough to close her eyes or rest, though any thought of sleep would be wasted while the battle rages throughout the night and into the first sun. In the fight, there are sometimes long stretches where nothing chances, and then another explosion catches her eye. The front of the engagement appears to move deeper beyond the Carvinga border. The twofooters are winning.

When the sun finally peeks over the crest, Iahel attempts to observe anything more in the brighter light and continues scanning the grassland as it reveals the surrounding area. There, behind her and maybe a mile to the south is a house. She studies the crest for any other homes and finds nothing else nearby. *That must be Crench's.*

With everything in her power, she focuses on that point. She looks at the shadow of her hand, knowing it will only give her a mild, if not flawed, indication of the right direction.

She climbs down and begins her trek toward the house, walking slowly and purposefully. This time, she keeps her palm in front of her. Her eyes and mind on nothing else. It takes about a half hour before the grasses begin to thin, and she glimpses the house through the foliage's cracks. She lowers her aching arm and hurries forward.

The grasses suddenly end and she stops. A denizen walks around the house, and Iahel finds that the tenfooter title is no grand invention. He stands twice her height, covered in fur from head to toe, wearing a ragged assembly of clothing. His facial features are barely visible within his mangled hair. He walks with a hunched back. The house itself accommodates the tenfooter's high stature, with doors and windows double the height of any she's ever seen. The roof is thatched with mud and multiple layers of grass. The sight is so outrageous, at first Iahel thinks she should instead run. Why is she meddling in the affairs of these dangerous denizens?

Before she's able to have another thought, another step, another decision, the tenfooter detects her. "Who's there?" His voice rumbles and vibrates with fury. He stomps toward her.

Iahel—no choice—steps out in the open, hands on head.

"Please, apory. I come in peace. I am a friend of Carson's."

The tenfooter stops. "How are you a friend of Carson's?"

Remembering, Iahel fumbles to retrieve the metal piece she was given and holds it out. The tenfooter reaches out his arm, easily the length of her entire body, and grabs the coin with his massive, fearsome hand. He turns the coin over in an examination and then swallows it.

Iahel gulps and waits.

"Are you the girl, Iahel?"

She nods, unable to look the tenfooter in the eye. She watches as his shadow, looming over her, stands and steps away.

"Come inside then."

Taking her first breath, she follows a few paces behind. He steps inside the haynest, leaving the towering door open behind him.

Inside is a mess of sticks and mud and fecal matter. The miasma inside the house is thick with a putrid whiff of urine and rotting foods. Iahel covers her mouth and swallows her gag reflex, unsure how the tenfooter would react to her retching in his living room. He turns and sits on a pile that crunches beneath him.

"Carson tells me you know where the other pieces of brass are?"

"I know where two are, yes."

"Did you bring them here?"

"No. A friend has them. In Yikshir."

"Yikshir? That's not far enough."

Iahel doesn't answer. The tenfooter picks up a mess of bones and begins to suck on them. They look to be her size.

"Do you know what the brass is for, Iahel?"

She shakes her head.

"The brass pieces form an ardroke's eye. If that brass is reunited and returned to Carvin's Grave, it will only mean the utter destruction of all us Carvingians. And then you Yikshirs. Of all the state's denizens. Even the passive little Radibians won't be safe." He waits. "You seem afraid of me. Imagine a frek one hundred times larger. Looming over the state with a strength to kill hundreds with a stroke of its arm. A stomp of its feet. Would you be afraid of that?" The tenfooter leans forward. His teeth and eyes lurk through thick, matted fur. They're black and yellow each. His breath reeks of death.

"Yes," Iahel says meekly.

He leans back. "I would be afraid of that. My fellow Carvingians think it's something to worship. Why they've spent generations sending back the weak, the short, the denizens like you. They're attempting to be as broad and vigorous as the ardrokes. It's a mad waste of time."

Drawing from Sanet's cold strength, she risks asking, "Why did you want to see me?"

"You need to warn them. Warn your friends. But you must be shown first. You must see it. To know what real dangers await this Land if the twofooters get their way." At this, he stands again. Though she knows how tall he is, the sight is still impossible to understand. Iahel steps backward, crunching mud and shnite beneath her feet.

He exits through the front again, Iahel gladly following. The air outside, the wind, and the chill are a welcome reprieve from the stifling odor of the tenfooter's haynest.

"My curam is Scover Crench. And I give you permission to climb onto my back so we may travel faster." He kneels on one knee. Iahel, apprehensive, steps closer, cautious but attempting to be brave.

Scover snaps his teeth at her, then laughs. "If I were going to bite you, girl, I would have done so when we first met."

She gulps and grabs on to him. His fur is wet and dirty. It has the lingering smell of his haynest. She holds his neck as he stands and begins to trudge through the grasslands.

"If we're caught, I can't cross that others won't want to eat you. They find young girls like you to be most delicious."

Scover continues along. His steps are broad and hurried. The wind at her face beats against her as she looks out across the grasslands. Within a few minors, they're passing the tree she rested in the night before. The battle far in the distance has faded some, even farther into the Carvinga state.

"The twofooters think they have the upper hand, but they don't know what's in for them once they've fully crossed those handmade bridges of theirs." Scover laughs at this. "That pathetic march is embarrassing. The leaders directed some of our weaklings to fight the first surge of them. Get them feeling cocky and brave. Unseat them from the safety of their valley fog."

The battle takes on a new shape. All those ingreves and getwishes. All the hatred and pride the twofooters are fighting for. *Useless.* Iahel hates the tenfooters. She hates Scover, even if he means to do the right thing.

They journey for a time until they come to an enormous stonetin, ten times larger and more ornate than the one buried deep in the tunnels below. From it, dozens of towers spiral to the sky. Scover stops and kneels. Iahel climb down but remains standing on his knee to keep a closer view to the top of the grass.

"There is one of our stonetins. Where we keep the remains of ardrokes. Do you see its shape?"

She looks at it more closely. It is symmetrical, with four main towers—two larger ones in the back corners, two shorter ones in the front corners—then many more between them and around.

"It looks a little like a throne?" she suggests.

"Exactly, girl. And do you know what a chair that size would be for?"

She looks back to the mammoth stonetin, imagining it to be a prodigious throne. A frek that could sit upon it would easily be the size of a mountain. The thought sends grenspimples down her spine. "Dustian."

"You'll need more than a god to save you if that brass finds its way to one of these."

She nods. "*One* of these? There are more?"

Scover laughs. "You think there's only one ardroke bell toll?"

Unsure of what he means by "bell toll," she still understands the dangers everyone is about to face. "Can you take me to the Yikshir border, to ensure I make it out of here?"

"I may. But it might be easier to just use my tapper. Do you know if your friends have one?"

She shakes her head, unsure.

"Scover. What are you doing here?" a voice booms to their east.

Iahel turns to see a group of tenfooters walking toward them, then quickly drops into the grass, out of sight.

"Run, girl. Or you'll never see another day."

On instinct, Iahel aches to run, but her feet don't move.

"Run, girl. Don't be mad."

And then, to her surprise, Iahel responds, "I'm... I'm staying."

Part Four

ETHAN

Chapter Twenty-Two
THE WOMAN WITHOUT A PAST

*M*ercet always falls asleep after Ethan reads the fourth page, likely because the first page takes more than a half hour to finish. Mercet needs time to settle into sleep. His process is to first use the relief room. Then to recite grats moon, a second time, to his mother. Nor can he forget to check for decomps or tenfooters in the closet. Eventually, the time comes when Ethan can begin reading. On this particular night, the cartoon details yet another seafaring venture of Dread Copla, the dashing and courageous captain, but before Ethan can turn to the fifth page, Mercet is fast asleep.

At the sight, Ethan pulls Mercet's sheets up, kisses him on his forehead, and leaves the room, keeping on a small neonlight that fills the room with a soft orange glow. This night's ritual, like countless others, is the same. Ethan even knows which spots to avoid on the floorboards that will squeak and wake Mercet. For the past few months, Ethan has been laboring on a regular and unchanging schedule, coming home in time for the same lyn-and-garon casserole, a duskmeal that has become so commonplace that he is reduced to seasoning it with varying amounts of hass and pestler. Sometimes a pinge of one or a gob of the other.

Returning to his own sleeping room, Ethan finds Undess already asleep herself. He walks up and removes the pair of clears she uses to read, pulling the novit from her soft and sleeping grip. This novit is entitled "You Had Better Not." *Another flam romance.*

The idea of her reading some salacious affair, with gliding bodies and unrealistic themes of single souls, digs irksomely into Ethan's skin. It has been a long while since the two of them have slipped together. Over the past years, she has let herself go and blamed it solely on their older son being sent left. But it isn't the appearance alone that keeps them from being together, though they do frequently grit on the subject. Ethan often suggested that she exercise and eat better, find new recipes perhaps to make for duskmeal or let him cook something for once. He liked to cook. But she declined. He insisted that constant, unchecked wallowing only sets an unbinding of friendship and of their single soul. She counters with accusations that he has a callous attitude toward their son's sudden sending and how much it unsettles her. She likes to double that Ethan is no fresh lyn himself. And their lack of conjugal intimacy isn't due to any of these rotating points, but specifically one figure: Cadwellion.

Ethan takes his nightly shower, relieving some pent-up hormones with the rough splash of the shower head. *She's reduced me to a horny adolescent.* He dries himself and creeps into their bed, kissing Undess quietly before turning over, sleeping with his back to her. He drifts a bit, forcing himself into a sleepless kiptale, before—

A knock.

He sits up, looking over at Undess in her peaceful sleep. Unstirred. He leaves the master, tossing on a robe, and steps softly down the hall to the front door. Their pet cog, Captain Reset, comes running underfoot. At the minor, the frek is a cautious-colored green.

Opening the door, he finds a female guard before him. Emotionless. The guard waits, dressed in dull-orange robes and a short cape. She is handsome, and if he remembers correctly, her curam is Amil.

"What are you doing here?" Ethan starts, looking over his shoulder.

"Cadwellion requires your assistance," the woman states plainly.

Ethan pulls his robe closer as a thin, crisp air presses into the house. He holds his tongue, not wanting to cause a scene in front of either Undess or Cadwellion's guards. "Give me a major to change then."

The woman nods and steps back as Ethan closes the door. He paces toward his master when Mercet steps through the hall, yawning and rubbing his eyes. Captain Reset bounces joyfully at Mercet, knocking over the two-year-old.

"Go away," Mercet whines as the cog hops backward. Ethan walks over and picks Mercet up in his arms and carries him back to his room. "Who's that, Daddy?"

"Cadwellion. You should go back to sleep."

"Are you leaving?" Mercet asks in stumbling words.

"Just for a minor." He sets Mercet back in his bed and attempts to pull the sheets over and tuck him in.

"I'm not tired."

"You are tired. You were yawning and rubbing your eyes."

"No, I wasn't."

Ethan huffs. "Hmm. I think we need to invite the tucking freks to help you."

"No!" Mercet laughs, swinging his arms wildly.

"I think the tucking freks are coming."

"No, Daddy, no!"

As Mercet protests, Ethan lifts his hands, holding them straight and flat. He begins to make a chugging sound as he flutters them toward Mercet. Mercet shakes and wiggles but is easily overcome by Ethan pressing and stuffing the sheets around the child, bundling him in tight and barely able to move.

"Apory, Mercet. You're all stuck."

Mercet giggles and squirms but is held firm by Ethan's hands tucked under him.

Ethan asks, "How do we get rid of tucking freks?"

Mercet immediately closes his eyes and starts to count. "One . . . two." He pauses.

"Three," Ethan helps.

"Free . . . four . . ."

As Mercet counts slowly, Ethan releases his grip. Mercet keeps trying to count. "Five," Ethan says.

"Five . . . six . . ." Mercet opens his eyes. "Grats moon, Daddy."

"Grats moon."

Ethan leaves the room as Mercet closes his eyes, counting again. "One . . ." As Ethan returns through the main room on his way to the master, another knock comes to the front door. *She's going to get me caught.* He hurries back to the master and picks out a set of clothes from his dresser and changes.

Undess wakes up as Ethan finishes buckling his belt and starts tying his shoe. "Where are you going at this hour?"

"Cadwellion needs something."

"Now?" Undess says, affronted.

Ethan shrugs. "Mercet woke up, but he's counting. He should be wisnok, but he may pop up in a few majors."

She huffs. "Fine. When will you be home?"

"Don't know. So don't wait up."

"I've gotten to an exciting part in my book, so I may." She smiles.

"Sounds nice. I'll see you on the morrow, I suppose."

He leaves the room as Undess grabs her novit and clears, commencing to read again. A third knock, this one more insistent than the others, pounds at the door as he approaches. He opens the door, grabbing his waist-length cloak from a nearby hanger. Amil stands in wait. "You're keeping him waiting." Her face bends in secret apory. *You can't kiss the girl, Ethan.*

"Apory, my son woke up." As he leaves, he kisses two fingers and touches them to the side of the door. *Lincoln protect me.*

The guard leads him to a large carriage. The wind outside sprays them with specks of red dust. Ethan wraps the orange cloak around himself, lifting an extended collar to protect his neck and half his face. The guard opens the door and Ethan steps inside where, to his surprise, Cadwellion waits.

"Cadwellion, I didn't know you were here."

The ranpart is an impressive body with his face hidden in the shadows beneath a thick overstretched hood. Impossibly thin, Cadwellion wears a black-and-orange robe draped loosely and unevenly over his frame. Cadwellion reaches out with an angular arm, grabbing for a small mug, and closes his elongated fingers, twice the length of Ethan's, around it. He drinks before speaking.

"What I found tonight is important. It cannot wait."

Ethan has known the ranpart for a while, their first encounter occurring in Ethan's early twenties back when he lived in Quemon. That was nearly ten years ago, and he's since labored as Cadwellion's acolyte, helping him research different phenomena and tricks of the Land. In that decade, Ethan has observed many incredible sights and findings, especially after Cadwellion would trek off on extended trips and bring back objects that seemingly had no significance but, after research and experimentation, were revealed to hold all sorts of unusual properties.

Over the last few years, Cadwellion has been particularly interested in Niance, the state beyond the eastern Merurro Sea, and particularly the last royal family from some three centuries ago. They speak often; or, more plainly, Ethan listens often to Cadwellion's disgust with the station of the various states, and his proclamations that the "peace" established after the Great Migration could not be sustained by the Three Laws on their own. He fears that even the smallest battle could escalate into all-out war, which in turn would finish off what the Last War almost did not: humankind.

After his declaration of importance, the remains of their ride to Cadwellion's stonetin are silent. Ethan has learned that it is best not to ask too many questions. His job is to act only as assistant to Cadwellion while he executes his researches.

Ranparts, in general, are feared across the Land; acolytes at times have to act as intermediaries in purchasing supplies or inquiring with various bodies on histories or accounts that interest a ranpart. Many believe that ranparts have abilities beyond normal bodies, but Ethan learned early on that it is only a trick to keep others at a distance and to keep a ranpart's experiments and knowledge secret. Ranparts prefer little interference from the peering eyes and minds of others.

The wind continues to accelerate in the cold and wintery night as they bump along, red sand peppering the windows in a nearly constant barrage. After an hour, they arrive at Cadwellion's foreboding stonetin, an impressive structure that overlooks the city of Salsman proper. In the full sun during clear and bright days, if you climb the back side's walls, a view could be had all the way to the Merurro Sea or, in another direction, across miles of the red desert sands. However, in the thick of winter, the dense sandstorms conceal the sight.

The first year of Ethan's labor with Cadwellion, the stonetin was ransacked by angry city bodies who were under the impression that Cadwellion was snipping children in the night. There was an expeditious trial, and it was found another body was guilty. But this verdict didn't subdue their suspicions, for if anything odd occurs in Salsman, it isn't long before Ethan's employer is at the center of the conspiracy.

Once they are parked, Ranpart Cadwellion gestures for Ethan to exit. Ethan steps outside and looks around. Thirty guards stand on various high walls, all dressed in similar drab-orange robes, around the stonetin. Each of them is armed with a crossbow loaded with flaming bolts that flutter in the high winds, and they wear headgear that shields them from the pelting sand.

After a minor, a set of guards deftly escorts Cadwellion from inside the carriage to the stonetin halls.

An air of paranoia lingers around the ranpart whenever he might be exposed to an open environment. Even within the protective walls of the stonetin, guards act as if enemies of the ranpart slink in the shadows. Ethan follows the entourage, welcoming the warmth of the fire-lit halls over the chilling sand winds outside.

Once in the safety of the stonetin, the lanky and towering Cadwellion pulls back his hood, exposing a sunken face inset with black and bloodshot eyes. His nose has long been cut down the middle and forms two split halves. Because so, Cadwellion carries hankers to wipe what is a perpetually running nose that, with any undue exertion of energy, bleeds a dark-blue blood. This off color is a result of experiments the ranpart performed on sneks when he was younger. Or so he's said.

"With me, Ethan," he sniggers, wiping his nose.

Cadwellion paces down the hall with long, slim steps, making Ethan jog behind him. They reach a staircase designed for the ranpart with steps larger than normal. Ethan considers these steps the sort of exercise he and Undess could use.

Reaching the top landing, they round a few corners and approach one of the ranpart's many sleeping chambers. Being the only living body in the stonetin, save for the many guards who reside below, the whole complex holds a cold and unwelcoming energy, one that counters the various guest and common rooms available. Cadwellion pulls out a small key and unlocks the door, then steps inside.

As Ethan enters, he finds a young woman, possibly in her midtwenties, passed out on a bed. He steps closer. She's a handsome woman with long black hair, nude, and covered in dirt.

"Who's this?" Ethan asks.

"One of my guards found her in an alley behind the Crescents bar."

Ethan steps up, first covering her with a sheet and then placing his finger under her nose. *She's breathing.* He lifts her eyelids and finds her eyes bloodshot. "She seems drugged."

"It would seem."

Ethan walks around the bed, examining her further, checking her pulse, between her fingers, and along the soles of her feet. He opens her mouth and checks her gums. "It looks like a violet overdose to me. Though she doesn't have signs of being a longtime user."

"Yes."

"I'm not sure I understand why you brought her here. There are many overusers in Salsman."

"This one is different."

Ethan turns back to the young woman, who remains comatose. He talks as he continues to assess her. "There's a chance she may not recover. Her heartbeat is slow. She's nearly sent."

"I didn't bring you here to tell me the woman has overused violet and is going left; I brought you here to heal her."

Cadwellion speaks with authority and displeasure. Whenever he speaks in this manner, Ethan senses the temperature in the room around him rise, creating a mood that's alien and unnatural. As if, in some way, Cadwellion becomes taller and more frightful.

"Yes, Sur." He returns to the young woman, checking her pulse again. "I'll need to retrieve a few instruments from my office."

"As you need. I'll be in my study until you have woken her." With a flick of his robe, the ranpart leaves the room.

Exasperated, Ethan is unsure how he's to wake the woman. If he's even able to. He leaves to gather a few medicinal supplies and returns to her after a few majors with even fewer ideas.

Over the next hours, Ethan proceeds to perform further tests, attempting to uncover anything he might use to draw her out of her current state. He starts by injecting her with fluids and vitams. The woman appears healthy, not like other overusers who fall into comas from being underfed or dehydrated, though the few unusual symptoms she displays only lead to the conclusion that she suffers from an overdose of violet and perhaps this is a reaction from a first-time user.

He pores over a few books from an extensive library downstairs and studies up on the most insidious effects of violet, seeking techniques others have employed to aid the recovery of victims in comatose states. Outside, the evening sandstorm has faded, just as the sun begins to peak over crest.

And then, without any warning or further actions, the woman takes a deep breath and sits up. Ethan is startled and stands in response.

She looks over at Ethan with confusion and shock, covering her chest. "Where am I?"

"Good morn. You're in, uh, Cadwellion's stonetin. You're safe. You were found in an alley." The woman acts confused and disoriented. "Let me get you a drink of water." He turns and pours some into a mug, and then hands it to her. She takes it, nodding in approsh.

He waits for a minor but decides to ask a few questions before informing Cadwellion. "Do you have any recollection of what happened? Do you remember taking violet?"

She shakes her head, lost in thought, her face distorted and her eyes closed. Thinking. "There was a black light, but I don't remember anything before that."

Black light? "What's your curam?"

She pauses. "I don't remember." She's frustrated as if she's trying to recollect something—thoughts that linger in front of the tongue but are wrapped in a stubborn fuzziness—but cannot.

"Have you ever used violet before?"

"Violet?"

"It's a drug. Bodies rub them into their gums. It can be dangerous in high doses, which is what I suppose happened to you."

"I don't remember that."

"That's not uncommon." He pours her a little more water. "Do you know where you're from? Do you live here in Salsman?"

"Where?"

"Salsman. In Yikshir."

She closes her eyes. "It sounds familiar, but I don't remember."

"Family? Parents who might know where you are? A husband? Wife?" The woman attempts to remember but shakes her head. "It's wisnok. You should rest. I'm sure you're not feeling your best."

She smiles—"Approsh"—and takes a deep breath.

"You're welcome. You're lucky that guard found you when he did. Not sure you were long for this Land."

"Who found me?"

"Oskar. He is a guard who labors for my ranpart, Sur Cadwellion. Now that you're awake, Cadwellion is eager to speak with you." She nods to Ethan, who smiles politely. "At the minor, I'll have a guard bring you some clothes."

"Approsh again." She sets the mug on a stand next to the bed and lies back down, pulling the covers over her.

Ethan leaves the room and ascends a staircase to the ranpart's study. After knocking, he opens the door to find Cadwellion hunched over a large desk, engrossed in a letter he's writing. "Excuse me, Sur, she's awake."

Cadwellion looks up from his letter. "Superb, Ethan. How is she?"

"She doesn't remember anything."

"As I thought. I was going to do this before she awoke, but I haven't had a chance. I need to follow up on another matter." He rises and walks across the room, leading Ethan back down the

274

staircase all the way to the basement. "You may accompany me, but I will not answer any questions." As is the normal.

Along the way, they come across several guards, who stiffen as Cadwellion passes. The two then arrive at the depths of the stonetin, where they find a wet and dark prison floor. Ethan knows about this area but has never actually been down or known that someone is here.

"You have someone priced?" The idea seems mad, especially with so many accusations against ranparts.

"He is my informant," Cadwellion quips without further explanation. "Please stand back, I told you no questions."

Ethan waits off to the side, watching Cadwellion from afar. The soft drip of water trickles from above as Cadwellion steps into one of the cells. From Ethan's angle and with the shadow, he's only able to see the faint outline of a naked man chained to the wall, huddled in the corner. As the ranpart steps up to him, he cowers in fear.

"Please, don't . . ." the man whimpers.

Cadwellion grabs on to his arm, lifting and examining him. He then stands the man up and rubs across his back. It's unclear what he's looking for or sees. After a major, Cadwellion leaves the cell and leads Ethan back upstairs. Ethan takes a last glance, and the man starts to snivel in the shadow.

Cadwellion turns to Ethan. "Your young and curious mind wants to ask questions. Wants to know more about what is going on here. You should forget what you've seen down there. I cross, the answers you find will not be to your liking, and I wish to impress on you that should you discover any answers, I will send you left without hesitation. Are the rules clear?"

Ethan swallows, taken aback at the bluntness with which Cadwellion speaks. He only nods in agreement.

"Very well, let's return to our guest."

They ascend the staircase to the sleeping room of the young woman, who lies quietly in bed. When the two enter, she sits up, covering herself.

Cadwellion's demeanor shifts when he sees her. "My child, welcome. How are you feeling?"

"Confused." She smiles weakly.

"We should get you some clothes. My apory for keeping you here. When we found you, you were unconscious."

"He said so." She nods toward Ethan. "Approsh to you and Oskar for finding me."

"It is of no consequence. In fact, it is my pleasure to meet you."

Cadwellion reaches out his long-fingered hand to shake the woman's. Ethan watches the exchange from a distance. Cadwellion's behavior is strange and unusually warm toward her.

"Do you know what happened to me?" she asks.

"I do not, my dear. Ethan here is my acolyte and supposes you were drugged on violet, but fortunately you were found before being sent left."

She nods, her eyes mistrusting toward Cadwellion. Even in his warm and soft behavior, the ranpart can be impassive.

"Ethan says you don't remember about where you're from?"

"I don't. I remember a black light, but nothing more than that."

"That's fine, dear. I, in fact, do know your curam."

The woman's eyes widen. Ethan unconsciously steps forward in surprise as well.

"You do?" she asks.

"Yes, dear. Your curam is Sanet."

Ethan looks on with more confusion. In the ten years he's known the ranpart, he's never heard him mention any woman curamed Sanet. *The man downstairs must know her.*

"Sanet?"

"Yes. Do you remember that curam?"

She thinks, but shakes her head.

"I know this all may seem so strange to you, but I believe you came to us with great purpose, and I am glad to finally have met you."

Sanet blushes. "I just want to know what happened."

"In due time; we all do. But, before then, I have much to teach you. Much to discuss with you. For now, though, you should rest."

She nods as Cadwellion stands to leave. Ethan turns toward the door as Sanet calls out.

"How did you know my curam? Do you know where I came from?"

"In truth, I'm not entirely sure. I only know that you have a son and it is in my interest to find him for you."

"A son?" Sanet asks.

"I'm afraid for him, however. There's nothing we can do now, but hopefully soon we can find him together."

With that, Cadwellion turns and leaves the room. Ethan stands by quietly in disbelief. He watches as Sanet sits dumbfounded in her bed and suddenly begins to cry. Ethan steps up and sits down next to her, rubbing her back.

"Apory, Sanet. I know this must be maddening."

"Who is he?" she asks, wiping her eyes.

"A ranpart. And it's a ranpart's way to walk in hidden knowledge and secrets. But if it's any consolation to you, I've worked with him for over ten years. He's a good man." Ethan smiles to comfort and console her.

Sanet wipes her eyes. "I have a son?" Her face speaks to his own emotion. Confusion in the unknown.

Chapter Twenty-Three
A WELCOME REUNION

*T*he novit was boring, to say the least. *I don't know how Undess reads these.* Since Cadwellion left six months ago, labor around the stonetin has been mind-numbingly monotonous. The guards have grown lax, which gives Ethan ample opportunity to wander the stonetin, peak to foundation. Though at times, he has to wait until the guards are asleep or have become so tipst they are completely unaware he's exploring in areas he shouldn't.

One of the areas he most likes to explore is the basement prison. He has long mulled over that night years ago when Cadwellion found Sanet and had kept someone here. The priced man living in this cell is never spoken of by any of the guards or even Cadwellion himself, and had inexplicably disappeared only a year ago—though it remains unclear whether this happened with or without the ranpart's permission.

At home, things continue to be the same. It is Mercet's ninth paseday on the morrow. Undess chooses not to celebrate pasedays, believing they take away from the worship of Dustian. This absurd practice doesn't stop Ethan from taking Mercet out for a walk and, in secret, presenting him with a gift. This year, Mercet wants a Yantak playset, the arch nemesis of Dread Copla.

Ethan has the playset swathed in silver wrapping, waiting at the stonetin. Though Undess knows that Ethan enjoys giving presents and celebrating with Mercet, she closes her eyes to the "sin of gifts." But for months afterward, she'll grit on any number of irritations and annoyances as a way of punishing him. She lives to divert her real feelings. Mercet's paseday always makes the house a little smaller, and because so, since Cadwellion will still be gone for a few months, Ethan makes plans to bring Mercet to the stonetin overnight, and they'll celebrate his day in grand fashion.

Beyond the respite of present shopping, Ethan takes a lot of naps and tries to keep in better shape running up and down the staircases. These upstairs-downstairs jogs halt short at the ranpart's steps, which are too tall to conquer without tripping or catching a side stitch. This burst of health and exercise came to him as he grew agitated over Undess's lack of aspiration to better herself. As she grew larger and more sedentary in the years since Kevin's passing, Ethan began to lose some of his life weight. Still, he reminds himself: *Long way to go, Ethan. Long way.*

It is a particularly sweet morn with the midsummer cools ramping up when Ethan sets out to walk the upper stonetin walls. Reaching the open air, he takes in the refreshing breeze on a day, now past the full sun, remaining a magnificent clear blue. In the distance, the endless sea lies as placidly as a duskmeal round, where farther out, a fleet of kleeps sail leisurely across the waters. A drum of jarjers fly above them, completing the perfect major.

He wanders to the southern wall and looks down across the shifting sands, catching a glimpse of a lone horsal plodding along. The frek and whomever it's carrying, Ethan guesses, are possibly a few hours from the Salsman redrock and another hour or so from the top of the steep switchback-laden climb to the city gate.

Curious and bored, he pulls a large magnifier from a resting pitch and looks down the barrel at the flat-backed horsal, where he sees an odd couple. On it sits a slightly older yet handsome man with hass and pestler hair and a peculiar-looking cog vaulting back and forth across his shoulders. And then beside him is a dark-haired woman—

My Lincoln, it's Sanet. He drops the magnifier into the pitch and hurries down the stonetin staircase. *She's back. She's back? I wonder if she found them?* The day has been so lazy, and suddenly there are a thousand things to do. He makes his way down to the guards 'quarters to speak with the officer in charge.

"Sanet's returned. We should prepare for her arrival."

The officer, hearing Sanet's curam, quickly stands, his demeanor shifting from absolute apathy to undiluted joy and anticipation.

So, now they're ready to labor.

Within minors, the entire stonetin is alive with activity. Guards and servicemen rush about. The dirt and grime of the building suddenly become wholly apparent. Ethan himself showers and dresses. *I'll need to pick up Mercet, and then I can meet Sanet at the gates.* Guessing she would arrive at dusk, he relays the plan to the entrance guards that he'll return with his son, Sanet, and her companion later that eve. The guard staff scoffs at the idea of her bringing back a partner. Ethan rolls his eyes. *She can't be in single souls with the whole of you.*

Taking one of the ranpart's many carriages, he journeys back to his haynest. Perhaps it is the sudden shift in events, but Sanet's return seems like a grand affair. Mercet always enjoys Sanet as well. *What a lovely paseday surprise for him.* Undess isn't the biggest gully for her and will most likely sneer at Mercet and Ethan for leaving for the night. She's become unbearable over the years. It's been ten years now since Kevin's death, and she's only become more irritable, quicker to anger, and less . . . amused. To see Undess smile would be like seeing a tenfooter dance the Green Palco.

After the hour's journey, Ethan enters his haynest to find Undess sitting in her usual chair, reading while consuming coffee sticks between pellets of green brackleberries. *Next, she'll be on violet.* "Where's Mercet?"

"Dustian to you too, Ethan." Undess speaks without lifting her eyes from the page. "He's in his room."

Ethan shakes his head and paces to Mercet's room. The boy is lying stomach down and flipping through cartoons. Ethan sits down next to him.

"Evening, Mercet." Mercet looks away. "What's the matter?"

"Nothing."

"Mercet, look at me." Mercet turns his head, and in the dim light, Ethan can see that he wears a huge bruise over his west eye. "What happened to you?"

"Nothing. Jeroff being a shnite." Mercet sits up in defiance, putting on a thin air of confidence and indifference.

"Careful with your words, son."

"But he is." This is the fourth time this year that the children at his boaler have sent Mercet home with a blue's eye. Ethan isn't entirely sure why Mercet is picked on out of the others. He isn't awkward or antisocial, though he enjoys cartoons over championships, as do many others his age.

"Well, what would you say if we spent the evening at Cadwellion's?"

"Really?" His eyes light up.

"And I have another surprise, but we can't tell your mother," Ethan whispers.

Mercet and Undess don't get along much. She tends to treat him as an extra in the house. It isn't that she dislikes Mercet. Far from it. She has it stuck in her mind that, somehow, she is the cause of their first child's death and she's afraid of getting too close to Mercet—in case he, too, meets the same fate. She confesses this often after grits about nothing between her and Ethan.

At the prospect of leaving for the stonetin and more surprises, Mercet quickly gathers a bag of clothes and his toothbrush before rushing out of his room to wave goodbye to Undess.

"Leaving for the whole night, are you?"

"Thought we'd take a night out, yes," Ethan states plainly.

"Mercet, I know your father doesn't believe, but Dustian always knows when you're lying to your mother. When you're a liar to Him." Ethan huffs. *Always with her fatalistic nothing-matters-but-Dustian nonsense.* "Be kind in your day. Approsh the sun. Approsh the moon." She kisses him on both cheeks.

"I will, Mom." He hugs her and then turns his back, rolling his eyes in view of Ethan.

Ethan stops him. "Don't roll your eyes. Appize to your mother."

Embarrassed to be caught, Mercet's face distorts. He turns, sheepish. "Apory, Mom."

"I told you, you can't hide from Dustian."

"Dad's not Dustian," Mercet replies sarcastically.

"Certainly not, child. Certainly not."

The boy giggles and leaves the room, followed by Ethan.

"Have a blessed night, Undess," Ethan says as he walks away.

She closes her lips and breathes with disapproval.

Outside, Mercet hops into the carriage before Ethan enters and closes the door behind them. They set off. Mercet behaves as if enamored at the turn of events and watches as they pass various bodies and small horsals along the cobblestone streets. "We're not headed to the stonetin?" he questions as he pokes his head out.

"We're meeting someone."

"Who?"

"Soon enough."

At this, Mercet rolls his eyes once more. "You're incorrigible."

"Incorrigible? Where'd you learn that?"

"My teacher said that's what I was."

At this, Ethan laughs heartily. They continue along until they reach the Salsman Gates, where they park along the side road. Mercet jumps from the carriage and rushes through the massive city doors. On the other side, a cliff overlooks the shifting sands and a setting sun. Almost dusk.

"Can you tell me now?" Mercet asks.

"They'll be here soon enough."

Unimpressed, Mercet looks around. He hops over to a small boulder to see farther down the trail but catches nothing. After a major, the gates open and a large horsal with short brown matted fur wanders by, carrying a large family of six on its broad, flat back. It pads quietly along the road winding down toward the sands.

Mercet grows impatient. "Where are they?" And then he spots her as they come around a corner. He starts to run.

"Mercet, watch out now."

He doesn't listen and Ethan dashes after him. With Mercet being quicker and younger, Ethan quickly gives up the chase. The city's night bells ring out as the sun disappears over the crest.

When Sanet catches sight of Mercet running, she hurdles off their little horsal and greets him, grabbing him up in her arms and swinging him in a great circle. Ethan eventually catches up. Sanet looks as magnificent and fresh as she always did, wearing her signature green hood.

"Sur Ethan, a pleasure." They embrace.

"Is that your cog?" Mercet points to a strange looking frek sitting on the shoulder of the older gentleman.

"This is Brute," the man states. "Not a cog. He's a creshwillow."

A creshwillow? Aren't those the pets of protnuks?

"This is Bernard. Bernard, this is Ethan and his son Mercet."

Bernard stands and hops down off the horsal. Up close, Bernard looks much younger than he appeared from afar, athletic with thick, muscular arms. He holds the air of the Land about him. *A Radibian, if I had to guess.*

Sanet continues, "We met in the Highlands. He's helped me find the brass."

She did find it. His mouth forms a wide and beaming smile as he speaks, "We now have two things to celebrate."

"It's also my paseday," Mercet interrupts.

"Paseday?" Bernard questions.

Mercet answers with indignation, "Yeah, it's my paseday."

Sanet interjects, "To celebrate the day you're chosen."

Bernard nods with understanding. "Well, hopefully, your paseday doesn't end in a bunch of fire." He ruffles Mercet's hair.

"Don't ask," Sanet responds to Ethan's confused expression.

The ride to Cadwellion's stonetin is lively. Sanet and Bernard recount their journey, detailing the abnormal pattern of the tormisand and the frightful encounter with welkings inside a temple of monstrous krakes. Mercet and Brute have fallen into a battle of wits, as Mercet attempts to hide parcels of meat from the creshwillow and Brute grows more and more agitated.

When they arrive at the stonetin, it stands ready with a grand welcome, the guards standing tall and quiet. Firelight and neon illuminate the walls in soft orange and yellow as the officer in charge greets them at the front gate and escorts them into the main hall.

"Shall we eat?" Ethan asks.

"That'd be wondrous," Sanet answers.

Ethan looks to Bernard, whose eyes scatter from corner to corner. "Impressive?"

"Quite. I've heard of stonetins, been in a few since I've trekked out, but this is by far the most elaborate."

Ethan looks around. Ornate windows, intricate tapestries over the walls. It is notable but perhaps much less so, at least to him, after his years of laboring inside.

Duskmeal is served. Lyn, mashings, and vegs with plenty of ale. Ethan allows Mercet to have a sip of the ale, which he spits out, after a toast to Sanet: "To your safe return. To new friends and celebrations of your success."

As the evening draws out, Mercet is sent to sleep. And though he begs and protests the denial, Brute refuses to follow him.

They continue the night in a smoking room, Bernard and Sanet passing green.

"Sanet, you have to show me," Ethan states, unable to wait any longer.

With an eager grin, Sanet nods and leaves the room. Bernard and Ethan sit alone for a major. The Radibian remains soundless, as he has been throughout the night, from his veneration of the stonetin. If anything, it is charming. Ethan is about to ask Bernard about the brown leather mitts he wears when Sanet returns, carrying a large fragment of brass.

She polishes it a bit before handing it to Ethan, who takes it cautiously in his hand. "Lincoln, I didn't think it would be this large." It's nearly the size of his fist.

"This was found in the krake's stonetin in the Carvinga Tunnels. With that key you replicated."

"How marvelous. And the other one? The one at the manor in Misipit?"

Sanet pauses for a second. "Someone else found it."

"Oh. Shame." Ethan looks back down to the brass, turning it in his hands. It is inexplicably pedestrian after so much buildup around it. And then there's a knock on the table. He looks up and sees Bernard holding a smaller sliver of brass.

"What is that?"

"I told you . . . someone else found it." Sanet smiles.

"You? How?"

Bernard then recounts his trouble with the neox and how he met Sanet soon after. Sanet continues with her experience with the crimson men and chasing the neox through Carvinga. Ethan sits back in amazement. Never in his kiptales would he have made such travels. He spent hours and days on the pages of research, in conversations with odd and unsavory bodies. To go forth and see the Land seemed absurd and dangerous.

"Well, now that I've had a few drinks and Sanet plainly refuses to ask, I want to know why," Bernard says.

"Why?"

"Why these are so unispar?"

Sanet sits back in her chair. "I told him it wasn't our bargain."

"I have to confess, I know little myself," Ethan starts. His research did give him a little hint, but in truth Cadwellion knows much more about their significance, and he seems to like it that way. "That said, I do have some notions."

"Well?"

"Well, they form a larger orb. You see here," Ethan leans in and rubs a smoother side of the slightly rounded brass, "this is likely the outside of it. And here," he holds his hand out to take the smaller second sliver from Bernard, who hands it to him, "I bet you these two . . ." He begins to press them together as if they were engineered puzzle pieces. After a minor, they snap together, making a small *clink* as they do. It surprises all three.

"Lincoln," Bernard blurts out, standing to get a closer look.

Ethan examines where the two pieces came together and finds he's unable to distinguish a crack or even the slightest line. "Lincoln indeed," he repeats.

"We had both those pieces all this time." Bernard shakes his head. "So, it's one big orb, but for what?"

"That's the riddle, isn't it?" Ethan stands. "I should show you something."

He leaves the dining hall. Sanet and Bernard follow, and they make their way up the stonetin stairwell to Cadwellion's study. After they enter, Ethan closes the door behind them.

"You see, here is where Cadwellion keeps his own orb." He moves to a cabinet and opens it. Along its empty shelf is a small rounded indentation. "A ranpart's orb is used for many reasons. It's what gives them their alleged power, though I haven't seen any evidence of it. And some believe that ranparts can't do anything out of the ordinary. That the whole bargain of being a ranpart is drawing power from fear and misinformation."

Sanet shifts her stance. Ethan isn't sure where his flippant dismissal of Cadwellion comes from—*too many drinks*—but he continues nonetheless. "In any case, the assumption here is that these fragments are part of a larger orb. And judging by this piece, it's not something that's the size of one's hand, like his. This one could be . . ." He looks at the brass fragment once more. "Well, this could be over eight feet across."

Bernard's eyes widen, then he recalls, "You know, when we were in Smith Tunston's shop, I saw an orb."

"You saw an orb like this?" Ethan says curiously.

"It wasn't eight feet, of course, but a smaller one like your ranpart's." He points to the empty case. "If I remember correctly, it was black. It had that same shimmer as the stonetin of krakes."

"Fascinating. Finding an orb without its ranpart is rare. Where did you say you found it?"

Sanet answers, "There's a smith in Radiba."

"A smith? I've not met one of those. None here in Salsman. I hear they're quite the entertainment though."

"You could say that." Bernard and Sanet share a knowing look. "So, you're saying that this orb could bring power?"

"Perhaps. If anything, it'll make for a nice collector's item. But all this said, I do believe there's a reward for its recover."

Ethan leads them to another room with a desk. He places the brass piece down and pulls out an enormous note-lined ledger. He writes in it and then walks over to a locked cabinet and pulls from it a few bags of coin. "Sanet, my dear, you're going to be a heavy girl."

Sanet beams.

He hands her the coin, and she immediately passes a significant portion of it to Bernard.

"This is as much yours as it is mine," she says.

Bernard rolls it in his hand. "And Logan's and Iahel's."

"Of course, but you did hunt a neox for eighteen hours."

"Eighteen hours?" *He's quadruple the man I am,* thinks Ethan.

A voice says from behind them, "Apory to interrupt, but you received an urgent tap." One of the guards stands at the doorway. In his hand is a small note. Ethan reaches for it, but the guard motions away from him. "Apory, Sur Mershner, but this is addressed to Sur Wells."

Surprised, Sanet nods and takes the note. She reads it to herself before looking up at Ethan and Bernard with a look of puzzlement.

"It's from Iahel. She says she's in Carvinga and that there's a battle between the tenfooters and Misipit. And she wants us to secure the brass. To keep it safe and as far away from Carvinga as possible."

"A battle between states?" Bernard questions. "How can that be? That's . . . well, that's illegal, isn't it?"

Ethan watches the two, his heart skipping a beat. "It's not just illegal, it's downright apocalyptic."

Chapter Twenty-Four

ETHAN AND THE WEONSLOW

*T*he tap from Sanet's friend Iahel, warning them of the conflict between Misipit and Carvinga, bewilders Ethan. Though the Three Laws do not explicitly proclaim that one state could not invade or attack another, their entire charge is to prevent war altogether. The revelation feels as if someone has gut-punched him with a daggered knuckle.

Once he's read the note himself, Ethan looks up and suggests they part ways until the next day, as it is sure to bring on a series of lengthy discussions about what their next actions must be. "It's best to get a good night's rest."

After escorting them to separate rooms, Bernard tittering at the elegant accommodations, Ethan retires to a sleeping room next to Mercet's. Before slipping off to sleep, there's a sudden and quiet knock at his door, which opens and then gently closes. He squints in the dark and makes out the familiar outline of Amil, one of Cadwellion's guards. Ethan sits up as Amil walks in and, without much ado, removes the top layers of her uniform before getting into the bed next to him.

"Tonight's not a good night, Amil."

"Mercet's asleep. And I don't think Sanet or the new sur will mind." Amil says this as she leans over and kisses him.

The act itself gives him a bit of a rise, and he instinctively, unceremoniously, kisses her back. He immediately regrets it, stopping and pushing away. "Apory, it's been an eventful day. I forgot we talked about tonight."

At his remark, Amil sits up. "I can leave if you'd like."

"No, appize. Stay." He kisses her again. "Stay. I need a distraction."

She smiles, a sight that still gives Ethan grenspimples, even after four years. He knows that at some point he and Undess will have to break things off. But he also knows that Amil is much too young for him, and beyond a good slip, they don't have much in common. But Amil is kind and easygoing. A welcome reprieve from the uptight and difficult relationship with Undess.

"Do you want to talk about it?"

"No, I just need to think."

"The other guards are saying that Sanet received a tap. That some battle is brewing in Carvinga. Is that true?"

"She did receive a tap, from a friend who said she was in Carvinga, but it's hard to believe she was able to survive around tenfooters, and it's also hard to believe that the Misipit would be flam enough to start a war. So, it's difficult to discern what's true."

"That's wild." Amil says this more to herself than Ethan. She reaches out and takes his hand, squeezing and rubbing it as she sinks under the blankets.

With the thought of war and Cadwellion's secrets returning to the front of his mind, Ethan is unable to sleep. "Amil?" He squeezes her hand.

She opens her eyes, big and brown and innocent. "Do you think you could, perhaps get me a key to Cadwellion's office?"

Amil sits up at the words. "Now?"

"If you can. I mean, if you can't, don't worry about it. It was just a thought—"

But before Ethan's able to finish, Amil hops up from the bed, tosses on her uniform, and disappears into the hall. *She's wonderful.* He sits in the quiet, unsure of what he aspires to find.

Looking out his sleeping room window, he sees the moon lying in perfect alignment against the sand-lined crest.

A few majors later, Amil creeps back through the door, waving for Ethan to follow her out. Not ready to leave, he gets up and quickly dresses, with Amil waving her hand for him to hurry.

"Apory, I didn't think this would happen so soon."

"You know I relish this kind of thing." She beams a flam and enthusiastic grin.

"I owe you a bargain."

"I'm sure you'll deliver. Now let's go. Ren won't be happy if he finds out I took his personal key."

"You took Ren's?" He shudders at the thought of the husky guard's guaranteed overreaction.

"He ate like a prenog tonight. He's going to sleep past alarm."

At this, Ethan calms a bit and follows Amil outside. They sneak along the hall and up the tall staircase to Cadwellion's master. Amil unlocks the solid burnished-iron door and turns to Ethan. "I'll wait out here, in case anyone comes along."

He nods before moving in. "I do appize for how I treat you. If the Land rotated west to east—"

"Just go, you big cog."

Ethan smiles with tightly pressed lips and turns into the room.

Unlike the ranpart's study, where guards and Ethan himself roam in and out, here is where Cadwellion keeps his most-guarded writings and memoranda. Ethan makes his way over to a large desk covered in inks and papers written in old and coded languages. He also finds illustrations and maps that do not correlate with any states he's studied or in fact can remember as part of the hundred and thirty-three. Lines scratched across the maps resemble what might be words or letters but that look more like the sketches of a three-year-old child learning to write their curam.

The pile, organized in no intelligent manner, is sure to equate to each of the various mysteries: the impending assault in Carvinga; the pieces and fragments of the brass orb; the meetings between Sanet and Cadwellion without him. Even if Cadwellion is an absolute fraud, he at least has his reasons. A purpose to the madness. And then, underneath even more writings and letters that riddle along another road, Ethan discovers a promising lead . . .

❖ ❖ ❖

Over mornmeal, everyone wishes Mercet the happiest of pasedays. The traditional meal of one's paseday centers on a serving of flaps that number in the years one has folded. In Mercet's case: nine. As one grows older, the flaps are supposed to shrink in size, making a stack of thirty or forty flaps manageable when compared to a childhood stack of three or four. However, this stack of nine set before the group is at first a convivial challenge, but quickly evolves into complete agony among them.

"I'm fuller than a prenog on Sharpen's Day," Mercet cries out, rubbing his stomach in an exaggerated gesture. The others chuckle at Mercet's small voice sputtering some old-man's adage, followed by their own groans of overstuffed pain.

Ethan presents Mercet with a big silver gift. The nine-year-old unwraps it to find a Yantak action set and lets out an unfiltered yelp. Without pause, Mercet dismisses himself to unpack and play, giving the others a chance to begin dissecting the previous night's tap from Iahel.

"I can't believe there's a skirmish between states," Bernard starts. "And what are these, appize the term, twofooters thinking if they assume they can take on the Carvingians? Those friends are massive. I ran into only one and barely survived."

"It's odd for sure. I just hope it doesn't escalate into anything further. And Lincoln forgive me, but if it's an all-out slaughter, it might be for the best," Sanet continues.

Ethan listens and then adds, "It's odd that after twenty-five hundred years of peace, the Misipiants would suddenly decide to post a march into Carvinga."

"Do you think someone instigated this? This ranpart, maybe?" Bernard asks.

"Wellion isn't the type to start wars," Sanet insists.

"I wouldn't dismiss him so easily," Ethan says, pointing his finger at Sanet. "In fact, I was doing some investigating last night and found that Cadwellion's been seeing a weonslow."

"A what?" Bernard asks.

"A weonslow." He pauses a minor. "You've both met a smith, right? They're similar, except instead of designing gear or armor, weonslows . . . weave information from the Land. They have an unusual understanding of old languages and ancient histories." Ethan looks around, noting which guards are within earshot. He then leans in close to the two and whispers, "Cadwellion used to have a secret prisoner here. Years ago. He would sneak downstairs after dusk and speak with him for hours and take extensive notes."

"For what?" Bernard wonders.

"If Wellion was keeping him a secret, how do you know about him?" Sanet asks.

"The night we found you, Cadwellion had me follow him downstairs while he spoke with him. I wasn't allowed to get close, but he inspected the prisoner's body and whispered something to him. That priced man was down there for years. Unfortunately, I never had a reason to speak with him personally or even see him out of the shadow. I tried to find a way to sneak down there, but it was always guarded, which surprises me, as I've been allowed to go nearly everywhere within this stonetin. But he's gone now or been sent left. I last heard of him about a year ago when a guard told me the prison downstairs was vacated."

"I never knew any priced were kept here," Sanet says mainly to herself.

Ethan continues, "The strangest part is that the prisoner knew your curam. That's how Cadwellion knew who you were when you didn't, and about your supposed son or not son or whatever the foretale is now."

"Your son?" Bernard exclaims.

"A long tale." Sanet dismisses him.

The subject is sore for her, causing what Ethan perceived as a growing rift between her and Cadwellion, especially once the ranpart redacted the notion she had a son. Sanet still believes in him, however. Still trusts her ranpart.

"In any case, I think this prisoner is the one who told him about the brass, and I think he also forewarned him about the war. Which is why I believe he sought out this weonslow," Ethan finishes.

"Has Cadwellion found any other pieces?" Bernard asks.

"According to his notes," he whispers the next few words, "that I shouldn't have," Ethan then pulls out a few pieces of a pad, watching nervously any guards who might spy on them before smiling, "according to these translations, there are only seven pieces. The two you found and three somewhere over in the western states, which is where Cadwellion has been the past six months."

"And where do you think the other two are?" Bernard asks, curious.

"That I couldn't find, which is why I want to visit Cadwellion's weonslow." Ethan sits back, folding the writings back into his pocket. Nervousness and excitement compete inside him.

"Isn't the crux of our situation whether or not we should be uniting this brass and not finding more of it?" Bernard adds.

"If Cadwellion believes joining them would end the war, shouldn't we try and do that? Isn't that what we should attempt to do?" Sanet offers.

"If Iahel's letter is right, she's saying to keep the pieces apart," Bernard counters.

"I think speaking with the weonslow will help us understand what this all means. In truth, I don't trust Cadwellion with Mercet's life. Or, frankly, my own. I want to know what he knows and then either we can continue to help him . . . or we stop him."

"Why would we want to prevent him from ending the war?" Sanet asks.

Bernard answers, "In this Land, you're never sure what motives drive a friend. I agree with Ethan: the more we know, the better." The three sit back in silence as an air of hesitation rests between them.

✧ ✧ ✧

At the break of dusk, they pull up to Ethan's haynest, and Ethan escorts Mercet to the front door.

"Approsh for the acers paseday, Dad."

"You're doubled welcome, Sur Mercet Good Sur." Ethan ruffles Mercet's hair as Undess greets them at the door, her face contorted from crying. Ethan huffs, unwilling to start another grit with her. "What's wrong now?"

"It's over, Ethan."

At the words, Ethan closes his eyes and takes a deep breath. It's been "over" many times before. He turns to Sanet and Bernard in the carriage and holds up a single finger for them to wait a minor while he steps into the house.

"Mercet, why don't you go to your room?" Mercet rolls his eyes before running off and around the hall corner. To Undess, he says, "So, tell me how it's over again," then huffs.

"It's clear you don't love me anymore, Ethan. You've made that obvious over and over."

"You don't make this easy for me, Undess. I try to help you through your grief, but it's been ten years now. You can't believe this is healthy for us. Or for Mercet."

"How can you be so cruel? He was my first child. He was our first child. And you're off celebrating with Mercet like Kevin's sending is nothing."

"You don't want to celebrate Mercet's paseday. You want him to just wallow in grief with you. You want us all to sit around in a constant sadness."

"Our lives on this Land are nothing compared to what awaits those who believe. Our lives are just a speck before the Eternal Future. We are sent here as tests of our faith. And Dustian shall judge our lives as lived."

"Undess, I can't have a religious conversation with you right now."

"Oh, you never have time for a religious talk with me. You go on with your flam Lincolnism, like everyone else who barely believes, and you give nothing back to Him."

Ethan takes a deep breath, resigned. "I need to go." He spins and moves to exit.

"If you walk out that door, you better never come back."

Ethan stops. He turns. "There is no ultimatum here. This is as much my haynest as it is yours. If you want to end our union over a religious disagreement or your refusal to let go of the past, then, by all means, it's over. But you can't threaten my son or my haynest."

She steps forward. "You're just going to walk out that door?"

Ethan stands firm. "We are two very different people, Undess. You've made that clear."

She slaps him. "I know about Amil. I know you're slipping with her. And to have Mercet there. It disgusts me."

Ethan's heart jumps. He has been careful. He knows how wrong it is for him. But Amil is soft and warm. *It is wrong.* At this minor, he hates Undess. He raises his hand to his warm cheek and sees Mercet peering around the corner. "It's done then. Mercet, get your things."

Mercet steps out.

Undess turns. "Mercet, go back to your room. This has nothing to do with you." She turns back to Ethan. "He is my son first."

"How does that make any sense? He's our son. We chose him together."

"You walk out that door, and you'll never see him again."

Ethan closes his eyes. The threats are always the same. He opens his eyes. "I am leaving, but I will be back."

Undess, not speaking, presses her lips tightly together.

"And I'm telling you," he raises a finger to her, "if you do anything to him, I will never forgive you."

"As Dustian will never forgive you," she counters.

"Oh, you shnite woman, just stop."

She smirks at his inability to counter her. Instead, Ethan turns and leaves the house, slamming the door. He stomps over to the carriage and steps up to one of the guards. "I need you to stay here and keep watch on my son. Make sure she doesn't leave with him."

"And if she does, Sur?" the guard asks.

"Just make sure I can find him when I return."

The guard nods. Undess has acted out from exasperation at times, but she is never rash. She acts this way whenever Mercet shows more affection to Ethan. She sees a power struggle between him and her. *I should never have started things with Amil. I lost my moral high ground.* Ethan puts his head in his hands.

In the carriage, after Sanet asks if everything is wisnok and Ethan remains silent, they ride as such for the duration. Sanet places her hand on Ethan's. He pats it as he looks over at Bernard, who ignores the thickness of the carriage's air and instead stares outside with the same wide-eyed wonderment as Mercet.

To be that simple again.

❖ ❖ ❖

They arrive at the weonslow's haynest a little after the full moon. A small breeze climbs over the hilltop they've been ascending for the past hour and winds through a line of vacant houses.

Ethan informs them, "We're in a part of town most don't live in, but this is where she supposedly lives." The three look out toward the haynest, seeing a modest building with a soft flickering light inside.

Stepping off the carriage and up to the door, they find it's carved to resemble various famous bodies of Salsman, one of them a poor interpretation of Cadwellion. There are other depictions of Salsman life: winter sandstorms, serial sendlefts, the massive council building.

Ethan knocks politely, and Sanet and Bernard stand at the ready behind him. He turns to see Bernard with his mitt on a dagger. "Don't think we're in for a fight," Ethan smiles.

"I've seen enough since I've left Radiba. You'd be surprised."

The door creaks open, revealing what at first appears to be a wrinkled woman, but the sight's undone by a triple set of eyes, each stacked on top of the other, and two hands without thumbs but instead uncommonly long fingers that wrap in and on themselves. She speaks in a slithery and strange language, which Ethan understands, a language from Yikshir's past and one that Cadwellion had insisted he learn.

"*Good vigil, Ethan,*" the woman says without pause.

"*Good eve. We wanted to speak with you,*" he responds in the same language.

"I was expecting you. Please, come in." Ethan wonders how she knew he'd come. He turns to Sanet and Bernard and translates. She opens the door fully and invites them into the old haynest.

Stepping inside, they find a dimly lit and pleasing space with a small crackling fire in a stone hearth and a set of tea mugs waiting on a table. Ethan notes three place settings.

The woman looks between them. *"I would have set a fourth had known you'd bring a fourth."* She glares at Bernard while Ethan translates.

"Bernard Babek," Bernard responds, reaching out to shake hands despite her long, twisted fingers. She looks him over cautiously and turns back to the kitchen, without shaking. Bernard lowers his mitt.

"Let me find another setting. Please, sit down." Ethan translates everything she says to Sanet and Bernard and motions for them to sit. They watch the weonslow's fingers unravel in and on themselves as she digs through a cluttered cabinet. With only three seats, Bernard pulls a chair from across the room and sits down in it backward.

"Drink, drink," the weonslow encourages. Ethan and Sanet take a sip, but Bernard holds back, his eyes darting cautiously around the room.

When the weonslow returns with a mug, she pours herself a sip and begins to drink with them. As Ethan watches the weonslow's fingers nimbly wrap around a few sugar cubes to dip in her mug, he starts. *"So, why were you expecting us?"*

"It was Cadwellion's bargain that I wait for you. That when Sanet," she nods to the woman in the green hood, *"returned, we were to speak. I've been waiting for you to visit for..."* She looks to be counting in her head with each number tied to amplified frustration. *"A full month now."* She takes a tremendous sip of her tea. After Ethan translates, Sanet speaks up.

"Is this about the brass?"

"Yes, dear. But more to the point, it is about the War." She pours herself a bit more tea.

"The war between Misipit and Carvinga?" Ethan questions.

"Ah. The opening salvo."

"There's more?" Bernard gasps, hearing the translation. Ethan's mind races to his studies of the Last War and tales of the great explosions and the sending of millions.

"Yes, stranger who was not invited. And the only way to control the War is to reunite the brass. Sur Cadwellion's plan is now as such, and it is why he's traveled to find the remaining pieces in the west."

"There're seven collectively, right?" Ethan asks.

"Yes. When the Merigen brass orb was shattered into seven pieces, each of the fragments was placed in a discreet stonetin around the continent, with the largest of the pieces transported to Carvinga, where the Carvingians have been protecting it for over a hundred years. They were chosen to protect this most notable piece because of their closed border. I have no doubt this attack from the Misipiants is a distraction to, in the chaos of battle, procure it."

"But Cadwellion is trying to end all this?" Sanet asks.

"His aim, as it has always been, is to protect the Land."

"But what's this orb for?" Bernard asks.

"As much as there's written about it, we know that it is an orb of calling. To give people the strength and confidence to fight. And it gives them the strength to die for a cause."

At her answer, Ethan attempts to understand the logic of her position. *"Isn't it paradoxical to rally people to a war you intend to end? Or am I missing something?"*

"My boy, as I have said, it is only an opening salvo."

"What did he want you to tell us?" Sanet asks. "What does he want us to do?"

"He wants you to meet him in Carvinga in a month's time. And, if you were successful in your task, to bring Logan Hunst with you. There, he will reunite the brass orb."

Ethan's mind races among all the scenarios, all the various bits and pieces of information he's gathered over the past years and past months. Nothing sums to anything true. *"I'm still not understanding how some orb will stop this confrontation from happening."*

"Cadwellion believes that whoever controls this orb controls the War. Ending or starting a skirmish is not part of his concern. The War is coming, regardless of some... distraction south." The weonslow sips her tea again in a giant gulp. The answers were still unclear. Ethan decides against his better judgment, feeling the weonslow won't be much of a threat, and shares their secret.

"I must confess that Sanet and Bernard recovered two of the pieces. So, I have to ask, if the final fragment is in Carvinga and Cadwellion found three of them out west, where is the last piece?" Ethan speaks without translating, unsure he wants Sanet to know of his confession.

The weonslow's fingers curl tightly in on themselves at this revelation, as if what she's heard was not the way the discussion was to go. Her eyes dart most prominently to Bernard, who's upsetting everything she's prepared.

After a major, she speaks again. Reluctant. *"It is in* Trimod.*"*

"Trimod?" Ethan responds.

"Trimod? What is that?" Bernard asks.

Ethan answers. "It's an island. Halfway across the Merurro Sea. It was one of the first states abandoned after an endless row of tormisands decades back. Bodies believe that now it's a place of lost souls. Where no one goes if they have their head spun straight."

"But the crimson men are sure to go. We have to stop them. We have to get there first." Sanet states.

"Cadwellion already has bodies recovering this final piece. This task is of no concern to you. He was clear with me that you should set straight for Carvinga. You're already behind his schedule." The weonslow commands.

"Who is he trusting to recover them? Why not do it himself if these pieces are so unispar." Ethan asks.

"He has risked many lives to retrieve these fragments. He has entrusted his research and faith to procure the final piece in Trimod. It is too far east and too far away to go himself."

"Don't translate this, but I'd like to step in here and say that if someone is going to possess these fragments, I'd rather it be us," Bernard says.

"Chasing off to Trimod? You know there're likely monsters there? Big ones," Ethan protests.

"I agree with Bernard. And we're not asking you to go."

"I go? I'm not going. I'm telling you that you shouldn't go." As Ethan's temper steams, the weonslow stands and walks back to the kitchen to grab a few biscons from her cabinet. She returns and passes them out simultaneously. Ethan takes one in a huff, flabbergasted that sailing on the sea to Trimod is something anyone would seriously consider. He snaps into the biscon and bites his lip, cursing to himself.

Ethan continues, keeping the conversation between the three. "Obviously, someone is wrong here. If this friend of yours, Iahel, says we shouldn't bring the brass anywhere near Carvinga, and Cadwellion wants the opposite, we can agree that Cadwellion is the one with an ulterior motive. Why risk sailing across nowhere for a war he may or may not be starting?" Ethan implores Sanet.

Bernard suggests, "Why don't we rid ourselves of the fragments we have? We're the only ones who know we have them." Ethan says nothing.

"Iahel knows. And Logan," Sanet states, exasperated. "Look, you can't convince me that we shouldn't go after this last piece. And if we hide them, who knows what those crimson men will do to find them. They could come after you or your son. They've already tried to send us left."

"Come after me? I have nothing to do with it. If anything, they'd come after Cadwellion. And who would be shnite enough to take on a ranpart?"

"It's decided, Ethan. I hear your protests, and I approsh your sentiment, but even if Wellion doesn't trust me, I still trust him. I believe that reuniting this orb could end this battle. It seems mad to think Wellion would go through all this trouble not to want that as well."

The weonslow, having sat in quiet while Sanet and Ethan grit, reaches out, wrapping her fingers around Ethan's hand. *"I have ill news for you, Sur Mershner,"* she begins. *"If she attempts to go into that stonetin, you must be with her. It won't be as simple as the others. There are tricks inside."*

Ethan listens but doesn't translate the weonslow's warning. Bernard and Sanet wait. *"You understand us?"* The weonslow nods. *"Why would I care to do that?"* he asks her, continuing to leave Sanet and Bernard out of the conversation.

"She will be sent if she travels there on her own. I don't know anything of this other man, but it is the way of Trimod. It does not take kind to the naive. It has been foretold Sanet will be sent left in a most hideous way. And without you, Trimod may be the reason why."

Exasperated, Ethan rips away from the weonslow and walks out of the room. He turns into a hallway where he places his head on the wall and closes his eyes. *I can't go traipsing off across the sea.* He hates the sea. And the idea of monstrous freks. He also hates the idea of leaving Mercet. *But Sanet being sent?* The woman who only desires to know who she is. And what if he's sent left? How would Undess feel? How would Mercet? And why is Sanet so adamant on going? Trying to prove herself. It was a flam idea. This whole shnite plan is flam. Chasing after foretales and orbs. It's only children's tricks and lies.

Sanet steps up behind him and puts her hand on his shoulder. "What's wrong?" Ethan looks up.

"She says I have to go. That without me, you'd be sent left." He pauses. Sanet has no answer. Or easy response. He continues. "I don't trust Cadwellion. And you don't trust these crimson men. And I don't think either of us can trust that woman or midfrek in there."

"Ethan. We should be the ones who recover these pieces. When we have them, we have the control. It's our choice. Isn't that why you slid me that key? If we have them, we can do whatever we want. We can toss them into the sea and just let the whole thing fade away. Maybe it is all ranpart tricks. But, if it's not. And Cadwellion *is* doing good. Then we're helping him save the Land. We're preventing war. We can't let anyone else get them. Because you're right. We can't trust anyone else." Sanet holds Ethan by the shoulders.

"I wish I knew the right choice."

"I know you don't believe these things, but 'the Land sets its course, and we are merely its passengers. Lincoln guides our path, on Land. And upon our leavings left, let Them guide us home.'"

"Now see here, Undess. While that's a sweet sentiment, it's as flat as saying Dustians." Ethan smirks.

Sanet shrugs him off. "I believe in doing what's right. I was brought into this without my say. I was woken up without a memory. All I know is what I've been told and taught over these past seven years. What happened has to mean something. It must. Bodies don't just wake up without a past for nothing."

Ethan waits. A woman without a past but with eyes on a hopeful, greater future. If only he could feel that way. *It is foretold she will be sent left.* "I can't let you go alone. If you're there and get sent, I'd never appize that."

Sanet smiles. "You've always hated the sea."

"And freks," Ethan adds. "I hate the freks. Even hate cogs. Except Captain Reset—"

Sanet pushes her finger to his lip. "I'm sure I've seen the worst of them, and I'm still here."

"I'd bargain you haven't."

"Then how exciting it is." She smiles.

Ethan shivers at the thought.

Chapter Twenty-Five

ACROSS THE SANDS OF YIKSHIR

*E*than arrives back at his haynest where he dismisses the guard keeping watch over his son. The guard returns to the carriage, which departs with Sanet and Bernard on their lengthy trip back to Cadwellion's stonetin. As the carriage disappears over a misty crest, the last words of the weonslow repeat in Ethan's head, making for a confusing and bizarre departure that he shrugs off for other concerns. At the minor, that's sleep.

Stepping up to the door, he goes to open it, but it's locked. Frustrated, he pulls his key from his jacket and tries the lock. It turns but when he attempts to open the door he finds it's barred shut by a large piece of furniture pushed in the way. Angry and exhausted, Ethan begins to knock loudly on the door. "Undess, this is ridiculous. Open the door."

There's no answer. He bangs louder. More silence.

After a major, a shadow appears at the door. Mercet. Ethan kneels to his level, just barely able to see his face through the crack. "What did your mother do?"

"She doesn't want you to come inside," Mercet whispers.

"She's being pretty flam right now."

"I know."

"Can you help me out?"

A minor passes. "Maybe you shouldn't come inside?" Mercet says as quietly as he's able.

"What?"

"You make her angry. She's not nice when you're around."

Ethan hurts. *Amil.* "I don't mean to make her that way, Mercet."

"I know, but she said she's not happy."

"Are you not happy?" Ethan asks, afraid.

"A little."

His heart drops. He had thought all along that his relationship with Mercet was stronger, even knowing how much Mercet hated when he and Undess fought.

"Maybe it would be better if you weren't here for a while," Mercet murmurs.

"Mercet, I'm your father."

The boy's eyes start to well. "I don't know, Daddy. I don't like seeing her sad."

Ethan wants to answer, but all he really wants at the minor is to hug his son. To squeeze out the fear and sadness inside him. He reaches through the crack in the doorway, but his hand is only able to wipe Mercet's cheek, wet with tears.

"Single souls, my son."

"I know, Dad."

Mercet smiles for a minor before turning away and disappearing into the darkness. Ethan sits back on the porch floor. Alone. He returns his head to hands. And cries.

He has tried to be a kind and understanding father. The thought of traveling makes him feel small and insignificant in this major, even as the Land swells with the scent of war. Even as the Land calls upon him to save it from tumbling into chaos. He would forgo the whole affair for a minor hug with his sons.

Over the night, Ethan wanders the streets of Salsman. The city itself is of medium size, not as big as Philsburg in the west or Porsans in the north, but respectable. The defining factor of Yikshir cities is an ever-present layer of red dirt over the windows and walls and roads. For a time, Ethan follows a set of footprints, wondering who they might belong to. *What troubles or joys did they have on this eve?*

For a long while, Ethan has led a normal life. He labors and has a haynest. He has his wife and child, but when his first was sent left, it had upended their natural trajectory. When they chose Mercet a year later, it only exacerbated the divide between him and Undess. He has enjoyed his labor with Ranpart Cadwellion, who often returned from his travels with many striking and wild objects. The Land outside of Salsman is beyond Ethan's comprehension. After leaving Quemon, Ethan lived squarely between home and Cadwellion's stonetin, traveling only the sand seas to neighboring cities. Once he was on a kleep for a small and much needed respite, but the trip was shortened after ferocious storms nearly shattered it. Coupled with his fears of the deep sea and monstrous freks, the whole trip ahead amounted to nothing more than a constant source of anxiety and panic. Ethan was a thinker, not a traveler.

The long night passes as Ethan's thoughts drift across his past, his future, and the present. Before long, the sun peeks over the crest, and he can see that the stonetin is only a mile away. He approaches it and is greeted by the entrance guards, who take him in, escorting him to his sleeping room. It's not long before Ethan falls into a kiptaleless sleep.

❖ ❖ ❖

A knock wakes him. As his eyes flutter open, Sanet walks in with a round of mornmeal. "Late night?" she says as she sets the tray down.

Ethan props himself up and quickly grabs for a coffee stick. The hot food goes down well and comforts what feels like a drinkless hangover. "A terrible night." He takes another bite.

"Bernard and I were going to spend the morn packing and resupplying before heading out. You don't have to go. I know that weonslow believes you should, but I know we'll be fine."

Ethan's thoughts return to Mercet, and how Undess had turned their son against him. "I don't know what to do."

"If things aren't going well at haynest, perhaps some time away would make it better?" Sanet suggests.

The idea, as simple as it is, is true. "I still hate the sea." Ethan smirks.

Sanet stands. "Well, I'll have the guard put together a bag for you just in case."

She leaves and Ethan looks around the room. Sparse and cool. Stone brick walls twenty feet high. Red and orange tapestries outlining the city of Salsman. He leaves bed and looks out the tall, thin windows and across the yard below. The green grass grows in opposition to the red sands outside the stonetin. Mercet wanders into his mind again, and Ethan wants to wallow. Like Undess . . .

He stops himself. He shakes his head and hands, waking himself up. The mood has to change. He starts to run in place. *You're young. You have much to learn, much to do. If that older guy can hang with Sanet, so can I.* Ethan knows that he has to approach these new circumstances without somberness but with excitement. There is nothing he can do at this major with his haynest life. Instead, he should put his time into his labor, into stopping whatever the crimson men had started.

He turns, still running in place, and finds Amil staring at him. "You're up in the mood, today."

Ethan stops, blushing. Amil walks over to a dresser and starts to pull out clothing.

"I'm trying."

She continues to pack as she talks. "So, you're leaving with Sanet?" A quiet concern drips across her question.

"I am." Ethan takes a deep breath. "Amil, I need to ask a favor of you. Something, you can't share with anyone else."

"Of course." She turns, her face bright and young and eager.

"There's something stirring. And I'm not sure it's real or not, but I'm afraid that Mercet could be in danger, should things escalate."

Without him saying another word, Amil walks over to him. "Mercet is in safe arms. As Rainmen watch, so shall I. My cross to you." She kisses his nose.

❖ ❖ ❖

By an hour past the full sun, the three are settled into a carriage. They decide to head toward the northern gates and hire a horsal to travel across the wavering sands to the ports in the city of Porsans. There they hope to secure a kleep to sail east across the Merurro Sea and to the island state of Trimod. After waving their goodbyes to the guards, who seem more saddened by Sanet's departure than by Ethan's, they set off.

At the gates, Ethan rents a larger horsal to carry not only the three of them but also their equipment and luggage for the few weeks' journey at sea. This frek looks friendly enough, giving them plenty of room to lie down for rest. The journey to Porsans, which isn't more than a full day and full night's ride, should pass without a stop.

The horsal plods down the winding switchback of the redrock, and after an hour's time, the gang hits the sand of the coast. Sitting under a comfortable shade, Ethan looks back at the city above and toward Cadwellion's stonetin, which stands with an unnerving defiance against battered rock walls. Bernard's little frek, Brute, bounces around and on occasion decides to sit on Ethan's lap. Brute is an unusual frek. It seems to have a personality beyond the loyal, mindless following of colored cogs.

"Seems to like you," Bernard states. Ethan looks down and pets the creshwillow, who purrs on his lap.

Salsman becomes a small speck in the distant south when the sun sets against the sand's crest to the west. With the moon a slim crescent, the sand turns black in shadow, and high above an endless, white-dotted blanket develops. With Ethan's every passing glance, more and more stars appear in the night sky. As he listens to Sanet and Bernard converse about someone curamed Sur Taron and erupt into titters, Ethan is rocked off to sleep with the aid of the softly blowing breeze and swaying steps of the quiet horsal.

"Wake up."

Sanet shakes Ethan. He opens his eyes and sees her and Bernard both standing. The horsal has stopped. In the distance, three getwishes head toward them. The dark night makes it difficult to discern who's riding, but their trajectory appears to be straight for them.

"Who are they?"

"Crimson men, if I had to guess," Bernard answers.

Ethan sits up completely at the answer. He's never been in a fight before. When Mercet would come home with a blue eye or bruise, Ethan's response was to "always inform the adults," advice he's sure has led to even further humiliations.

The three riders grow closer as Sanet raises her crossbow and Bernard his rifle. Ethan remembers when Sanet first trained with the guards to use a crossbow. How quickly she excelled at it, how impressive she was. *As if she had done it before.*

"Stop there," Bernard calls out.

The three shadowed figures slow to a stop a hundred strides away. The one in the middle screams across the sands, "Give us the brass and we'll leave you wisnok."

Ethan's heart skips. *I've barely left the city, and I'm already being sent.*

"Pretty sure you could ask your compatriots if they're wisnok," Sanet retorts.

"Don't antagonize them," Ethan pleads in a whisper.

At this, the three whip the reins of their getwishes and plod forward again. Steady. Cautious.

"We said don't move," Sanet calls out.

Steady. Cautious.

Bernard takes a step and cocks his rifle exaggeratedly. Ethan's eyes vault between the three men and Sanet and Bernard. Steady. Cautious. As they get closer still, he catches the crimson men raising their weapons.

"Get down."

The voice comes from Sanet, who's shifted her weight and swung her bow toward Ethan. Without hesitation, Ethan cowers and hears the *shunk* of her bolt crossing over him. He turns to see a fourth crimson man shot, a flaming bolt flickering from his chest, and sprawled across the sands. Gunshots ring out, and the horsal rears on its side, tossing the three and all their luggage to the ground. Bernard grabs Ethan, pulling him with ease out of gun range and behind the overturned, sent horsal. *Shnite, he's strong.*

"Come out, you bastards!" one of them shouts.

Sanet responds by standing and unloading another bolt, which is followed by a scream. "One left," she says.

"Don't send them all," Ethan stammers. "They have information."

Bernard holds his gun with a nervous shake. He takes a breath, then screams across the horsal at the remaining man. "No more shooting. Let's talk." The man answers by shooting the horsal with a reverberating thud. Bernard turns. "Not sure he's going to talk."

Ethan tries shouting. "Look, we have two pieces. How about we give you one of them? You're not leaving empty-handed . . ."

As the flam words pour out, Ethan quiets Bernard's and Sanet's confused faces. "I'm just keeping him talking," he whispers.

"Kind offer. But I'd just as well have both," the man calls out.

"Let's not send each other left out here in the sands. Why don't we discuss this calmly?" Ethan calls out.

"Oh, shut your face." The man shoots twice more, the weapon's report followed by the one-two thud at their backs.

"He's out."

Bernard looks to Sanet, who confirms. In step, they both spin from cover and shoot. The man shrieks. Alone behind the horsal, Ethan peers around the corner before stepping out to see the last crimson man on the sand holding his knee and bleeding out.

Sanet moves toward him, reassuring, "You'll be wisnok, don't piss in the mud." The man spits up at her. Sanet wipes her face. "You're all raised in sweetening, I gather?"

Ethan and Bernard join her. The man, defeated, turns his head away as Sanet begins treating his wound. Ethan turns and searches the overturned luggage to find wraps for the man's leg. As he does, he notices each of the mounts has been sent. *I guess we're walking.*

Returning, Ethan speaks to the man. "The morrow's going to be fun. Approsh to you."

The man doesn't answer and instead closes his eyes as Sanet squeezes his wound. *Maybe not that hard, Sanet.* With little else to say, Ethan joins Bernard, who's gathering the luggage and piling it all together. He then pulls cans of food from a bag and transfers them into his own rucksack. "We'll need to sort through what we can carry. We should continue traveling tonight and then find shelter in the morn. That summer sun won't be kind in these sands."

"Agreed," Ethan says, dropping a particularly heavy case onto the larger pile. "I should also give my approsh for pulling me to cover."

Bernard shrugs. "Anytime, friend."

"You've got some pull." Ethan nods to Bernard's mitts.

"Oh well, another long story," he says, flexing his fingers.

❖❖❖

With their bags organized and the man bandaged, they position him against the horsal. "I think it's time we get to know each other," Ethan starts.

"Suck my cog's cock." His face is set in defiance.

Sanet pushes in. "Why are you here? Who told you about us? About the brass?"

The man hesitates for a minor before she kicks him in his bandage. He hunches over and screams, "What the shnite, woman?"

"Who told you we had brass?" Ethan doubles.

Bernard stands back smoking green, with Brute on his shoulder.

The man snarls before answering. "We received an urgent tap you were leaving Salsman."

"From who?"

"They don't tell us who. It's only a tap."

"Where's the tap?"

The man doesn't answer. Sanet begins to riffle through his clothes.

"Careful woman, you might turn me up." He smirks.

Sanet, currently digging through his pants pocket, grabs ahold of something and pulls, causing him to clench his teeth and groan.

Ethan continues, "Come on, you can't be that dull."

Sanet lets go and searches him further before pulling a piece of paper from his shirt pocket. She reads it and after a minor looks up. "It's from Wellion."

She hands it to Ethan, who reads it aloud:

Peter,

Sanet is leaving tonight escorted by my acolyte and her accomplice, a man who goes by the curam Stone Fingers—the same man who sent Franz left. She will have two pieces of brass that I wish for you to recover and return to me. It is imperative that you do not harm her. She is of great importance to me, and if she were to meet an uncertain time, I will skin you before your wife and children.

Do not disappoint.

Ranpart Cadwellion

Sanet steps backward. "How . . . why?" she stammers.

Ethan folds the letter and places it in his pocket.

Bernard tosses the cig away. "What do we do now?"

"Is there really a piece of brass in Trimod?" Ethan turns to the man they now know is Peter.

"Not for long." Peter smiles.

"He can't do much without the pieces we have," Bernard says. "Why don't we just leave the state with them? Go into hiding?"

Sanet acts as if dazed. "How does he know everything? He's not even here."

Ethan is eager to step in. "He doesn't know everything. What does he know? You have a son . . . but you don't? That your curam is Sanet? He's been controlling your mind for seven years."

"I'm not sure this is something we need to figure out now," Bernard interrupts. "The question is what we're going to do. We're in the middle of the sands here, and when that sun comes up, it won't be pleasant."

Ethan looks around. "I'd say we're equidistant from Salsman and Porsans. If you still think sailing to Trimod is the right decision?" he questions.

"How does he know everything?" Sanet asks again.

"He may not. That weonslow could have easily drafted a tap after our visit. Just adding Cadwellion's curam."

"You sure it's not just you?" Bernard accuses Ethan.

"Me?" Ethan looks offended. "I didn't even want to go. I don't trust that body. Everything about him reeks of betrayal."

"Well, this friend of yours seems more and more delightful." Bernard swirls his hand in the air, then lights another cig.

Sanet looks still lost in her thoughts as if working out the facts she's facing. "He's always told me that there are things that must take place to save the Land. That there is order. That he was not always right. He told me about Logan. This brass has to be important..." she continues to puzzle out the facts before them.

Peter speaks up. "Shnite your ranpart's order. The Roar is what saves the Land. That's what Franz wanted. And it's why Ranpart Cadwellion believes. He's just afraid of you . . ." Peter points to Bernard.

"Me? Because I killed one of his men?"

"Everyone knows you're a Dark Valor. That you're upsetting what's been foretold."

At this, Bernard rolls his eyes, taking a deep drag of his cig "I have ill news, friend—nothing is foretold. If Franz and his friends hadn't burned my haynest down, hadn't sent Jame, we wouldn't be bargaining right here in the middle of a proshing desert. No. It wasn't foretales. It was those fires they lit. It was their actions. Their choices." As Bernard speaks, his voice grows gruff from holding back conflicting feelings of fury and sadness.

"Everyone, let's . . . calm down. Bernard is right. We do have to decide what to do. We could die out here in that sunlight."

Bernard lets the air sit in silence a minor before speaking again. "I say we get this last piece of brass and we don't return.

We continue sailing across the Merurro. Away from Merigen altogether."

"I can't leave my son. We'll have to come back," Ethan asserts.

"And what about Logan? If Wellion wanted him in Yikshir, what's to say he won't find him west?" Sanet says.

"Logan made his decision; he chose to be on his own. If that's not what Wellion wanted, then I think that's the best thing for now," Bernard states.

While they continue to debate, Peter lunges at Bernard, attempting to knock him to the ground, his face contorted in pure hatred.

"You betrayed Franz. You betrayed the Roar!"

From below, Bernard grabs Peter by the neck and tosses him to the side like a twig, crushing his neck as he does. Peter lands motionless and sent left. "Why did you do that." Bernard screams at Peter's sent body. He falls to his knees are cries, mumbling to himself.

"I know you're not one for the plan, but having more of this brass in our possession is our only option. We can't trust anyone else with it." Sanet says to Ethan as she kneels next to Bernard. "Are you wisnok?" Bernard doesn't answer.

Ethan, resigned and staring at the brave bodies before him, stands up straight. "Then let's untell a ranpart's ridiculous foretales, shall we?" Sanet looks up and nods in approval.

Lincoln help us.

Chapter Twenty-Six
JOHAN'S BLONDE SEA HORSAL

*B*ernard, burying his emotions, attempts to keep the group moving throughout the night but Ethan and Sanet lag behind. He reminds them on a constant loop that he recently turned fifty and there is no excuse for being tired.

"Eighteen hours I hunted that neox," he calls back to them as they shuffle their feet in the sand. "And you chased that frek for months!" Looking directly at Sanet, who waves him off, shuffling through the sand. But as the sky shifts from dark, speckled night to a cog-fur pink, their pace quickens with the threat of heat outweighing their exhaustion.

"Is this what it's like to trek with the two of you?" Ethan shouts between deep breaths. "Because I've already been nearly sent left and we haven't even left the sands. The sea is where I'm supposed to be the most afraid."

Bernard's hand, mimicking Sanet's, waves out in the air with a huff and dismissal.

They continue to trudge through the sands as dirt grinds on their ankles and their muscles cramp from hours upon hours spent on the unstable, uneven land beneath them. The sun, rising ahead and to the east, continues to threaten a long day ahead. Soon Bernard removes his leather jacket and wraps it around his waist. Brute has hidden himself within Bernard's rucksack since the previous night. Shortly after Bernard, Sanet follows suit and removes her green hood.

As the morn sun leaves crest, the day's heat intensifies, and Bernard loses his shirt altogether. Sanet strips to her unders. Ethan hesitates for a major but loses the battle of shame over sweat. Besides Undess, not many people have seen Ethan without his shirt. Bernard's muscular frame and tan skin radiate a controlled masculinity, while Sanet's athletic build stands with confidence and beauty. In comparison, Ethan's soft and pudgy pale skin seem to almost weigh him down. It is not just his weight that causes his reluctance to strip in front of others but a large pasemark that slashes across his back and stomach. The orange mark, with no distinctive shape, nothing exotic to note other than highlighting his abnormality, marks him with a badge of humiliation. Taking off his shirt, Ethan steps back to keep Bernard and Sanet in front of him. He holds the shirt in his hand, ready to slip it back on as soon as Porsans comes to view.

At nearly full sun, the three have begun to cover themselves in a white oilment, Bernard helping Sanet and Sanet helping him in return. Ethan continues to hold back and rubs his own arms and chest. Bernard turns to him, causing Ethan to suck in his stomach. Bernard grins as he rubs a bit of oilment on his own hands.

"Let me get your back, friend."

Ethan remains quiet as Bernard steps behind him, rubbing his back. Bernard's touch is firm and coarse, his stone fingers felt through the thin brown leather mitts.

"Let me know if I'm too rough," Bernard says as he continues to slather Ethan's back.

"I guess I understand the curam Stone Fingers," Ethan jests, attempting to hide the red blush and humiliation as Bernard's hard touch bores into him.

Bernard finishes up and grabs one of the rucksacks. "Still not used to it, but they're becoming a part of me, I guess." He flexes his fingers and continues forth.

Sanet grabs her own bag and they continue. The day passes, and eventually, there in the distance lies Porsans. The three of them dress again, to Ethan's relief. *Clothes are the skins of whom we wish we were.*

Unlike many of the other cities in Yikshir Sands, Porsans acts as a sizable port city, a trading community for some of the far north states and across the sea. Though redrocks grow around Porsans, the city itself is built on the coast. As they trek closer, more and more bodies come into view. Some leave the city, while others enter through tall white-and-red-stained gate walls. Like Salsman, the city is surrounded by a single rock wall, guarded and watched.

A drum of horsals passes them as they cross into the open gates. Several guards walk the perimeter.

"Does Porsans have its own ranpart?" Bernard asks.

"I think there's a council here. The bigger cities usually have elected officials," Ethan answers. "The docks are over there. Hopefully, we'll be able to find someone willing to sail to Trimod."

Porsans may be at sea level, but it does not lack for high views. Many of the buildings stand stories high. Apartments reach several hundred measures upward, some more dilapidated than others. The sea breeze flows around them while tumbling trash, and wild cogs roam in the hustle and commotion of the streets. The city bustles with life: vendors, shoppers, passersby; bits of yelling; arguments; soft conversations and laughter.

Kleeps of all sizes are tied at the docks. Sailors and captains hike up and down ramps, loading and unloading. Ethan guides them along as they begin to ask around if anyone might be interested in sailing east, but the day nearly ends without an offer to take them, as most scoff at the destination. *No one goes to Trimod.*

Over duskmeal, as the mood remains soured, a handsome body walks over to them. Tall, blond, and with a roguish smile, the man speaks directly to Sanet. "I hear you're headed to Trimod?"

"We are." Sanet smiles back.

"I can get you there. For a price, of course." The man smirks.

"We offer five hundred up front with five hundred on the return," Ethan states.

The man sits down at the table. "Quite the price. Which begs me to ask what's so special about an abandoned state?"

"Not answering that is part of the price, I'm afraid." Sanet smiles again, placing her hand on the man's shoulder, rubbing her thumb softly near his neck.

He smirks again and leans back, putting his hands on the back of his head. "Bargain, then. When are we leaving?"

"When are you ready?" Ethan sits up, surprised by the man's brazenness. *Or perhaps it's a lack of poise with Sanet.*

"On the morrow. I need to settle a few things." He reaches out his hand to Sanet. "Johan's my curam."

Sanet clasps his hand to shake, but he pulls her in to kiss the back of her hand, then stands and nods to the others, tipping an invisible cap. "Good eve." He leaves.

"Well, I guess we could have had an actual decomp for captain," Bernard comments in shade.

Sanet laughs. "Oh, he'll be a good little cog. It wasn't like we were in store for a hero of the Land."

Ethan is unimpressed. "Truth told, I don't care who takes us. My only hope is calm seas."

❖ ❖ ❖

Ethan and Sanet vomit off the side of the small kleep, christened the *Blonde Sea Horsal*, which bobs up and down and up and down against the choppy sea.

Ethan holds on to the edge, white knuckled as he upchucks for the fifth time. "Lincoln, what have I done?"

Sanet turns to him, patting him on his back. She attempts to say something but retches herself. They both stumble backward and look toward Johan, who's currently at the wheel, steering through the small but buoyant waves. "Those are your biggest smiles yet," he yells across the deck, the odious phrase he's adopted for their sickness.

Ethan waves him off as they enter the main cabin. Bernard and Brute are relaxed on a couch, Brute lying on Bernard's chest as he reads a novit.

Bernard sits up. "Friends, have a bit of green. Relax." Another wave hits against the kleep, and they're tossed across the room. Bernard catches Ethan. "Careful, friend."

"Approsh, Bernard. How are you not—" Ethan's barely able to speak.

"Guess, I have a better constitution. You both should be fine after a few days." The kleep continues to rock up and down. Up and down. Up and down.

Up.

And down.

Days pass before Sanet can keep down food and her color returns to normal. Ethan, on the other hand, can't seem to swallow without it coming back up. "Lincoln, I hate the sea." He spends most of the days on the floor of the cabin, sharing handholding with Sanet and Bernard. Brute at times attempts to sleep next to Ethan, but the effort ends after Ethan hurls all over the mortified frek.

The seas calm after a week of sailing, and the kleep subsides to a soft rocking. Ethan finds that he can breathe to the motion of the sea. Deep breath in and up, deep breath out and down. The rhythm works, and eventually the whole Land stops spinning.

"I think I'm nearing wisnok," Ethan states over duskmeal, but the brief look at food causes his stomach to tumble.

Appealing to Ethan's essential needs, Bernard pushes over a mug. "At least drink some water, Ethan."

"Approsh."

On the deck, the sea and sky are clear across the crest. No Land or frek in sight. "Still on course?" Sanet asks, walking up to Johan.

He nods. Ethan watches as Sanet laughs and giggles with him, and after he grins wider than any man should, Ethan thinks ill of his intents. *That man is as fake as a ranpart's tricks.*

Over the next few days, Ethan's stomach returns. And for the first time, he can look out and admire the might and beauty of the sea. In every direction, an endless view of white-capped waters. Johan, manning the small kleep himself, tells them that, now that everyone can enjoy it, he's making them his famous hash duskmeal.

Throughout the day, he passes around some home-brewed sea ale. "It makes the hash taste better," he says with every given shot.

Sitting on the deck, lying in the sun, the breeze floating through the air, Ethan is peaceful. *I wish Mercet could have come. He would have loved this.* On the bow of the kleep, Bernard looks out to sea, something of a morn ritual for him. Ethan walks over.

Standing next to him and resting his elbows, Ethan watches off the crest. To the east, the sun has fully risen. Above, a doubled sail flaps in the wind. In the waters below swim a school of laughing earniks, friendly and colorful freks who some believe come from the souls of the drowned. They're mainly distinguished, however, by the noises they make, which sound a bit like gurgled laughter.

"How long have they been leading the kleep?"

"Seems like a few days. Unless these are a different school than the first ones I saw," Bernard answers, pulling out another green cig.

"You sure smoke a lot."

"It calms me."

"You've said." Ethan turns around, looking across the main deck. Johan at the wheel, drinking morn coffee. "You know, now that we're away from the threat of the crimson and before we reach whatever's out there," he points into the distance, "this is paradimo. If Mercet were here, it would be perfect."

"I feel the same about Jame," Bernard says with a whisper and more to the sea than to Ethan.

To that, Ethan has little to say. He still has Mercet to go home to. And even though things aren't the best between them, at least he has a chance to fix it. Without knowing much about Bernard or his past, he does feel a deep sympathy for him. They stand quietly for the rest of the morn with the rhythmic splash and swim of the laughing earniks echoing below them.

By duskmeal, the four bodies are jarent, laughing and talking decibels too loud. Ethan's heart suddenly feels . . . free. At one point, he leaves for the main cabin and screams out into the night and the half-moon twinkling off the sea's waters. He returns to the other three in silence, and they watch him for a minor. Feeling sheepish and flam, he slinks back into his seat before Sanet bursts into a laugh, followed quickly by the others. Ethan realizes he's safe here. Without judgment. These bodies are kind and happy, to a point, and he is wanted. Like with Amil. Ethan realizes he just misses the goodness in bodies.

With this sudden outburst of kindness, he reaches out to kiss Sanet, whose eyes widen in a smile.

"Ethan, you're so friendly when you're tipst," she says, and Ethan laughs.

"No singles for me?" Bernard calls out.

"Oh, Lincoln, why not." Ethan leans in and kisses Bernard, whose scruffy beard is an odd and new sensation for him.

Bernard reaches around and holds Ethan's head for a major before they stop. Johan and Sanet clap and cheer. Johan then goes in for a kiss with Sanet, who stops him, finger to his lips.

"Oh, so I'm the one who's left cold?" Johan whines.

Ethan speaks up. "Prosh it, bring it in." He stands, leaning across the table hands outstretched.

"No desires. I'll stick to the lady in kind over here."

"Frigid, Sur. Make a man feel real unispar." Ethan sits back down in a bloated huff.

At that, Johan stands up to retrieve the meal and serves Ethan first, then Bernard, then himself. He starts to move away when Sanet rolls her eyes.

"You're a child, aren't you?"

"Apory, sur, I didn't see you there behind that cold, frigid heart."

He serves her the smallest of portions. Bernard and Ethan giggle.

"Serve me well now, Captain Johan, and perhaps you'll get more than a kiss." Before she finishes the sentence, Johan plops the rest of the hash onto her round, splashing it on everyone, which only brings on more laughter.

The meal is delicious, though Sanet comments that the day's worth of sea ale was the best ingredient. Johan doesn't protest. Afterward, Ethan gathers the rounds and prongs to wash while Sanet mentions how full she is and starts to waddle out of the cabin. Johan follows her, reminding her of the cross she's made. She hits him playfully as their conversation leaves the room. Bernard helps Ethan finish, and they stand foot to foot while they clean dishes.

The kleep seems to be rocking a bit more, and suddenly, Ethan's stomach starts to turn. "I think the sea ale's coming back."

Bernard catches him as he stumbles to the floor, laying him on his back. He reaches over for a pillow off the bench and places it under Ethan's head.

"Perhaps you should rest for the night," Bernard suggests.

Ethan smiles. "Approsh, Undess." With closed, concentrated eyes, he pats Bernard on his beard. "Oh, Undess, you need a razor."

❖ ❖ ❖

Ethan staggers out of the main cabin the next morn, and he has to shield his eyes from the bright sunshine. They adjust, and he sees a shirtless Bernard diving off the port rail and into the waters below. Still waking up, he stumbles forward in shock only to find Sanet and Johan are already swimming with a school of earniks. Sanet screams as one passes between her legs. She hoots and dips under the water as the earniks pop in and out in fits of laughing babel.

Bernard waves. "Come in, Ethan."

The sea looks dangerous. "How deep is it?" Ethan asks.

Johan looks down. "Thousand measures? Can't you swim?"

"I can swim." *I can, can't I?* He doesn't remember exactly when he was last in the water—especially water that runs deep enough to swallow a mountain.

"Then jump in. You'll never get a time like this again."

He watches the three, all eyes on him. At this point, there is no way he can back down.

"Fine. Fine."

Ethan steps back as the others cheer and begin calling out his curam. *What flamboy am I to jump into the sea? If Undess could see me now.* He removes his shirt. Shame, once again, ignored. *Mercet would have already been in there.* With a deep breath, he starts to run, and at the last minor, he jumps in the air but slips, knocking his knee into the side of the kleep. He tumbles toward the water, hearing the "oh!" and "ah!" from the others.

He splashes in headfirst, disoriented, bubbles and shapes zipping past him. After a major something pulls him above water, and he takes his first breath.

Bernard holds him up. "That was incredible to see, Sur Mershner. Just unbelievable."

Johan claims, "You could be a champion with that dive."

"The sincerest of approsh, Captain."

Bernard looks to him. "You wisnok, friend?"

"Just hit my knee. I'll be fine."

At this, Bernard lets go and swims a stride away.

"I'm in the sea. Here I am. Swimming"—an earnik floats past him, rubbing its smooth skin against his—"holy shnite, what was that?"

The earnik peeks above water and laughs. Ethan splashes at it, and it pops back underwater. He then dips his own head under and swims down. The sea is clear and aqua green. A beam of sunshine angles down into the darkest reaches of the water. Swimming in and through it are dozens of laughing earniks, whisking by in all directions. They're laughing a muffled echo underwater. It is a sight both wholly frightening and entirely beautiful.

Returning to the main deck, Johan adjusts course, setting the sails. "We should be reaching Trimod by dusk," he informs them.

Ethan takes pause at the reminder. The whole purpose of the trip—and the dangers that await them—had left him. As had the war brimming in Carvinga. Ranpart Cadwellion. The brass orb. The crimson men. He looks ahead, and in an outlying distance, he sees a darkened cloud. As the day goes along, the clouds blacken, and the waters begin to ruffle with a return of whitecaps.

"Gents, be ready for a bit of a rough sea," Johan informs the gang, pointing ahead. Looking forward, he notes a strange blue-and-red glow come into view. Over the side, the school of earniks has long since disappeared.

Though the sun still has an hour before setting, it's blocked completely by storm clouds. Lightning flashes and rain begins to pour. The kleep bobs up and down, Johan using the whole of his strength at the wheel to keep on course. Squalls of wind send waves crashing onto the main deck. And then, in random views, minuscule archipelago islands, no more than two hundred strides in length, poke out of the waters like tiny fingers, causing Johan to swerve and weave around them, timing it with the waves.

Though Johan is a crass body, his sailing skills are on full display. He bellows out commands. "You'll need to push off this coming rock, Stone Fingers," he yells to Bernard.

Bernard leans over the side, held by Sanet and Ethan, as a giant rock comes at them full speed, and with an ease coupled with a struggled grunt, he pushes off it.

"Good show, old man."

Thunder booms around them through the red-and-blue glow. The kleep creaks. Above them, the mast swings and sails luff wildly in the wind and rain. The deck floors are slick with water, forcing the three to hold on to various rails and cleats.

"There, up ahead!" Sanet yells to Johan.

Ethan sees the enormous island, its size hidden in the mists, the murky storm, and black clouds. As lightning strikes, a giant mountain can be seen, perhaps once a volcak.

Johan steers the kleep through a few more small island rocks before the sea clears up. Lightning and thunder boom out again, increasing with every passing minor. The wind is constant at this point. Ethan and the others are soaked from head to toe from a steady barrage of waves crashing tens of feet above them.

And then, as if they've passed an invisible wall, the storm lets up. The winds ceases instantaneously, and the waves, though still white-capped, begin to calm. The mist remains in thin tufted lines. Behind them, the storm continues, but in front, the island sits in wait.

The odd glow, in and around the island, has no origin. It floats in the air like ribbons of mist. Johan guides the kleep to shore, setting anchor just as the beach comes into view. "Won't be able to get any closer."

"Looks shallow enough here," Sanet suggests, looking overboard.

She jumps over the side, climbs down a rope ladder, and hops into the water, which at this point is about chest deep. Bernard exits next after tossing the single rucksack they packed for their trip into Trimod to Sanet. She holds it above her head while Bernard hops in. Ethan and Johan follow.

"You don't have to come with us onto the island, Johan," Ethan states.

"Oh, I'll be seeing what's so unispar about your little trip."

Ethan exchanges looks with Sanet, but the debate is settled. And with that, they trek through the waters and toward the mysterious island state.

Chapter Twenty-Seven

IN THE JUNGLE OF TRIMOD

*T*he gang decides to camp on the beach for the night to dry out and be wholly rested before the trek into Trimod. The storm circling Trimod is unusual, clear as night, then as rough and tempestuous as a tormisand. Ethan tries to rest and close his eyes, but panic sets in. *What lies in wait in there?*

The next morn, they pack up camp and head inward. Ahead of them lies a thick, damp jungle, the leaves glistening in humid air. A constant airstream tickles the trees and wiggles their branches and leaves. With no visible trail, they take a path least covered by branch and trunk.

The inside of the jungle calls out in a cacophony of hoots and hollers, both distant and straight above them. They hear the songs of exotic jarjers and the reverberating howling of keymos, furry eight-armed freks that swing and hang on branches. They use webbing from their limbs to stick to and climb the trees and occasionally to catch smaller prey. Light cuts through the jungle and countless trees and branches, still colored by the ever-present wisps of red and blue.

"Where should we even look?" Bernard asks.

"Because this is a smaller state, luckily it's only about a two-day hike across. That said, I assume we start in on one of the larger villages near that mountain," Ethan responds.

"Are we sure that everyone here was sent left?"

"Other bodies have explored this state, but they only found the remains of buildings and . . ." Ethan trails off.

They continue, occasionally hacking through a bushel of leaves or a small trunk in the way. It's then that a bright-yellow light illuminates the entire jungle all around them as if someone has shone a giant neonlight from above. They look upward to witness a long and slithering frek floating by in the canopy. Its stomach, facing the Land, bursts with bright yellow.

Ethan falls backward in fright. "Wha . . . what is that?"

The frek continues to worm along, its yellow light fading as it floats away. Shadows move in an upward motion before they return to the usual darkness of the jungle.

Bernard steps forward and gives Ethan a hand as he stands up. "I've never seen such a thing. I don't even know how something like that works."

Ethan brushes himself off. "Getting to be a habit of yours, always picking me up."

"Don't mention it," Bernard says, waving his hand. "So, friends, I think we should follow that thing."

"Follow it?" Ethan asks fearfully.

"It's bound to be near something. I can't imagine it roams an empty jungle. What does it eat?" Bernard answers.

"I'm not interested in learning that," Johan states.

They continue forth, chopping leaves and stomping through mud. Occasionally, they find themselves in a clearing and eventually come across a brightly lit circle of flowers and color. They cross it and make their way back into the jungle. After an hour's trek, they spot a settlement. Or what's left of one. The buildings have long since been abandoned, overgrown with creepers, most without roofs. Brute takes off toward the sight. The jungle opens here to a central road that divides the buildings. The four bodies walk along to the main square spotted with simple carved rectangular columns, which at one point might have held up a larger second floor.

"Looks like this might have been a bargaining square?" Sanet says, walking through. Johan follows her after swiping away remnant drops of rain falling from an broken roof.

"Over here," Bernard shouts. They gather to the north end of the square and look to where Bernard points. "There."

On a small hill on the farthest stretch of the settlement is a small, plainly made stonetin with four towers.

"That looks like the one that was in the Tunnels," Sanet says.

"Could be the right place." Bernard smiles.

With eager energy and a destination, the gang picks up their pace just before the flying yellow frek again lights their path. They look upward as the worm-like frek, massive in size, ten feet wide and hundreds of strides long, wiggles along in the air above. The shadows beneath them and across the buildings move back and forth as it glides through the air.

"Let's keep out of sight of that thing," Ethan suggests.

The others agree and move against the buildings and down some smaller alleyways. The frek floats along and turns, going back toward the square behind them. Bernard waves them forward.

The stonetin ahead is perhaps a third of the size of Cadwellion's and has writings carved into it in one of the old languages. As they step closer, Ethan recognizes some of the words from the studies he has done for the ranpart. Pulling out a bit of pad and stick, he translates.

"You can read that?" Sanet asks.

"I think so." Ethan concentrates. He finishes and reads it to the others. "'Trimod Stonetin, built 402338 for Mane George VI to house the safety and security of the Land.'"

"Three thirty-eight? That's over two hundred years. Didn't you once say the royal family ended three hundred ago?" Sanet asks.

"They did. That's part of what Cadwellion had me researching. He believed that after Niance rebelled against the

Lion, the family disbanded and went into hiding in various states. No one has heard from any of them. But, yes, that was in two fifty-two. Mane George was maybe fifteen at the time, so it would be unlikely that he would have lived to see this built after a hundred years."

"Maybe they started to build it after his sending or something?" Bernard suggests.

"Perhaps." Ethan looks closer at the walls. "The other stonetin, with the brass, did it have writings, like this one?"

"I believe so, yes, but I can't say it was the same."

"The Niance rebellion started after the Lion was persuaded by a ranpart who encouraged them to debit the underbodies to finance the ranpart's various researches. Of course, the bodies of Niance did not take kindly to the idea, feeling oppressed by the Lion, so they rebelled against them and sent many of the royal family left. It's unclear who escaped in all of it. And who survived. What that ranpart was studying was what Cadwellion wanted to figure out."

"Seems flam to hire a bunch of coinhires to recover what's clearly something very valuable," Bernard states, his vehemence for Cadwellion continuing to grow since the reading of the tap back in Yikshir.

"True. We don't really know his motives," Ethan doubles again. "I think his concern is getting these fragments no matter what. If you throw enough bodies at the problem, it's sure to be accomplished."

"You think this royal family back then was looking for the orb?" Bernard asks.

"I think they already had the brass orb, and they decided after the rebellion that it would be best kept out of any underbodies' hands. I can't imagine they weren't the ones who broke the orb into its seven pieces and had these stonetins built to house them."

"Well," Johan speaks up, "if they've kept whatever this thing you're looking for locked away across sea and state, why in Dustian are you digging it up?"

"I think our hand is being forced, no? It's either Cadwellion or us," Sanet says.

"I'd rather us. Let's get inside. I'm afraid our floating friend over there will be back soon."

Bernard steps up to the door. Johan and Sanet follow. Bernard tries the door, but it doesn't budge.

"Help me out here." He motions for Johan.

Together they push with their shoulders but manage no movement of the door. Sanet and Ethan join in, and the four of them each drive on the count of three. Nothing. They look up and around. No other doors and no windows.

Ethan moves his hand along the door, which is covered in slick algae. There are small divots about halfway down.

"Looks like there's a mechanism here. Not a key per se, but something similar."

Sanet confirms what he's found. "Looks like you can press something into there to turn it."

They each dig around the door and find the divots make six concentric circles. "Must be some sort of gear."

"Where are we going to find that?" Johan says, defeated.

Ethan looks around the stonetin walls again. "There're little reliefs carved into the walls here. Maybe they have a map or direction?"

He examines them, pushing aside moss and uncovering illustrations of the settlement with a huge and looming frek battling another frek that's emerging from the water brandishing dozens of tentacles. Another relief shows the orb glowing in the first frek's eye. A third shows the settlement putting the orb pieces together. The last of the series shows a body using a big gear. The large man turning the gear is wearing what looks to be an apron.

"Looks like a smith built this mechanism. So if we can find where his shop is, there might be something to help us there." Ethan stands and looks back toward the settlement.

"Last smith we visited didn't go so well," Bernard recalls.

"I can't imagine we have to worry about meeting anyone still alive on this island."

"Besides that." Johan points to the floating frek in the far distance. They all begin descending the small hill toward the settlement.

"I think we should explore each of these old buildings. Hopefully, we can find something," Ethan suggests.

And so, the search begins. Ethan starts on the buildings farther west. Bernard follows, and Sanet and Johan commence on the east buildings. As they make their way from building to building, they avoid the yellow frek overhead, which on occasion passes by the broken windows or directly above them where the roofs are either caved in or entirely absent.

The first few buildings look like haynests, with old beds and dressers. Little ricks scamper underneath the furnishings, causing Ethan to jump more often than he thinks he should.

"Who do you think lived here?" Bernard asks, rubbing his finger across an old, faded painting. The painting depicts two people standing side by side, stoic and somber.

"If Mane George lived here, perhaps his stewards. Or guards. Acolytes?" Ethan looks around, pushing aside pieces of furniture. The yellow glow slides across the room, causing Bernard and Ethan to push against the walls.

"Do you think that thing is aggressive?"

"Not sure I want to find out. Let's head to the next building."

They continue searching building after building with no luck. Occasionally, the two shout across the road when they see Sanet and Johan through a window. "Anything?" They shake their heads in disappointment.

Farther on, Johan calls out to them, "I think there's something here."

Ethan and Bernard hurry down a staircase and out to the road. Above them and down the street the yellow frek floats around a corner and disappears. They enter a large room with a burned-out forge.

"What do you think of this?" Johan asks, pulling aside some lumber. Behind it is a giant wheel. "This could work, I think. Help me look."

It's heavy and takes Johan's and Ethan's considerable strength to take hold of it. Bernard walks over and takes one of the sides, and suddenly the wheel feels like a children's frontop.

"Quite the grip there, lad," Johan comments. "This might work, actually. Let's get this up the hill before that thing flies by again."

Walking slowly, the three friends carry it up the hill. Sanet keeps watch, having them duck off to the side whenever the frek passes over.

"I'm going to feel pretty foolish when this little frek turns out to be as friendly as Brute," Bernard states.

"Where is your creshwillow, anyway?" Ethan asks.

"Brute? Oh, he's an explorer. He'll show up before we leave. He has good sense like that."

Once they clear the buildings, the climb up the hill is the most precarious, with open air between them and the front door of the stonetin.

"We'll have to make a run for it," Sanet says. "That frek turned south, so we should have a few majors before it returns. Ready?"

The others nod and run up the hill. When they are about halfway up, the yellow glowing frek turns down the street. They continue onward as Sanet walks backward, keeping a close eye, detailing how near it is.

"Four hundred strides . . . three hundred." They're only about fifty from the door. "Two hundred."

Reaching the door, they spin around and guide the pins of the wheel into the divots dug out by Ethan. Ethan oversees the other two. "Little west. Little east."

"One hundred. I think it's seen us."

"Little more. There. Push." They do, and with a sharp *thud*, it bumps into place. "Let's turn it." The three try to turn the wheel. It doesn't move.

Sanet warns, "It's starting to glow."

Ethan turns. "Doesn't it already glow?" The frek's light is completely white at this point. Ethan shouts to the others to run.

In turn, they look toward the flying monstrosity before leaping out of its way just as a beam of light ejects from its underside. It then slithers to the ground and makes a sudden screech. They all cover their ears, falling to the ground. No discernible face to it, the frek begins to glow again and aims its front end, this time toward Ethan and Bernard, who run around the side of the stonetin. A beam of light screams past them, blasting into a tree, which topples over.

"Holy shnite, what is that thing?" Bernard yells.

Ethan shakes his head in disbelief. Its natural light moves, and they watch shadows begin to recede from around the corner.

"Looks like it's flying again."

"We're going to need to get inside. Not sure we can shoot that thing down."

They creep around the corner and see Sanet pointing her crossbow at it. She lets a flaming bolt fly, and it hits the frek straight in its stomach. The bolt evaporates on impact.

"Worth a try." Sanet shrugs, spins, and runs back around the side of the stonetin.

"Try to distract it while we turn the wheel," Ethan calls out from around the corner, hoping Sanet and Johan hear. He sees

Johan running away toward the buildings downhill. The frek sees him too and spins its head.

"That's either brave or completely flam," Ethan says to himself.

Bernard runs and grabs for the wheel. "Quick, help me turn it."

Ethan shakes himself back and follows. Sanet comes around the corner, and within a minor, they each grab ahold and spin the wheel. It budges.

"Only a bit more . . ." It shifts again, and the door slowly opens. Dust and debris rain down on them. "Keep going."

The door is now a stride open and Sanet tries to squeeze herself in. She pushes as Bernard and Ethan spin the wheel. Then, she's in. "Come on, Ethan."

Ethan squeezes in but looks back at the sound of a gunshot in time to see Johan fall to the ground. In the far distance is a trio of crimson men, one with a shotgun. The frek sees them and heads toward them. They shoot up at it but turn back in retreat. From Johan's body, a red-and-blue mist rises.

Bernard, without thinking, yanks off the wheel and tosses it in the air. It flies a distance beyond any rational comprehension and smashes into the frek, which loses balance and crashes into one of the buildings, toppling it to the ground. Bernard pushes Ethan into the stonetin and grabs the door, shutting it with massive force behind them.

"They just sent Johan left," Sanet says, wide-eyed, trying to leave.

Bernard holds her back. "We can't help him now."

"We can—"

"Sanet, he's already sent," Ethan mutters.

"Prosh those men!" Sanet yells to the closed doors.

"Well, they'll likely be sent left as well when that frek comes to. What's best is that we focus on why we're here," Ethan says, trying to calm her.

Sanet takes a deep breath and bites her lip, turning away from the others.

After a minor, Bernard says softly, "We can't help him now, Sanet. Let's get what we came for and hopefully be out of here before those crimsons figure out how to get in."

She says nothing but has ceased to struggle. Accepting what seems to be her surrender, Ethan nods and looks around into the high cathedral chamber.

"Where now?" he calls into the empty room.

Chapter Twenty-Eight

MONCH, BROON, SOUL

*T*he inside of the nave is unexpectedly well kept. The pews are lined and clean, and there's an unusual lack of dust and grime. The three walk down the aisle toward the apse.

"When we found the other fragment, it was down a staircase behind a statue like that one," Sanet says, pointing to one standing tall behind a tablatur.

"You don't chance to still have that key, do you?" Ethan hopes.

"No. Left it back in the other stonetin," Sanet says.

Ethan nods. "Well, hopefully, that won't be necessary here." In the rafters, he sees Brute and points. "How'd he get in here?"

Bernard and Sanet look up. "That's not Brute," Bernard states. The creshwillow tilts its head and hops carefully, plank to plank, downward. "You don't think that bodes for another protnuk?"

"Let's hope not," Sanet says, gripping her crossbow. She wipes her eye. "Not sure I can handle yet another of their foretales."

"It's heading in there." Bernard points as the creshwillow disappears into a small hole halfway up the western wall.

"You don't think we need to go in through there?" Ethan says, stepping closer. The hole is about two measures up and would easily need cautious lifting or a rope to reach.

"Let's look around first—before dropping into dark holes. Sure there's something here."

They wander the cathedral floor, pressing against walls, pushing and pulling dents and indents. Sanet moves behind the tablatur to the statue, this one detailing a human with four arms. She calls for the other two to help her push. The scrape of the statue's base echoes across the large cathedral, and behind it, they find a clean and unbroken wall. "Worth a try."

"Just a minor." Ethan's eye catches irregular grooves along the wall behind the statue. "Here, help me brush the dirt from these."

Eager for a lead, they dig their fingers into the lines and curves of the wall. What initially seemed like a few outlier spots and scores soon emerge as an illustration of the entire stonetin with three layers beneath it. Stepping back, Ethan takes in the whole design.

"What is it?" Bernard asks.

"It looks like the stonetin's lower levels, under this cathedral. Each one has written here what the level contains. The first, just underneath us, is for the monch. The second there is," Ethan looks closer, wiping more grime from the wall, "broon. And it appears like the final level, the lowest level, is soul. Monch. Broon. Soul."

"I don't know any of those words but soul," Sanet says.

"They're old words. For the mind, body, and soul. After the Great Migration, bodies created a universal language, Merigen, so that everyone would be able to easily communicate. The population was so small then, it wasn't that difficult. Though there are a few differences between states now, like how we bodies address each other: friends, folk, denizens, souls."

"So, what does it mean?"

"I'm sure whoever wanted to protect what lies beneath us designed this stonetin to test our worthiness. We're in for a bit of a trial it seems."

"Grats. How do we get into the first level?"

"It doesn't say."

"Perhaps we *do* go in there." Bernard points to the hole in the wall and suggests, "I could give you guys a lift?"

Ethan looks. "Maybe. We didn't see anything else?"

Bernard and Sanet shake their heads. And so they step closer to the small opening, only a half-stride wide. "You first?" Bernard looks to Sanet, who agrees.

With his back to the wall, Bernard holds out his mitted hand, and Sanet steps on. He lifts her up, barely gritting his teeth as she reaches for the hole.

"Little more." Sanet's fingers are inches away. Bernard raises her as high as he can. "Got it." She grabs on to the hole and lifts herself up and in, then reemerges. "Ethan, you're next."

Ethan steps forward as Bernard holds his mitts together. As if Ethan weighs close to nothing, Bernard lifts him upward until he grabs Sanet's hand and holds himself tightly on the ledge.

"Now take my leg," Ethan calls down to Bernard, who reaches out and proceeds to take hold.

Sanet pulls, Ethan lifts, Bernard assists, and after some considerable awkwardness, the three stumble into the small hole, grinning slightly at their improbable situation.

"We're like giant children," Bernard comments.

Inside, they scan their surroundings. The hole leads down into a small tunnel, requiring the three to crawl on hands and knees. It's dark and lit only by bits of light beaming in from the cathedral behind them. The tunnel curves to the east and downward and comes to an abrupt drop. Sanet exits first, then Ethan, followed by Bernard. After Bernard lands, he retrieves and lights a frontz torch from his rucksack.

"This is good, this is likely the first level," Ethan notes.

Sanet reaches out and squeezes his shoulder. "I guess it is good you're here."

The air is colder here. The trail leads in two directions between walls made of jagged rock and crystal. It widens most toward its eastern direction. They all agree, silently, to head that way. After a few strides, the path slopes downward, curving slightly around a gentle bend. A few majors pass, and they turn to each other, wondering if perhaps the western direction would have been a better choice, as their current track presents nothing but more rock and trail.

"Let's see it through," Bernard encourages.

Soon they arrive in a chamber with a large cylindrical stone, nearly twenty measures high, standing in wait in its middle. A singular wall emerges from either side of the chamber that blocks any attempt around. This wall rises to the ceiling, curving around the top of the rounded stone. After they step into the room, Ethan paces around in thought. Ahead, cut into the middle and bottom of the circular stone, is a hollowed-out opening, large enough for a single person to crawl through. Inside, the opening leads only a few strides inward but is otherwise meaningless. On both sides of the chamber, narrow vertical levers are built inside the outer wall.

"Bernard, can you pull on one of those?" Ethan instructs.

Bernard agrees and steps over to the west wall. He grabs the lever with two hands and pulls it downward. Nothing happens.

"Try pushing it?" Ethan suggests.

Bernard's effort shifts the lever back to its original position and beyond.

A gruff moan reverberates across the room. Sanet calls out behind them, "Sounds like something's happening inside."

She points to the small middle opening near the floor. Ethan peeks inside and watches as a back wall shifts to the east to reveal a small closet-sized opening. Sanet peers inside as well.

He looks again and says, "I don't think we should go in there. I wouldn't want us getting stuck or possibly crushed."

She waves him off. "Bernard, how far can you push it?"

Without hesitation, Bernard pushes the lever upward. In response, the entire stone column begins to rumble, dust snowing from its upper side.

Ethan begins to work out that the lever is somehow adjusting unseen walls inside the rounded stone. "It's an enigmit. Testing our monch."

Bernard stops. "That's as far as it goes."

"The panel closed off that little room, Ethan," Sanet says, her eyes still on the opening.

"Wisnok. Bernard, pull it back. Sanet, keep an eye on it and let us know when it's completely open."

Sanet holds thumb to finger as Bernard takes the lever again and begins to pull down once more, slowly and steadily. He listens to the grind inside the walls and Sanet crouches on hands and knees to watch.

"Stop," she calls out. Bernard stops. "I'm going in."

Ethan's heart skips. *What are we doing here?* With reluctance, he agrees. "Be careful."

"Always, Sur Mershner."

She crawls forward and disappears into the dark. Ethan drops to his knees to see if he can watch where she goes, but without light, there's only the echo of her voice.

"It's a small room. Not big enough for you two." After a minor, a flicker of neon illuminates the inside. "Lincoln, there's a lever here too."

Though something feels odd about the entire room, without a better lead, Ethan decides against his best judgment. "Sanet, try to push or pull it." He waits.

After a major, the stone shifts again and the hole through which Sanet crawled produces another panel that closes it off. "What happened?" she calls out, her voice muffled through the stone.

To Ethan's west, Bernard yells out, "You opened a door here. I think I can fit inside."

This news brightens Ethan's mood. *Clever contraption.*

"Should I?" Bernard waits for Ethan's approval.

Before answering, Ethan works out the logistics. "I think you'll have to. But we should be sure we do this with purpose. If we push when we're supposed to pull, we could crush each other."

Bernard nods and squeezes his way into the new opening, turning sideways and wriggling his way inside.

Ethan asks, "How are you doing, Sanet?"

"Fine. It's hot."

"Hopefully this won't take long."

Bernard, whose voice is also muffled, yells through the stone, "There's a handle here. Do I push or pull?"

Without answering, Ethan steps back, searching the chamber for something he might have missed. Looking up, he spots a set of crystalline rocks in the ceiling reflecting light from the frontz torch Bernard left. They are aligned west to east, with the first set arrowed west, then the next arrowed east. The third set points east as well, with the last pointing west once again. "Sanet, which way to did you move your lever?"

"I pulled it."

"Grats. Bernard, you have to pull the handle."

"You got it, friend."

A minor passes as the stone moves again. Sanet cries out. "The walls are closing in! Wait. Wisnok, I can step up. Keep going. Slowly."

Ethan paces back and forth, rubbing the back of his neck and feeling useless, staring at the center stone rumbling in the dark, lit only by Bernard's left-behind torch. "There's nothing here. Don't see any handles."

"Should I have pushed it?" Bernard shouts.

Ethan wanders to the other side of the chamber to find an opening in the stone's east wall. He grins to himself. "Looks like there's a third opening. I'm going in." Before doing so, he glances back up to confirm the direction he's to move the lever. *Push. Pull. Pull. Push.* Nodding to himself, he steps inside the narrow walls until he's barely able to move. He shifts himself, squeezing in his stomach and reaching forward, grasping on to an inner wall for leverage.

"How are you doing, Ethan?" Sanet calls out, her voice barely audible within the stone walls.

He grunts as he presses farther inside the room. It becomes clear that just beyond this narrow slit, the stone walls open. And in the opening, across the small room, another lever sits in wait. Using both hands now, he continues to struggle, scraping skin and clothes until he falls to the ground in a blubbering mess. *What a flab of meat I am.* He stands up, brushing his knees and crouching before a low ceiling.

"I'm in. Barely. Going to push now. You both ready?"

"Ready," Sanet responds.

"Ready for you, too." Bernard's voice is even more muted.

With that, Ethan takes hold of the lever and pushes. At his hands, he can feel the vibration of the stone walls' movement as dust showers down on him.

"There's an opening on my side now," Bernard says in an eager, excited tone.

"Me too. Going through now." Sanet pauses a minor before calling out again. "And I'm back where we started."

"I'm on the other side. There's another tunnel." Ethan turns to see a newly revealed opening. He steps over, squeezing through, to find Bernard. Brushing himself off, he yells across the stone toward Sanet. "Anything open over there? Any new doors?"

"No, it looks exactly like it did when we got in here."

"Shnite. What do you want to do?" Bernard asks.

Sanet continues, "I'll head back to keep watch. I'm sure those crimson freks will be making their way down here. I can hold them off while you two continue down."

"I don't like the idea of us splitting up," Ethan yells back.

"Unless you want to spend another hour figuring out this puzzle . . ."

He knows she's right; time isn't kind to the cause. "Don't do anything rash, Sanet," he commands.

"I'm your Green Valor. Who says I'm rash?"

Ethan smiles at her words. Bernard's face contorts at the comment.

"Long story."

"Valors." Bernard huffs with dismissal.

With Sanet gone, the two of them continue forward into the new tunnel, the mood between them turning quiet without Sanet's connective presence. The new trail descends deeper, to the west, and soon opens into a fresh chamber. Here, they find a thick rope threaded through large metal hooks that stand just under a measure high. They circle out from the center, creating an increasingly larger spiral that ends at the edge of the wall. Bernard steps in over the first line of the rope. Ethan follows.

Bernard looks around and asks, "What do you think this is all about?"

"If the first level tested our monch, I assume this chamber tests the broon."

At Ethan's assessment, Bernard nods. Ethan hops over the ropes, making his way to the center, where he finds a carved circular panel. "Looks like this may move." He brushes aside a bit of soft dirt and traces the rope to a hole in the floor. "Where does the line end?"

Bernard follows the line, stepping over the rope as it curves around and around toward the outer wall. He stops at its end and finds a large knot that is held back by a small metal loop. "It's here."

"Should we pull it?" Ethan asks.

Without answering, Bernard takes the knot in his mitts and begins to walk backward with it. His arms tense as he creeps back. The chamber groans as the rope threads through each of the metal hooks. Ethan stands away from the center panel, which begins to slide away and reveal a downward ladder. Bernard at the minor is shaking and at the end of his strength.

Ethan encourages him. "You got this."

"Not for long. Is it open?"

The panel has slid completely underside. "It's open."

"Thumb to fingers." Bernard lets go, and the panel, with the rope, slams closed.

"No, no, no!" Ethan hurries over and nearly crushes his fingers. He bangs his fist on the closed panel door. "Prosh. I think we'll have to hold the rope to keep it open."

"If that's true, you're going down there on your own."

"Maybe I can pull the rope and you can hold the panel when it opens?" Ethan suggests.

"Not to piss on the plan, but I could barely pull it. This may be something designed for three or more to pull. Many people working for the one, perhaps."

Ethan hates the words. "Absolutely not."

"Should we turn back? We could try going through that stone chamber again, return to Sanet?" Bernard attempts to soothe the growing agitation at the situation, but Ethan understands the next step.

"I'm going to have to go down there alone, aren't I?"

"What's the last level supposed to be again?"

"Soul."

"That won't be difficult, will it?"

"Who's to know?" He rubs the back of his neck and takes a deep breath.

"Are you ready?"

"No?" he says, uncertain.

"You're ready. Just remember, I'm always there to catch you."

"Not this time."

"If it's for the soul, I will be. We'll both be there."

Ethan is not one for the spiritual, for religion and things that can't be backed up with fact and research and reality. The things of the sky, the things unexplained are not things to worship but to investigate and attempt to explain. There is always an explanation.

"If the time is now."

Bernard doesn't answer but instead nods, shaking his mitts and cracking his neck. He takes hold of the knot, returned to its place against the hook. In the next minor, he pulls and the room groans once more. The panel creaks open again.

"You're going to be wisnok, Bernard?"

"Never worry about the life of an old man," Bernard growls through his teeth.

Ethan smiles to himself and waits, watching the darkness unfold before him. When the panel has slid out of the way, he climbs inside.

The hole curves almost immediately, creating a short slide that dumps him out onto a trail. From behind him comes the sound of the panel slamming shut. *Hopefully, Bernard's able to make his way back through that stone room by himself.*

Ethan moves along, pulling a neonlight from his pocket to light the way. The path broadens as it spirals downward, curving this time to the east. After a few majors, he comes to what he hopes is the last chamber.

Circular in shape, it resembles an upside-down cone, with a small sunlit opening at its tip, some two or three hundred measures up. Broken paths with open rails circle the room, spiraling upward. And in the middle of the chamber, a small boy stands, lit by the opening above. At the sight of the boy, Ethan is brought to his knees. "Kevin?"

"Hi, Daddy."

Creshwillows hang on all sides of the chamber, off the railings and along the floor. They're in various states of awake and asleep. Ethan knows it's not Kevin, his son having been sent nearly ten years ago, but the resemblance is uncanny. He appears older than when he was sent, and Ethan's instinct is to run across the room and embrace his son. To hold him again. But it isn't Kevin. It is only a trick of the eye. *A protnuk's trick.* Kevin walks out of the light and then back into it, this time as a man with wild hair and white eyes.

"You seem tense? You come all this way to harm an unarmed man?" The man raises his hands, palms out, fingers extended.

"I'm looking for something. Don't mean to be a bother," Ethan states calmly as his heart beats nearly out of his chest.

"A bit of brass, perhaps?" The wild-haired man pulls from his pocket a small flicker of brass. "I've been wondering when someone might come down here to take this from me." He holds it out as if to hand it to Ethan.

Ethan steps forward. "You're just going to give it to me? No riddles or foretales?"

"You'd like a riddle? How delightful." Almost unseen, the man retracts the brass, slipping it back into his pocket. He lifts on his toes and then his heels before walking the inner chamber in a small circle. Ethan counters the movement.

"To think. To think. How about—" He begins by speaking in the old language. *"When the orb is reunited, it fulfills the exarmadasis."*

"Exarmadasis?"

The wild-haired man sneers at Ethan. "A smart one, then." He says another riddle, this one in a language Ethan can't understand.

When he finishes, Ethan holds up his hand. "You've blocked me on that one. Haven't studied in that language. So, you've won. May I have the brass anyway? It would be much approshed."

"Did you like my yellow derange? It loves to chomp on all those pleasant souls."

Ethan recalls the flying frek with its bright-yellow light. The blue-and-red streams from Johan's sent body. "Oh yes, very much. It welcomed us well. Please . . . the brass?"

"I feel you're using me. Don't you want to be a friend, Quemon?" The man's voice deepens.

"Just hand over the brass. I've made it all the way down here, shouldn't I at least be rewarded with something?"

"Who do you think you are? Do you think you're someone worthy? Are you part of my Lion? Do you belong to my family?" He starts to circle Ethan, sniffing the air. "You don't look like what's foretold. You don't sound like my Roar." Ethan sees the man's fingers begin to lengthen. "Why did you disturb my nest?" The man's body continues to shift and grow as it squirms and wiggles around Ethan. And then he stops and continues to sniff the air. Ethan stands back.

With a deeper, menacing voice, the old man says, "You're with that Dark Valor."

"Please, I mean you no harm. I'm just here for the brass," Ethan states plainly. Calmly.

"You think he's been called by the Land?" The man's size nearly doubles, and he hunches over, crawling on long hands and feet, with two other limbs emerging from his clothing, which rips at the seams. He seems enamored with Ethan, and sneers and growls.

"Please, I've no weapons against you," Ethan stammers.

The protnuk's head grows, and it's no more than a minor before he, now an it, is a hulking orange frek. Its voice is modulated and reverberates in a deep wail. "You think he must protect the Land, this Dark Valor. Protect it from me!" Its mouth snaps at Ethan, saliva dripping and flinging on him.

Ethan attempts to remain calm. *I'm absolute mad to stand here. Move.* As the protnuk continues to transform, it drops the brass, its attention and focus exclusively on Ethan. And then, out of the corner of Ethan's eye, he spies Brute, which seizes the brass fragment as the protnuk's back is turned. The other creshwillows eye the new frek as it disappears into a small alcove.

Ethan, considering it time to leave, steps backward toward the tunnel he entered from, keeping his focus on the protnuk's movement. Every passing minor, the protnuk grows more and more agitated but hesitates to attack. As soon as Ethan turns his head, the protnuk roars, filling the chamber with a great thunder, before giving chase. It swipes with one of its massive underclaws, by inches missing Ethan, who slams himself against the tunnel wall. He picks himself up and runs again along the narrowing path. After a few strides, the protnuk is unable to reach him and crams its body into the upward tunnel, its broad shoulders held back by either side. Its mouth chomps, spittle flinging into the air.

Ethan runs as fast as he can, upward and around the bends of the path. In the shadows and darkness, the protnuk's voice echoes: "You can't protect the Land from me."

Without stopping, Ethan finds his way back to the area he dropped down into and bends over, hands on knees, exhausted and breathing heavily. He looks around in the darkness, realizing he lost the neonlight back in the protnuk's chamber. He then hears scratching above him. Cowering, covering his head, he freezes before seeing Brute pop out of a small hole.

"Where'd you come from?" Ethan stutters, out of breath. Brute disappears into the hole and then reappears, yelping out a quiet whimper, likely as loud as it can. "You want me to follow you?" It then dips back inside. Without another option at the ready, he follows Brute, pulling himself up into the hole.

Inside, it is dark and cramped, forcing Ethan to crawl. The small tunnel winds around and around until a dim light appears ahead of him. He hurries toward it and finds it drops down into another tunnel. The light grows. Relieved, he climbs faster toward it and discovers he's near the other hole that exits into the cathedral. *A proshing shortcut.* He crawls with haste and hops down, causing a great stomping echo to bounce across the cathedral's nave. Sitting in one of the pews, Bernard and Sanet turn and stand, then hurry over and embrace him.

"Ethan, you brave madman, you're alive."

"Can you believe it? Brute just came out here and handed this to us." Bernard holds the protnuk's piece of brass. "Funny thing, we probably didn't need to go in there at all. Seems Brute found a whole tiny tunnel system. It led me out from the rope room. I bet those other creshwillows dug them out over the years."

Ethan grins at the thought, still shuddering at what he encountered below.

"What did you find down there?" Sanet asks.

"As you both say, long story."

At this, they turn the corner toward the exit and find the front entrance door cracked open—and a severely injured crimson man pointing his gun at them.

He shoots.

The three take cover behind a pew. Sanet loads a bolt and moves to send the man left before Ethan stops her. "Don't. We need someone who can sail Johan's kleep."

"Come out. Don't hide you shnite bastards," the man yells across the nave before blasting another round of fire.

"I don't do well with these friends. You'll need to negotiate," Bernard says to Ethan, who nods.

"Wisnok." Ethan raises his hands, and instantly a gunshot explodes behind him. He lowers them. "Please, stop shooting."

"What'd you say?" the man yells back.

Calling out from behind the pew, Ethan says, "Let's talk. Obviously, there're three of us; no way you'd survive if we try to send each other left."

"What's there to talk about? Why don't you give me that brass, and I'll let you live alone on this island?"

"Why don't you sail us back to Yikshir, and we can bargain with the brass when we're back?" Ethan squints. *A real negotiator.*

"You think I'm flam? You think Cadwellion would want me to let you bodies off this island without consequence?"

"We have Sanet. I know Cadwellion doesn't want you to harm her."

The man fires another shot, stomping toward them.

"I've heard enough," Sanet says exasperatedly. She stands and shoots.

The man screams. Ethan turns around and sees the man lying on the ground, grabbing at his knee.

"You like doing that, don't you?" Bernard says, sprinting toward the crimson man.

Sanet's words are cold. "I'd aim for his heart if he had one."

"I was getting there. We didn't have to shoot the man," Ethan stammers.

Neither respond, and Sanet assists Bernard in propping the man up as he yells and curses at them.

"Now now, no reason to shout," Bernard tells him, his mitt holding the man by the back of his collar with a grip that keeps him motionless. "This is good for all of us."

Pushing the injured man ahead, they leave the cathedral stonetin. Outside, the village below lies quiet.

"What happened to that yellow derange?" Ethan asks the man.

Still held by Bernard, the man seems angry, if not saddened by the event. "The what? That flying frek didn't recover from being knocked out, but not before it shot that light at my brothers. It slithered back into the jungle." The crimson man spits, pointing to the empty trees.

Sanet hurries ahead of them toward Johan's body and flips him over.

Ethan follows her and catches a look at the sailor's corpse, now covered in moss. His cheeks are sallow and sunken. "No time for the left here, is there?" he murmurs.

"He was a good man. Greasy, but good." Sanet stands up, wistful.

Ethan takes a last glance behind him at the silent stonetin on the hill. The fleeting image of Kevin and the creeping presence of the orange protnuk are still with him. Below him lies Johan's corpse. *How could I have ever protected Mercet here?*

The three take turns carrying the whimpering crimson man through the jungle and eventually to the beach, where two small kleeps are roped and anchored.

"You think you can sail that one?" Sanet asks, pointing to Johan's kleep.

"It's all the same to me," the man says, defeated.

"Great, we're sailing back to Yikshir," Ethan says, his words a demand.

"Whatever you want, friends," the man says through snarling teeth, glowering at Bernard.

Part Five

SANET

Chapter Twenty-Nine
CADWELLION'S POWER

Once Ethan leaves for the evening with his wife and child, Sanet slips off to her sleeping room. The heavy duskmeal of barmeal pies settles comfortably over her like a thick blanket. Lying contentedly, with eyes closed and kiptales trickling in, she stirs when a knock comes at the door. At first, she disregards the visitor, rolling over and clasping a pillow over her head. But with hesitant impatience, the knock comes again in three rugged raps.

She gets up, staring across the quiet room at the half-dim and faded neonlights and the window overlooking a moonlit and placid sea. With her robe on, she steps to the door to find Nico standing on the other side, sheepish and quiet. He's a garish guard who labors as Sanet's personal acolyte. He taught her the ways of crossbows and stonetin etiquette and has accompanied her on a few treks beyond Salsman and the Yikshir borders. Though Ethan takes on a role as the usual liaison between her and Wellion, Nico gives her outside details, things that Wellion most likely doesn't want her to know.

"Apory to wake you, Sur Wells, but I was asked to bring you up to Cadwellion's."

Sanet closes her robe as a breeze seeps in from outside. "Did he say why? I was hoping to get a night's rest before I leave in the morn."

"He did not, Sur, only that I was to find you once Ethan returned to haynest."

"Very well, I'll be up in a minor."

Nico nods and stands at wait as Sanet closes the door and redresses. There's always an enigmit way with Wellion. *Why didn't he just find me at dinner or in the smoking room?* Once dressed, she opens the door again to find Nico waiting, standing tall and proper. He smiles at her and leads her upstairs.

Down the hall, they approach the ranpart's staircase, taking the high steps to the upper floor to Wellion's master. Nico steps to the door, knocks, and they wait for an answer. "Did you have a nice duskmeal, Sur Wells?"

"I did. Approsh, Nico."

Wellion opens the door and smiles at the sight of Sanet. He wipes his doubled nose and waves Nico away. "Come in, dear, come in."

Leaving the door open, he steps back into his master, and Sanet walks inside. Nico, conflicted at the minor whether to come in despite Wellion's motion not to, decides against it, and remains eager and hungry for attention just outside the door. After Sanet steps through, Wellion turns and motions with his hand, closing the door with the gesture.

"Apory to have interrupted your sleep. I know you're trying to get rest before you travel tomorrow, but I came across something that I found painfully relevant."

The years living in Wellion's stonetin have been odd. On the one hand, it's been an engaging and cheerful period. Everyone finds her to be the most enthralling body in the room, always smiling and watching her eagerly, attending to her every whim. Nico, with his pure infatuation, treads a line between honeyed charm and exasperation. And Ethan has become a close friend, someone she's able to divulge her secret reservations about Wellion to—finding his own run far deeper.

To her, Wellion is kind and gentle. He has become accustomed to calling her his daughter, which she assumes is due more to his oddity as a ranpart than anything ominous. Ethan once elucidated that ranparts are not common in the Land and not much has been written about them beyond their great awareness of past histories and tricks. In fact, Ethan has only heard of three: Wellion; one living alone atop a tall, narrow pillar in Guloren; and another who left centuries ago, when they labored for the now-exterminated Lion. It's theorized that their preoccupation with enigmits leads to an unnecessary suspicion of them as some sort of supernatural midfrek, eating and mauling the Land's bodies. *A folk tale.*

Her experience has shown that Wellion is not the devious body one tends to read about. Whenever she returns from long treks, he listens to all her enthralling tales of places she's seen and freks she's met, even though she knows they are nothing worth mentioning. Whether it's true or not, he believes she is foretold for many great things and worries for her safety. He often comments about how lucky he is to have found her, that in some ways she saved him as much as he hoped he had saved her. There is a sweetness to him underneath his cold exterior. When she inquired about becoming a valor, he ensured she had lessons on the right weapons, of which she chose to specialize in using a crossbow with flaming bolts. When she wanted to learn more about the other states, he sent her off to the Tunnels, through Misipit and even to where Ethan studied, a boaler located in Quemon.

She has been given stacks of records on the many strange freks and bodies of the Land, of tenfooters and protnuks. And even as these studies sometimes run tedious and rarely lead to real-Land engagements, she appreciates learning more and being more prepared for the Land around her, which she believes will be valuable if she is to ascertain her forgotten past.

Over this past year, her studies and training have shifted in focus to a collection of missing brass fragments. There is a piece in a lost stonetin deep within the Tunnels. Another is rumored to reside alongside other ancient objects inside a lone manor on one of the Misipit plateaus. Others, less known, are hidden in states farther west. She asks on occasion about what they are meant for but is met with much hesitation when given answers. An instrument of some sort is as much as she can get out of either Ethan or Wellion.

When she heard that Wellion was going to leave with a few of his most trusted guards in search of the fragments, she begged to join him but was met with complete opposition to the idea. In fact, his behavior contradicted how Wellion usually treated her, as he usually seemed pleased with her when she was engaged with his strange and secret curiosities. The mood soured between them after his outright denial, and she began to believe her fate would be to live aimlessly in this lonely stonetin of Salsman.

That was until a few weeks ago, when she was brought to his master in a manner similar to tonight, and Wellion gave her the task of recovering two of the brass fragments. That night and that discussion were much darker and more serious in tone than any of their previous. He seemed almost defeated by the decision, as if he'd been pushed into it. Which suited her; she'd like to believe it was her tenacity. Since then, she's taken the opportunity with momentous determination to apply everything within her to ensure the brasses' safe return.

Their relationship has shifted since that conversation. Wellion watches Sanet during training sessions and steps in intermediately to correct her posture or decision-making, insulting even the smallest of mistakes. When he does, Sanet controls her temper and concentrates harder. The closer it comes to her leaving, the more he treats her like a valor he barely trusts instead of his innocent daughter. It is vital that she demonstrates she is worthy of the labor.

Wellion moves across his master to a small table and chair, where he motions for Sanet to sit. She does. "I'm proud of how well you've taken to your task. Nico has told me many excellent things about your training, and Ethan says that your studies have also gone satisfactorily."

"Approsh," Sanet says.

"I know it has been strange over these years to be treated like a child."

It is true that she often lashes out at the guards when they treat her like a teenager. It is also true that Sanet doesn't remember her past or where she came from, her family, or her childhood. Based on some initial studies, blood samples and various marks, they estimated that when they found her, she was around twenty-six, which was seven years ago.

Her entire life sits in a black shadow, with her unable to remember a single detail about bodies of the past. She can speak. She can read. She can recall basic things about the Land, but big details are lost. She knows there was a Last War, but she doesn't know of the Three Laws. She knows about cogs, but not about protnuks. And when it comes to an actual body, there is nothing. No curams, not even her own. No relationships. No memories whatsoever.

"I've come across new information about your son," Wellion continues.

Sanet's breath catches. The subject hasn't been brought up much over the last few years, and whenever it is, there is nothing new to report, no news of where or who her son is. "You have?"

"Yes, but I'm afraid I was . . . wrong. It's been made clearer that you, in fact, do not have a son."

"What?" Wellion doesn't answer immediately. She stands, crossing her arms, and paces in front of him. "I don't understand. I don't have a son?"

"I know this may be very frustrating; it is for me as well. But when dealing with the past and the future, things are not always unblemished. What may seem like the shadow of a man when looking to the ground may indeed only be the lifeless limbs of a tree."

The news is heartbreaking. Sanet's only tie to the past, the only thing she knows about her past, is that she has a son. A boy who, somewhere out there in the Land, is hers. At the thought of losing this, Sanet begins to cry.

"Oh dear, Sanet. I must appize to have to tell you this." He glides over to her, resting his long fingers across her back. "Let's step into the fresh air." He wipes his nose again with a hanker before leading her out to the porch overlooking the city of Salsman. After a major, Sanet calms. Her chest still tight. Her heart still crushed.

"I believe, however, that this news of your son is not completely unfounded. I think I merely misinterpreted the foretale. That it was not a son that you already had, it was one that you will have. And that is why I asked you to join me here tonight. I am dreadfully afraid that this trek of yours may . . . upset its unfolding."

"Finding the brass?"

"Yes. You see, the father of your son is on the road now, returning from Organsia, and I believe that your time would be best spent looking for this man instead."

"The father? How do you know who's the father?"

"In my research to learn more about you and your past, of your son, it appears that what I thought was your son, was in fact not. And that your son hasn't been chosen yet. That the only one out there now is the father."

"But what about the brass fragments?"

"I have already secured a legion of coinhires to assist me with the brass. I believe history will be best served by this new task. I do not wish for you to seek out the brass." Sanet wipes her face, her mood shifting from that of heartbreak to insult.

"You never wanted me to be your valor. You just expect me to be a prisoner. And what? Find someone to choose a child with? What's the point of that?"

She feels demoralized. Of all the men in the yard, she is nearly the best shot. Nico himself has commented on how easily she's taken to archery. Wellion has continually treated her like a glass object, ready to break at the slightest pressure; now he's found yet another reason to keep her restrained and unlearned.

"How do I know that you're right about this? That this isn't another mistake. Another misinterpreted shadow."

"It is my great displeasure that I can never know if I am wholly correct. I can only move in the direction the Land guides me. Like fog in the valley." His voice seems disappointed at this truth.

"This still feels like you're attempting to keep me here. As you have since the beginning. You're playing with me."

"This is no game we play, Sanet."

"I know it's not a game. I'm not trying to insult you. I'm only trying to understand. I want to do what is right. I want to find these brass pieces. Not just for you, but for me. I want to be worth something. I want to have a purpose. And I don't want it to be me as some," she pauses, "haynest mother."

Wellion ignores her vexation and turns to the cityscape of Salsman before speaking. "In a Land where the ground is firm and the air is thin and never shall the two intertwine, it is easy to believe that this is the way it is in all of time and forever. But since I can remember, I've questioned why the Land lives as it does. You believe it's mad, that I think you serve the Land best by finding this father and not seeking out the fragments. That, in a way, this presses you into a purposeless existence, but in truth, it may be the greatest thing that ever could chance. But suppose we forget this. And you leave to find these fragments on your own, and you find a body on the road. Handsome, kind, sweet, who falls in single souls with you, who you slip with because the road is long and lonely. Together you choose a child. Would that be so strange?"

"Now? Of course, it would be. Because you're telling me that's what I'm supposed to do."

"But only because you know it. Meeting someone and raising a child together is strange and odd and beautiful, but it is not mad."

"It is if someone foretells you. If it's not my choice."

Wellion takes a deep breath. "At times you have shown great courage and intellect, and yet tonight you're showing me how little you've learned. I believe this foretale is the key to your past. I believe that finding this body, the one who will one day be the father of this boy, could be an answer to everything."

The past. Sanet bites her lip, feeling his manipulation. After a pause to contemplate what is clearly important to Wellion, but to her is only flam, she says, "If I seek out this body, perhaps only to bring him back here, I'd still like to uncover the brass."

Wellion hesitates to answer. "I'm afraid that both tasks may not coincide. I've already sent my legion. There's no reason for you to seek them. It is already not an easy task to track down someone on the long and empty roads, nor easy to uncover the fragments."

"That's the bargain I offer." Sanet stands firm, knowing she's pressing her luck. Wellion watches her a minor, wipes his nose, and then turns away.

For an extended major, he stares at the cityscape. The few lit torches. The occasional soft echo of laughter and talking. He spins back to her, resigned. "It's a bargain then. I will send you the details in a note on the morrow, as I am leaving this eve."

Sanet smiles to herself. She knows he doesn't trust her to go on her own with the brass, but she will prove him wrong. *Prove to myself he's wrong.* For all the things that Wellion does, there is something about him that feels like good intentions. It's as if his mind holds so many thoughts and pieces of knowledge that he's almost incapable of communicating the severity of his tasks. The idea of finding a man to have a child with is mad. Though its purpose she isn't wholly opposed to learning more of. *Who is he? And why? What makes him so unispar to me? And is he the key to my past?*

Though many questions remain unsatisfied, it is clear the conversation has ended. Sanet excuses herself to Wellion, who's turned back to his overlook without a word. She makes her way back down to her sleeping room, Nico in tow.

"Is everything wisnok, Sur Wells?"

"I don't know. Wellion's intentions are always covered in oil, and I can't pin him down on what he's actually after."

"Always the way of ranparts, spending their entire lives in the past and on subjects us ordinary bodies can barely understand. But, by the crest of morn, his passion is for the Land and all of us who inhabit it."

"I'll have to take your word for it, Nico." When they reach her sleeping room, Nico holds the door for her. "Approsh and grats moon."

"Can I get you anything further, Sanet?"

"No. Just tired." She nods and grabs the door to close it.

Nico stands in the way. "Let me make you a bit of steamed tea, perhaps? It always helps me sleep."

"I'm wisnok, Nico. Truly."

"Of course."

Nico steps back as Sanet closes the door. Sometimes he can be odder than Wellion. She turns down the lights in the room and undresses, and slips into bed to close her eyes for the night.

❖ ❖ ❖

In the dark, she hears a door open. The sound comes from miles away, across the desert sands, across waters and rain. Then, footsteps echoing across grasslands and through the mists. In the bowels of a raging volcak. Then—a hand across her throat.

She opens her eyes to see Nico. She tries to call out to him—
What are you doing here?—but her throat is being squeezed and
she's barely able to breathe. Sitting up, she attempts to push his
arm back. His face looks maddened. She tries to take a deep
breath, and with great delight Nico squeezes harder. Sanet starts
to cough, making airless spitting noises.

Then, using every muscle, she spins herself onto the ground.
Using the fall's momentum, she pulls him onto her and, with her
legs free, knees him in the crotch. He doubles up but catches her
with his other hand on her neck. They roll across the floor, Sanet
tossing herself one way, Nico throwing her the other. The room
and he go cloudy, and everything slows when suddenly a gasp of
air comes to her, and through her faded sight, she sees Nico slam
halfway up and against the wall and stay there, flailing his arms.

As everything comes back into view, coughing and spitting,
she looks over her shoulder to see Wellion standing in the room,
one hand outstretched and pointing toward Nico while the other
is held back, a small glass orb floating in the air inches from his
palm. Wellion then clinches his hand aimed at Nico, who emits a
high scream and crunch of bone. Sanet turns her head to see Nico
folded in on himself, bones of his legs and arms protruding, blood
spattered across the wall, dripping below. She covers her mouth
as he suddenly flies from the wall and crashes through the
window before it all ends in a distant thud. *I'm in no kiptale.*

"Are you well, Sanet?" Wellion states, stepping up to her.
Near emotionless. *As if this already happened and he is running the
circuit.*

She turns back to him and finds his outstretched long-
fingered hand awaiting her. Taking it and standing, she notes the
glass orb has vanished, even as her body shakes and she draws
deep, wild breaths. "Why . . . why did he do that?"

"He was afraid you were going to leave him, I suppose,"
Wellion says.

Sanet rubs her neck and steps over to the window to see Nico's crumpled body lying across the lawn below. Other guards have gathered around.

"Once you are dressed, it's important that I see you one last time before I depart."

"I don't believe it," Sanet says. Wellion spins, preparing to leave the room, and before he exits, Sanet calls after him, "Approsh on my life, Wellion."

"Of course, Sur Wells. You have an important task ahead of you. I believe the Land requires that you stay alive longer than some unrequited soul."

He leaves the room. Around her are spread the ruffled sheets, the upturned rug, the crack in the stonetin wall. *Nico has been with me for six years. Why would he decide suddenly to send me left?*

❖ ❖ ❖

In the morn, she hurries down the ranpart stairwell to find Ethan and Wellion sitting at a table, served mornmeal. While Wellion eats, Ethan's face pales and quiets.

"Sanet, join us," Wellion says, waving her over. She sits at the table as one of the guards serves her a round of food. "Eat, dear, eat. The first day on the road is always exhausting."

She looks down at the eggs under and bacon. With her throat still sore, she passes. "I'll take it to go, I think," she says to the guard, who nods and reaches for the round.

"I said eat!" Wellion yells, slamming his hand on the table. Ethan and Sanet remain silent as the ranpart watches them both, narrowing his eyes. "Wisnok, do as you like." He waves her off.

The guard, hesitant at first, creeps in and grabs the round.

Sanet speaks up. "I thought you were leaving last night?"

"The plan has changed. You are no longer to seek the brass. And you will be punished severely should you." He presses his hanker to his mouth, and then wipes his nose, which is bleeding a thick blue blood. He spits the food that remains in his mouth into the hanker and then pushes his plate aside. "Good travels." He stands and leaves the room empty, colder, and now ten times the larger.

❖❖❖

Later that morn, Ethan walks Sanet to the entrance gates. When they're out of earshot of guard and ranpart, he whispers, "Are you wisnok, Sanet?"

"I think so. My throat is sore, but I think I'm more shocked than hurt."

"He did bruise your neck a bit, it seems," Ethan says, looking at her neck. "The oilment I packed for you should work well."

"I don't understand. I've known Nico for six years."

"I've known him since I started here ten years ago, and I can't say more than this, but don't trust everything that happens at face value. Nico was a good man."

"Then you think that it wasn't him?"

"It was Nico, I just don't believe it was . . . Nico. I'm only glad you were able to defend yourself. It makes me feel better about you leaving on your own. When you return, I hope to have much more to discuss, but for now, I can only say to be wary of whom you trust. And," he pulls a small key from his jacket, "this is the thing we spoke about last week. I know you're not supposed to have it now..."

Sanet smiles, pocketing it in secret. "You're going to get me sent, Ethan Mershner. And I will. I'm learning all too well the shadows are not what they seem." She kisses two fingers and sets them upon Ethan's chest. "You as well, be safe."

"Lucky for me, Cadwellion is headed west until summer. Things might grow so boring I'll end up reading one of Undess's romance books." Sanet laughs at the thought.

"I wish you would come with me."

"Mercet wouldn't like that. And even so, it would be the most unlikely of Lands to see me setting off on such an adventure."

"After last night, I don't think anything is unlikely." The carriage pulls up and she enters, setting off, unsure of how to arrange the past hours, if not the past seven years.

Chapter Thirty
BENEATH THEM, UNCERTAINTY

*T*he snarling crimson man, who nickens himself Ponce, sails Johan's Blonde Sea Horsal through Trimod's encircling storm, needing only a half-try skill, indicating his unfortunate necessity if the gang expects a safe return to Yikshir. To double on the disappointment, his insults and annoyances with every rock and wind and wave are sure to make the voyage considerably longer. As they drift farther from the island state, its gray-stained clouds ease with the fade of the sea's whitecap rollers. The blue-and-red glow, the mountain that punches through a forever fog, all of what became of Trimod shrink in the distance, at once an unsung happening.

Sanet's view of the island causes her heart to skip a minor at the thought of Johan, a man who happened upon a one-way trip. A man who wore the smarmiest of grins and a body filled by crass ingenuousness. A man with his own morals. Though the thought that he followed her like a cog onto that island eases her culpability, Sanet takes a full share's blame for his sending. Over the past seven years, she's found she possesses an unprovoked magnetism with other bodies. First with Oskar, and then Nico, then Logan, who approached her in the forest highland. And ultimately, Johan. Even Iahel lost a glance to her on more than one occasion while trekking through those interminable Tunnels. Most times, she didn't mind using their weakness to her advantage. But beyond a lingering guilt, her heart hangs indifferently for these other bodies. Instead, her interest lies in what is beyond her obligation to the ranpart. If not one objective, it is something else she is encouraged to attain. Nothing of her own choosing.

Despite Wellion's warning, the attack from Nico just before leaving Salsman forced her intention to retrieve the brass fragments to become undivided, their recovery a test of her devotion. *Wellion saved me, after all.* It has become a means by which she can measure her worth. Over the past years, reading and learning expressly about the Land, and yet little of herself, caused an unquenchable need to uncover something that may prove who she is or, more importantly, why she is.

Her expedition began southwest of Yikshir, in the state of Misipit and its infamous foggy canyons. But those early excitements soon drift into the memories of staying in Wellion's stonetin, to the countless combat techniques Nico instructed her in—*which, ironically, I used against him*—to the wild histories of the continent of Merigen and the entire planet of Homen that Ethan taught her. She recalls the sleeping room she stayed in, the same one she awoke in nearly seven years prior. All the admiration and affection from the guard staff for the stranger without a past. But thoughts of the stonetin inevitably bring her to thoughts of Wellion himself.

Before witnessing him so easily crush Nico, she was beginning to believe Ethan's theory that Wellion was only a fraud. But afterward, even the small orb that he carries around terrifies her. And now, they possess three pieces of a brass orb that's tenfold larger. She fears Wellion's control over that amount of power would include his coolly academic approach to experimentation and reaction. She fears that if bodies end up sent in pursuit of uncovering a truth, his attitude will simply be: So shall it be. The idea of turning the brass over to him, even for peace among them, doesn't seem the right of endings. Though

Wellion's appetite, as he says, is to protect the Land, by hiring these vehement crimson men, it means at any cost.

Sanet snipped the first fragment without much incident. It was kept in a large manor belonging to a family who had no need to lock their doors at night, no reason to guard an innocuous sliver of brass left unprotected among dozens of other antiquated artifacts. The long chase after, first by that crimson man who snipped it from her and then after that proshing neox skittering all the way into Radiba, tested her further. Where at first she relished the idea of being a hunter of treasures, it quickly distorted into a hopeless, heaving slog, with tireless exhaustion and the pain of a slow, interminable burn.

Which set the scene and a welcome reprieve meeting the handsome Radibian man. When he alleged his curam was Logan, it felt like a kiptale. Was Wellion's foretale true, that he would become her son's father? But even as her mind lurches into another of Wellion's biddings, the reality remains: every choice has been chosen for her.

When confronted with Logan's charming appearance, it wasn't difficult to deny Wellion's task. It was easy to see why bodies wanted to hold him or be held by him. His soft eyes and wide frame emitted an unintentional sexual allure. An all-encompassing masculinity. As if he were a walking-man's demvirst. That first major, when he looked at her as if he already knew they were in single souls and she heard his curam, she wanted to reject Wellion's wild proclamation that this man, this stranger in the woods, would choose a child with her. At the same time, she was curious to let the foretale play out. And in doing so, resume Wellion's order. Logan was persuasive and straightforward, and he'd found her when she was psychologically spent. She would later wonder if those weeks of minimal sleep and intense single-mindedness prior had not been a contributing factor in allowing Logan to so easily attract her.

The serendipitous circumstances of their encounter clouded her judgment, and it wasn't until she gained a full night's rest and marked the looming tormisand that she would recall the neox and the brass. After leaving Logan's haynest that morn, she had no intention to ever see him again, whether Wellion wanted her to or not. And with that thought came thoughts of Bernard. The Dark Valor who emerged from that cave as an innocent bystander and by his actions brought her back to Logan.

But truthfully, it was after her interaction with the protnuk, transformed as a young girl, that her unwavering commitment to Wellion formed. To choosing a child with Logan. Yet another portent about her future, a riddle entailing Dark Valors and nines and more, only added to her frustrations about the lack of knowing anything of her past. The Land's way had become infuriating over curious. After the protnuk's riddle, she left the cave in a state of absolute frustration. She decided she would wait for the sleeping man to leave and convince him to give her that sliver of brass. From such a thing came this.

The thought had occurred to her to just snip it in his sleep, but she wasn't sure what sort of man he was or how dangerous. She laughs now at the thought of Bernard being dangerous. *The burned man knows.* Looking back, she knows she also hesitated because, if he did not have it, if it was not inside that neox, her entire trip south, the entirety of the past few months, would have been for naught. And after misplacing the steel stonetin key that Ethan slid to her when she left Salsman, while chasing the neox up through the Carvinga Treasures, she was close to losing both pieces in the same decision. *Failing a neox hunt is bad luck.*

But, as with all things Bernard, he was unexpected. And while she waited, he did not leave. And didn't leave. And didn't leave. And so, Sanet had to either wander back into the cave or never know the fate of the brass. Afterward, when he walked out and handed her the very thing she held so precious in the months before, without care or worry, she believed. Her mind so focused, so determined to do it herself. And yet, this old man, handed it to her.

That minor, made her believe in him and the protnuk's foretale. Bernard sending the crimson man, the act of a Dark Valor, was only confirmation. Sanet believed then that the Land was larger than her and that all its things flow in a design to serve a grander purpose, making her desire to know what had happened to her fade like the setting sun. And perhaps what Wellion said was to be believed. He was serving the Land. Or, at the very least, he was aware of something she was not. *I can trust him.* His foretale could be as true as those of that protnuk in the cave.

With fate-filled eyes, she understood her fascination with the myths of valors. Valors are bodies chosen by the Land to course-correct when required, when tensions rise, when the Land feels threatened. They are categorized by color, each with their own purpose. Green Valors, whom Ethan describes as warriors, are possessors of might and ferocity, protectors. Sanet, since waking from her violet coma, has trained to be such a fighter, and her skill, as commented on by much of the stonetin guard, is impressive and innate. She is driven by the independence of the warrior, someone capable of holding one's own. She hates that something has taken nearly twenty-five years of her life. That everything before has been erased. She wants to be strong and bold and independent. A Green Valor. She wants to prove she is worth something.

In the corner of a page on valors, she once spotted a small handwritten note describing something called the Dark Valors. Which, it suggested, means they are the last remedy called upon when the Land feels at its most vulnerable, when the common valors are no longer enough. Morals, and what is right and what is wrong, stand separate from the duties of the Dark Valor. When Bernard sent that crimson leader, when he missed nine but one more, it all dropped into place. There is darkness in sending someone left. Bernard acted out in anger and fury, to a zealot, yes, but in the end, he chose to feed the emotion. He was no hero. No Logan. Or even Ethan. It wasn't intellectualism or logic that drove him. It was primal and of the Land.

Sanet has given in. If Logan is to be the father of her child, she is going to allow it. Not fight it. Logan is handsome and kind and sweet. Generous and eager. It isn't difficult to like the boy. When he left without a wave, it hurt. And regardless of her accepting this foretale of a father, for reasons she couldn't articulate, she didn't feel in single souls with him.

Her thoughts continue to drift as she looks out toward the calm sea, Trimod long gone from crest. Bernard steps up to her.

"What are we going to do with Ponce?" He looks over his shoulder back at the wheel where Ponce stands. At the minor, Ethan is inside the small cabin, sure to be sick again.

"I think our bigger concern is where he's actually going to sail us. I'm not skilled enough to know how to correct a kleep's heading. Or to know which direction we're sailing, save east to west."

"If I were him, I would sail us straight to Carvinga, toward wherever Wellion is," Bernard says. "I'm going to watch how he sails for a few days, and once I feel I have the hang, we can bind him and hopefully navigate elsewhere."

"I know Ethan wants to get back to his son, but I think it's better we get away from the Merigen states. Sail east, toward Eerim. Niance is sure to give us more answers than anywhere else. Especially if this last royal family had bargains with the brass," Sanet says after some contemplation.

Bernard twiddles his thumbs and sighs. "You may be right."

In the quiet, he starts to leave, but Sanet holds his shoulder. "Are you wisnok?"

"Yes. A little tired, perhaps. The thrill of the travels has faded some. I miss haynest. And Jame."

"You think we should sail to Radiba instead?"

"Selfishly, of course. But that doesn't allay the worries and claims of a war. While I still don't believe your thinking I'm some Dark Valor, I can't say that there isn't something inside me that knows going haynest and sleeping under the blankets is the wrong plot."

"The only thing worth trusting is yourself."

"That could be a problem." Bernard smirks and returns to the cabin.

Sanet turns and watches Ponce before walking across the deck toward him. She steps up toward the wheel.

"What do you want, woman?" Ponce spews.

"Still paranoid?"

"I know that old cog of yours is eager to send me left. Not difficult to feel a pinge of concern around 'im."

"When the redrocks come about crest instead of a war-torn grassland, I think we'll all breathe a bit easier," Sanet answers plainly.

"Redrocks over grasslands. The men of Yikshir are as ready to find you as the drums in Carvinga," Ponce sneers. "You're safest at the bottom of the sea."

Sanet presses her lips in a smile. "A pleasant chat as always." With a quick glance at the compass, currently pointing west, she returns inside the cabin and finds Ethan and Bernard talking.

"I don't feel as woozy as I did before, which is a good sign. Hopefully, my sea legs will chance sooner this time." Ethan smiles.

"That's good to hear. Watching him, I don't think it's going be too difficult to steer the thing. My fear is we'll be hit by a storm," Bernard comments.

Sanet sits down with them. "He supposes that no matter where we beach, we'll be found. Which I'm sure is meant to be a threat, but I can't imagine he's not right."

"I'm scared Cadwellion will act against Mercet and Undess soon, once he knows we have the final piece," Ethan remarks, his expression drawn. "I need to make sure they're safe. Once I can get them, we could possibly head over to stay with family of mine in Quemon. It's populated enough there that it would be difficult for Cadwellion to find us."

"We were talking a major ago," Bernard starts, "and thought perhaps instead we should head to . . . Niance."

"A month across the sea? In the other direction? Madness," Ethan says dismissively.

"There'd be more answers to what this brass is for there than in Quemon," Sanet doubles.

"I thought our only goal here was to keep our three pieces away from Cadwellion."

"Yes, but what if what he's looking to do with the brass is actually the right thing? The right thing in the wrong hands, but the right thing." Sanet offers again, still unsettled by the letter to Peter. Still not ready to cast Wellion a villain.

Bernard interjects, "I can't believe that's true. We can't know what's proper to do with it until we know more about it. And until then, it should be as far away from others as possible."

Neither Sanet nor Ethan can grit against his case.

Sanet continues, "I agree that, for now, we keep it away from Carvinga. And we should also keep this new fragment from snapping together with the other two. If you want to go to Quemon, while we research in Niance, that keeps them seas apart. Which, until we can understand what it does, is our best plan." Settled for the major, Bernard stands and begins to put together a duskmeal.

Outside, the sun sets into the sea, and after an hour, Ponce enters the cabin. Bernard serves everyone, with Ponce getting the smallest portion, and they all sit around in quiet. Brute, having found his way back to the kleep before the others, sits off in the corner atop a cabinet. Ponce rolls his eyes at the frek.

"Your little cog is eyeing me again."

"Not a cog. It's a creshwillow, and it's probably sure you're in need of watching," Bernard says without looking.

Ponce huffs through his chewing. "Can't we at least be friendly with each other? Obviously, I can't do anything but sail this kleep. I'm sure once we're landed, we'll grit and bargain against each other, but for the next few weeks no reason we can't be happy little kleepmates."

"I think this civility is as about as warm as we're getting," Sanet says.

"Not going to persuade me to come to your side? To see things your way?"

"And leave your labor as a shnite beast?" Bernard grins, looking him in the eye.

"Well, with that opening offer, you're putting me on the defensive."

"I've had the pleasure of interacting with your sort four times now. Each time has had the same result. No reason to believe you're different."

"I could be. The ranpart sent us on an assignment that's clearly failed. Why wouldn't I switch sides? We're but merely coinhires."

"How are there sides? What are there sides for?" Ethan asks.

Ponce responds, halfhearted and annoyed. "You clearly have no intentions of reuniting the brass, invoking the war, and saving the Land. You don't believe in the advent of the Roar."

At this, Bernard stands and wipes his face. "I've heard enough of this nonsense; I'm getting some air." He leaves the room.

"Sensitive fellow, he is." Ponce smiles, taking another boorish bite of food.

"How does war save the Land? Did you all forget the Last War? The one that destroyed everybody?" Ethan continues.

"That was eons ago," Ponce says dismissively. He then points his lyn bone at Ethan. "Do you garden?"

"I don't."

"Well, if you never prune your veggies, then all the dead leaves and excessive limbs extract all the nutrients from the younger, healthier parts, and it kills the entire plant. We've spent eons in this perpetual state of peace, allowing a festering of priced and classism. Do you know that the Yikshir councils regularly purge the lower classes? Just a few weeks ago, they nearly destroyed everyone in Balton. For what? Because they have a large lower class? They sent thousands left without much more discussion than how they'll do it. The tenfooters bind and toss those they find too small and ineffective in some dark pit where they either drown or are eaten by who-knows-what below. In Organsia, the Victors are so entrenched in the debts of its citizens that the entire state is practically priced. It all needs to be cleaned. To be pruned. We all need to refocus the nutrients of our own humanity. War gives us this perspective so that no longer are we caught up in small personal gains, in our own needs, but instead we fight for the whole. For what's important."

"Why set homes on fire? Send innocent people?" Sanet asks.

"To wake the states up. To rile them to war. Isn't your old cog riled? Isn't he ready to fight? You see, we don't care which side you're on, as long as you're fighting." Ponce smirks. "But, please, convince me to come to your side."

Ethan grabs his empty round and walks to the sink. "What I don't understand is this Roar. How is a child a call for war?"

"It's been foretold that seven from the advent is the start of war."

"Seven weeks?" Ethan asks.

"Is there not a war begun?"

"So, which is it? The brass or the Roar?"

"The Roar was the call. The brass is the answer," Ponce states.

Ethan looks to Sanet and returns to the table, drinking from his mug.

"Even if what you're saying is right, which in truth, I can't believe, what happens when the war leads to our complete destruction?"

"Is that not what the Land demands? Have we not overstayed our welcome here? The Quemon and Yikshir populations are far beyond what was allowed by the Laws. What good are we doing here? What purpose do our lives have and how do they matter to the Land?"

"Why not kill yourself then, if you find the Land so burdened?"

"I will," Ponce grins, "but I plan on taking as many bodies with me as I can when I do."

Sanet takes a deep breath. "It's unsettling to witness your lack of sympathy for the sent. Especially for something that's at best a thought experiment."

Ponce shrugs. "Who could care what you think?"

He stands and walks over to drop his round into the sink, and as he walks back, he pushes Sanet into the table. Despite the shock, she recovers herself, but not before Ponce is able to take hold of her pistol. He points it at them.

"Stand back!" he shouts.

Ethan and Sanet stand, hands on head.

"There's no reason to do anything rash here. Bernard will surely come in and send you left. We can't stop him if you shoot us," Sanet states.

"He can't send me before I take one of you out. My finger is on the trigger, Bernard!" Ponce shouts this louder just as a rifle appears at the door, with Bernard stepping through behind it.

"Lower the gun, Ponce. My lack of sailing skills is far less convincing a decision than my desire to pull this trigger. Don't let me make the choice." Bernard crosses completely into the cabin and presses the rifle against Ponce's head.

"Bernard, friend, no need to worry. I have no intentions of shooting your friends here."

Ponce lowers the gun to his side. Bernard eyes Sanet and motions for her to take the gun. She steps forward, but Ponce shoots three times into the floor before Bernard blasts his head clear apart, spraying blood and mind across the cabin walls.

Sanet lowers her arms from shielding herself and watches as Ponce's sent body slumps across the floor, blood pouring from his neck and blown head. But what's most alarming is not the puddle of blood but the water deluging in from three holes in the cabin floor.

"We need to get them covered immediately!" she yells.

Bernard pushes Ponce's body aside to find the three springs. Ethan quickly takes off his jacket and shirt, rolls the latter, and shoves it into one of the holes.

"We should grab a towel or something. And see if Johan has some wood plugs around."

Bernard nods at Ethan's quick suggestion and runs from the cabin. Sanet steps over Ponce's body and into the growing puddle. She pulls a towel from the shelf above and tosses it to Ethan, who quickly rolls it and begins plugging the second hole. Ethan then rips the shirt from Ponce's body to fill the third.

"This won't last long. We'll need some plugs fast," he states.

Sanet nods and runs from the cabin. Across the deck, Bernard is looking through a small room under the wheel deck. He's tossing tools and bars over his shoulder, a hanging neonlight swinging frantically above him.

She runs over. "Anything?"

"Nothing. I assume it looks like some cone or something?" Bernard keeps looking.

Sanet steps up to the wheel deck and sees that the compass has been smashed. *That beast knew he was going to drown us.* The wheel is also spinning out of control. She takes hold of it.

Bernard stands back from the room and looks to Sanet as she yells, "He's smashed the compass! We won't know which direction we're headed until morn."

Bernard shakes his head. "Should have sent that man left back at the stonetin." He hurries back to the cabin.

She locks the wheel in place and follows. "Anything?"

Bernard shakes his head again. "What was he thinking? If we die out here in the sea, the brass goes down with us."

"I don't think men like that think."

"There's no time to assume we know the intentions of the sent, we need to find something on this kleep to plug those holes. Maybe we can chop down some of the cabin?" Ethan suggests.

"I saw some black oilment. If we can get a large enough cover, we could seal the edges?" Bernard suggests.

"That could work, let's make it happen. Glass may work better." Ethan points.

At this, the three work together, using a crowbar and ax to remove a pane from the cabin's window that is large enough to cover all three holes. Bernard holds it in place while Ethan seals the edges. Sanet begins removing the flooding seawater with a mug and a pot, throwing it over the kleep rails. As she does, she feels the first droplets of rain. After twenty minutes, the holes are sealed. The three then all take efforts to remove the inches of water from the cabin floor. Without ceremony, they toss Ponce's body overboard as the rainstorm picks up.

Bernard takes a position at the wheel, deciding that the best course of action is to keep it steady. Sanet and Ethan, meanwhile, take the sails down to mitigate the kleep's toss and thrust in heightened winds. The sea's whitecaps begin to bob the entire kleep up and down, sending Ethan to his knees, vomiting over the edge.

Sanet starts to feel her stomach toss as well but attempts to ride the kleep, holding onto the cabin's doorway. "How's it going, Bernard?"

"I'm hoping this isn't that big a storm coming," Bernard yells across the deck. But the rain picks up in intensity.

Ethan falls backward and hits his head on the floor when the kleep tosses to the east, a massive wave crashing over them. Sanet steps forward, reaching her hand out.

Bernard calls to them, "You friends should go inside. It's not safe out here."

Sanet nods and grabs Ethan's hand. His face is pale and his steps reel.

Inside the cabin, walls still covered in Ponce's blood, Ethan holds on to the table, his eyes closed, his face in concentration. Sanet holds on to him and the table, watching the neonlight above them swing wildly from side to side before it smashes into the ceiling and goes out. The cabin falls to darkness, the kleep and storm outside the only things visible. Rain pours in from the missing glass pane, and Brute huddles below them, hiding. Lightning and thunder roar across the deck. Out in the distance, the moon is temporarily blocked by . . . *Lincoln, that's a massive wave.* The wave towers over the kleep, rushing toward them. The cabin tilts away as it rallies closer. And behind the dark wall of water, for only the smallest of glimpses, a pair of large glowing red eyes.

Sanet grips the table, bracing herself for what she's sure will destroy the entire kleep. She tries to see across the deck toward Bernard. "Hold your breath, Ethan, this is going to—"

The whole kleep crashes to its side. Sanet is lifted from her seat, Ethan and Brute rising up with her. Within minors, she smashes her head against the roof and feels the brunt of water and wood crash into her body. And then, the momentum hits her again, tossing her body in the other direction, water gushing into her nose and mouth. She closes her eyes, holds her breath, and braces herself for the second impact. She feels a crack in her shoulder.

And then nothing.

Chapter Thirty-One
PRISONERS OF PAULO

S anet wakes up drifting in the sea, the full sun bearing down on her skin, roasting her red and hot as water strikes her cheek in rhythmic lapping. She's slumped over a broken section of the kleep with the letters *D E   S E A* written across it. Craning her neck and squinting, she peers around at other shattered portions of the kleep dipping up and down in the soft, rippling waters and sees Bernard across the way, hugging his own piece of driftwood. She calls out to him in a raspy voice, and he shifts his head toward her, lifting his mitted hand in a slight wave. *Now, where's Ethan?*

Scanning the sea, she finds only more drifting wood and debris. An attempt to look behind her sends a sting of pain through her shoulder. Looking down, she catches a glimpse of a long and oozing swath of blood on her shirt. She closes her eyes and takes a breath to bury the pain before paddling and kicking her way toward Bernard, slowly and painfully.

He looks at her and smiles. "Apory for my poor sailing."

She reaches out to brush his hair. "My little madman. Have you seen Ethan?"

He nods, pointing over his shoulder toward the far distance. There, Ethan floats gently on his back with Brute sitting on his chest peering around curiously. Her eyes widen and breath holds at the sight.

"Is he—" she asks.

"He's wisnok. Broke a leg, so I put him on the biggest piece of wood I could find. Also," he lifts his other hand from the water and shows Sanet her rucksack, "I managed to keep hold of this shnite brass."

She laughs. "You're incredible."

"As I've been told." Bernard smiles again before resting his head back, closing his eyes in the sun.

Sanet paddles over to Ethan, dipping her head under the water every few strokes to relieve herself from the heat.

Drawing closer, she calls out to him, and he turns his head slowly toward her, squinting. "Shnite this sea and everything in it," he curses.

Seeing Sanet, Brute jumps into the water and swims clumsily over, hopping onto her small section of wood. The frek's weight shifts it and sends another throb of pain into her shoulder.

"Careful, Brute. I'm hurt."

The creature tilts its head. The sea remains calm and clear, save for the three of them and the few dozen drifts of wood. Any optimism for continued safety, sudden Land, or passing kleeps would be downright flam.

"We should stick together before we drift farther apart," she tells Ethan.

"Apory, but I can't move much. I'm afraid to fall off this little piece, and I'm not a great swimmer even without a broken leg," he laments.

Sanet agrees and waves her hand, calling for Bernard to join them. Without pause, Bernard paddles himself and his driftwood toward them. Brute catches sight of Bernard and hops off Sanet, sending her wood into the water and further pains through her shoulder. *That shnite little frek.* He swims eagerly for Bernard, hopping up onto his habitual residence on his shoulder. Once the three are together, they bob along the water as Bernard holds on to Sanet and her rucksack and Sanet holds on to Ethan.

Time passes.

"What's the next step in our grand travels?" Bernard asks.

"Since we're far from any land, not sure that's an option. I think the best we can hope for is a passing kleep." Saying it aloud makes Sanet's heart flutter. As they float in the sun and in the wide sweeping sea, the likelihood of someone passing them feels a thousand to one.

Time passes.

"Don't move too much, your arm is completely dislocated. I should probably try to pop it back in," Bernard says. Sanet tries to adjust herself and splashes water on her burned face.

"I'll take my chances," she says, her shoulder pulsing in pain with every heartbeat.

Time passes.

In late hours, a school of earniks swim playfully around them, poking their heads out of the water and splashing their faces with their colorful nostrils, urging the three to dive and swim with them. The gang instead lies quiet and injured and without interaction. The earniks swim away, unimpressed.

Time passes.

Sanet checks her fingers, which are wrinkled and itching. She rubs them across her face and feels the bumps and ridges. Drops of hass water trickle into her mouth. She closes her eyes and lays her cheek to the wood, letting water splatter against her face and blip into her ear.

Time passes.

A soft breeze brushes over her cheek, a welcome relief from the sun. She splashes a bit of water onto her face again. Ethan is unconscious and brightly red. Sanet turns his head, spilling seawater over him, trying to keep him cool.

Time passes.

Every few minutes, Brute hops into the water and dives down, swimming around the three before hopping back onto one of their planks.

"Well, this is boring, any new ideas?" Bernard asks.

Sanet shakes her head in defeat. "Are you having fun seeing the Land with me?"

"If we're being honest here, I'd say this isn't my favorite day of the journey," Bernard says, closing his eyes and splashing his own face. "I can also say that I keep drinking a little bit of the water and it's downright terrible."

"Now you stop that. It'll only make you thirstier."

"Yeah, yeah."

They fall back into silence as time passes. The sea dips them up and down. Ethan turns his head and dry heaves. Sanet squeezes his arm.

"You know, there was a major I thought Mercet would have liked sailing," Ethan says to himself. He titters quietly before falling back asleep. The sun slinks across the sky.

"It's going to be cold tonight," Sanet comments as the sun drops closer and closer to crest. No one answers. She watches through squinted eyes as the sun sinks and sinks and then— perhaps it's not real—she spies a small dot in the distance. Her head pops up. "Is that—" She shakes Ethan. "Do you see that?"

Ethan lifts his head slightly.

"I don't. Wait, I think . . . is it?"

She squints. The sky is a candy-colored orange and quickly darkening, making it difficult to discern reality from hope.

"Bernard, look."

Bernard peers over them. "Maybe. You think if it is, they'll find us?"

"We should swim toward them. Get as close as we can before dark," Sanet suggests.

Bernard nods in agreement, and they both start to kick and paddle. Ethan flips onto his stomach, wincing as he shifts his broken leg, and starts to paddle with them. The kleep, luckily, is headed toward them, and by the time the sun hits crest, it's only three hundred strides away. As it draws closer, the three begin to scream out, calling for help and waving their arms, splashing in the water. The kleep continues its course toward them.

"Does it see us?" Sanet says, hopeful.

"They have to," Bernard hammers his mitts into the water harder, "we're so close."

Together, the three continue to scream and shout and splash to gain the attention of the incoming kleep. It draws closer in the darkening air, its size three times that of Johan's, and Sanet catches the first glimpse of one of its crew members. Her heart sinks. *Crimson men.*

They shine a neonlight on them. One of the men, dressed in their familiar red cape, points to them from the port bow. His cape is short, falling no farther than his upper shoulders.

When Ethan catches a glimpse of them, he curses to himself, "Of all the bodies out at sea."

"Ponce must have known they were out here. Why, he knew he could sink us," Sanet whispers. "But there's nothing we can do now. It's either them or drown out here."

"Not sure which is worse," Bernard comments.

The kleep sails next to them, the man who first spotted them directing the crew to slow before tossing down a ladder. "Come on, get yourselves up," he shouts at them.

"Two of us are injured. We'll need help," Bernard says.

At this, another of the crimson men dives overboard, swims to them, and helps wrangle some rope and harnesses over Ethan and then Sanet. It takes a few majors, but once they're out of the water, it comes as a welcome relief. The three are given blankets. Sanet looks around and sees the main deck populated by a dozen crimson men watching them intently.

From the crowd, a notably larger man, with the longest cape, steps up and kneels in front of them. "How long were you in the water?" he asks.

"Only the day," Sanet answers.

"You're lucky we came looking for you then," the man states. "What happened to my men who went to Trimod?"

"Sent." Sanet grins.

The man grins back, showing pointed yellow teeth. "You must be Sanet. My curam is Paulo. Is this my approshment gift?"

He motions to another crimson boy, no more than eighteen, who attempts to pull the rucksack from Bernard's grip. At first, Bernard is easily too strong for the young boy's pull, but Sanet shakes her head. Bernard, rolling his eyes, releases the rucksack, sending the obstinate boy backward and the crew into fits of laughter.

Recovering, the young boy curses and brushes himself off before reaching haughtily into the rucksack. He tosses aside wet clothing and Sanet's pad—*all those ruined thoughts*—before pulling out two pieces of brass: the small fragment they found in Trimod and the other larger part they formed from the first two. Paulo reaches for the two pieces. He examines them and, without show, clinks them together, creating a single rounded piece from all three.

"Sur Cadwellion will be pleased. Take them below and set course for Carvinga."

He walks off as they're lifted away. Ethan yelps as they drag him by his broken leg, and Sanet swallows her pain as they yank her by the shoulder.

"Careful, Cadwellion will not approsh if you treat her ill," Bernard warns.

Paulo sneers as they're shoved across the deck to the darkened brig below.

❖ ❖ ❖

They're placed into a holding cell below deck, and when the two crimson men leave, Bernard shifts his focus to Sanet's shoulder. "It's pretty bad. We're going to need to pop it in soon."

Sanet closes her eyes, taking a deep breath. "Please, I can't cope with that right now."

She opens her eyes again to see Bernard staring quietly. He nods with understanding.

Ethan sets himself against the back wall, pushing out his leg, mangled and bent. He tears off the upper portion of his pant leg to see a chunk of bone extending out. "Lincoln, that doesn't look right." Ethan leans his head back, focused solely on breathing.

After a few majors, an older crimson man with a cape halfway down his back climbs down the stairs carrying a small purse.

"Hello, good souls." He opens the cell door. "Please, do not try anything heroic. I'm here only to see to your injuries and have no intention to harm any of you." He steps inside and locks the cell door behind him. Bernard moves aside as the crimson man looks Ethan over first, then Sanet. Eventually, he turns to Bernard. "And how are you doing, Bernard is it?"

"It's them who need help."

"Yes, I can see." He pulls from his purse some instruments and bandages. "I'll need you to help me. Do you trust that I'm here only as a nurse?"

Bernard hesitates. Sanet knows his seething hatred for the crimson men, but he nods nonetheless.

"Then you'll need to follow my instructions carefully."

He begins on Ethan's leg, having Bernard hold Ethan still, keeping him calm as he winces and screams between the cracks and pulls of the nurse's treatment. Bernard attempts to talk to Ethan, asking him about Mercet and Undess.

"Of all people, I don't want to talk about her," Ethan says through his screams. The nurse continues to set the bone and finally wraps his leg. After Ethan, he turns to Sanet, checking her shoulder.

"Not as bad. We'll need to pop it back in."

Sanet looks Bernard in the eye and shakes her head. "Don't say anything."

Bernard presses his lips in a soft smile.

The nurse clutches her softly by the neck and either side of her body and snaps her shoulder, to which Sanet exhales a full-bodied scream. After more treatment, he wraps her arm in a brace and hands them both small balls of red medicines to swallow. In the end, he gives Bernard a tube of white oilment for their burned skin. He also hands him some red oilment for the swelling and deep bone fractures. "You three should rub both in every few hours, over your arms and faces. I'll check on you in the morn, but you should rest for now."

The nurse repacks his purse as Bernard looks over the containers of oilment. "Could this red oilment have worked on emorteen poison?"

"Perhaps. The cures of oilments are still new to most of us. We're learning as we go what works and what doesn't." Bernard doesn't respond.

The nurse leaves the cell and returns up the staircase. The kleep rocks softly in the drift, and Sanet, tired from the long day lost at sea, rests her head on Bernard's shoulder and fades to sleep.

❖❖❖

Over the next few days, Sanet and Ethan heal acceptably to the nurse, who returns every morn and dusk to stretch them and check on their progress, insisting they keep applying the oilment to their burned faces. They're fed small meals, which are enough to keep them alive, but not enough to keep them from being hungry. They drift in and out of sleep, with dawn and dusk jumbled. Sanet turns down repeated plans to escape or fight their way to take over the kleep. Bernard grows restless and bored and so sends Brute out the small window across the room while he listens to the crewmates holler and howl at the little frek stealing their food and small tools. On more than one occasion, Paulo comes down to the cell to threaten sending the creshwillow left.

"All for nothing, I guess?" Ethan states one morn, as he practices hobbling across the cell. "We could have done absolutely nothing, and it would have made no difference."

"At least we know where the brass is, and I'm sure there's still something we could do," Sanet states encouragingly.

"How galling. I could be haynest with my son, instead of on this needless trip."

There is no answer or response to Ethan's lament. Like everything Sanet has been asked to do, it all comes back to feelings of manipulation and loss of control.

A week later, Paulo greets them, waking them from their sleep. "Come with me. We've something to celebrate." They're led outside to find the whole crew in various states of jarentness, laughter, and celebration. The moon is full, and the sea is calm. One of the men sets off a burst of celebratory lights into the sky.

"By now, the Roar should have made his way into Carvinga and the war started." Around them, there are great cheers and calls for celebration. The three are given mugs of ale. "Drink, drink, we should all be celebrating!"

Sanet and Bernard exchange looks, taking small sips. Ethan, defiant, pours his out.

"Now that's a waste there, boy," Paulo says.

Sanet puts her hand on Ethan's shoulder. She looks around and sees Brute hanging on one of the crimson men's shoulders, digging through his hair. A feeling of helplessness courses through her. Neither Ethan's defiance or Brute's indifference seem to fit her mood. *Perhaps, I just want to live the simplicity of Bernard's night gardening.*

"Since it's been a few weeks," Paulo continues, raising his mug, "I've decided to allow each of you to roam my kleep freely. Of course, if you try anything, I'll be forced to send you left. But it'll be you first," he points to Ethan, "then the old man. And finally, we'll have to keep you below decks," Paulo finishes, staring directly at Sanet. "Sur Cadwellion doesn't want his daughter sent left anytime soon." He grins without teeth.

Brute suddenly catches sight of Bernard and dashes over to hug Bernard's neck. "On seconds, it'll be that cog of yours that's sent first, old man," Paulo says with indignation.

"Not a cog," Bernard grits beneath his breath.

Paulo shrugs and calls for another round of drinking.

❖ ❖ ❖

The kleep continues along for another two weeks, sailing in various weather states, but with more control and stability than Johan's. Ethan continues to recover, first needing full crutches and then only the help of others to move around. Eventually, he's able to limp across the deck on his own. The crimson men laugh and jest and cheer him as he does. He waves them off.

Over duskmeals, Paulo is cheerful and pleasant, inviting the three to dine with him. He implores them to share their stories of obtaining the brass pieces. They respond with hasty and uninspired tales. Bernard continues to plot what they might be able to do once they arrive on the shores of Carvinga, each scenario madder than the other. It would require unexpected luck and most likely end in someone being sent.

Ethan suggests that at some point they should find the brass and toss it over, but at every turn around the kleep, they're being watched with a careful eye. Every hour, every minute, a crew member has eyes on them, and when caught, they nod with knowing smiles.

After days of trying, Paulo makes Sanet laugh. He jokes about the ranpart's incompetence, and she comes to discover that these crimson men are half believers and half coinhires. Sanet asks Paulo about his thoughts on the Roar, but he gives her little information. Just as she's unwilling to part with any truths she knows, Paulo treats her with the same distrust. Bernard is still disgusted by the whole of the crew and looks ready to strangle them all.

"Why do you even follow the ranpart?" Bernard asks Paulo.

"I don't follow him. The man pays me. And if that's the labor, I don't question his action. That's the choice I've made, and because I'm good at it, I'm content," Paulo says with little modesty.

"But the man sends people left. He's killed for his own twisted foretales. Do you want to be associated with someone like that?" Sanet asks.

Paulo doesn't answer and instead shrugs off her question with another sip of ale.

❖ ❖ ❖

On another morn, Sanet becomes sick and spends the evening in a relief chamber. She sits alone in the room for hours on end feeling nauseous as the room spins unceasingly. She mentions this dizziness to Ethan, who holds her hand and, unexpectedly, rubs her small rounded stomach. "Do you mind? Have you felt any different lately? Physically, I mean?" She nods. In the past few weeks, her stomach has felt fuller, even though her appetite has increased. Ethan, at first, takes the disclosure without answer, then speaks. "It's likely just a bout of Johan smiles." He brushes a piece of hair over her ear. "Nothing to worry about."

Days later, on an unusually warm morn, a thin sea mist burns away to reveal the shoreline in the far distance. The men aboard cheer and yell, enthusiastic to finally see the Land. The rest of the day is full of chatter about sleeping without a rocking bed and the foods and men and women they're going to indulge in. Paulo is the only one to lament the sight, clear his joy is with the sea. Ethan, fully recovered, races crew members across the main deck, the tensions of boredom and being among enemies thin and untraceable.

"We'll need to put you back in the cell," Paulo tells them.

"Afraid we'll escape?" Bernard smirks.

"Like you wouldn't?" Paulo nods for a few crewmates to bring them down below.

The three are then led into their familiar cell and small metal bracers are placed over their wrists. Once the crewmates lock the cell door and leave them alone, Bernard begins to pace once more. "So, what's the plan?" He looks to the others with hopeful, eager eyes.

"Pretty sure that's going to be all up to what happens when we get to shore," Ethan states.

Bernard is unimpressed with such uninspired logic.

They wait, unable to view any details from the small window on the other side of the room. After a few hours, they dock as the entire kleep wobbles and then comes to a diminished rocking.

A commotion rises outside, and they hear crewmates start to jump kleep, splashing down into the waters below. The sound of a large *thunk* hits the main deck, echoing across the room, and things draw quiet after everyone has left.

Bernard steps up to the cell door and begins to shake it.

"Keep calm, Bernard. They won't keep us down here," Sanet says, holding Bernard by the shoulder.

"I could probably pry this door off if we need too," Bernard states plainly, turning back to them.

"I don't think that's necessary."

"Only saying I probably could." He grips the door slightly, which creaks at his touch. "Definitely could."

Sanet shakes her head. "Listen." A muffled conversation is taking place upstairs. "They're coming down."

The voices grow louder as the door to the main deck opens and daylight beams down into the brig. Sanet shields her eyes as the silhouette of a tall and lean body blocks the sun. *Ranpart Cadwellion*. The figure steps down to them, and as it does, the three of them back away from the cell door. Wellion stands imposing and taller than the others around him.

"Sanet, dear, how sad to see you here. Guards, unlock them."

Two guards maneuver around Wellion and hastily open the cell door. Sanet stands against the back wall as they swing it open.

"Come, dear, follow me."

He turns and begins up the staircase. The three hesitate for a minor before they follow behind, passing the guards, who take up the rear. Reaching the main deck, they find the kleep lined up along a makeshift dock and a ramp that leads down to the beach. All along the shoreline and around the surrounding grasslands are tens on tens of ingreves, with getwishes standing between them, and mounted on all the large and smaller freks are onlooking twofooters.

"Guards, remove these bracers from my daughter and her friends." Wellion extends his long fingers, then walks along the ramp leading to the beach.

The guards push for the three to follow. On the beach, the surrounding march looks even more intimidating. All eyes are on them. Ranpart Cadwellion turns to Paulo, who steps forward, handing Wellion the large brass fragment. Wellion turns it over in his hands and beams.

"How did I know you'd disobey me, Sanet?" Like being scolded by a father, Sanet has a sudden flush of guilt. Wellion spins back to address the entire march. "Fellow Misipiants, we have found the remaining pieces of the brass. We are now poised for success in our undertakings against the Carvingians. No longer shall you live in fear of them. No longer shall they send your brothers and sisters, your wives and husbands, your children left. You shall be the conquerors. You shall conquer . . . with this!" He holds the brass up, and at its sight, everyone cheers. Sanet scans the massive march. Paulo is unimpressed. "At dawn, we will continue our march upon the tenfooters' stonetin. We will reunite the brass and we will . . . win . . . this . . . war!" A final cheer goes out across the crowd, sending the getwishes rearing backward.

And then the tenfooters attack.

The first sign comes when some of the twofooters take shots to the back, falling off the ingreves and rolling, sent left onto the sands. "We're being attacked!" shouts one of the twofooters.

Sanet watches as suddenly a gang of tenfooters smashes through the tall grasses. They have clubs and arrows and slings. The ingreves turn as twofooters make their attack.

Bernard grabs Sanet by the shoulder. "I think this is our major." Bernard waves to Ethan, pointing his mitted hand to the grasslands.

"In there?" Ethan asks, concerned.

"Better idea?"

Ethan looks around and, shaking his head, follows Bernard, who leads the way into the grasses. Sanet hesitates for a minor, the chaos around her growing by the minor. Looking into the blades, she recalls her long, exhaustive chase of the neox. With a deep breath, she follows the two and crashes back into the tall grass. The pursued where once she was the pursuer.

Chapter Thirty-Two

A BATTLE BETWEEN
TWOS & TENS

*T*he thwack of thick green blades hits Sanet instantly, and she presses her hands forward, trying to keep track of Bernard and Ethan, who disappeared into the blades before her. The sounds of the skirmish are all around her. Screams and yells and curses fill the air, and then she feels the rush behind her. Over her shoulder, a large ingreve opens its vertical mouth wide, releasing a deep rumbling growl before charging at her. She turns forward and continues to run.

"Bernard! Ethan!" she screams.

No answer, and the chaos of battle, the whirls and whizzing of bolts and arrows, guns and rifles, makes it even harder to hear if they are calling back to her.

Afraid to lose them, but also afraid to be caught by whatever might be in pursuit, she cuts slightly east as the ingreve brushes past her, whacking grass blades into her back. She races through the blades and spots a clearing ahead. She pushes a few remaining blades aside to find herself before three ingreves surrounding a barwolf. This monstrous frek, thirty measures high, is currently unrolled, showing massive claws that are ten feet wide and dug into the dirt below. It opens its mouth, wide as its body, and chomps at one of the ingreves, tossing five twofooters off it and sending them thudding to the ground. As they scramble to stand, a tenfooter straddled atop the barwolf leaps down with a spear aimed to stab one of the twofooters. In a swift, deft swing, he slings the spear east, throwing the impaled twofooter into the others. Behind him, the barwolf curls in on itself, creating a massive woolly ball that bowls and crashes into the ingreves. One of the fallen twofooters attempts to crawl away, but the tenfooter, without mercy, stomps over and pierces him with the spear. Letting out a guttural scream, he spins to Sanet.

As she's about to run, Wellion appears from a side of the clearing, his hand outstretched and his glass orb floating inches above it. His other hand points at the tenfooter and squeezes into a fist, crumbling the body before her. *All sent without cause.* Before he catches her presence, Sanet disappears into the grasses.

She runs ahead blindly, registering the whoosh of passing bodies—tenfooters and twofooters, getwishes and barwolves—all of them emitting rage, distress, or fear. She continues to run and uses what little perception she must to hear if anything is in front of her or to her sides. She cuts east. Then west. Then east for a major. Then straight.

After majors pass, she finds herself ascending a small hill where the blades around her shorten and she's able to witness the first glimpse of war. Across the grasslands of Carvinga, in every direction, stands destruction. Smoke and fire rise from oversized settlements. Buildings are blown in half. There is a smattering of large throne-shaped stonetins, one close and others farther, much farther, in the distance. Her eyes catch eight barwolves rolling through the grasses like giant caustic boulders plowing over everything in front of them. A group of twofooters hangs from a couple of ingreves, shooting arrows and rifles at the incoming barwolves with no success. Sanet scans around and, to her surprise, hears the voice of Bernard. She turns and sees him waving his arms at her. Relieved, she waves back and hurries down toward him back into the tall grasses. "Bernard!" she screams aloud in response and hears the muffled sound of her curam. She continues in the same direction until, finally, he grabs her by the shoulders.

"Approsh Lincoln, I thought I lost you."

They hug and squeeze with abandon.

Bernard asks, "Ethan?"

"I haven't seen him. He was behind you, but in front of me."

"We'll find him. We need to get out of this fight. There're outright sendlefts around here. No wonder friends hate war."

Sanet nods and takes Bernard by the mitt as they start to move again through the thick grass. As they do, they pass a gang of tenfooters, who upon seeing them lunge and scream. Their massive hairy bodies are horrifying to glimpse and cause them both to jump backward into the fray. As they run from the tenfooters, they bump into an ingreve mounted by twofooters, who point and yell at them but are immediately attacked by the chasing tenfooters. At this, Bernard and Sanet disappear into the grass. They continue to run until they arrive in a tenfooter settlement.

The buildings, once haynests to the tenfooters, are constructed twice the size of what Sanet has grown to know. They have doors twelve feet high and upper floors starting twice her own height. This settlement, which contains more than three dozen buildings, sits razed and burning. Moans and screams and blood litter the streets. Decomps raid the recently sent. Twofooters and tenfooters alike crawl against the sides of buildings, clinging to comrades, crying and shouting into the air for help or cursing the other side. One twofooter repeatedly stabs a tenfooter long since sent left. Ahead, a floor collapses as twofooters gather around it, pulling a rope and revealing a family of hiding tenfooters whose arms are around their younger children, already taller and more intimidating than the attacking twofooters. When they're exposed, they scream in retreat and surrender but instead are met with guns and bolts, sent left within minors.

"Lincoln," Bernard whispers.

They continue to dodge and weave through the buildings, hopping corpses of both states and doing everything they can to remain invisible to the pandemonium.

Reaching the other side of the settlement, they charge into the grasslands once more, unsure of where they're going, but hoping at some point they'll leave the battlements. They continue along for another hour before the sounds of battle, the screams, the horror, the gunfire, start to fade. Their pace lightens and eventually they feel safe walking, pushing the blades aside with careful gentle motions.

"We have to leave this state," Bernard declares.

Eventually, they come to another small settlement, this one destroyed but already abandoned. The smell of rotting corpses and the fog of dust and collapsed buildings carry through the air.

"Let's find a place here to hole up. Catch our breath before we decide what to do," Sanet suggests.

They wander the devastated town until they find a building that is mostly intact, where others have massive missing walls or crumpled ceilings. They push through the front door, which is already cracked open. Inside, they find the oversized furnishings of a tenfooter family. A pile of clean picked bones sits neatly in a corner. A rotting unknown smell hangs in the air. Sanet collapses onto one of the tough, hard couches. She closes her eyes. At once, the silence feels odd and invasive. For the morn, she has been bombarded with a cacophony of horror. Flashes of terrified faces cross her mind. The conflict of ire and wrath. The tenfooter who slaughtered twofooters. The twofooters showing no compassion to the bystander family.

Bernard searches the house for dangers, and when he returns, he sits next to Sanet. "I hope Ethan is safe. Wish we didn't get separated."

Sanet sits up. "I wish I knew where in Carvinga we are. Don't know if we're closer south near Radiba or up north near Yikshir."

The house remains silent and still as movement arises outside. They stand and walk over to the window, catching a tenfooter walking the streets, holding a giant spear. It looks toward them as they duck out of the way. "Did he see us?"

"Don't think so," Bernard says.

She peeks, and the tenfooter is gone. "We should leave."

Bernard agrees, and they make their way toward the back of the giant house, where an older tenfooter enters, carrying a smaller child. Sanet and Bernard turn to run as the tenfooter cries out to them.

"What's you doing in my house?"

They stop, raising hands on head. "Apory. We mean no harm. We're trying to stay out of the fight." Sanet pleads, fearful of being so close to the towering tenfooter.

"Are yous with the caped denizens?" the tenfooter asks, setting his child down. The young one immediately starts walking toward them.

Sanet shakes her hand. "We are not. We'll leave in peace."

"Now, now, yous don't need to. It's dangerous outs there. My brethren are ons a rampage. If you're seen by them . . ." The tenfooter's speech trails off as he heads toward his kitchen. The child stares inquisitively at Sanet and Bernard, chewing on its finger a minor before spinning and following its father into the kitchen. The two exchange a look before stepping forward. "Can we offer yous something to drink?" the tenfooter calls out.

Taken aback, but grateful, Bernard answers, "That would be much approshed." They wait as the tenfooter returns with large mugs of red coffee.

"Please, haves a seat." The tenfooter motions toward the couch as he sets down the mugs. He then moves toward the window and pulls its curtain closed and flips on a lamp. The small tenfooter child starts upstairs, remarking that he wants to play with his toys. Alone in the room save for Sanet and Bernard, the tenfooter takes the mug and drinks before speaking. "What side are yous fighting for?"

"In truth, we were taken as prisoners and came off a kleep when the Carvingians attacked our captors."

"The twofooters were your captors?"

"The crimson men. And the ranpart."

"Oh, yes, that's what you call that midfrek," the tenfooter says with a pinge of disdain in his voice. "Why did they capture you, fighting for us were you?"

"We were in possession of items they sought."

"I see. Does this have to do with the ardroke that midfrek is attempting to resurrect?"

"Ardroke?" Bernard asks.

"The ardrokes who roamed the Land long before us. Theys were our rulers. Yous call us tenfooters because we have spent generations attempting to extend ourselves in respect and worship of them. You think you insult us with the term, but it is a badge of honor. We will be ready when they return."

"So, you want them to return?"

"Their return would mean the end of things. But, nones the less, we must be ready. Wees closed our borders to protect his grave, but the twofooters who've destroyed our state seems to be looking for this ardroke Carvin." Sanet and Bernard shake their head at the curam. "The first ardroke and the bell toll of the Zantiphy. When our ancestors subdued him, they buried him beneath Carvinga and built other stonetins around the state as temples of worship, but Carvin lies in only one of them. Most Carvingians don't know it's only the one. Only him."

Sanet sits forward. "Buried where? And if he is something to be subdued, something to be feared, why do you worship him?"

"He's a symbol of power. Of might. But in truth, it was nots our decision. The other states united under the fight against the ardrokes. Carvin was taken down here in our state. Leaving us as these twofooters have, in disarrays and in indescribable destruction. They left us with nothings but the ardroke's corpse. The disrespect other denizens have for us and theirs judgment against our regard for the ardroke made us close the borders to yous. We no longer want anything to do with the likes of yous." He says this with a snivel, drool dripping from his mouth. "We worship the ardroke as the truths, and in doing so have beguns our march toward becoming like him. Like Carvin. We, like the ardrokes before us, must protect the Land."

"Perhaps that's why the Misipiants want him back," Bernard surmises.

"They believe the ardroke would help destroy us. That the ardroke would be jealous of our size and fight for the twofooters instead, but thats is perfect flambanes. The ardroke would destroy everything."

Bernard stands up, turning to Sanet. "What is Cadwellion's plan here? To bring back some massive frek and destroy the states?"

Sanet thinks a major. "If he was studying the royal family, perhaps he wants to unite the states again. If he creates a disaster, a war, he's forcing the states to merge. Which is what the crimson men want."

"To unite behind the Roar," Bernard says with annoyance.

"A new royal family," Sanet states.

"Why would he wants to destroy the Land, only to brings it together?" the tenfooter asks.

"That is the question. I know there are people who believe in a united states. That too many are pricing its people, sending the lower classes left; but it's rather extreme to start a war to free a bunch of bodies," Sanet works out.

"If anythings, why starts the war here? Why put our denizens in danger? Wees have lived in peace for alls time. The Laws keeps us in peace."

"Radiba, too, has been in peace. Seems presumptuous to think that we all want to be under the banner of one rule," Bernard doubles.

Sanet becomes heated. "Because you and you are safe? Happy? What about those who are not? What about Logan? What about the bodies of Balton, who were cleansed for no reason other than to keep the Law of Population?"

"No one has to stay in those states with such statutes and practices. They can leave," the tenfooter says plainly.

"Those are their haynests. And Logan isn't from Organsia. He's from Radiba. And the Carvinga have been sending its own bodies left. We saw them being thrown into the pits, to drown or be eaten by krakes. Why? Because they weren't big enough? What about what you did to the Misipiants," Sanet states.

The tenfooter retorts. Standing and pacing about, raising the tension of the room. "Then yous agree with this war? Yous agree with these spineless twofooters marching into our state and setting it on fire?"

"That's not the answer, of course not. Nor is bringing back some colossal weapon, but we should do something to stop these atrocities, shouldn't we?"

"Yous idealism smothers reality, girl. The ancestors knews better than us. They knews that denizens need their freedom from others' morals. They knews we needed space to practice and freedom to roam. These were the tenets of the Land. Any deviation from these are paths to our undoing." The tenfooter takes a final sip before refilling. "It's been a long day. I'm going to get mees Fran to sleep. You are welcome to stay." With that, the tenfooter bows and retires upstairs.

After he leaves, Bernard turns to Sanet. "Regardless of who is right, what are we going to do about it?"

"To be honest, I don't know. I don't know because I'm not even sure why I'm here. My entire life so far has been in training for this. The whole of these past seven years has been to help Wellion reunite this brass."

"You can't believe that."

"In some ways. I feel as trapped as Logan did. I don't want to do what Wellion wants because he found me. I don't owe him my life. He helped me, but I'm not going to be some servant for the rest of my life."

"You don't need to be his servant. Leave. Let's go back to Radiba."

"But what if these protnuks are right? What if what Wellion wants is right, but he's doing it wrong? Ethan said that the protnuk told him, 'Reunite the brass and fulfill the exarmadasis.' But I don't think Wellion is the one who's supposed to reunite the brass. I believe you are," Sanet says, staring at Bernard.

"Me? I'm just a gardener. I'm a man who chased a neox and lost a partner."

"And I've been controlled, pushed and told and trained and given instruction. I've had my life taken from me. I don't think it was violet that did it. I don't even have a taste for it. I think Wellion did something to me. He's been forcing this on me. And I believe that you weren't in this plan of his. That man who was giving him all these answers—you weren't part of that. I feel that's what makes you the Dark Valor. The one he couldn't see. The man in the shadow."

"It's flam. And even if I were, what am I going to do? Walk up to Wellion and demand he give me the brass?"

"I don't know. I don't. I only know that I can't let some ranpart control me anymore."

"He doesn't. You can leave now. We can travel south and let this whole battle play itself out."

"And if that brass does bring back some giant monster, some great destruction . . . then it was me who sent all these bodies left. I recovered that brass." *You weren't supposed to, Sanet.*

"There's nothing we can do, though."

"Yes. You. You are the Dark Valor. We can make a choice to change the foretale. You said you wanted to let your soul have its way. That you've let the careful warnings of your parents and your partner hold you back. Perhaps now is the time to make a choice as well. You've gone this far . . ." Sanet sits closer, taking Bernard by the hand. "It's time we take our own paths."

"You're sounding like a little Roar yourself."

"In truth, it's what feels right. Doesn't it?"

There's a minor when Bernard doesn't answer. His mind seems to reflect on their past few months together. *I'm sure Jame is weighing in on his decision.* "Wisnok. How shall we upset your friend Cadwellion?" Bernard asks.

Sanet answers plainly, "We find Carvin's Grave . . . and we take back our brass. Somehow."

❖ ❖ ❖

Sanet and Bernard set out onto the street, careful to avoid the eyes of others. Bernard notes the unusualness of kind tenfooters, to which Sanet replies, "The Land is full of surprises."

The new plan is to track the destruction. To follow the march of Wellion and, hopefully, find some means to steal back some of the brass. The idea feels absurd, but for some reason, Sanet feels it is right. Bernard is unispar, different from the rest. In some ways, she had thrust him into this role, forced him to believe in the hymn of a hungry frek. But perhaps it didn't matter. Bernard is clearly capable. The smith's mitts have given him confidence and abilities she couldn't imagine. She is also afraid of Bernard. He has a growing rage inside him, one that lacks compassion for the crimson men. One she thinks she should rein in. *Jame isn't here to give him counsel. He can't see that Paulo is kind, driven by coin over fanaticism.* There were nights in the cell when Bernard seemed eager and ready to send the entire crew left.

Convincing Bernard also feels selfish. In some way, she is rebelling against Wellion because that's all she knows. He had taken her, she was sure of it, from her haynest. From wherever she came from. From her mother and father. From her life. And then he'd convinced her that she had no past. There is a fury inside her for what Wellion did to her, for so boldly lying to her.

They continue through the settlement before heading back into the tall grasses, walking along through the blades for a few hours before coming to a clearing. It contains another small settlement with no more than six buildings, one of which has been recently set afire. Abandoned. As they walk along, they catch a glimpse of some wandering getwishes.

Bernard turns to Sanet. "We should use those as mounts through the grass."

Sanet agrees. They hurry toward the getwishes and then flank them, Sanet going west and Bernard east. Bernard walks up to one, holding out his hand with a bit of granola. "There, there." The getwish, with its odd elongated head and long knobby knees, steps backward. "There, there, little frek," Bernard states.

He stops in place, and the getwish steps forward, dipping its head and taking a small bite from his hand. He waves to Sanet, who walks out from the side of a building. The getwish perks its head up at seeing her but then returns to nibbling the granola. Sanet pulls from her pouch a bit of granola as well, holding her hand out toward the other getwish. It legs over to her and begins to munch, its wet beak and soft pinches tickling her palm. She pets the abnormal frek as she sees Bernard grab the neck of the one he's lured and hops on.

"Mount it, they're used to it."

Sanet turns back, grabbing the getwish's neck and lifting herself on. It bows a bit under her weight but quickly recovers, lifting her upward. The sensation of its round and wide back spreading her legs apart is odd. Intuiting the frek has already had some experience with being reined, she takes ahold and leads the getwish behind Bernard. They set off.

Heading through the grass now gives them much more to see. The Land is vast and open. Pockets of smoke surround them from various battles taking place in areas miles away. And then to their northwest, they see a great stonetin, the largest Sanet has ever seen, which holds quite the commotion around it.

Bernard turns back to her. "Think that's the place?"

"When I was on that hill, there were dozens that I could see. But this one does seem the largest of them," she says, looking back at it.

Bernard nods and turns back, flicking the reins on the getwish to pick up pace. Sanet follows suit, and soon they're galloping through the grasses toward the monolithic throne-shaped stonetin.

Chapter Thirty-Three
THE GRAVE OF CARVIN

*D*rawing closer to the stonetin, Bernard and Sanet catch sight of a tenfooters' march camped across the grassland almost a mile away. Barwolves wander through rows of oversized tents, with some rolling and others trotting over the heads of the tenfooters, who duck beneath their crossing bodies. Bernard leads Sanet and their getwishes toward a large boulder away from the camp and ties off the tall freks so they can move in closer without being seen. As they step through the thick, dimly lit blades toward the noise of the camp, they pick up bits of conversation.

With relief, they discover that Wellion is at the minor inside the stonetin where they all believe Carvin's Grave lies. Throughout the camp, tenfooters offer conflicting thoughts in their discussions about whether Wellion's ability to resurrect Carvin is even possible. Most seem assured it is. Some of the tenfooters want to move in before he's able to release the ardroke, but the stonetin's defenses, now in the control of the twofooters, would likely send most left. Fear that Wellion is planning to complete the ritual this very evening permeates through the camp. And there are no disagreements that the ranpart's only reason to initiate these skirmishes from the Misipit state line to the Carvingian coast was to seek out and conquer Carvin's Grave.

After listening for a half hour, Bernard and Sanet return to the getwishes. "Looks like we know where we need to go."

"But how do we get inside?" she asks.

"Back into the grass and then over there, I'd reckon," Bernard whispers, pointing to the back of the stonetin, where flickering red lights emit from a line of thin horizontal openings carved near its base.

She nods and they guide their getwishes away and around the tenfooters' long camp. As they pull closer to the stonetin, its magnificent size rises farther into the air, growing larger and more impressive with their every stride. Atop each of the four towers, dozens of twofooters pace back and forth, taking stock of the Land beneath them.

"We should drop into the grass," Bernard calls back as he hops down from his getwish.

Sanet agrees, stepping off her own. The minor she's in the blades, her getwish makes a high-pitched squeal before tumbling backward, shot in the neck with an arrow. This startles Bernard's getwish, who legs itself into the blades beyond, leaving Bernard and Sanet plunging to their stomachs, hands over head. *Shnite!*

Looking up, Sanet slinks over to Bernard, and he takes her by the hand. After a triple count, he nods, and they stand and begin running, keeping the prominent stonetin in their sights along the tips of the grasses above. Every few steps, arrows *shink* past their shoulders and legs.

Bernard offers, "I think they've spied us."

"We'll lose them ahead. Hopefully."

They continue to run and—after what feels like forever—find themselves reaching the stonetin wall. The structure is colossal, with gray bricks built on bricks, each five feet tall. The overgrown grass grows all the way to the stonetin's foundation, allowing Bernard and Sanet to remain partially hidden from where they'll begin climbing.

"Look there." Bernard points. Above them, twenty measures upward, is the row of openings, presumably light and air holes. "Ready to climb up this brick?"

Sanet nods, following Bernard's lead. He steps up to the wall, reaches for the first block, and digs his fingers into the crack. Hand over hand, he climbs with ease. *Not a single drop of sweat.* Sanet follows behind, using the holes left behind by his stone fingers, keeping her eyes directly above for any down-looking twofooters.

Bernard reaches the window first and helps Sanet with the last few feet. From the opening's ledge, they view a glowing red stonetin lit by hundreds of torches. An oppressive heat blows past them into the darkness behind them. Brute finishes climbing and perches on Bernard's shoulder. The hall ahead is empty, though they still wait a major before dropping in. When they do, their impact echoes across the corridor. Sanet points ahead to a doorway, and they scamper across the spacious hall and then dive into the relatively small room. Immediately they notice how every object and furnishing stands nearly twice its normal size, including doors and torches, and tables and chairs. The effect is dizzying.

This antechamber looks to be a document room of sorts lined with shelves and shelves of paperwork. The room itself doesn't appear to have been used for many years, with dust and debris collecting on the papers. Everything in the antechamber is designed near twice in size. Sanet peeks out in the hall once again, looking down the long corridor. Still empty. She motions to Bernard, and they sneak out, sliding along the wall, keeping low, and attempting to minimize their footsteps' echoes.

Halfway down the hall, they come across a grander room where columns around its center mark a descending, half-crooked staircase. The walls inside this room present an enormous relief carving of a large, four-armed frek, each hand holding a substantial block hammer. Echoes of movement ascend from below. Sanet and Bernard continue until they reach the head of the large staircase, where they observe exaggerated shadows moving across the lower floor and walls. Sanet eyes Bernard, who acknowledges what she's seeing. They begin stepping down the tall staircase.

It's not long before an underground chamber comes into view, and they witness the shadows and bodies of twofooters and crimson men alike, all facing inward. Sanet scans this outer room and spots another overlooking ledge, similar in style to the earlier one. Slowly and cautiously, they step toward it before climbing the jutted wall protruding at the foot of the staircase. Upon reaching the upper ledge, they take their first glimpse of the space below.

Ranpart Cadwellion is in the middle of the chamber and stepping toward a tall cube-shaped tablatur. The entire room is populated by hundreds of varied bodies: twofooters on artificial legs, a few others without, crimson men. Paulo and some of the crew members are there as well as Ethan, whose hands are tied in front of him. At either shoulder stand familiar guards of Cadwellion's, one male and the other female. On the far end of the room stands a small tent with eight guards surrounding it. The tent is red, similar in hue to the cloaks of the crimson men, and an ornate letter Y is sewn on both sides of it. Cadwellion demands beholding as he steps up to the high tablatur and addresses the crowd.

"Bodies of Misipit, heroes of the Land, we are gathered here to commence the first stage of our unification." At this word, the crowd cheers. "For too long, the Land has grown perilous without a leader. Without a ruler to keep us free from the tyranny of our coming oppressors. Your Roar, your voice, has arrived!"

The crowd cheers again, their focus and heads turning toward the tent. From it a small boy, no more than six years old, emerges. He wears a deep red veil over his face. The boy walks about ten strides in front of the tent and then raises both arms, sending the crowd into a remarkable fit.

Cadwellion chants, "The advent of the Roar brings the union of the Land. The advent of the Roar brings the union of the Land."

Everyone continues to cheer and shout, repeating the chant at the boy.

And then the boy speaks, in what feels a practiced cadence, his voice small and quivering. "I, Yannick, am your servant. I will protect you from our enemies. I will bring the Land together. I am your Roar!" He holds his hands up again, and the crowd is sent into even further fervent chants and hollers.

Sanet turns to Bernard. "I thought this Roar was a baby. Wasn't he found only a few months ago?"

Bernard shrugs, his face growing angry. From the crowd, Paulo steps forward, pulls a knife, and tosses it at the boy. The audience gasps in amazement as the knife whizzes by them and then stops midair. The boy is unaffected, unmoved; across the room, Cadwellion's hand is outstretched, the small glass orb floating beside him. Paulo screams, pushed to his knees by an unseen force. The knife, still floating in the air, spins and points at Paulo. It slowly begins gliding toward him, and he squirms and struggles against invisible bonds. The boy turns away and returns to his tent while a silent crowd watches breathlessly as the knife reaches Paulo's throat and pierces through without slowing. He gurgles and spits blood, and when sent left thumps to the ground.

The air is chilled. Where minors ago everyone felt energized and eager to celebrate, a darkness now looms over the attempted assassination of the small boy curamed Yannick.

Cadwellion scans the room, then asks, "Are there any other defectors among us?"

Sanet has a notion to say something. For too long she has sat along the coastlines, letting the sea's tide wash over her. Wellion stands there, vulnerable, and it is time to act. But something inside stops her, a voice telling her to wait. That her safety is more important than vengeance. *When have I ever feared my sending?* She senses Bernard's muscles tense at Wellion's call but holds him back.

"Not yet," she whispers.

Wellion looks around the room, and Ethan steps forward. *Ethan, you cog man, what are you doing?* He raises his bound hands.

"This is madness. Resurrecting an ardroke is madness. Their only use is to destroy everything."

As Ethan pleads for sanity and logic, the crowd begins to hiss. Wellion steps closer to him. Surprisingly, the female guard steps between Ethan and the ranpart.

"Don't hurt him," the woman shouts.

"Amil, don't!" Ethan reaches forward, grabbing her by the arm just as Wellion rips her away, twisting her body and flinging her across the room. *Sent.*

Ethan's eyes well and he falls to his knees.

Wellion sneers through his teeth, wiping his bleeding nose. "My dear acolyte, have I taught you nothing? Has history taught you nothing? We are on the verge of the total annihilation of mankind. We are not destroying it . . . we are saving it."

Ethan looks up at Wellion, fury in his eyes.

"Flam to stand up to that friend like that," Bernard whispers. "Brave, but flam."

"It is no matter, acolyte. Your short-sided perspective has no bearing here. Does it, my bodies?" Wellion raises his hands and receives a welcoming agreement. Cheers and shouts. "Now, for the unification."

From the opposite corner of the chamber, four guards carry a considerable chest. The crowd quiets as the guards step across the large hall and set the chest down beside Wellion, who has returned to his place before the front of the cube-shaped tablatur. The guards step to either end of the tablatur and pull on two large rings built into the stone and wood. It snaps apart, sending a deep boom throughout the chamber. The crowd stiffens into nervous hums of awe and fear. As the tablatur opens, it reveals a large brass orb with a serpentine chunk missing from its side. The orb floats in the air above a large hole, once hidden by the tablatur. The orb is almost ten feet in width, just a fraction smaller than the hole it floats above. Once each side of the tablatur is pulled clear, the guards stand back. Their faces look outright terrified. Wellion's sharp yellow teeth appear in a thin, twisted smile.

He steps over to the chest and opens it up, pulling from it what is clearly the missing piece of the orb.

"He's about to do it," Bernard states. "What are we going to do?"

Sanet doesn't know. It feels too late. They're too high; there're too many others. They'd never be able to run down there and stop him. And the six pieces, the three they found and the three Wellion gathered, are already together, too large to carry out single-handedly.

"I don't know." The helplessness overcomes her again as well as an instinct to protect herself over anyone else. Who is she? A woman without a past believing she could somehow alter fate and lead a revolt with an old man with broken fingers. Instead, she sits in silence. In wait as it unfolds before her.

As they watch, Wellion uses his glass orb to float the soon-to-be-unified seventh fragment into place within the larger brass orb. Anticipation sweeps across the crowd as the piece draws closer and closer to the orb. Then, without fanfare, within a whisper, the piece moves into place with a clean *clinking* snap. The crowd doesn't react. Breathless. Fearing something about to happen. Wellion steps forward and puts his elongated fingers across the now-smooth reunited brass orb. He begins to whisper something in an old language. Sanet glances over at Ethan, who begins to step backward into the crowd, as if prepared to run. Wellion continues to circle the orb, chanting something under his breath, his eyes now closed. The guards have all stepped back.

The orb begins to sink into the hole under it. This causes a stir in the crowd.

"What's happening?" someone shouts.

Wellion doesn't answer but instead continues to caress the orb with his fingers and chant with his eyes closed. The orb continues to descend, farther and farther into the floor, and soon, it falls out of Wellion's reach. He opens his eyes. "It is done."

With these words, the guards suddenly react. Two of them run into the tent and take the boy Yannick. The remaining guards, some within the crowd, some near the ranpart, all turn on the twofooters and crimson men. They attack, shooting and slicing them down. Blood and screams fill the entire chamber. Sanet covers her mouth in shock. Bernard's eyes widen.

"We have to go now," Bernard states.

There's no more time to wait. Sanet pulls her crossbow and flicks the switch on top, igniting one of the bolts. She aims squarely for Ranpart Cadwellion and pulls the trigger. The bolt fires across the chamber but freezes before hitting him. Cadwellion spins in place as the bolt falls innocuously to the floor. He points to Sanet, and she suddenly feels her insides being pushed. She falls backward off the ledge. Bernard catches her as she slams her back against the wall below, losing her breath. Out of Wellion's sight, she regains feeling in her body and reorients to gain a grip on the wall.

"I have it."

"Wisnok. I'll come down after you."

She lets Bernard's firm grip go and begins descending the wall. Above her, Bernard fires his rifle. To her side, Brute is clinging to the wall, and below her, she hears the screams and running footsteps of crimson men and twofooters alike. She can see a few of them. Some are blood-soaked; others are carrying bodies already sent left. It's complete bedlam, bodies pushing past each other like a tumbling river just as the entire stonetin starts to reverberate. Huge stone bricks from above crash down onto the staircase, smashing against some of those trying to escape, causing even more screams and yells. Sanet reaches the ground and pushes against the crowd, trying to get into the main chamber. She sees Bernard finally making his way down.

Inside, the bulk of the crowd has escaped the large room, but there are no signs of Wellion. Guards and twofooters are still fighting what looks to be an uneven match. The guards are much more skilled, taking out four or five twofooters at a time. The crimson men are in even greater shock. They're young bodies. At the major, Sanet feels apory for them. Eager, flam coinhires betrayed by Wellion without effort or strain. *He treats everyone the same. With complete disregard of their lives.* More brick and dust come tumbling from above, filling the air with a thick fog.

"Bernard! Ethan!" she screams into the chaos.

Bernard grabs her by the shoulder. "We should get that brass."

"It's already done. We have to leave."

"No. You brought me here, that's what we're going to do!" Bernard exhorts her over the yells and screams.

"How?"

He doesn't answer. Behind her, there's a pronounced crash in the wall of the stonetin, and the crowd shifts its focus. Tenfooters, mounted on barwolves and carrying gigantic axes and hammers as well as spears and guns, smash through, causing a huge wave of air to billow into the room, dropping its temperature. The smoke quickly clears as Sanet turns her attention back to Bernard, who's made his way to the large hole in the ground, where streams of blood drip down below like rivulets. He jumps in and disappears. Brute follows behind him.

"Bernard!" Sanet runs forward, trying to catch Bernard, who almost immediately rises upward, Brute on his shoulder.

Some of the others witness this, and it becomes clear after a major that Bernard stands atop a platform rising from the hole. The platform, too large for the small opening, slams through the floor, causing everyone to react in shock and fall backward, fearing what's taking place. The crash makes Bernard bend over, holding tight onto the light-tan platform as it continues upward

420

out of the hole. The higher it rises, the more its true form becomes apparent.

It's a hand.

Sanet steps backward. *It's real.* The hand, followed by a wrist, bends downward, causing Bernard to jump clear and roll shoulder over waist on the ground. Brute leaps forward into the crowd and zips in and out of the scattering legs. Sanet tries to hurry toward Bernard, but the large hand smashes down between the two, positioning itself as if something below is ready to climb out. At this, the entire clash devolves into a retreat. Twofooters, guards, crimson men, tenfooters all turn to cover. The ground beneath them cracks.

Sanet runs around it and jumps over the growing fissure. She pulls on Bernard, who stumbles up, shaking his head. "We have to go. We have to run." She looks down into the fissure and catches her first glimpse of the monstrous size of the ardroke below. "Bernard, run!"

Chapter Thirty-Four
OVERTURE OF
THE DARK VALOR

*D*ust clouds discharge from the stonetin as the panicked crowd emerges, climbing up from the underground chamber into the grasslands above. The setting sun transmits a muted cerise red across the burning prairie. Sanet, shuffled within the crowd, turns to catch her first glimpse of the colossal frek still pulling itself from the ground below. After an entire arm surfaces, clawing for a nearby column, shattering its outer layer of brick, a second arm appears. It drives straight for the same column, bricks tumbling in its wake. Together, they pull the frek out—and what appears is wholly unnatural. It is repulsion incarnate wrapped in vulgar strands of fur braided into a thousand smaller ones and creating an endless hypnotic loop.

It pulls and drags itself from the depths, emanating a dread that seeps into the soul, leaving Sanet motionless, overwhelmed with panic. The monstrous head of the ardroke, now appearing from underground as Carvin's chamber continues to shatter and collapse in on itself, also swirls in this matted fur, dripping with what looks to be caked mud. Its long worm mouth can barely hold in rows and rows of barbed yellow and black fangs. A purple tongue slithers across its lips as if it were its own living beast.

And then there are the eyes: one a vacant gray with thick blue veins pulsing with its heartbeat; the other the brass orb set perfectly in its socket. The orb that must have been shattered years ago to prevent its return. The ground smashes open even more, revealing two other arms, which it uses to complete its emancipation from the grave. It opens its mouth, issuing a raucous bay that steals down Sanet's gaping throat and leaves a toxic knot within her stomach. It is death. It is the end of all things.

Running in all directions away from the stonetin, the crowd shrieks and bawls, the noise swelling erratically as Carvin unfolds itself and stretches upright, striking the stonetin roof and launching a pair of twofooters to the grasses below.

Released upon the Land, the four-armed ardroke stands a thousand feet high, towering above even the stonetin. A young crimson boy next to Sanet falls to the ground as he crawls backward while attempting to gawk upward. The ardroke steps forward, stomping down among the crowd, crushing twofooters and crimson men alike. The crunch of bones and wet splattering carry through the air, drowned only by the cries of panic. One of its four arms reaches down and rips from the root a nearby tree as if it were a flimsy branch stuck in the dirt. Carvin then tosses it aside, slamming it against more of the fleeing crowd. More sent.

To Sanet's west, a gang of tenfooters fires guns at the ardroke, their bullets pelting the thick, matted fur—but the act is futile. They're unable to distract the frek from its forward course. Sanet turns her head to locate Bernard, gone within the crowd.

She continues to be pressed away from the stonetin, hands and wisps of yelling voices passing by her. She's caught in the rattled current, forced to run and glance over her shoulder. Ahead, a small tenfooter child is shrieking, standing in a trail made from the recent fleeing of the tenfooters. As she passes the young tenfooter, her instinct is to protect him. He reaches out his arms, needing someone to save him. But no one claims the small child. Something kicks inside Sanet, and without hesitation she turns back and grabs the little one, who stands three feet tall and impossibly thin.

In her arms, the child hugs around her neck, squeezing, and cries in her ear. The tenfooter's soft and furry arms brush against her skin. Turning back, she sees Carvin has now begun reaching out for various bodies, grabbing and crushing them in its great hands, bones snapping like twigs before it tosses them in its mouth, masticates, and swallows them. It bellows again before the escaping mob, causing some to collapse to their knees in a paralyzing fear.

Sanet squeezes the tenfooter in her arms, her eyes scanning the various bodies, hoping to find someone looking for the youth. She can feel her shoulder soaking with his tears, and his whimpers and sniffles hammer in her ear. She squeezes him harder. *Where is Bernard?* The farther she makes her way from the stonetin, the thinner the crowd becomes. She calls out. "Bernard? Bernard, where are you?" And then she looks backward, toward the ardroke's large flat foot, and sees Bernard and Brute running toward it. She starts forward—*toward my friend*—but stops and looks around when she hears a familiar voice.

"Sanet!" Ethan calls from the crowd. "Sanet, what is he doing?"

She looks back and sees Bernard reach the frek's foot and jump onto it, Brute following behind him. *Lincoln, what is he doing?* She screams out, stepping forward, "Bernard, stop!"

Her sight is hampered by whiffs of smoke and dust, but she can't help but watch as Bernard unsheathes his dagger and stabs the beast while pulling himself up using the knife and clumps of its fur to climb its east leg. Brute, too, climbs the beast as if it were a tree.

"What is he doing?" Ethan yells once more.

Some of the others turn to see this small old man ascending the ankle of the ardroke, now nearly twenty feet up.

Another gang of tenfooters fire a round of shots at the frek, this time aiming for its head. One shot hits inside its mouth, and the ardroke reacts, spinning wildly. It howls, causing everyone to cover their ears and hunch over. Sanet steps backward, brushing and attempting to comfort and console the young tenfooter she embraces. Ethan has taken her by the elbow and guides her backward. Carvin steps forward again, lit only by the surrounding grass fires and blackening pink sky. She ducks from the elevated frek as it passes her and others and looks up in time to witness Bernard on the back of the ardroke's long leg. Brute is farther up. *That man is mad. I encouraged a madman.* Others notice Bernard and point and call out to him.

A small gang of twofooters are enamored with the looming ardroke standing before them. They call out to it as if it were their god: "O' Carvin! Your ascension is our blessing!"

The ardroke doesn't acknowledge them but instead steps past, and on, the worshippers below. It ambles along the prairie, grabbing at trees and grasses, howling at the air. Sanet, with her eyes fixed on Bernard, attempts to chase the ardroke, following the downed grasses of its footsteps. Ethan is behind her, along with others who are bewitched by the frek. Still others run in the reverse direction, dread seething among them.

Bernard and Brute continue upward, provoking no reaction from the ardroke. Its massive body must be unable to feel Bernard's grabbing and stabbing along its upper back. And then tenfooters emerge from the grasses ahead, discharging cannons they'd pulled to the battle. The cannonballs merely brush the ardroke's arm. One cannonball nearly hits Bernard. *Shnite, be careful.* Carvin turns, causing Sanet to lose sight of Bernard. It reaches down with one of its four arms and grabs a cannon, crushing it in its hand.

The line of tenfooters at the cannons offers an unexpected sight: Iahel sits upon one's shoulders and yells. *Is she calling out orders?* For the duration of their travels through the Tunnels, she thought of Iahel as meek. A follower. Someone ready to fade into the shadows of her own personal space. Seeing her among the tenfooters is odd. And inspiring.

Carvin howls again, and the tenfooters cower before it. It spins. "It seems me," she says aloud, "I'm going to be sent. My child!" And without thinking, she grabs for her stomach and squeezes the tenfooter in her arms. The ardroke glares at Sanet and the crowd surrounding her before commencing to stomp toward them. *My sending has come.*

Sanet steps backward before turning and running, her grasp firm on the tenfooter child, whose cry has grown to a wail. The ground beneath her reverberates with each footstep smashing down behind her. *It's above me. It's crashing down around me. There's nothing left in anything.* From the corner of her eye, she sees the ardroke's hand reach forward to a passing tenfooter and crimson man, who both screech, breath stolen, as they're lifted and yanked backward. Ethan is ahead of her, running for his life. He should be in Yikshir reading to his son. To his remaining child.

The ardroke's hand returns, reaching for her.

"Ethan, turn off the path!"

Without a minor's pause, both she and Ethan roll sideways and leap out of the way as the brush of Carvin's hand misses her and instead claims a twofooter. Sanet, flat on her back, turns and watches as the ardroke lobs the twofooter down its throat, spitting out its mechanical legs. *There's nothing left in anything.* The small tenfooter has fallen from her arms and attempts to help Sanet back to her feet while still crying out for its mother.

And there is Bernard, climbing along the frek's neck, which the ardroke senses. Bernard and Brute continue, hand over hand, paw over paw, as quick as they can, gripping the ardroke's facial fur and drawing closer to their destination: the brass eye.

The closer Bernard gets, the more the ardroke begins swiping at its face, though its arms are unable to reach, able only to swipe past them. At each swipe, Bernard swings his arm out and slices into the ardroke's finger. It responds with a howl and shakes its hand. Brute, the fearless frek, leaps from the ardroke's face onto its upper eastern hand. It bites and scratches and scrambles around, distracting the ardroke, giving Bernard time to advance once more toward the brass eye.

The whole of this insane sight, of a small man and a red creshwillow climbing on this mountainous ardroke, has now caught everyone's attention. Carvin has completely stopped and is solely motivated to remove its two intruders. Sanet stands firm, biting her lip. *You have this.* The crowd itself waits in silence. Ethan steps up beside her and grabs her shoulder. The child tenfooter reaches out to be picked up again as the three watch breathlessly.

And then Bernard reaches the brass eye, bracing one hand against its eyelid and pulling the other hand back.

With an almighty grunt, he punches the ardroke in its eye.

The ting of impact is heard a minor later ringing across the grassland. The act makes little sense at first until someone from the crowd cries out, "He's cracking its eye!" The words cause Sanet to step unconsciously forward as Bernard punches the ardroke's eye again. It howls again, spinning wildly in place before falling to its knees. Bernard loses his grip, falls back, and hangs loosely from the ardroke's eyelid. Brute, halfway down Carvin's lower arm, falls to the ground, limp.

"Bernard!" Sanet screams out.

"Bernard!" another shouts.

And then everyone begins to bellow in unison, in support and encouragement. Bernard recovers and without pause punches the ardroke's eye again—and this time, a light radiates from the cracks. Bernard shields himself.

"Bernard!" the crowd screams again.

Bernard punches the eye a fourth time and, at this, totally dismantles the orb, sending pieces flying out. The force tosses Bernard backward, down and down and down, before he clumps, like a snapped wooden staff, to the ground.

"Bernard!" Sanet shrieks, running toward him, Ethan close behind.

The rest of the crowd rushes forward. Above them, the ardroke sways for a major before falling backward and crashing to the ground and releasing a tremendous boom as dirt and dust billow out.

Sanet reaches Bernard and, setting the small tenfooter down, pulls him to the side, pushing through the agitated crowd and holding him in her arms. "Bernard, are you wisnok? Bernard, say something."

There's nothing to his expression but emptiness. Stillness. The crowd grows, gathering around them.

"Stand back! Stand. Back!" Ethan demands, stepping through. He kneels before Bernard, whose head gushes blood. He checks his pulse and holds two fingers over his mouth, then looks up at Sanet. "He's still breathing."

"Lincoln, you brave beast." She squeezes Bernard's arms. "You shnite little beast, why'd you do that?"

There is no answer.

"Carvin's dead. That man sent an ardroke left!" a tenfooter yells out.

"His curam is Bernard!" another shouts.

Sanet continues to hold Bernard tight while Ethan squeezes and rubs Bernard's forearm. His face, wrinkled and spotted, looks worn. Old. The Dark Valor called. The Dark Valor answered.

"We'll need to get him somewhere calm and quiet," Sanet says to Ethan.

Ethan stands. "Does anyone have somewhere we can rest this hero?"

A tenfooter steps forward from the crowd. "My haynest is near." She raises her hand. At this, the small tenfooter near Sanet calls out for its mother. When the tenfooter sees her child, she hurries forward, taking the little body in her arms. Sanet, for a minor, feels unexpectedly abandoned.

"Wisnok. We need to carry him there," Ethan states.

"I'll help!" yells a twofooter.

"I will as well," calls out another, a young crimson man.

"We need a bed to carry him," says another—Iahel. Her eyes are bloodshot with tears.

The crowd works together to find a flat surface to place Bernard on, and after a few majors, he's lifted into the air and carried away by Sanet, Ethan, Iahel, the tenfooter mother, and a crimson man. A twofooter has found Brute and places the tiny frek on top of Bernard. Both remain still. As they transport Bernard, the crowd reaches out to touch him, sending a prayer and approsh over him. Dustians. Lincolns. Rainmen. Or simply, sympathy for a friend. A whisper for the Dark Valor. Sanet catches Ethan's eyes, filled with tears.

"I'll carry you, my friend," he says quietly.

The crowd travels for a few miles through the fire and grasslands in uncommon silence and with unknown camaraderie before reaching a small haynest.

Inside, Bernard is set to rest in an oversized bed. Sanet wipes his brow of sweat and dirt and blood. She stands and walks over to the window to witness the crowd outside staring up at her. The Land united. In some twisted way, Wellion made everything happen the way he wanted. She steps back into the room and waits for Bernard to wake. Ethan sits quietly at his side while Brute lies motionless next to him.

Chapter Thirty-Five
ADVENT OF THE ROAR

*T*he smell of garons fill the house. Sanet pulls a roasted lyn from the oven, setting it aside to cool. Mercet enters the kitchen flying his Yantak toy through the air with a series of loops along imaginary hills and valleys. He stops after smelling the warm lyn and looks it over. "Duskmeal's ready?"

"It is."

"Yum." He smiles before returning to flying his toy farther along and out the other side of the room.

It's when she's alone again that Sanet senses an incredible sting. She massages her stomach and calls out for Ethan. "I think it's coming."

Ethan races into the room. "Really? Are you wisnok? Are you ready?"

"No." Sanet shakes her head. "Is there a choice?"

"Don't think so." Ethan reaches out and takes her by the arm, leading her down the hall into a spare sleeping room.

Mercet joins them as they make their way over to bed. "I thought we were about to have duskmeal."

"I think someone else is coming before that. Can you get me the blanket and that pot of water? The one we talked about?" Ethan asks calmly.

Sanet's stomach begins to cramp more than it ever has before. She groans. "Lincoln, I'm not ready. I'm not ready, Ethan."

"You're ready. You've been through worse," Ethan says, calming her as she lies on her back and he props her feet up.

Bernard enters the room, Brute on his shoulder, wearing his usual leather garb. He smiles and sets Sanet's mood at ease. Wellion might have wanted to call her his daughter, but seeing Bernard now, stoic and calm, protective and unreserved is as close to having her father walking in as anyone else.

"You trying to have this baby without me?"

Holding back tears, she jests, "You're welcome to have it." Sanet grits her teeth while Bernard steps forward and takes her hand.

"I wouldn't dare steal that joy from you." He sits by her side.

Mercet returns with blankets and a small pot of water and sets them down next to Ethan.

"Mercet, now go wait outside."

"Why?"

"Because, I don't want you to see this."

"But *I* want to."

"Mercet, please. Go."

Mercet rolls his eyes and stomps out of the room. Pain hits Sanet in her lower back and stomach. She squeezes Bernard's hand.

"Sanet, this is where you'll need to breathe. In through the nose." Sanet breathes in. "Out through the mouth." She breathes out. "Remember. Re—in . . . and then—lax out. Re. Lax. In. Out."

She concentrates. In through the nose. Out through the mouth. In through the nose. More pain shoots up her back, and she squeezes Bernard's hand, his fingers solid as stones, but in this instance unusually warm. "Apory."

"You can't hurt me. Squeeze all you like." Bernard smiles, patting her hand.

She grits her teeth again. *Re. Lax. Re. Lax.*

"Wisnok, Sanet, relax. Do not push yet. Be calm and safe and still."

Sanet continues to breathe. Ethan watches her below. She starts to feel a little nauseous, the room spinning, her legs shaking. They continue to wait, breathing and talking. The time passes. And passes. Breathing and breathing. Bernard attempts to bring up Sur Taron again. Sanet laughs and then snarls at him. Breathing in—

"Wisnok, Sanet, now push."

At this, Sanet's eyes widen, not ready, her whole body numb. She squeezes Bernard's hand and screams out, pushing. Sweat pours down her forehead and Bernard massages her hand with the ease and tenderness of a father. Her hips feel as if they're being torn apart. She pushes and breathes, Ethan giving her the rhythm.

"Follow me. Breathe. Push. That's right."

She continues, the room fading into black.

"Stay with me, Sanet. Push. Push."

Pressure. Tearing. Ripping. Stretching—

And then the entire pain is gone, followed immediately by the scream of a newborn. Sanet begins to cry, looking over to Bernard, who also has tears in his eyes. Ethan takes the baby, wipes it down, and cuts a long cord. After a few minutes, he walks over with it, wrinkled and small, and hands it to Sanet.

"Grats on your new baby boy."

Sanet looks down at him, shocked and awed. He has a thin layer of black hair, and his face looks as if it were a baby-faced Logan. She wipes it as he whines, eyes closed, and wiggles his hand. Mercet sneaks back into the room and walks over to them.

"It's a boy?" Mercet asks. Sanet nods. "What's his curam?"

"This is Jame," she says.

At the curam, Bernard squeezes her arm. He kisses Sanet on the forehead, and in the quiet, he breathes, "You're kind." With those words, he nods and leaves the room wiping his eyes.

"Can I hold him?" Mercet asks.

"Not yet. Let Sanet have a minor, can you?"

"Fine."

"Why don't you go see Bernard? I think he needs a friend right now."

"Wisnok." Mercet leaves reluctantly.

Ethan, patting her brow dry, "Do you need anything. Water?"

"No. Everything's just right."

Ethan wipes his hands and gathers the towels and pot, then leaves the room, leaving Sanet alone with her newborn baby boy.

Wellion had his way in a way. Uniting the states. Having this child with Logan. But did he know it would be born and not chosen? She caresses Jame, who at the minor has fallen asleep. *Where is Logan now?* She wonders if he has any sense that his son has been born all the way across Merigen. *I hope he knows.* Bernard told her a few weeks ago that once she had the baby, he would make the trip to Organsia to discuss releasing Logan. "By force if necessary," he said with a grin. With their coin from the brass somewhere at the bottom of the sea and no longer an option to pay Logan's debts, Bernard hopes he might figure another way.

As she lies back, feeling sore yet surprisingly content, gently stroking the silky head of her son, her mind drifts over all she's witnessed over the past year and what's become of this small circle of friends.

Bernard—he's the one who's most changed. There is a confidence in him since the Two Tens Battle. Once Bernard grew well, the gang sneaked away south to Radiba, where they decided to rebuild his haynest. Ethan returned to Salsman and ended his marriage with Undess, then took Mercet away with him. He had taken the sending of his friend Amil hard and wanted nothing to do with Wellion or decidedly the entire state of Yikshir.

When Ethan and Mercet arrived back in Radiba, the four spent the next few months finishing Bernard's haynest rebuild. After the stress and immediacy of their past travels, they found welcome simplicity in the woodwork and painting. *Pitch back the old, catch front the new.*

They took a meandering marvelous trek to southern Radiba and purchased new furnishings. The new house, though principally the same, was planned to include additional rooms because it would now be haynest to Sanet, Ethan, and Mercet. After releasing Logan—if they could—they planned for Ethan and Mercet to make haynest somewhere nearby and for Sanet and Logan to move into their own. *Should Logan forgive me . . .*

The baby stirs, burbles in his sleep, and stills. Sanet smiles. Rumors of Wellion and the young Yannick boy have thinned since the return of the ardroke and the battle before it. In the wake of the ardroke's death, a sudden peace spread through Carvinga and reconstruction began across the state. The anger and blame for the fight rested entirely on the ranpart after the Misipiants executed a formal appizement and sent resources to assist in rebuilding. Most surprisingly, the Carvingians opened their borders, and rumors say the Tunnels beneath have fallen into economic turmoil. Gossip at Bomwigs has it that a group of nefarious coinhires have taken over Greren and Tapsters after the sending of the demvirst. *Where once was a place of natural lasciviousness, now has partners in a darker, more sinister denizen.*

Underneath his confidence, Bernard doesn't express much of his feelings about what happened to him. When he woke up in the Carvingian's haynest, his only desire was to return to Radiba. He missed the Highlands, and to Sanet, the idea of returning was excellent. For the past seven years, she had been unplugged. Removed from herself and left on the path of Wellion's control. Even though she still didn't know her history, didn't have an idea from where she came, it was freeing to be out from under Wellion's eye. To live where she wanted without the looming threat of a cataclysmic event to tend to. Her joy was that now she could learn to night garden and forget her skills and training as some Green Valor. She grins at the reference.

Despite their remote location, there is a looming dread that Wellion might seek her out. And she's had more than enough kiptales of Wellion slinking into her sleeping room at night to snip her son. His presence looms in the shadows of the haynest, even as at the minor she knows she's safe. Alone. Quiet. Her chosen family in the other room, ready to protect her.

After a few hours, Ethan returns with a solemn expression. "Doing wisnok, Sanet?"

She nods, brushing Jame's head.

"Can we talk? Now that you've had Jame, now that we know it is possible. I think there is something important to discuss."

"What is it?" Sanet asks, sitting up in bed.

Ethan pulls up a seat from across the room and sits beside her. "As you know, this child is . . . unispar. More than just being yours. But, having him. The way you did." Sanet knows. No one can have a child the way she did. "And it's important to keep him safe. And away from . . . well, I think Wellion's foretale about your son was true, but not in the way he originally believed. Which is why he kept changing his understanding about it. He had information that was right, but didn't seem so. I think when he discovers the truth, he will come for him."

"But do you know how this is possible?" She says this, unconsciously holding Jame closer. "If no one can have a child, if everyone is created through the Paseco, then how could I?"

Ethan waits before speaking again. "When our foreparents crafted the Three Laws, they assigned Protectors to the Laws. The Law of Population's Protector is the Paseco. What it does, or what it is, is lost or hidden with time. But the fact remains that no family or woman has been able to have children since the Last War. Instead, the children's squares provide them."

"And no one knows where who what this Paseco is?"

"I don't believe so. Whatever it is was forgotten over the millennia or was made to be forgotten. What we do know is that every year children are brought to children's squares around the states, and bodies go and choose their sons and daughters there. When children who are not chosen turn five, they are sent left. All a means to protect the Law of Population. Of course, this doesn't stop people from traversing from one state to the next, making some more populated than others. That's still a problem that even a Paseco could not stop."

"Why are friends so concerned with population?"

"With so many bodies to feed. So many bodies consuming the resources of the Land, there grows conflict. It is what nearly destroyed us. It is a fact hard to grasp. We all want life. We all want to live happily. And long. And we want our families to grow and be well. Which is why most don't talk in detail about the Law. Only the broad stroke. No more than ten thousand. The bigger point of this is that he," he points to Jame, "is something quite extraordinary. And we'll need to protect him."

"Why didn't you tell me this sooner?"

"In truth, I didn't believe it could be. That you were, as they once said, pregnant. And I didn't know if Jame would or could be born. When I thought it might happen, on Paulo's kleep, when you were sick, Bernard and I decided it would be better to keep you here. Keep things small and quiet. I didn't want you to stress. To only focus on being healthy. Jame may be the first natural-born baby in two and a half thousand years."

"But what about Wellion's Roar?"

"Perhaps that's why everyone made such a big deal of him. But that child was at least six when we saw him. I think wherever Cadwellion found him, he was not born naturally. That Roar, that little boy, is only a machine for propaganda. For whatever thing Wellion's trying to accomplish."

Sanet looks down at Jame with new eyes. The first in two and a half millennia. *Perhaps here's the true advent of the Roar.*

❖ ❖ ❖

A few weeks later, Ethan calls the family to duskmeal. Sanet walks in from the sleeping room with Jame nestled in a wrap. A knock comes at the door, and Sanet steps over to answer, finding Iahel and Ruth standing there. "Sanet!"

"You made it!" Sanet exclaims, hugging Iahel.

"We did. And is this the little one?"

"Yes, this is Jame."

"Jame, how sweet." She peeks in through the wrap. "Oh, he's the tiniest." Ruth peeks in as well as Iahel introduces her. "This is Ruth. Sanet, Ruth."

Sanet smiles. "Nice to meet you officially. We were just sitting down for duskmeal."

"Well, we're both starved, so this makes a perfect minor," Ruth states. They step in as Bernard comes around the corner.

"Iahel, nice to see you." They embrace.

"The Dark Valor, how are you." Iahel grins.

"You can call me Stone Fingers, apposh."

"I think it's best you remain our little madman," Sanet doubles.

With an exchange of laughter, they return to the kitchen, where Iahel introduces Ruth to Ethan and Mercet.

The gang sits and eats and laughs and tells stories. Iahel talks about the reconstruction of Carvinga and how much different the tenfooters' attitudes are toward passersby and travelers.

"It's like going through Radiba," she says. Ruth and Iahel are now leaders at Radnicks after the owner retired.

Bernard goes on again about meeting Jame in the forest when his leg was caught in the trap. They lift mugs in memory of Bernard's late partner.

The night goes deep past full moon, with Bernard carrying Mercet off to bed earlier. Iahel and Ruth are completely jarent, but not more so than Ethan, who appizes every few sentences, especially to his sleeping son, who found the whole evening with the adults to be "absolutely hilarious."

When Bernard doesn't return, Sanet stands up and wanders the house, finding him outside tending his garden. She rocks Jame back and forth in her arms and watches Bernard for a few majors. When he looks up, he smiles brightly.

"Doing a bit of night gardening?"

Bernard chuckles. "Yes. I think it's what I do. When Jame would fall asleep, I would come out here. Relax and reflect on the day. Enjoy the fresh night air." His talk fades a bit. "I'm also nervous I didn't bury this far enough."

As he says this, he pulls a large fragment of brass from the ground before returning it to another deeper hole. The gang had decided to give the remains of the shattered brass pieces to each of the factions that participated in the Two Tens Battle: the Carvingians, the Misipiants, and even a piece to the crimson men, over Bernard's disagreement. If everyone had one of the pieces, they believed no one group would be able to reunite the brass.

A shuffle comes from the wood as Brute emerges from the trees. Behind him darts a second and smaller creshwillow. "Brute, what are you up to?"

"Another little Roar, it seems." Sanet laughs.

Brute hurries over and hops onto Bernard's shoulder. The other creshwillow steps into the yard and grabs on to Bernard's feet.

"Not sure I want two of you," Bernard says to Brute, who suddenly begins to jump up and down. "What are you going on about now?"

It hops down onto the short fence, squealing wordlessly at something in the wood. Sanet looks across the lawn, and to her surprise, she spots a neox standing in wait. *Lincoln.* Bernard doesn't recognize it at first, and as he turns toward the neox, it quickly disappears into the forest.

"Was that another neox? Isn't it bad luck to let one go?" Sanet asks.

Bernard turns to her, and for a minor, it looks as if he's thinking about all the chasing the neox might entail. The dangers it carries. Their trek through the Tunnels, into Yikshir, across the sea to Trimod. The battle in Carvinga. Their losses and their gains. *Jame.*

And then, with a quiet breath and simple shrug, he answers, "And leave my friend again?" He presses his lips into a soft smile just before a droplet of rain hits Sanet's shoulder.

She ignores it.

EPILOGUE

*I*n the dark of night many years ago, a large woman with wild red hair walked in the forest. This didn't often chance, as over the past few years, tormisands in Radiba had gotten longer and longer, and the time between them had grown shorter and shorter. So, when it came to be that the rain stopped, the woman took every opportunity she could. Her husband, sleeping at their haynest, didn't like walks. He thought his long treks across the states were exercise enough. The moon on this night was particularly bright, and there was a chill in the air, the autumn showing its first breaths.

Across the Lothatin Bridge and along the winding paths past the young Babek's haynest, the woman thought that perhaps it was time to turn back, knowing it would be an hour's walk back haynest. But her decision was interrupted by a small cry. It was soft at first, then rang out through the gentle breeze of the Highlands. There was a haunting sound to it. Curious, she followed the sound, wondering who in the Land would be out here this time of night. As the cry amplified, she determined that it was the clamor of a young boy. She quickened her pace, trying to orient herself to the noise, and grew worried that whoever—or whatever—was making the noise might be some frek that attracted its victims to a trap; but for all her readings, she couldn't recall any frek that would mimic the voice of a child.

She continued along and suddenly found a slight luminosity in the forest ahead. The cry here was louder as she proceeded toward the leaves glowing in the night. Looking closer, she determined that they seemed burned away at the edges with a thin light, like a neonlight, outlining where they were burned. As she looked around, she found that the thin lines created what amounted to a giant and perfectly round sphere, which encircled a space all the way to the upper canopy. A strange and unusual sight.

Sitting in the middle of this sphere of light was a small boy. Naked and alone. Crying. She stepped up to the boy, unsure at first, but quickly scooped him up in her arm. She scanned the area, wondering where the person who brought him here might be. She called out across the forest without an answer. The boy instantly took to her, clinging to her neck.

The air in the area of the sphere was hot, and her skin started to sweat as soon as she stepped into the circle. When she stepped back out of it, the Land returned to its evening chill, which the young boy reacted to by squeezing her even harder. She wrapped her shawl around him to keep him warm.

She walked back toward her haynest, only once turning back to where she'd found the boy. The glowing sphere had disappeared. She hugged the boy tighter at the sight, the major holding a sense of foreboding and dread.

In some ways, the boy was Lincoln-sent, as she and her husband had never taken the time or effort to choose their own child, despite her longing for a son or daughter. The trek to the Radiba children's square was nearly two weeks long, a trip her husband refused to take.

Reaching haynest, she decided to give the boy a warm soap and rinse to wash the dirt and grime of the forest from him, but she found in the bright relief room light that he was already perfectly clean. Despite this, she washed him anyway, if anything to warm him up. After the long walk and being in the warmth of her haynest, the boy seemed to calm and even gave her a wide and heart-melting smile.

After a major, her husband, a short, balding man, woke and walked into the relief room. "What are you still—who is that?"

"Don't be angry, Lester, but I found him in the forest. All alone and crying."

"Whose is he?"

At this, she shrugged.

"What are you going to do with him? You're not going to keep him, are you?"

"I don't know. But there's nowhere to take him tonight. He was all alone out there."

The husband stood at the entrance to the room as the little boy raked his arms back and forth in the water, giggling and laughing.

"Does he have a curam?"

The woman turned back to the small boy. "Do you know your curam?"

The boy looked at her with an expression of confusion and then shook his head.

"Do you know how old you are?" He shook his head no. "Do you know where your parents are?"

He shook his head no again.

"He looks like my uncle," the husband stated. "Maybe he left him there knowing you'd find him."

"He was pretty far south. If your uncle did this, he would have put him on the porch."

"Maybe."

"I think he looks like a Logan," the woman stated, combing the boy's hair from his face. "Do you like that curam, Logan?"

The boy grinned and nodded yes.

Acknowledgements for
ADVENT OF THE ROAR

I wrote the first chapter of "Advent of the Roar" on March 28th, 2016. It was a Monday. And it was only going to be a creative past time. A hobby. I was going to write a chapter, think about it, and then, if inspiration struck, write another.

I wrote the next chapter on March 29th. A Tuesday. And in that section, instead of going home, Bernard decided to go back into the cave where he met Zabjed the protnuk. And the riddle he received in this interaction intrigued me enough that I spent the next two days uncovering its mystery and forming the outline of a seven book series.

On Friday, April 1st, I wrote the third chapter and within ten weeks finished the first draft. Over the next two years, I read and adjusted. Sent to friends. Got feedback and became obsessed with everything about it. I fell in love with the monsters, the characters, and the mystery.

This story is a culmination of everything that's drawn me to art and entertainment. And I could not have finished it without some incredible and amazing people helping me along the way. I'd like to thank them here:

NINA, VICTORIA, ERIC, KELLY, & TOM
the first readers who gave me the confidence to finish

TAMMY SALYER
Line Editor
www.inspiredinkediting.com

CHRISTINA PALAIA
Copy Editor
&
NAOMI EAGLESON
Editorial Director, *The Artful Editor*
www.artfuleditor.com

JAMIE TAO
Cover Illustration & Design
www.jamietao.com

ERIC ERNST
Back Cover Synopsis & Best Bud

About the Author
BENJAMIN M PIETY
www.bitmapx.com

A failed magician since eighth grade, Ben instead graduated with a film degree from the University of Central Florida. In 2006, he moved to Los Angeles, California to pursue a career in filmmaking and over the next few years, his short film work was exhibited in film festivals worldwide, including the 2008 Sundance Film Festival and winning a 2007 Special Jury Prize for experimental short at SXSW in Austin, Texas.

But these creative acts came to a standstill on February 28th, 2008 after testing positive for HIV and sending him into a regressive and inward journey.

On the ten year anniversary of this news, February 28th, 2018, his life changed again when he published his first novel, "Advent of the Roar." A fantasy adventure as part of a larger series of books entitled "The Land Old, Untouched" forming a curious question about what the next decade will bring.

Book Two
THE LAND OLD, UNTOUCHED

REIGN

OF THE

PASECO

releasing 2020

❖❖❖

A SPECIAL FAVOR TO ASK OF YOU AWESOME READERS:

First, thank you! As a self-publish and independently financed novel, it's crucial to receive real and honest feedback. If you enjoyed this book, please take a moment of your time to rate & review "Advent of the Roar" on Amazon and Goodreads. And, even better, spread the word.